A DANGEROUS BREED

ALSO BY GLEN ERIK HAMILTON

Past Crimes
Hard Cold Winter
Every Day Above Ground
Mercy River

A DANGEROUS BREED

A NOVEL

GLEN ERIK HAMILTON

WILLIAM MORROW
An Imprint of HarperCollinsPublishers

A DANGEROUS BREED. Copyright © 2020 by Glen Erik Hamilton. All rights reserved. Printed in the United States of America. No part of this book may be used or reproduced in any manner whatsoever without written permission except in the case of brief quotations embodied in critical articles and reviews. For information, address HarperCollins Publishers, 195 Broadway, New York, NY 10007.

HarperCollins books may be purchased for educational, business, or sales promotional use. For information, please email the Special Markets Department at SPsales@harpercollins.com.

FIRST EDITION

Designed by Kyle O'Brien

Art by nexus7/Shutterstock, Inc.

Library of Congress Cataloging-in-Publication Data has been applied for.

ISBN 978-0-06-297851-6

20 21 22 23 24   LSC   10 9 8 7 6 5 4 3 2 1

For Bruce and Marjorie,
who raised a large and wonderful family, and made room for one more

A DANGEROUS BREED

PROLOGUE

W<small>E WERE IN THE AIR</small>, falling backward. The black water of Puget Sound coursed ten feet below, glints of moonlight defining gentle waves. For an instant there was no sound at all.

Then the police car hit hard and speared below the surface, bobbing swiftly back up to slap the waves flat. The impact threw me face-first into the clear plastic barrier separating the rear of the car from the empty driver's seat. Blood erupted from my lip.

I yanked myself upright, hampered by handcuffs that bound my wrists behind my back and the heavy bulk of the man lying half across me. The car window pressed his head into an awkward angle, deforming his cheek. A puff of breath condensed on the glass.

He was alive. For now.

We began to dip forward, borne down by the mass of the cruiser's V-8. Seawater bubbled and splashed into the front compartment. In seconds it had swamped the pedals. A briny reek overwhelmed the tang of blood in my mouth. I twisted in my seat, trying to feel for the tiny piece of bent metal I'd dropped in our fall.

The car leaned toward the icy deep as if eager for its embrace. Half a minute, maybe less, before the roiling water would fill the interior.

I pushed at the unconscious man with my shoulder, trying to gain a few more inches of space, but there was nowhere for his body to move. The cold lent a razor sting to every gasp of air. My grasping fingers brushed the hard plastic seat, only to slide away again.

Heavy diesels churned nearby. The barge from which we had fallen began moving away from the sinking car and toward the shore. Four miles off, the city sparkled in the clear night. I had one final glimpse of those glittering lights before the waves shrouded the windshield outside and darkness consumed both of us.

Me, and the man I'd met for the first time barely one week before. A week of violence and death—and the hard proof about the identity of the man about to drown alongside me.

My father.

ONE

Thirteen days ago

B ULLY BETTY'S GRAND REOPENING WAS a triumph threatening to collapse into tragedy. By midnight the main room of the bar was almost bulging at the seams, a crush of two dozen warm bodies past any sensible capacity.

Word about the new location had spread, and then some. Betty's first weekend on Capitol Hill attracted her kind of crowd. Queer techies. Theater vamps wearing tailored tartan suits. Horn-rimmed creatives with enough side hustles to fill a résumé. A combined target demo that might be narrow anywhere but Seattle. All the revelers temporarily free from their holiday obligations and end-of-year deadlines. Ready to shake themselves slack.

"Van." A-Plus, shouting from ten feet away. I read her perfectly glossed lips more than I heard the words over the din of a hundred other voices: "Two sour ales, three tequila shots with lime, two house bourbon." She flashed French-manicured fingers to make sure I caught the count.

A-Plus and the other bartenders handled the showy job of making cocktails. I pulled all the pints and poured bottles with both hands to keep the river of well drinks flowing. Factory work. The arrangement suited both sides. They kept the tips, and I didn't have to make small talk.

Betty had allowed a few concessions to her loyalists in the new place. At the corner of the bar nearest me, a muted television streamed a rerun of the U-Dub women's basketball game against Oregon State. The Huskies had an ace power forward this year who was expected to turn pro a year early. I knew all this because the knot of women glued to the action had been singing the player's praises since tip-off.

"All that technical crap, like executing the game plan," one fan in a sleeveless T-shirt proclaimed. "The team can learn that shit from the coach. But *that*." She jabbed a finger at the screen. "That's fuckin' *mean*. You can't learn mean." Her nugget of wisdom prompted affirming whoops from the others.

Betty had noticed my self-imposed exile, of course. She'd thrown me the side-eye, but that was all she had time for. Too busy keeping order, nostrils flared for anyone vaping, making sure Maurice on the door was confirming that every pretty face matched with an ID photo.

"I'll have a gin fizz," a woman said to my back, over the babble of the crowd.

I knew the voice and angled my gaze downward before I turned around.

The bar counter was tall. Addy Proctor was not. Only her head and shoulders could be seen above the edge. Her cherubic crinkled face poked out from the hood of a cherry-red quilted parka lined with fake fur. A scowling circle.

"Do I look like I know how to make a gin fizz?" I said.

"No more than I look like I belong here." Her neck trapped in the parka, Addy turned her whole body to examine the throng that moved like wheat stalks in wind every time the door opened to admit just a couple more. Drops of rain suspended from her fur collar broke loose. "I'm a gnome among mermaids. Look at these children. It's marvelous."

"I'm working," I said.

"You can spare a minute for an old woman up past her bedtime. If you can't make a decent drink, pour me a vodka. Something that pairs nicely with a fixed income."

I ignored Addy's restriction and pulled the Woody Creek Reserve from the top shelf to fill a shot glass for my former neighbor. A-Plus brought another stack of orders. I waved her toward the taps to fend for herself, ignoring the gorgeous pout she fired my way.

"You haven't returned my phone calls," Addy said, sniffing at the vodka.

"It's been busy." I nodded to the bar. "Betty lost her lease. We wanted to relocate before the end of the season."

She frowned. "That's not the cause. You've been a damn ghost since you got back from Oregon, and that was over two months ago."

I didn't want to talk about Oregon. I had been practicing hard to not even think about what had happened there, and I had finally reached the point where I managed the trick most hours of the day.

"I've come by your house," I said. "At Thanksgiving, with Cyndra." Cyn was Addy's foster kid.

"You came, you brought a pie, big whoop. You spoke about ten words, Van. It hurt her feelings. I know Luce getting married must have been tough for you—"

"What do you want, Addy?"

"Fine. Cyndra went to L.A. to have Christmas with her father. Which means she spent the holiday in a convalescent home with Mickey, who is nowhere near a suitable host for her, dad or not. She'll be on the morning flight back. You're going to help me welcome Cyndra home and make sure she has some fun. Starting with taking her to her team practice to-morrow afternoon." To underline her point, Addy downed half of the shot glass.

Betty had spotted our conversation and angled her path toward us through the crowd. I was reminded of an icebreaker, its armored prow shoving aside tons of frozen floes.

"If I say yes, are we done?" I said to Addy.

"For now," she muttered, understandably distracted by a seven-foot sylph in green sparkle makeup using the bar mirror to freshen their mascara.

"Bring your next luncheon group here," I teased.

"Please," Addy said. "I lived through Haight-Ashbury."

Betty reached us. She had no problem making room for herself at the counter. Besides wielding shoulders as wide as mine, twin ebony boulders covered in purple tattoos advertising the combined Aztec and Ghanaian heritage she claimed, Betty possessed a force of personality that encouraged the world to make way, or else.

"You got to be Addy. Hello," Betty said, giving our parka-encased guest the once-over.

"I must be. I'm surprised Van has mentioned me. Congratulations on your new place."

"I'll exhale when it's still standing in the morning. I'd forgotten how wild the Hill can get." Betty turned to me. "Maurice is taking over the taps."

I shook my head. "He made me a deal. He's on the door. I close up."

"Big Mo doesn't frighten off drunks. Dickless wonders keep cruising past and hollering shit at the clientele."

"That's harassment. Can't the police help?" said Addy.

Betty and I both looked at her.

"Or is that a foolish question?" Addy finished, eyeing me.

She knew enough of my personal history to predict my opinion. Being raised by my grandfather, a professional thief and onetime armed robber, had lent me a different true north on my personal compass. Betty had suffered her own challenges with the cops, like pretty much anyone black and queer and raised in poverty. Maybe that shared suspicion toward the rest of the world was why she and I got along.

"I'll take care of it," I told Betty.

"Don't forget about Cyndra," Addy said. "Tomorrow morning. And we're not done talking about this."

Betty offered me a penlight to use when checking licenses. "No one paying you for conversation here. Go scare somebody."

I retrieved my jacket and gloves from the back room.

Addy wanted to know what had been bothering me since my return. She'd assumed it was my ex-girlfriend, Luce, tying the knot earlier that month. Wrong guess, Addy. Thanks for playing.

I had made some choices in Oregon that I couldn't ignore, or walk back, if I had cared to try. I hadn't. Living day by day had been tough enough these past weeks without worrying about something as ephemeral as atonement.

On my way out into the cold, I reflected that the basketball fan had been dead wrong, too.

Someone *could* learn to be mean. Start as young as I had, and there was no limit.

TWO

ONE NIGHT JUST BEFORE THE start of the school year, Cyndra had found a movie on cable about young women competing in roller derby. She used her own money to buy a digital copy that same night and pasted her nose to the screen, watching the film six more times before Monday rolled around.

Within a week her skateboard had given way to quad-wheel boots. Cyndra would have worn the skates to bed if Addy had allowed it. They found a junior league team called the Screaming Mimis. When I arrived at Addy's on Sunday morning to pick up Cyn for practice, she was already outside in the cold, gear bag over her shoulder for added weight as she did calf raises on the porch step. She heard my car pulling up and sprinted to meet it.

The Mimis' derby league was flat-track, meaning the skaters competed on smooth concrete. Parents had arranged a fund drive to have a new floor poured in an old cinder-block warehouse near Northgate. I'd handed Addy a short stack of cash to donate. She knew better than to ask where the money had come from.

At fourteen and undernourished much of her childhood, Cyndra weighed about as much as a loaded sack of groceries. But what she lacked in size she made up for with speed. She was a favorite jammer among the newer players, the fresh meat. Jammers scored points by making it past the opposing team's blockers, who did their level best to knock the jammers on their asses. Sportingly.

I sat against the sage green blocks of the warehouse wall, watching Cyn lean into the curve, picking up velocity, angling for the inside, and then suddenly juking right to find daylight between two blockers who hadn't linked arms. She whooped elatedly. A fraction too early, as her skate caught another player's and she fell, skidding two yards, her plastic kneepads and wrist guards rasping harshly on the concrete. I winced. But Cyndra popped back up as if the impact had been a cool breeze.

Speed, and guts.

The instructor, a slim woman with a dark braid and a band of tattoos spiraling up her right arm, blew her whistle to bring the girls in for a lesson. They gathered with a clomping of wheels like pony hooves on hard dirt.

I turned my attention to the stack of mail Addy had given me. My old house, the home I'd shared with my grandfather Dono as a boy, had been up the block from Addy's. Mail still trickled in at that address. The family that had bought the property and built their own house on the land left anything sent to the Shaws under Addy's welcome mat.

Grocery fliers and tool catalogs made up most of the stack. One expiration notice of union membership for nonpayment of dues, forwarded by a mailing service to Dono—or, more accurately, one of Dono's aliases. My grandfather had always maintained a couple of identities. Handy for emergencies, and for purchasing items unavailable to people with felony rap sheets.

I nearly missed the last envelope, which had been tucked into a bulk-mail magazine of coupons. I glanced at the handwritten address. And then stared at the name.

Moira Shaw, it read.

My mother.

My mother had died when I was six years old. A distracted driver tapped the wrong pedal at the wrong moment and jumped the curb in downtown Seattle. I wasn't there. My daycare worker brought me to the hospital. No one had really told me what was going on. Not until Dono arrived. He took me to his home that same night, and there I stayed.

Moira Shaw. I barely remembered her. Dono hadn't kept pictures. Hardly ever spoke of his only child. Seeing her name again, for the first time in I couldn't remember, felt like I'd swallowed a small but very sharp icicle.

I headed outside, ducking under the rolling door the Mimis kept partway open to allow some ventilation in the airless warehouse. Drizzling rain, a near-constant in December Seattle, coated my face and hair. I opened my car to sit in the driver's seat.

The return address at the top corner of the envelope was a stick-on label with a Christmas theme, green holly and candy canes. From a John and Josephine Mixon in Redmond. Our house address had been handwritten on the envelope in purple ballpoint.

I opened the envelope and removed the single sheet of paper. Only the salutation and a phone number at the bottom had been written with the same purple pen. The rest of the text was a typed copy.

> *Dear Moira,*
>
> *I hope this note finds you! We are just starting to plan the Emmett Watson High 30th Reunion (WOW!) for sometime next summer, and would love to include you. Please call me at the number below to let us know!*
>
> *Go Paladins!*
>
> *Sincerely,*
> *Jo Mixon (Gerrold!)*

Just a form letter, sent by someone so far out of the alumni loop that she hadn't even heard Moira Shaw had died almost a quarter of a century before.

I had only a few sparse facts about Moira's life. Her own mother, Dono's wife, Finnoula, had also died while Moira was still young. The Shaw women traveled tough, short roads. Moira had gotten pregnant and left Dono's house a few years after that.

So far as I knew, she'd never spoken a word about who had knocked her up. Out of shame, or maybe to keep Dono from murdering the guy. Probably the latter. That secrecy had driven a wedge between father and daughter.

Cyndra's practice was about to end. I tossed the letter from Jo Mixon on the passenger's seat and stepped out into the cold mist.

GRANDDAD KNELT TO WRESTLE THE *heavy bench grinder free from the other tools crowded under his worktable. He muttered curse words with every tug. My homeroom teacher, Ms. Heffler, had put the word involuntary on last week's spelling assignment, and Granddad's swearing was the first example that came to my mind. I didn't write that down for my practice sentence, though. I wasn't that dumb.*

While Granddad set up the grinder, I opened the cardboard box of papers he'd told me to sort. We were making space. We called the little room carved into the hill below our house the garage, but only about half of Granddad's truck would have fit inside. Mostly the garage was his workshop and a storage place for whatever he didn't want in the house. The box of papers he'd given me was so full, it bulged at the sides. The cardboard was soft to the touch and smelled like rags left out in the rain.

Make three piles, he'd said. One for records from his contracting business, one for home stuff, and one for instruction manuals or anything else that didn't fit the other two piles. I pulled out a handful of papers and started looking through them.

"Finish that fast," Granddad said as he tightened bolts through the work-table to hold the grinder in place, "and I'll teach you to use this. About time you worked with something other than hand tools."

"What are you making?" I said. He had brought a sack of metal rods from the hardware store.

"Some disposable punches. For knocking out hinges and locks and the like."

"What locks?"

"Never mind that. Get to it."

I turned back to the papers. It wasn't tough to sort them. Usually the first page of each bunch told me what pile the papers belonged to.

Then I found one lone page, stuck in the middle of a manual for a power wrench. A lined sheet of notebook paper, with a girl's handwriting.

Moira Shaw
Ms. Cullen, Room 17
Native American Tribes of the Northwest

Mom?

I stared at the loops and slants of the letters. This had been hers. She had written it, touched the paper with her own hand.

Paragraphs in the same writing covered both sides. She'd gotten an A on the paper. If there had been more pages to it, they were missing. The top corner of the paper was torn, probably where a staple used to be.

I knew Ms. Cullen. She taught fifth grade at Bertha Landes Elementary. My school.

"Did Mom go to Landes?" I said.

"Eh?" Granddad looked up. "What's that?"

"It's Mom's. Was Mom's." I showed him. He took the page from me. "Did she go to my school?"

"She did." Granddad's eye moved over the paper.

"You never said."

He didn't answer. Just held the page by his fingertips, like it would rip if he pressed any harder. Granddad had big hands, even for somebody as tall as he was, and I was suddenly worried he would decide to crumple the fragile page to dust.

"Was she at Hovick Middle School too?" I said quickly. "That's where I'll be going."

"Next year. I'm aware." Granddad set the homework sheet on the upper shelf with his router set.

"Because maybe some of the teachers remember her—"

"You've work to do."

I knew better than to keep talking. I went back to the box, rummaging through the stack even faster than before, hoping to discover more of Mom's stuff. Our house didn't have anything of hers inside, not even a photo of Mom as a kid.

But I reached the bottom of the box without finding anything else of hers.

The realization made a lump in my chest. I looked around the garage. Maybe there was another pile of old papers. Or books or toys or anything that might have been hers. All I saw was more of Granddad's tools and a lot of paint and varnish cans.

"How come we don't have any pictures?" I said. "Of Mom, or Grandma Fi? Or anybody?"

"Because I don't want them around."

"Why not?"

"Pictures are false. Better my haziest memory than the clearest photograph."
He hadn't turned away from his task of putting a new wheel on the grinder.

Weird. But then a lot of things Granddad did were strange. Or scary. My friends from school didn't like to come to our house. Only Davey Tolan was brave enough, and that's because his home wasn't much better.

Later, when Granddad went up the stone steps to the house to grab us coffee and a Coke, I stood on a stepladder to reach the upper shelf and Mom's school paper. I folded the page into a square and slipped it into my back pocket.

When kids at school talked about their parents, I avoided the subject. If they didn't get the hint or a teacher asked me a direct question, I just told them my mom and dad were dead and that usually shut them up fast. At least half of that answer was true, anyway. Maybe all of it.

Granddad wasn't going to say any more. But Ms. Cullen or some of the other teachers might. They'd met her. Mom. I wanted to learn whatever they could tell me.

Anything would be more than I knew now.

IN THE WAREHOUSE, THE WHOLE derby squad was on the track, doing laps. Their trainer with the thick dark braid of hair stood in the center, shouting out the elapsed time from a stopwatch. Two minutes. Two-thirty. The skaters pushed harder, racing to achieve some goal unknown to me. The older teens skated in a line, with long fluid strides that ate up the track, weaving like a Chinese parade dragon around kids like Cyndra, who doggedly ground out their own laps in disorganized and gasping clumps.

Impossible to say who tripped first. One girl went down on the far side of the track, and then three and four, most of them just tapping the concrete with their kneepads before bouncing right back up.

Cyndra stayed down, cradling her arm. In an instant I was running the length of the hangar.

The trainer reached her first. Two members of the squad around Cyndra's age hovered anxiously as the woman helped Cyndra stand and roll to the outside of the track.

"I'm sorry," one of the girls kept saying.

"Not your fault, Jaycie," the trainer said. "Take my stopwatch and call out when they hit five minutes." The girls reluctantly skated back to the track. The woman held out her hand to Cyndra. "Let me see."

Cyndra uncurled her arm. Her fingers were bright pink, the same color as her face, and scraped raw. "I'm fine," she said. The reflexive answer of any kid embarrassed by sudden attention.

"Uh huh. Make a fist." Cyndra did, carefully. "Good. Wiggle your fingers."

"What happened?" I said.

"Somebody ran over it," Cyn said. "It's okay." She used her other hand to quickly wipe her eyes.

"It is," the trainer agreed, "though you need some antibiotic. C'mere." She led us over to the bench, the two of them floating on wheels, me thudding behind. When the woman knelt to fish an equipment bag from under the bench, her black-coffee braid fell to one side, revealing her derby name stenciled in block white letters on the back of her ebony tank top: PAIN AUSTEN.

"What do we always say, Mortal Cyn?" she asked.

"Fall small," Cyndra answered, giggling despite herself.

"Got that. Best way to protect your extremities." The trainer sprayed Neosporin on Cyndra's knuckles. "I haven't seen you here before," she said to me.

Cyn remembered the manners Addy had been working so hard to instill. "This is Van. He's . . ." She hesitated. What was I, exactly?

"Family," I said.

Cyndra nodded vigorously. "Yeah. An' this is Pain."

It was the trainer's turn to grin. It was a good grin. A little crooked, a little self-mocking. She was long of leg and strong-looking in the way naturally slender athletes develop over time, as much sinew as muscle fiber. Kneeling with one leg up and balanced on her skate's toe-stop seemed to be no effort for her at all.

This close, the spiral of tattoos on her arm and shoulder was identifiable as a loose line of small birds in flight. Each bird varied slightly in size and radically in style, from photorealistic black and gray to eye-poppingly bright cartoon. The flock winged its way from her wrist all the way up and under the strap of her tight tank top. Her skin beneath the ink was tan, whether by genes or the sun. Not every part of her figure was slim.

She caught me looking. "My name's Wren," she said, nodding at the bird tattoos before turning back to Cyndra. "Teddy bears or pop art?"

"Art," Cyndra said. Wren took two bandages with Warhol soup cans and Elvises printed on them and applied them to Cyn's ointment-covered knuckles. "There. Better than new."

"Can I finish?" Cyndra said, looking at the track. The other skaters had collected by the aluminum bleachers to stretch and rehydrate.

"You better. You owe me laps."

Cyn dashed away, injury forgotten.

"She's fast," Wren said as we watched her bank hard into the curve, "for being so new to it."

"Making up time," I said.

"You're her stepbrother or something?" said Wren, eyeing me. I knew what she meant: that Cyndra and I looked nothing alike. Cyn was small and blue-eyed and fair, at least when her hair wasn't dyed. I was none of those things. I'd inherited Dono's Black Irish looks through Moira.

"It's an unusual situation," I said. "You've met Addy? Cyndra's guardian?"

"Talk about unusual. She's amazing. She told me she had a tryout with the Bay Bombers back in like nineteen-sixty-something."

I hadn't known that but didn't doubt it. Addy seemed to have lived enough lives for a dozen octogenarians.

"None of us have other relatives," I said, "except for Cyndra's dad, who's down in California. Addy was a neighbor of my grandfather's. We all sort of adopted each other."

"Chosen families can be the best. If you want to help out Mortal

Cyn, she could use some resistance training. You look like you've seen the inside of a gym."

"Once or twice."

"Show her how to use the weights. Nothing too heavy. Just build up the endurance in her back and legs."

"Core strength. To get up every time she falls."

"You got it." Wren's eyes were a lighter shade of brown than her hair, a splash of cream mixed in the coffee. With tiny flecks of gold near the center. "Come to practice again. Let me know how it goes."

"I'll do that."

She glided away to join the girls, who had collected by the aluminum bleachers to shed their gear and goof around, not in that order. One of the older teens handed out popsicles from a cooler. Wren waited until Cyndra had finished her laps, then she had the skaters shout out the team name three times to close practice. Kids or not, they could yell like drill sergeants.

RAIN PELTED DOWN, BOUNCING LIKE hail off every hard surface. Cyndra and I ran for the car with me carrying her gear bag. She shook water out of her hair while I turned the defroster on full blast.

"You want food?" I said.

"Uh huh."

"Dumb question."

"What's this?" Cyn said, taking the letter to Moira off the seat.

"Junk mail." The AC had cleared the fog of condensation from the bottom few inches of windshield. Good enough to see the road. We pulled out of the lot, the Barracuda's wheels splashing through a newborn river of water in the gutter.

"Are you gonna call this person?" Cyndra pointed at Jo Mixon's number.

"I'm not going to the reunion."

"Yeah, but . . . your mom, right? This woman knew her."

"If she really knew my mom she'd know Moira was dead."

Cyn frowned. Whatever point she was making, I was obviously too dense to grasp it. "Well, what about your dad? You said you never met him. She could know."

"Not likely."

"But there's a chance. Like, you have to call her."

I should have expected this. Ever since I'd made the mistake of telling Cyndra about my unknown parentage, she'd romanticized it into thinking I might be the love child of an exiled duke.

"Cyndra," I said. "Give it a rest."

"Promise me."

"Yeah. I'll call her. But no more about it."

"And you have to tell me everything she says."

"You want to walk home?"

She sat back, satisfied.

A gust of wind rocked the car. At the next stoplight I pulled up the NOAA weather streaming app, letting the monotone male voice of the running forecast play while we drove. After a few minutes the looped recording cycled around to report on the coastal stations nearest Puget Sound. Winds up to forty knots with a small craft advisory in effect for everything south of Port Townsend.

"I have to go to the marina," I said. "Do you want me to drop you off first?"

She looked alarmed. "But food."

"On it."

The rain hadn't discouraged many diners from the eternal line outside Dick's on Broadway. I left Cyn in the warm car playing on her phone while I snagged us two burger-and-shake combos. Double patties for both of us. Cyn could eat nearly as much as me.

We parked in front of Addy's quaint yellow house and ate in the car, dumping our fries into a collective pile in the cardboard tray. Cyndra held her Deluxe with one hand and deftly texted with the other.

"Your trainer Wren says I should teach you how to lift weights," I said. "Cross-training, you know?"

"When?"

"Whenever we want. I can take you to my gym. Once we know what size weights you need, we'll figure out something to use at home."

"D'you like Wren?" she said around her next mouthful.

"I just met Wren five minutes ago."

"But she's pretty, right?"

"You want to tell me about Elias?" Elias was a name I'd heard Addy mention at Thanksgiving. Mention only once, because the topic had made Cyndra flush bright pink from her hairline to her throat, as she started to now. "Okay, then."

Détente assured, I told Cyn to give Addy's dog, Stanley, the last bite of my burger and to tell him it was from me. She hauled her bag out of the back and kicked open the fence gate to run to the front door. Addy, ever prepared, opened it before Cyndra reached the porch. I waved to them and pulled away.

The letter to Moira slipped off the dashboard on the first turn and fell onto the steering column. Refusing to be ignored.

Addy and Cyndra weren't my relatives, but neither were my brothers in the Rangers. Both were a kind of chosen family. The difference was that Addy and Cyndra and I had chosen each other, and the Army had chosen the guys in the 75th Regiment, after we'd survived the levels of hell that made up the selection process.

Blood, though. Dono had been the only blood relation in my life that I had known, beyond scattered and unreliable impressions of my mother.

Moira had become pregnant at barely sixteen. She hadn't told Dono about her boyfriend, but it was possible that she'd trusted a friend. And anyone who was that close a friend had probably gone to Watson High with her.

This might be my best shot at ever learning who my father was. If I wanted to know. I'd gone a long time and done just fine without that knowledge.

Air blowing from the car's vent caught the letter and sent it flying. I snatched it out of the air without thinking. Like I'd been terrified to lose it.

THREE

I RACED THE RAPIDLY SETTING SUN toward the west. About as far west as it was possible to go in Seattle, to the big marina at Shilshole Bay. The gale warning on the NOAA broadcast meant enough wind after nightfall to bang boats against docks and maybe shake them free from their moorings. My speedboat was one of the last possessions of my grandfather's that I still owned, and I didn't want it sunk by a storm.

The wind wasn't waiting for darkness, already pushing the rain half sideways and the Barracuda insistently to the left, as the muscle car's wide tires sluiced through the streams flowing across Leary Way. The copper-colored Barracuda was a recent acquisition. It still felt disconcertingly low to the ground compared to Dono's old Dodge pickup, which time and wear had finally forced me to set out to pasture, if an exorbitantly priced space in a long-term garage could be called pasture.

I parked in the marina lot and dialed the number written in purple pen on the letter.

"Hello?" A woman's voice, sounding rushed, like she'd snatched the phone up while dashing between rooms.

I explained who I was and about how the reunion letter had found its way to me. The voice belonged to Jo Mixon. She made appropriate sounds of dismay when I informed her that Moira had died long ago.

"Why I'm calling," I said, when her torrent of words slowed, "I was wondering if you could put me in touch with anyone who knew Moira then. A school friend, or even a teacher."

"Oh. Let me think."

The noise of rain on the car roof and kids arguing in the background on her side provided a strange kind of hold music.

"Here we are," she said finally. "I had the yearbook out as part of all the work for the reunion. This is who I was trying to remember. Stasia Llewellyn. She and Moira were joined at the hip, you know?"

"A yearbook? Is there a photograph of Moira?"

"With the seniors?" I heard her flipping pages. "No, I don't see that. She *was* in school."

But maybe she had been pregnant with me when class-picture time came around. Not keen to capture the moment.

"I don't have any contact information for Stasia," Jo Mixon said. "I'm sorry."

I told her that was fine and asked her to spell Stasia Llewellyn's name. As we said goodbye, I was already pulling up a browser to search for Moira's friend.

Luck was with me: a Stasia Llewellyn-Wiler on Facebook, from Seattle and now living in Philadelphia. Her family pictures focused almost exclusively on a flock of children who ranged from grade school to college. A job profile on two networking sites listed her as a senior comptroller, whatever that was.

I sent Stasia a message, repeating the basic information I'd given to Jo Mixon and asking her to call me whenever it was convenient.

At dusk on a wet Sunday the marina was nearly deserted. The floating docks bobbed well below the parking level. I had to watch my step on the wet ramp. Cabin lights of a few liveaboards gleamed through the masts and radio antennae like lanterns in a forest.

One bright cabin belonged to Hollis Brant on the *Francesca*, two docks over. I'd just reached the speedboat when he stepped out from the aft door and waved one broad hand in greeting. He may have shouted something as well; it was hard to tell from a hundred yards away over the drumroll of rain pelting on my jacket hood. I waved back, aware that

I'd been avoiding Hollis as much as I had Addy and Cyndra lately. He'd broken things off with his latest girlfriend, Gloria, too. Small wonder he might be craving any company, even as lousy as mine was these days.

The narrow spearhead bow of my twenty-foot speedboat rode high at rest. A consequence of the big Mercury outboard weighing down its stern. Dono had installed the engine and its muffled exhaust not long before his death. The boat had no name, only the registration numbers on the sides. It was painted shark-gray and originally intended for very fast and quiet runs across the Sound and up into the San Juan Islands, usually in the dead of night.

In the weeks since Oregon, it had become my refuge. When the apartment grew small and people became loud, I busied myself with scut work aboard or day trips out on the Sound, even sleeping some nights in the shallow triangular sarcophagus of its tiny cabin. The rhythm of the waves eased my restlessness.

I tied two more fenders as an extra defense between the boat and the dock and had begun checking that each snap of the canvas covering the cockpit was secure when Hollis came rumbling down the ramp. His sole acknowledgment of the foul weather was a canary-yellow slicker thrown over his T-shirt and shorts. Water dripped from it onto his short ruddy legs and sandals. Hollis gave the impression of being ninety percent upper body, all chest and shoulders with a hard round belly and ape-like arms. Even his hair under the slicker's hood was a shade an elder orangutan would admire.

"Hullo," he said as he hurriedly closed the last steps. "It's something when the Sound gets angry, isn't it?"

"Easy to enjoy a storm when you're in the harbor."

"Now that's a bit of truth. But this is the exception that proves the rule. I'm damned glad you're here."

"What's wrong?"

"Best I explain where it's dry. If your hatches are sufficiently battened, let's get the hell inside, shall we?"

We walked through the mounting rain to his dock, Hollis taking every third step double-time, as if to urge me to move even faster. Something was chipping away at his normally carefree façade. By the time we boarded the *Francesca*, he was practically jogging.

Hollis's home was a fifty-foot Carver, outfitted for comfort and modified to hide many things that were better left unseen by harbormasters and customs officials. Hollis was a smuggler, an expert one. He'd been a frequent accomplice of my grandfather's as well as his closest friend.

I hung my dripping coat in the enclosed aft section as Hollis opened the door and almost rushed into the main cabin, leaving a trail of rainwater across the faux teak parquet.

"Hollis—" I began, and then I saw what held his concern.

A tall heavyset white man with bristly brown hair lay on the main settee. He was shirtless, his left rib cage covered with a flat rectangle of folded cloth. Blood had seeped through at least two spots at the lower edge of the thick pad. He didn't stir at our approach.

Hollis grabbed a waterproof first aid kit from the table and unlatched it to take out a roll of clean gauze, winding it rapidly around his hand to make another pad.

"The damn wound's still bleeding," he said. "I've tried taping it shut, but no."

"I'll look. You start talking sense. Did you do this?"

"Hell no. The man's a friend of mine."

I knelt down beside the wounded man. His airway and breathing both checked out normal, and his pulse was steady. Pupil reaction when I lifted his eyelids looked fine, too. I didn't see any sign of an injury to his head.

"How long's he been out?" I said.

"Almost since I found him. He was more asleep than awake. I managed to get him up and walk with him onto the boat, but then he went out completely. That's when I took off his coat and saw how much he was bleeding. Scared the hell out of me."

I set the man's arm carefully to one side. The cloth pad turned out to be two of Hollis's undershirts, folded and held to the man's abdomen by strips of athletic tape, which I peeled away. Underneath, more tape and wads of gauze made a red clotted lump. A sharp smell and yellow streaks on the skin underneath were evidence that Hollis had done what he could with iodine as antiseptic. As I looked, a drop of blood escaped the sodden bandage and fell onto the settee's blue upholstery.

"His name's Jaak," Hollis said, "a sailor on the Finnish freighter *Stellar Jewel*. I sailed out on the Sound earlier this afternoon to meet him. Just a bit of information and a sample product to show me, nothing major. He was supposed to borrow a boat and meet me in Smith Cove. Instead I found one of the freighter's launches drifting near shore, with Jaak lying inside. Out cold. It took all I had to drag him aboard."

Pulling back the bandage with a finger, I saw a long seeping cut across Jaak's side, with a wider puncture at one end. A blade had stuttered along the hard ribs until it found the softer flesh below.

"Stab wound," I said.

"That much I know."

"So why aren't we talking to paramedics right now?"

"Because the man's got no sailor's card on him, no visa to be onshore. If I take him to a hospital he'll be reported as illegally entering the country. At the very least he loses his job, and maybe the poor fool spends some time in jail here *and* in Helsinki to boot. But if we can get him back to the *Stellar Jewel* in one piece, his mates can cover for him. I'm sure of it."

"Well, I'm sure that he needs surgery. Soon. Look here." Hollis stepped forward, and I showed him a purplish blotch where blood was pooling below the puncture, blurring the skin down almost to Jaak's kidneys.

"He's hemorrhaging inside," I said, grabbing latex gloves from Hollis's kit. "We have to staunch the bleeding as much as we can. I need clean sponges. And duct tape."

"Tape's with the tools here," Hollis said, removing a small tackle box from shelves in the galley. "I think I've some new sponges in the cleaning supplies."

"Tear them up into pieces. About the size of a marble. Wash your hands well first."

He hurried to comply.

"I can patch him, but field medicine doesn't cover sewing up whatever's sliced inside." Keeping light pressure on the wound, I used my other hand and my teeth to tear off strips of duct tape, setting each one aside. I couldn't figure why Jaak was unconscious. He wasn't especially pale, and his pulse was solid. Not so much blood loss that a man his size should pass out. "He needs a doctor."

"I have an alternative to visiting an E.R." Hollis nodded. "I was about to give up on the idea, but then you arrived. Evidence of a grand design." He brought me a cereal bowl filled with small ragged chunks of orange sponge.

"Hold the towel there," I said to Hollis, indicating below the wound. "This will be messy."

When I took pressure off, the stab wound opened again. Blood flowed down Jaak's stomach, even as I swiftly began packing the puncture with pieces of sponge. The orange bits immediately swelled and grew saturated with blood. I pressed each of them gently into Jaak's body, counting on the swollen weight of the massed sponges to slow his internal bleeding. Six pieces, seven, and then the wound would take no more.

I pinched the two halves of the puncture together and used the last chunks of sponge to mop most of the blood from his skin. The last of the gauze went on next. It would keep the wound clean of duct tape residue. I layered the strips of tape in Xs, counting on them to keep the skin over Jaak's ribs from pulling apart. If the injured sailor was going to have surgery within the next couple of hours, I didn't want to attempt suturing the wound and risk tearing his lacerated skin further. My makeshift bandage would stem the flow. If it held.

Hollis climbed to the helm on the flybridge above the cabin and started the *Francesca*'s engines. A moment later his VHF radio began blaring the same weather broadcast I'd heard only an hour before. I looked out the cabin window. Between the rain clouds and the dusk, the sky was already a step beyond black. Wind buffeted the masts outside, making their halyards clang like muffled gongs.

"Hollis," I called.

"I know, I know. But we only need to sail as far as Vashon Island."

"In a gale."

"If you don't want to get involved—"

"Come on." Hollis and I had known each other long enough that the question was insulting. "What's on Vashon?"

"A physician called Claybeck, in a lovely beachfront home with its own dock."

"Tell the doctor to get ready," I said, peeling off the gloves. Jaak's blood had changed the latex from sky blue to deep violet.

"Thanks," Hollis said. "I'll cast off."

"*I'll* cast off. You get us moving. The faster we get across the Sound, the less chance we'll all finish this day by drowning."

FOUR

I T TOOK AN HOUR TO cross the furious Sound to Vashon Island. A full
sixty minutes, as each ten-foot swell coming from the north lifted the
Francesca like a bubble to speed beneath us, leaving the boat heeling pre-
cariously to starboard as it fell into the trough behind. Hollis did what he
could to follow a course that kept the stern at an angle to the current.
Allowing the looming walls of water to slam straight into the transom
might have swamped us.

"How's he doing?" Hollis shouted from the flybridge above. I caught
the gist more than his actual words, smothered as they were by the laboring of the diesels and the latest wave's reverberating boom against
the hull.

I felt Jaak's throat for his pulse while keeping a tight grip on the rope
I'd used to lash the unconscious man to the settee. One hand for yourself,
one hand for the ship, always. Especially when the weather was trying its
hardest to toss you on your head.

"The same," I yelled back. I checked Jaak's pupils one more time. No
dilation. His leg had twitched against the rolling of the boat a moment
before, so I was halfway sure the sailor wasn't about to slip into a coma.
But there was no way to know how much blood he might be losing inside.

Small blessing that he was out cold. The boat's rocking was almost painful even without a knife wound in your gut.

"Five minutes," Hollis said. "Then we should be 'round the point and out of the worst of this."

"What about the doctor?" I said, leaving Jaak and climbing the step to join Hollis at the wheel. He held his balance against the ship's motion as if the seas were as smooth as glass. "Can he meet us at the boat?"

"She," Hollis corrected. "Claybeck's a woman. I've been trying to reach her. No cell signal way out here but I've tried her on the satellite phone, and still nothing."

"But she knows we're coming."

"She knows I might turn up with a patient."

"Christ, Hollis."

"Options were limited, lad. I called Dr. Claybeck straightaway once I found Jaak. She told me she'd be at her house after nightfall. But with the storm and Jaak passed out, I had nearly resigned myself to calling an ambulance and giving them some half-assed story about finding him unconscious at the marina."

And then I showed up and Hollis decided to gamble on Claybeck being home. God help the sailor if we crossed the Sound in a storm only to find an empty house.

"What's your business with a freighter from Helsinki?" I said.

"You'll laugh. Video game controllers. A new model, with built-in memory and some sort of kinetic whatsit for the player's movements. People will spend thousands on the latest generation to get the edge on their competition. What do they call it?"

"E-sports."

"Right. South Korea's crazy for those. An acquaintance of mine in Vantaa found a couple of dozen extra controllers lying about their R&D department and got them to Jaak, who was going to show me a sample today. If all looked proper, I'd buy the rest tomorrow. But then—" He shrugged and glanced toward the cabin where the unconscious sailor was secured to his blood-dappled settee. "Fate had other plans."

I looked at the indistinct shape of Vashon Island, off our starboard.

The scattering of lights onshore helped differentiate the black of the land-mass from the dark sea below and clouded sky above. We hadn't rounded the point yet, but already the waves rolling the *Francesca* were decreasing in size.

"Doc Claybeck's home is just four miles along," Hollis said, reaching for the satellite phone he'd tucked into the chart holder. He let the phone ring as he nudged the throttle forward. The *Francesca* responded as if she'd been waiting for the moment, her bow lifting to keep pace with the rapid current. No one answered the call. I went below to ready Jaak to move.

I guessed the sailor's weight at about two hundred and fifty pounds. I could conceivably get him off the boat and into Claybeck's place, but only by lifting his substantial bulk in a fireman's carry over my shoulders. That would put a lot of pressure on his gut, which sounded like a bad idea. Hollis and I would have to try hauling Jaak using a blanket. I went below to the *Francesca*'s staterooms and found a duvet that looked thick enough to handle the load without tearing.

By the time I'd readied the makeshift stretcher, Hollis was easing back on the *Francesca*'s speed and turning us sharply toward shore. Through the windshield I could see a stubby dock outlined by footlights every few feet along its length. Beyond the dock, a broad house stood at the top of a rise. A lamp glowed from behind one long picture window. The rest of the house was dark.

"Not promising," I said, loudly enough for Hollis to hear me.

"But the dock lights are on." I could imagine Hollis gesticulating encouragingly. "Tie us off and I'll try calling the doctor one more time."

I stepped out the aft door into the driving rain—the island did nothing to block that—and made my way carefully along the narrow side deck to kick the fenders to hang over the rail before picking up the coiled and sopping bowline. As Hollis brought the *Francesca* alongside the dock, I jumped down and wrapped the line around the nearest cleat. A surge shoved the ten-ton boat into the floating dock, crushing the fenders between nearly flat. The planks groaned with the pressure. I hurried to tie off the stern. My head was already soaked, hood or no.

"Anything?" I called to Hollis. He began to shout a reply from up on the bridge, but my attention was distracted by movement from the rise leading to the house.

Dogs. Large dogs, running at top speed. Running at me. Their claws made hasty scrabbling clicks on the first wooden planks of the short dock as they lunged, fangs bared.

FIVE

I MOVED AS QUICKLY AS I ever had in my life, jumping high to catch hold of the *Francesca*'s deck rail and vaulting in a single motion onto the boat. Without pausing I reached up to grab the chrome handrail on the side of the flybridge above me and practically ran vertically up the cabin windows, hooking a foot on the handrail and hauling myself upward.

Below me, the dogs jumped to snap menacingly at the air and ran in circles on the dock. The side deck of the *Francesca* was only a foot wide—too narrow for the beasts to leap aboard easily, but their jaws could reach just fine. Every jump brought them close enough for me to count their teeth. They looked like some sort of shepherd or Malinois mix, big-chested with pointed ears and tawny fur and black faces. Big enough to tear off a man's limb if they wanted to. They wanted to. They didn't bark but instead whined with spine-chilling eagerness.

I was perched in a crouch with my feet on the slick metal handrail and my arms holding on to the side of the boat for dear life. Like a treed cat. Me on the outside of the flybridge, Hollis gaping at me from the other side of the polyurethane window.

"Van?" he said.

"You might have mentioned the damn dogs," I shouted.

"I didn't know," Hollis said. "They weren't around the only other time I've been here."

I risked standing up on the slippery handrail to climb to the aft of the boat for a better grip. I was stuck between the dogs and the pouring rain, but at least I wasn't in danger of falling to the dock. My escape seemed to urge the hounds into trying to leap aboard, their claws scraping the fiberglass hull with every attempt.

"I've got an air horn," said Hollis. "And a gun, if we need it. But—"

"We're not shooting the dogs. Any other ideas?"

My phone rang. I wasn't in a position to reach for it.

"Look there." Hollis pointed.

Another light had appeared up at Dr. Claybeck's house. The right size and shape for an open door, down at ground level.

The dogs stopped jumping. In another instant, they were running as fast as they had come, up the dock and the short hill and presumably into the house. The rectangular light went out. I hadn't heard a whistle or any other signal.

After a moment I climbed down to the side deck. Hollis met me outside. We both kept a wary eye on where the dogs had gone.

"The doctor must have called them off," he said, turning to put the satellite phone to his ear. "Maybe I can reach her."

"No need." I nodded toward the house. In the dim, a distant figure of a tall person in pale clothes stood out like a phantom. The figure raised one arm and held it aloft.

"That her?" I said.

"Let's say yes," said Hollis. "Jaak can't wait forever."

We lifted the unconscious sailor onto the duvet and wrapped him like a tamale. Only his face showed from the folds. With Hollis taking his legs and me at his head, we carried Jaak aft—both of us grunting with effort—and down onto the swim platform, from where we could step to the dock and begin making our slow way toward the house. The pale figure stayed where it was. No sign of the dogs. My forearms ached with the effort of gripping the duvet.

Flagstones in the lawn helped us climb the hill to the house. Hollis's breath was coming short and fast.

"We can rest if you want," he said. Then another two gasps later: "Better than dropping him."

I nodded and we set Jaak down gently on the soaked grass. We were close enough now for me to be sure the figure in the cream-colored rain jacket was a woman. Hollis waved exhaustedly to her. In her middle years and over six feet tall, she had curls that might be ash-blond under the jacket's ivory hood. She hovered outside the closed door, barely shielded from the weather by a stunted overhang.

"Doctor," Hollis managed.

"You shouldn't have come," the woman said. "Take him to a hospital."

"We're here now," Hollis said. Rain dappled Jaak's slack face. "At least have a look—"

"He's not my concern. Leave." Claybeck held herself stiff upright, as if guarding against the cold and the occasional gust that splashed water over her boots.

"Why tell us now?" I said. "Hollis has been trying to call you for hours."

"I'll let the dogs loose again."

"He could die before we reach the mainland. If we go back to the boat, it'll be to call nine-one-one. You're in this now. Help him."

Before she could answer, the door swung open behind her. A slim man with a thigh-length tan leather coat and a hard expression on his darker face appeared from one side of the doorway. He pointed the blunt barrel of a machine pistol at me. Hollis stepped back reflexively.

For an instant, nobody moved. I watched the gun, anticipating the minute flex of the man's trigger finger that would send half a dozen rounds tearing through my center mass.

A young woman stepped past the gunman, blocking his field of fire. Her platinum hair had been highlighted with blue tips that brushed the shoulders of her trench coat. She took in the sodden sight of us for a moment before nodding assent to some private decision.

"I have a better idea," she said. "Come in out of the rain."

SIX

THEY MADE US LEAVE JAAK on the wet lawn while the glowering man patted Hollis and me down. His leather coat had a band collar and only buttoned partway down his chest, as much poncho as jacket. I guessed him to be Indian or Pakistani, or some nation close to those borders. He removed my wallet and multitool and even the change from my pockets. Then he knelt to check Jaak himself.

When they were satisfied, the white woman with the bicolor dye job ordered us to carry Jaak into the house. Dr. Claybeck remained at a distance, observing our progress without comment.

We hefted Jaak's limp form through a mudroom lined with cedar planks and into a finished basement, though unlike any basement I'd ever seen before.

The square room had been outfitted like a very small but completely modern emergency care clinic. Two hospital beds and one steel-topped surface that might serve as an operating table took center stage. A rack on one wall held equipment like defibrillators and vital-signs monitors that I recognized, and a lot more that I didn't. Cabinets and refrigerators completely covered the far side of the room. Each shelf was fully stocked with a pharmacy's worth of pill bottles, surgical tools, and other supplies.

One of the beds was occupied. A man, fully clothed in an expensive-looking metallic gray suit and fawn shirt, and a ventilator mask covering most of his face. Elastic bands around his forehead and neck held the clear plastic wedge in place. Tubes connecting the mask's valve to the ventilator flexed and shuddered minutely with every breath. A sweep of brown hair started high on his scalp and reached down to his shoulders. His eyes were closed.

"Set him on the table," Dr. Claybeck said to us. It was her first utterance since the blonde and the gunman had appeared. Hollis and I made one last heave to set Jaak carefully on the steel surface.

"Leave him." The blonde strode across to grab Claybeck's arm. "See to Bilal."

"Bilal is stable—" the doctor protested, as the blonde shoved her toward the man in the ventilator mask.

"Then keep him that way."

Claybeck looked on the verge of spitting right back. She didn't give the impression of a woman who would be pushed around, literally or otherwise. But she made work for herself by checking the ventilator machine.

"What the hell's going on, Paula?" Hollis said. "Setting your animals on us and now this?"

"I'm sorry." Claybeck spared a glance for him. "Saleem and Aura let my dogs loose to try and force you to leave." She indicated the man with the machine gun and the blonde. "I convinced them that unless I turned you away directly, you'd keep trying. I underestimated your stubbornness."

"Sorry we didn't take the hint," Hollis growled at the blonde, Aura. "This is madness. Why not tend to both of them?"

Because there was no point, I had realized. Whoever the man called Bilal was, his presence here was meant to be kept secret. Now that we had seen him, Saleem and Aura might have no intention of letting us leave.

The man called Bilal opened his eyes. Wide eyes, very dark and completely alert. The mask and tubes gave the impression of a large translucent snake against his face. It was unclear who was eating whom.

He motioned to the mask, and Aura began to remove it.

"He needs that," Claybeck said. They ignored her.

Saleem motioned toward the opposite side of the room with his gun. "There. Sit down there," he said in a heavy South Asian accent.

Hollis and I sat on stools against the wall. The stools weren't metal, like the table, but they were solid enough chunks of wood. Aura seemed distracted with Bilal. If Saleem came close, I would have a fair chance of putting his lights out with the stool and taking his gun before Aura could effectively retaliate.

Except Saleem was a watchful fucker. He kept his distance from Hollis and me. His Steyr machine pistol was more than capable of cutting us both in two from across the room.

Aura helped Bilal prop himself up on one elbow. His bronze face was long and square and creased with temporary furrows left by the mask and permanent ones that spoke of heavy concerns. He took a long breath, maybe testing his lungs. I guessed Bilal's age at late forties. His brown mane showed no gray. Maybe he went to the same salon as his girlfriend, who must be twenty years younger.

"Your names, please?" Bilal said to Hollis and me. His voice was deep and casual, with the same accent as Saleem's, though not nearly as pronounced.

Saleem answered for us. "The old man is Hollis Brant, who the doctor told us about. The big one with the marks is Donovan Shaw." He stepped forward to offer Bilal my driver's license. The picture on the license didn't show my marks—the scars that divided my left cheek into three distinct sections, and the smaller ones that bisected my eyebrow and creased my jaw on that same side—as starkly as real life.

Bilal tapped the license with a blunt finger.

"Donovan Shaw," he said. He met my gaze. "Perhaps you shorten that? To Van?"

An answer wasn't required. Bilal knew me, or at least recognized my name. Which was unsettling, since I'd never seen the man before.

Bilal nodded to the unconscious Jaak. "Who is the man on the table?"

"Only a merchant sailor," Hollis said, doing enough nervous fidgeting for both of us.

"And if he dies? What is that to you?" Bilal sat up, swinging his feet to touch each woven leather shoe gingerly to the tile floor. Aura stood prepared to catch him if he tottered.

Hollis grunted. "He's a friend."

Bilal stood up with almost exaggerated slowness and buttoned his suit jacket. "You go to considerable risk for your friend. Sailing through storms. Friendship is important to you. Correct?"

"Yes," said Hollis. He glanced at me, maybe feeling the same apprehension I had about the direction of Bilal's questioning.

"Good. Friends are very useful. I would like to be your friend. Yours and Mr. Shaw's."

"Let the doctor look after our guy," I said, "and I'll buy the first fucking round."

Saleem spat a threat. No translation required.

"Everyone may leave the doctor's home healthy tonight," said Bilal, as if neither of us had spoken.

"In exchange for what?" I said.

"Two necessities. One is that you will not mention our meeting here. To anyone, in any capacity. You have never heard of my name."

"I'd be happy to forget the whole damned night," Hollis said, "you especially."

Bilal looked at me. I nodded agreement. He murmured something to Aura, who walked out of the room. Her steps retreated swiftly up a flight of stairs.

"My second condition is a transaction," Bilal continued. "The doctor is in my employ tonight. Exclusively. I've paid well for this. If she saves your sailor friend, then it stands to reason I should be recompensed for her time and effort."

"How much do you want?" Hollis said.

"Not money," I answered for Bilal, who was looking at me with the same focused expression as when he'd clicked on my name.

"Not money," he agreed. "I have a task for you, Mr. Van Shaw. For this service, all three of you will have your lives. A good exchange, I think. Until then—"

Aura's quick steps tapped back down the stairs and into the room. She carried a computer sleeve under one arm. Saleem crossed to hand her my cell phone. Aura removed a tablet from the sleeve and plugged my phone into it with connecting cables. Her face showed absolute concentration, as if we'd all gone for a walk in the storm and left her alone to work. It was a face I might have found cute in different circumstances, heart-shaped and with a snub of a nose between blue eyes that matched Bilal's for size. But the circumstances did a lot to ugly her up.

After a minute she handed the tablet to Bilal and pointed to the screen. "They're the primaries."

Bilal nodded as he read. "Addy Proctor. Cyndra O'Hasson. And"—he looked up at Hollis—"Mr. Brant."

My scalp felt like worms were crawling over it. Saleem noticed and smirked.

"These are the people with whom you are most in contact," Bilal continued. "People you care about. I could list more."

"You've made your point. Here's mine: If you touch them, you're dead." I glanced at Saleem. "I'll go through this one and anyone else like fucking butter to get to you."

"You misunderstand. I do not need to touch them. This"—he tapped the tablet—"is a toy. Useful, but not the extent of my capabilities."

Aura had glowered slightly when Bilal dismissed the tablet. Had it been her work?

He continued to scroll down the screen. "You have biometric sign-in for your bank account. Foolish. Though perhaps not so big a fool. You have a surprising amount of money for someone employed at a tavern, Mr. Shaw."

Bilal said it like a shared joke, like we both already knew the punchline. Damn.

"I can harm your friends without resorting to violence," Bilal continued. "Without even being in the country. Without even being *alive*, Mr. Shaw. My team could carry on ably, should anything happen to me. Debit accounts. Retirement savings. Legal status. Even medical records. Imagine Mrs. Proctor going to her doctor and being prescribed the wrong medicine. Or incriminating texts from Miss Cyndra appearing on the phone of someone arrested for selling drugs. These are simple things. It can get much worse."

I stayed silent. I didn't trust myself not to snarl like one of Claybeck's attack dogs.

"Good," said Bilal. "You understand."

He extended a hand and Saleem passed him a cell phone. Bilal held it out to me.

"You will keep this close. It must be answered when I call."

"What's the job?" I said.

"I will tell you the particulars when time allows. Soon."

I still didn't move to take the phone. To the left of us, Saleem stiffened. Aura shifted into view on Bilal's other side, the pistol back in her hand.

"Van," Hollis urged.

"If I don't like the job, I won't do it," I said to Bilal.

"Then we will renegotiate," he said, as if he'd expected that very answer. He looked pointedly at Hollis. "I'm certain we can agree on terms."

"Mr. Nath," Dr. Claybeck said, one hand on the wheeled cart of instruments. "The patient."

"Of course. See to him."

The doctor checked Jaak's breathing and pulse, then took scissors from her cart to begin cutting his bandage away. Bilal and the others moved to the door. He motioned for Aura to go ahead of him and then paused in the doorway. Saleem tossed the items he'd taken from us on the spare patient bed.

"You cannot clap with one hand. Do you know this expression?" Bilal said. "It means out of assistance comes great things. We are associates now. We cooperate."

Or else, I thought.

The gunman, Saleem, took the rear, his eyes on us until his boss reached the top of the stairs. Then he, too, was gone.

SEVEN

HOLLIS AND I GATHERED OUR possessions and joined Claybeck at the steel table.

"Who the hell was that bastard?" Hollis said to her.

"Priorities." Claybeck had donned gloves and a surgical apron. She peeled away the tape and gauze that had held Jaak's wound closed over the massed wad of sponge pieces. "What happened?"

"His name's Jaak," said Hollis. "He passed out shortly after I found him, stabbed. Almost four hours now."

"My work," I said, indicating the bandage. "I'd guess Jaak had lost at least a pint of blood by then. Maybe more inside him."

She frowned as she began to pick out the crimson-soaked bits of sponge with tweezers, dropping each one to the floor. "Military, I suppose."

"How's his blood pressure?"

"Still there. Now leave, please. Wait upstairs." The doctor's voice cracked slightly, but her hands moved without pause.

We followed the same path that Bilal and his soldiers had taken. The stairs led to a living area so long it was practically a meeting hall. The picture windows we'd seen from the dock offered a view of the Sound and the distant lights of Dash Point on the mainland, all blurred by rain washing over the glass with every gust of wind. Crepe paper streamers adorned the room in preparation for what might be an early New Year's party, if that year was 1963. Every low-slung chair and walnut credenza screamed Camelot. Only the computer monitor sitting on an elegantly curved desk in the corner fit this century.

"A time capsule," Hollis said, delighted by the display in spite of what we'd just been through.

A whine and fervent scratching from the opposite side of a nearby door revealed where Claybeck's dogs had gone. We beat a fast retreat to the farthest end of the living room. Hollis headed for the loaded bar cart and clanged through the bottles to see what was on hand. The cart was identical to the one downstairs with the surgical tools. I looked out the window at the evergreens. Their top reaches lashed to and fro like bullwhips. The cell phone Bilal had given me made a heavy lump in my pocket.

"Your choice of health care sucks, Hollis," I said.

"Don't you think if I'd known—" Hollis started. "Never mind. I'm sorry. Let's have a drink and start the fucking healing process."

He poured two generous quantities of a brown liquor and brought them over to sit on the seafoam-blue couch. After a moment I took the matching chair and accepted the glass from him. We drank. Rye, smooth enough to soothe a consumptive's cough.

"This isn't her fault," Hollis said after a few moments. "Doc Claybeck. She's trapped."

"Trapped by what?"

"By who. The doctor had—still has, my mistake—a daughter. That poor girl was born with a devil's truckload of what we used to call birth defects. I don't know what the kinder term is now, but whatever you choose to say, the child is afflicted, even though she's long since grown. Vision and hearing troubles, mental and sometimes emotional troubles, too, since her brain stopped developing after a point. She needed a lot of care. More than the doctor and her eventual ex-husband could pay for."

"So Claybeck borrowed."

"After a fashion. Paula Claybeck had an acquaintance from Seattle's social elite. This person offered to hire the doctor at an exorbitant salary to be on call as a private physician. For whomever the acquaintance chose."

"For people like Bilal. Get there quicker, Hollis; I don't need a damn yarn right now. What are you not telling me?"

"Fine, fine. Doc Claybeck's benefactor"—Hollis layered some uncharacteristic venom into the word—"is Ondine Long."

I stared at him.

"Exactly." Hollis nodded. "Once in, Paula was in all the way."

Ondine Long was a broker. A facilitator. She might not deal directly in drugs or gambling or flesh or set up scores herself, but she knew who could and would make the introductions for a percentage. Her connections reached from corner boys to the legislature. She donated generously to symphonies and charities and the right politicians. A spider, if the spider never had to leave the center of her lavish web to feast on a morsel from every insect that happened along.

Ondine and I had crossed paths before. After the dust had settled, we had both tacitly agreed to give one another a wide berth.

"How are you in the know on Claybeck's story?" I asked.

"All that medical equipment you saw downstairs? I was the one Ondine tasked with obtaining it for Paula. Best if the AMA didn't start asking why a surgeon would be outfitting her home like a trauma center."

I had to chuckle. "And you held on to Claybeck's number."

"Who knows when a man might need a physician? Besides." Hollis looked a little sheepish. "She's a handsome woman. Though I never did call her, until tonight."

"Hell of a first date, Hollis."

He sighed. "At least Bilal is gone. Do you think he can do what he claims? Empty everyone's bank account and all that cyber witchery?"

I wasn't certain. Bilal's trick of phone hacking had been impressive. He might have made an educated guess at my net worth from text notifications of past deposits still in my history. The rest of his assertions sounded a few ticks above knocking down the privacy barriers on a cell phone. But his knowing everyone in my contact list was enough to me to take Bilal at face value.

The doctor had spoken his last name: Nath. A place to start. I'd have to learn everything I could about the man and find something that would allow my own brand of renegotiation.

We turned at the sound of Dr. Claybeck coming up the stairs. She had taken off the apron and was wiping her hands on a paper towel.

"Jaak was very fortunate," she said before she reached the top step. "No penetration of the organs that I can determine. But it's a serious puncture. Something thicker than the average pocketknife. Do you know what it was?"

"No," said Hollis. "Some of the sailors carry fixed blades for their jobs. Those can be sturdy."

"I've sewn up his subcutaneous tissue and the surface laceration separately, with some staples, given how jagged the injury was. I've also typed him and given him a unit of blood. Plus antibiotics." She shook her head in judgment of my field care. "If anything kills him it will be the imminent infection. His vitals are good but we'll have to watch him through the night to make certain."

"We?" Hollis said. "I'm no medic."

"You can manage to work a blood pressure cuff," the doctor said, dry as parchment, "and check his pupils. I'm not confident that he doesn't have a concussion. It's disturbing that he's been unconscious most of the night. That's not normal, even for someone in shock from being stabbed."

"What's wrong with Bilal Nath?" I said.

Claybeck looked uncertain. "I can't—"

"I promised the fucker I would forget he was ever here. That includes forgetting you said anything about him. Why would he pay Ondine Long to see you?"

She glanced reprovingly at Hollis. He'd been indiscreet. "Nath has ALS."

"Lou Gehrig's disease."

Claybeck nodded. "He had an attack last night and couldn't breathe properly. And for whatever reason, he refused hospital care."

"Perhaps he doesn't want anyone knowing he's sick," Hollis mused.

"That's possible. Or he won't admit it to himself. He's on riluzole and other medications, but he's going to go downhill quickly without full treatment."

"How quickly?" I said.

The doctor raised an eyebrow at my tone. "Hoping your problem will solve itself?"

I grunted. "I won't be that lucky. Bilal has something specific in mind for me. He won't waste a second if he's going to die soon."

"The progression of ALS can vary hugely. Stephen Hawking lived for over fifty years after his diagnosis. But"—Claybeck shrugged—"most patients succumb within five. I believe Bilal was diagnosed at least three years ago, and his limbs are showing signs of recent atrophy. My best guess is that he has a year at most."

"So we all take a long vacation," Hollis said, trying to break the mood. "Maybe Jaak can arrange a sea voyage. Speaking of our friend . . ."

"I'll take first watch," I said.

"No," said Claybeck. "I won't be sleeping anytime soon. And I want to stay close to the patient for another couple of hours in case he needs another unit of blood."

I wasn't so sure sleep was in the cards for me, either. But after the doctor led us past the door with her ravenous dogs and down the hall to the house's spare rooms, I lay down on one of the beds and closed my eyes. An old habit from the Rangers: Rest whenever you can, because the next opportunity might be a long time coming.

EIGHT

D R. CLAYBECK SHOOK ME AWAKE. Her face so slack with fatigue I thought she might collapse onto the bed next to me.

"Jaak is stable," she said. "You shouldn't have to do more than check his pressure every hour. You know how?"

I did. The doctor left immediately for her own room, her dogs padding after her. I washed my face in the guest bathroom sink and headed downstairs.

Jaak looked about the same as when I'd last seen him, save for a much cleaner bandage strapped to his side. He was snoring lightly. I took that for a good thing.

My watch read five minutes past three in the morning. I checked my phone and remembered that it had rung earlier in the night, during all the chaos. Stasia Llewellyn-Wiler, from Philadelphia. Moira's school friend had left a brief voice mail saying she was happy I'd gotten in touch and that she'd try me again tomorrow. Which was today. I texted to let her know I was awake on the West Coast.

The other cell phone, the one Bilal had given me, felt hot in my chest pocket. Right over my heart.

Goddamn it. A day ago I had my life in order. A tenuous state, but at least I was putting the recent past behind me. Now I was keeping watch on one of Hollis's smuggling cronies and owed a favor to some gangster connected to Ondine Long, of all people. What the fuck was I doing wrong?

Maybe it was karma. My ex, Luce, for all her pragmatism, had liked the idea of karmic balance. Do some good, and trust in the ripple effect to benefit you and yours somehow. I didn't believe justice worked so efficiently.

I didn't believe in ghosts, either. But somehow the men I'd killed in Oregon managed to haunt me, at least a little.

My pocket buzzed. For an instant I thought it was Bilal, wasting no time in putting me to work. But the vibration came from the other pocket, and my own phone. Stasia, calling back right away.

"It's Van," I said. "Moira's son." Those last two words sounded very strange coming out of my mouth.

"Van, it's Stasia Wiler. This is amazing. Truly. It might sound very odd to you, but I've thought of you so many times over the past twenty years or so. Almost every time I remembered Moira. How are you? Or maybe *who are you* would be a better question, after so long."

"I'm good," I broke in. "I wanted to ask you some questions about Moira."

"Naturally. I could talk for an hour about she and I and barely scratch the surface. Wait—" Stasia interrupted herself. "All I can think about is how much you might look like her. Could we switch to video?"

Her call was already sending a request to activate my camera. Best that Stasia didn't see Dr. Claybeck's clinic and the sleeping trauma patient. "Give me a second," I said.

I'd spotted a set of baby monitors on the rack of medical equipment earlier in the night—an odd fit with the rest of the gear—and now I had an inkling of how Claybeck used them. I set the monitor next to the sleeping Jaak and brought the parent unit with me as I jogged back up to the cavernous living room to turn on the lights. If his snoring changed, I'd come running.

I accepted the video request. Stasia's face came into the frame. Lean and equine, with subtle makeup in place despite the early hour and auburn locks barely tamed with a large tortoiseshell clip. Her eyebrows popped into view over the lenses of her glasses.

"Oh, my God!" Stasia said. "You are very definitely Moira's boy. Your hair. And something in the mouth, too. Those are so her. Not your eyes. Hers were brown, too, but not nearly so dark . . ."

"The eyes skipped a generation."

"Her father, yes, yes. Donny? Is he still alive?"

"Dono. Donovan, I'm named for him. He died a couple of years ago."

Stasia rubbed her forehead with a fingertip. Behind her, I could make out a bookshelf loaded with thick three-ring binders and framed degrees on the wall next to family photos. A home office, maybe. "I'm very sorry." She sighed. "Man. Moira's dad. He was . . . an intimidating guy. Of all the ways Moira impressed me, the biggest might have been standing up to her father."

"When she became pregnant? I was also hoping you knew something about her boyfriend back then. Dono—and I—never found out who he was."

She laughed, a little shakily. "Well, nothing like starting a conversation with the easy topics. I don't know how much you know about Moira—"

"Just north of zip. Don't worry about offending me."

"Then I'll begin at the beginning. Moira and I met in middle school. She was very smart. We both liked to get good grades and had our hands raised in class constantly, even if the teachers called on the boys nine times out of ten." Stasia paused to reflect.

The storm outside had finally passed. A low cloud cover cast an ashen pall over the night sky.

"We were closest then," Stasia said. "High school sort of tugged us apart. Even though she'd already skipped a grade in elementary, Moira was enrolled in AP courses. And there were boys."

"She dated a lot?"

"Not her, me. I had the hormone crazies and didn't make as much time for Moira. We still saw each other, but . . ." Stasia made a face. "Between my having fun and her being such a private person, it wasn't the same. She sort of withdrew."

That was the Shaw way. Keep to yourself and guard your flank. My own circle of friends in school could have been counted on the tines of a pitchfork.

"Not your fault," I said. "Kids drift around."

"That's why it was so surprising when Moira asked if she could come stay with me and my family, just before our senior year. I was stunned. But happy she'd asked, even if I didn't really know why. All she would tell me was that she couldn't live at home anymore. That she and Dono were arguing all the time. She implied without actually lying to me that their fights were about whether Moira would go to college right away or take some time off."

"And you took her in." My glass of rye whiskey was still sitting on the coffee table, half full. I picked it up, less to drink than to feel its solidity.

"My parents were fine with Moira living with us for a while. She was still pulling all As and they considered her a good influence, you know? And they might have been nervous to talk to Dono about what was going on."

"I could see that."

"So we started school and came home each day and that was pretty much all for two weeks. Then I found Moira crying in the closet, not for the first time, and I told her I was going to go to the police unless she told me what was happening. That did it. She fessed up that she was four months pregnant. Of course I insisted that she tell me who the boy was, but no way. She hadn't even told Dono who he was. Hence her extended visit."

"Dono kicked her out." My fingers were tight around the whiskey glass. I made myself set it down.

"No. At least I don't think so. My guess is that their fights were about him pressuring Moira to give up the boy's name. She seemed scared of what Dono might do."

I could understand that, too. My grandfather was scary enough when he was calm.

"And she never hinted at who he was?" I said.

"No. Not for lack of my asking. But Moira wrote letters. I found her scribbling feverishly at my desk once, and she swept the letter into her backpack and made me promise that I'd never go hunting through her stuff. And I never did. She was so furious. I'd already seen the words at the top of the page but pretended I hadn't: '*Dear Sean. I'm sorry but I can't. If Dad ever asks you—*' That was all I caught."

Sean. My father's name was—might be—Sean.

Then the *other* critical point hit me.

"'*If Dad ever asks you*'?" I said. "So Dono knew this kid?"

"I suppose he must have. But that doesn't mean Dono ever realized Sean was dating Moira. I remember thinking about that and mentally going through every boy I had ever met, trying to recall one named Sean. I'd promised Moira I wouldn't look through her things, but not that I wouldn't try my best to figure out who her secret boyfriend was. It was pointless. Eventually I accepted that if I wanted to stay friends with Moira I had to let it drop."

Dono would have done the same, I realized. Considered every boy in Moira's life, trying to figure out who was to blame. Moira must have been damn good at keeping her life private.

"Moira stayed with us first semester," Stasia said. "She kept up with school, too, even though—people were cruel. Students and even some of the teachers. I don't know how she stood it. But the longer it went on, the tougher Moira seemed to get. She was so brave. I remember she was going to church every week. I suppose that helped her."

"Church?" I said. "Like, Catholic?"

"Yes. We were Presbyterian, so I don't know if we're talking about attending full Mass, or if Moira was just going to a cathedral to sit and contemplate. It was new for her. Discovering or rediscovering her faith. Did she take you to church as a boy?"

"I don't think so. At least I don't remember that." Dono had rejected religion early on, a collision of tough corporal schooling and his tougher defiance. I suppose Grandma Fi might have been closer to the church. And that Moira would have been christened or baptized or whatever it was when she was a baby.

Damn, maybe I had been, too.

"Wait, you said Moira stayed with you first semester?" I said. "Where was she after that?"

"Her own place. Before Christmas, when she was just a few weeks away from popping, Moira told my parents and me that she'd be getting an apartment starting in January. We thought that was crazy. She was still sixteen. How could she live alone? How could she pay for it? But there it was."

"It must have been Dono's doing. A compromise, if Moira wouldn't return to their house on Roy Street."

"You're probably right. I couldn't change her mind about moving out. Moira's apartment was only a few blocks away from school. I visited her at least once every week through the rest of the year. Partly to see the baby—you—but also to study. It wasn't completely selfless: I brought her homework when she had to skip, and Moira got me through Physics." Stasia shook her head. "She was so proud of you. Babies don't do much during their first months, but man, she talked to you like you could understand every word. You'd babble back and she'd pretend you were interrogating her like on a cop show. I would fall over laughing. She could be very funny, Moira. Very wry."

More droll than Stasia knew. Dono had played a game like that with me, too, one where he was the cop and I had to avoid being trapped by questions. It had been good practice. Had he taught Moira the same lessons?

"What about other friends?" I hoped my mother had another confidante, anyone she might have talked to about Sean.

"If there was anyone, I never met them. I'm sorry."

"And Sean never came around."

"No. I don't think he did. Perhaps Moira thought she was better off without him."

Perhaps. Dono knew Sean: my thoughts kept circling back to that. Most of the people Dono had known were not straight citizens.

Stasia asked me what I'd been doing with myself since I'd learned to walk. I gave her a sanitized version of my life, as quickly as politeness allowed, and turned the conversation back to my mother.

"After graduation things trailed off," Stasia explained. "I headed to college at Penn. I know Moira was aiming for college herself when you were a little older, but I don't recall her ever taking any classes." Her voice trailed off.

"Before she died," I finished for her.

"When I heard, I was so upset. I called around and someone told me Dono had taken you in, so I assumed that Moira and Dono had healed their relationship."

No way to ask either of them now.

"Oh, wait," Stasia said quickly. "You'll want to see this." She left the frame for a moment. "Here. From our junior year, before all the trouble started."

She held up an open book to the camera lens. A yearbook, the head-shots of the students in black and white. It took some trial and error for Stasia to position the heavy book so that I had a clear view of the second row, last picture.

Moira Shaw.

Dono hadn't kept family photos. I was seeing my mother's face for the first time all over again. She was fifteen years old, and a stranger to me.

Except. The black hair and the cheekbones and just the way she was smiling at the camera, with a hint of *can-you-believe-we're-doing-this* in her tilted eyebrow, rang as true as a sledgehammer on a gong. Embarrassed and awkward and beautiful in spite of and because of all those things.

"I'll take a picture and send it to you," Stasia was saying, "and if I find any others—"

"Thanks," I said, my voice thick. And then again: "Thanks."

"You never got to know her." Stasia caught a tear as it rolled from under her glasses. "You should have."

I coughed to clear my throat. Stasia Llewellyn-Wiler and I both took a moment.

Stasia wished me a happy new year. I returned the sentiment. We ended the call. I picked up the glass of whiskey and downed its contents without tasting a drop.

My mother. Barely half the age I was now, with an infant son, living on her own and finishing high school. Whatever trials I'd conquered in my own personal life, they were vying for second place behind Moira's survival.

———————

"MIZ CULLEN?" I SAID.

She looked up from the stack of math assignments on her desk. "Hello, Van. Davey wasn't here today." Ms. Cullen was my best friend Davey's homeroom teacher. I had Mr. Rigby this year.

"No. I mean, I know. I wanted to—" I glanced outside at the hallway, making sure again that it was empty. "Um. You knew my mom? When she was here? Moira Shaw?"

Ms. Cullen blinked. "Moira?" She looked past me at the open door to the hallway herself. "Well, yes. Of course."

"And, did she—was she, like, good in school?"

Ms. Cullen looked at me for a moment, then motioned to the door. "Why don't you close that, Van? We can talk better."

I didn't really want to shut the door, though I wasn't sure why. Maybe because if it stayed open I could turn around and leave faster. But I closed it anyway and sat down in the first row where Ms. Cullen pointed.

"Your mom was a very good student," Ms. Cullen started. "She liked to read a lot. You read, too, don't you?"

I nodded. Granddad made me, keeping the TV off, but I probably would have read, anyway. We had a lot of books in the house.

"Well, Moira was especially good at book reports. She would tell the class about scenes she had read and get other children excited to read the same book. That was a real gift." Ms. Cullen took her glasses off, which made her squint a little. She opened her drawer to get a cloth and began cleaning the lenses. "Moira's father: Do you live with him now? I think I heard that."

"Uh huh."

"I see." She finished wiping the glasses and set the cloth down. She cleared her throat. "Do you and he ever talk about your mother? Or your grandmother?"

I shook my head.

"Can't pretend I'm surprised. I met your grandmother a few times, at parent-teacher conferences. She was—very smart. Very direct. She wanted to make sure Moira had everything she needed in school. She dressed very well. A lovely green linen dress one day. And she wore her hair up, with chopsticks for hairpins. It's very funny, what people remember after so long. Oh, Van." She *got up and took a Kleenex from the box on her desk and handed it to me. "Blow your nose, sweetie."*

I did, and I wiped my eyes on my wrist.

"It's okay, dear. Of course you want to know about Moira, and your grandma. Do you want to keep talking now?"

"No."

"That's all right. I'll see if I can remember more. It was—well, there have been a lot of students but I'm sure there's more in the back of my head. You come back when you're ready."

I nodded, already hurrying to get out.

"And Van? I won't mention this to your grandfather. Okay?"

I hadn't even thought *about Granddad. Man, if he learned what I was doing, I was toast.*

"Thanks," I managed. I opened the door and closed it tight behind me before I ran down the hall.

I STRODE DOWN THE HALL to Dr. Claybeck's second spare bedroom. Like the living area, it was of another age. Hollis made an unkempt lump under retro Mondrian sheets.

"Hollis," I said, clicking on the bedside lamp. The bulb glowed beneath a fabric lampshade patterned with starbursts. "Wake up."

"Whazzit? My turn?"

"No. Did Dono know anybody named Sean? Back when Moira was a teenager. A young guy, I'm guessing."

"Who's—wait. What are we talking about now?"

I forced myself to rewind and told Hollis about Moira's reunion letter, and my conversation with Stasia. The room smelled of Lemon Pledge and faintly of Hollis himself. I must have needed a shower just as much.

When I finished, he was sitting upright, his eyes wide.

"Jesus God. You think this lad could be—"

"Sean," I pressed. "Did Dono know someone named that?"

"Your man didn't socialize much. You know as well as I do. Much less with young people. Most of the men he met were in our line of work, one way or another."

"So what jobs was Dono pulling that spring? Was he into house scores? Smuggling anything with you?"

"Easy now, I'm thinking." He leaned back against the robin's-egg headboard and scratched his tousled head. "That was during one of the big tech booms. I remember Dono stole a truckload of stuff from Microsoft right off the loading dock. Housing prices going up, lots of expensive development materials. And new players in town . . . Oh."

"Hollis."

"Give me a moment. Fats. No. Gut."

"Gut?"

"Gut Burke. He was a fat man, hence the nickname, though I don't know if anyone dared call him that to his face. Fergus Burke, or Gus or Gut. A very bad sort. He had been some kind of muscle for one of the families. I think he was new in Seattle, from back east."

"And Dono worked with him?"

My grandfather had kept himself at a long distance from organized crime, as a rule. It was the main reason he and Grandma Fi had left Boston for Seattle in the first place. The East Coast was too mobbed up for an independent operator like Dono.

"Or Gut Burke was buying something. Don't recall exactly what that might have been. The point is, Burke had brought his son with him. A teenager. I can't swear to it, but the boy might have been named Sean."

"You're not sure."

"It was thirty years ago, Van. And your grandfather told me all of this secondhand. But Moira was around. Burke and his lad came to the house unexpectedly, which pissed your grandfather off to no end, let me tell you. He never liked conducting business with family nearby. If he hadn't been so royally furious and ranted to high heaven about it, I might not have remembered the incident at all."

"So they met: Moira and Sean. If it was Sean."

"They must have. Dono and I talked about the strangeness of Gut Burke taking his son along on the errand. Learning on the job."

Just like I had with Dono. I wondered what sort of skills Sean had perfected as Gut Burke's apprentice.

"You've got a contact in the FBI field office downtown, right?"

"Yes." Hollis's voice was cautious.

"I want to meet him. After he's pulled everything he can find on Gut Burke and his son. And," I amended, "on Bilal Nath and his soldiers, too. Might as well get all of my shopping done at once."

"Van, that's not—I've been a long time earning my man's trust. He's a jumpy fellow. He can't just type in names and have NCIC spit information out without people noticing. They track these things. You're asking a lot."

"Less than a sharp poke." I nodded toward the stairs leading down to the clinic.

Hollis flushed. "I suppose I do owe you for tonight. It's Monday. I might be able to reach him this morning."

"Call him now. I'll make it worth his while if he comes through. A bonus if it's fast." I had come into a lot of money early in the year, through circumstances that required me to spend the cash quietly. I still had some of that slush fund left for emergencies. And this had been one rainy goddamn day.

Hollis got up to put his pants and sweater on over his sleeping attire of boxers and undershirt. I idled impatiently in the hall.

"Did you sleep?" he said.

"Some."

"I imagine . . . since you came back, that hasn't come easy."

My pacing stopped. "What do you mean?"

He hitched up his trousers, a kind of embarrassed shrug. "You've told me your combat experiences gave you nightmares for a long while." Hollis glanced down the hall and lowered his voice another notch. "After what happened with those maniacs in Oregon, it stands to reason you'd have some trouble putting that aside. In your dreams, I mean."

I looked at him, understanding. That *would* be the normal response. It just hadn't been mine.

"My dreams aren't troubling me, Hollis," I said. "The thing that troubles me is that I haven't been dreaming at all. Not since I came back. I killed those men and I've been sleeping like a baby ever since."

I couldn't put an exact name to Hollis's reaction, but the closest expression might have been wariness. Like realizing the docile neighborhood mongrel was showing flecks of foam around its jaws today.

NINE

JAAK REGAINED CONSCIOUSNESS SHORTLY AFTER dawn. I roused Hollis and
Dr. Claybeck. The sailor's English was limited but serviceable, which
was a grace as none of us knew any Finnish and Hollis only a few phrases
of Swedish, most of them dealing with the possibility of being arrested
and protesting innocence. But we all collaborated to piece together the
story of what had happened to Jaak the evening before.

He had been preparing to sneak off the *Stellar Jewel* to meet Hollis
when a ship's petty officer named Kauko had caught him. Instead of turning Jaak in, Kauko had offered a deal. Kauko had been planning to take
one of the freighter's launches to pick up other sailors north of where the
Jewel was docked on Harbor Island. He offered to hide Jaak in the launch
and ferry him to meet Hollis. In return, Jaak would share the profit from
the deal. Trapped, Jaak couldn't refuse.

Things had taken a turn. During the ride on the launch, Kauko had
pressed Jaak to share drinks from a flask. Jaak began to feel groggy. By
the time he realized he'd been drugged, it was too late. He had a rough
memory of staggering toward Kauko and the petty officer looking at him
in terror. Then nothing. Dr. Claybeck theorized that Kauko had doped
Jaak with Rohypnol or some similar benzo compound.

Kauko's motives were less clear to all of us. Jaak told us that Kauko had stolen his entry visa. Perhaps that had been his intent all along, to filch the document to make his way onshore and maybe use Jaak's name to start a life in America. But when the roofie hadn't knocked the large Jaak out quickly, Kauko had panicked and stabbed him in self-defense. Thinking his shipmate dead and himself a murderer, the petty officer had bolted.

Claybeck okayed Jaak to be moved, and Hollis agreed to take the sailor back to his freighter. If Kauko had returned to the *Stellar Jewel*, Jaak would confront him and take whatever punishment came for leaving the ship.

"What do we owe you?" Hollis asked Claybeck.

"Peace and quiet," she said. After her short sleep the doctor looked slightly refreshed, if just as aloof. Only Jaak received any hint of warmth. "Make sure your ship's doctor takes you to a hospital," she reminded him.

We left. I risked Claybeck's ire to leave my number and asked her to get in touch if she heard from Bilal again. She didn't refuse outright, which was as much as I could hope.

A rippling chop greeted us on the Sound, but compared to the previous night, the *Francesca* barely felt the waves. Hollis dropped me off at a marina in West Seattle. After dozing through a Lyft ride, I was back in my own car and headed for home. I needed rest and food before I met with Hollis's FBI contact later in the day.

And, I decided, I needed to talk to someone who could tell me if I was insane for even considering digging up family secrets. For wanting to know who my father was, if the son of a bitch had abandoned Moira and me thirty years ago.

"YOUR *FATHER*?" ADDY SAID. THE pan she was removing from under the oven clanged against its drawer. "That's tremendous!"

"Keep it down," I said. A glance into the living room confirmed that Cyndra was still engrossed in a *Fortnite* mission with other gamers around the world, her over-ear headphones in place. Addy's excitement was enough; I didn't need Cyn getting overstimulated, too. She'd think the whole situation was romantic. The long-lost family, reunited. "I don't know if Sean Burke is my father. Just that he might have known my mother."

"How could you not have mentioned this before? That you were tracing your roots?"

"I've barely started. And if Burke isn't the guy, I might be finished just as fast." I wasn't even positive yet that Gut Burke's son and Moira's Sean were one and the same.

"Don't downplay this. You might actually find a blood relative. Someone other than your grandfather, for the first time since you were small. It's huge."

I went back to dicing potatoes. When I'd first met Addy, her antique set of Henckels kitchen knives had been so dull they were more useful as bookmarks than cutting tools. Addy was a good cook but terrible at maintaining things around the house. I had borrowed a manual sharpener from Luce's bar to hone the blunted edges of the knives and bought Addy a sharpening steel to use regularly. She never touched it, but the steel was there when I visited.

"What are you going to say to him?" Addy said as she plopped a roast into the pan. The three of us were having a pre–New Year's Eve dinner together, since she and Cyn would be joining one of Addy's coterie for the holiday itself.

"That's the big question," I said. " '*Hey, did you knock up Moira Shaw when she was statutory?*' "

"They were children. Teens make mistakes."

"A mistake Sean Burke had years to make up for."

"How do you know he didn't try? The only way to find out is to talk to the man. I'm sure you've already searched online."

I had. There was no shortage of Sean Burkes in the world, and a handful on the West Coast who might be the right age. But the field would narrow once I learned more about Fergus Burke. Gut's only online presence was a two-line notice of a conviction in Everett for DUI and solicitation, almost twenty years ago. A great anecdote to tell about my possible paternal grandfather.

"It's only a big deal if I let it be," I said.

A deal I would be smart to postpone. My shadowy bloodline wasn't important right now. Not with Bilal Nath holding me at his beck and call. That had to be my priority.

"Addy," I said, "how long are you and Cyndra staying with Dorothy?"

She paused in her grinding of peppercorns and rosemary. "Just sleeping over at her home after the ball drops, and then breakfast on New Year's Day."

"Could you extend it?"

"What's going on?"

"It would be better if you and Cyn were out of this house for a while." I took a breath. "Somebody with hostile intentions hacked my phone. There's no direct threat. But I'd feel better if you were harder to locate for a few days."

Addy set the mortar and pestle down. A small action, but Addy pausing her bustling flow sent as much signal as a shout. "Any threat feels direct enough, Van. If you don't see that, I don't know what I can do for you."

"I just want to take precautions."

"This is a caution. A *pre*-caution would be avoiding situations like this in the first place. And you seem incapable of doing that. No, don't say anything." She held up a hand. "I accept the part of you that's prone to trouble. You know that. You also know it's not me or you I'm concerned for."

"I do."

She looked toward the living room, and Cyndra. "I will ask Dorothy if we might stay a couple of days. It'll give us a chance to go through some donation ideas she's been on me about."

"Thanks."

"You'll recall I once did some volunteer work with addiction therapy. Friends and family support groups."

Surprised by what seemed like a swerve in topic, I blinked. "Yeah."

"Something we always taught: the first and primary reason that a family member should cut ties with a loved one is when safety is jeopardized," Addy said.

From the backyard, a crow cawed its harsh laughter.

"It's foolish of me to expect you to change," Addy continued. "But if your choices mean Cyndra is forced to live with any kind of fear, or risk to herself? That's an easy decision to travel a hard path, as my Magnus used to say. That girl has experienced enough trauma."

I nodded. What else was there to say? I would take that path, too, if I were in Addy's place.

TEN

RUNNING WITH ADDY'S DOG, STANLEY, was like being tethered to an enthusiastic horse. Not only did the huge mixed breed resemble an especially pale and muscular pony, but I was also very conscious that if Stanley suddenly chose to switch directions, there wasn't a hell of a lot I could do about it.

Fortunately, Stanley limited himself to occasional arm-yanking tugs at the leash as we jogged. He probably wondered why our pace was so leisurely. He knew I could run faster, even if it would never be as fast as he would prefer. But I didn't want to be early. So we had taken the long way from Addy's house, coasting down the steep slope of 24th Ave and winding around Interlaken, descending even farther to arrive at the edge of the arboretum, our breaths making steam-engine puffs in the late afternoon air. Traffic was light but rushed. I kept a watchful eye for cars slaloming through the boulevard as fast as the curves allowed.

In another five minutes we reached the Japanese garden. I bought a ticket and let Stanley investigate the lawn before we entered. Normally he'd mark his territory, but he'd depleted himself during the first mile of our run.

Inside, the garden was nearly empty. Just me and Stanley and a few families with young children. Hollis's friend from the FBI hadn't arrived yet.

Within a few months the garden would be a riot of colors and scents. I wasn't much on horticulture, but I remembered the vibrant pinks of the azalea bushes and an almost bittersweet lush smell of the cherry trees in full bloom from walks I'd taken as a kid, whenever the big house I shared with Dono became uncomfortably cramped. Now the garden looked subdued, patiently waiting for the celebration of spring to start.

A small boy, encased in a puffy coat and pompom hat, screwed up his courage to take two steps away from his parents and toward Stanley, who wagged his tail in greeting. I made him sit, and the boy reached out. Stanley landed a lick on his hand before the boy began scratching the dog's tea-saucer-sized ear. A blue Prius, so new it shone like a sapphire, pulled into the parking lot.

I led Stanley down the long path that looped around the narrow park. On the far side was an open-air shelter, overlooking the largest of the garden's ponds. I sat on one of its benches and waited. The owner of the Prius made his cautious way through the gate and eventually toward us.

Stanley huffed as the man drew nearer. I patted the dog's side and fished in the pockets of his harness for a bully stick. The harness held everything from waste bags to hand wipes. Stanley could have easily carried a cooler full of beer, too, but Addy drew the line at that. I gave the stick to Stanley. He seemed assuaged as he lay down and began to gnaw at the rawhide.

I removed a small receiver from the other side of his harness, switched it on, and put it in the pocket of my running jacket.

"What kind of dog is that?" the man said, stopping ten yards away. The comforting mass of a rhododendron still between us.

"Part mastiff, part Komodo dragon," I said.

The man nodded, not really listening, his head moving to and fro as he scanned the park. He was skinny enough to seem taller than he actually was, with old-fashioned glasses that reminded me of Scrooge counting pence.

"We're alone," I said. "Unless there's a police diver hiding in the koi pond."

He actually glanced at the surface of the water. His name was Panni. For the purposes of our meeting, I was told to call him Mark if I had to say his name out loud. Hollis had said Panni would be more comfortable if we used aliases, and I was trying to make friends here. Panni was probably only a year or two out of grad school, finding his criminology degree of limited use in a low-level position in the Records department of the FBI's Seattle branch office.

After another moment of reconnoitering the lily pads, Panni sat down on the bench beside me. While his jaw was so hairless that it might never have seen a razor, his embroidered skullcap bulged with long locks tucked beneath it.

"How do I know you're not wearing a wire?" he said.

"You can check if you want."

He thought about it. Maybe it had already occurred to him that if OPR, the Bureau's version of Internal Affairs, were on to him, they would have busted him the moment he tried to leave the field office with confidential files.

"Never mind," he said.

"And I'll trust you, too." The little receiver in my pocket hadn't emitted the buzz alerting me to any cellular or two-way signals within a dozen feet. Panni wasn't wired.

"I don't know why we couldn't go through our mutual friend," he said, sitting next to me on the bench.

"Because our friend isn't always available," I said, "and if I need information quickly in the future, it's better that you and I know each other." I patted Panni on the back.

"I can't do this a lot," he said. I wasn't sure if he meant logistically or emotionally.

"Let's just take care of today."

"So how do we . . ."

"You leave what you brought on the bench. Then you go to your car and find yourself a party."

He frowned. "What about the rest?"

"It's already in your pocket, Mark."

He pressed his elbow against his North Face ski jacket and was rewarded with the crackle of paper from the folded envelope I'd placed there. His eyes widened.

"Happy New Year," I said.

Panni fumbled in his jeans pocket and set a black thumb drive on the bench. He managed to take long strides on his way back out of the garden, despite being clenched enough to hold a broomstick lodged where I couldn't see it.

I scratched Stanley's flank as I reached into his harness again for an adapter cable. I plugged the thumb drive into my phone and began to read the files Panni had brought.

The first document was Bilal Nath's travel visa to the United States, including an image of his passport. He was a citizen of Pakistan, with a listed residence in London. He'd entered the country on a flight from Heathrow to Miami in mid-November. The next two pages of search results confirmed Bilal had no arrest record in the United States and a check with Interpol had drawn a similar blank.

But the next file was a surprise. A State of Florida marriage license. Bilal Nath and Aura Kincaid had been married in Miami only a week after Bilal had arrived in America. The gangster and his girl were newlyweds.

Aura's record wasn't quite as clean as her husband's. Arrests for identity theft in her home state of Washington, and again in Florida, which also included a count of wire fraud. Cybercrimes. Unsurprising, given that code she'd created to strip-mine my phone for all its data. She hadn't been indicted on the first rap and had gotten off with probation for the second.

The sentencing statement noted that the judge had been lenient given Ms. Kincaid's ongoing health concerns. It didn't elaborate on what those problems had been, but if they'd been serious enough to make a Dade County judge pause, I guessed Aura had been afflicted with more than a hangnail.

She'd been married once before Bilal, too, I noticed. To a Timothy Gorlick, while she was still living in Washington. Their divorce had been finalized right before her move to Miami.

That was the sum total of information on my new and unwanted acquaintance. I had gleaned a few biographical facts, but nothing that might give me any leverage to shake Bilal loose. Stanley caught my angry curse and raised his head.

Bilal had hired Dr. Claybeck through Ondine Long. It was a sure bet Ondine was also the person who had first dropped my name to Bilal, although I had no idea why. Nothing good, that was equally certain. Whatever motive that witch might have had for mentioning me, my best interest wouldn't be a factor.

I closed the files on Bilal to open the second folder. The information Panni had been able to find on Fergus Burke.

Gut Burke's federal rap sheet was the largest file. It had been linked to records in various counties and states. I didn't know if that efficiency was Panni's good work or courtesy of Homeland Security tying information across sources.

Fergus William Burke, aka Big Gus, aka Gut Burke, aka George Bergin. White male, six-foot-one, 260 pounds. Born New York City, died twelve years ago in Longview, Washington, only days shy of age sixty.

So he was dead. If Gut Burke had been my paternal grandfather, he was just another relation lost to time, never to be known.

But that was making the very big assumption that Burke had any connection to me at all. I scrolled ahead, looking for his family and known associates.

There. Three relatives. Wife Iva Burke, divorced with no year listed. Daughter Kathleen, deceased. She had her own criminal sheet as a separate file on Panni's drive. Katie Burke had been arrested in Berkeley twice for possession of heroin and died of an overdose at age twenty.

And son Sean. Sean Burke.

Hollis's memory had been spot-on. My mother, Moira, had known him.

The news was big enough that I let the file labeled SEAN_WILLIAM_ BURKE _09790467A sit unopened and full of its own portent, while I read more about his father, Gus.

Gut Burke had racked up enough arrests to force me to scroll down twice to see the whole list. He'd been in handcuffs before he'd had his first zit. Assault, burglary, armed robbery, possession with intent, suspicion of extortion, suspicion of kidnapping, suspicion of murder more than once.

Leaving aside a host of short jail terms, two of those arrests had earned Burke prison time. Four years in Sing Sing for manslaughter, six in San Quentin for selling cocaine. East Coast, West Coast.

Mug shots of Burke at various ages showed a man who was almost fully grown and next door to good-looking at sixteen, with a strong nose and chin and dark wavy hair, who had slid downhill fast. Like a time-lapse of Dorian Gray's portrait. It wasn't just the weight gain that ballooned his already thick neck. The skin on his cheeks blossomed into rosacea and his countenance became darker in a different way.

Burke looked exactly like what he was: a thug, a crook, a killer.

The attached Bureau dossier gave me some color commentary to back up all the stats. Gut Burke had been an enforcer for the Westies, the Irish-American mob in Hell's Kitchen, who started as competitors of the Italians and ended as little more than attack dogs working for the Gambino family. Seeing the writing on the wall, Burke had pulled up stakes and fled to California in the early 1980s. The Feds had tried to make him turn state's evidence when they nabbed him for trafficking drugs, but Gut hadn't taken the deal.

Burke had moved again, to Washington State, just after his parole from SQ ended. The dossier showed registered addresses in Olympia, Longview, Tacoma. Never anywhere longer than five or six years. And no arrests after his relocation to the Northwest. Had he suddenly quit? Or changed his methods?

Which renewed my curiosity about what business Burke might have had with Dono thirty years ago. Despite a few similar notes in the melody of their criminal records, the two men didn't have much in common. Burke was a few years older than my grandfather had been, and from NYC, while Dono had come to the States through Boston. Dono was a thief, with no interest in dealing narcotics and especially not in murder for hire, which looked to be Gut Burke's specialties. And Dono had assiduously avoided working with gangs. If crime could have hermits, that would have been my grandfather.

My fingers hesitated over Sean's file. The more I learned about the Burkes, even reading between the emotionless lines of the official record, the less I liked.

My grandfather had raised me to be just like him. A thief. Dono Shaw wasn't without his own scruples, and he'd loved me. I'd bought into the idea—the delusion—that he and I were justified in what we did. That I was a good person despite my crimes.

I'd grown out of that way of thinking.

Gut Burke couldn't by any stretch of the imagination be considered good, not ever. Was his son the same?

I opened his file.

Sean Burke's driver's license and two passport copies were on the first pages. He was forty-seven. He traveled internationally with enough frequency that he'd filled the first of the passports within a few years. Trips to Canada and Russia, mostly, and a handful of former Eastern Bloc nations as well.

I studied Burke's face. The photos were straight-on and impassive, as with most DMV and passport pictures. It was a squarer face than his father's but with the same strong features and the same pugnacious set to the jaw.

He didn't look a ton like me, except for the shape of his skull and perhaps the ears. Dark hair and eyes, sure, but not so dark as the Shaw bloodline with their black hair, and eyes close enough to that shade that a drunk girl in a bar near Fort Benning had once poked me in the chest and proclaimed them obsidian. I'd known my whole life that my looks resembled Dono's. Everyone who'd seen us together had remarked on it.

Burke and I were similarly sized, though. Over six feet, and big in the shoulders and chest from what I could gauge from his headshots and his license. That hadn't been the case for Dono. My grandfather had been even taller, but rangy. More a wiry strength than the muscle mass that came naturally to me. I noted Sean had kept his weight down as he'd aged. No one was likely to call him Gut after his dad.

He was also married. To Natalia Burke née Morozova, no children. Real estate records showed they owned a house right here in Seattle, a two-bedroom suburban in Bitter Lake bought ten years ago for four hundred and ten thousand and probably worth twice that now, thanks to Seattle's insane real estate boom.

Married, and settled. That surprised me, and the fact that I was surprised made me wonder whether I was trying too hard to fit Sean Burke into a preconceived notion. I exhaled a breath I hadn't realized I'd been holding. Maybe Sean had escaped the pull of his father's gravity, as I'd more or less escaped Dono's.

I continued to page through his records and stopped abruptly, thinking at first that the copies of Burke's U.S. travel documents had been duplicated.

But no. I was looking at a copy of a second passport for Burke. With the red-and-gold cover of the Russian Federation.

That must have taken some doing, even with a Russian wife. Did Burke somehow arrange for dual citizenship? Was that even recognized by both countries? It hadn't seemed to set off any red flags during travel. He'd logged at least two trips to Asia per year, with entry points at Pushkin International in Moscow and also to Kiev in the Ukraine. Family visits? Or working?

Sean held a Washington State business license under the name SWB Consultants. I clicked away from the file to make a fast search. If the business was still operating, it was unusual. I couldn't find any online presence for SWB or Sean Burke. No social media, no company website, not even a Yelp review.

He did have a criminal record. A single arrest by the SPD, for suspicion of assault when he was barely eighteen. I checked the date against Gut Burke's file. Sure enough, father and son had been busted together. Neither man had been indicted.

The last part of his rap sheet was especially curious, an appended section of only two sentences. Sean Burke had been questioned by the ATF two years ago. Any inquiries were directed to the federal agency's Seattle field office. No further details on the investigation were provided. I suspected that the official record had been classified, which would make sense if the case was still considered open.

Burke might be a suspect. Or a witness, or even just a technical expert the Feds had consulted for information. No way of knowing. But those two lines had become a cloud obscuring any clear picture of Sean Burke.

The final three pages were almost identical, each one a federal fire-arm transaction form. Burke had purchased two SIG Sauer M17 pistols, and one bolt-action SSG 3000 rifle by the same maker, all within the past four years. I knew the M17, had even tried it out on the range in the Army when the model was in contention to replace our standard issue Beretta. SIG Sauer had eventually won that bid. The M17 was rolling out by the tens of thousands to Army and Air Force personnel.

Burke wasn't a veteran. Why pay top retail to own pistols that would become as common as weeds within a couple of years?

The SIG rifle struck me as even stranger. A sniper rifle used by law enforcement, and an odd choice for the casual gun enthusiast.

I recalled something else about the rifle. Something that turned the nagging tap at my mind to frantic scratching. The SSG 3000 had a rare feature, a barrel that could be replaced in just a few minutes. Useful, if you wanted to try out different calibers.

Or maybe swap out the rifle's original barrel to muddy the results of a ballistics test.

I could think of at least one private sector occupation that would find that feature useful. A job that might reward tactical proficiency with a model of handgun you could acquire with comparative ease almost anywhere in the world.

Combine those facts with frequent travel. A vague registered business. And a family history shadowy enough to make mine look like a bunch of Peace Corps volunteers.

A shooter. Not a grunt like Gut Burke, weighted down with a rap sheet that would attract attention in any town he settled in. But a professional killer, careful and prepared.

Had Sean Burke gone straight? Or, like Dono after his young wild years, had he refined his approach over time to become much better at the work he'd done all his life?

Hell. I was probably building an elaborate house of cards. Maybe Sean Burke had buddies in the Army whom he liked to go shooting with, or he had found some price break on weapons from his favorite manufacturer.

And he lived in Seattle. My possible next of kin, my father, might have been living less than ten miles away from me all these years.

Ten miles, a drive of no more than twenty minutes. I could be at Sean Burke's house just that fast.

I unplugged the drive and filled Stanley's harness with the various pieces of electronics once more. The bully stick long since devoured, he hopped up, keen to be on the move.

So was I, I realized. I had enough raw energy suddenly firing my blood to sprint like a wolf chasing prey.

I just wasn't sure which direction I should go.

ELEVEN

CYNDRA WAS THE FIRST TO hear Bilal's phone ringing. I got up from the little circular table Addy used for sit-down meals, which had become more frequent occurrences now that Cyn lived with her, and retrieved the phone from my jacket pocket.

"Yeah," I said.

"This is Shaw?" Bilal's gunman, Saleem, I guessed, based on the accent.

"You give these phones out to a lot of people?"

He paused, maybe uncertain whether he was being mocked. "We are at Eastlake and Roanoke. Come here."

"Later. I'm busy."

Another delay as the line went completely quiet. Maybe Saleem covered the phone with his hand while he conferred with Bilal or Bilal's new wife, Aura.

"We can come and find you," Saleem said finally, "at the Proctor house."

My jaw tightened. I had to give them intimidation points for efficiency. Bilal could track the phone's location, and he'd already matched it to Addy's home. Sure as shit I didn't want these assholes anywhere near Roy Street.

"Half an hour," I said, and hung up. I could be terse, too.

"Who was that?" Addy said from over her sliver of mince pie. Addy liked food, would try a bit of everything, but she claimed she'd reached the age where she couldn't eat as heartily as she once enjoyed.

"Someone I have to see." I returned to the table and tucked in to the last of the roast. "Start the movie without me. I'll come back to catch the end if I can."

"But it's Mad Max," Cyndra said. "And Furiosa."

"I've seen it before. We all have."

"Too much for me," said Addy. "So much violence." Her tone implying something other than the film.

"It's not that bad," I said, answering her question. "Save me some dessert. Cherry, not that weird spiced stuff you call pie."

Addy didn't rise to the joke, lame as it was. Cyn didn't look entertained, either.

"You're still off school." I nodded to Cyndra's gear bag lying in the corner of the living room. "How about you and me go to the gym in the morning? Like Wren said?"

"Okay," she answered, only half looking up from her plate.

"I'll be back as soon as I can."

Neither of them said anything to that. I swallowed the final bite and took my dishes to the kitchen before leaving. Setting a fine example.

I KNEW THE INTERSECTION OF Eastlake and Roanoke. About a block away was a good Italian restaurant called Pomodoro that stayed open until midnight. I'd taken Luce Boylan there once. And another woman much more recently, on a date that had ended in a one-night stand. The meal was worth seconds, the sex not so much. We'd both agreed to feast elsewhere.

As I drew near, Bilal's phone rang again. Probably tracking my progress. My electronic leash had a fucking choke collar on it.

"I see you in your car." Saleem again. "Leave it and come down to the corner." I spotted him in his leather coat on the stone steps leading to the tennis courts at Rogers Playground. I'd played some baseball on the diamond there as a kid. Never enough time on any league team for me to become much of a batter; life with Dono had interfered with the schedule demands of organized sports. But I could run fast enough and throw hard enough to get by at center field, the same position my idol, Ken Griffey Jr., played. The notion of beaning Saleem with a fastball gave me an ounce of pleasure.

I left the Barracuda two blocks from the park and walked down. Saleem stayed on the steps, maybe to keep us eye to eye. His jacket was open, and his right hand hovered near the buckle of his braided belt.

"Nervous?" I said.

Saleem's only reaction was in his eyes, which blazed. His chiseled face might have approached handsome if it ever relaxed. But there was an intensity, maybe lifelong, that had drawn the fine ligaments under his skin taut, like the rage within was consuming him.

He angled his head at Eastlake. "There."

I looked. A Mercedes G-class utility vehicle in glossy lunar blue idled at a fire hydrant. The rear door opened and Bilal Nath stepped out. Aura, a white winter cap covering her azure-tipped hair, joined him. Another man I couldn't see clearly through the tinted windows sat in the driver's seat.

"We can walk from here," Bilal said, as if he was looking forward to the exercise.

"Walk where?" I said. No one bothered to answer.

Aura took Bilal's arm and they crossed the street, headed down the slope toward Lake Union. Saleem didn't move until I did. I followed Bilal and Aura, Saleem followed me, and after a moment the rumbling Mercedes made a caboose to our little train.

"You were born here. In this city," Bilal said. "Is it still home, after all of the travels serving your nation?"

An unsubtle flex. Bilal had done some homework on me, maybe by asking Ondine Long. Between tracking my location and this, it was clear that my new acquaintance liked to show off.

"Where's home to you?" I said. My own background check on Bilal Nath could remain my secret.

"Karachi, originally. I, too, am a city person. But so much larger a place. Seattle seems a small town to me."

Aura squeezed his arm. "It's your way. You want everything available, every hour of the day or night."

"Yes, I do. Here."

We reached the end of the block. There had once been a small marina here, one of a handful on this side of the lake, along with the community of houseboats just a hundred yards south. In place of the former docks, a swath of water had been filled with tons of rock and sand to extend the land and construct a building. A new enough project that the sign of the architectural firm was still planted proudly outside, above shrubs that retained their unnatural geometric squareness straight from the nursery. The building's exterior cladding carried the look of brushed steel. With most of its lights on inside, the whole structure gleamed like a pale opal in a dim room.

CERES BIOTECHNOLOGIES, the angled silver letters above the fourth story read, over a symbol that was a combination DNA helix and sheaf of wheat.

Aura and Bilal looked at the building. Their expressions took me a moment to place. Hostile, certainly, and tinged with something close to loathing. The temperature on the street dipped another ten degrees each time a breeze whipped off the water. Neither of them took any notice.

Bilal pointed to the building's upper stories.

"Ceres holds something which I require. You will take it from them, and then I will consider your debt paid," he said.

"What is it?"

"That is not your concern right now. Your task is to gain access to the building. And to disable any protective countermeasures."

Countermeasures? Like booby traps? What could a biotech firm have that a gangster might find valuable?

"Not a chance," I said.

"This is your answer? I can send Saleem and Juwad to discuss better terms with your friend Addy, perhaps."

"I'm not bargaining. I'm telling you that this whole idea is dead on the starting line. Look." I nodded at the building. "There's a guard at the front desk at this hour, and another man just walked past that window on the third floor. So we can assume twenty-four-seven security. There are cameras and keycard entry. That's what we can see from here. There are bound to be other barriers inside, especially in restricted areas. Fingerprint access. Voice recognition."

I was laying it on thick. Angling for whatever advantage that might give.

Aura looked at me with the same antipathy she'd given the shining offices of Ceres. "You're supposed to be good."

"Good enough to know a bad thing. If Ceres handles government contracts, they could have a direct patch to the FBI. Any vaccines and viruses, they'll have extra precautions."

"We do not want viruses," Bilal said. "I am not a terrorist."

"It's not a disease we're after. Or a weapon," said Aura.

I glanced at the Ceres building and back at them, my doubt readily apparent.

Not a disease, but perhaps a cure. Bilal was sick and going downhill fast. Was Ceres working on a vaccine for ALS?

"How valuable is this thing?" I said. "Why is Ceres so worried about theft?"

"The safeguards are to prevent accidents, not theft," Aura said.

"Wife," Bilal said to her.

"He'll know eventually, Bilal," she replied. "Better to tell him now, so he can be ready."

She turned to me. "What we need is on the fourth floor. In cryobank storage. Extreme cold. Ceres does keep some materials on-site that might be infectious. So each individual storage tank has a safeguard. A controlled burn that will destroy the contents in the event that the tank is ruptured, before its contents can thaw."

"If you know all this, why do you need me?"

"Knowing is different than being able to do something," she said. "I promise you: what we want will not hurt anyone."

"Then there shouldn't be any problem telling me what it is."

"No." Bilal put his hands in his pockets. He looked drawn. Either the nighttime walk or our argument was pushing the limits of his energy.

I wanted to tell them to fuck off. That if they were foolish enough to come after Addy or Hollis or anyone near me, I'd dump their carcasses into the trunk of their hundred-K Mercedes along with Saleem or whoever else got in my way and bury them all in concrete.

But that would be the wrong play. Something in Bilal's and Aura's shared attitude resonated that they didn't just *want* whatever was locked away in Ceres, they *needed* it. An edge of desperation. They might not flinch if I forced their hand.

And that urgency was a crack in their armor. A place to start prying, if I could find enough time.

"It'll take research," I said. "I'll need the building blueprints, and make my own version of the external alarm, for practice. See if I can reverse-engineer it to figure out what might be waiting inside. I'll have to watch the building to learn the guards' patterns."

"Wednesday night," Bilal said.

Forty-eight hours. New Year's Eve. "Impossible."

"I do not care," he said. "This is as much time as you have. If you require a team, I will provide them. Take it by force if you must. But do not fail. Do not try to evade this. I will avenge any disobedience on you and every person in your life. Do you understand?"

Saleem was behind me. I didn't have to look to know he had a hand hovering near his Steyr machine pistol. The driver of the idling Mercedes might be aiming a second gun at my head right this second.

And despite the odds, I was still angry enough to be half a tick from making a move.

"We're clear," I said through my teeth.

Bilal nodded. "There is a number programmed into the phone I gave you. Call that when you are ready."

"Don't wait," Aura said. "Find out what you can tonight, while you're here."

The driver, Juwad, rolled down the driver's window. He had a phone to his ear. "Sir. The restaurant valet has called."

"Our table." Bilal shrugged. "I suppose everyone is short on patience tonight. Tell them two minutes."

He stepped to the Mercedes and held the rear door open for Aura—a damn gentleman—and went around the other side to board himself. Saleem stayed where he was.

"I do not trust you," he said to me when the doors of the big car had closed.

"Likewise," I said.

"Bilal and his *wife*"—Saleem bit off the word like a piece of rot from an apple—"believe they require you, as if you have magic. They are wrong. I can take what he wants from this building without you. And I will be ready to kill you. I will enjoy it."

He might have meant he *would* enjoy it, if I stepped out of line and Bilal gave the order.

Then again, maybe the gunman's vision of the future was clearer than mine.

TWELVE

THE BIG MERCEDES PULLED AWAY. I waited until it was out of sight around the curve of the road before taking out my phone.

Aura had one thing right: I should learn whatever I could, right away.

Faregame was a rideshare company I'd used before. Local and a little more flexible than the bigger providers. I requested a car. Within ten minutes, a baby-food-green Chevy Volt covered the last block on Eastlake doing forty and stopped within an inch of the curb.

"Hey," I said, leaning into the back. The driver was a young dude, with a wall of curled hair and a mustache bushy enough to outstretch the tip of his nose in profile. "I got a problem. My friend left her phone and I have to stay here." I held out Bilal's phone with a fifty-dollar bill and a scrap paper receipt from Analog Coffee I'd found in my pocket wrapped around it. "Take this to the destination I wrote down and keep the fifty."

"I don't know, man."

"Same as dropping me off. Only instead of a person, it's the phone. Read the note."

He looked at the piece of scrap paper. I'd written: *Addy: Call me on your phone to let me know this arrived safe. Thanks. V.*

I pointed at the driver. "Once she calls I'll tip another fifty. Right?"

"Shit. Okay, I guess."

"Thanks. You're saving my life."

The Volt sped off, and the phone with it. Bilal could track my movements all he damn well wanted tonight.

I backtracked to the Barracuda to retrieve some tools. My car was known to Bilal and way too noticeable. I needed another ride.

Within a month after the Barracuda had come into my possession, I had constructed flat hidden compartments between the trunk space and the backseat. One compartment held my kit of various electronics, including a cigarette-pack-sized transponder that could get me arrested just for owning it in the United States.

It wasn't by chance that I'd modified the car, or that I owned the illegal gadget. Over the past few weeks I'd been investing a lot of time and money in building the kind of tool collection that Dono might have once used, with me working right alongside him. Call it preparedness. Since I'd returned to Seattle from the Army, I'd been in situations where the right gear might have made a difference. If I wasn't going to change my life, I could at least update my methods.

Halfway up the block, a dusty white Camry was reversing, the driver having spotted an open space at the curb. He began to parallel park.

I preset the transponder for the low frequency common to that generation of Camry sedans as I walked toward him. The device started by mimicking the car. It sent a signal, and the smart key in the driver's pocket dutifully replied with its unique ID, which the transponder captured. Reverse the process, and the transponder would act as the key itself. All before the driver had set the parking brake.

Once he'd hustled away, burdened with his briefcase and what looked like groceries for dinner, I pressed the transmit button. The car unlocked and its engine started.

I had to admit using the transponder wasn't as much fun as boosting older cars by hotwiring their ignitions, but you couldn't beat it for expediency.

While waiting for the Faregame driver, I'd searched online for restaurants. Specifically eateries with valet parking, within only a couple of minutes' drive of Ceres Biotech. I was counting on Bilal's penchant for precision and his demonstrated taste for the finer things.

There weren't many top-end dining options this far from downtown. Two at the south tip of the lake were closest. I drove the Camry one mile down Fairview and pulled into the parking lot shared by the restaurants.

Luck was on my side tonight. The big Mercedes GLE was easy to spot in the reserved parking section of a steakhouse. I waved no thanks to the approaching valet and U-turned to find a spot in the self-park lot that allowed a view of the restaurant entrance.

My phone rang. Addy.

"You have a strange version of sending flowers," she said.

"I would have if there had been time. Thanks."

"The young man delivering your phone seemed very perplexed. I take it you're not coming home soon."

"No," I confessed. "At least one more errand to run. If that phone I sent rings, don't answer it."

"I wouldn't dream," Addy said.

I sat in the white Camry, its engine running, watching the restaurant. Now I knew why Bilal had been talking to Ondine Long, and how my name had come up: he'd needed a thief.

A fractional part of me, a shadier part, felt some pride that the criminal broker with all her connections had placed me in the top echelon. But, then, I didn't know the criteria. Maybe I was only in the top tier of guys with professional burglary skills whom she also considered disposable. She sure as hell wouldn't shed any tears if Bilal had me aced.

Bilal and Aura kept dinner short. Within an hour, the valet pulled the Mercedes out of its parking spot. I kept the Camry's headlights off as I slowly drifted toward the exit to the street.

Saleem and Juwad were the first out the door of the steakhouse. Juwad was an inch taller and much heavier than his slender partner, with the blocky build of a powerlifter and hair gelled so liberally I could see its shine from forty yards away. Saleem tipped the valet and let the man open the door for Bilal and Aura when they joined the party. He and Juwad kept watch on the surroundings. I was glad the Camry was partly concealed behind the Chandler's Cove sign and its ornamental bushes, and that the engine's purr was soft. Only when their master and mistress were safely within the car did the two bodyguards climb in.

A careful team. I would have to be equally cautious. I waited until the Mercedes was half a block away before following.

Bilal was only in Seattle for a while, he'd said. That implied a hotel. I hoped it would be one of the larger chains downtown, where I might have a better chance of following his team on foot without being spotted, at least far enough to determine which floor their room was on.

But instead the Mercedes jogged left onto Boren Ave, cruising through the easy late evening traffic. I stayed three blocks back, confident in the Toyota's smaller size and my knowledge of the city to allow me to catch up if I became trapped at a stoplight or they made an unexpected turn. Boren took us both over the interstate and diagonally up the west side of my home turf of Capitol Hill.

I nearly lost them, anyway. Juwad turned right on Madison. When I followed fifteen seconds later there was no sight of the big car, even though I had a clear view down three full blocks of the wide street. I craned my neck from side to side, slowing to a crawl even as cars angrily revved to drive around me.

There. In the tight turnaround in front of the Hotel Neapolitan, their Mercedes partly hidden behind hedges that shielded the hotel entrance from the busy intersection.

I kept rolling down Madison and left the Toyota in an alley just behind the hotel, then ran back toward the entrance. Bilal and Aura and the rest were already inside.

It had been a long time since I'd seen the small lobby of the Neapolitan. At least one full remodel ago. If I strolled in unprepared I might run smack into any one of Bilal's crew.

This would have to do for now. I knew their car and their hotel and at least two of their soldiers. More intel would follow soon.

Very soon. I'd just burned two of my allotted forty-eight hours. I could almost hear the tick of that clock over the stolen Camry's purr.

Bilal had suggested hiring a team to knock over Ceres Biotech. I liked that idea. I could make good use of the right people. Even if their goal wasn't quite what the venomous Mr. Bilal Nath had in mind.

THIRTEEN

I WAS TOO AMPED UP AFTER my confrontation with Bilal to consider rest. Bitter Lake, and the home owned by Sean Burke, was only a few short miles up the freeway. And the night was overcast and dark. Ideal for reconnaissance.

The Camry had served its purpose. I drove it back to Roanoke and marveled at the small miracle of the same spot at the curb being available as I parallel-parked and turned the wheels to touch the curb on the incline, just as they'd been when I first saw them. If the owner was especially observant, he might puzzle over how the odometer had gone up and the gas gauge had gone down overnight. But the placement of his car would offer no clues.

After driving the boosted Camry so gingerly, it was a pleasure to make the Barracuda growl as it merged onto the freeway. I supposed I would get habituated to the muscle car before long, but for now it had that new toy feel. Its former owner, for all his sins, had kept the engine in fighting trim.

Burke's address was walking distance from the lake itself, midway along a short street called Amsbury that ended in a cul-de-sac of homes. Each eighth of an acre allowed for a swath of front lawn beside a two-car driveway and an unassuming strip of backyard behind each house. Almost aggressive in its normalcy.

The residential street meant I could cruise at a slow pace without drawing attention. I drifted by the Burke home—what Dono would have called a ranch house, one story, low-slung, and shaped like a shallow L— and followed the curve of the cul-de-sac at the end of Amsbury to return for another pass.

No cars in the driveway. One light on behind curtains at the far tip of the L, probably a bedroom. No security company sign. Standard deadbolt on the door, maybe a Schlage. The lawn was so well groomed I suspected weekly landscaping rather than an owner's touch.

I drove away from the street, in case anyone had been tracking the Barracuda's progress from their living-room window, and parked to examine my toolkits in the trunk for the second time that night.

The houses on Amsbury Street had no mailboxes. USPS had consolidated delivery for its own convenience into a stand of metal postboxes emblazoned with the familiar blue-and-white eagle logo at the end of the road. A Douglas fir, its drooping branches still holding zealously to its needles in winter, sheltered the mail stand from view of the houses. From the truck I removed a lockpick gun and traded the transponder I'd used on the Camry for a larger wireless scanner. I pocketed the scanner. The pick gun I could make use of immediately.

The mail stand offered three sizes of postboxes, ranging from envelope width for standard mail to large enough to suit residents who didn't want packages left on their doorsteps. A label on one of the bigger mailboxes matched Burke's house number. Maybe he collected stamps and received an entire bushel of correspondence from around the world every day. Or maybe he bought his ammunition online.

USPS didn't invest heavily in the latest lock engineering. I had the pins clicking into place in less time than it had taken me to walk from the car to the mail stand. The little metal door swung open.

I'd expected to see an empty box, or at most a couple of letters. Sufficient to fulfill a burglar's standard precaution and verify whether the Burkes had been home recently.

Instead I had to extend a quick hand to stop a short tower of paper from tumbling out onto the wet ground. Loads of mail. Junk circulars, political fliers, coupon books, enough volume to fill half the available square footage.

The postmarks at the bottom of the pile were from more than a week ago. I had hit the jackpot. The Burkes must be on vacation for the holidays.

Then I just as quickly revised my guess. Vacation would mean a hold on their mail, not renting a bigger postbox. This must be a common thing for Burke and his wife, being away from home for long periods.

He had his Russian passport. Maybe they were abroad. Conducting whatever business paid for ranch houses and large postboxes in a sleepy neighborhood.

My quick memorization of the environs from online maps told me Burke's house bumped up against one of the trails leading down to the lake. I walked up the street to find a gap in the treeline. One leap over a sodden ditch to the trail, and a fast stroll through the dark, and I was looking at Burke's slash of backyard, its fence shrouded by blackberry brambles and creeping ivy.

The same single light still shone from the house, increasing the depth of the shadows in the yard. I saw no cameras or motion sensors or other signs of security beyond the simple lock on the sliding-glass door. The Burkes kept their curtains drawn. They had planted rows of short cypress trees on either side of the property, as a privacy screen from their immediate neighbors. All the better for me. No water dishes or chew toys or fecal land mines on the grass that signaled a dog, either. This was about as clear a coast as I could hope for.

I was nervous, and I realized why. Burke could be my father. A narrow chance, but a chance nonetheless. A better person than me might consider breaking into his immediate relation's home to be crossing a moral line.

Burke might also be someone who put bullets into people for money. That was a more pressing reason to be jumpy.

Trail maintenance near the lake didn't include limbing up the lower branches of the fir trees. It was much easier to climb one of the tall evergreens and drop ten feet down into the backyard than to fight through the brambles. I landed on the strip of bark that bordered the lawn, just a soft rustle above silent.

For a moment, I didn't move. The house remained equally still.

My first stop was the window with the light shining behind it. A deep blue curtain obscured the interior of the room. I watched, and listened, until I was ninety percent confident that despite that lamp's claim, the room was empty. And likely the entire house with it.

At the sliding door, I removed the scanner from my pocket. A slender silver box the same size and shape as a surge protector, the scanner was similar to the receiver I'd used when meeting Panni from the FBI at the Japanese garden. It made a sweep of low-band wireless frequencies, nothing more than 900 MHz, looking for a spike in activity. Low frequencies are best at penetrating walls and furniture, ideal for silent alarms. The scanner's digital readout remained blank as I swept it across the edges of the doorframe.

I made a visual check as well. No telltale contact pads around the sliding door or the nearby window. No motion sensors under the eaves. Peering through the glass I could see straight through to the front door on the other side of the slim house, partly illuminated by the streetlamps on Amsbury shining through a vertical strip of pebbled glass at the doorframe. I didn't see an alarm keypad on the nearest wall. Could it be this easy?

There was still a tiny possibility that someone was in the house, asleep. I rapped softly on the glass. A minute went by before I used the pick gun to unlock the door. It slid open with the slightest of shudders.

The scanner in my hand stayed dormant. I slipped my wet running shoes off and stepped inside.

Spotless. Both my entry, and the home as well. The Burkes must have a housecleaner as well as a landscaper.

It wasn't a flashy house, like Dr. Claybeck's midcentury marvel. Most of the furnishings looked like they had been acquired through catalogs, and not so long ago. The watercolors on the walls, too. As clean and uncontroversial as a home prepared by a Realtor to show prospective buyers. All the dishes put away. No clutter on the countertops. One lone raincoat hanging on the line of pegs by the front door, but no messy shoes below. Even the roll of paper towels on the kitchen wall looked fresh from the plastic, the first sheet still stuck to the ones below. Only the black-painted ceiling beams offered a hint of individuality.

I left the back door open—in the event I had to suddenly bolt—and stepped softly down the hall.

The bathroom and two identical bedrooms followed the same pattern. Very clean, very colorless. Men's toiletries in the bathroom, but not so much as a whisker stub in the bone-dry sink or soap scum in the tub. The dresser drawers and closets held men's clothes. Not enough of them to fill many washing machines at the laundromat. Sweaters, mostly XL, a couple of sport coats in 46R, and two pairs of lace-up dress shoes, one brown and one black, sized eleven-and-a-half. Same size as the sneakers I'd just removed.

Most of the clothes looked lightly used, but not enough that any of the garments were truly broken in. Even the socks neatly folded in the dresser had their creases from the original packaging.

From Panni's records I knew Burke had bought the house ten years ago. He might have moved in yesterday, for all it showed. And he'd apparently left his wife, Natalia, back in Smolensk or wherever she was from.

I spent a few more minutes searching through hall closets and under kitchen counters. There were only a handful of things beyond the expected linens and appliances. Some camping gear and old stereo equipment was about as intriguing as it got. The spare bedroom lived up to the name. Spare. No filing cabinet or computer or other personal records. In a kitchen drawer I found bills from the past quarter for the house's water and power, its trash pickup, its landscaping. I used my phone to snag a picture of each.

Locking the back door behind me, I put on my shoes and left the Burke home—no longer an accurate word for the place, I was sure—via the side of the house to Amsbury Street. A quick walk put me back at the Barracuda.

I took a moment to sit and muse about the strangeness of it all.

The house was spitting distance from deserted. For what reason? Had Burke moved, separated from his wife, and now the house on Amsbury was just an investment waiting for the market to bubble again? Was it a safe house in case he needed to crash somewhere in an emergency? That didn't match. It didn't make sense to use his address of record as a refuge.

But the idea redirected my thoughts back to the stack of mail I'd seen in Burke's postbox. No magazine subscriptions. No bank statements. No cards or personal letters. Only junk that might as well have been addressed to Occupant.

I recalled my impression of Burke's home being ready for an open house showing. Realtors had a word for that: staged. That was what Sean Burke's house was. Just a bare façade of a dwelling, there to provide an impression but nothing more. Soulless.

As I drove down Amsbury Street one last time, my skin prickled. It took me a few seconds to catch up to why.

Burke's house had contained no photographs at all.

That simple fact shouldn't have surprised me, not with how impersonal the rest of the interior had been. But the similarity to the home I had once shared with my grandfather was positively spooky.

FOURTEEN

I'D DISCOVERED MY GYM THROUGH a Facebook group that provided community info and general bullshit sessions for the 2nd Ranger Battalion at Fort Lewis. Most of the group's posts concentrated on activities near the base, but there was usually a mention when a brother got something going in Seattle. One of those Rangers was a former second lieutenant from 1st Bat named Twelvetrees, and one of those somethings was his venture into training MMA fighters.

The LT's business had suffered a rough start. His first location had been burglarized of all its brand-new equipment. When Twelvetrees had posted on the battalion group, it was to ask if any brothers had old punching bags or dumbbells or gloves they could spare, or at least lend, while his stable of fighters got ready for their upcoming bouts.

My curiosity had been piqued. I exchanged messages with Twelvetrees online. He'd said he hoped the cops were able to trace the gear; that he'd etched *12T* on every piece. I wasn't as optimistic, given the smaller scale of the theft and the manpower constraints of the SPD, but I kept that to myself. I told the lieutenant I'd do some hunting.

Almost everything that had been stolen was heavy. The punching bags—the largest of them two hundred pounds—would have required more than one person to take down and carry. It didn't take intuitive genius to guess a truck or van had pulled right up to the door, with two or three men inside. At least one of them had been familiar enough with the gym to know it was worth knocking over.

The free weights would be worth far more if sold as a set. I tried eBay and Craigslist and other sources for new listings. I checked pawnshops I knew might not give a crap about the provenance of their inventories. I came up blank.

Then it dawned on me: Who would want a metric ton of fighting gear?

I asked Twelvetrees if he'd had any prospective clients who'd come from other gyms but never signed on. He remembered a guy from Lacey who claimed to have a few pro fights and was looking to become a trainer. The guy had told Twelvetrees that he would come back to work out and talk more, but that was the last the LT had seen him. With a little mental digging, Twelvetrees recalled the dude's name—Hepp—and that he'd had a shaved head and a tattoo of flames on the side of his neck. It gave me somewhere to start.

A gym called World Class Warriors had opened two weeks prior in Lacey. It had a basic webpage with address and hours and photos. One of the photos showed an instructor working with kids, his flame tattoo stretched as he extended his neck to call out instructions.

I took a drive. World Class Warriors was open. Hepp's bullet head was visible toward the back, leading a group in abdominal exercises. I paid ten bucks for a pass and waited until the evening class let out.

Hepp caught me scratching at the red paint on the dumbbells, exposing the etching underneath. *12T*. He protested, vehemently. I knocked him down, twice, along with one of his more foolhardy middleweight fighters, before holding a seventy-pound dumbbell suspended over Hepp's throat while I explained to him how he was going to spend his night. The alternative would be a squad of highly motivated Rangers making an impromptu sortie to Lacey.

It took Hepp three hard hours to load my truck with the stolen gear, working alone. By the end, all of the fight was out of him. I let him keep the ten bucks' gym fee but warned him that if Twelvetrees so much as saw a cockroach in his newest place, it would be Hepp's fault.

Two days easy work, and I'd earned myself a lifetime membership, along with a key to unlock Twelvetrees Fitness at any hour.

Which was how Cyndra and I found ourselves in the former auto-body shop at nine in the morning, working on the basics of the deadlift. In the opposite corner of the gym, two fighters named Oscar and Cannonball shadowboxed in the ring. I showed Cyn what the movement looked like before rolling a ten-kilogram barbell with no plates on it in front of her toes.

"Keep your spine straight," I said, "and pull a little on the bar. Feel the muscles in your back engage?"

"Uh huh. I just pick it up?"

"Push with your legs. Let them do the work of getting the bar off the ground."

She did. We refined the motion a few times before I put a five-pound plate on either side of the bar. Twelvetrees had positioned the plate racks to conceal bolts still jutting from the concrete floor, remnants of the auto shop's hydraulic lifts. The gym still smelled faintly of oil from its past life.

"I can lift more than *that*," Cyn said.

"Sure. But try this ten times first. Take it slow."

She did. By the last rep her face was crimson and she had to concentrate every second to keep her back from arching.

"What's it for?" she said after a couple of breaths.

"Darn near everything. But especially your back and legs. Perfect for derby. Get some water; we'll try bench press next."

"I can do more."

"You'll feel it tomorrow as is. Tell me about Los Angeles."

"Huh? It was fine."

"'Fine' like fun, or 'fine' like you got through it?"

"Mostly got through it. Dad's happy. And I got to see some of the kids I used to live with."

In their foster homes. "Are they solid?" Meaning were they leading what most people would consider law-abiding lives. Cyndra was the daughter of a former crook and, just like me, had grown up with a skewed perspective. Hell, mine was still skewed. I was just aware of it. And trying to keep Cyndra from falling into her old habits.

"Yes," she said. "Farrah got a job at the Northridge mall. She sells big pretzels."

I grinned. "How many'd you eat while you were there?"

"Like six."

My phone rang. I practically leapt across the rubberized mats to grab it off the apron of the ring.

Willard. Finally. I had reached out to my grandfather's onetime criminal cohort last night, letting him know it was urgent. With every hour that had ticked by since, I'd grown more convinced that Willard was occupied with his own work and wouldn't respond.

I told Cyndra to practice her flexed-arm hang on the pull-up bar while I took the call.

"Got your messages," he said in his meat-grinder voice. "All three of 'em. You ever sleep?"

"When there's time." The two fighters in the ring had begun working with the mitts. I walked toward the entrance so I could hear Willard over the pop of Cannonball's fists on leather.

"Time you don't have. That came through loud and clear, during your second voice mail, I think."

"It kept cutting me off. I figured the faster you had the details, the faster you could get to work."

Willard rumbled his discontent. "*If.* If I get to work. This is a long list you gave me. Genesee Architectural Cooperative. H&L Construction. Blueprints, electrical plans . . ."

"They built Ceres Biotech within the last year. And I need whatever specs you can find on their security company. By this time tomorrow."

"It's the holidays, Van."

I wondered if my grandfather had had an equally difficult time getting Willard to commit to a job. Not that the huge man was unwilling. Just deliberate to a fault.

"No rest for the wicked," I said. "I can give you eight grand for the intel, and another twelve if you'll back me up during the score."

"A fool and his money, huh?"

My cash reserves from my unexpected windfall had dwindled rapidly.

Getting my neck out of the noose seemed a good reason to blow the last of it.

"Give me a couple of hours," Willard said. "By then I'll know if any of this is even possible."

"As long as I'm pushing my credit, there's other help I need." I took a breath. "From Elana."

"Fuck you," Willard said, loud enough I glanced up to see if Cyndra had overheard. She'd grown bored of hanging from the chin-up bar and had gone back to more deadlifts, with more weight. "You keep my niece out of this."

"It's just some snoop work. Hollis or I would be recognized."

"Let me do it."

"You stand out like a bowling ball in a fish tank," I said. "Elana can be there and gone fast enough."

"Are you asking or telling me?"

"Call it a courtesy notice."

"Some courtesy. Every time you call me I get the same feeling. As though I'm reaching into a garbage disposal to fish something out, and your finger is poised over the switch."

He hung up.

When I turned around, Cyndra took a flash picture of me. "There."

"I should have put your phone at the top of the climbing wall. Least you'd have to work for it."

She held out the phone to show me. Video of her lifting the barbell, already on TikTok. She swiped the screen and I saw myself, looking startled, for an instant before Cyndra pulled it away to continue tapping messages in the app.

"Wren says hi," Cyndra said. With enough innocence for a platoon of angels.

"Say hi back."

"You should. Here. Text her."

"I'll text her you're slacking off to DM your whole school. You'll be doing laps for a week."

Cyn scowled. "That's not fair."

"Fair is what you make out of what you get. Let's go to work."

JUNIOR YEAR, PART ONE

I was late for registration at the start of the second semester, having overslept because Dono and I had been out late the night before to case a gated community in Magnolia. All of the shop electives I had wanted were full. Technical theater with Ms. Nasgate was the best of what was left.

I figured I'd just make the most of it, work the spotlight, and maybe practice my rewiring skills on the electricals in Watson High's auditorium. If I wanted Dono to teach me more about greasing home security systems, I had to master the basics, and I was forbidden from messing with our house since I'd accidentally shorted everything out over winter break.

But on the third week, when we were breaking out into different teams for the spring show, Ms. Nasgate had a different plan.

"Costumes?" I said.

Yvette Friel next to me laughed. Enjoying my pain.

"You'll be good at it, Van," Ms. Nasgate said. "I saw how quickly you sewed on that button during our orientation week. Very deft. Imagine what you can do with a machine."

Jesus, had that been some kind of audition? I kicked myself for doing the job so fast. "Yeah, but . . ."

"No nonsense about costumes being just for girls," she replied, though I wasn't going to say that. *Think* it, maybe.

Ms. Nasgate turned to our group of ten. She'd had the students move our desks into rough circles for each team. Theater in the round, which we'd just learned about, as she gave instructions.

"We'll start with fixing some of the basic pieces that need some TLC. In theater, we always try to repair and modify, not to replace. It's cheaper and it requires more ingenuity." She showed us plastic storage bins labeled VESTS and PETTICOATS and other costume bits. "Then we'll move into using those pieces to design costumes for the show."

Damn it. A whole month of frills and frocks.

Yvette was whispering something to her friend Kayla, both of them glancing my way. They noticed that I had noticed.

"You should really wash your hands first," Yvette whispered to me, like she was sharing an important secret. And of course I was dumb enough to look at them, which prompted more laughter. They weren't wrong; I had dirt under my nails. Not the point.

I guess my disappointment showed, because halfway through stitching a rip in a pants seam, Ms. Nasgate called me to her desk. She brushed the ends of her scarf behind her shoulder. She always wore a silk scarf around her neck, and the scarves always had gold in them, I guess to go with her short straw-colored hair.

"I know you're not happy with this assignment, Van," she said. "Do a good job, and I'll let you take your pick of teams for the senior variety show."

"Okay."

"You really might be good at costuming. Your mother was."

That brought me up so short I almost fell over. "What?"

"That's right. She had my class and she volunteered

for one of her graduating class's projects. A quilt that used to hang in the library, with squares from every student who worked on it. You've seen that."

I was struggling to keep up. Teachers just didn't mention my mom out of the blue like this. Sure she'd been in a lot of the same classes as I took now. But she was dead, which always made people nervous. Plus I knew she'd been pregnant with me while in school. That *really* closed teachers' mouths, at least around me. Pregnant during her last year, because she'd skipped a grade and graduated just after she turned seventeen.

Which meant . . .

"When she was on the senior project, was she, um . . ." I put my grimy hands out like a pregnant belly, praying that Yvette and Kayla weren't watching.

"She was. Never let that slow her down much. Now finish fixing those trousers, and I'll ask Marli to walk you through setting up a sewing machine before end of class."

"Wait. You said the quilt used to hang in the library?"

"Oh. I'm afraid it went missing last year. I'm very sorry." Her face fell. Maybe realizing no one had thought to mention to me that something my mom had made was just hanging there all this time.

"Missing like stolen?" I said.

Ms. Nasgate hesitated. "We're not sure." Which meant yes.

I went back to my seat. My fingers worked on the stitching while my brain tried to picture what the quilt had looked like. I *kinda* remembered it, hanging above low shelves near the dictionary stand, but who looks at junk on the walls in the library? I hadn't even clocked that it was gone. It wasn't like I spent a ton of time there, anyway.

Kayla and Yvette were already slacking off, talking through plans for the party Yvette was going to throw this weekend after the school's midwinter carnival. I knew about her parties, though no way I'd ever been to one. If you weren't rich or in Yvette's drama clique or able to help her popularity in some fashion, forget getting on that list.

Mom had made a quilt. Or at least part of one. I wished I'd known that before. And why the hell would somebody steal a quilt? Some of those antique ones from like Amish people went for a lot of money—Dono had considered taking a quilt during a house score last year before rejecting it as too traceable—but this was a fucking high school project. Who cared? I mean, *shit*.

My fingers tightened on the needle and it slipped and jabbed me through my jeans. It hurt. I didn't mind. Pain could be better than feeling.

FIFTEEN

AFTER DROPPING CYNDRA OFF WITH Addy I invested two hours casing Ceres Biotech. My eyes tracked the patterns of movement around the building while my brain gnawed bitterly on the problem of finding a way into the cryobank on its fourth floor without getting myself or any of the Ceres employees killed. I didn't doubt that Bilal Nath meant what he'd said. If I couldn't crack Ceres by stealth, he'd resort to force. The security guards were armed. They might be dumb enough to resist. It wasn't tough to imagine the ever-angry Saleem going to town with his Steyr, cutting through any opposition like a scythe.

When I got the message from Elana Coll, the distraction was a relief. *Meet Neapolitan lobby at 4. Dress right.*

Dress right? I guessed Elana meant I should look like someone who belonged at a four-star hotel. I didn't own business clothes. The best I could manage would be chinos without noticeable stains and a better shirt than the flannel I had on now.

I was due to meet Willard at noon. He'd chosen to combine business with his midday meal. That meant Zane+Wylie's steakhouse downtown, and me picking up the tab.

The hostess at the Z+W reception was too classy to look askance at my barn jacket and workboots ensemble.

"Reservations?" she asked.

"Loads," I said, scanning the tables on either side of the elongated bar running down the center of the restaurant. The guy I was looking for was easy enough to find. I just looked for a wall wearing a suit and tie.

Willard was the kind of size that people remembered, long enough to tell their grandchildren about. He was tall, sure, and broad and thick in an ancient world sort of way, when muscles came from hard labor and harder warfare. But beyond those stats there was a solidity to Willard, a colossal weight of presence that made him more awe-inspiring than any individual statistic.

He had chosen a seat at the back, taking up a full half of a four-top table. On the wall behind him a giant black-and-white photograph formed a mural. The photographer had captured a trio of cowboys riding away from the viewer in three-quarter profile. Willard's suits were custom-made, by necessity. This one was houndstooth in brown, giving his shoulders the look of a fence that the horses had just leapt.

"How's the prime rib?" I said, sliding into one of the chairs opposite.

"Lean," Willard rumbled, "like my prospects."

"What happened to that roadshow casino you were running?"

He grunted. "Some muttonchopped little jagoff in Portland lost forty grand in one night and went crying to daddy. A city councilman. So low on the political ladder that a quick donation kept my name out of the official record. But it wiped half my capital. No more traveling circus for the foreseeable."

"Menu, sir?" the waiter asked, looking as selectively impartial as the hostess.

"A shot of rye straight up, please," I said. Dr. Claybeck's liquor selection was about my only good memory of that night. Willard nodded assent. The waiter left, pants cuffs flapping in haste.

"The card games will come around," I said. "People need their vices."

"Your vice seems to be the same as your granddad's." Willard cut into his ribeye. "Crazy schemes."

"Don't tell me you never made a profit with Dono."

"I made out fine. But I also flirted with a fucking ulcer." He swallowed his bite of steak. "Ceres Biotech. We might have some headway there. Ceres built their new headquarters on artificial landfill and on the water. That raised the hackles of some local activist groups. They pushed the city's environmental review board, which forced the members to put the building plans under a microscope. And then they had to share those plans with the EPA and Public Relations, given the stink. So there's no shortage of copies floating around City Hall."

"Blueprints?" I said.

"Blueprints, electrical, hazmat evaluations. A lot of it is public documentation. A citizen could put in a request and get most of it in two or three months."

I saw where he was heading. "How much to get it today?"

"Three large to the right guy. He'll spread it around a little. I'll pick the papers up from him late tonight."

Crime really didn't pay. "All right." I put an envelope on the table, which Willard made disappear with superb dexterity for a guy with hands the approximate size of shovel blades. "That's your eight. Take the palm oil from that and I'll make it up on the back end."

Willard took another small bite, his lantern jaw barely moving to chew. "And what are you gonna do, while I'm attempting all this legwork?"

"I'll be talking to a couple of people. Ondine Long was the one who gave my name to Bilal Nath. I want to know why."

He lowered his fork. Willard didn't give away much—he was probably a hell of a poker player, along with running illegal gambling joints—but his misgivings were plain enough.

"Bad on top of worse," he said.

"You know, that might be the first time I've seen you nervous."

"Ondine'll kill you before Bilal Nath can if she thinks you're any kind of risk."

"So I'll have to count on my charm."

"Stupid." Willard frowned. "Ondine's not why you're hiring Elana." It sounded like an order.

"No. I wouldn't put your niece near Ondine."

"Elana." He made a rumbling sound in his throat, half sigh and half growl. "I got her a straight job last summer. This guy owed me a favor.

His firm was a headhunter for pharmaceutical reps. You know those women who talk doctors into buying products? Elana's smart, attractive, knows how to read people. I figured she'd be good at it."

"She turned it down?"

"No, she signed on. Took it serious. She memorized the shit out of the product catalog in just a couple of weeks, and the clients fucking loved her. Then she quit after two months. She said of all the things she'd ever done, pushing drugs was the lowest." Willard drank the last of his wine. "Maybe she took the job just to prove she could do it. To me or to herself. I dunno."

"I'll find Ondine on my own."

"She moved somewheres out by Broadmoor, I think. But tonight she'll be at SAM."

"Sam's a boyfriend?"

"SAM. The art museum, genius." He pointed in its direction, just a handful of blocks away. "The trustees are throwing some big gala for benefactors or some shit tonight. Ondine goes every year. Hell, you can find her name on the wall of diamond-level donors, or whatever they call it."

If Ondine was attending an event surrounded by the wealthy and powerful, it wasn't for the pleasure of their company. Patronizing the museum at her level must mean elite privileges, special access. And special influence.

"I'll talk to her there," I said.

Willard actually laughed. It sounded like a stump grinder in action. "They wouldn't let you onto the front steps. It's black-tie, Van. Do you have a tuxedo?"

I'd never even *worn* a tuxedo. My expression confessed as much.

"What I thought," Willard said. "Plus it's invitation only. God knows how much you have to donate to get on that list. Forget it."

"Who does your suits?" I said.

"Go to hell."

"Just a tux off the rack will do."

"You say the words *off the rack* to my guy, he'll kill you. Or himself, or both. This'll cost you." When I didn't flinch, Willard grumbled again and took out his phone.

"I need a business suit, too," I said, remembering Elana's text.

"Jesus. You really have to find the limit, don't you? Hang on."

He began texting someone. The waiter brought the bill in a calfskin folder. I had just enough in my wallet to cover it.

SIXTEEN

MADE A QUICK STOP AT the Barracuda to retrieve more cash from another of my hiding places, this one inside the driver's seat. The address Willard had given me for his tailor was off Blanchard, close enough that a fast walk would get me there sooner than driving. Lines of pedestrians snaked to and from their holiday plans, everyone's urgency matching my pace. I skirted the light at 4th Ave to the next block.

Forty yards behind me, a weighty guy in a zip-front running jacket and matching black pants jogged across Stewart to beat the traffic. Active wear or not, he didn't look like jogging came natural to him. His jowls bounced a bit as he hustled along.

I turned onto 3rd. He did, too, matching my pace exactly. A block later I paused at Virginia as if deciding which way to go. Jowls stopped, instantly preoccupied with his phone.

He wasn't alone. Another man, this one with a shock of sandy hair looking like a lit matchstick atop his puffy blue hiking coat, had halted abruptly on the other side of the avenue. He gazed with furious interest at the window display for an eyeglass store.

When I moved, they moved. I rounded the corner onto Virginia and immediately sprinted to stretch the distance between us.

Bilal's people? These were white guys, and excepting his wife, Aura, all of Bilal's soldiers I'd seen so far were South Asian. I considered leading the two men on a roundabout chase, maybe corner one and get some answers, but I was in a hurry.

At the next block a thick column of people had formed outside the Moore Theatre, waiting for entry. The marquee read: DEC 30 / 2 SHOWS: CRATER + SKATING POLLY. I wasn't clued in to the bands, but they had drawn a big enough audience that the line for the matinee filled the sidewalk from wall to curb, all the way down the block and onto the next. I dove into the first rows.

"Hey," a woman said.

"Sorry, dropped my keys somewhere," I said, shuffling past and removing my barn jacket while keeping an eye on the corner. My pursuers appeared on the opposite sidewalk. I kept my head down as they scanned the streets, the crowd of theatergoers, and then the streets again with increasing desperation. I kept up my sham of searching the pavement as I edged farther back into the throng.

After another thirty seconds Jowls pointed, and his lean partner speedwalked down Virginia toward the water, in the direction they'd last seen me going. My friend in the tracksuit took a more deliberate route, walking along the avenue for a closer look at the crowd. But the mass of people had started to move, and I let myself shuffle along with it, no one giving a damn if I was cutting in line so long as they got inside themselves.

Jowls gave up and hurried after his partner. A little extra exercise for him tonight. I waited until he was out of sight, then bolted up the avenue.

Who were these guys? They could be cops—Jowls had that plainclothes vibe, not quite matching the vibe of the civilians around him—and they knew at least the basics of tailing someone, even if they needed more men or more practice. But there was no reason for cops to be following me.

At least no reason that I knew.

Which flipped me back to the other side of the coin. Bilal might have wanted me followed, to make sure I was complying with the plan to break into Ceres Biotech. Maybe he'd hired help, knowing his men would be recognized. I might not be the only one building a team.

The more worrisome question was how they had tracked me here. Had they been watching the car? Or Willard? I kept to the shadows, metaphorically speaking, on my way to the bespoke tailor.

His shop was called Giuseppe's, and it was shaped like a wide hallway between two much grander Belltown stores. The wizened Italian guy who unlocked the shop for me either spoke little English or was so angry at being rousted from his home to fit me for a tuxedo he refused to speak. He just pointed.

I put on the black tux with the notched lapels he had indicated. He pinned the hem and the sleeves within a flat minute, and disappeared with the jacket and pants into the back of the shop.

By the time I'd used my phone to read what I could learn about the Seattle Art Museum gala online, Giuseppe had returned, placing two zippered clear garment bags on the counter along with a pair of black patent-leather shoes. He hadn't asked my shoe size. He hadn't measured me for a shirt, either, and I could see the top edge of a white collar on a second hanger under the tux.

I glanced at the second garment bag. A two-button suit in light wool, in slate blue with a subtle gray check paired with another white shirt and a tie the color of rust on iron.

"Should I try them on?" I said. Giuseppe's glance was withering. It softened marginally when I put fifty hundred-dollar bills beside the register.

As he locked the door again, I surreptitiously opened the zipper and glanced at one of the suit sleeves, to make sure I wasn't being conned. There had been no sound of a sewing machine from the back room. The cuffs had been hand-stitched, each loop precisely the same distance from the last. The old tailor would be hell at lockpicking if he chose to change professions.

I took a circuitous route back to the Barracuda, buying a pair of shoes to match the blue suit and slipping out the back of the store. Spent ten minutes checking the surroundings before approaching my car. And another twenty examining both interior and exterior with a penlight for tracking devices. I wasn't certain that Jowls and his matchstick buddy had started tailing me at the car, but if they knew my ride and were trying to find me again, the Barracuda would be an easy choice. I even checked my own hidden compartments, in case they'd used those against me.

When I drove away, I circled the blocks around Belltown until I was sure I was alone. The feeling that I wasn't safe proved impossible to shake.

SEVENTEEN

E LANA COLL LOOKED AS COMFORTABLE in the lobby of the Neapolitan as if she were a guest in their Marchesa Suite every night. It wasn't hard to imagine the owners making some arrangement with her whereby Elana would adorn the lobby during peak hours just to add some millennial appeal to the classical surroundings. She had the right look: very tall, very green-eyed, and swathed in an LBD that flirted with being too L.

If the owners knew how often those green eyes focused on the jewelry of other guests, they would rethink their options. Elana was Luce's best friend, which said something about her magnetism all by itself. Luce was about as ethical as a human could get. Elana was never happier than when she was breaking a law.

"Hey." She looked me up and down as I approached, my new shoes squeaking. "You took me serious."

"As a heart attack. Why are we standing where every person and camera can see us?"

"Because guests of the hotel have no reason to hide." She held up a wine-colored keycard between her first two fingers. "Room 502."

"You checked in?" I sat down in the gold velveteen chair opposite hers.

"Technically Solange did. Personal assistant to Mr. Gilles Foster."

I tamped down my impatience. Elana would have her fun.

"Mr. Foster has a number of personal assistants in various cities," she said, with the tiniest of smiles. "One of them is my friend Winnifred, whose professional name is Solange."

"Okay. And Foster stays here when in Seattle?"

"He usually stays at the Fairmont, but Solange made a special request. She finds the Neapolitan much sexier."

"Where are the lovebirds now?"

"Gilles's plane arrives from Montreal in two hours. Solange checked in early to make herself presentable. Two keys. Your friend Bilal and his wife are in suite 501, and his two angry-looking associates are in the adjoining room 503."

"What else?" Elana looked too smug.

She waggled the key. "502 is the room on the other side of 501. Solange told Gilles she likes the eastern view. The Neapolitan has it so that entire families—or celebrity entourages—can occupy a floor without ever stepping into the hall."

The lock of a connecting-room door would be a whole lot simpler to open than the door off the hall. And much more private. "Nice."

"Say it."

"You're very good. Do you also know if Bilal and his team are at home?"

"I was with Winnifred half an hour ago when they left. We went down to the lobby after them. They took their car."

I winced inside. "How much have you told Winnifred?"

"Just that Bilal is a bad guy and I promised we wouldn't steal anything. Strictly fact-finding. And we need a lookout."

"You're the lookout."

"Hell I am. I'm going in." Elana stood up before I could protest further. "Besides, you need me to make introductions."

The Neapolitan's elevators had retained their old brass accordion gates as accent pieces after their modernization. Elana paused as I opened the gate for her.

"You're going to be cool, right? About Winnifred?" she said.

"Yeah."

"Some dudes get all flustered around sex workers. Just don't embarrass me."

"I'll try not to faint."

Suite 501 was at the end of the short hall, flanked by 502 and 503 on opposite sides of the corridor. Elana tapped softly on the door to 502. Winnifred-slash-Solange answered her knock immediately. She was nearly as tall as Elana, every inch the corporate businesswoman. Her blouse and skirt would have passed the dress code of any bank. As she glanced my way, a slight magnification of her blue eyes revealed her glasses weren't just for costume.

"Van, Winnifred," Elana said, striding into the room.

"Hello," I said. "Elana said she talked you into keeping watch."

"I offered," Winnifred replied. "Just tell me what you need."

A murmur at the back of my brain wondered if that would have sounded provocative even if I hadn't known her profession. "Set up in the lobby where you have a view of the entrance. You've seen their Mercedes. Text Elana if it pulls up."

"That's all? I expected something more . . . covert."

"The simplest plans are the best." I was already examining the deadbolt on the adjoining door. A thumb turn allowed me to unlock our side. There would be a similar knob in Bilal's suite. As a backup for the hotel, there was also a keyhole that would spring both mechanisms. I set to work with my lockpicks and drew the bolt back.

"Whoa!" Winnifred said at the sound of the click. She was still putting on her shoes.

"We won't be long," Elana said. Winnifred nodded and hurried to the hall. We waited three minutes before Elana's phone buzzed to signal that Secret Agent Solange was in position.

Aura and Bilal had evidently told housekeeping to let the room alone. A twisted rope of bedsheets lay at the foot of the California king, and the soft pillows still showed deep depressions from their most recent nap. The towels on the floor of the bathroom were damp and the air in the small tiled space humid. They had showered before heading out for the day.

"Don't touch anything," I said. "They can't know we were here."

"What are you looking for?" Elana said.

Anything that might give me some chance of slipping the leash Bilal had fastened around my neck. Something that could help me stall him for a while or get him arrested and booted out of the country. A box of plutonium would be nice. Call the FBI with an anonymous tip and let them take over.

It didn't take long to check every drawer and every piece of luggage in their room. Nothing unusual, not even a gun. The room safe under the dresser was open and empty. On the nightstands were books—two in what might be Urdu, with translated promotional quotes on the back from prominent European politicians. The books on Aura's side were slightly flashier—a paperback suspense novel and a thick well-thumbed tome on health and pregnancy. Looked like the newlyweds weren't wasting any of Bilal's limited time.

In the bathroom, I found half a dozen prescription bottles from a Miami pharmacy for Bilal, treatment for his ALS. An evil part of me whispered that I could return and doctor the pills just a little. But Bilal had warned me that even death wouldn't stop his vengeance if I crossed him. Even if I could set aside my scruples—*no different than Oregon*, the insidious voice whispered—it wouldn't set me free.

Aura was taking a prescription as well. The largest of the bottles held fifty or more cream-colored time release capsules. A drug called olaparib. I was familiar with a wide variety of pharmaceuticals thanks to time spent in Army hospitals and in therapy, but olaparib was new to me.

The judge that had granted Aura probation on her identity theft charge had referred to health concerns. I'd considered whether Bilal might be sending me to steal a vaccine for his incurable disease. But maybe Aura's own troubles were their real motive.

The only items of interest were two new-looking HP laptops on the desk. Bilal might be conducting business while on the road. If he'd been at all careless, the computers could be hard evidence. But I had no way of hacking past their log-in screens here, on the fly. I'd have to leave them. The idea of abandoning something so potentially useful made me grind my teeth.

Elana was admiring a set of black pearl earrings Aura had left on the room's lone table. "What did you say this guy does? Hacking?"

"Something related to that. I don't have a handle on him yet," I said, running my fingertips over the back of the dresser to see if anything had been taped there. A last-ditch effort. "He's more skilled than the average black hat."

She tilted her head to see the pearls from another angle. "Must be. These could pay my rent for a year."

A high-end hacker must have high-end enemies. Small wonder Saleem and Juwad went everywhere Bilal and Aura did. Saleem struck me as someone with advanced training—maybe maroon berets or some other Special Service branch of the Pakistani armed forces. And devoted to his boss's continued good health, at least against anything that could be cured by a well-aimed bullet.

The connecting door to 503 was unlocked. Saleem and his buddy kept their room considerably neater, though again without a hotel maid's help. The blankets on both twin beds had been pulled back into place, and the surfaces of the dresser and table were bare. I set about searching, faster now. We'd already spent more time in the rooms than I'd intended.

The safe in Saleem's room was closed. I punched the LOCK button twice to enter administrative mode, then tried 9999 as the factory default. It didn't work. I tried all zeroes and then all ones, with the same result.

"Shit," Elana said, thinking we were stymied. I pulled the safe out slightly to see the top. A small metal plate stamped with the safe company's name decorated the center of the front edge, fastened in place with two hex screws. I used my multitool to remove one screw and swung the little plate aside to reveal a tiny cross-shaped keyhole.

I grinned. A manufacturer's lock, to open the safe if guests forgot their codes. Elana leaned over my shoulder as I began to work the lock with the slimmest of Dono's old picks.

Her phone buzzed, making us both jump.

"They're at the valet," she said.

Dammit. The lock clicked and the door came open with a whine of the bolts drawing back.

"Get ready to run," I said, as I scanned the safe's contents.

Boxes of 9 mm ammo. Two empty magazines for Saleem's Steyr. All squeezed to one side. Filling most of the safe's cubic foot was a white cylinder with a narrower top, like a large metal water bottle. A logo on its side read CXS-3001. I took the bottle from the safe.

"In the lobby now," Elana said, waiting by the adjoining door.

The top of the bottle unscrewed. Removing it drew out a green plastic plug. The rest of the interior was filled with some kind of soft insulating foam.

"Van," said Elana.

No time to take pictures. I replaced its screw top and set the bottle back in the safe, held the thick door shut, and began tweaking the lock with one hand. Elana cracked the door to 503 to peer down the hallway. The lock gave way and the servomotors buzzed as the bolts glided back into place.

A ping came from down the hall. The elevator, reaching our floor.

"Go," I said, screwing the metal plate down with my fingertips. Elana closed the hallway door and raced to Aura and Bilal's room. I shoved the safe back into position and almost leapt after her, closing the adjoining door and crossing in a rush to meet her in 502.

Relocking the connecting door gave me more trouble than it should have. From the hallway we heard the scuff of feet on carpet and light thumps as the door to the suite opened. Saleem's voice, asking a question. I made myself relax. The mechanism gave a faint click as the deadbolt sprung back into the frame.

Neither Elana nor I moved. Just listened, as Bilal's door thumped closed, followed seconds later by the sound of Saleem and Juwad opening their own room.

We slipped out to the hall and padded silently to the stairs. It was three flights before Elana spoke.

"That was perfect."

"You have a strange dictionary."

"I meant the timing. This might be the best holiday treat I've ever had. What's next?"

We reached the lobby. I gave Elana a moment to talk to Winnifred privately. I was busy with thoughts of the insulated bottle in Saleem's hotel safe.

It had clearly been designed to transport something under extreme cold, which made sense for biological material. Whatever Bilal wanted me to steal from Ceres, I was going to carry it away in that.

Reason it out: Bilal Nath is a hacker, dealing in information. Maybe Ceres made a breakthrough and Bilal found out about it. He's stealing a sample to sell, or to ransom.

Elana interrupted my conjectures. Her emerald eyes sparkled with enthusiasm.

"When I asked what's next, I meant it," she said. "Willard let on that you have a score tomorrow night. I'm there."

"No. It's a one-person job. And dangerous."

"Willard also said that limpdick will kill you if you don't do it and might kill you if you do. So you obviously need friends."

What I needed was a minor miracle. For Bilal to have a heart attack, or suddenly get religion, or become homesick for Karachi. But none of that was going to happen. Whatever was protected in Ceres's cryobank had brought him to Seattle, and it would remain Bilal's singular focus until he'd acquired it. I'd seen his and his wife's expressions when they looked at the biotech company.

None of my options were sunny. Run, and Bilal would come after my people, either by sending his killer Saleem or through more devious online attacks. Hand over the goods and I would be beyond expendable. Ensuring my silence would become the new priority, at least for the few moments until Saleem squeezed the trigger.

The sun had gone down while Elana and I had been inside the Neapolitan. It wouldn't be long before the museum gala opened its doors. I still had to figure a way to storm the gates and find one particular benefactor.

Ondine. She knew Bilal; she'd set him up with Dr. Claybeck. Odds were good that she also knew something about his plans on her home turf.

Crashing the gala would be a challenge. Convincing Ondine Long to help me might be impossible.

EIGHTEEN

I CHOSE A PARKING GARAGE A block away from the museum and drove up the ramps until I reached the top level. A modicum of privacy for me to change clothes for the second time that day.

The tailor's efficiency hadn't stopped at the shirt. Hanging along with the tuxedo pants under the jacket I found a black silk cummerbund and bow tie. The cummerbund I could figure out. The bow tie was beyond my ken. It took a quarter of an hour and a couple of YouTube instructional videos for me to finally get it tied to where it didn't look like a bat had squashed itself against my throat.

The tux made me the most overdressed guy at the Starbucks on 1st Ave. Watching the SAM entrance from across the street, I saw museum staff—employees drafted into putting on their finest and working the holiday—just inside the arched portico, using scanners to read QR codes off paper invitations and cell phones submitted by the guests. Security in blue blazers stood discreetly to one side.

There were cops, too. During my passes along the sidewalk, I'd seen a team of uniforms on the long low flight of granite steps inside the museum, pausing to chat by the Chinese statues of seated rams with the nonchalance of patrolmen on easy duty. I wouldn't be sneaking in.

A knot of revelers waited at the crosswalk. Doyennes and dignitaries who had noticeably started their evening at dinner, with wine. Their dress was formal, their laughter considerably less starched. The ivory edge of an invitation showed from one pooh-bah's tuxedo pocket.

Tempting, but risky. If the code on the invitation was unique to the guest, or their name was printed on the card, I might be finished before I started. These people looked like longtime supporters who might be known to museum staff.

Someone closer to my age, maybe. Like the half-dozen suited-up college kids under the legs of the Hammering Man statue, having a last vape before going inside. Maybe their families were donors, or maybe they were tech prodigies with a yen for modern art. Just so long as they had their invitations.

I tossed the dregs of my Sumatra and crossed the avenue, pretending to be as engrossed in my phone as most of them were. In the half light of the winter street, it was an easy task to review their screens as I paced. A blast of wind off the harbor steps made the nearest girl shiver.

"Let's go," she said, her teeth chattering either by natural reaction or to deliberately emphasize her point.

Her date nodded without looking up. She nudged him impatiently before his screen changed to display the black mottled square of the QR.

"Could you grab my picture?" I said, abruptly holding out my phone. "I promised my folks they'd see me in the tux."

They looked startled but the boy complied, and he even angled himself where he'd capture the moving statue in the background.

"Thanks a lot," I said as he handed the phone back. "Have fun tonight."

I looked at my phone and swiped away from the picture of me grinning sheepishly to see another app. The black square of the invitation code appeared, every pixel as crisp as the original.

It was a simple program on the surface. Simple, but highly illegal. Similar to the old applications that traded contact information or photos when two enabled phones bumped each other, this function stole a screenshot from the nearest unlocked phone on command. In this case, an image of the kid's invitation code. I'd bought the app off an anonymous hacker from Hong Kong, thinking it would be useful for snagging texts or emails should I ever have need. But I could be flexible.

I quick-marched to the entrance, wanting to make sure my copy was the first one seen. A pass of the scanner gun over the phone resulted in a satisfying ping. All good.

The docent secured a black plastic bracelet with the SAM logo around my wrist.

"That's your pass," she explained, showing me the strip of flexible metal on the underside. "You can come and go now if you like. Don't forget the director's presentation at eight o'clock in the forum."

I examined the bracelet. Classier than an ink stamp at a club. I wondered if its metal band also signaled if a guest was permitted in the VIP sections. There was bound to be a private room somewhere. Rich people loved exclusivity. The more select their daily lives were, the more they coveted reaching that next level. Ondine lived on the next level.

A loose line of volunteers—flanked by SPD officers in crisp navy—ushered all of the entrants to the nearest escalator and up to the museum's main forum, the launching pad of the party. I went with the flow.

It was early yet. Most guests hadn't advanced beyond the forum, enmeshed in politely chatting clusters. A coat-check service in the corner was doing brisk business. I wove around the knots of people.

Elana would have coveted the jewelry adorning the necks and earlobes of many of the matrons. She could pass for a member of this class, probably creating a whole backstory about being the heiress to a lumber empire. My sharp tuxedo aside, I would have more trouble blending.

The forum took up half the length of the long block on 1st Ave, a room as tall as a terminal in a regional airport. There were a few nods to the season in the holly branches placed on the front desks and at the corners of video screens behind the receptionists. Restrained, unlike the art installation that had many of the two hundred guests craning their necks upward.

A representation of an old-growth tree, suspended horizontally. One hundred feet or more from its fan-shaped roots to the wiry upper branches at the far end of the hall. Its trunk had been segmented every fifteen feet or so, and the pieces rocked fractionally on their guywires in response to some movement in the air above us. It made the longest branches appear to be stretching toward the high windows of the lobby. As if straining to rejoin nature.

A plaque on the wall told me the piece was crafted from over a million pieces of reclaimed cedar, off a plaster cast of a living tree. But the dappled surface looked less like wood to me than the skin of some great snake, cast off and wrapped around crooked tubes. Elegant and eerie.

The thought of serpents brought me back to my purpose here. I went hunting for Ondine.

On the third floor, the galleries had been opened to allow guests to wander freely about the twisting metal sculptures and abstract images in oil and aluminum filling the walls.

Hard to envision Ondine gazing at modern art, unless it was brought directly before her after being liberated from a private collection by someone like my grandfather.

Up to the fourth level. More galleries, with bristly costumes and ceremonial masks from Africa. More guards, too, wandering with slack expressions between rooms.

One of the more imposing sentinels held his post by a red velour curtain that had been set up to block a wide entryway off the rear hall. A glowing screen past his shoulder read WYCKOFF PORCELAIN ROOM. As I watched, a crisp white-haired member of the gentry approached. The guard moved the curtain aside to admit him before the man had to break his stride, without so much as a nod exchanged.

That would be the place. But from the look of the guard, I wasn't going to bluff my way inside.

I still carried the burner backup phone I'd been using since Bilal had hacked mine. I stepped into one of the side galleries to mess with the burner's settings and downloaded a Migos song that Cyndra had been playing in her room before dinner the other night, until Addy had protested about the lyrics searing the paint from the walls.

Down the hall from the Porcelain Room, past a collection of Catholic triptychs, I found a gallery dedicated to textiles from the Restoration Era, or replicas thereof. Gowns ten times as elaborate as any on the museum guests. I waited until the nearby guards circled away to check the adjoining exhibits before slipping the burner into the folds of an especially lavish bodice.

Nothing I could do about the cameras, which would have caught my tuxedoed image near the gown and my profile leaving the gallery. But then I didn't plan to stay and admire the culture all evening.

One minute later the timer I'd set went off, and Cardi B's voice-over began to echo through the galleries at the highest volume the little phone could manage. It was a shame I hadn't had time to patch into the museum's sound system. Cardi's words were hard to make out from the adjoining hallway, but I imagine most guests got the tone if not the precise words describing her riding her man like a BMX bike.

Guards hurried toward the textile gallery as if hot coals were frying their feet. Curious patrons joined the rush. The sentinel at the Porcelain Room resisted the pull for a slow count of three, then strode across and into the gallery, looking ready to crush the offending device in his meaty fist. I was through the red curtain in seconds.

True to its name, the room was like being inside the world's largest and most expensive china cabinet. Each dish and cup and tureen individually mounted within slim cocoa-brown display cases. Whatever viewing benches the room usually housed had been replaced by chairs and couches with velvet upholstery, arranged into seating areas around hexagonal glass coffee tables.

On a loveseat at the far side was Ondine Long.

She'd spotted me before the curtain had stopped swaying. Her soft smile for her companion—the stiff gentleman I'd seen enter the room earlier—didn't change, but her eyes held mine for an extra second before turning back.

If I gave her a few minutes, she might gracefully extricate herself from the conversation. Minutes I didn't have. I wove through the standing knots of guests, absorbed in their close discussions over drinks they had acquired from some unseen server.

"Ondine," I said.

The starched man looked up, thrown by the intrusion. Was I some impertinent waiter?

Ondine hardly moved. She wore a green dress made of some kind of silk, high-necked and so restrained in its cut that it had to cost as much as a decent used car. Her hair was coiled in an equally minimal arrangement. Only her makeup was a touch too visible. I wasn't precisely sure of Ondine's age—her blend of Asian and Western heritages and the very best surgery complicated any attempt at analysis—but suspected that she'd had a professional apply her mask, and the artist's hand showed in the work.

"Good evening," said Ondine, as if she'd been expecting my visit for the past week. "Van, this is State Senator Werring. Senator, Donovan Shaw."

"Hello," the senator said, without another glance at me. "Ondine, I think if you'll consider the party's point of view, you'll understand why your support—"

"I promise you I'll consider every perspective, Lyle. And I'll have an answer for you by Monday. If you'll excuse me."

"Of course. I'm overdue to check in with my campaign staff." Werring stood up, adroitly turning the dismissal into the next move of a man of action. "Mr. Shaw."

I nodded, choosing the seat on Ondine's right rather than the chair directly opposite. The angle let me keep half an eye on the entryway.

"I'll be astounded if you've begun patronizing the arts, Van," Ondine said. Her words and expression and tone all projecting calm politesse. I wasn't fooled.

"You've branched out, too. Playing kingmaker." I nodded to the chair the senator had recently occupied.

"The recall election. Many candidates and very few days before February."

"Time is short all around. Tell me about Bilal Nath."

The corners of Ondine's mouth twitched, which passed for disapproval.

"I didn't realize you two had met," she said.

Apparently neither Bilal nor Dr. Claybeck had shared the details of that stormy night with Ondine. No point in pulling Claybeck further into quicksand.

"He tracked me down," I said, "with the offer of a lifetime."

"I'm willing to discuss this matter tomorrow."

"Tomorrow I'll be busy dealing with the grenade you've dropped in my lap. We'll talk right here."

Her direct gaze might have unnerved a more anxious guy. Or a less angry one. Having me tossed out of the museum would attract the kind of attention not in keeping with her stature. And she couldn't be sure I wouldn't tell the cops about the connection between her and Nath. Even if they didn't believe me, it would be on record, and Ondine would find that unacceptable.

"Start at the start," I said. "Why did Nath hear my name?"

"He inquired about people with your skill set. I gave him my top recommendation. But he wasn't satisfied. He needed someone immediately and wanted options. I provided him with a short list of names—including yours—but cautioned that for various reasons they may not be to his liking. You, specifically. I told him that you weren't manageable."

"So why mention me at all?"

"What is it that Bilal wants to acquire?" she said, instead of answering.

"He didn't tell you?"

"No. He was very closed about his intentions, even though it might have helped me find the best contractor for the job."

Contractor. Like I would be remodeling Nath's kitchen.

"He won't tell me what he's after, either," I said. "What's he into? His regular business?"

"That's not relevant."

"I'll decide what's useful. If Nath is my problem, then I'm yours."

"You are not as formidable as you imagine."

"Try me."

Ondine waited, still as one of the porcelain figurines in the nearby display case, until a tangle of guests had moved out of earshot.

"Bilal Nath started as an early online entrepreneur. Mining personal search histories to encourage small payments from individuals, in the days before the Internet had many ramparts in place."

Even with Ondine's oblique language, I grasped the extortion. *Send $500 or we will email everyone in your contact list these sick webpages you've* *visited. Everyone will know you're a pervert.* A scam with a very low success rate, but minimal cost and no risk at all if carried out from beyond the reach of U.S. authorities. Run the job on a few million addresses, and even if only a tiny portion of one percent paid up, you'd still be rich.

"I already knew Bilal was a hacker," I said.

"On a higher level than most, if not all. He transitioned into more targeted ventures before long," Ondine said, "aimed at celebrities and public figures. I'm told he has a team in Lahore, which he hires out to acquire private information for political movements in South Asia and perhaps elsewhere. Nath is very adept at circumventing defenses."

She didn't make it sound like a compliment. An inkling that where Bilal Nath was concerned, Ondine's customary detachment might be shaded with something else.

"Yeah, I had a demonstration of his skills," I said. "So what does an international blackmailer need that he can't buy or coerce?"

Ondine turned over one palm, as if considering the question moot. "You may have also noticed that Bilal is ill. Perhaps he desires something of emotional value."

I thought of the cryo bottle I'd seen in their hotel room. Something personal?

The door to the Porcelain Room opened and the thick-necked sentinel strode in, along with an equally brawny guy in a black suit and tie. He looked at Ondine. And me.

"Yours?" I said, looking at the grunt in the funeral wear.

"My driver."

"Surprised he wasn't lurking near the soup tureens to protect you."

"I have Jessica for that." I looked where she indicated. A fortyish Latina woman wearing a claret-colored dress and more sensible shoes than a formal party demanded stood off my left shoulder. Her hand rested, relaxed, at the open top to her Kate Spade handbag.

"Diversity in bodyguards," I said. "Good for you."

"Our time is up," Ondine said.

The museum guard was holding the burner phone I'd left in the antique French gown. A glance at his ruddy glowering face told me he'd seen the security video and identified me.

"So it is," I said.

I stood up. Jessica moved to a position beside Ondine's loveseat.

"How's the employee health plan?" I asked her. "Just in case I hire on."

"Profit sharing is the real draw," she said. "Nice tux."

"Let's go." The guard, at my elbow.

"Can't take me anywhere," I said. Jessica smiled minutely. Ondine looked undisturbed by anything around her, like she might already be weighing the merits of contributing to Senator Werring's campaign.

I walked out the open door, past Ondine's driver. The guard followed close enough behind to pick lint off my collar. Two more guards joined our procession as we paraded down the escalators to the portico where I'd first come in.

"Your wristband, asshole," the guard said.

He wanted to take a swing at me so badly it was making his fingers twitch. I held enough pent-up rage myself that I was tempted to ask him if he wanted to take it outside, where he could make a move free from any cameras or easily horrified party guests.

But I'd started the trouble tonight. And this poor furious goon wasn't my enemy. I tore off the wristband and handed it to him and left.

Outside, the hammer of the giant statue rose and fell, rose and fell. I finally turned toward University Street and began walking. Just a well-dressed mutt, looking a whole lot better than he felt.

I was tired. Which was no excuse for not having spotted Ondine's bodyguard Jessica, despite the signifiers of her practical shoes and the handbag large enough to hold her piece and as many extra magazines as she could want. Sloppy.

I unraveled my bow tie and unbuttoned the top buttons of the tuxedo shirt, grateful that I didn't hold a job where a necktie was a daily require-ment. I barely held a job at all. My gig at Bully Betty's was just marking time. Betty had recognized it before I had. I didn't need the income—though I would soon, the way I was burning through my savings—and as much as I liked the people at the bar, pulling drinks and keeping the peace weren't any challenge.

Bilal was a threat. And threats were a kind of challenge. The kind that kept me sharp, focused on something important, feeling the way I wanted to feel. I wasn't suicidal, but I would have to be dense not to recognize the pattern of my own behavior. I liked the action.

My grandfather had, too. Dono was never happier than when he was planning a score. Afterward, when the excitement and urgency had abated, he'd sink into what he called his black dog days. Growing morose and surly for no accountable reason.

Screw it. Solve the problem right in front of you, Shaw. Get Bilal Nath off your back. Then you can sweat the small stuff, like the rest of your life.

On a normal night, the garage where I'd left the Barracuda would have been nearly empty. But with half the hotels and restaurants at the heart of the city hosting end-of-year events, every parking space from the stadiums to Belltown was filled. I wound my way through the packed rows on the sloping roof level. I was five yards from my car when a tapping sound came from the dark at my nine, pebble on pavement.

I dodged to one side, ducking down behind a blue minivan. Was it Bilal, or Saleem? How had they tracked me here?

"Hold it." A man's voice, on my opposite side. Very close. He'd suckered me. "Get your hands up. Now."

I showed my palms. The man stepped out from the shadows of the elevator stand.

Sean Burke. In the flesh. With an arctic expression on his face and one of his recently acquired SIG Sauer pistols in his hand. A suppressor extended the barrel like an accusing finger, pointing dead square at my head.

NINETEEN

BURKE WAVED ME TOWARD THE other side of the elevator stand. Where someone returning to their car would be less likely to spot him holding me at gunpoint. Or emptying his clip into my heart.

He walked steadily sideways as I approached, keeping at least a dozen feet between us. When I reached a spot in the center of the nearest handicapped space, with an SUV blocking us from the rest of the lot, he motioned for me to stop.

"If you want my wallet, man, you can have it," I said.

With his left hand he removed something from his pocket and flicked it so that it landed at my feet. A thick square of folded paper.

"Pick it up," he said.

I did, and unfolded it.

It was a picture of me in black and white, taken from a foot or two above the level of my head. The distance was tricky to gauge due to the fish-eye lens. But there was no mistaking my face, with my concentrated expression and every scar sharply detailed as I came toward the lens. Taking my first shoeless step through the sliding-glass door of Burke's cul-de-sac home in Bitter Lake.

There were more papers, more pictures. Me in Burke's hallway, rifling through the closet. Me in the bedroom, opening a dresser drawer.

Each image taken from roughly the same elevation. Each a prosecutor's dream.

Not that I thought Burke had any intention of involving the cops.

"In the ceiling beams," I said.

Burke nodded. "Triggered by pressure plates in the floor." If he had much emotion about our situation, he was keeping it to himself.

The black paint on the beams had struck me as odd at the time. Now I knew why. It would have been almost impossible for me to spot a tiny camera lens in rough wood painted black. Especially at night. The part of me that wasn't screaming at myself for fucking up admired the simplicity.

"You're not a shooter," Burke said. "You didn't bring a gun to the house. Who are you, Shaw?" he said.

He knew my name. Son of a bitch.

"Hey, I was just looking for cash, man. It won't happen again, I swear."

"Burglars don't leave flat-screens and stereos behind. And your car is registered to some dead shitheel in Oregon." Burke lowered his pistol until it pointed at my left knee. "Last chance. Who do you work for?"

The elevator motor started. Neither of us moved.

Burke wasn't bluffing. I tensed, waiting for the hot round to fracture my kneecap and shred the ligaments around it into wet mush.

A car alarm beeped and parking lights flashed from the lower slope. In the instant Burke's eyes flicked in that direction, I dove and rolled under the SUV. I came up on the other side and kept moving, bolting for deeper cover. Expecting gunfire to follow at any second. I heard laughter instead, and happy curses, as a small group of teenagers made their loping way off the elevator. On the row below us, the car whose alarm had beeped roared to life.

I risked a look over the nearest hood. Burke was gone.

Maybe he had stepped into the open elevator. Or maybe he was waiting until the new arrivals had left to emerge and finish me off. I ran to the Barracuda, diving into the driver's seat, leaving thick black stripes on the asphalt in my haste to be away.

Driving out of the garage gave no relief. I expected Burke to appear from behind every car, around each corner. Only when I was on the street and roaring south did I unclench.

How had he found me? How the hell did he know who I *was*, even with the pictures from his camera trap at the house? It had been less than twenty-four hours since I'd darkened his doorstep. *Goddamn.*

Once I'd passed the stadiums and was sure no one was following, I pulled over and stepped out of the car. The way I was going I'd smash into a lamppost, or get busted for reckless endangerment.

My new tuxedo was beyond repair, torn and stained by my roll across the oily pavement. I could feel my knee seeping blood. I tore off the jacket and shirt and replaced them with the old flannel I'd started the night with.

Idiot. The only reason I wasn't ending the night in a hospital or a morgue was dumb luck, emphasis on the *dumb*. I had been a step too slow in every single dance tonight.

I called Hollis. Maybe misery could do with company.

"You alone?" I said.

"For the moment. Matty and Fran from J dock are on their way over. We've a trip planned south to Cannon Beach after the new year."

"I just met Sean Burke."

"The man who might be—"

"The man who might be. We didn't get into that."

"So what's he like?"

"Calmer than me. But he was the one holding the gun." I told Hollis what had happened.

"Sly devil," Hollis said, "with his hidden cameras."

"In a home that might as well be a worm on a hook. An entire house, set up just to see who comes knocking."

"Who does that?"

Somebody with serious enemies. If I had walked into Burke's house with a gun in my hand, he'd have assumed I had broken in to kill him. In which case he might have ended me straight off, no need for interrogation.

"I can't get distracted by Sean Burke right now," I said, more to myself than Hollis. "Bilal Nath is still dead set on forcing me to crack Ceres Biotech tomorrow night. It's more than just business for him, I'm sure. And I don't think I can shake him loose in time."

"And you need help."

"I need a third option."

I told Hollis what I had in mind.

"That's possible," he said, "but are you sure you won't want a little—what do you soldiers call it—fire support?"

"Willard will be there if things get hot. My last resort."

"Matty just stepped aboard," Hollis said. "I can come by your apartment in the morning."

"I'll come to you."

"You all right?"

"I'm rattled. Between Bilal knowing where all my friends live and Sean Burke tracking me down hell knows how, I'm not sure where safe ground is. Better to keep on the move."

"Get some rest, lad," Hollis said. "We'll sort it out."

He hung up. I knew he was right. I'd been on the move and on edge all day, and tomorrow would be worse.

The last day of the year. Time for resolutions. And fireworks.

JUNIOR YEAR, PART TWO

Seeing my friend Davey Tolan in the library was like spotting a coyote at the off-leash dog park. Out of place, and very likely up to no good. He was alone at one of the study tables, reading or pretending to read our English assignment of *Brave New World*. Really he was drawing robots and shit in his notebook like always.

"Davey," I said, sliding into the chair opposite him. "The fuck?"

He smiled like he already knew the punchline to a joke I was telling and flicked his eyes toward a group of girls at another table I'd passed on the way in. "Kate Barra."

"Huh?" I knew who Kate was. Honor Society, in every AP course ever invented and probably creating more they hadn't. High-Quality Life. "You're not horny for her."

Davey leaned in so far he practically lay across the table. His dark hair flopped over his face. "I am since I saw her running in gym class. Katie Girl's exercise necessitates an industrial-strength sports bra."

I snorted. Davey's dick was like a compass with a magnet nearby. Unpredictable. "She'll never go for it."

"You have no faith at all. One, Kate has agreed to help me

with algebra. Two, she broke up with Pel Rosario last weekend. Time is ripe and so is she."

How did Davey track all this stuff? Every time I thought he and I were roughly equivalent in our social status— somewhere north of the burnouts and south of everyone else—he proved he was tapped in. And despite my scoffing, I knew damn well Kate Barra might be in his range. Davey had those kinds of looks. Girls had been into him since before we knew what girls were.

"So that's why I'm in the library . . ." Davey said, nudging.

"You remember a quilt? Used to hang on the wall right there." I pointed to where a bunch of watercolors from Ms. Pico's art class now covered the wall.

"That is maybe the weirdest question you've ever asked me."

"Do you?"

"Whoa." He mimed raising his hands to ward off a blow. "Yeah, sure I do. It got ripped off last year. So?"

"My mom made part of it."

"Oh. And it's gone now. Man, that sucks." He thought about it as I stared angrily at the watercolors. The library smelled a little like old wool, even though the school had dehumidifiers running all year long to keep mold away.

"You talk to Colten?"

"Who? Colten Gulas?"

"He got fucking reamed by Mr. Lindhoff when the quilt disappeared. 'Cause I guess Colten was watching the library, part of his detention or some shit. So either Colten left when he wasn't supposed to, or he knew who took the quilt and wouldn't squeal."

Mr. Lindhoff was the guidance counselor. I didn't like him, and I probably wasn't one of his favorite people, either. "Why's Lindhoff care so much?"

"Dude!" Davey laughed. "He cares 'cause Ms. Nasgate cares. They're boning, man. How do you not know this?"

Because I rarely gave a thought to school, except to finish it and get away. I was starting to see the downside.

"I'll find Colten," I said.

"I figured. You got that look, like you're biting on aluminum foil. But you'll have to wait. The dork's been out of class past three days."

"He sick?"

"Dunno."

"You know where he lives?"

"Man, you are caffeinated today. I don't. He sometimes skips last period to hang with Singer Boeman's Club for Shitheads, so maybe he's skipping the whole week."

I remembered Singer. The school's dealer of tiny bags of pot or coke or whatever pills he'd been able to steal from somebody's parents' bathroom. Boeman and most of his bunch had graduated or finished their credits during summer makeup sessions last year.

"Kate's friends are leaving," Davey said, shrugging into his black leather jacket. My cue to make space. "I'm gonna see if she wants to go to Yvette Friel's party this weekend."

"Bet you don't even get a hand in her sweater," I said, standing up.

"You *should* have my back, dude," he said. "Kate says Eden Adler likes you. I might be in a position to make that miracle happen."

"Bullshit."

"I mean it," he said. "Swear to God. She's no Kate"—he subtly mimed huge globes on his chest—"but if that's your type, go for it."

Eden Adler did not require a double-whatever-letter bra. Eden Adler didn't require anything but being Eden Adler. And Davey really was just trying to help.

"Thanks, man," I said.

"If we all go out, you're payin'."

It was a Wednesday, which meant Mr. Lindhoff was in his office. Early in the school year he had come around to all the homerooms to introduce himself and had mentioned that most guidance counselors served two or three high schools depending on size. He meant the size of the schools, but I guessed it could also mean the size of the district budget.

Probably because he wasn't there more often, his office was for crap. More a long closet with a high window, like a jail cell, and so narrow he would have to turn sideways to go between the wall and his desk, which was not exactly huge itself. Below the window, a hanging magazine rack was packed solid with brochures on universities and voc-tech schools, instructional packets for writing college essays, GED forms for students dropping out, and reams of other stuff I'd likely never give two shits about.

Lindhoff's eyebrows popped over his bifocals as I entered. The idea of him and Ms. Nasgate as a couple was weird. She wasn't young or anything, she'd been at the school for like twenty-five years. But Lindhoff seemed old. Like dentures old.

"Mr. Shaw?" he said. "Rethinking our talk about colleges?"

Right. Lindhoff had said something to me about my grades holding up for two-year colleges and maybe state school if I applied myself. I had forgotten what I'd said to get away from him at the time.

"Sure, but . . . I wanted to ask about the quilt from the library. The one that got stolen."

"Ask what, precisely?"

"Did Colten Gulas ever say who took it?"

He removed the glasses entirely now. I'd gotten his attention, which may not be the best thing.

"Why," he said, "do you want to know?"

Oh shit. I saw the leap he'd made. Now Lindhoff thought I was worried Colten had ratted me out.

Sometimes the truth really does set you free.

"My mom. She's dead." I let that hang in the air for a moment. Lindhoff nodded impatiently, but his expression eased back a little. "She made one of the squares, Miz Nasgate told me." *A one-two punch for sympathy, throwing out my mom and your girlfriend, dude.*

"I see. And you're hoping to recover it." He cleared his throat. "I'm afraid that's a dead end, Mr. Shaw. Colten said he never saw who took it."

Which was different than not knowing. I caught that, and Lindhoff saw me catch it.

"At this point it would be best to consider it lost," he said. "That's my belief as well as the school's. Do you grasp my meaning?"

"Yeah." *Don't go beating up Colten for answers, or the guidance counselor will guide me right into a suspension.*

"Good. And I'm sorry. I remember your mother. Moira, wasn't it?"

"Yes."

"Unusual name here in the States. She and I talked about college options for her, even after her surprise." He nodded toward me. "A very good student. I think she was looking at community schools, something that might allow her flexible hours. Do you know if she ever went?"

"No."

"'No, you don't know,' or 'No, she never attended college'?"

Lindhoff could be such a dickwad. "I don't know."

"Hmm. Priorities, perhaps. Still, a bright young woman." He turned back to his paperwork. I left him.

At least Lindhoff hadn't given me the old speech about doing a good job because Mom would have wanted that.

People had been telling me that shit my entire life, like they'd known her at all.

And he hadn't been convinced by Colt's story. While I didn't like Lindhoff much, I had to admit he wasn't a dummy. If he thought Colten Gulas knew something about the quilt, then I'd bet he was right. Suspension or no suspension, I was going to find out what that something was.

TWENTY

RETURNING TO MY APARTMENT WAS too big a risk. Even though I'd kept my name off the lease, Bilal Nath had access to enough information that he might conceivably track me to my overpriced studio off Broadway. And there was no telling where Sean Burke and his silenced SIG might pop up again. Or the pair of men who had tailed me earlier in the day.

Less than a week ago, my biggest concern was how to mend fences with Addy. Now I was dodging at least three different menaces while setting up a score that might get me killed. I needed a new life plan.

The speedboat should be safe ground. Officially I'd sold the boat after Dono's death and it was registered to a marine supply company in Everett. Which in turn was owned by a real corporation in Hong Kong, although those papers were false. I was subletting its moorage with cash. That made enough of a smoke screen that I could close both eyes to sleep.

In the morning, I rose to find the cloud cover had lightened to the point where I could at least guess at the position of the sun. The docks smelled of Canada geese and algae and clean ocean air every time the breeze picked up.

The *Francesca* wasn't in its slip. Hollis might be offshore, out of the reach of Bilal. I texted him the number **16** and tuned the VHF radio to that hailing channel. I'd finished changing clothes when his voice came through the tinny speaker.

"Benning Boy, this is *Francesca*." Fort Benning in Georgia was the home of the Ranger Regiment.

"*Francesca*, this is Benning Boy. Reply seven-one."

"Seven-one," he confirmed. We switched frequencies.

"Smart thinking calling on the radio," Hollis said once we'd exchanged call signs again. "I've been nervous about using my cell phone since that—" He stopped himself from cursing over the airwaves. "Since our spot of trouble."

"Where are you?"

"A few miles north. Have you heard from our large friend?"

I'd received a text from Willard overnight.

"I'm meeting him at ten," I said. "You remember the place where Albie used to watch the ponies?"

There was a moment's pause. "I do. It's still around?"

"Sort of."

"I can tie up at a guest slip in Edmonds and probably get there by then."

"See you there. And thanks."

"Don't thank me. My head might just as well be on that same chopping block, you know."

At a diner on Seaview Avenue, I drank too much coffee and picked at an egg breakfast, as I concentrated on reading details online about the CXS-3001 container I'd seen in Saleem's hotel safe.

I'd been right about it being designed to transport biological material. The CXS-3001 was touted by the manufacturer as a new generation intended for small-scale transport, and top of the line. The heavy base of the aluminum bottle could receive a pressurized cartridge of liquid nitrogen that would charge the foam inside within minutes instead of the hours necessary for larger, older models, the advertising claimed. So charged, the bottle's insulation and vacuum plug would maintain the temperature south of one-hundred-fifty degrees below zero, Celsius, keeping its contents viable for at least ten days.

Time enough for Bilal to escape. Far out of the reach of any law. He'd claimed he wasn't after anything that would cause harm, but I trusted that about as far as I could fastball the runny egg yolk on my plate. Even if I were stealing some prototype vaccine that might help him avoid a slow death from ALS, who knew how that theft might set back research at Ceres, or how many lives a lost cure would impact?

I had to go through with the job or suffer the consequences. That, or call the FBI now and have them ready to bust all of us the moment I stepped over Ceres's gleaming threshold. I'd keep Hollis and Paula Claybeck out of the story if I could. But if that was impossible, so be it. Better to have them in a cell than dead, or enabling the deaths of who knew how many others.

Would calling the cops even solve the problem? We'd all be stuck in holding tanks until Bilal's lawyers arranged to cut him loose. Probably much sooner than I would be arraigned and make bail. He could be out and making his next move within hours, and I'd be trapped, unable to protect anyone.

Yet I couldn't let Bilal Nath get hold of whatever he was after. Regardless of the risk to me or Hollis or even Addy and Cyndra.

The whole puzzle was giving me a headache. I swallowed two aspirin from my pocket, which reminded me of Bilal and Aura's lineup of prescription bottles in their hotel bathroom. What had Aura's been?

Olaparib. I looked it up. A cancer cell inhibitor. Commonly taken as a long-term maintenance drug to help prevent recurrence. The description I read mentioned particular use for patients with advanced ovarian cancer after prior lines of chemotherapy, once the tumor had diminished or disappeared.

I knew just enough to understand heavy chemotherapy could impact or even end a woman's fertility. A book on pregnancy had been on Aura's nightstand. Was she healthy now, or waiting until her body could handle carrying a baby to term? Were they racing against time with Bilal's worsening health? Any way it shook out, I didn't see how knowing she was afflicted could help my problem.

First things first. I'd meet Willard and Hollis, and we'd see how tough a nut Ceres would be. Then, unless I had some brilliant idea before nightfall, I'd drop by the FBI field office downtown and hand whatever agent had pulled holiday duty a shiny gift for the new year.

LUCE'S LATE UNCLE ALBIE BOYLAN had loved to gamble. He never had enough money or credit to get himself deeply into hock, but he seemed to get as much joy out of betting five dollars as five hundred. The bar he'd fronted for my grandfather—who had called the shots behind the scenes—didn't carry the cable channel showing the action at the old Longacres track. So to watch whatever horse race he'd bet that week's spare change against, Albie would toddle down to Alaskan Way and a billiard hall nestled under the viaduct.

Over the years the pool hall had been sold and partitioned, with half the space becoming a coffeehouse, which was eventually halved again into a sort of lunch bodega for commuters and tourists coming off the ferries and looking to grab a fast bite. But the television stayed in roughly the same place on the wall, upgraded to a flat screen now and showing a singing competition on Telemundo. I bought a Coke to claim space at the window counter.

Willard crossed the street at Marion, walking without hurry. He carried a long cardboard mailing tube, which looked a little like a drinking straw in his fingers. I joined him at a bench outside, for privacy. Willard's ass wouldn't have fit on one of the bodega counter stools, anyway.

He opened the mailing tube and slid a thick roll of papers out. The blueprints were the largest, but some of the other plans were nearly poster-sized as well.

"You've already looked," I said.

"Sure. And the headline is: Don't Do It. Check this." He unrolled the stack and leafed through to pick one batch of pages. Eleven-by-seventeen sheets, and thick. Electrical schematics.

He flipped to an interior page and held it out to me. "Fourth floor. Everything's pretty much normal until you see that they've wired the cameras separately. I think that's because this section"—he pointed to one quarter of the building—"has got its own power supply that switches on in case of an outage."

"That'll be the cryogenic storage bank," I said. "Can't have things melting during a blackout."

"Well, that room's cameras and alarm are completely enclosed. Even if you manage to patch into the building system somehow from outside, or make the lights go out, that piece of real estate keeps right on humming. The guards downstairs can still see everything that happens in that section. And I gotta assume the system can still make a cellular call to nine-one-one, too."

"Aura Nath said that Ceres has controlled burn safeguards to destroy their biological matter in case of a breach."

Willard actually smacked his heavy brow. "Controlled burn. That explains it. I was trying to figure why they had this." He flipped to another page. "It's a tiny room off the cryogenic unit. Hypoxic air generator, the label says."

"Fire suppression," I realized. "The oxygen level in the cryo unit is kept low. In case a controlled burn is set off. The flames destroy the virus or whatever it is, then sputter out from lack of oh-two before anything else catches on fire. I saw hypoxic chambers in the Army. They have them for high-altitude training. And computer data centers, so they don't have to use water sprinklers."

"So you can't breathe inside the cryo room?"

"There's enough oxygen in the air for humans. Might give you a headache after a while."

"Christ. Now I get why Nath wanted a pro."

I sat with the thought. Being a professional meant being a realist. And realistically, Ceres was a bitch.

Gulls cried overhead. Just a few weeks ago their caws might have been drowned out by a constant sonorous drone of traffic right over our heads. But the old viaduct was closed. If I listened hard, I could hear the scrape and crunch of the claw machines south of us as they tore down the two-story highway. Route 99 now went far under our feet. It had taken billions of dollars and nearly that many delays, along with the biggest drill in the world, to bore two miles of tunnel through the heart of the city. The whole waterfront would soon be repaved and redesigned, once the highway was gone. I guessed it wouldn't be long before market forces pushed the bodega out, too. Maybe the perpetual TV would carry on as a marker.

I thumbed through the schematics Willard had brought. The challenge with complex defenses, overlapping means of security, is that they add extra wrinkles that can go wrong. Your backups wind up needing backups. Somewhere in Ceres's design there was a flaw. Maybe systematic, maybe human. But what could I exploit with just a few hours to prep?

Nothing. Time to face facts. I had to bring in the law. Maybe I could convince them that I wasn't a terrorist myself.

I heard Hollis coming before I saw him. He was breathing hard and sweating lightly, even with the morning chill.

"I misremembered which block," he said, before coughing violently into his hand. "Thought you might have left already."

"Ceres is a wash, anyway," said Willard.

"Van?" Hollis asked.

I shrugged. "With time, it's beatable. But Bilal Nath is expecting me to show up in nine hours."

Hollis settled onto the bench with a sigh. "I hesitate to suggest it, but there is the nuclear option."

"Killing Nath," Willard said.

I'd thought about that, more than once. It was an option. Even if it made my mouth taste bile.

"I know he claims to have an axe ready to fall on your head if he suddenly dies," said Hollis, "but do you believe him?"

"Ondine gave me Nath's bona fides. Even she respects him. And Bilal has a whole team to avenge him, not counting Aura."

"So he means what he says," Willard noted. "There's a contract on you, unless he cancels it personally."

"And I can't force him to do that. He's already dying. I don't know what he fears."

"He loves his wife, you told me."

"Yeah," I said. "But going after Aura is a fool move, even if I could stomach it. Threaten Aura, and Bilal will just spirit her off to Karachi or Indonesia or anywhere else out of our reach. Kidnap her and Nath comes after Cyndra or Addy in return. There are too many ways for him to retaliate."

"Which leads us back to Ceres Biotech," Hollis said, glancing at the blueprints. "What about a takedown? Masks and shouting and make one of the guards hand over the goods?"

"That stinks," Willard said. "What if there's employees working late, or another guard wandering the building?"

"I know it's a lousy idea," said Hollis. "I'm not a damned beginner. But we're down to the dregs here."

"Here's an employee roster," Willard said, finding a stapled bunch of sheets in the pile. "All the security is contracted through Markham Protective. I've got some history with that company. They're good, but they follow the same procedures with every client. We could pull the old gag of telling the guard we've got thugs watching his family."

I glanced at the top sheet, less because I was honestly weighing Willard's idea than to grasp at straws. The roster started at the Ceres executive board and went down by department and rank from there.

One name, just below those of the CEO and the president, caught my eye: Timothy Gorlick, MD, PhD. Chief medical officer, co-founder.

Gorlick. I'd seen that name before. On Aura Kincaid's civil records from my new buddy Panni at the FBI.

Aura had been married to Timothy Gorlick shortly before Bilal Nath. And she'd fought ovarian cancer. Had she been struck with it before she and Gorlick were divorced?

"You all right?" Willard said to me.

"We'll figure a way out of this, lad," said Hollis.

I barely heard them. I was getting an inkling of what Bilal Nath wanted. Why he and Aura were so ruthless in their determination.

And, more important, how I could turn that against them.

"Willard," I said, "walk me through everything you have on Markham Protective. Start with their camera circuits."

TWENTY-ONE

Two hours later, I left Hollis and Willard to the tasks we'd agreed
upon. For me, that started with retrieving gear I kept hidden in storage.

My apartment was a studio. Hiding burglary tools there was out of
the question. During the past weeks I'd set up a workshop inside a mul-
tistory storage unit on the Hill. Not in my own name, of course. There
were plenty of DIYers using their units for home repair jobs and side
businesses, so nobody looked twice at the occasional whine of a drill or
the shriek of metal being cut coming from my own space. I'd slipped the
manager extra to clear out a unit way at the back, with plenty of privacy.

I wasn't blind to the ways my life had begun to echo my grandfather's. Hidden places, extra identities. I hadn't chosen Dono's life of
crime for profit. I'd carved my own path, winding as it might be. But the
methods I used were the ones he'd taught me. Plus my own innovations,
some courtesy of my Ranger training.

Duffel bags and backpacks of various sizes lined shelves I'd built
from two-by-fours and plywood. I opened four of the bags to retrieve
items from within. A keycard programmer. A set of fiber-optic cables
and splicing tools. A laptop computer, and a wireless transmitter similar
to those used in home theaters. A device that looked very much like a
paintball gun. And a short prybar, in case brute force was called for.

Burke. I hadn't given much thought to the man during the past few hours, which was a freakishly odd thing to say about a guy who'd aimed a gun at my face the night before. There was no question in my mind that he would have shot me, save for my extremely good fortune that he'd been interrupted.

He hadn't gotten the answers he'd demanded. He'd try again. Although Burke knew my name, it was my motive for seeking him out that really concerned him.

Burke was a killer. So was I, if I were being honest with myself. Besides the rough similarity of our dark hair and size, he and I had violence in common.

Like me and Dono, Burke had apparently started on the same path as his brutal elder. Gut Burke had been a murderer and enforcer. Whoever Sean worked for now, himself or some racket, he was operating on a higher level than roughing up shopkeepers who had fallen behind on their protection payments. Which made him that much more dangerous.

If Burke learned he might be my father, would he be less likely to murder me, or more?

The keycard programmer looked like an oversized calculator. In the side pocket of one of the duffels I kept a bag of blank RFID keycards. I distracted myself from further thoughts of Sean Burke by getting to work with the programmer and the specs Willard had acquired on Markham Protective Services. I'd have to hope Markham had stuck to their cut-and-paste approach to installation. If Ceres had sprung for an extra level of security, those bells and whistles might bring every guard running the moment we stepped inside.

When that task was complete, I spent another half hour double-checking my plans. Ceres's system was good. I could be better.

Finally, I packed the tools I'd chosen into a rucksack, wrapping each piece in a towel as padding. It would be heavy but manageable once strapped to my back. And silent, which was at least as important.

The rucksack rested on the passenger seat as I drove the old blue Dodge down Interstate 5. Rattles and pings all the way. The truck saying it was grumpy at having its rest disturbed, or peeved at being left alone so long. Maybe both. Maybe it was confused.

I switched on my blinker to move out of the fast lane, taking advantage of a gap in traffic to glide over three lanes in one go. A hundred yards behind me, a low silver Acura moved, too, abruptly jogging one lane to his right and then holding, as if the car had reacted reflexively. He dropped back as I accelerated.

Another half mile along, I moved into an exit-only lane for the next ramp. After a slow five-count, the Acura steadily crept over the last two lanes, until he was on my tail.

I drifted out of the exit lane, and of course the Acura followed.

Damn it. Who was this guy? My gut said police. He followed like police, like he had the basics of mobile surveillance down. Patient enough to keep his distance in the easy sightlines of the freeway, but maybe more accustomed to being one of two or more cars in a rotating pattern, plus air support. Hell, he might have exactly that kind of backup, and there was a police radar plane tracking me right now.

And me with a rucksack full of suspicious tools on the seat next to me, some of them worth a Class 3 felony. If my new admirer realized that I'd clocked him, his next move might be to pull me over. All my plans for Bilal Nath and Ceres Biotech would be smoked.

So my new first priority was to ditch this sucker before he got smart.

The next exit led to Highway 518 and SeaTac. I drifted onto the ramp without changing speed in the slightest, letting the Acura have plenty of notice. He followed me as I merged onto 518 and off again almost immediately, following the exit for International Boulevard.

This close to the airport, long-term parking lots dominated the landscape. I chose one called Renny's FastPass Parking—*The Business Traveler's Best Friend!*—and pressed the button at the gate to receive a ticket. The gate lifted, and I sped inside.

I would have to count on my pursuer hesitating. Should he follow me inside or wait and see if I left? What if I boarded a shuttle for the airport? I swung the Dodge around and up the ramps to the third level and into an open space in a row of parked cars. In an instant I had my door open and was grabbing the rucksack with my other hand. I dropped to the ground and began to low-crawl under the cars in the row, as fast as I could, dragging the ruck with me.

At the fifth car, I turned faceup and shimmied so that I could reach the exhaust pipes leading to the mufflers. I unclipped the rucksack straps and fastened them around the pipes, pulling them tight so the ruck was suspended off the ground. It would have to do. I crawled back to the Dodge, whose engine still idled expectantly.

As I walked to the stairs, I glanced at the fifth car from the truck. A Nissan Altima, not that I'd been able to tell that from just its undercarriage. The rucksack below was essentially invisible, unless someone leaned way over and looked for it.

I made it down one flight of stairs. Two plainclothes cops—as recognizable by their flat affects as from their aggressively business-casual shirts and trousers and sport coats on a holiday—met me at the second landing.

"Mr. Shaw," said the one in the lead. "Come with us."

TWENTY-TWO

THEY DIDN'T HAVE TO SHOW identification for me to know they were legit, but I asked them to do it, anyway. The bigger one, the cop who'd first spoken, tugged his ID off his belt to flash it for a full two seconds. Walter Podraski. A detective sergeant with the state. A big guy, almost as large as Bilal's goon Juwad, but with the added spread of middle age.

And jowled. Podraski had been the man tailing me on foot after my lunch with Willard. His partner's sandy hair was less windswept now that they were off the downtown streets.

"What's this about?" I said.

"Nothing serious," the partner said. In addition to being much leaner, he was slightly better dressed than Podraski. Nordstrom Rack instead of JCPenney. His hair and stature were boyish, but up close I realized both men were the same age, well north of forty. He hadn't offered his ID and he wasn't showing much deference to Podraski in answering my question. My antenna buzzed Fed.

"Driver's license," Podraski said. I took it out of my wallet and showed it to him. "This is your current address?"

"I sold the property. I'm staying with a neighbor down the block."

"Where are you headed?" the federal cop said.

"To that Thai place up the road." Name and address and where I was going officially exhausted, what they could demand of me, or bust me for if they caught me in a lie.

"So why not park there?" the Fed asked.

"Am I under arrest?"

"This won't have to go that way," said Podraski. "We just want to clear some things up."

On another day, I would have smiled. They'd already decided to haul me in. Playing nice was just to dangle a carrot and get me talking. One way or another, I wasn't walking free. Which meant bad things for my appointment with Bilal Nath in just a few hours.

If I made a show of cooperating, maybe I could figure out what this was about. A state detective and a Fed was an odd combination to be tailing anybody.

"All right," I said. "Where we goin'?"

Just up the boulevard, as it turned out. They stuck me in the backseat of the Acura—undoubtedly the Fed's personal car, as he was driving and there were stale Cheerios wedged into the rear seatbelt buckle—and drove a quarter mile to a WSP station right off 518.

While Podraski stayed behind to clear things with the admitting officer, the Fed ushered me through a long room of cubicles that might have been any office in America, save for the PSA posters and the holstered weapons on the uniformed desk workers. Our destination was an interview room with three chairs and one camera, high on the wall.

"I didn't catch your name," I said to him once we were seated. The room was cramped. They are always cramped, and hot, and boring, increasing pressure on the interviewee every way possible. There was no table between us. The better to get personal, establish a rapport.

"It's Rick. What do you do for a living, Mr. Shaw?"

"I just sold that property, Rick."

"So you're between things?"

"You don't need to wait for your partner?" I nodded toward the closed door.

He shook his head. "What have you been doing the past couple of days?"

"Enjoying the holiday."

"A day off from all that free time, being between jobs and all." Rick the Fed grinned, like I was clearly making the right choices in life.

Podraski opened the door, closed it behind him, and took the last chair. No notebooks, no visible badges or guns or other signs of authority. Just us dudes, hanging out.

"You don't look like someone who sits at home playing PS4 all night," Rick continued.

"I'm more of an Xbox guy."

"First-person shooters? Since you don't have the real thing anymore?" Podraski said, taking over the lead. "I know another vet when I see one."

Making friends already. "You?"

He smiled. "A long time ago."

"Let me guess," I said. "MPs."

"Nope, just plain old Eleven Bravo." Infantry. "You do any contract work after serving? A lot of guys sign up for that now, I hear. Private security. Bodyguarding."

"Not yet."

"If I was as tough as you, I'd be cashing in."

"Could you tell us where you were two nights ago?" Rick said.

And there it was. Two nights ago I'd been breaking into Sean Burke's house.

"Sure," I said.

"So where was that?"

"I probably should have a lawyer, right? If we're talking about a crime?"

"We're not accusing you of anything, Van," Rick said. "Maybe you saw something we should know."

The lure, sparkling in the water. Detectives love for perps to try and fool them. *I was there, yeah, but it was this other guy . . .*

"What would I have seen?" I said.

"We just need some facts and then you can go. Where were you again?"

"'Cause this sounds like I'm a suspect. What happened?"

"It's probably a mistake," Podraski broke in. "People ID the wrong guy all the time."

I was supposed to ask who saw me, where they saw me, jump up and down protesting my innocence. Innocent people protest. Guilty ones get quiet.

"We just want to help," said Rick.

Podraski nodded assurance. "You're a combat vet. I know what it's like coming home after being downrange. It ain't easy. You have to find your place again."

"Gotta have a purpose," I said.

"So we're on your side here. Whatever you're into, we can put in the right word for you. If you need protection, you've got it. If you help us in return."

Protect me. From whom? From Burke?

"I'll call my lawyer," I said, "and he'll come here and then we'll talk."

"You don't need to do that," Podraski said.

Rick held up a hand. "Your lawyer might not be on your side. Who pays for his services?"

Now that was an odd question.

I took out my phone. "I'm calling."

"Bad choice," said Podraski. He stood and plucked the phone out of my hand. "Now we have to stick you in a cell until you get smarter. Stand up."

I complied and we went through the business of frisking. The cold strategic part of my brain noted that Podraski was overconfident. He had his main piece clipped over his right kidney. I could have relieved him of his weapon and shot both men before they had Chance One. But I wasn't a lunatic. I stood quietly while the state detective emptied my pockets and handcuffed me. They left the interview room.

My immediate future was clear: They would toss me into a holding tank, drag their feet through the booking process, and then allow me to call for a lawyer once everyone had left for New Year's Eve and I would be guaranteed a long uncomfortable stay. My lawyer was Ephraim Ganz, who had been Dono's attorney for a long time. Ganz was damn good at his job, but the last time I'd left him, he'd been delighted to see me go. I wasn't positive he'd even take my call.

I was going to be a no-show at Ceres Biotech tonight. That was a given. I could only pray Bilal Nath didn't immediately leap to hunting down my friends in retribution.

An hour later they returned. Ready to try a new tack. Podraski read me my rights, signifying that their questioning was about to become official. I confirmed I understood. Podraski took the chair this time, Rick at the door.

"You were in Bitter Lake three nights ago," Podraski said.

"I want to call my lawyer," I repeated.

"We've got witnesses."

This was curious. And a little unsettling. Once I'd asked for an attorney, the cops should have shut down their fishing trip. Unless they'd decided to ignore the rules.

I glanced at the camera on the wall.

"Just us talking," Rick confirmed.

"Now maybe you were only casing the place," Podraski said. "That's barely trespassing. You could get off with a warning. Were you there?"

I counted the checks on the chest pocket of the detective's blue jacket.

"A guy with your service record for his country, any judge will probably go easy. Just talk to us."

Thirty-two stitches. I counted them twice more as the silence stretched out. Silence makes most people uncomfortable. They rush to fill it. I was happy to meditate on Podraski's fabric halfway to forever, just to see how long it took them to give up.

"With the holiday it could be three days before you make bail. We haven't booked you yet. There's still a way out of here."

The more they are desperate for you to talk, the more lenient they'll pretend to be. One of Dono's lessons.

"Somebody hired you," Rick said. "He's the one we want."

"Forget it," Podraski said. "This guy's an idiot. His granddaddy was a moron, too."

I'd have lost a bet with myself on how long it took them to bring up Dono. I'd have guessed the next round of questioning.

"Grandpa had multiple falls," the detective continued. "One of which sent our poor baby here to foster care. Boo hoo. Surprising they didn't keep you in the system for good, instead of throwing you back into the lion's den."

That had been the path I'd been on. A life shuffling between overtaxed foster families. But social workers could be bribed as readily as any under-paid government employee. Dono had found a way to get me home.

Podraski pointed at my chest. "Bet your granddaddy taught you some stuff about B&E, didn't he? In between fondling you at night, I mean. That why you went into the Army? To get away from that sick freak?"

Get them scared, get them angry, get them talking. I pretended I was holding an ace-high straight and willing Podraski to throw in his chips.

"Maybe you liked it," he said. "Maybe you want to go to jail, get another taste of that."

A sharp knock at the door made Rick jump. He stuck his head out and the desk officer murmured in his ear. The Fed's expression fell in surprise. He left the room without another word.

"Just between you and me," Podraski said, once the door was closed. "You kill a lot of guys?"

He sat a little crooked in his chair, the result of the piece pressing into his back. If he'd been at his desk or in his car, he would have removed it for comfort.

"Were you good at it?" he continued. "Maybe I've got you wrong. Maybe you're a stone-ass motherfucker. That what you are?"

I denied him the tough-guy stare he was so clearly expecting.

"Okay. Silent Sam. Stay quiet and take the fall. Nobody's gonna pay you for it."

The door opened and Rick came back in. Followed by a familiar face. Familiar, if not entirely friendly. John Guerin, SPD.

"Shaw," he said, nodding at me. He still had the mustache, which was a shade darker than his prematurely white hair. In his glasses and crisp dress shirt he looked less conspicuously like a cop than either of the other two men. More like a very intense bonds trader. I guessed a lot of crooks were fooled by that, until it was too late.

"Detective," I said.

"Lieutenant," he corrected.

"Congratulations."

"What the fuck is this?" Podraski said.

"I've had the same question, Sergeant Podraski," said Guerin, "ever since I got your call yesterday asking for background on Mr. Shaw here. You didn't give me much context. Then I catch wind that two of our patrolmen ran into you in Bitter Lake a few nights ago, where you were conducting what they were told was a routine interview."

"You're out of line. This is a state matter."

"So you said over the phone. I called Captain Fisher in District Two just to make sure we were coordinating our efforts effectively. He told me he wasn't familiar with this particular joint operation, but that he was sure you'd be in contact with our North Precinct soon, so they could understand why you were conducting investigations in SPD's yard."

Podraski looked like he was about to retort before Rick the Fed cut him off.

"This isn't worth your time, Lieutenant." He waved a hand. "Or the trouble it will bring."

"See, now that could be interpreted as a threat," Guerin said. "I wouldn't want to get the wrong impression. Why don't we leave Mr. Shaw here and make sure we're all on the same page."

He held the door open. After a moment they acquiesced and left the room.

"Don't suppose you can get them to take these off?" I nodded to the handcuffs behind my back.

"I'm not sure you don't belong in them," Guerin said, and he closed the door.

I might see the sky again today after all. I didn't know what kind of jurisdictional dance Guerin was doing, but it was clear enough that Podraski and Rick had overreached somehow.

But right this minute, I had nothing but time. I thought back to the schematic I'd seen of the Markham security system, how the alarms on the cryobank worked, and the controlled burn safeguards for the bank's contents. I rehearsed each step in my mind and considered contingencies. A lot was riding on Hollis and Willard. And Elana. I'd found a role for her to play after all.

Two hours, I decided. That was how much time I would need before going anywhere near Ceres's cryo chamber. An hour to access the utility shed on the roof, then another hour of work there before I dared to go inside the building itself.

It would be getting dark outside now. My spare minutes were burning fast.

The door opened. Podraski came in, tossed a gallon Ziploc with my personal effects in it on the table, and removed my handcuffs. Then he left again, leaving the door open.

I pocketed my things. Bilal hadn't tried to call me while my phones were in police hands, which was a minor blessing. A state trooper waited for me just outside the room. "That way," he said, pointing toward the exit at the far end of the cubicle farm. I obliged.

My two hosts, Rick and Podraski, had vanished somewhere, along with Guerin. Passing by a conference room, I heard voices, fragments of overlapping sentences dueling in anger—*that's not what I—hang on a damned minute—might wind up like Santora with—*

It would be poking the bear to intrude. But I was too curious about the whole episode, not least why they had suddenly let me go without booking me. I opened the door and stuck my head in.

Podraski and the Fed stood in close and what looked like intense conversation with another man in a blue suit and conservative tie. A much better suit than Rick's, just as Rick's had been better than Podraski's. His suit and the professional styling of his silvered brown hair added up to brass. Rick the Fed's boss, maybe, or someone even higher up the chain.

All three men turned. The combined force of their surprised glares almost made me grin. Instead, I said, "Sorry, wrong door," and vamoosed.

Guerin was waiting in the lobby. I was feeling like a relay baton, passed from one cop to the next.

"How'd you know I was here?" I said as we left the building and followed the entrance roundabout to the station lot. A brilliant stripe of magenta filled the western sky, backlighting the hills between the station and the airport just beyond. Far-off jet engines combined into a constant whispery moan.

"Friends. After Podraski called me yesterday, digging into your sordid history, I was curious. Then more so once I learned he was running some job on Seattle turf. I asked a contact of mine in WSP dispatch to watch for your name. Podraski may play loose with jurisdictions but he's not an idiot. Before they pulled you over, he called it in."

I grasped what Guerin meant. I had a family background and military record that would make any cop extra vigilant. If I'd turned out to be some trigger-happy head case, maybe even left Podraski and Rick the Fed dead at the scene, at least their compatriots would know who was responsible.

"Guess I owe you some thanks," I said.

"Save your gratitude. Tell me what you were doing in Bitter Lake."

"Question is, What do *they* think I was doing in Bitter Lake? They seemed convinced somebody hired me to be there."

"They don't know you like I do. You work for yourself." His eyes narrowed behind the rimless glasses. "Like your grandfather."

"And they didn't book me," I said, looking back at the patrol station. "They could have held me for at least a day and done their best to put me through the ringer if they'd gone through with putting me on the record. That strike you as weird?"

"Whatever you're chasing, drop it," said Guerin. "It will not end well."

"Who's the Fed?" I said. "FBI?"

"That's exactly the kind of thing I mean. I won't be around next time to stir up shit."

"They warned you off, too," I said, realizing. "How does that happen?"

He exhaled, a soft whisper of breath out of his nose. On Guerin, that might have been a shout.

"Okay," I said, raising a hand to signal a truce. "Let's trust each other. I'll tell you why I might have had reason to be in Bitter Lake, and you tell me what kind of minefield I've apparently wandered into."

"Your problem, Shaw, is that you imagine you're my equal. Podraski and me, we're cops. You're a repeat offender, with no fixed income or residence. And even that assessment is generous."

"What if my answer changes your mind? About trusting me?"

"Only one way to find out. Talk."

"Thirteen Coins. Tomorrow. I'll call you with the time."

"Bullshit."

"Best I can do. I have a hot date tonight."

Guerin frowned. He knew I wasn't lying when I offered to share information. He also knew I wouldn't be pushed into doing so sooner than I wanted to.

"Tomorrow," he said. "Don't make me hunt you down."

Enough people were doing that already. "Deal."

"I feel sorry for the girl." He walked away.

Renny's FastPass was close enough for me to jog back. The run blew off some excess energy from being trapped in the stifling interview room. And it gave me room to reset my mind toward Ceres Biotech. Two more hours before I was due to meet up with Hollis and Willard. I could just make it.

Back on the top parking level, I made sure I was alone and ducked under the Nissan to retrieve my rucksack. At least the owners hadn't returned and driven it home with them. That would have been the last nail in my coffin.

I paid my ticket at the machine and pulled out of the FastPass lot, only to realize how close that comparison had been. The lot lay directly across from a cemetery.

My Dodge pickup was old, without any hands-free phone functions or Bluetooth or even a CD player. I waited until the next light to call Hollis.

"You're late," he said.

I didn't want to tell Hollis I'd been arrested. He got edgy enough before a job.

"I need a license-plate check," I said. "Silver Acura TL, probably owned by a guy in federal law enforcement. First name Rick, unless he was bullshitting me." I read Hollis the number of Rick the Fed's car.

"FBI? Is this some other horrible problem for us to handle before tonight?"

"Nothing to do with Bilal. I think this team might be on to Sean Burke."

"Ah. Well." Hollis hesitated. What does one say when talking to a friend about a possible-father-and-probable-hired-killer? "Personal information will be restricted from DMV if he's federal law. Our friend Panni might have the right access. But he might not be around until after the holiday."

I said that was fine. We had more pressing concerns. Like surviving Bilal Nath long enough to see the new year.

But back on the highway, my brain wouldn't stop chewing on what had just happened. A weird kind of catch-and-release, with Rick and Podraski hauling me in only to change their minds at the last minute. Was that solely Guerin's doing? Or had something else prompted them to cut me loose?

The superior who'd been reaming the two cops had looked familiar. A little overly groomed, too. Like he spent time with the media. A slick suit. Athletic, but in the way that a youngish CEO might be fit, thanks to diligent personal trainers and nutritionists rather than pursuing any sport.

Then it hit me where I'd seen him before. On television. The slick guy was one of the candidates for governor in the recall election. I couldn't remember his name, but knew he was some kind of federal attorney. Holy shit.

It made for easy arithmetic. Federal prosecutors plus special agents plus state detectives added up to major trouble for Sean Burke. And anyone dumb enough to be close to him.

JUNIOR YEAR, PART THREE

I waited until Mr. Grennon, coach for the Watson Paladins' not so lauded baseball team, was deep in conversation with the batter on deck about reading the slider or some shit like that before I leaned out from under the bleachers to tap Davey in the back of the head with a thrown pebble.

He whipped around. When he spotted me skulking, he had a hard time not cracking up as he meandered to take a seat in front of me. It was a preseason workout, nominally voluntary. None of the players carried themselves with the intensity of real practice. Recent rain had turned the baseball diamond into clay. It smelled like I imagined a newly turned farmer's field would, all loam and earthworms.

"I got your message," I said. "What's up?"

Instead of answering, Davey just grinned wider and looked off to right field. Past the fence, Singer Boeman and his pack were hanging by their twin Pontiacs. First time I'd seen that bunch in over a year. They were spread out. Watching cars leave the lot, and the students drift out of the main entrance.

"Those morons," Davey said, scraping dirt out of his cleats. "What the hell are they doing here? They graduated. Or almost."

Leaving school had lost them their pissant revenue stream. Singer himself had tagged me as a kid who could probably keep his mouth shut during my freshman year. He'd sidled up, all chill, asking if I wanted to buy a little somethin' for me or maybe to share with my friends. I hadn't.

Later that first semester, Singer had made me a different offer. To deliver a bag for him and keep ten bucks as my fee. I'd almost laughed, his approach was so lame. He was at least bright enough not to make a big thing of it when I turned him down a second time. No point in making an enemy when your whole business model relied on being approachable.

Colten Gulas had started hanging with Singer's group the next year. And then Singer and most of his buds graduated. Maybe Colten had become their go-between for Watson High.

"Think they're waiting for Colt?" Davey said, echoing my thoughts.

"Or hunting for him."

"Hey, where you goin'?"

Across the field. If these dipshits were looking for Colten, we had at least one thing in common.

The outfield had been mown just before the last rain. By the time I jumped the fence, my sneakers were covered in wet green clumps of grass.

Singer Boeman sat on the hood of his car, which was discernible from the other white GTO because of the large rust-speckled dent in the driver's door.

"Hey," I said. "You seen Colten?"

"What the fuck you want?"

Which I'd just told him. "Colten. Where is he?"

"You seen him?"

Jesus. I was starting to think Singer hadn't graduated at all, just frustrated the school to the point where they handed him a paper with writing on it and told him it was a diploma.

"I owe him money," I said.

"Shit, he owes us." Singer's guys had noticed our conversation and begun to walk from each end of the short block toward us. Whatever we were doing had to be more interesting than watching the crowd. Burn Burkley was one of their gang. The only one of the four still enrolled at Watson. He saw Yvette Friel off and on, and it was a toss-up which of the two of them was less appealing. Good faces and rotten insides.

"Dudes," Singer said to the bunch. "He's looking for Coltie, too. Paying his debts like a man." He pounded the car hood in mock glee. Singer had been a running back for Watson's football team, and he still had the compact muscularity that seemed to extend all the way to his close-cropped brown curls.

"Give us the money," Burn said. "Cut out the middleman."

"What about Candace? You seen her?" one of the others asked.

"No," I said. Candace was a friend of Colten's; they hung out behind the portables smoking. Which was probably also where Davey got most of his news. It made sense that Singer's boys would look for one to find the other.

That might work for me, too. I knew another crowd Candace hung out with.

"Forget it," I said, walking away.

"Hey," Burn said, moving to intercept. "The money."

Singer stayed on his car, but the two others instinctively edged closer with Burn. Pack mentality. Younger or not, I was sure I could take any one of them. Singer was strong but smaller than me, and Burn tall but not much else. And I knew I was meaner. But four on one, forget it. They'd pound me like bread dough. I coiled, ready to hurt the first idiot who got close and then run like hell.

A whistle sounded from nearby on the baseball field. The guys surrounding me flinched back at the signal of authority. Grennon had gathered the team in the outfield for wind sprints.

Davey was watching our little drama, a look of concern on his face.

I ambled away before Burn got his courage back. Davey looped near the fence after his first sprint. Not breathing hard yet; he could run like a rabbit.

"Anything?" he said.

"Maybe. We saw Candace on Broadway last week, right? Hanging with the street kids by the Rite Aid?"

"Yeah. Oh, Candy and Colten. They've been hooking up. You think she knows where he is?"

"Where he's hiding. Singer and the others are looking to get paid. Money or blood. Normally I wouldn't care, but I want my shot first."

"I'll come with you—shit, I can't. Ma and Michael have this thing at the church tonight, I gotta go, too. And dinner after."

"Don't sweat it. Candace and Colten might not even be around."

And besides, this was something I wanted to do alone. Family business.

TWENTY-THREE

CERES BIOTECH'S CHUNK OF MAN-MADE land extended out from the natural shore about thirty yards. The lake side of the building blazed with another of their slanting silver logos at the very top, big and bright enough to be seen from the opposite shore of Lake Union. Environmentally friendly LED lamps on the corners of the roof cast wide cones of light over the face of Ceres. And created equally broad contrasting shadows. At the building's north side, the dilapidated marina looked like a rotting stump in a polished smile.

Hollis guided the speedboat past the remnants of docks and pilings as I tightened the chest straps on my rucksack. We'd placed black electrical tape over the running lights. Sailing low and dark and quieter than a car engine, thanks to Dono's muffled outboard. Water traffic was heavy tonight farther out on the lake. Boaters readying to watch the fireworks display at midnight at the south end.

Ceres Biotech had constructed a patio area made of all-weather planks spanning the rear of the building, for employees to lunch outside and indulge in the view when weather permitted. The patio extended out over the water. Hollis nodded to me and slowed the boat to a drift.

I jumped from the bow to the composite slats of the deck and sprinted toward the side of the building opposite the abandoned marina. The south side, the one facing the houseboat community next door, was out of the question. It wouldn't do to have some host or his holiday guests step out on the balcony for a toke and see a guy scaling the building next door.

Four corporate stories and related sublevels made at least ninety feet from ground to roof ledge. It looked even taller from where I was standing, looking straight up.

Given a rope and a little training, climbing a sheer surface isn't that hard. The Army had given me all the practice I could want and more on hard terrain, including but not limited to inching up and rappelling down icy mountains in Georgia during Ranger School.

A black 9.9 mm rope made a thick bundle at the top of my ruck. I couldn't use pitons and a hammer on the building wall. But the thick lampposts extending a yard from the roof offered another method.

I had packed a cable string launcher under the rope. Cable installers used launchers to shoot pull lines through tight spaces in ceilings and under floors, or across wide gaps. The launcher looked almost identical to a paintball gun, up to and including the laser sight and the thick cylinder under its barrel. But instead of paint capsules, the cylinder held a spool of coiled filament. The end of the filament was fixed to a plastic dart like a crossbow quarrel. The launcher could shoot the dart half the length of a football field. Shoot the filament, tie its line to the heavy cable, and pull the cable through from the other side.

The launcher would work equally well for my needs. I hoped.

No doors on this side of the Ceres building meant no need for cameras. I turned on the cable launcher's laser sight, aimed it at a spot just above the horizontal lamppost four tall stories above me, and pulled the trigger. The launcher made a sound like a partly deflated balloon popping, and the red filament flashed into the air with a descending whistle.

It took me a moment to spot the dart in the shadows, now dangling twenty feet below the lamppost. I fed it more filament, and the dart gradually lowered to meet me on the grass.

It was a quick task to attach my climbing rope and pull the rope up and over the thick pipe of the lamppost and down to the ground again. I held the two ends and yanked hard, then leaned with all my weight. The lamppost didn't waver.

I checked my watch. Eight-forty. Twenty minutes wasn't enough time to scale the roof and complete my preparations up top. I'd have to meet Bilal first.

Without my rucksack. I didn't want Nath or his devoted retinue getting the idea to examine its contents. I tied the loop of climbing rope to the ruck and hauled it skyward. Its bulk created a dark lump under the lamppost, like a shy gargoyle.

Somewhere just out of reach of the lights from shore, Hollis waited in the speedboat, idling while he watched my progress through binoculars. If there was any sign of police presence, he would signal me. Willard was watching the other side of the building from a hiding place along the lakefront paths. That was as much backup as I would have. If trouble erupted inside, I would be on my own.

The phone in my chest pocket buzzed. Bilal. He was early. Maybe edgy.

"I'm here," I said.

"Two blocks south." Saleem's voice, sounding as usual like speaking to me was beneath him. "Opposite a place called Zoo. Now."

I knew the Zoo Tavern. I'd boosted a Harley Shovelhead on consignment for one of their regulars when I was a teenager, working side gigs without Dono's knowledge. That job had gone smoothly. Maybe this was a good omen.

I walked the two blocks on Fairview, just another Seattle dude in a fitted black jacket, gray jeans, and black jungle boots. Half the people in the city dressed like they were about to go for an extended hike. Tactical wear for burglary fit right in.

Bilal's Mercedes SUV waited at the lot's accordion fence. Juwad hoisted his heavy frame from the driver's seat and gestured for me to raise my arms. He removed items from my pockets as Aura and Bilal stepped from the rear of the car.

Saleem was already out. He'd been watching me from the opposite side of the road for the past hundred yards.

"You are ready, I trust?" Bilal said. Juwad handed him the short lengths of climbing cord and the large steel carabiners he'd taken from my jacket. "What are these?"

"That's how I'm getting inside. I still don't know what I'm supposed to do once I'm in there," I said, taking the cords back. "Time to level with me. What is it you're after?"

"We're changing the plan," said Aura. She motioned to Saleem, who approached. "Saleem will go with you. He knows what we need."

I stopped. "That's not possible. This is a one-person job."

"Make it possible," Bilal said.

Saleem had a small rucksack of his own. Its rounded contours told me he was carrying the CXS-3001 cold-storage bottle I'd seen in their hotel room. The bulge under his coat was evidence that his machine pistol would be along for the ride, too.

"Look," I said, "if you want this job to go right, I can't be dragging your man through the whole building like some fucking toddler."

"You think I'm a child?" Saleem said. "Say that again and I will see you dead."

"Stop," said Bilal. "There is no question: Saleem will accompany you. Once you have given him entrance to the fourth floor, he will take over."

"We can't trust you," Aura said. "But you will have to trust us. Get Saleem inside, and once you're done, you and your friends will be safe. I swear."

She was either a damned good actress or telling me what she thought was the truth. Maybe her husband had convinced her I'd be allowed to skip merrily away once the job was done.

Shit. My plan had been to grab Bilal's prize from the cryo chamber and make a very hasty exit out the other side of the building, to Hollis and the speedboat. Leaving Aura and Bilal and his thugs literally staring up a rope, waiting in vain for me to climb back down. I had bet the farm that what Bilal and his wife wanted was so valuable to them, so irreplaceable, they would be desperate to make a deal once I had it in my hands.

Adapt, Shaw. You know more than they do. Use that.

I looked at Saleem. "I hope to hell you can climb." His lip curled in contempt.

"We will be nearby," Bilal said. "Do not disappoint me."

Disappointment was the least of my intentions. I repocketed the cords and carabiners.

"Come on," I said to Saleem. We retraced my path up Fairview. I paused before approaching the building.

"Do not stall," Saleem warned.

"Shut up." I watched the lobby of Ceres Biotech, and the floors above. New Year's Eve meant no regular employees were around, and the cleaning crews had completed their jobs earlier that night. Only the pair of guards held the fort. I checked the time. Twelve minutes past nine o'clock.

"Why are we waiting?" said Saleem, shifting his weight from side to side.

"That," I said. One of the guards passed in front of the windows on the third floor.

Hollis's surveillance yesterday and today had confirmed the guards made their rounds once every hour on the hour, taking the north stairwell all the way up to the fourth floor, making a loop, and going down the south stairwell to the next floor and continuing that pattern to the ground level. The other guard would be stationed at the front desk, so that someone was on the monitors at all times.

The fourth floor should be clear for most of the next hour.

"Let's go," I said.

He followed me around by the old marina and onto Ceres property, to the shadows of the back corner. I had the momentary urge to bounce his skull off the building wall and carry on by my lonesome, but only Saleem knew exactly what Bilal wanted. And what Bilal wanted, I needed.

I tied two of the cords from my pocket into Prusik knots around the climbing rope, one cord with a loop for my foot.

"This is not—" Saleem began. He was staring with wide eyes at the sheer face of the building.

"I told you to shut up. Pay attention." I made him stand with legs apart as I used the last and longest length of rope to tie a rappel seat around Saleem's waist and thighs. It was undignified as hell for him, made worse by the thought of what he was about to attempt. I clicked the carabiners at his waist, then grabbed the lower cord on the climbing rope to show Saleem.

"Like this," I whispered, putting my boot in the loop and pushing down until it was tight. Holding the climbing rope and top cord with my hands, I used the loop like a step to climb off the ground. I showed Saleem how to alternate between the two cords, shifting weight from hands to feet to move each cord a foot or two at a time and climb the rope.

It was steady progress if you knew what to do and stayed calm. Otherwise it was exhausting as well as treacherous. Saleem would at least have the rappel seat to keep him from plummeting to the ground. I jumped down and slid the two knots down to knee level and held them out to him.

"There must be another way," he said.

"You wanted to join the party," I said, threading the rope through the carabiners at his waist. "We go in through the roof."

"But if I have this"—Saleem shook the rappel seat—"how will you climb?"

Nice of the shithead to worry. He might have considered the question before now.

"The hard way," I said. I tied another Prusik above the two already around the rope. Better to have the stronger climber up top, to lend help if needed. Assuming I made it to the top.

I put on my climbing gloves, half-fingered gauntlets with thickly padded palms and edges that would save my skin if not my neck. With the nitrile gloves to prevent fingerprints making a second layer underneath, at least there was no risk of my hands getting cold.

The ninety feet above me looked like nine hundred in the dark. Damn it. I could do this. One vertical step at a time.

I put my boot in the new loop, pulled it tight, and lifted myself two feet off the ground. Winding the loose rope below around my other leg let me take some weight off the loop and shift it higher. Not much higher. Maybe six inches. This would be a tough go.

When I was ten feet off the ground, I motioned to Saleem to get moving. With a moment's fumbling he got his foot into the loop and began to make upward progress. I left him to it and concentrated on my own climb.

Ten more feet. Twenty. The guards would both be back in the lobby now, passing the time, so there was little chance they might look out an upper window and see two figures spidering up the side of the building. But we were slow. Slow enough that it would be a race to see if Saleem and I would make it to the roof before the guard began his next round.

From blocks away, zippering pops from a string of firecrackers rent the air. Harbingers of the bigger show to come. As long as no one was looking our way, I'd take it.

I heard a whispered exclamation from Saleem below me and smiled. I had tied the rappel seat loose enough that it would creep up and squeeze his balls like a vise. A dick move, but I was feeling ungenerous.

At the third story I spared a glance at my watch. Nine-forty-six. Shit. I moved faster, risking holding more weight with my arms to get an extra few inches with every move of the loop. A gust off the lake, honed by cold to a knife edge, made the rope sway. My breath was fast and rasping in my throat. After another few minutes of back-straining effort I pushed the hanging rucksack aside to touch the thick bar of the horizontal lamppost.

Now for the really dangerous part. I shook the corded loop loose from my foot and hauled myself up, hooking a knee over the post. The roof ledge with its silvery alloy weatherproofing was within reach. I grabbed it with one hand and with a grunt heaved my upper body onto the ledge.

Mostly. I began to slide backward, scrabbling at the ledge for a solid grip, finally finding it and rolling my body onto the roof's gritty surface.

No time to celebrate. I stood and looked over the edge. Saleem was still back at the start of the third floor.

Too slow. I clutched the climbing rope with my gloved hands and pushed at the roof ledge with my foot, hauling Saleem upward three feet in one yank. I heard his faint gasp of alarm. I pulled again, moving fast before my arms had a chance to give up in angry protest. In another minute Saleem's head appeared at the edge, his hands reaching frantically for the ledge. I grabbed his shoulders and almost threw him onto the roof.

We were still for a moment, me standing, Saleem on his ass, both of us breathing too hard to speak.

"You are—" Saleem attempted, then let his malevolent stare finish the thought. I leaned over the ledge to untie the rucksack.

At the center of the roof, a steel shed with its large satellite dish looked like a square head wearing an especially wide-brimmed hat at a rakish angle. The shed housed telecom and transmission equipment for the dish and its nearby cellular tower. I carried the ruck to the shed.

Saleem watched as I picked the lock. "The way in is over there."

"With cameras on the other side. Be my guest."

I opened the door. A series of hinged metal housings like large fuse boxes lined the walls of the shed. I searched for one specific box and opened it to reveal a forest of cables inside, each with a tag denoting its purpose. At least the Ceres engineers knew their jobs. I began unloading my gear from the rucksack.

"What are you doing?" Saleem pressed.

I cursed silently. Answering would at least keep him from talking more.

"The security cameras and alarm around the cryo chamber are completely enclosed inside the room, including their own power source," I said as I stripped the rubberized covers off three of the coaxial cables within the box. "But keeping the two systems physically separate means that the chamber's cameras are forced to transmit their images wirelessly. That's hard to do through an entire building. Impossible with medical equipment around, and there's a few tons of that downstairs. That's why hospitals restrict cell phone use in some wards."

I tapped a wireless transceiver below the cable. "So what Markham Protective does is send that wireless signal from the cameras here instead. The cryo chamber is right below us. This transceiver grabs the signal and feeds it into the main system. The guards see the image on the monitors. What we're doing"—I connected my own fiber-optic band to the stripped cable—"is tapping into that same signal, copying the still image, and feeding that to the monitors instead."

I wasn't sure Saleem understood. But he stayed quiet as I opened a laptop and plugged it into the transmitter I'd taken from my storage unit. Markham liked a cookie-cutter approach to their systems. I'd soon know for sure if they used the same frequency for all their wireless cameras. A screen came to life on the laptop, allowing me to fine-tune the transmitter's frequency using the keyboard.

And there it was. A full-color view of a plexiglass door, with a clear plastic bar handle and words stenciled in white on the surface. Only in reverse. We were looking at the image from the camera inside the room, pointed outward. The mirror-image words read: CRYOGENIC FACILITY—AUTHORIZED ADMITTANCE ONLY—NO PHONE, COMPUTER, OR OTHER ELECTRONIC DEVICE USE PERMITTED.

Two other cameras on the same frequency broadcast images of different corners of the chamber. It was the work of a minute to capture the images and feed them to the cable I'd spliced into the system. The monitor downstairs would cycle through the three incoming feeds, showing each in turn. Now the guards would see a chamber as placidly unoccupied as it had been all night. So long as we could make it into the cryobank without being caught on the building's hallway cameras, we'd be invisible. And I had a plan for that.

Saleem had regained his energy and squandered it by shifting from side to side. "We must go."

"We begin after I've disabled the alarms," I said. "If you're bored, check the perimeter. Make sure the guards haven't found our rope."

The Ceres guards didn't patrol outside, but Saleem didn't know that. Watching me type was only increasing his stress. After a moment, he strode to the edge of the roof.

That's it, you jackoff. Take your time.

I pulled up the output from a different network cable. Despite what I'd told Saleem, it wasn't the cryo chamber alarms. Thanks to Willard's homework, I already had a way past those. What I was working on now was something new to me.

Ceres Biotech boasted cutting-edge environmental controls, monitoring and fine-tuning every inch of their building's climate via a central source. Green and clean, including the cryo chamber. And its fire-suppression system.

It took me twenty minutes before I was sure I had the functions tweaked to work the way I intended.

Reasonably sure. I'd never tried a stunt like this before, and there would be no rehearsal. Saleem was back at the shed.

My ruck was mostly empty now, save for some basic tools. The laptop would stay behind, happily fulfilling the tasks I'd set in motion. Eleven-twenty now. The guard should be done with his latest round of the fourth floor.

I texted Hollis. **Confirm clear?** A moment later the magic word **Clear** appeared on my phone.

The lock on the roof door offered less resistance than the one on the telecom shed, and it wasn't alarmed. I reached out a hand to stop Saleem. "Not yet."

My next text was to Willard: **Ready for delivery.**

The wait was longer this time. I ran the mental movie of what would be happening four flights below us.

Elana, dressed in a FedEx polo and probably one of her many wigs, walking up to the main door. The guard, seeing a delivery person dropping off a package at a late hour on a holiday—not unheard of in the age of twenty-four-seven service—and leaving his post to take receipt.

Saleem's very short patience ended. He grabbed my shoulder, his grip surprisingly strong for a slender guy.

"Do not play games," he said. "I know you are planning to betray us. I will leave you dead right here."

"Your bosses promised I'd live."

Delivery now, Willard's text confirmed. Saleem eyed it suspiciously.

"Bilal will not weep for you. And I do not care what the woman says. Go."

I opened the door and hurried down the stairs. Saleem followed. The cold-storage container in his backpack thumped lightly with every step.

His other hand rested inside his unzipped coat. Quick access to his machine pistol. Positively salivating to rip me to pieces, once my duty to his master was complete.

TWENTY-FOUR

A T THE FOURTH-FLOOR LANDING, I stuck my head out to check the surroundings. Branching hallways curved gently in three directions, each with its own array of conference rooms. Every second ceiling light was out, conserving energy after hours. I could make out the entrance to an atrium halfway down the center hall. That should be the fastest path to the cryo chamber. I ran toward it, Saleem on my heels.

Elana would detain the guard as long as she could manage, which was considerable given her looks and charm. She'd take her time ascertaining that Timothy Gorlick, MD, PhD, chief medical officer, did in fact work at Ceres Biotech. She would bid the guard to sign here, initial here and also here, and did his family have any plans for New Year's Day?

I didn't pause at the atrium, trusting my memory of the blueprint. Right, and then left, and the chamber should be at the far end. Yes, there was the clear glass door. We raced to it. The second guard would be returning to the lobby before much longer. One glance at the monitors and he was sure to notice Saleem and me, dashing around the halls like mice in a maze.

The black square of a standard RFID keycard reader waited beside the clear door, its light blinking red. I could beat the reader with only a few minutes' work, but thanks to Willard's intel on Markham Protective,

I didn't have to take the time. The keycard I'd programmed at my storage unit had Markham's proprietary master code. One swipe to make the light flash green as the magnetic locks on the door opened with a satisfying clunk.

I stopped to take in the sight of the cryogenic chamber. Oblong tanks, each about thirty inches high and painted a dull olive green, squatted in loose rows. Tubes connected each tank to the power station and a central cooling unit, maintaining their interiors at far below freezing. The machinery gave off a rumble that got down to the bones, like the lowest note on a double bassoon, playing forever.

Stickers in four languages warned of extreme temperatures and danger to exposed skin. More signs on the walls prompted employees to follow safety procedures—masks, glasses, aprons. An eye-wash station occupied one corner.

On the western wall, air vents made a row of black meshed columns. That would be the hypoxic air generator. The chamber's air smelled of something akin to menthol, maybe a byproduct of the constant adjustment to the oxygen levels.

I checked my watch. Eleven-thirty-eight.

Deep breath, Shaw. This would be close.

"You're on," I said. "Show me which tank." Saleem reached into his pocket to remove what looked like a stun gun. My instinctive tension eased when he used the device to scan the bar code label under the lip of the closest tank. He moved on to the second, then a third.

"This one," Saleem said. He stepped back to give me access to the tank. The lid read WARNING—PYROGUARD SEAL B-16—REMOVE ONLY WITH AUTHORIZATION. A list of instructions followed.

"I can remove it," I said, "but there might be a failsafe inside. Don't make any quick moves. One mistake and this thing will torch every microbe in the tank."

He nodded irritably.

The truth was the lid was designed to activate in the event of breakage, not wired with an alarm like a combination safe. Removing it was just a matter of releasing the pressure seal in the proper order as indicated. But I didn't let Saleem in on that. I took another deep inhalation, as if I were nervous that the entire room would explode any second, and began removing screws.

In another minute I had pried the lid loose. A swirl of white vapor escaped from under the lip, cold that made my fingertips tingle even through the gloves.

Under the red lid, around the lip of the cryo tank, were six numbered indentations, most of them holding a hook at the end of a slim metal rod that extended down into the vat of supercooled nitrogen.

"Okay," I said. "Here's the tricky part. Show me which card is the queen."

Saleem got the gist if not the reference. "Move over there," he said.

"I have to check the inside of the tank—"

"I am not a fool. There is no other alarm. Stand by the wall." He drew the Steyr to make his point.

I went, cursing to myself with every step. Would he finish me right here? Once Saleem found the right vial, once he was sure of what he had, my odds of leaving this room were as low as the core temperature in the tanks.

How much time would it take? It was already eleven-forty-four. I made myself relax. Tensing up was the last thing I wanted now.

Saleem holstered the pistol and opened his backpack to remove the CXS-3001 container. When he lifted the cap a translucent wisp rose along with the vacuum plug. He set the container aside to draw a rod out of the cryo tank. At the other end of the rod was a rack of metal trays, dripping with liquid nitrogen. Tendrils of vapor swirled around the exposed tray as if trying to draw it back down into the tank.

Using a pair of rubberized tongs, Saleem selected one slim vial—like a crystal straw—from the tray and slid it with infinite care into the container.

I felt a sharp pain like someone pressing the tip of a blunt pencil between my eyes. That was the first hint. The rest of the symptoms came fast on its heels. An unconscious quickening of my breath. A slight blurring of my vision around the edges.

I concentrated on Saleem. He managed to set the cryo container down before heeling to one side. I shoved off the wall to launch myself toward him. He heard me coming and turned. His hand drew the machine pistol.

Too slow. I caught his wrist in my left hand and gripped tight, pressing the pistol against his stomach. He had realized what was happening, and his eyes were insane with fury.

We stood locked for a moment as he strained to aim the gun and I fought equally hard to keep that from happening. I let go of his shoulder with my right hand and punched him in the solar plexus. It wasn't a great punch. I was already weakening. But it was enough. Saleem grunted and his lungs expelled the last of his air.

My legs began to buckle. Saleem's gave out first. He slumped to the floor, his brain shutting down from hypoxia. I clumsily grasped his gun and staggered with it toward the entrance to the room. Fell to one knee. Black rushed in from the sides of my eyes.

Come on. Move. It's right there.

I crawled the final two yards and dropped Saleem's gun to press both hands on the door and push it to one side. The plexiglass slid open a crack.

I fell with my face at the gap and drew in huge lungfuls of air. It was warm and stale, and nothing could have tasted better in that instant.

My plan had cut things too close. Almost fatally. But I'd had no chance to practice, just guessing at the direction the wheels I'd set spinning would roll. I'd used Ceres's environment controls to override the hypoxic generator. At eleven-forty, my laptop had ordered the generator to make the chamber's oxygen level plummet from its usual sixteen percent down to zero. Within five minutes, the chamber was lethal. Within ten, we'd have both been dead.

I couldn't rest. Saleem might regain consciousness any second. I picked up his gun and stood, carefully, to walk with increasing confidence back to the open vat of liquid nitro. As good a place as any for the machine pistol. I dropped the gun into the foggy mix and watched as it sank to the bottom.

The cryo bottle waited on the counter. I glanced inside it, at the delicate vial that had led to all this trouble, before screwing the cap back on.

Saleem coughed and sat up. I hit him again, much harder this time, with an elbow to the side of his head. He crumpled back to the tiled floor.

I was tempted to leave him where he lay. But that would be short-sighted. He was a foreigner caught in a secure biotechnology facility. Homeland Security would grill him like a cheap steak, and maybe the NSA would have their turn, too. It wouldn't take long before he gave up my name.

Instead I wadded up a pink protective glove from the counter to stuff into Saleem's mouth, and I bound his wrists and ankles with electrical cord cut from peripheral equipment around the cryobank. When I was sure he couldn't worm his way loose, I dialed a number on my burner phone and let it ring while I pocketed the phone again.

It would take about ten seconds. I hoisted Saleem over my shoulder. I waited an extra count of ten more, to be sure, before opening the door.

Downstairs, the package Elana had dropped off with the front desk would be hissing and smoking. The guards, if they had any sense, would get far, far away from it. And the monitors.

I ran for the north stairwell, Saleem over one shoulder and the cryo bottle tucked under my arm like a football.

It was a balancing act, moving as fast as I could down three flights without dropping either burden or falling ass over teakettle. At the very bottom of the stairs was a fire exit. I was past caring if I set off any alarms. I slammed the pushbar with my hip and ran for the water.

Hollis saw me coming. Before I had reached Ceres Biotech's rear patio deck, I heard the muffled rumble of the speedboat's engine and the splashes of water thrown up by her propeller as the boat surged forward.

Saleem had revived. He began to struggle madly against his bonds, and I let him drop. He landed on the slats of the deck with a pained grunt. He couldn't talk with the wad of pink glove in his mouth. But the frenzied rage in his eyes spoke volumes.

The deck ended at the water. I stopped, gasping for the air that my body still seemed desperate for after the trauma of the chamber.

"Shaw!"

The shout came on the wind. I turned to see Bilal at the corner of the building, fifty yards away. Aura joined him, coming into view almost at a run herself.

She took in the sight of me, of the boat drawing near the dock, of the precious cryo bottle in my hand. She dropped her bag and sprinted toward the dock. Hollis drew alongside and I stepped aboard. Her scream of *No!* was as much lupine howl as human voice.

"Go," I said. I could make out Bilal continuing to shout, maybe to his wife, maybe to me. Then the waves slapping the hull drowned them both out as we sped away.

To our port side, a salvo of brilliant, strobing explosions filled the shoreline. White first, then yellow and blue curlicues snaking upward. The delighted whoops and screams of spectators on their boats carried over the muffled bangs of the pyrotechnics. Midnight. The new year.

"Where to?" Hollis said over the growing cacophony. "Back to the *Francesca?*"

"No," I said. "Call Doc Claybeck. Tell her we're on our way."

"What happened? Christ, are you shot?"

"I'm fine." I hefted the thick bottle. Sudden starbursts of red and orange filling the sky gave its enameled sheen the look of a flaming torch. "I need a professional opinion. To confirm that what I just stole is as unique as I think it is."

TWENTY-FIVE

HOLLIS PILOTED THE SPEEDBOAT THROUGH the floating audience and billows of white smoke that drifted over the lake, taking us toward the locks. This night's crossing to Paula Claybeck's house was much faster than our previous trip and heralded by the explosive show. The highest rockets of the finale were visible as we exited the ship canal and entered the Sound.

Claybeck seemed no happier to see Hollis and me this time. We stood on the dock while her dogs sniffed us, until they were satisfied that we weren't an immediate threat. Claybeck warned us that the hounds were jumpy given the late hour and the unfamiliar noise of the fireworks. They growled faintly as if in agreement. Hollis looked like he was about to lose his latest meal.

Twenty minutes later, we were all in Claybeck's basement clinic—Hollis and me seated on the same bench where Saleem had held us at gunpoint, the two dogs sharing a padded bed, gnawing on chew bones that looked uncomfortably like human femurs. Claybeck's tall frame arched over a microscope as she examined the frozen contents of the cryo tube.

"I can't be certain without thawing them," she said, "which I can't do safely here."

"Best guess," I said.

Claybeck tapped the microscope. "Three mature human eggs. Unfertilized, and viable."

"Eggs?" Hollis said. "Like, for pregnancy and such?"

I nodded. "Aura's."

"Then why in hell—" Hollis snorted his exasperation. "Van, why would her eggs be in a biotech company? And why would she have to steal them?"

"I think because these are her last," I said. "Aura has a prescription for cancer cell inhibitors. The drug is most commonly used for cases of ovarian cancer."

"That's possible," Dr. Claybeck said, frowning. "Malignancy requires removal of the ovaries in nearly all cases. She might have harvested her eggs beforehand, knowing the risk."

"It's a theory that matches what we know, with some guesswork," I said. "Aura was married before Bilal. To a Timothy Gorlick, who happens to be the chief medical officer of Ceres Biotech. Maybe the divorce was an angry one. Maybe there's a custody battle over her eggs. For some reason they wound up at Ceres's secure facility rather than some easy-to-crack cryo facility somewhere."

Claybeck shook her head. "A custody dispute between exes might make sense if these were embryos. If they were created by both—Gorlick, you said?—by him and by Aura together. Then he might have a case. But unfertilized eggs should be her property alone."

"Should be. But Gorlick had them hidden. And Aura had to go to extreme measures to get them back." I rose and walked over to the sink at the wall to turn on the left tap. The flow might have run straight off an iceberg. I splashed the icy drops over my face and the back of my neck. The drips off my skin tasted like sweat and something more sour.

"Bilal deals in information," I said. "High-level hacking. If Gorlick somehow arranged to keep his ex-wife's eggs, out of spite or whatever reason, Bilal could figure out where they had been moved. And he would know how to hire somebody like me to steal them."

"Maybe that was the attraction," Hollis said dryly. "Aura's a lot younger and prettier than Bilal."

"He's dying. She can't have kids, except with the eggs. No wonder they're in a hurry."

"So what will you do with them?" Claybeck said, replacing the delicate vial into the thermoslike tube.

"Her eggs are irreplaceable," I said. "Bilal and Aura want them far more than they want me dead. We can cut a deal. Fast, before Bilal tries to grab anyone I know off the street to trade."

Hollis folded his arms. "Who's to say Bilal won't have you killed the second you hand the eggs over?"

I looked at Dr. Claybeck's dogs, gnawing on their bones.

"We'll enlist some help of our own," I said. "A bigger animal."

BILAL HAD TRIED TO REACH me, of course. Yanking desperately on the electronic leash. The log on the phone he'd given me showed unanswered calls starting two hours ago. He'd dialed the number every sixty seconds, then every five minutes, until about half an hour ago when he'd given up. I called him back on a burner phone from the speedboat.

"Where are you?" he said.

"Somewhere you can't trace the call."

"Return immediately. Or I will—"

"Aura's eggs look healthy," I interrupted. "So far as I can tell. I could let them sit on the counter for a while, see if they twitch a little after they thaw out."

He was silent.

"Right," I said. "Now you listen. No more threats. You want Aura's eggs, I want you gone. We're going to make a different agreement, with insurance to make sure you hold up your end."

"Please." Aura's voice. Not on speaker. She'd taken the phone from Bilal. "They won't last forever in the container—"

"I'm aware," I said. "Just like I know these are the only eggs like them on earth."

"We can pay you. Whatever you want."

"The things you love will stay safe, so long as everything I love stays safe. You get me?"

"Yes," she said. "I understand."

"I'll call and tell you where to meet."

I turned the phone off. Pocketed it. Walked back to Claybeck's house while I tried to quell the churning in my gut.

I was the aggrieved party here. No question. Bilal and Aura had fired the first shots. And they would be merciless if it got them what they wanted.

That didn't make me feel much better about holding a cancer survivor's only hope for children over her head.

Back in the basement clinic, I took the cryo tube from Claybeck. "Thanks," I said.

"Normally I would bill you, but I'd rather be free of this entire situation immediately." She turned off the microscope and went to sit on the floor with her dogs, who shifted themselves to lean against her before slipping back into their postsnack dozes. "With a guarantee of no more midnight visits."

"I'll lose your number," I said.

"Would you mind if I didn't, Paula?" Hollis said. "So long as I promise to call at a more civilized hour?"

Dr. Claybeck looked at him. "And for a more civilized reason."

"Of course."

She nodded fractionally. Hollis's smile could have woken the dogs, it was so bright.

TWENTY-SIX

I SLEPT ON THE SETTEE IN the cabin of the *Francesca*, waking at midmorning. Much later than I'd intended. My eyes felt nearly as gritty as my mouth. The action of the previous two days had wrung me dry.

Hollis's snores from the main stateroom below almost made the plates in the cupboards rattle. He'd left a note on the galley counter in his large loopy scrawl. *License plate Richard Martens, ATF.*

Rick the Fed was ATF. Not the FBI after all.

I knew enough about the ATF to know that the modern bureau focused primarily on the last two components of its complete name: firearms and explosives. I also knew the ATF was tiny compared to other branches of federal law, with only about fifty active agents for every state, on average. A victim of the U.S.'s tortuous gun laws—no politician who wanted to keep their job could argue for more funding for a bureau that half the country considered a sworn enemy to their civil rights.

So what was Sean Burke into that could be worth Special Agent Rick Martens's time, given the severe manpower constraints of the Seattle field office?

I showered and brewed a pot of coffee, downing two large mugs and an equal amount of water before I approached feeling human. Raiding

Hollis's dresser, I found a T-shirt advertising Baja California Sur that was relatively stain-free.

I texted Guerin that I was headed for 13 Coins. He would know without asking that I meant the one near Union Station.

Growing up, I'd taken full advantage of the twenty-four-hour restaurant in its old location on Boren, where it had been since before my grandfather had come to town as a young man. At fifteen years old I was as likely to get kicked out of the place for making a nuisance as be allowed to order a Monte Cristo at three in the morning.

The new location retained a few familiar touches, just like Bully Betty's had when the bar was moved. Swivel chairs at the counter, and the absurdly tall booths with quilted leather backs. But it lacked the amiable seediness of the old place. Too wholesome.

On the holiday, between the breakfast and lunch hours, I had my pick of seats. I chose the swivel chair at the farthest end, where the counter curved and I could watch for Guerin to come in.

I checked the news while I waited. The break-in at Ceres Biotech had earned a few lines from most of the local outlets, most of them quoting the SPD spokesperson that police were confident suspects would be apprehended before long. Ceres had officially stated that nothing in the facility had been taken or damaged during the attempt.

Which was a lie. But did the people at Ceres know it was a lie? Had Timothy Gorlick, MD, etc., hidden his ex-wife's eggs in Ceres's cryo chamber without anyone at the company being aware?

The top story on most webpages was the tightening race in the recall election for governor. It was the Democratic candidate whom I'd seen at the state patrol station, giving hell to ATF agent Martens and Detective Podraski. U.S. Attorney Palmer Stratton.

I looked up Stratton's specifics. Seattle native, son of a long-term congressman and grandson of a female state senator. A graduate of Whitaker Academy, one of Seattle's toniest prep schools, followed by Cornell for undergrad and law. Photos from a quarter century ago showed Stratton at college wrestling tournaments and standing proud in an NROTC uniform. Stratton served five years with Naval JAG, which seemed to be a family tradition after his father and grandpappy. Then back to Washington State to fight for good and right.

The Strattons went back a long way. From the looks of it they'd been rich and connected every step. Boards of directors, charity funds, hosting events for the Seattle archdiocese. I found numerous photos showing Margaret Stratton, the candidate's mother and wife of the late congressman, as the regular guest of honor at an annual sailing regatta named for the family.

The scion Palmer had gone the public service route in becoming a federal prosecutor, but that was plainly just a stepping-stone to the family business of politics. In another few weeks he might be governor. Onward and upward.

Guerin walked in at half past ten, surveying the room with the almost arrogant confidence I associated with cops. Some of them lost that swagger when they stopped wearing the badge. I suspected Guerin had it before he'd even entered the academy.

"Lieutenant," I said, as he took the chair next to me.

"Let's keep this tight," he said. "I spent enough time yesterday fielding phone calls about you."

"Phone calls from whom?"

He flagged down the server and ordered coffee and a plate of egg whites and wheat toast. I ordered the Italian scramble, just to balance out the level of cholesterol in our party.

"You first," he said. "Bitter Lake: Why were you there?"

"Sean Burke," I said.

He very nearly blinked. Enough of a reaction that I knew the direct approach had surprised him. But I wasn't done yet.

I showed Guerin the letter from Jo Mixon about the reunion. "This got me following a trail. About Moira—my mother—and maybe my father, too."

Guerin stared. It took a lot to throw the veteran cop, but I might have managed it.

"Burke is your father?" he said.

I waited until the waitress had placed our mugs of coffee in front of us. Neither of us moved to pick them up.

"I don't know," I said. "Dono had dealings with Sean Burke's father, Fergus, around that time. I know through a school friend of Moira's that she knew Sean. They seem to have had a relationship of some kind, enough that Moira wrote him letters. Beyond that . . ." I shrugged.

"Good Lord Almighty," Guerin said. We both sat for a moment.

"Dealings," he said at last, "with Gut Burke. You happen to know what kind?"

"Whatever they were, the statute of limitations is gone in the rearview. Plus the fact that they're both dead. Makes a conviction tough."

I tried the coffee. It was hot enough to kill any taste buds that dared to take a whack at it. "If you know Gut Burke's name, you must be up to speed on Sean. Your turn, Lieutenant."

"Not so fast," he said. "Let's go back to why you were around Burke's house."

"Learning what I could," I said.

"From the view standing on the sidewalk, I'm sure."

"Anything else would be trespassing."

Guerin shot me a flat look. "I don't like cute."

"Then don't ask when you already know how I'll answer. If you're just going to stonewall me, I'll get my breakfast to go and save us both some fucking time."

My attitude didn't piss Guerin off. Like any cop who worked for a living, he took abuse almost every day. The smart ones learned how to let it wash off their backs while they continued to look for an angle.

And Guerin must have had some idea of the emotions fueling my outburst.

"You're going to keep looking into Burke," he said.

I was waiting with the fork in my hand when the server put the plates down. Ravenous. I took a bite of the scramble and washed it down.

"All right," Guerin said. "I can tell you a limited amount. Maybe you already know what I know, thanks to those two hauling you in yesterday. But it's all you'll get."

I nodded.

"Burke has eyes on him," Guerin said. "High enough that there's a special joint task force. It's small and very contained. Podraski is state. There's federal involvement, too."

"ATF," I said.

He fixed me with a look. "However the hell you found that out, I can neither confirm nor deny it. SPD is out of the loop. But that doesn't mean I'm free to conjecture. Right?"

"Go on."

"Do you know who Gut Burke worked for, a few years after he made the move west?"

"Some mob. That's all people remember from thirty years ago."

"If you dug deeper into Seattle history and arrest records and bought some old print journalists a few beers, somebody might connect Burke to the name Liashko. Ever heard it?"

"Nuh-uh," I said around a mouthful. My hand and mouth managing the food while my mind was completely focused on Guerin.

"Anatoly Liashko," he said. "Ukrainian, originally, but raised mostly in western Russia. The eldest son of a homegrown mobster who started making inroads here in the Northwest just before the Wall came down, when things were going to shit for the Soviets."

"Running what?"

"Human trafficking to start, then drugs on a limited scale, whatever the slime could dredge up. After the collapse, young Anatoly expanded. Eventually into weapons during the Chechen wars. His eventual arms concession—legitimized thanks to the Russian oligarchs—made him a hundred times richer, with political influence to match. A lot of that money and clout evaporated when Putin started consolidating power. Maybe Liashko didn't bribe the right people at the right time."

"Did he still have connections over here? If he couldn't sell his goods at home . . ."

Guerin touched his nose. I'd hit the mark. The server came over and asked Guerin if there was anything wrong with his plate, which he hadn't touched. He shook his head and picked up his fork.

"Liashko doesn't come to the States often," he said. "He'll visit Vancouver, where most of his—'dealings,' you called them—seem to be centralized. But he's wary. You sure you don't know what business your grandfather was into with Gut Burke?"

"Dono didn't work for crime families."

"So you say. At any rate, Liashko still has American citizens on his payroll, too."

"Doing what? Arms smuggling?"

He ignored the question. "Podraski and his partner hauled you in yesterday to try and figure out who you work for. Liashko, or one of his enemies. They thought they could squeeze you."

From Guerin, that was almost a compliment.

"When it became clear that you wouldn't bend, they had a choice," he said. "They could book you for suspected B&E at Burke's house. You'd hide behind a lawyer and sooner or later they would have to explain to a judge why they are watching Burke. That could risk their whole operation, and one burglar just isn't worth it. So you walked. But if you cross their paths again, they will go back to Door Number One and stick you in a box for as long as they can twist the system to keep you there. They are motivated."

Guerin finally took a bite of his egg whites. "We've reached the end of story time. The point, in case you missed it, is that you would be all kinds of smart to stay the hell away from Sean Burke. For reasons both legal and familial." He raised his eyebrows. "If you really are related, the less you let this scum into your life, the better."

I still had a third of my meal left. I didn't want it.

"One last question," I said. "The doors in the patrol station aren't as thick as they could be. I caught the name Santora when Podraski and the ATF guy were arguing. Something about winding up like Santora."

The lieutenant stopped chewing. "I told you the department was out of the loop."

"Doesn't mean you don't recognize the name."

"Which you might also find background on, if you dug hard enough. Which you would. Damn it." He scowled. "Marcus Santora. An ATF agent. He's been missing and presumed dead for the past two years. No funeral yet, because the family is still holding out hope. His bureau isn't. When an agent disappears while on undercover assignment, there aren't a lot of alternative theories to the obvious one. We can only hope to find his body someday and give the family some peace. That's another reason why I don't want you kicking up dust."

"Santora was undercover on Liashko?" I stopped myself. "Forget it; I know. Neither confirm nor deny. I can piece it together."

"Not quite." He tapped a fingertip on the counter. "Liashko was the target. But it was Sean Burke who's the prime suspect in killing Agent Santora. Burke also looks good for the murders of at least two more people we know of, on Liashko's orders. The Feds may not have evidence to prove it—not yet—but they'll get there soon enough."

Guerin pushed his plate away. Maybe his appetite had vanished as quickly as mine had.

"Burke is an assassin, Shaw. He's Liashko's gun in the United States and maybe elsewhere, and he will absolutely end anyone who gets too close. Anyone at all. You'd best keep that reality front and center in your head."

I couldn't think of one damn thing to say to that.

JUNIOR YEAR, PART FOUR

Broadway was home ground for street kids. The permanent homeless had Pioneer Square and the tent cities along I-5, but teenagers had gravitated to the Hill since before I was born, Dono once told me. They still did. Something about the compactness of the neighborhood, lots of people, lots of little shops, combined with the length of the street itself. Nearly a mile on the main drag left a lot of space if somebody ordered them to move along.

Prime panhandling was wherever foot traffic was thickest, off the bus stops and by the main intersections. The parking lot of the B of A was popular. Good foot traffic, easy to see cops coming. A couple of kids about my age had parked themselves there, mumbling the litany of "spare change" to every passerby. They weren't so high that I couldn't get a response out of them. I asked if they'd seen Candace tonight. The space cases didn't recognize her name right off, but after a quick description they knew what girl I meant.

Candace was what my granddad would call a do-gooder. He didn't mean it as a compliment, though I was never sure why not. If Candace wanted to spend her spare time talking with street kids, who gave a fuck? At least they could trust her not to rip them off.

After half an hour, I'd walked the length of Broadway until it started to curve at the north end. Nobody lucid had run into Candace tonight. I crossed the street and started back on the other side.

By the strip of shops called the Alley, I hit pay dirt. Candace herself, squatting outside a sushi place with another girl and her Chihuahua dog. The girl said "change" by reflex as I hunkered down next to them. Both her hair and her crusted eyes needed a rinse.

"Hey, Van," Candace said. "Good to see you." She sounded as though she meant it, like always. That was Candace. Ultra-skinny and scattered and she dressed like she'd picked the clothes randomly out of someone else's laundry, but you'd have to work damned hard to dislike her.

"You, too," I said. "I gotta talk to you. About Colten."

Alarm widened her hazel eyes, and I held up my hand. "I'm not with Singer Boeman. Swear."

"Okay." Her fear hadn't completely left. The fried girl caught the tense vibe and curled up around her dog.

"Singer's looking for him. And his gang. You know that, right?"

Candace nodded.

"I'll help. But I have to talk to Colten. Tonight."

"I can't."

"Candy. This isn't going to go away. At least tell me why Singer's so pissed off."

She glanced at her friend, who might as well have been on Venus. "Colt . . . He had some stuff to sell around school. Nothing really bad. I've told him to stop but he has such a hard time saying no to them . . ."

"What stuff?"

"Poppers. A whole bag of them, like two hundred. But someone stole the bag, and now they're blaming Colten."

"Okay." Davey had mentioned seeing little nitrite vials at a party he'd crashed recently, students mixing them with coke for a bigger rush. We figured it was the latest trend, old shit becoming new again. "So what's Colten's plan now?"

"I don't know." Candace was near to crying. "He can't go to his parents. They're terrible."

"Let me talk to him. I won't let anyone else know where he is. Promise. Cross my heart and hope to die."

The childish vow hit home. Candace said a few words to the girl, and we left. Half a block on, Candy pointed another group of teens she seemed to know well in the girl's direction, asking them to look after her. Then she led me on a long walk down the slope of Olive. Even with the breeze, the exhaust fumes of the constant traffic lingered in between blocks. She slowed at the little King of the Hill market, eyes wandering over the selection inside.

"You hungry?" I said.

She nodded, and we went in long enough to buy micro-wave burritos. Candace heated two up on the spot and ate one as we carried on.

We finally stopped at an ivy-covered apartment complex called the Biltmore, shaped like a block-letter C. The deep inside of the C formed the brick-accented entryway, lined with shrubs and small trees. While the brick exterior looked grand, like something built a hundred years ago, music from three different stereos on upper floors competed for dominance, and I could hear voices arguing from the nearest windows.

"My aunt lives here," Candace explained. "We're going to crash after she leaves for work." She turned to call out toward the apartments. "Colt?"

Colten Gulas emerged from behind a stand of trees at the far side. He was dressed for the cold in a tatty ski parka, gloves, and thick hoodie, but he didn't look comfortable at all. The only color on his drawn face came from his pink nose and red eyes. Baked, and maybe crying, too.

"Wha's he doing here?" Colten said.

"He's come to help," Candace said, handing him the warmed burrito she'd carried in her pocket. He didn't acknowledge it.

"How you doing, Colt?" I said, thinking that was the sort of thing Candace might say, and maybe I'd get further with kindness.

"Shitty, man."

"Candy told me about the poppers," I said. "That sucks."

"Fuck, Candace, why you have to talk?" he whined.

"I need to know something," I pressed. "And if you tell me, I'll see if I can help you like Candace said."

"Wha'd you want?"

"The quilt that went missing from the library last year. Who took it?"

"Aw, shit, man. That's not—nobody knows, man."

"You do. Straight trade. Tell me, and you've got me on your side."

"Help me first, then maybe." His bloodshot eyes looking as close to sly as they could get, being so clouded. I held myself back from grabbing Colten and shaking him like a bull terrier on a rat.

"Colten," said Candace, placing her hand on his chest, which managed to be hollow even with the parka. "This is a good deal." The way she said it made me suspect she knew more about the theft of the quilt than I did, but Colten was our focus right now.

"Tell me what happened with the poppers," I said.

Colten shrugged. "I picked them up. I went to school. When I came out, they were gone from my trunk. That's it."

"Came out where? To your car?"

"Yeah." Like that was obvious.

"Who knew they were there? Who saw you?"

"Nobody *saw* me, man. Somebody busted in. They kinda

pushed the window down and opened the trunk and took them."

"But they didn't take anything else," I said. Colten shrugged. I took that for a yes. "Who'd you pick them up from?"

He shuffled his feet, reluctant to squeal. "Burn. He gave all the poppers to me that morning."

"Just Burn? No one else was around?"

"No way. I'm not stupid."

You passed stupid on the way to dumbfuck, I thought.

"You think Burn took them?" Candace said to me. "But he had the poppers in the first place."

And Burn wanted them, so he made Colten the scape-goat, giving him the poppers just long enough to hang their disappearance on him. But Burn hadn't been bright enough to reason that if he was the only one who saw Colten put them in his trunk, he would be the prime suspect. Granddad always told me ninety percent of crooks were dead in the head. Singer and his boys looked like poster children.

Moreover, I had a pretty good guess why Burn might have wanted to steal his own gang's supply.

"I can get you off the hook with Singer," I said, "but no going back on our deal."

"Sure," Colten said, shifting his feet again.

"Colt." I waited until his bleary eyes got a focus on me. "I'm a lot worse than Singer or Burn. A lot smarter. You'll tell me who took the quilt or I will make what you're going through now seem like summer vacation. Yeah?"

"Yeah. Okay."

I nodded.

"You didn't have to bully him," Candace said as I walked away.

Maybe not. But call it a little extra insurance. I was about to take a big gamble for Colten, and even if he didn't appreciate it, he'd sure as shit pay for my grief.

TWENTY-SEVEN

AFTER LEAVING GUERIN, I MADE a phone call. It was answered by a service. The lady at the other end took my name and number and said, with superb diction, that she would pass my information along to the party requested. No promises made or implied of any further contact.

I'd held the cryo bottle with its own promise of Aura's future children for twelve full hours now. I was conscious of that clock ticking, perhaps almost as much as Aura must be herself. If we couldn't make a deal within the next few days, what would I do? Rent space in some cryogenic bank somewhere? Tough job filling out those forms and explaining how I'd come into possession of human eggs.

Nothing for it but to set my only plan in motion, and find out if my persuasion skills were on par with my survival instincts.

ADDY'S FRIEND DOROTHY LIVED NEAR Lincoln Park in West Seattle, the kind of location that Realtors would tout as being mere steps away from majestic views. When I pulled up to the odd house—like someone had placed a Craftsman bungalow as a cap on two additional stories to maximize vertical space—the only view I had was of similar homes squashed into their own cramped lots.

Cyndra was playing with Stanley in the side yard, taking advantage of the unusually bright and dry winter day. The yard wasn't nearly big enough for a game of fetch, so she tossed a tennis ball high into the air and Stanley would try to catch it as it came down. More often than not the ball bounced off his nose or noggin, which didn't discourage him. He'd snatch it off the ground and run in happy circles, tearing through the bark landscaping until Cyndra ordered him to drop the toy so she could throw it again. Slobber spun from the thrown ball like rain off a whirling pinwheel.

"Look," Cyn said, once Stanley was running loops again. "Dorothy had those in her basement. She heard I was lifting weights and she made us take them." Boxes on the porch held pairs of dumbbells, each pair coated in pink or purple nonslip neoprene, in various weights up to eight pounds.

"You're already stronger than these," I said.

"I know," she said. "Isn't that cool? I'm gonna give them to the team."

I grinned and left her to Stanley, who was rolling on the ball like he wanted to fuse it with his pelt.

My knock at the door was answered by Addy's shout to let myself in. Inside, past a knickknack-laden sitting room still strewn with confetti from the night before, I found her puttering around the kitchen putting things in order. Like me, Ms. Proctor was not one for sitting idle. She'd find something that required adjustment, at least to her way of thinking, and set to work.

"Where's Dorothy?" I said.

"She'd already made plans with her children for the day, so we have the house to ourselves for a few hours. A relief after staying up so late. Is there any news?"

I understood what she meant. "Still working on clearing the coast. But you and Cyn should be able to go home within a day or two."

Addy nodded but didn't look away from her work rinsing dishes.

"I'm sorry," I said. "It's not fair to either of you."

"As hideouts go, this could be shabbier," she said. "I'm too tired to debate you right now. Have you learned any more about who your father might be?"

"Nothing good." I told her all I had uncovered about Sean Burke and the murders he'd committed for his gangster boss. I didn't have to sugarcoat it for Addy. Or for myself. She settled on a blue divan in the living room. After another minute of pacing I made myself sit on the couch.

"Worse than you feared," she said when I'd finished talking.

"Yeah."

There were levels of bad, like shades of night. Dono had not been a good man, even if he'd tried to be a decent parent to me most of the time. I was somewhere on the murkier end of that spectrum myself.

But Burke was something else. Somewhere past what I, even with my sorry background and questionable choices, could justify. *Unredeemable* was the closest I could come to putting a name to it.

"So what now?" Addy said. "Do you let it go?"

"Everything tells me I should," I said. "That it would be smart to be Zen about the whole damn thing and release it to the universe, or whatever the hell the phrase is."

"But."

"But I still don't know if Burke is my father. And I hate not knowing. I have always hated not knowing." I clenched a fist. "At least with a definite answer, I won't have the question burning a hole in me."

"Could you talk to him? Or"—she shrugged—"get his DNA somehow? You could send it to one of those labs that verifies family relations. Just because you learn the truth doesn't mean Sean Burke has to."

I'd had that idea, even before breaking into Burke's house in Bitter Lake. That place had been so clean I'd wondered whether he intentionally kept it scoured of all genetic evidence.

"To do that," I said, "we'd have to at least meet."

"Something tells me I'm a step behind," Addy said.

"Only just."

Burke had found me once. I'd have to make sure our second encounter was on my terms.

"Pain is here!" Cyndra, calling from the porch.

It took me a second to grasp what she'd said. I looked out the window. Cyn's derby trainer—Wren, aka Pain Austen—stood on the sidewalk, holding a hand out for Stanley to sniff and lick in greeting. Her right hand, on the arm with the winding spiral of birds. Wren's hair was free of its braid today, the black-coffee waves cascading down to end just above the small of her back.

"I forgot to tell you," Addy said. "Cyndra invited Wren over to pick up the weights before tonight's beginner class."

"Uh huh," I said, knowing there was more to Cyn's motives than that. Maybe Addy's, too. I was suddenly aware that I hadn't shaved today, and I was still wearing Hollis's T-shirt touting tourism in Mexico.

We stepped out onto the porch. Cyn had ordered Stanley to sit and behave while Wren opened the gate and joined us.

"Happy New Year," Addy greeted her.

"Happy New Year, and hello," Wren said to me. "Cyn didn't tell me you'd be here."

"There's a lot she's neglecting to mention today," I said.

Cyndra covered her sudden blush by asking if we'd all care for something to drink, automatically using the same inflection Addy would have used. We sat in three Mission-style chairs on the porch while Cyn escaped to the kitchen. Wren asked Addy how she'd spent the holiday, and Addy wove adventures of her faction of very active retirees.

Addy talked. Wren listened. I tried to do the same. But I was struck with a feeling of separation, of watching myself from outside my body with disbelief. The night before I'd been scaling a building and scrambling to keep Saleem from blowing my head off. Today I was sipping iced tea on a porch.

Returning home after a deployment overseas created a similar shock to the system. Between rotations I would dampen that blow to my psyche by staying immersed in Ranger life and training around Benning. If I never fully wound down, I never had the challenge of gearing back up. But there was no escaping the anchor-like drag of civilian life.

Maybe that was a learned skill. Living in peacetime. I'd never had a chance to practice it much, even in childhood. Now that an opportunity for the quiet life presented itself, I was finding that I was a lousy student.

"Van?" Addy said, bringing me back to the now. "Did we lose you?"

"Sorry," I said. "New Year's Eve was rough."

"I kept my partying to a minimum. This time." Wren grinned. "Last year I felt like you do for three whole days."

"Speaking of recovery," Addy said, "there's nothing in the pantry. Cyndra dear, grab my keys and we'll visit the grocery store while it's quiet. Come on."

She headed off Cyn's protests, handing me a house key and bustling the kid to the driveway and into Addy's Subaru. They were gone as efficiently as if a helicopter had snatched them into the sky on a SPIE rope.

"That was awkward," I said.

Wren laughed. "Mortal Cyn is playing Tinder."

"Yeah. Sorry again. She's good at ambushing."

"I don't mind. And I've been stuck inside all weekend. Are you regretting last night too much for a walk?"

"It's not a hangover. And yeah, let's go."

Stanley would have battered down the door if we'd left him behind. I buckled the giant hound into his harness and we set off toward Lincoln Park. Wren was dressed lightly for the cool day in green cotton pants with slim cargo pockets, and a white polo and fleece vest that contrasted nicely with her skin.

"Cyn said you grew up here in Seattle," Wren said.

"Capitol Hill, born and raised. You?"

"Might as well throw a dart at a map. I was born in Algiers. Then when I started school we moved to my father's home in Marseilles. We came to the United States when I was ten. Since then, seven different states, if you only count the places we stayed longer than a year."

"Whoa. So you're—French Moroccan?"

"I'm American, like you. But I have my French citizenship as well."

I was reminded of Sean Burke's Russian passport, acquired no doubt to facilitate his work for Anatoly Liashko. I mentally shoved the intrusion away.

"I'm Irish," I said, "but that's the American version of Irish, which can be More Irish Than."

Wren laughed. "Performative heritage?"

"Exactly. My grandfather was the real thing, from Belfast. He got out during the bad times in the 1970s and made his way here."

An ambulance flew past as we reached Fauntleroy Way. I tugged at Stanley's lead. He wanted to race after the howling beast.

We crossed the road to enter the park and chose a trail that led to railroad-tie steps, down through the sparse forest of ferns and ponderosa pine. Scores of kids running and shouting on the nearby playing field sounded like colliding streams, splashing and bubbling with chaos.

"Seven different states, huh? And counting?" I said.

She looked at me, one dark eyebrow cocked. "Do you always find the heart of things so quickly?"

"I withdraw the question."

"No, it's all right. It's only—I've been thinking hard about that same question. I'll have been in Seattle for three years this spring. The first place I've lived, the longest I've been anywhere, without any of my family nearby. Most of them are in New Mexico now. I miss them. It's a good life here, though."

"But you're not sure if it's a permanent fit."

"Nothing is permanent, except change. I'm just deciding whether to make change happen, or let it happen on its own." Wren grinned. "You know about that kind of choice. When did you leave the military?"

"Cyndra told you?"

"No. One of my brothers is stationed down at Pendleton. There's a way of moving. Like"—she motioned—"the backpack is still there, and you're too light without it. Did you know you walk on the balls of your feet?"

It was my turn to laugh. "That's kinda witchy."

"A real witch could tell which kind of fighter you were. The Marines?"

"Army Rangers. I rolled out about a year ago." The thought made me stop. "Almost exactly one year, in fact."

"Your anniversary. And your birthday soon, too. Cyn did tell me that."

"Next week. I haven't had much time to think on it."

We reached the shore. A graded path ran along the rocky beach. We strolled north, letting Stanley sniff at each bush and random stick. The wind was in our faces, carrying the smells of salt and seaweed abandoned by the low tide.

Wren described growing up with her extended family, the bunch of them going wherever her father's job as a solar engineer took them, then continuing that nomadic life into adulthood. I gave her a very abbreviated and slightly sanitized history of my own upbringing with Dono. I said he'd been to prison and I'd been a foster kid for a time before we came back together.

And, suddenly, I found myself telling Wren about Moira.

"I'm curious about her in a way I never was growing up," I said. "Instead of what she was like when she was with me, I'm wondering what she had planned for herself."

"As a person, not just your mother."

"Right. She was twenty-two when she died. I was about to start school. Was she finally going to college? Starting a career?" I shook my head. "All those things she never got to do."

"Of course. You're working on your own direction, seeing a reflection in her."

"Did you pick up a psych degree in your travels?"

"I've spent enough on therapy," she said, nudging me with her elbow. "I might as well get something from it."

We turned inland, finding another path that would take us out of the park. This trail was narrower than the first. Hiking up the easy slope, Wren's shoulder brushed mine every few steps.

"Your birds." I touched a fingertip to her arm and its tattoos in flight. Despite the breeze, her skin was hot. "From your name?"

She nodded. "A new one every time I migrate. Sometimes two. It's not a strict rule. Wren is a nickname for Raina." She pronounced it as if there were an accent over the *n*: *Rain-ya*.

"'Van' is short for 'Donovan.' My grandfather's name."

"And yours. You own it. Donovan. It's strong." She tilted her head. "What do you want for your birthday, Donovan Shaw?"

"I don't know your last name," I said, a little embarrassed at the realization.

"Marchand. That was an easy gift."

"Friday night, then," I said, "if you're free."

Wren considered. "I could be. I have something early in the evening, but it won't take long. You could meet me there."

Back at the house, we traded numbers and she said she'd be in touch about the time and place. She declined my offer of help and hefted the box of free weights without much effort. As she reached the sidewalk, Wren paused and turned back, pivoting as gracefully on one foot as if she wore her skates.

"Friday. The whole night?" she said, with a touch of a smile.

"Or as long as you can stand my company."

"We'll have to find out." She walked away and climbed into a well-dented camel-colored Jeep to drive away.

Damn. Maybe Hollis knew something I didn't. He had managed to make inroads with Doc Claybeck. And I was wearing Hollis's shirt today. I'd never make fun of his fashion choices again.

TWENTY-EIGHT

JUST AFTER TWO O'CLOCK, FOUR of us met at Willard's house near Green Lake: me, Hollis, Elana, and Willard himself. The big man had owned the place for decades. Or maybe it would be more accurate to say he'd owned the land, as the house had been rebuilt from the ground up within the past three years. What used to be little more than a cottage—cozy for most, positively cramped for Willard—was now a two-story gabled home with solar panels on its bronzed metal roof.

I arrived in time to see Hollis's sky-blue Cadillac sailing down the street in search of a parking spot. The convertible top was up today. He waved a hand as he coasted past. Elana sat on a dining chair outside the front door, long legs crossed and propped on a garden planter as she vaped lightly from an ivory pen.

"No smoking inside," she said, "in case you were inclined."

"Good thing that's my resolution this year," I said.

I let myself in. The first story had been made an open design to maximize square footage. From the entry I could see the living room with a fireplace, dining area, and part of the kitchen beyond. Most of the furnishings were steel and cedar, and all of them were large enough to accommodate Willard's frame. The walls were papered in a putty-colored bamboo pattern that shouldn't have worked but somehow did. A tang of dark tea filled the space.

Willard came down the stairs, buttoning the cuffs of his shirt.

"Place looks good," I said.

"I had help."

"Interior designer?"

He shook his head. "Sonny. A friend with an eye. You want coffee? Tea?"

"Either." Passing by the mantel, I stopped to look at framed pictures of Elana and her parents when she was younger. And one of a tall, lean black man with a ring of silver hair around his temples. I guessed him for Willard's friend Sonny. Willard had always been very circumspect about his private life. His confirmed bachelorhood an open secret, but never stated, as if it were fifty years ago. I assumed that discretion worked for him. For them both, maybe.

Hollis and Elana came in, Elana exhaling her last drag in the rough direction of outside before closing the door. I set my rucksack down and extracted the cryo bottle with Aura's eggs.

"That's it?" Elana took it from me, weighing it in her hands. "Huh. I figured it would be heavier."

"Mostly padding and vapor," I said.

"And three lives," Hollis said. "Imagine."

We joined Willard at the dining table. He'd set a pot of coffee on a trivet and passed out mugs.

"I can't think about it that way," I said. "Like the eggs have any value beyond what Aura and Bilal give them."

Willard gave me a flat look. "So if you can't agree on a deal with them, you'll toss her eggs in the trash?"

"They'll deal. They'll never be more willing."

"You don't have to hand all three eggs over," Elana said. "Give them one. Keep the other two as insurance."

Willard looked at his niece like she'd sprouted horns. "That might be even colder."

She shrugged. "They started this."

"They did," I agreed, "and I thought about splitting up the eggs, too. But all three might be destroyed in the attempt. Even if we did it right, if Bilal and Aura are successful in having a kid with their first try, I've lost my leverage. If they can't, we're right back where we started. I don't want to do this again in a few months."

"Haven't these dickweeds heard of adoption?" Elana muttered.

Hollis hummed as he swallowed a mouthful of coffee. "I have to admire his commitment to her."

"You would," said Willard.

"It's true," Hollis protested. "Aura might only have one option, to get her eggs back. But Bilal doesn't. He could go off and have a kid with any willing woman before he kicks off if that's so damned important to him. Hell, he could sire a whole brood."

I stopped in midpour. "You're right."

"Of course I'm right. I know how children get made."

"About Aura being in a corner. She's the one who's truly desperate." I was looking out the window but not really seeing anything beyond the idea that was taking shape. "She's the one who'll be left alone when Bilal dies."

"Alone raising a brat," Elana said.

Hollis grimaced. "What is it you're thinking, Van?"

"Bilal has the money and the soldiers. But it's Aura I'll need to reach an agreement with," I said.

My first thought had been to talk face-to-face with Bilal and Aura, once I'd figured out exactly how to ensure my continued safety. Now I was peering down a path I hadn't spied before.

"We'll have to arrange a meeting," I said, as the idea occurred, "and let Bilal come heavy."

Willard rumbled. "Well, that sounds like ten kinds of crazy. You know if he sees a chance, he'll grab you and torture you until you surrender the eggs. After that . . ."

"That's what I'm counting on. Him seeing a chance. I'll need you and Hollis to be my eyes."

"You're not cutting me out again," said Elana.

"Nope. You'll be critical"—I stopped Willard before he started—"and out of the line of fire. You'll all be away from the heat."

"Speaking for myself, lad," Hollis said, "you walking in alone to meet those two and all the muscle they can hire is just mad-dog cowboy shit."

"Rabid, reckless, and all the rest," I agreed. "Let's pray Bilal Nath thinks so, too."

TWENTY-NINE

A FTER LEAVING WILLARD'S, I DROVE around the lake and wound my way toward downtown, the side roads giving me time to puzzle over a different problem, and a different threat. All my careful maneuvers with Aura and Bilal might come to an abrupt end if Sean Burke appeared and caught me by surprise once more.

My subconscious had been picking at the tangled knot of just how Burke had tracked me to the parking garage on the night of the museum gala. I had an inkling—my only idea this side of crazy notions like Burke following my car with a team of flying drones—but its implications were unnerving.

I'd used my personal credit card to purchase an evening pass when entering the garage that night. Burke knew my name and my car. If he'd somehow put a trace on my accounts, he might have known where I was within minutes. Perhaps even before I'd chosen a parking space.

Was that even possible? Burke's Russian boss, Liashko, had money, and pull. Did his reach extend to flunkies inside major American banks? Guerin had said the arms dealer wielded enough power to control his interests without setting foot on our shores. Wielded through men like Burke.

I was as realistic—Addy would say cynical—as anyone about the corruption of those in power. Hell, I'd bribed an FBI employee less than a week ago. But Liashko having that level of influence at his command gave me one very long pause.

And a theory I could put to the test.

Some car juggling was required. I drove my truck downtown. On the holiday, the streets were halfway to deserted and I had my choice of metered parking spots. I left the truck at the curb, not far from the museum. Caught a rideshare back to Addy's to retrieve the Barracuda. And drove the muscle car right back to the garage where Burke had aimed his gun at me. With intent, as the law would say.

I used the same credit card to buy a two-hour ticket. Wondering if, somewhere, the charge on the card was even now sending a flag to alert whoever might be watching.

Five minutes later the Barracuda sat nestled in a spot on the second level, copper paint gleaming in the low January sun, and I was back at street level, sitting in the truck. Watching the garage entrance.

I'd set the shiny lure. Now came the waiting.

If I was right, Burke had waited for me to return to the Barracuda after my visit to the museum. The more I thought about that, the less I figured he had stood outside on the roof of the garage, exposed to the cold and to witnesses. He'd have kept watch from a car of his own. Not his personal vehicle. Something untraceable to him, in the chance that he would have to leave me dead, with my rapidly cooling blood flowing down the slope of the garage ramp.

My phone rang, with the number of the answering service I had called early in the morning.

"It's Jessica," said a contralto voice. "You remember?" Ondine's bodyguard from the museum.

"Sensible shoes and a lethal purse," I said. "Can you speak for your boss, or are you just relaying messages?"

"This line's secure."

I took that to mean Jessica had some authority beyond being Ondine's flyswatter.

"Good. Let's cut to it. I need to set up a meeting with Bilal Nath. He knows it's coming. I figure he'll circle back to you to recruit more soldiers. Maybe he already has."

"Go on."

"Your boss told Nath I was unmanageable. Play that up. Make me out like some rabid dog. Encourage him to bring along a full team, racked and ready."

"Why?"

"That's my business."

"I'll state the obvious," Jessica said. "We don't take orders from you."

"No. But you are taking commands from Nath right now. Right? What's it worth to get Bilal off your back for good?"

I waited through the silence that followed. Jessica might be conferring with Ondine.

I'd sounded much more confident than I really was. In truth, I was playing a hunch, based on my hard-won experience with Ondine Long.

She had shared Bilal Nath's biography with me far too easily. My confronting her at the museum had been like an opening bid, and she hadn't responded with a counteroffer. Instead she'd folded, telling me what she knew, and quickly, before the guards showed up to end our conversation.

So why would the most mercenary woman in Seattle be willing to give me intel on Bilal for free? Her client, who'd paid her for Claybeck's services?

Unless he wasn't a client. Bilal was very adept, Ondine had said. A bitter aftertaste in her statement. Maybe Nath had a leash around Ondine's neck, just as he had on mine. Had she been gambling a little herself, on the off chance my thrashing against Bilal might solve a problem for her?

Jessica came back on the line.

"Bilal has to stay alive," she said. "If he dies . . ."

"Agreed. This isn't that kind of op."

"But you want him protected?"

"I want him ready for a war. And if he demands a kidnap team to make me disappear, give him that, too."

Another moment passed.

"We can make that happen," Jessica said, "though we can't control what the teams do once they're in motion."

Meaning I was digging my own grave, from their perspective.

"It's on you if this goes wrong," Jessica continued. "In any way at all. Understand?"

"I'll tell Bilal where and when. Sometime tomorrow."

She hummed reflectively. "Whatever you have planned, I hope it's not as stupid as it looks from here."

I grinned. This was Jessica talking for herself, not as Ondine's mouthpiece.

"Nice to know you care," I said, and hung up.

During our call, a few cars had driven into the garage. A minivan with kids in the backseat watching movies on the fold-down screen. Teenagers in a Honda Civic adorned with the cheapest racing mods available from their local O'Reilly Auto, heavy beat pulsing the windows. Nothing that fit the right profile.

Until a black Ford F-250 with a bright silver toolbox across the full width of its bed, like a stripe over a thick beetle's wings, turned off Seneca and cruised slowly to the garage. Smoked windows obscured the interior.

The Ford stopped for a moment at the entrance, as if smelling the air, before pulling through the gate.

Five minutes passed, then another ten. No one walked out from the garage.

Okay. I hadn't seen Burke in the flesh. But I was sure he was there. Like the scent of another predator at the watering hole.

I was prepared. I had sandwiches from Addy's and water, and an open-necked bottle if I had to relieve myself. Mostly I had a lot of practice in waiting and watching. Casing jobs with Dono, back when I was a fidgety teen. Recon of targets in the Rangers, when moving at the wrong moment might bring a hell-storm of opposing fire.

My parking ticket had only been for two hours. I wondered if Burke knew that. He'd paused at the gate, maybe reading the hourly prices and comparing them to the small charge on my credit card. He might be expecting me to return to the Barracuda at any minute.

I hoped so. The more frustrated he became, the better.

While my eyes did the work, my thoughts strayed to Wren. I didn't know much about the woman yet. But what I did made me want to learn a lot more. She was intuitive as hell. And forthright. There hadn't been any question she'd been flirting with me, and I could admit I wasn't always the best at reading women's signals.

And sexy. Damn, Wren Marchand was an absolute smoke show. I wasn't positive which of us had asked the other out in the end, but I was glad either way.

I ate a sandwich made from Addy's leftover roast and some provolone. Sipped at the water. It had stayed plenty cold just from the ambient temperature. This time of year, the shade between downtown buildings was nearly round the clock. Even sheltered from the wind in the Dodge, I kept my watch cap on my head.

The Barracuda's parking pass had long since expired. Maybe an attendant had already placed a ticket under the wiper, informing me I'd have to pay for the full day. Maybe Burke had seen that and realized that I might not be returning as promptly as he'd imagined.

Another hour ticked by. The edges of the buildings around me began to soften, melding with the twilight sky. Their interior lights defined stripes and squares that grew ever brighter in contrast. Fewer lights than on a normal workday, so that each side of the avenue looked patchwork, incomplete.

The headlights coming down the garage ramp revealed the Ford's presence seconds before the truck itself hove into view. It stopped at the gate, which rose obediently to allow passage. As the Ford pulled out onto the avenue, beams from a passing delivery truck shone directly through the windshield, overcoming the tinted glass and giving me an instant's glimpse of the driver.

Sean Burke. Gotcha, asshole.

He turned left onto Spring Street. I U-turned to follow, staying at least one block behind and giving Burke plenty of room as he turned again onto 6th Ave and we made our way uptown.

Not far, as I soon learned. Burke pulled into a lot near the Westin. I drifted past, coming to a stop in a loading zone, watching in the rearview. A sign at the front of the lot had touted monthly parking rates. If the Ford was Burke's clean machine for work purposes, maybe this was where he kept it.

In another minute, a Lexus GS sedan in granite gray appeared from the lot. It continued on the same route, passing me and shimmering its way up 6th. Burke's broad frame was visible through the rear window.

I didn't follow right away. Burke might have marked the Dodge from his own truck. Pulling out behind him now could be a dead giveaway, accent on the *dead*.

He went left on Bell. In another second, I hurried after him. I passed through the intersection in time to see the Lexus cross under the monorail track at 5th and turn into an alleyway on the next block.

I stopped before the alley. Too easy to spot me in those close quarters. I left the truck at the curb and ran ahead to look down its length. The back of the Lexus was just vanishing from sight into a wide brightly lit rectangle. As I watched, the rectangle compressed until it was gone entirely. An automatic door had shut behind Burke's car.

After a slow count of twenty, I risked walking down the alley. The wide door was painted with the name EMPYREA.

I retraced my steps to the front of the block, on 4th Ave. The alley ran behind the Cinerama theater and a luminous high-rise, maybe forty stories or more.

The Empyrea. A newer addition to Seattle's skyline. Its lower six floors had been clad in backlit glass that shone a verdigris green. The same pale green highlighted each floor of the looming tower above. Discreet signs in the windows advertised units still available. On the other side of the doors, posters of happy families and conspicuously affluent professionals, enjoying the amenities within. The lower floors of the tower operated as a hotel under the same name.

I sent a text to a friend. More of a work acquaintance, really. I included the license plate number of Burke's Lexus GS. I'd had to lean on my newer colleague Panni to trace Special Agent Rick Martens's license. But for DMV checks on regular citizens, I had my own sources.

Ten minutes later the name Garrett Costello and an address matching the Empyrea Tower added to our text thread. Unit 3105. High living. I spent two more minutes wiring my acquaintance his fee for the service. Pays to know people.

Garrett Costello. A buddy of Burke's, lending him his car? Or the name Burke lived his daily life under, to keep people like me off his track?

I wasn't inclined to wait to find out. The security of the average hotel was no challenge. I made my way in through a utility door off the alley and then cut across at the quiet mezzanine level to find the elevator.

The elevator required a keycard to access the residential floors. I ignored the swipe pad. In my lockpick kit I carried a firefighter's service key, which allowed me to open the Phase 2 panel inside the elevator and override the keycard controls. The button for the thirty-first floor lit up on the first try.

Apartment 3105 was halfway down the hall, likely boasting unobstructed views of the southern skyline and the water beyond.

I listened at the door. I could hear faint voices from a television, a news channel. I debated whether to pick the deadbolt or to coax Burke into coming out somehow, maybe by leaving a package at the front desk. The television went quiet.

Then I heard muffled footsteps, close and coming closer, and had just enough time to get my hand on my Beretta before the door opened.

Burke. Dressed for going out, and with a look of stunned surprise. A gift horse with a gaping mouth. I shoved him back into the dark interior of the apartment and drew the gun.

"Hands," I said, kicking the door closed behind me. "Up."

He froze. I pointed the gun at his knee, just as he had to me, to underline the point. He laced his fingertips on top of his head.

I spun him around and quick-marched him up against the wall of the living room. His leg banged the glass table beside a black leather couch, knocking a full tumbler of water to the carpet.

My left hand patted him down while the right aimed the Beretta at his spine. I stayed off to one side with a few inches of extra space. No point signaling to him exactly where the gun was, inviting an attempt to disarm me. And I wasn't positive we were alone in the apartment. If anyone else suddenly appeared, I wanted Burke as a shield.

He had a small squarish automatic, maybe a Walther by the feel of it, in a soft concealed carry holster over his right kidney. A gravity knife with a four-inch blade in the pocket of his overcoat. And a backup piece, a subcompact Glock on his right ankle. Armed for a damned standoff. I tossed all the weapons toward the door. Fury radiated from Burke like heat off a reactor core.

"Get it over with," he said.

"You said it yourself: I'm not a shooter. But I will put a round through you if you step out of line."

"Then what the fuck is this?"

"My turn for picture time."

I tapped his shoulder with a half sheet of cardstock and the penlight from my pocket. Slowly, he reached a hand from his head to take them. I drifted back to give myself some space. This high in the sky, the city lights made more of a soft undertone to the darkness in the room than any illumination we could see by. The shadows worked to my advantage.

When he turned on the penlight, the beam bounced off the glossy print and into his face like a suntan reflector catching rays. Slashes of shadow trapped in the crags of his square face just served to emphasize his look of shock.

I said what we both already knew.

"Moira."

He didn't take his eyes from her yearbook picture. As his gaze moved slowly over the contours of Moira's image, motes of flashlight beam glimmered in his eyes.

"How do you have this?" he said. Something like wonder in his voice.

"She's my mother."

Burke turned the flashlight my way. I had anticipated the glare. With twelve feet between us, his blinding me and jumping to attack wasn't a practical option. Not that he seemed inclined. Flat-footed in both stance and attitude.

"You and Moira were friends," I said. "When you were both teenagers."

"And?"

I took a breath. "And I want to know if you're my father."

He stared at me for a long moment, before his lip curled in a snarling grin. If the laugh that followed had any humor in it, it was the kind that revealed itself when watching a video of someone you didn't like taking a nasty fall.

"You asking if I laid her? That it?"

"That's a first step."

"To what? Child support? Shit, you're bigger than I am."

"Did you?"

"Man, you really believe this. Dumb fuck." Burke shifted, his heel squashing on the wet carpet. "I never got in the bitch's pants. And without that, there's nothing. I haven't given two shits about her since. Happy?"

"Not yet. I want proof."

"Proof?"

"A hair sample. Including the roots."

The grin evaporated. "I should have known this was a cop trick." He dropped Moira's picture to the floor.

"I'm no cop."

"Oh, I heard that. You're just some snitch they told to break into my house to nab some DNA. What do they got over you? Another burglary rap?"

"You're wrong."

"Go fuck yourself. The only sample you're taking from me is blood." He nodded at the gun. "You got the stones?"

I did. On any other day. Popping one through the outer meat of Burke's thigh—a volcano of pain but nothing fatal, so long as he got help soon—and yanking out a fistful of his hair while he writhed on the floor might have been easy work. I didn't even have to go that far. Burke was strong, but I could whip him across the head with the Beretta and continue from there.

Except.

Except I'd seen the way Burke had looked at Moira's photo. Like you'd look at a childhood treasure you'd long believed lost.

Except he hadn't asked about Moira, or told me to take my fool questions to her. He already knew she was dead. Which meant he was lying about never giving her another thought.

There was something stopping me from hurting Burke. It didn't take a flash of genius to figure out what that was.

"Here." I took a burner phone from my pocket and tossed it to him. He caught it one-handed.

"In case you want to talk to Daddy?" he said, the predatory smile back in place.

"In case you decide to stop bullshitting me. Until then I've got other things to do."

"Other contenders, huh? Mom spread it around a little?"

I wasn't going to give Burke the pleasure of seeing my anger.

"Stay away from me, Shaw," he said, "or I'll finish this."

I backed toward the front door. Burke didn't bother shining the penlight in my direction. He stood with the beam illuminating the cuffs of his trousers and his shoes, and the white edge of Moira's photo on the frost-blue living room carpet. His shadowy outline only shifted once I began to close the door.

I left the Empyrea via the lobby. As I joined a stream of people letting out from a show at the movie theater, I had to step around a long-limbed dude inclined with almost sagging relaxation against a post, a cigarette like a piece of smudged chalk stuck in the black sand of his heavy beard stubble.

A few feet farther on, I caught the smoke. A pungent, deep-tar punch.

No way that was an American brand, not even hand-rolled.

I kept walking to the corner before looking back. The lean dude with the black overcoat and blacker stubble was still hanging there, eyeing the hotel lobby. He glanced vaguely in my direction. Then assiduously avoided doing so again.

Maybe Burke had been leaving to meet him. Or maybe the dude was watching the lobby, intent on following Burke when he left.

Podraski and Martens, the task force cops, had implied someone might have hired me to break into Burke's house. Burke himself had demanded to know who I worked for. And if the smoking dude wasn't from Eastern Europe, I was a Martian. Was Burke somehow on the wrong side of his boss, Liashko?

I took my time returning to my truck, to make sure the smoking dude wasn't on *my* tail, and to take a moment to think about my last sight of Sean Burke.

As I had closed the door to 3105, he had moved. It had been hard to know for certain in the gloom, but I thought I'd seen Burke reaching down, rescuing the picture of my mother from the sodden floor.

JUNIOR YEAR, PART FIVE

I didn't skip classes often, not nearly as much as Davey. Part of my arrangement with Dono was that I could work with him so long as my grades maintained at least a three-point average and I stayed out of detention and other trouble. But today was a special case.

Not having a car of my own, I had to hide in the trees that bordered the school parking lots while I waited for first bell. Lurking like some perv. At least the woods smelled good, more like cedar than the spruce trees I guessed them to be from their mossy, scale-like bark. I wanted coffee and breakfast but I'd had to make do with a Coke grabbed from the fridge early this morning and some wintergreen gum.

When the lots were empty of students, I went looking. Burn Burkley's white GTO was in the farther lot, between a pickup truck and a Ford SUV. Perfect. No one could see me from the school as I used one of Dono's tools to pop the trunk.

No alarm sounded. Maybe Burn didn't have one, or he had installed some aftermarket brand on his shitmobile that only went off if someone unlocked the doors. It wouldn't have mattered. What I was searching for took me ten seconds to find.

Under the spare tire, a plastic Safeway bag filled with pinkie-sized bottles wrapped in gold foil. A quick glance at one told me the little flasks had been mass-produced in England, where I guessed poppers must be legal. Maybe Singer or Burn had a relative willing to mail them over.

Twenty-two minutes until the end of first period. Time enough. I made one stop in the 400 block of classrooms, and another to wash my hands carefully in the bathroom. By the time the bell rang I was at my locker, picking up books as if it would be a nice, normal day ahead.

Word was all over school by lunchtime. Vice Principal Rik-kard had opened up Burn Burkley's locker, and whatever he'd found there—rumors ranged from a sack full of airplane liquor bottles to a kilo of heroin—it had prompted a visit from not one but two police cars and the cops pulling Burn out of third period. No one had seen him since, but Lane March said he saw Burn in the back of one of the cop cars as they left, all snot-nosed and sweaty.

Yvette Friel didn't look much better. Like she was about to hurl, or had just hurled, or both. As I passed her in the hall at lunch I couldn't resist twisting the knife a little.

"Sorry about your party favors," I said.

She gaped at me like I'd grown fangs. Which it kinda felt like I had.

I'd puzzled over why Burn would steal the poppers back from Colten Gulas, when his whole sales market was in the high school. He couldn't have sold them at Watson without someone in Singer Boeman's circle noticing and making the connection.

But he could give them away. Maybe pour the liquid into dollar-store bottles for shampoo first so it wasn't so apparent they were the same supply. And Burn's sometime girlfriend Yvette was about to throw a huge bash tomorrow night. That was, if she didn't end up in a police station answering questions all weekend. I didn't put it past Burn to claim it was all Yvette's idea.

Colten and Candace met me after school, by the weird metal sculpture that the school had installed sometime during the 1970s. It was iron-gray and looked like sine waves had collided and broken into pieces. Like the artist had had a bad time in math class and wanted everyone to know it.

"What," Candace said before even saying hello, "*happened?* I mean, God. Everyone says there was an anonymous call to the fire department about a bomb or something. Or that the custodian found a puddle under Burn's locker."

"Spillage," I said. "Stuff leaked all over the floor in 400."

"You did it. How?"

"Doesn't matter. What matters is that by now even Singer has heard that Burn was busted with the goods. Colten is home free."

"I thought you were going to give them back to me," he said, hunching his shoulders so that his backpack rode up around his head. "That would have been better."

I waited. Stared.

"Colt, I think Van's done his part," Candace said.

Colten sighed.

"Who took the quilt?" I said.

Another sigh. "I did. Rebecca Hoff said she really liked it, and I thought she really liked me, and . . ."

"And you took it to give to her."

"She was graduating. If she had the quilt, she'd remember me. No one *cares* about the stupid thing, anyway."

I was back to staring. Keeping myself calm. Candace spoke even faster than before.

"Van clearly does, honey. Go on."

Colten took off the backpack and unzipped it. "Here."

He handed a thick folded mass to me. It was stained and tattered in multiple places, and nearly pulled apart in others, but unmistakably a handmade quilt.

"We had it as a dog blanket," he said. "Fenster chewed a little."

Even if Colten hadn't said anything, I would have known that. The quilt reeked of canine.

"Go away," I said.

"I'm sorry," Candace said.

None of this was her fault, but I guess the look on my face must have spooked her a little, because she got Colten up and moving like he was on fire.

When they were out of sight, I unfolded the quilt. A couple of the fabric squares had representations of people, but most stuck to patterns of diamonds and triangles and smaller interlocked squares. I remembered the quilt better now that I saw it. Reminiscent of Easter, pastel colors like pinks and sky blues and soft yellows.

But I'd never seen the back before. Each student had stitched their name.

There it was: MOIRA SHAW, in green thread. One of the interior squares that weren't as frayed as the edges. I turned the quilt over to examine her square. It, too, was made in shades of green, with a central square and triangles angling off it like a sunburst. I liked it. I ran my fingers over it lightly, feeling the ripples in the fabric and the stitching. She'd had me in her belly when she made this.

I liked it a lot.

Ms. Nasgate and Mr. Lindhoff were together in her classroom. A nicer meeting place than his cramped office, I guessed.

"I found this," I said, placing the folded quilt on one of the sewing tables. Ms. Nasgate was on her feet in an instant.

"Oh my," she said. "Look."

Lindhoff frowned. "Where'd you get that, Mr. Shaw?"

I pointed to the quilt's edge. "A dog's chewed on it."

"I asked you a question."

"That's no real concern, Milt," Ms. Nasgate said to him. She was already unfolding the quilt, spreading it to drape smoothly over the table. "It's very dirty, but the fabric we used is forgiving. A lot of these stains will come out." She spoke breathlessly to herself. "I think we can rescue most of them with a little patching. Which one was your mother's?"

"This one," I said. The speed of my answer wasn't lost on Lindhoff.

Ms. Nasgate smoothed the quilt's cloth with her hand, like she was soothing a nervous animal.

"Now, I wouldn't normally break up a project, Van, but this is a special circumstance," she said. "Would you like to keep your mother's square? We'll be reassembling much of this, anyway."

I shook my head. I'd taken some pictures of it. They would be enough.

"She made it to be part of something," I said.

"Well, thank you very, very much. You know this is the only senior project since I've been here that was lost? We'll take good care of it. And put it back in a place of honor."

"Mr. Shaw?" said Lindhoff. I inhaled, waiting for the shoe to drop. "I trust . . . no one was harmed in the recovery of this?"

Ms. Nasgate looked very puzzled by the question. I shrugged.

"No," I said, "but they deserved to be."

He chewed on that. "Then I suppose everything ended well."

Well as can be.

I left them there to talk over whatever they needed to talk over. I'd done all I could. Somewhere, Mom would know that.

THIRTY

WILLARD AND I STOOD IN an unleased floor of an office building, across the street from a similarly empty and even more rundown warehouse on Seattle's north end. Rundown, but hardly quiet.

"You see them?" Willard said. "In the repair van."

I did. I had an even better view than Willard, once I'd adjusted the focus on my binoculars. Two men sitting in the front seat, and at least one more in the enclosed rear of the high-ceilinged van. The vehicle tilted slightly as the unseen third moved around.

Ondine had provided Bilal Nath with plenty of resources. All men in casual clothes, all moving with purpose, and every one of them armed. I'd counted four so far, carrying duffels long enough to allow for carbines or shotguns. They hadn't arrived all at once. The team had been taking positions around the warehouse since eight this morning, less than one hour after I'd texted him the address along with the time to meet: High noon.

They had set pairs of operatives at the corners of each intersection and already entered the warehouse. More than likely they were also on the roof of the building Willard and I were watching from.

I'd chosen our meeting place after searching through commercial listings. I didn't care much about the neglected warehouse itself. But I loved that the office building across the busy street had space available, giving us an excellent vantage point. And that its occupied floors were dedicated mostly to single-business suites, psychologists and massage therapists and chiropractic clinics, which buzzed with appointments after the holiday break. Lots of comings and goings. Lots of people for Bilal's team to try and keep track of.

It was a reasonable assumption that the repair van was planned for me. The kidnap team. Once they had me trapped, the team would bring the van around and they would efficiently force me out the side door of the warehouse and into the vehicle. What would happen after that wasn't worth thinking about.

Willard scanned the streets. "I'm up to eighteen so far. Think Ondine gave Bilal a bulk rate?"

I took my eyes away from the lenses. "A joke. From you. Amazing."

"Laughing in the face of death."

"Look at it this way: the more of them that are here, the better."

Eleven o'clock now. One hour to go. I called Elana.

"They haven't left the hotel," she said immediately. "But their Mercedes is in the roundabout, with two tight-asses in suits and crappy haircuts hanging at the entrance. How's the meeting spot?"

"Might as well have a giant bull's-eye painted on it."

We held the line open until something changed. It took less than ten minutes.

"He's here," Elana said, her voice an octave higher than usual. "Bilal. He and the two rejects and that bodyguard with the angry face are getting into their car."

"That's Saleem. No Aura?"

"No Aura."

"We're on our way."

Willard and I took the elevator to the ground-floor parking level. Hollis was in the passenger seat of Willard's Continental, from which he had been watching the eastern side of the warehouse.

"Are you sure it's too late to call in your Army compatriots?" he said as he climbed out and stretched. "I'm sure one of those lads carried a no-bullshit machine gun through that door."

"Keep your distance," I said, taking his seat. "And text me—"

"Once your man arrives. I'm on it. Good luck, boyo. I hope you know what you're doing."

Willard and I pulled out on the rear side of the office building and gave the warehouse a wide berth on our way to the interstate. I kept watch on the oncoming lanes as Willard sped south, on the off chance we'd spot Bilal's Mercedes as it passed. We didn't, but it didn't shake my confidence that Nath was headed where I wanted him.

Elana met us at the gate of the Neapolitan.

"I forgot to tell you: I haven't seen that walking cement truck who works for Bilal."

"Juwad. He's probably guarding Aura." I turned to Willard. "Think you can keep him from twisting my head off?"

Willard smiled. Humor didn't look at all natural for his Cro-Magnon features. As if a rock suddenly rippled like water.

"You're up," I said to Elana.

She smoothed her white blouse. Combined with the conservative skirt and efficient black pumps, and her hair drawn into a neat bun, she looked the very model of a hospitality professional. From the waistband of the skirt she removed a Neapolitan Hotel name pin that read NANCIE.

"Where'd you get that?" Willard asked.

"From Nancie, of course." She tapped the pin with her nails. "I'll put it on in the elevator."

"See you inside," I said.

Elana pivoted and walked away, a distinct spring in her step. Willard and I gave her a minute's head start before walking into the lobby and directly across to the hotel bar. It was lunchtime, and the handful of business travelers and affluent vacationers were doing their best to start the weekend a little early.

The Neapolitan's bar had a back room available for rental to parties of up to twenty people. It was closed for a private function. Ours. Hollis had reserved the space yesterday.

I left the door to the room ajar and chose a booth out of the direct line of sight. Willard stood outside at the bar as if waiting to order.

Elana would be knocking on the door of Bilal's suite by now.

Helpful Nancie, conveying the message to Aura or, more likely, Juwad that Mr. Nath had mentioned on the way out that he would prefer they wait at the back of the hotel bar, and would Mrs. Nath please bring her computer and tablet in case they were required, and was there anything else she could do to make their stay more pleasant?

Aura might call her husband to check. Or maybe she would assume radio silence while Bilal was supposedly dealing with me. We had to roll the dice on that. She would have Juwad and the midday crowd in the nearby lobby for reassurance. Safe as houses, as Hollis would have said.

I set the cryo bottle at the edge of the booth's table, where it could be seen from the doorway, and watched the bar in the stripe of mirror that ran along the top of the artfully tiled wall.

We didn't have to wait long. Aura appeared in the entrance to the back room, her aqua-tipped blond hair framed by the broad expanse of Juwad's chest behind her. Both scanned the room. Her eyes lit on the cryo bottle. She rushed forward as if to stop the container from falling.

I placed my hand on it before Aura could reach the table.

"Let's talk," I said.

Juwad came up fast behind her, barreling toward me. Before he reached the table, Willard was there, draping a gigantic arm over the powerlifter's wide shoulders and taking hold of Juwad's bicep with the other hand. Juwad's neck muscles grew taut as he strained to pull away. Willard's fingers tightened. They stood, neither of them moving, two titans locked in an uncertain contest. Juwad's face contorted. Willard smiled grimly.

"You're safe," I said to Aura, "and if everybody stays calm, you and I can make a deal for these." I drummed my fingers on the bottle, looking pointedly at her guardian.

"Juwad," she said. "Please."

Willard stepped back. Juwad almost slumped into the booth, but he righted himself. His brow was shiny with sweat.

"Bilal is waiting for you by now," Aura said, her eyes on the cryo tube.

"Let him wait. These are yours, not his."

"What is it you want?"

"The same thing you do. A future for me and my family. Can we agree on that?"

She sat down opposite me in the booth, almost tossing her tablet and laptop aside, eyes flickering between me and the container. "You want our word you won't be touched."

"I want mutually assured destruction." I hefted the bottle. It was amazing, in a minor key, that only an inch of material separated my fingers from cold that would shatter them like peanut brittle. "I want enough hard evidence to send you and Bilal to jail forever, enough to make sure your future children are taken from you if it comes to light. If I have that, then I'll sleep soundly."

She blanched. "That's impossible."

"That's my price."

Aura touched her teeth together. The bottle pulled her gaze back as if her eyes were physically stitched to the slender tube. "Bilal has—clients. I could give you their names, and the materials he has on them."

"Not even close." I set my phone on the table, leaning against the cryo tube, angled so its lens would capture Aura's every expression and gesture. "Three eggs, three stories. You, Bilal, and Ondine, too."

"Ondine? Why?"

"That's my business."

"Bilal—"

"He'll understand. But even if he doesn't, you'll have your children."

That was enough for Aura to look at me. "If you're lying to me, or if my eggs are already gone, I won't be able to stop him. I won't want to."

"I accept that, Aura. So let's figure out how to get past this."

After a moment, she leaned back. "I can—I can tell you about me."

I nodded. Baby steps.

"Timothy, my ex-husband. We were together when I was first diagnosed with cancer. He suggested harvesting my eggs. Our marriage was already—" She frowned. "It doesn't matter. The whys."

"Go ahead."

"Timothy oversaw my procedure. The head of the clinic, Jackson, was a friend of his. A friend of *ours*, I thought. We didn't have any money of our own—Timothy owed nearly a million dollars just for his school loans, all those crazy degrees, and everything was tied up in trying to get Ceres launched—so it was all done as a favor. I was so desperate, I was dumb. I never signed papers or even told my insurance company, just to keep it all under the table."

Aura closed her eyes, maybe berating herself out of habit.

"It wasn't long after that when I told Timothy I wanted out of the marriage. We fought, and when I saw that he was determined to draw our separation out for as long as possible, I demanded my eggs."

"He refused?"

"They told me that there had been an accident, that my eggs had been destroyed. I was sure at first that Timothy had arranged with Jackson to make the whole matter go away. They could have both lost their licenses if I went public."

"Why didn't you?"

"I had no proof. I have a criminal record, and time spent in psychiatric facilities when I was a teenager. Who would believe me compared to them? I'd already decided to fight back another way." Aura touched the sleeve that held her laptop. "It wasn't hard to hack into Jackson's home and work computers. I made some false trails, just to make it look right."

Her breath caught. I kept my mouth shut, allowing her space to say the next part.

"Pornography," she said. "Of children. There are horrible, horrible things available, just—out there. For the sick freaks who want it."

"You framed Jackson."

"I left one trail where it would be found. It was enough. The court sentenced him to six years." Aura's eyes flicked to the camera lens, to the cryo tube holding her eggs, to me. "Jackson didn't know about my skills, and I don't think he ever suspected me. But Timothy did, of course. He knew that I'd gone after Jackson first just to make him sweat it out. That he would be next."

I raised my eyebrows. Aura was, in her way, as merciless as her extortionist husband. "And that's when he told you he still had your eggs."

"I should have realized it sooner. If you're not with Timothy, you're against him. He would never destroy something that gave him so much control over me, even if it might save his career. And now he could use my eggs to keep me from ripping his life apart."

"You were trapped," I said. "Both of you."

"Until I met Bilal. I took some work with him, hacking into companies here in the States. When he came to Miami for treatment, we met in person. Our relationship was already serious. With his illness he didn't have time to spare, and I wanted him to be able to stay in the country. So we got married. I confessed to Bilal what I'd done. Ceres had completed construction of their new building by then. It made sense to us that he would hide my eggs there. Bilal's team and I searched through the company, looking for any coded items in their records without a paper trail back to R&D or vendors. Timothy wasn't as clever as he imagined."

I wondered again if that had been part of Aura's attraction to Bilal. Power, wealth. A chance for revenge against her abusive ex. And to be completely cold about it, only a temporary commitment, with Nath already showing signs of ALS.

"So now you know," Aura said. "If the police found out, I would take Jackson's place in prison."

"I have to have actual evidence." I pointed at my phone and its camera. "Something to back up your story."

I had expected Aura to kick at the final step, but she removed her laptop from its sleeve.

"There are the original logs and the ones I doctored to put on Jackson's computer," she said, "plus the hacked account from where I stole the—the pictures. Tell me where to send them, and they're yours."

Give her this: the woman was decisive as hell. We spoke for another thirty minutes while Willard kept watch on the entrance and Juwad grew increasingly agitated. The battery on my phone ran dangerously low as it videoed Aura's entire confession.

I learned about Bilal Nath fixing a provincial election in Pakistan, and two other instances where he'd bribed territorial leaders to get charges dropped against his informants. Aura also told me that Ondine Long had jumped a little too quickly to act on whispers of a company going public, with email messages that would be highly embarrassing at best and lead to charges of insider trading if the DA chose to make an example of her.

Aura was one of Bilal's best operatives, as well as his wife. She sent the evidence of their transgressions to the shared drop site I gave her. I'd already arranged that anything placed on that location would be automatically copied to a second private site in the cloud. Trust, but only so far.

"Ondine," I said to Aura. "I own the goods on her now. Forget you know her name."

"That's everything," she said. "Everything I have."

"Not quite," I said. I touched the white tablet that she'd used to hack my phone at Dr. Claybeck's. "I want this handy gadget."

Aura looked perplexed. "It's not perfect. And it requires recoding every time a phone model pushes an upgrade to its OS. Without updates, it will be obsolete within a month or two."

"I'll take it, anyway."

I turned off my camera and handed her the cryo tube. "It's safe to open it."

She did, as if the tube held the antidote to a poison already consuming her. I gave her a glove, and she used it like a rag to extract the slim steel rod with the vial of her eggs attached to its end. Wisps of escaping vapor curled almost protectively around the tiny crystal straw.

"Store them somewhere more permanent within two days," I said.

Aura nodded, but I was uncertain if she was paying full attention. I signaled Willard, who moved to the doorway separating the bar from the back room. Juwad remained on his stool as I stood up.

"Goodbye," I said to Aura.

"If Bilal sees you again," she said, delicately turning the seal to close the tube, "I don't know how he'll react."

"Then convince him to leave town," I said. "For your kids' sake, if not yours."

She nodded, as if she'd already thought of that. "Yes. I want to be gone. Tonight."

Willard and I walked through the bar to a utility hall that led to the alley behind the hotel. His Continental waited there, its engine idling, with Elana at the wheel.

"All good?" she said as we climbed in.

"Not all bad," I said. Elana hit the gas, and we were out of the alley before I took another breath.

THIRTY-ONE

I DIDN'T TAKE AURA'S WORD, OF course. Willard and I took opposite corners of the block to watch the hotel entrance, Willard from the comfortable driver's seat of his car, and me from an apartment-block entryway that did little to block an adamant wind that smelled of impending ice sheer and car exhaust fumes.

Within half an hour, Bilal Nath's lunar blue Mercedes returned to the hotel roundabout. The vehicle bounced an extra inch as it nudged the curb, its suspension tested by all that hired muscle inside. Bilal's men quickly disembarked before Nath himself appeared from the rear seat. With his thin frame and cowl of dark hair, he looked like a chess-set bishop surrounded by bricks.

My phone buzzed. I didn't have to look to know who was calling.

"Ondine," I said.

"I imagine you already know that Nath has left the meeting place," she said. Her voice so calm, like the drop in air pressure just before a tornado hits.

"Yeah," I said. The rear guard of Bilal's host vanished into the lobby, leaving the SUV to the scurrying valet.

"Explain yourself."

"I'll cut to the finish. Aura Nath and I have reached an agreement. She and Bilal will be leaving town."

"With what guarantee of your safety?"

"That's my business. I've got everything I require. So will you, if we can cooperate."

"Meaning?"

"Insider trading must seem like small potatoes to a guy like Bilal. I wouldn't have thought you needed the dough."

Ondine's silence stretched long enough to read a page of hexes.

"What is your intention?" she said.

"I don't really give a crap about your stock market dabbling. Leave Dr. Claybeck out of any future business, and we can forget the whole thing."

Listening over the wind, I could almost hear the gears gnashing as Ondine pieced together how I could have met Paula Claybeck.

"You go too far," she said.

"Come on. Of all the things I might demand, this is easy."

"I'll be forced to take your word on it, I suppose?"

"So long as I stay hale and hearty, no one will ever know. And think how great it will be to never hear from Bilal Nath again."

"If I were truly fortunate, that would extend to you as well."

"We can dream," I said, and hung up.

I'd let Hollis tell Dr. Claybeck the good news. A token of his affection.

Shit, it was Friday. I was supposed to meet Wren tonight. She'd sent a text earlier this morning. I'd seen it but had been focused on Bilal and the warehouse.

8 o'clock @ Clifford's in SODO okay?

I replied with an apology that it had taken me so long and, yes, I'd meet her there.

Two hours later, as the wind worked on freezing my nose shut, the valet brought Bilal's SUV back. Only two of the blocky goons flanked Bilal and Aura this time, with Juwad taking the driver's seat.

The goons carried suitcases. Aura carried a black leather Gladstone bag, cradled under one arm. I could guess what was inside.

Saleem brought up the rear. He walked past the Mercedes and stopped to scan the street beyond the Neapolitan's gate. I knew I was invisible in the sheltered entryway, but it still felt as though his furious gaze paused on me for a moment. Did he suspect I'd be watching? A deep violet bruise marred the side of Saleem's face where I'd struck him. After another moment, he turned on his heel and stalked back to the car.

Within a minute they pulled away from the hotel. I called Willard.

"I'm on them," he said.

"Boeing Field," I said. "I'll bet a buck on it."

If I'd successfully convinced Aura to leave us alone. And if she had convinced Bilal. That was the trickier part. I wished we'd had time to bug their room. Having a fly on that particular wall might have helped me relax.

No point in continuing to freeze my ass off. I walked up Madison and found a pizza place that served lunch to the neighboring office workers locking its doors for the evening. A twenty convinced them to give me an unclaimed white pie and a bottle of Peroni lager to go. Not wanting to wait, I ate the warmish slices across the street in the partial shelter of a bus stop.

A scarlet sign on the building wall above the pizza place directed emergency vehicles to go around the block to access the E.R. at Virginia Mason.

That's where she died, a voice told me.

Moira. I hadn't even known that memory was in my skull. But there it was, as unyielding as any foundation block. After she'd been run over by the car downtown, the ambulance had taken her to the Mason E.R. Where the daycare worker had taken me. Where I got my earliest firm recollection of Dono, as he told me as plainly as he could manage that my mother, his daughter, was gone.

Willard called back. I tossed the remaining pizza and the unopened beer in the trash.

"I owe you a buck," Willard said. "Bilal just took the exit to BFI. The guy must have some pull to charter a flight this fast."

"He was prepared to leave tonight, no matter how it went down."

"I'll hang around until I'm sure he's gone."

"Thanks. Hey. You never knew Moira, right? My mother?"

There was a silence, which didn't prevent Willard's puzzlement from coming through loud and clear. "Naw. I started working with Dono not long after you were born, but I never met your mom. Hollis said something the other day about you tracing your roots."

"Did Dono ever mention what Moira did after she left high school? Besides raising me?"

"Dono never mentioned shit. He wasn't the kind for small talk, unless he was soused, and I hardly ever had tickets for that show. I remember we had some extra cash after one of our first scores together. He asked me to drop an envelope with some paperwork and a few bills off at a school on my way home. I think that was for Moira."

"What school?"

"Hell, Central? I don't know. One of the college buildings by Broadway. There was a woman's name on the envelope, but don't even try asking me what it was. Maybe just one of Dono's girlfriends."

Maybe.

"Thanks," I said. "I'll talk to you tomorrow."

"Keep your head on straight. Sure as shit this ain't over."

My apartment was a twenty-minute walk from the Neapolitan. I used every step of it to shake off the unpleasant energy that was powering me now. A combination of leftover adrenaline, too much stress during the past days, and the frustration of crossing paths twice with Sean Burke, both times with guns involved. I needed a shower and a catnap and food with some actual nutrition.

A mile later I caught myself grinning. I'd realized my jittery feelings weren't stemming completely from bad soil.

I was excited to go meet a girl. For the first time since Luce. Was it really that simple?

THIRTY-TWO

FOUND MY WAY TO CLIFFORD'S Brewing Company without needing to check the address. South of the stadiums, near Holgate Street and the loose row of cannabis shops on the avenue competing for who could offer the widest variety of edibles. I'd driven past the brewery's neon orange sign with its yellow flames dancing where the apostrophe would be at least a dozen times but had never been inside.

Most of the weed purveyors were open late, their green crosses ablaze as if warding off Clifford's devilish fire. I left the Barracuda in an empty lot of a wholesale food distributor a block away and jogged toward the flames.

Friday night had the bar packed shoulder-to-shoulder, including the people smoking on the sidewalk. I bobbed and weaved through the door and went looking for Wren Marchand. It took a while, shuffling through the throng without knocking anyone's drink out of their hands or getting overly familiar. One girl in a sundress—maybe she'd planned for the crushing humidity in the crowd—laughed and raised her longneck bottle over her head to let me by. We about brushed noses as I edged past, and she winked.

Life was famine or feast. I seemed to be on the verge of the better half.

I'd just about completed my circuit when a combined shout of voices rolled out from somewhere beyond what I had thought was the back of the bar. Loud enough to carry over the freight-engine rumble of a hundred conversations. I changed direction, knowing somehow that Wren would be where the action was.

Halfway down a short hallway—also packed, here with people waiting for a restroom—I heard the THUMP of something very solid striking wood. The crowd in the room ahead groaned, but all I could make out were more people. I pressed closer. The throng shifted, and I saw what I was missing.

At the right side of the room, tall sheets of plywood lined the wall, each sheet painted with a classic target in blue, red, and yellow concentric circles. An instant later a short axe sailed through the air, landing with a THOCK this time as the blade hit properly and stuck. The audience whooped encouragement.

In another moment the mass of spectators undulated like an amoeba, and my guess was confirmed. Wren, grinning and holding a silver-bladed hatchet aloft like the cover of a fantasy novel, if warrior women wore black jeans and T-shirts advertising Cubana Perfecto cigars.

Her opponent looked much more the stereotype to wield an axe, in short-sleeved plaid flannel tight over his biceps and a full beard cut square at the bottom. A paisley handkerchief had been tied around his head as a blindfold.

Wren grasped his shoulders to turn him toward the target and handed him the hatchet. I couldn't say the crowd exactly hushed, but the din at least hit a lower register. The lumberjack drew back his arm and threw in a practiced, almost casual motion. His blade spun twice and hit home between the yellow center and the red stripe. The resultant roar caused beverages to slop from every glass.

The end of the match, it seemed. A Clifford's employee in his safety-orange polo began to collect the axes into a large bucket. Spectators drifted back toward the main room, and I found myself swimming upstream just to stay in place. In another minute I could make headway toward Wren and a circle of friends, still at the throwing line.

"You made it," Wren said.

"I'd have been here sooner but I didn't bring a bulldozer," I said, matching her volume to hear myself.

"This is Ulf." She squeezed the arm of the bearded axeman, who took the bucket of hatchets. "And Sara, Estrid, and Bo."

Bo arrived carrying two pints of ale, with another Clifford's staff member behind him toting four more. They began passing them out. I wound up with one somehow.

Ulf was selecting specific axes from the bucket, examining their edges for nicks before slipping the weapons into a leather carrying case. "Beer," he said. "Finally."

"'Drink and throw, lose a toe,'" Estrid said at my questioning look. "They don't serve until we're done."

"And done I am, beautiful people," said Wren, draping a leather jacket over her shoulders. "Thanks for the game." She toasted the group with her pint with one hand and took me lightly by the wrist with the other.

We snaked our way to a heavy wooden door, beyond which was a large enclosed patio handling overflow from the bar. Less crowded than the inside, thanks to the nighttime temperature, which threatened a frost before midnight. Wren set her pint on a flat plank railing to don her jacket. The heat lamps Clifford's had set on the patio kept the immediate surroundings thawed but a long way from warm.

"Hell of a show," I said.

"You caught me on a good night. I'm still getting the hang of it."

"Is it a league, like with roller derby?"

"Just with friends. I stumbled into it one night. Since my date was already throwing, I wanted to try it for myself."

"You and Ulf?"

"Me and Estrid. For a while." She gave me an assessing look. "I see who I want to see, and I don't apologize. Anyone I like. You cool with that?"

"Works for me."

"Okay. I'm glad."

"And I'm glad it's not Ulf. Never cross a guy who brings his own axe."

She laughed. We touched glasses.

"I don't know what you do," I said, "besides crush every sport you try."

"I'm an herbalist."

"That's . . . plants as medicine?"

"Botany, right. Everything from digestion to chronic pain relief. I have some private clients and classes now, but my friend Lettie and I are working on opening an online shop. It's the clinical part I really enjoy. Like with pharmaceuticals, you have to understand someone's history to consider what treatment might work for them, and know what drugs they might already be taking. You have to work with modern medicine, not against it."

"You like your job."

She shot me that self-aware grin. "I'm talking a lot, huh? It stokes me. We share a plot of land up in Skykomish where I grow what I can in this climate. I'll make the cures and consult with the patients, and Lettie will handle the inventory."

"I've used some of those remedies before. Addy has them. Calming essence drops, under the tongue when I don't want to knock myself out with trazodone or something like that."

"Do you have trouble sleeping?"

Not at all. But I couldn't explain to Wren why.

"Not as often anymore," I said.

"Can I ask something personal?"

"About my face?"

She dipped her chin, not quite daring a nod.

"It happened during my first deployment with the Rangers. Rock shrapnel off an RPG—a grenade—blowing up near us."

"Your first deployment? You had more after?"

"Lots. I was in the Army for ten years. Our rotations were usually around four months long each time. It adds up."

"How old were you?" Wren said, not to be deflected.

"Twenty."

"God. That's so young. I knew the wound must have happened when you were an adult, but I just assumed it was the reason you left the Army. Childhood scars look different. See?"

She turned around and pulled up her jacket and shirt to show me the small of her back. A slim pinkish line traced the soft humps of her lower vertebrae, vertically from her pelvis halfway to her shoulder blades. The scar was slightly wider at the middle, with tiny white notches every inch or so along the edges. On my pale Irish skin the line would have barely made an impression, but Wren's richer complexion gave it contrast.

"Spinal surgery, when I was eleven," she explained, "to correct a defect in my discs."

"That must have been terrifying as a kid."

"Yes. But it was very painful before, living with the condition. I was old enough to understand why I needed the operation. And that it wouldn't be a magic cure. Even if the surgery helped, it might not help forever. They fused three of the bones together back there. The recovery period was awful. Then it got better."

"Does it hurt now?"

"No, not at all. And every day I get up and I use my body. While it lasts." Wren smiled. It wasn't a rueful smile at all. She'd found honest joy in the reprieve.

Wren touched the lowest scar, the thin line along my jawbone. "Do you feel yours?"

"The opposite. My face is slightly numb on those spots." I tapped my bisected eyebrow and the Y-shaped furrows at my cheekbone. "They filled in some of the bone and my back teeth with Bioglass. I can't grow a decent beard anymore."

"You're joking. How long were you in the hospital?"

"A week or two in country. Then they sent me to Italy for more cosmetic surgery. I rotated back to my platoon after a couple of months."

"So fast. And you were barely out of your teens. It's horrible."

"I wanted to get back to work. Waiting around was driving me batshit."

"No, I understand that part. Having to take control. To do something for yourself. I meant it was horrible being so young and having such—" She stopped herself. "How did you feel then?"

I took a moment to find the words. It had been almost the full ten years since I'd spoken out loud about that time after my injury, and I'd only said anything then because the Army made wounded soldiers jump through psych hoops before they would cut you loose. We all knew what to tell them. Feeling good, feeling strong, ready to go, Doc.

Which wasn't at all what I had really felt. Not since that first look in the mirror, once the doctor was done slathering me with caveats like *This will look much better once the swelling's down,* and *There's more we can do once your natural bone bonds to the new materials.* He'd finally removed the bandages and allowed me to see for myself.

A horrid puffed mass of purple and pink and black covered the left side of my face. So swollen that I could make out those livid colors at the corner of my eye without needing the mirror. Dozens of individual stitches protruded like tiny spines from a deep-sea creature. And an awful hollowness beneath it all, my face unable to feel, or refusing to accept, the alien material under the shredded flesh.

"I felt like a door had been slammed," I said to Wren. "Like normal life wasn't ever going to happen for me. So I might as well throw myself into my job."

"You couldn't be a regular person again. Because of your face."

I nodded. "I avoided mirrors. For a year or two, what I was seeing wasn't what I was seeing. Even after I'd healed, if that makes any sense."

"Body dysmorphia. Like what anorexics have, seeing themselves as fat no matter how thin they've become."

"Yeah. How was it for you? You were just a kid."

She shifted closer, tucking her head against the chill breeze. "I wouldn't show my back to anyone, all during school. I'd change shirts in the bathroom stalls if I had to, and I was late for P.E. all the time. It wasn't until I was in college that I dared to wear a bikini to go swimming. No one said a thing. And after a while I stopped being so self-conscious. But you"—Wren frowned—"you couldn't hide at all."

"Overseas, it didn't matter. There were plenty of other casualties around, some a lot worse than mine. Guys missing limbs and still doing their part. My Ranger buddies would maybe crack a joke. Happy it didn't happen to them, yeah, but so long as I could do the job, no one gave a shit."

"Acceptance." She tilted her head, considering. "You couldn't stay overseas forever. What happened when they sent you home on vacation?"

"Leave," I corrected automatically. "Our battalion would deploy, rotate home for weeks of rest and training, and then do it again. So I didn't have to spend long stretches of time stateside. I usually hung around the barracks. Bachelor enlisted guys live on base."

"My brother lived at the bars near Pendleton." Wren laughed. "You can't tell me you never went out. Never wanted a girl."

I smiled. "I gave it a shot. I'd go drinking with my team, looking to hook up like anybody else. But . . . I could feel eyes on me. Whether people were really staring or not. After two beers, I'd make some excuse and head home."

"I'm sorry."

"That was a long time ago."

"You got over it eventually." She looked at me through her dark lashes. "I trust."

"Yes."

"How? A girlfriend?"

"Now, that's really getting personal."

Wren laughed. "I'll trade you secrets, then. Ask me anything you want. And just to be up front, I'm not going to bed with you tonight."

"No?"

"No. So whatever you tell me, you don't have to worry about it ruining your chances. Or that I won't see you again."

"You first?" She smirked agreement. I thought about it for a minute, my fingers prickling around the cold pint. "Okay. What are you most afraid of?"

Wren leaned back against the rail. "Here I was sure you were going to ask me a sex question."

"That would be too easy for you."

"You're right." She folded her arms. "I'm scared of playing things too safe. Of never knowing what's around the corner, because I didn't dare see it for myself. You know the Kipling book, with the mongoose and the cobras? There's a line from that: *The motto of all the mongoose family is, 'Run and find out.'* I loved that story."

"So you move around a lot."

"So I move around a lot." Wren nodded. "Your turn, Donovan Shaw. How'd you rejoin impolite society?"

"By seeking professional help."

"That's a cheat. I wasn't talking about your therapy."

"Me, either."

It took her a second. "You . . ."

"Hired a girl. Yeah. It was down to two days before my next deploy-ment and I couldn't face going out to a bar again. I went online. Found a woman in the classifieds and wrote her about me, so she'd know what she was dealing with, wouldn't run away screaming. We met at a hotel a hundred miles from Benning, just to make sure no one I knew would see us."

"And how was it?" Wren looked more entertained than astounded.

"Businesslike. But she was kind. That's what I needed more than any-thing. It got me—"

"Over the hump."

"I was not going to say that."

"Sure you weren't."

"By the time our battalion rotated back again, I was more myself. Or at least I cared less what people saw when they looked at me."

Wren raised her glass. "Here's to remedies."

"And understanding. Thanks."

"My pleasure. You want another round?"

I surely did.

THIRTY-THREE

I SPENT PART OF SATURDAY MORNING on the phone. It took a few calls to track down the person I was looking for, but fewer than I'd imagined. Even with a hundred other options there are still phone books, real and virtual, and plenty of people, especially of an older generation, still have their landlines listed.

My last call was to a retirement home in Mill Creek called Highland Hearth. The receptionist assured me that visitors were more than welcome between the hours of eight and four. I told him I'd be there within the hour. It took me less than half that before I was knocking on the open door of a room on the ground floor.

"Mr. Lindhoff?" I said.

The orderly behind me tapped my elbow. "You have to speak up. Mebbe go there in front of him, so he can see."

I took his advice, pulling the wicker guest chair from beside the narrow bedstead with its safety rails to a place in front of Milt Lindhoff's recliner. His eyes worked from behind his glasses to gain a focus on me. In the thirteen years since I'd seen him the lenses had widened and thickened, as if to balance the thinner, heavily creased face behind it. This close to him, a nostril-stinging smell of analgesic was strong and mixed with a sweeter note, like overripe fruit.

"You're not Louis," he said. His voice was husky, perhaps age or just from dryness. I didn't remember what it had used to sound like.

"I'm not," I said, louder than before. "My name is Van Shaw. I was a student at Watson High."

Lindhoff cleared his throat. Looked out the window of the little room at the path and kidney-shaped patch of lawn with its single crab apple tree, leafless now in winter. Single tree to match the room's single bed, single dresser, single recliner with attached folding tray where Lindhoff could take his meals when he wasn't up to joining the other residents in the dining room. On the walls and tucked up against the mirror on the dresser were paintings of people, all from the shoulders up, all on ten-by-ten prestretched canvases without frames. The paintings weren't sophisticated but were still intriguing. All of the people looked back at you with something like misgiving in their gaze.

"I got a lost quilt back for you once," I said. "You and Ms. Nasgate."

"Della."

"Right. Della." This had been a mistake. Lindhoff was not what he once was. "Sorry to have disturbed you."

"The tough boy," Lindhoff said. "The quiet one."

I eased back onto the thin pillow of the chair. "Do you remember me?"

"Sure. The only kid Harshbarger wouldn't yell at. Little creep was scared'a you."

Harshbarger had been the composition teacher. Short and short-tempered.

"My memory's slow. Not gone," Lindhoff said. "But I can't hear for a damn, son, so don't be afraid to rattle the windows. How'd you find me?"

"Ms. Nasgate's sister. You and Ms. N. got married, I found out."

"Second time for both of us. Ten good years 'fore she passed on."

"I'm sorry."

He waved the sentiment away. "Whatcha here for?"

"My mother, Moira, went to Watson before I did. That would be thirty years ago. Around the time you started."

"Jesus. If you say so. Thirty years ago I could still run marathons."

"Do you remember her at all? Dark hair like mine, very pretty. She was good at English and wanted to go to college before I came along.

When I was a student you told me you'd talked to her about community college, and—a friend of mine remembers dropping off what might have been tuition later at Seattle Central." I held out my phone with the image of Moira from the yearbook.

Lindhoff peered at the phone. I wasn't sure if his cataracts allowed him much of a view. His hand, gnarled but clear of liver spots or lesions, worried at where the crease of his pants might have been.

"No," he said finally. "I know the girl you mean. Got pregnant." He waved it off again. "With you, I know. That kind of thing didn't happen so often I wouldn't remember. But I don't know her face. Central, you said?"

"Yeah."

"Then it's Shelly Rudkin you want. Shelly was the rep for the Seattle community colleges, came around to Watson twice every year. Usually stopped for dinner with me and Della. Call Della's sister June back. She'll have Shelly's number in the book."

He motioned for me to comply. I did. June Nasgate, perplexed but willing, looked up the contact information. I copied it down.

"Shelly's a good saleswoman," Lindhoff said once I'd hung up. "I expect if your mom went to Central, they would have had a talk at some point before that."

"Thanks," I said.

"I may not remember her, but I remember you some," he said. "The talk that went around the teachers' lounge about you. Odds on whether you'd wind up in jail before long. Didja?"

"Army," I said. "Right after graduation."

He grunted. "Good. You might be suited to that. Your mother finished her senior year at Watson, is that right? Pregnant and all?"

"Yes."

"Thought so. That kind of thing didn't happen often, girls expecting and staying in school. I already said that." The hand fluttered again and pointed at me. "Hell. That must have been a lot for her to handle. She wouldn't have sacrificed so much if she hadn't thought it worth the fight."

"Guess not."

"That quilt," he said, as if remembering for the first time. "One of Della's projects."

"Yes. My mom had worked on it."

"Della loved those sorts of undertakings. Said people working together to create something good was our highest calling. Art especially. You do any art?"

"Nope. You?" I already had the answer, of course.

"Painting, when the brush'll stay in my hand. I like portraits, but mine never look like the subjects much. Doesn't matter. I just say I'm capturing their inner self, like the brush is possessed or something. Nine times out of ten they buy it." He shook his head. "You believe that? Angels and all that horseshit?"

"Not anymore," I said.

Lindhoff coughed, and it took me a second to realize he was laughing.

"Not anymore. Isn't that the living truth?" he cackled. "Isn't that just true of everything?"

SHELLY RUDKIN STILL WORKED FOR Seattle Colleges, and she was dedicating her Saturday afternoon preparing for the new quarter starting the next week. She told me over the phone that if I could make it to her office off Harvard Avenue within the next hour, she would speak with me today. The address was barely two blocks from Bully Betty's. I knew exactly which lights to run to make it there with time to spare.

"Your question put me right into the Wayback Machine," she said once she'd let me into the building and we'd shaken hands. "The high school circuit was my very first job with the district. By the time Moira contacted me a few years later, I had transferred to Admissions. Good timing for her, I must say."

I had to stretch my stride to keep up with Rudkin; she walked like she was trying to keep pace with her words. She had pale hair and paler skin, but her eyes were nearly as dark as mine, in a face shaped like a generous heart.

"Do you remember Moira?" I said.

"I do. We only spoke a few times, but I processed her application. The school hasn't transferred all our backlog from twenty-five years ago to the new system, but transcripts and student registrations? Those we have. Schools prioritize money and credits. Here we are."

She sidestepped through a shared office crowded by at least one more desk than the room had been intended to hold. Rudkin had stacked copier-paper boxes on her desk to elevate the monitor and keyboard, creating a standing workspace. The absence of a chair gave her another foot of elbow room. I hovered to one side as she typed ferociously with two fingers, then swiveled the monitor to show me. It was Moira's transcript, with columns for dates and course codes and grades and credits earned.

"She completed two quarters and had registered for a third," Rudkin said.

I looked at the span of dates. Moira had died before the spring quarter began. To have something else to think about, I pointed to the list of codes. "What are these classes?"

"The course IDs are out of date, but that one was Intro to Public Policy. And that one in the second quarter is Group Counseling."

"Like what, psychology?"

"Social work. Moira was on a track to eventually earn an MSW. I know because of this."

She scrolled down to show a scanned document. A letter of recommendation, addressed to SCC Admissions, from the director of something called New Road Outreach. It was a lengthy letter. Moira had been volunteering her time, and the NRO director had written two paragraphs about her empathy and aptitude and resilience in dealing with some of the tougher cases in their program.

A program for the children of prison inmates.

Rudkin hummed thoughtfully. "That's unusual. My guess was that Moira was applying for grants for her education, and the letter was to help make her case."

Grants. Maybe Moira hadn't been comfortable having Dono pay her freight. "Do you know these people? New Road?"

"I used to. It's defunct, has been for at least twenty years. A victim of budget cuts and competition for charity and who knows. Their director left for Austin or someplace not long after. New Road served at-risk kids, most of them in foster care or stuck somewhere else in the system. Some in juvenile detention. Or kids just needing counseling with one or more parents incarcerated."

Kids from criminal families.

Just like Moira. Just like me.

"Would you make a copy of these?" I asked. My voice more hushed than I'd expected.

Rudkin spun the monitor back and got to typing. "Normally there would be a formal request and a fee for a transcript, but honestly, who has more right to it than you?"

A printer in the hallway between offices hissed and buzzed. I followed Rudkin out to take the papers off the tray as they appeared. Each sheet warm from the rollers.

"Hope this was what you were looking for," she said.

I looked at the copy of the letter, sent by a long-shuttered charity on behalf of a woman who had been killed only a few weeks after. Both more and less than what I'd imagined I might find here. An idea of what Moira had wanted to do with her life, and the dead end I'd known would come eventually.

THIRTY-FOUR

I T HAD BEEN A FULL week since I'd been to work at Bully Betty's. The crowd placid enough now that the holidays were over that no one on either side of the bar was moving at more than half speed. A-Plus granted me a half-lidded gaze of curiosity at my unexpected appearance, showing off her brilliant blue eye shadow, as I walked behind the counter to take over the taps and the menial work.

As my hands got to cleaning, I thought back to what Milt Lindhoff had told me. That Moira wouldn't have sacrificed so much if she hadn't thought it worth the struggle. The *it* being me, her baby boy.

His implication was clear enough: Did you grow into a person worth everything she gave up?

Those concerns passed the time, going around and around in my head, until late in the evening, when my phone rang with a blocked number.

"Shaw?" a man's voice said. I waited. "This is the guy who met you at the airport lot. Yeah?"

Yeah. I grasped the voice now. Rick Martens, the ATF Fed. Working very late, apparently.

"I remember," I said.

"Let's meet. It's good news."

Sure it was. "I'm busy."

"No bullshit. This is something you want to hear. I'm on Queen Anne at a place called Uncle C's. You know it?"

A cop bar. "Pass."

He chuckled. "Guess you do know it. Okay, then where?"

Martens's insistence annoyed me. And I had to admit, I couldn't guess what he thought was so urgent that he needed to find me after midnight.

"You know where I work," I said. He probably had my file open in front of him, including Betty's W-2 filing for employee taxes.

"Uh, yeah. Cap Hill, right?" Martens must have transferred to Seattle from another division. I'd never heard anyone call it that.

"I'll be here for another hour."

Out in the main room, a dozen night owls roosted in the booths. Two other birds of undefined gender made out at one of the center tables while their friend went on with their story, seemingly oblivious. The Fed would stand out like a terrier here, and perhaps be just as skittish.

I stuck my head out the door to wake up Mo.

"You'll see a white guy here before long, looking like he just strolled off the driving range."

"Should I hiss at his spikes?"

I grinned. "Just let him in. Even if we're past last call."

Martens made it before that. I'd taken over dishware duties for closing, letting A-Plus finish stocking the stirrers and toothpicks and parasols with hasty dexterity, before gliding away with the entourage that always materialized to greet her when she went off duty. She blew me a kiss, as Martens turned sideways to gawk at the passing bevy of magazine-gloss perfections.

"Holy shit. Who was that?" he said, taking a stool at the counter.

"The most beautiful bartender in Seattle, according to the *Weekly*. And the *Stranger*." Though the *Stranger* had tactfully called A-Plus their "Favorite," probably to avoid accusations of objectification.

"And she's—uh—here?" Martens glanced around at the bar's late-night menagerie and the ceiling beam with its line of human hair braids and ponytails, souvenirs of the old location. I set the tumblers out of the dishwasher in rows to dry overnight. The middle-aged Fed was attracting a few baffled looks himself. Maybe it was the Brooks Brothers tie. So up-tight it was almost ironic.

"When I learned you worked at a bar, I was picturing something different," he said. "MGD on tap and MMA on the screen."

"We got a regular here who's seven-and-one in her pro fights, if that's your type." I took a last pull off the bottle of Reuben's Porter I'd been nursing and tossed it into the recycling bucket with a clank.

"Sorry I said it. Can I get a cola? So damn cold outside I need some caffeine to get my blood going." As I drew one from the soda gun, Martens took off his blue jacket and folded it neatly to place it on the counter. "And get yourself whatever you want. On me."

When cops are this polite, start sniffing for the trap. Mo flicked the lights to signal last call. Quiana at the other end of the bar made a couple of dirty martinis for the lovebirds while a few customers made half-hearted moves toward the exit. Martens fetched a paper napkin from the rack A-Plus had just filled. There was no one within hearing range of us.

I finished with the dishware and poured myself a healthy shot of Redbreast. "Once this is empty, I'm gone."

"Fine, fine. Here's what it's about: Podraski and I pulled you in the other day because you were spotted in Bitter Lake." He held up a hand. "I won't rehash our debate from the other day, I promise. But can we at least agree that Podraski and I were *told* that you were seen? Whether or not it was really you?"

I waited.

"So let's build on that," Martens continued. "Let's say that if some-one was in Bitter Lake that night, breaking into a particular house, then perhaps that wasn't a random burglary. Perhaps this very skilled dude was hired to do that job."

He took a sip of his Coke while looking pointedly at my shot of whiskey. "I don't have to tell you how these things work. We aren't inter-ested in the hired hand in this scenario. We want his boss, the guy at the top. Especially if that boss has a lot of other activities rolling that pique our interest."

"You want a snitch."

The agent's mouth twisted in a rueful frown. "A snitch squeals on everything and everyone, hoping to shake himself loose from jail time. We're looking for a man on the inside. If his information is gold, he might write his own ticket. Immunity from prosecution. Perhaps a few dollars in his pocket, too. You aren't drinking."

I sipped at the shot, taking a few ticks to think about Martens's setup. He followed the progress of my glass all the way back to the counter. My radar pinged Recovering Alcoholic. No one else was so focused on another man's booze.

"What happens when there's enough information to lower the hammer?" I said.

"Then we bring that sucker down. But for our man, he's free and clear. Protection and a new life if he thinks he needs it."

"A hell of a deal," I said.

"All of this hinges on whether our man has the kind of information we need. That's where I'd need some proof."

"What sort?"

"Start with a name. If it's the right name, we're off and running."

I finished my whiskey. How far to pull this thread? I wasn't the hired gun Martens imagined me to be.

But there might be an advantage to his task force thinking I was. At least long enough to confirm once and for all whether Sean Burke was as poisonous as his rep suggested.

"Liashko." I mouthed the word, on the off chance that there was a cell phone recording our talk from Martens's jacket, placed so conveniently between us.

"There we go," Martens said.

"And as far as we go. Until I see the details in writing."

"We will make that happen." Martens pointed. He scooped his suit coat. "I gotta visit the can, meet you at the door."

I killed the chili-pepper lights and walked around to check that no one had left their belongings in the booths. Quiana let the last straggle of customers out. I bolted the emergency exit at the side for the night. Martens rejoined me at the door.

"I'll call you tomorrow. We're moving fast on this," he said, plunging out into the cold.

I watched him cross the street and hurry to his Acura, hunched against the wind.

Something was seriously warped here. I didn't fully buy Special Agent Martens's offer to make me a confidential informant, out of the blue. Even odder, I was halfway to certain that he didn't believe me when I'd told him I'd take the deal. So why in hell had he come all this way in the dead of night?

I decided to take the truck from its space near Bully Betty's and crash tonight at the marina, in my speedboat. Maybe talking to Hollis in the morning could help me make sense of this. I fetched my coat and said good night.

My long-term parking spot for the Dodge was on Union, serving denizens of new residential buildings that had been built or converted to condominiums on the west side of the hill during the past couple of years. As my truck rattled down the ramp and onto the street, I passed a metallic-green Buick sedan, which had stopped to let a long-limbed dude hop into its backseat.

I'd seen the guy before. This time he was wearing a hat pulled low and had the jacket collar popped to ward off the cold, but it wasn't enough to fully hide his thick shadow of beard stubble. He'd been outside Sean Burke's apartment building two nights before, smoking foreign cigarettes and watching the lobby.

The smoker wasn't alone this time. The Buick pulled out again, a hundred yards behind me. And closing.

THIRTY-FIVE

WHO WERE THESE BASTARDS? BURKE'S crew? Or working for Liashko him-self?

Whoever they were, I wasn't going to let them follow me home. Shaking the Buick would be tough on the nearly empty roads at two in the morning. The grid of one-way streets in downtown might be my best chance. I turned left and at the next intersection jogged one block west to Boren. Not pushing my speed. Not yet. The Buick stayed with me, green paint glittering under the streetlamps. Like a blowfly keen to find a carcass. The Beretta in my pocket made a comforting weight.

They followed me over the freeway and into downtown, drifting southward. I knew of an alley off Columbia that ran for two long blocks. If I could put some extra yards between me and the Buick, I'd veer into the alley without them spotting me and have my choice of half a dozen escape routes at the other end.

I turned down the slope of Columbia. Two intersections away, the stoplight flashed red at 2nd Ave. The Buick drifted confidently behind me, one block back. I looked for a gap in the traffic, ready to run the light and leave them hanging.

A black Taurus launched itself from the curb and past me in an instant, turning sharply to block my path. I jogged right by reflex. The truck's grill slid off the Taurus's fender with an agonized scrape.

My engine sputtered and nearly stalled. The gas pedal felt as soft as butter. I downshifted and managed to keep the old Dodge moving, down the hill, more coasting than driving. Men were out of the Taurus now. Running to catch up. The truck's engine finally gulped fuel and the Dodge lunged forward.

The green Buick roared past me, trying to cut off my escape. I turned hard left and nearly brained myself on the ceiling as the truck bounded onto the sidewalk, then swung right again before I crashed into the building. The truck flew off the curb, screaming across 2nd, the Buick roaring after me through a blare of frightened car horns.

The black Taurus caught up to me on my left side, the Buick now on the right. I couldn't outrun them in the old Dodge.

And ahead, a nightmare: Columbia Street closed to all traffic by a chain-link fence, readying for the viaduct demolition. If I stopped I was dead.

I swung the wheel right. The side of the truck banged off the green Buick, once, twice, but the heavy car barely moved.

I was out of road. All the way out.

A chained gate blocked the on-ramp to the viaduct. The Dodge crashed through, sending the gate half off its hinges and links of chain flying like fastballs. I shifted again and the truck howled in protest as it tore up the ramp. Behind me, a screech and a low crunch of impact as the Taurus slammed into a solid plastic barrier at the side of the gate.

The truck climbed, so slowly that I yelled at it out loud. Headlights in the rearview. They were coming.

The on-ramp curved left to become the lower level of the abandoned highway, the southbound lanes. Demolition had already begun. I swung the wheel to avoid a pile of concrete rubble torn from the lanes above and left in pieces on this level for salvage teams to cart away.

Another heap of debris ahead, a larger one. The truck bounced as I hit a loose chunk of old asphalt. Moonlight streamed through missing portions of the upper level, where tearing down the guardrails had also demolished huge shark bites of the pavement underneath.

At the other end of the viaduct, a mile south, there must be another gate. A way out. The headlights of the Buick were closer now, the faster car eating up the distance despite the ragged road.

I'd picked the wrong instant to check the rearview. The truck struck another chunk of highway and the wheel spun. Only stomping on the brake kept me from hitting the guardrail. I sped forward again, but the Buick was right on top of me.

Ahead, just coming into full view in my headlights, a short wall of smashed concrete and twisted rebar blocked the entire road.

No way around. No way over. The truck could never climb that crumbling, spiky mass, not even with all four wheels churning.

I could make it on foot. I swung right to put the truck between me and the Buick. As I slammed the brake, the Beretta skidded from the seat where it had jostled from my pocket during the havoc and onto the floor of the truck. I unclipped my seatbelt to reach for it.

A bullet shattered the passenger window, making me flinch from the flying shards. A second round punctured the door. I ducked and rolled away from the barrage, falling out of the truck to land next to the wall of destroyed highway.

Shouts in what might be Russian or Ukrainian followed me as I half ran, half crawled up and over the bank of rubble, loose hunks tumbling and crumbling under my feet. One chunk tipped over, threatening to crush my ankle beneath it. I sprung away and fell to my hands and knees on the other side of the wreckage.

Demolition of the highway was further along in this section. The road in front of me had become more a collection of huge mounds of cracked pavement than any kind of passable route. The night sky showed in patches ahead. I was up and running, even as I heard another pistol shot and more shouts from behind.

The mounds of concrete would offer some cover. How many men would be chasing me? Four, maybe five. Too many to fight even if I still had the Beretta. I'd have to run for it, all the way to the far end. Pray none of these thugs were competitive marathoners when they weren't busy killing people for Burke and Liashko.

No, I realized as I sprinted. Running was no good. There was no way to get off the viaduct until it ended all the way down near the stadium. Too far away, too many minutes to get there. They would send half their team with the car to head me off at the other gate. Maybe they already had.

I was boxed in, just as surely as a bull in a slaughterhouse chute.

Continuing to run would just exhaust my energy. Already my breath was tight in my chest, lactic acid building in my legs, the adrenal rush from the ambush having peaked. I needed a place to hide. Get a second wind. Attack with surprise and take a weapon from one of their crew.

There. A taller pile of rubble than most, broken sections of roadside barrier heaped on their sides against one another, forming a crude low pyramid. I looked behind me to make sure none of my pursuers were in sight before I ducked behind the pile.

I concentrated on slowing my breath. To ready myself for a fight, and so that I might hear something more than the pounding of my own heart. I peered between the leaning chunks of crumbled pavement to watch the road. Dust of decades-old cement filled my nose, as powdery as clouds from a chalkboard.

They came at a fast walk. Two of them, one on either side of the four-lane highway. Both with handguns. Scuttling like spiders from mound to mound and avoiding the brighter spots of moonlit road. Searching. Maybe they'd found the Beretta and were more confident that I was unarmed. They circled each mound separately to flank anyone on the other side. Like me.

I felt strangely calm. The part of my mind that emotionlessly calculated tactical options narrowed that list to one and ordered the rest of me to get on with it.

I reached down to pick up a heart-sized chunk of rubble. With melting slowness, I made myself as flat as I could at the base of the outer side of the pyramid, near the guardrail, one leg coiled underneath.

The two men were moving too fast to be silent. Each footfall made a distinct scrape on the pebble-strewn pavement. Twenty yards away now, checking the nearest mound of debris. Coming toward mine.

They would move together around the pyramid where I lay. I listened as each rustling step closed the distance.

A shoe landed three feet from my head. I sprung up, half blindly swinging the chunk of rubble in my fist with all my force to where his head should be. It nearly missed, striking the man high on his skull, tearing the fabric of his hood. He went sideways with a cry of pain and terror, almost leaping away in his panic. Away from me, and over the rail. He vanished.

A second cry then, shorter and ending cruelly. There was surely a sound when he hit the street thirty feet below, but it did not carry.

The other man shouted, "Stop!" behind me. Any instant now his bullets would rip through me, turning my heart and lungs into so much paste.

They didn't come. I turned. The lean dude with the midnight stubble stood twelve feet away, his face a sweated mask of hate.

"You. Down," he said, in heavily accented English.

I stayed where I was. Might as well die on my feet.

"Down."

I waited. He didn't move, either. Maybe too smart to get close.

Our little contest of wills didn't last. A single headlight appeared to the south, weaving between the piles of debris. Their team had come through the gate at the far end. The Taurus stopped, its lone beam illuminating my angry foe and me, the other headlight and a good portion of the front grill crumpled by whatever the car had struck earlier.

Three men scrambled from the car. All of them drawing guns, training them on me.

A fourth emerged from the passenger's seat. I didn't need the moonlight to recognize his dark visage immediately.

Sean Burke.

He looked at me. The killer with the permanent five o'clock shadow said something to him in Russian. Burke walked to the rail and looked down at the body of his soldier on the street below.

"Take him," Burke said. His man stepped forward to whip a leather sap I hadn't seen across my forehead.

He got his wish. I went down, all the way. The last that any of my senses registered was a scouring rasp of grit against my cheek, and the strange sweet taste of powder from ammunition.

THIRTY-SIX

I WOKE TO A SHRIEK OF metal against metal. Far enough into consciousness that I felt the brush of fabric shrouding my head. Hands grabbed me, lifted me out of a car—the clunk of the door closing, a thousand miles off—and the toe of my boot scraping dirt as they dragged me along.

But I wasn't truly alert until they threw me onto a table. Its surface frigid and so hard that the tap of my wristbone against it sent a crackle of pain up to my elbow. My bound elbow. My arms and hands were stuck tight to my sides. The stutter of duct tape coming off a roll snapped me to full attention.

And brought the first wave of panic. I bit down on the rag that filled my mouth, stifling an instinctive cry of alarm. Where had they taken me? A more frightening question followed close on that thought: Why wasn't I dead yet?

The cloth bag over my head was infused with the sickly powder I'd tasted before blacking out. Powder from pistols, recently fired. The scent had filled my nose past the point of smelling it directly, to where I felt it like a physical mass in my forehead, pressing back against the ache of where I'd been sapped.

A metal toolbox clanged down on the table by my ear. I tried moving my feet, without success. More tape at my ankles. Another pressure now, over my thighs, tightened until my quadricep muscles were crushed against bone. They were strapping me down. I sat up, lunging against the bindings. Futile. A hand gripped my throat and shoved me down so abruptly that my head bounced off the steel surface of the table. Before the impact stopped shooting sparks into my brain, they had me immobilized.

Then came a ratcheting click. My feet rose, my head lowered. I yelled into the gag, a rasping caw barely audible above the machine sound. The table stopped halfway to vertical. Halfway to upside-down, my blood pounding my head from the inside.

Someone pulled the bag off. I turned to see the tip-tilted world.

Two men in twill workpants and zip-front athletic jackets pushed at a heavy rolling door, closing it. The squeal of tortured metal returned as the door's wheels ground against their track. A visible square of night narrowed quickly to a sliver and was gone with a bang.

Someone behind me swore in English. The lean killer with the heavy stubble came around where I could see him. He glared and yanked the rag from my mouth before walking away.

The room was large, maybe twenty feet by more, depending on how far it went back behind me. Even craning my head, I couldn't make out the far end of the room in my peripheral. Wooden rafters, high overhead, and a sloped roof like a barn. A floor of poured concrete.

And a huge vat behind and to my left, pipes running from the vat into the wall. An acrid reek wafted from its direction, sharp enough to carve away the last of the powder smell.

Think, Shaw. Two exits, one beside the rolling door and one to my left. No windows. I might have seen a flash of the green Buick before they'd closed the rolling door. If I could get free . . . They had removed my jacket and pullover, leaving only my T-shirt. Was my multitool with its blade still in the pocket of my jeans? I squirmed, trying to press my hip against my arm to feel it.

The door to the outside opened and Burke walked in, another man with him. That made five. Burke was more sharply dressed than his thugs, in an ash-gray suit and black shirt.

"Stepan. Have you called it in?" he said to the man with the stubble.

"No."

"I'll do it. Don't start on him until I return. Anatoly may want to hear what this punk has to say, straight from the rat's mouth."

Stepan nodded assent. Burke motioned to two of the other men and the three of them left through the side door, to what I perceived was deeper into the interior.

When Burke was gone, Stepan exhaled minutely. Burke's reputation must have extended across both sides of the Pacific.

"Scared?" I said.

Stepan said something I assumed was another curse. "No one here is frightened of you."

"But you're not all here, are you? At least one missing."

He glared balefully at me. Maybe deciding whether to cut my throat and be done with it. Instead he walked away to a table against the wall. I had to work to focus, the upside-down angle messing with my eyes.

Stepan's partner, a gangly man with a hoop earring in his right lobe, watched him and grinned. When Stepan returned he carried what looked like a gallon paint can. He set the can down close to my head. A puff of the bitter fumes I'd smelled before seared my nostrils.

"Gennady was a good boy," Stepan said. "Very excited about visiting America. His first time."

"A hunting trip."

"You joke. This is not funny."

"So do something about it. Cut me loose, and you and your buddy can beat the shit out of me like real men. If you've got any guts, even two against one."

"Not funny yet," he clarified, waving a finger and then drawing a circle in the air to indicate the room. "Burke tells us about this place. Where he makes people go away. Even policemen."

Guerin had told me about the ATF agent who'd disappeared while working undercover on Liashko. Marcus Santora. This had been his last stop.

"Look." Stepan drew something from his chest pocket to show me. An eyedropper. His hand dipped to the can and returned, the dropper held delicately between thumb and forefinger.

The open tip of the eyedropper showed a trace of milk-white fluid. A fresh reek rose from the disturbed can.

Some kind of lye compound, I guessed. Sodium hydroxide or a similar mix. Readily available and incredibly corrosive, especially when heated.

"Very bad," Stepan said, turning the dropper to make sure I would see the caustic liquid. "And much more, there." He pointed at the huge steel pressure vat.

That would be for later. To dispose of my body, after they'd wrung me dry.

"Starting before your boss gets here. Not smart," I said, the words threatening to catch in my throat.

"For Gennady," he said. He gripped my hair and jerked my head backward. My neck strained to pull away, to thrash, but I had no leverage.

I had a perfect view of the eyedropper, three inches from my eye. The rounded edge of the first pearlescent drop expanded, grew fat.

It fell onto my cheek. For a moment nothing changed. I had an instant's relief that they had gotten the mixture wrong, or that this had been some psych game to see if I broke down immediately.

Then the heat rose, shockingly fast. Like the red tip of a cigarette touched to my skin, but far from being smothered, the fire only increased with each second. My breath hissed through my teeth. The room went watery, tears rising as my body sought any way to expel the torment.

Another drop fell, adding to the first, the trickle now running up toward my clenched eye. My neck muscles strained to move, only succeeding in shivering and making the trickle run faster.

Stepan released my head. I shook violently, trying to throw any remaining lye away before it reached my eyelid. Beads of sweat popped from my scalp.

"Hold it." Burke's voice.

I blinked the water from my eyes as Burke and Stepan had a short, angry conversation in Russian. It ended with Stepan marching away to join his friend at the worktable, heels of his boots communicating fury with every step.

"I told you to stay the fuck away," Burke said to me. From upside down, his form looked monolithic against the barn ceiling.

"Message received," I said. "Let me walk and I'm gone."

He didn't bother to answer. Instead he leaned in to study the chemical burn on my cheek.

"Stepan doesn't think ahead," Burke said. "Normally, the face is where to start if we just want one piece of information. Melt a guy's nose off, fry one of his eyes, and the fear does half the work for you. But—" He shrugged. "Terror scrambles people's brains. They can't piece thoughts together and tell you anything complicated. And your face is pretty fucked up already. I'm surprised you can even feel much through that scar tissue."

If what I'd felt had been blunted, I couldn't imagine what the full treatment would be like.

"Just put a bullet in my head," I said. "There's nothing I know that you want your buddies to hear."

Burke moved to the center of the table to begin turning a crank. The table tilted back to horizontal and continued, my head rising.

"If Stepan had any sense he'd know it's better to start slow," Burke said. "With the feet."

He said something in Russian to Stepan and the other man. Stepan walked over to the wall of the room and began to uncoil a thick green hose from a reel on the wall. The man with the earring brought a deep steel tray and set it down on the floor under my boots before jogging to help Stepan.

Burke continued his lecture. "Not just leaving the victim's feet in the mix. That's for shit. Once a few drops of this gets into your blood, that's it—dead within minutes. No, you have to hose the feet down between dunks. The water helps activate the solution. Makes it even more corrosive. Painful, yeah, but it's seeing it work that makes magic happen. Nobody alive can stay quiet while they're watching their own feet drip off the bone."

I spoke under my breath: "If I talk, they'll know why I found you."

Burke gestured: *So what?*

"Even if you really were my kid," he said, "nothing I can do about it now."

Stepan and his buddy dragged the water hose close while his partner took out a paper painter's mask and pair of latex gloves. Burke didn't move to put them on.

"His shoes," Burke said, pointing. Stepan sneered, maybe at me, maybe at Burke, and knelt to start unlacing my boots. Burke said something in Russian, and the second man dropped the hose and picked up the roll of duct tape from the floor. He stepped behind me and began to unstrip the tape, winding a length around my shins to completely bind them to the table. There would be no thrashing and tipping over the tray during what was to follow.

Stepan pulled off one boot and looked up at me.

"After the feet we do your hands," he said. "Glug glug." His friend with the earring laughed as he came around in front to wind another loop over me.

Burke shot him in the back of the head. He fell forward, onto my legs.

Stepan turned at the sharp pop of the suppressed explosion. I saw his left eye widen in shock even as Burke's second round shattered his skull. A spray of blood and pieces more solid than blood blinded me. Hot in my mouth. I spat, reflexively.

"Hold still," Burke said, stopping me from trying to wipe my face with my shoulder.

I heard the whispery clink of a gravity blade and felt tension on the tape at my wrists as Burke sliced through it. I raised my hands to scrape the gore from my brow. I could see again. Stepan's blood was already growing sticky. I felt it thick on my lids with every blink.

Burke bent over the two bodies, checking. Stepan's leg twitched, but neither man would move again on their own.

"Why?" I croaked, my throat impossibly dry.

"I only had two bullets left," Burke said.

Not the question I was asking. He didn't elaborate, just resumed cutting me loose. The instant my ankles were free I stood up, tearing at the remaining tape, not waiting for him to finish. I wanted off that fucking table.

Burke crossed the room to a panel of gauges on the wall. I knelt to grab the hose. A spray nozzle at its end controlled the flow. I pulled the trigger and stuck my head under the gushing water. Through the splashing I made out the rhythmic clangs of Burke climbing a set of metal steps to the top of the vat.

By the time I was satisfied that the last of Stepan had been sluiced off me, he'd returned and was going through the pockets of the dead men, collecting their belongings in the same bag that had hooded me.

"Another ten minutes and the mix will be hot enough," he said.

"What are we doing?" I retrieved my boot that Stepan had removed.

"What does it look like? Getting rid of these assholes." He jabbed a thumb at the vat. "It's already heated up. For you. Twenty, thirty hours in there and these boys will be goop."

I started to protest, and then my brain caught up to reality. We sure as hell weren't going to call the cops and try to explain what had happened. Stepan and his buddy were dead, thanks to Burke.

Killed with what he'd said were his last two rounds. Where had the others gone?

I went to open the interior door. A smaller room lay behind it, an office space with smeared whiteboards and one aged desk in cracked blue plastic and peeling metal. No chairs.

Another door waited, opposite the one I'd just come through. I opened it, knowing what I would find.

The third and fourth men from Stepan's team lay on the smooth concrete floor of an empty two-car garage. Wide blooms of blood stained their running jackets; the chest of one, the spine of the other. The man who was faceup had had time to draw his gun. It lay a few feet from his outstretched hand.

Burke had killed these when he'd stepped out, supposedly to call Anatoly Liashko. He'd arranged for Stepan and the last man to have their backs to him, their hands busy, before he closed the deal on them, too.

He could have taken one of the pistols from the dead men. But maybe he only trusted his own weapon when it really counted. I followed that same rule.

THIRTY-SEVEN

I RETURNED TO THE VAT ROOM. Burke was using his knife to strip Stepan of his clothing.

"What is this place?" I said.

"Private property. The tank here came from a paint factory."

"And you . . . repurposed it."

"Gus did. He wanted a place out of the city nobody knew about, for this kinda work. It took him a couple of years to build. I've kept it up."

Jesus. The question of just how many bodies had found their way into the vat, melting into a caustic slurry, came into my head before I shoved it away. No point to dwelling on it. Not when we were about to add four more to the total.

"Your jacket and blade and shit are over there." Burke nodded to the table. "Cut the clothes off Iosef. The metal zipper and rivets won't break down in the vat. We'll bag 'em."

"What did you tell Liashko? Or did you call him at all?"

He looked up, his expression almost amused.

"You know about Anatoly, huh? Thought so. Maybe there's more to you dogging me than your little story about lookin' for Daddy." Burke brought his knife up the back of Stepan's shirt, parting the fabric like water.

"Stepan said they flew in this week. To kill me?"

"Don't flatter yourself. If this was just about killin' you, Liashko would have left it to me. Come on."

I helped Burke carry the bodies of the other two men from the empty garage into the main room. We stripped them and stuffed their shredded clothes into a heavy-duty plastic trash sack. All of the Russians' personal effects—passports, phones, wallets, knives, guns—Burke tossed into the bag. He removed the American cash from the wallets first.

Four naked bloody corpses lay in as neat a row as could be expected at the base of the vat. Christ. I inhaled, not caring about the smell of fresh death that was making its first appearance.

"I actually do gotta call Anatoly," Burke said. "He's waiting. Fuck knows what I'm going to tell him."

"Say that I killed them. And you killed me."

"Some shithead burglar killed all four of his boys? All Anatoly knows about you is that you busted into my place. Stepan's no lightweight. Liashko won't buy that story. Not without a news story showing the cops fishing your body out of the harbor."

I looked at the row of dead men. The idea that bloomed in my head was less a flower than a black, poisonous mold.

"What if he saw me for himself?" I said.

"Saw how?"

"If you have to call him." I stripped off my T-shirt. "You can send pictures, too."

"The fuck are you doing?"

He watched as I tossed my boots and socks aside, my jeans and underwear following just as quickly. Getting it over with. I walked barefoot over to Stepan. Burke's bullet had come out through the killer's left-rear skull, taking enough bone and brain along with it to fill a generous ice cream cone. I'd just washed some of it off my face. Now I dipped my fingers back into the gore.

Stepan's blood was cooling but still viscous. I scooped small globs of it onto my chest. Not wiping like paint, just daubing, trying to keep the horrible red as thick as possible. I could feel gritty flecks of bone matter on my fingertips. When I'd taken what I could from Stepan, I moved to Iosef, and then the others, stealing some from each.

Burke stared. I'd learned what it took to sicken a stone killer.

The lumpy red patina extended from the hollow of my throat to my armpit. It dried rapidly against the heat of my body. I shaped the larger blobs as best I could into a rough simulation of an exit wound, as if I'd been shot in the back and the round had exploded out through my breastbone. Trickles of watery pink dripped down my ribs to my groin and thigh. I ignored them, along with the voice in my head shouting to stop. I was busy.

When I'd done what I could, I lay down next to Stepan's body. The floor was cold enough to have made my skin prickle if my hair weren't already standing on end. Stepan's arm and leg felt like a partially deflated inner tube against my own limbs. Rubbery and cool. They warmed horribly against my flesh. I turned my head to one side and forced myself to relax.

"Do I pass for a cadaver?" I said, as much to distract myself as to ask.

"More than you wanna know." Burke stepped forward with his phone held high, to capture the moment. "Hold your breath. And move your arm, it looks too—living."

I half lidded my eyes and let them go out of focus. Burke shot pictures of the full row of bodies, then two of me, closer in. The flash blazed in my peripheral vision.

"Fuck me, that's creepy," Burke said, holding out the phone. I sat up to look.

My body was a shade darker than that of the dead Russians. The difference could be chalked up to genetics. The impressionistic artwork of viscera on my chest looked as violent as any of their fatal wounds. But my face in profile really hit home, the slackness and the rusty flecks around my mouth and neck that I'd missed with the hose. It looked as though my destroyed lungs had coughed out one final bloody breath. A final touch that sold the deception.

That, and my nakedness. The horrible indignity of being stripped and lined up like so many pigs for butchering. Even though that effect had been what I'd been aiming for, that my corpse must be real because no one would subject themselves to that primal disgrace, it still made me feel something close to shame.

I stood up and went to turn on the hose and spray myself clean for a second time.

"I'm calling him," Burke said after I'd rinsed the last of the red from my body. One of the Russians' shirts was clean of blood. I used it to towel off.

"Anatoly," Burke said into the phone. "We have to talk."

During the pause that followed, I gathered my clothes and mimed for Burke to turn up the volume.

"—where we may discuss," Liashko's voice came from the phone as I leaned closer. It was a resonant voice, even made tinny by the digital transformation. Careful enunciation cut through the thicker swaths of his accent. "Where is Stepan?"

"That's why I'm calling," Burke said. "Stepan is dead. So are Gennady and the others. They walked into a trap and that housebreaker you sent them after killed them."

"No." A flat refusal rather than an exclamation of shock. "I spoke to Stepan tonight. He said preparations were ready."

"And where was he going after that?" Burke asked dryly.

Liashko didn't answer.

Burke grunted to emphasize the point. "Gennady called me when they spotted Shaw. All hyper to run him down. When I got there the shooting was already over. Shaw was wounded. I finished him off."

"The police?"

"I got them out before any cops showed," Burke said. "Or most of them: Gennady took a fall and I couldn't reach him. I'm at the barn now. You remember?"

"Yes. Your father's place."

"Here." Burke pressed buttons on his phone. Sending his boss our impromptu photo shoot. "I have to put them in the vat, Anatoly. I'm sorry."

There was another pause, longer. I imagined Liashko studying the row of naked, grisly bodies, with mine making a kind of exclamation point at the end.

"I must tell Iosef's family," he said finally.

Burke grunted assent. "At least Shaw's dead."

"And who hired this man? This thief?"

"Near as I can tell, Shaw works for himself. The cops held him awhile back on suspicion in a diamond robbery. His grandfather used to pull the same kinda jobs. High-end burglary. And Anatoly," Burke chided, "you've put my name on a lot of those wire transfers under the import business, and had me withdrawing it in cash to grease a lot of palms. Somebody at the bank could be throwing up signals. Maybe alerting a partner like Shaw to check houses where there might be cash around. I've told you that's a risky way to move your money."

Liashko made a rumbling sound. Maybe disagreeing, maybe just chewing on the thought. "The police will investigate Gennady."

"I'll get rid of the traces tonight," Burke said. He glanced at me and walked away. "It's lousy, but we have bigger concerns," I heard before he stepped out of earshot.

I went to the table to gather my things. My wallet and multitool and everything from my pockets, including the Beretta I'd lost at the truck. One of the men must have fumbled the pistol into the rubble on the viaduct; it needed a serious cleaning to remove the grit in its barrel and works.

Burke had left the bag holding the belongings of the four killers on the floor nearby. On impulse, I slipped my hand inside to find the phone with a black enameled case we had taken off Stepan.

He'd said Liashko's team had flown here for more than just killing me. The arms dealer had something brewing in the States. Even with my clothes back on, I was still cold.

After hanging up, Burke stood at the corner of the barn for a moment. Staring at nothing. I pretended to be engrossed in checking the pockets of my jacket.

Was his hand shaking? Fear, or rage?

As if he sensed my attention, Burke stuffed his phone in his pocket and marched to a standing supply cabinet. He returned with two respirators, green masks with twin charcoal filters like stubby white tusks.

"Put this on," he said.

I didn't have to ask why. If I tried, I could still smell the lye residue on my cheek.

Burke had kept the dead men's belts separate when we'd stripped the bodies. He knotted two of them together, then did the same for the second pair. One makeshift leather rope he looped around Iosef's ankles. The other went around his chest. I had to lift the body by the head to allow Burke to fix the belts in place. When he was done, we had two crude handles for the corpse.

Without a word we lifted Iosef and carried his limp form up the stairs one careful step at a time. A thick hinged lid on the roof of the huge vat was held shut by twist handles and sealed with a rubberized gasket. It looked like a windowless porthole. Burke adjusted his mask before turning the handles to open the lid. He stepped back as he did so, letting the first billow of fumes have its space.

I looked at Iosef. "Small opening."

"Gus told me once he had to cut bigger guys up 'fore he put them in the mix."

I was sorry I'd said anything.

Iosef went in feet first, Burke removing the belt strap from around his ankles. I lifted the torso. Burke arranged his hands at his sides, almost delicately, like we were about to lay Iosef to rest in a coffin. But it was simply to allow his upper body to slide smoothly along the rubber gasket.

The surface of the caustic pool was five feet below, the vat only half full of the mixture. Iosef hit with a splash that echoed briefly off the stainless-steel walls.

Disposing of the other three men went faster. We were practiced now. The only hitch was Stepan, the last, whose shoulders caught briefly on the sides of the porthole. Burke held on to the railing and raised his foot to push hard on one shoulder, then the other, and finally on the top of the stubbled, bloody head until the body broke loose.

Stepan didn't make as large a splash as he struck the liquid. *Landed on his friends*, a voice whispered. Burke closed the lid and tightened the handles.

We walked down the stairs. I pulled my respirator off. Burke followed suit. The mask had left his face creased and drenched in sweat. He wiped his forehead on his sleeve.

"Once they're all the way gone, I drain the liquid into drums and bury those a long ways from here," he said. "The vat gets scoured. Floors, too. Nothing any lab could detect."

I hadn't asked. Burke was talking just to release tension, distract himself, whatever. It was my first hint of anything like human emotion from him, apart from anger or mockery.

He grabbed the trash sack of torn clothes and the bag of the Russians' possessions. I retrieved my jacket from the table. My T-shirt, stained with blood and worse, I rolled into a tight ball to carry away and dispose of later. I wouldn't put it with the other men's clothes.

"Why am I still alive?" I said.

"Because I didn't want you dead."

"That's no answer." I looked at the vat. "You've killed plenty, just on Liashko's orders. You've killed cops. I heard about Santora, the ATF agent. Why not me?"

Burke grimaced. "You think it's 'cause I'm your daddy? I already told you that's crap."

"So what's the reason?"

"Fuck off. That's the reason." Spit flew from Burke's mouth. "You owe me, Shaw. I just put my neck out for you. You owe it to me to be dead."

He pointed. "Your truck's outside. Take it and drive until you run out of land. Nobody sees you, hears you, smells you until I say so. I'll let you know when you can play fucking Lazarus. Take it before I change my goddamn mind and burn you down to nothing with the rest of them."

His right hand had drifted behind him. Nearer the holster on his belt. It might just be a reflex.

I left before I found out.

THIRTY-EIGHT

M Y SHAMBLING STEPS BROUGHT ME to the truck before my higher brain functions reminded me that I had no idea where I was. Or exactly when. It was still nighttime. Gut Burke's barn, his personal abattoir, was the only structure in sight, surrounded by acres of what looked like fallow farmland. To both my left and right, horizons of low black hills marked the borders of a valley.

My fingers fumbled with the phone. Just past five in the morning, and the map placed me in the southern part of Snohomish County. Stepan and his men had driven over an hour from where the luckless Gennady had fallen from the viaduct.

At least they'd brought the Dodge with them. Burke probably had a convenient way of disposing of cars, too.

My truck was missing most of a window and all of the air vent on the passenger's side. A crack the width of my thumb ran through the dashboard like a sideways lightning bolt. Fragments of glass and blue plastic littered the seat and floor.

But the engine started. And the truck moved when I touched the gas. And my hands and feet kept moving, too, just as mechanically.

Wind blasted through the destroyed window on the highway. I was desperately thirsty, but if I stopped now there was no guarantee I could start again. Momentum was everything.

Both the Dodge and I made it to the marina, though if someone were to ask me what route I'd chosen, they might as well have been asking me the way to the moon that had sluggishly sunk below the horizon during the drive.

Hollis nearly ran to meet me as I tottered toward the dock gate. Had I called him and forgotten?

"Did you know your headlight—" He stopped. "What happened to your face?"

I stared, not understanding. My scars?

"No, there." He tapped his own cheek. I felt my face and wished I hadn't. The burn line made by the trickling lye flamed anew.

"Long night," I said. I reached into my pocket for my keys and found Stepan's phone instead. The sight of it lent me a sudden surge of energy.

Stepan and his men had come to America. To handle important business for Anatoly Liashko. Lieutenant Guerin had told me Liashko was an arms trafficker. What had that business been? Or—I corrected myself—what was it still? Burke would surely pick up where Stepan had left off. Did the task force tracking Burke know about this yet?

"You look . . . like a coffee would help," Hollis said.

"Water. Thanks. Meet you there."

But he stayed put, watching me as I returned to the truck.

Good. Stepan's crew hadn't searched the Dodge. Aura Nath's tablet, her hacker's special, was still hidden under the backseat. I kept a USB and other charging cables in the center console. I grabbed them all and walked back, cords dangling from my fist like slain snakes.

Inside the *Francesca*, Hollis cleared a pile of clothes and random junk off the settee—a beach towel covered the cushion dappled with the Finnish sailor Jaak's blood—to allow me to sit down. I was already preoccupied with plugging Stepan's phone into the tablet.

The application within responded immediately, filling and refilling the tablet's screen with rows of information—contacts, search history, times of use. I had to hand it to Aura. Her tool even translated the Cyrillic letters on the phone's screen into English for my convenience.

Within two minutes, the tablet pinged to mark completion of its task. I looked first for emails or texts. The earliest dated from only a week ago. Stepan had kept his use of the phone to a minimum. Maybe a by-product of his boss, Liashko's, penchant for security.

"Paula was very pleased to know that Ondine won't require her services any longer," Hollis said, handing me a glass of water and putting a pitcher on the table.

I mumbled some vague agreement in response, all my concentration on the phone's single text message from an international number, consisting of fifteen characters: **BTZU 742669 0 22G1**.

The pattern of characters was familiar, though I couldn't place it right away. An account number? The text had been sent to Stepan yesterday morning, only hours before he and his crew had come after me. I wrote down the letters and numbers on a notepad.

Stepan hadn't used the phone's map feature to find his way around Seattle. I scrolled farther down the pages of data. The SIM card had dutifully recorded each cellular tower that the phone had pinged while active, and every corresponding update of the location services. It made for reams of information, much of which was numeric coordinates and cell tower authentication keys.

Most of the coordinates were the same. Stepan had remained stationary for at least half the day, and then he was on the move just after 3:00 P.M. local time. He'd stopped again one hour later, where he'd stayed until well after dark. I plugged those coordinates into my own phone. They matched the far south of the city, close by the Duwamish Waterway.

"What's the shipment?" Hollis said.

Off my puzzled glance he pointed to the fifteen characters I'd written on the notepad. "That's an ID for a freight container. A twenty-footer, general use model. See, you can tell from these numbers here."

I looked at him. "You're a genius. Can you tell where it is?"

"At least who owns it. BTZ, that'll be the company. The U just means standard freight. Hold on." He found his own phone. I finished the water in two gulps and refilled the glass while Hollis typed.

"Blacksea Tradepartners, a German firm," he said. "But I suspect what you really want to know is who's leased it. That's nearly impossible without having the company's own records."

"Maybe we can narrow it down." I sat down to show Hollis the coordinates by the waterway. "A ship near here."

He screwed up his face in mock pain. "It'll have to be a smaller freighter, if it's on the river. Or we could be looking for a train. Thousands of containers go through there every day."

Damn it. Of course that was true, in the heart of the city's international shipping. One twenty-foot steel box in a virtual sea of them.

"Can you tell me anything more?" Hollis pressed. "What's the cargo, or where it's from?"

"The owner is Ukrainian. The cargo is almost certainly weapons. I assume something packing more punch than small arms, if he bothered to send them all the way to the decadent West to sell them."

Hollis sat down. "You come across the most interesting people."

And sometimes I murdered them. A wave of fatigue threatened to knock me sideways.

"Are you all right, Van? Your hand?"

I looked. The glass Hollis had given me rested on my knee. Despite that, the surface of the water within bobbed and rippled as my forearm trembled in near synchronization.

"Grab a bunk down below," he said. "I'll see what my friends down the docks can tell me."

"I'll crash in the speedboat."

"You sure?"

I was. For one reason, the sun would be up soon. The enclosed interior of the small craft effectively blocked nearly all light from outside, making it ideal for rest at any hour.

For another, the sight of my shaking hand had brought back the memory of Stepan's arm, in the vat, being inexorably swallowed by the corrosive solution as the bodies beneath his own shifted and settled deeper.

It was entirely possible that I might start screaming, any second now.

"Call me if you learn anything," I said, carefully.

Hollis frowned. "Not too soon. You need downtime."

All the way off the *Francesca* and down the dock, I kept my jaw shut tight, in case any sound tried to escape.

THIRTY-NINE

M Y PHONE WAS RINGING, AND I fumbled to grab it from the radio shelf.

"Hollis?" I said automatically.

"No, it's Wren. Were you asleep?"

I blinked at my watch. In the pitch black of the speedboat cabin, its hands refused to resolve into anything more than a slim luminous triangle. "What time is it?"

"About six-thirty. I texted earlier."

I pulled my phone away from my ear to look. Two unread messages. I'd slept for nearly twelve hours.

"Shit," I said.

Wren laughed. "Well, I get now why you didn't message me back. You sound really out of it."

"Feels that way." I rubbed my face, trying to massage some sharpness back into my senses, and hissed at the sudden pain. The burn on my cheek had scabbed over during my hours of oblivion. The first rub cracked the scab wide open.

Then my brain finally kicked in to remind me why Wren was calling. "It's Sunday. We were supposed to get together."

"But that's not happening. Hey, another time."

"Wait," I said.

"You're not going to try to talk me into still hanging tonight."

"No. Just . . ." What was I doing? "Just hold on with me for a minute. At least until I can apologize like somebody normal."

She didn't say anything. During the pause I opened the cabin doors and slid back the hatch. Any warmth that had accumulated in the cabin from my body heat fled in a rush, replaced instantly by frigid evening air accentuated by the lightest possible drizzle, barely more than a fog. Welcome goose bumps popped to life on every inch of me.

"Okay," she said at last. "I'll ride along. Are you all right?"

"Getting there. I wasn't thinking I would sleep so long, and—" I paused for a second, even though I'd already made the decision to come clean. "And I spaced our date. Last night wasn't good."

"You want to tell me about it?"

I had my face raised to the sky. Could practically feel my parched skin soaking in the water.

"We don't know each other, not yet," I said. "I'd like to get there. Loading you down with a lot of my baggage might not be the way to start."

There was another pause. "I can stop just by hanging up. Hard to get safer than that."

"You know about me tracing my mother, Moira. I found a guy, here in Seattle, who might be my father."

"Oh. That's loaded."

"Yeah. He denies it, barely admits he ever knew Moira, but . . . it feels right. Which is the shitty part of the whole situation."

"How?"

"He's not one of the good guys. I don't know what to call him; he might be a full-on psychopath. Last night was violent. He wasn't coming after me but I saw up close what he was capable of. Sorry. I don't know why I'm telling you this."

"Because you need to tell somebody, and I'm almost a stranger. It's easier," she said, like the answer was obvious. "So now you know. What he is. And you never have to get near him again."

I didn't say anything.

"What?" Wren asked.

"I know him, yeah. I know part of him real well. The killing. Hard to keep him completely out of my life when that instinct is also a part of me."

"Do you mean what you did in the Army?"

I was sharing a lot with Wren. More than I'd thought I could. But there had to be a line.

"Right," I said, and I hated myself a little for it.

"Is . . . Is there somebody you talk to about that? Your time overseas? I know just enough to know when I'm over my head."

"There's a shrink I saw for a while. And I've talked with brothers from the regiment. But this—" I wasn't finding the right words. Maybe there weren't any, if I couldn't go all the way. "This is just new to me."

"You noticed what you and this man had in common. You must have differences, too."

"Yes. Hey, I learned something about Moira. She was taking college classes. In social work, maybe toward a job with kids in juvie or foster care."

"That's great." She sounded enthused. Or relieved that our conversation was on a more positive beat. "Did you know she had an interest in that?"

"I didn't know anything about her as an adult." And this might be all I'd ever learn. "It seems to fit. She was stubborn enough for the job."

"A trait she clearly passed on." I could hear Wren's smile.

"Thanks for not hanging up. If I can push my luck, can we try again?"

"I'm free Tuesday."

"I'll set an alarm this time."

"Damn right."

I kept the speedboat stocked with spare clothes and other essentials. Including ammunition of various calibers and a Colt Commander automatic I'd taken off a guy less trained and less restrained in proper handgun usage than me.

Liashko thought I was dead. That didn't mean I was safe. I clipped the holster to the back of my waistband and wore a heavy flannel shirt like a coat to conceal the weapon.

I was starved. The diner on Seaview might still be open, or I could hit Oaxaca in Ballard. My appetite could conquer an entire platter of pork with mole sauce, and beer.

But the cabin lights of the *Francesca* beckoned first. I wolfed a protein bar to keep my stomach from eating my liver and jogged over.

"Any word on the ship?" I said to Hollis from the dock.

"Ukrainian, you told me. I've checked with two different fellows who might know. They say the same: there are no Ukrainian vessels currently at port anywhere in Seattle."

"Dammit."

"Hold on, now. I'm warming up. There's a Moldovan freighter traveling under a Belize flag of convenience moored on the same stretch of shore you indicated. The *Oxana M.*"

"Moldova is next to the Ukraine."

"That much I knew. The name of the home port is beyond my ken. Gweer-goo-lesti?"

"Giurgiuleşti."

"Impressive. I expect the Army briefed you lads on all manner of fun places you might see. The ship sailed from Jeer-whatever the long way, out through the Black Sea and the Mediterranean, across the Atlantic, through the Canal, and back up again. Taking short-hop jobs as they went, as most of these small cargo freighters do."

"Any chance you can get your hands on the *Oxana M*'s cargo manifest?"

"A good chance, but that will be a long list. She's not a big ship, as they go. A hundred meters or so in length, no more than thirty thousand deadweight tonnes in her belly."

"All right, I get your point." It would take me half a week to search the *Oxana M*'s holds, even if I could do it in broad daylight. "Let's look at the manifest. Maybe lightning will strike."

As if in answer, my phone buzzed on Hollis's table. An incoming video call from a blocked number. An instant later, Aura Nath's face appeared on the screen.

We both stared at it. How the hell—?

I stopped my own thought; the answer was obvious: Aura and Bilal had an unsettling amount of tech wizardry. Of course they might be able to jack my phone's controls.

"Are you there?" she said, looking into the lens. From our side, all she might see was the ceiling of the *Francesca*'s cabin.

"What is it?" I said, picking up the phone.

"Thank God." Aura spoke softly. "I don't have much time. Saleem is missing. I think he might be coming after you."

Hollis and I exchanged a look.

"Why would your man do that," I said, "unless Bilal ordered him to?"

"No. Just the opposite." Aura's words came rushing one upon another. "Bilal and Saleem argued on our flight back to Miami. We told Saleem that we had what we needed now. Our time in Seattle is done. But Saleem insisted that you were an unacceptable risk, that you knew too much about us. He wanted to return. Bilal refused. Saleem became furious. I've never seen him like this. He's never challenged Bilal this way."

I remembered Saleem's maddened eyes when I dropped his hog-tied body onto the deck outside Ceres.

"And he left?" Hollis asked.

"Sometime during the night. He took Juwad's gun and some clothes."

Neither Hollis nor I said anything. I was wondering whether this could be some ploy. But even if Bilal and Aura had decided to renege on our deal, and risk their secrets coming to light, why warn me that their vicious servant was on his way to kill me?

Aura spoke again, maybe thinking we were still unconvinced. "Saleem left his phone behind. He probably expects we might track him that way."

"If he took the gun," I said, half to myself, "he must not be planning to fly. Does Saleem have a car?"

"Not one of his own. I suppose he could steal one."

A foreign visitor driving a stolen car across the continental U.S. I suspected Saleem was smarter than to try that.

"Does he know anyone in the States? Someone who could provide him with transport?"

Aura considered it. "He has relatives in New Jersey. Middlesex, I think."

Too far to drive down and pick up Saleem in Florida. But it was a place to start.

"Check them," I said. "Their accounts, their phones, whatever you can hack into. Do it fast. And anyone else Saleem might rely on."

She hesitated. "Bilal doesn't know I'm telling you this. He would— are you still there?"

My image had disappeared because I'd switched to a different app, to send something to Aura. I heard her phone beep as it arrived.

"What's this?" she asked.

"Who," I corrected. "Cyndra. She's one of the people Bilal threatened the first night I met you."

Aura was quiet. I switched back to the phone app and saw her staring, absorbed in the short clip Cyn had taken of herself, lifting weights and waving at the camera with that half-abashed, half-cocky grin on her face.

I leaned closer to the camera. "Saleem knows where this girl lives. She's what's at stake."

"I understand," Aura said.

"Find a way to find Saleem or everyone loses."

"Yes," she said again. "I'll make it happen."

She ended the call.

"We're a long way from Miami," Hollis said. "You sure Saleem is coming?"

I nodded. His eyes had told me. Too many humiliations for the volatile gunman. First his boss marrying Aura and having to take orders from her. Then Bilal choosing me to break into the biotech firm instead of trusting the job to his right-hand man. And the cherry on top: my knocking him cold and tying him like a rodeo calf in the cryobank. I could imagine all of those events fueling Saleem's resentful fire.

What did he know about me, besides where Addy's house was? He'd seen the *Francesca*, though without access to Aura's magic tablet he likely didn't know where it was moored. He may have seen the address of Bully Betty's where I worked. But Addy was the likeliest tack. Even if Saleem didn't find me there, he could still make good use of a hostage or two.

"That was a nice trick," Hollis said, tapping my phone and the video playing on repeat. The clip of Cyn deadlifting the barbell, setting it down, saluting ironically, over and over. "Showing her the girl. The soft touch, instead of pressuring her."

"It wasn't a trick," I said.

Aura understood my desperation to protect Cyn. She'd lived with that feeling for weeks while her unborn children had been used as collateral. First by her ex-husband and then by me. Now that our fortunes had reversed, an appeal to her empathy was my best shot at stopping Saleem.

And in case that went sideways, I had to get Addy and Cyn out of the line of fire. For the second time in a week.

Shit, Addy was going to eviscerate me.

FORTY

THE MORE I THOUGHT ABOUT the *Oxana M* on the drive to Addy's, the more I liked it. If Liashko had smuggled arms out of the conflict in the Ukraine, and if he was truly desperate to make this deal happen, he'd have played it very safe. Air travel was a nonstarter. Anything flying out of that war zone might have been searched down to the fuselage. He wouldn't have sent the arms by land across all of Asia to the Pacific. Too many hostile checkpoints, too many rolls of the dice.

Moldova was a friendly neighbor, and just a rock-skip away from the peninsula. Find a suitable freighter with a bribable captain—I couldn't imagine that had been tough—conceal the arms in a deep hold stacked under tons of identical shipping containers, and have patience while the *Oxana M* made its long journey halfway around the world to the western U.S.

Burke had ordered me to keep my head down. Implying whatever deal he had planned with Liashko was happening soon. And I already knew that Special Agent Martens's task force was aiming to catch Liashko on American ground.

If I could find the container that held the arms, I could pass that information along to Martens. The ATF could follow the weapons off the freighter and have a SWAT team ready to spring when Liashko arrived.

Closing the net on him, and on Sean Burke, too. I might have met my father just in time to see him imprisoned forever.

It was true that Burke had saved my life. But my life had limited value, even to me. I couldn't stick my head in the sand if a little recon work might mean ensuring Liashko's weapons never left the *Oxana M.*

ADDY SAT AT HER DINING-ROOM table, writing a note by hand. Probably a thank-you to Dorothy. From Cyndra's room I heard the competing discord of music and Cyndra talking to a friend who might have different music playing on her side.

The roller bag from their stay was still out, waiting on its wheels by the hall closet. I took it into the living room and unzipped it to lay it open.

"Are you packing?" Addy said.

"For you and Cyn. We have to relocate you for a while."

She slowly capped the pen and placed it in perfect alignment with the stationery. Her deliberate movement as palpable as a shout. "Absurd."

"I know it's bad news—"

"I mean you. What on earth is the matter with you?" She kept her voice low, so as not to alert Cyndra. Regardless, Stanley caught the shift in her tone and grumbled confusedly as he paced between the back door and the living room. "It wasn't a day ago that you told us it was safe to come back here. Now you're coming in like a rhinoceros, trying to charge right through any objections."

"We can argue later. Let's get you to a hotel. I'll explain on the way."

"No. If the situation is that dire, then we'll go to the police. I refuse to live on the run. Or to subject Cyndra to that. She starts school in the morning, for Lord's sake."

"Addy."

"I'm not having it, Van. I don't know what's happened lately, but you look twisted into knots. Certainly you're not in your right mind."

"I'm scared," I said.

"Well if you're frightened, how do you think I feel? Tell me what's going on."

I sat down on the floor next to Stanley. Laying my hand on the dog's panting ribs may not have given him much comfort, but it did some for me. As briefly as I could, I told Addy about Bilal Nath, and Aura and her eggs, and about the danger of Saleem returning.

"I don't know if Saleem will use you to get to me," I said, "but we have to plan for anything he might do."

"Anything and everything," Addy mused. "Small wonder you're twitchy. You can't protect everyone all the time."

"I don't care about everyone," I said.

"Yes, you do. Despite your many faults, you do give a damn, Van." She sighed. "Cyndra and I are going to go about our lives. I can tell the police we've had menacing telephone calls or somesuch, so they'll keep an eye on the house. We'll be careful."

A cop car cruising past every couple of hours wasn't going to make me breathe easier. "What if Hollis or Willard and I stay close the next couple of days? I can take Cyn to school and pick her up."

"Willard? He's your very large friend? I imagine any trouble would give him a wide berth."

"They're both smart. They'll know what to watch for."

"All right. I won't let my own obstinacy make things worse. But only for a day or two."

"I hope that's all I'll need."

"Where have I heard that before? And once Cyndra's home from school tomorrow, we'll both sit down with her and explain the situation. She's old enough, and it's unfair to keep her in the dark about her own life."

Old enough, and tough enough. Cyndra had come through harder times.

"Deal," I said. "I'll take the night watch and see if Hollis can relieve me tomorrow."

"Now I think we'll be sufficiently safe for twenty minutes while you make yourself useful and run Stanley around the block. Tire him out some so we can all sleep. Three days at Dorothy's and the poor boy is ready to dig a hole through the floor."

I sympathized. Every minute I would be guarding the house was a minute I wasn't solving the root cause of the problem. But it was what had to be done. What was I fighting so hard for, if not this cobbled-together duct-tape-and-baling-wire family we'd made?

FORTY-ONE

HARBOR ISLAND FORMED THE HEART of the city's commercial shipping, and the Duwamish River was its primary artery, winding from the terminals off West Seattle to taper and scrawl crazily into smaller waterways south of the city. Industries reliant on merchant vessels crowded its shores: landscaping materials, food products, biodiesel plants. And dozens more boatyards and maintenance docks to service the tugs, barges, and tankers that sailed at every hour of every day.

Hollis's notes on the *Oxana M* told me the freighter was moored south of the Georgetown reach, across the river in the industrial part of South Park. I drove half a mile farther to a stunted avenue ending in a high razor-wired fence. The closest any car could come to the water on a public street.

No company sign hung from the spiked gate. If you didn't know what the place was, you weren't supposed to be there. Past a collection of corrugated buildings, rust eating each of them from the ground up, I could see lifting cranes on cargo ships and multicolored stacks of twenty- and forty-foot steel containers, like a giant toddler's toy blocks left to fade in the sun.

Hollis had tracked down the *Oxana M*'s manifest, duly filed with U.S. Customs and Border Protection and a copy to the Port of Seattle. The freighter had arrived three days ago, offloading more than two hundred containers of industrial machinery and steel from Eastern Europe, textiles from North Africa, wooden furniture from Central America, and a thousand other goods. All from small companies, bartering on the cheap for a sliver of space in the *Oxana M*'s holds and accepting that it would arrive when it arrived, with no expectation of speed.

A check of the local map showed a small park just south of the shipping yard. I left the Barracuda and backtracked to find it. The half acre of community land had more dead grass than living, but it let me walk right up to the water. Looking north, I had a sidelong view of the shipyard.

Three freighters had been moored in a tight row along the yard's long concrete dock. The biggest was the *Oxana M*. Over three hundred feet long, the white block letters of her name at the bow stark against the black paint of her hull. Two loading cranes extending from her deck nearly touched at their highest points, like a praying mantis's forelegs. A white three-story-high superstructure enclosed the bridge and crew's quarters at her stern.

She floated high on the water, showing nearly as much red underbelly as black hull. Not completely empty of her burden. The container I wanted might still be aboard. If it was, it might be easier to find with the freighter's legit cargo already offloaded and out of the way.

Might, might, might. One assumption piled on all the others. I had nothing but a shipping container ID from a dead thug's texts. No proof that the *Oxana M* was the ship that had carried it, or that the container was still aboard, or even that Liashko was smuggling arms at all. I was chasing phantoms.

If I handed what little I knew over to Special Agent Martens, would it be enough to make the Feds hold to their deal and let Burke into WITSEC? Could I adequately explain where I'd gotten the shipping container code? Or would that be tainted evidence?

I hadn't signed any papers officially making me a C.I. for the task force. And no way could I tell Martens about the four men his good buddy Burke had murdered in saving my life, much less my own slaying of Gennady.

And if they believed me about the ship? And all of my guesswork turned out to be right? It was too easy to imagine U.S. Attorney Stratton weighing his options, opting for the safer bet, securing the smuggled weapons, and declaring victory. With a little spin the bust would undoubtedly lend him a rocket in the polls—"CANDIDATE FOILS TERROR PLOT" would be a dream headline for any politician—even without arresting Liashko.

An inner voice told me that would be best. Securing smuggled arms was a no-bullshit matter of national security. The life of one hitman couldn't compare. No matter what he might be to me.

I stayed in the small park and watched the freighter for the rest of the afternoon. Nothing was lifted on or off. Beyond the occasional ant-like speck of a sailor walking her deck, she might have been a ghost ship.

When the evening grew too dim to see more than the wan yellow deck lamps and the white arms of the cranes, I gave up. The only way to determine if the *Oxana M* carried anything of interest would be to take a much closer look. Which would require some thinking. I couldn't bluff my way aboard.

At a pub on Cloverdale I ordered a Cubano sandwich and a pint of brown ale while mulling over the problem. Before the food arrived, my phone chimed with a video chat request: Aura Nath. At least this time she waited before popping onto the screen, unasked. I mimed to the guy working the counter that I'd be right back and stepped outside to answer the call.

"I've got something," Aura said. Less hushed than her previous call; her husband must not be near. "Saleem's brother in New Jersey FedExed an overnight envelope not long after we arrived in Florida. His emails had the tracking number, so I was able to place it. The envelope went to a shipping outlet in a strip mall less than a mile from our hotel here."

"That must be it," I said. "Money, maybe, or identification."

"I'm ahead of you," Aura said. "The brother's credit card bought an Amtrak ticket here in Miami early yesterday morning. One adult in a Viewliner bedroom, going all the way to King Street Station in Seattle. Saleem must have boarded almost immediately."

Meaning Saleem had timed his departure to make a fast exit. Maybe he and his brother resembled each other enough that he could pass using the same ID and charge cards. Traveling by train fit my theory that Saleem wanted to hang on to the gun he'd lifted from his buddy Juwad. "Where's the train now?"

Aura paused while she looked over her notes. "Outside Washington, D.C. It'll go through Chicago and Salt Lake on its way to Seattle. Arriving Wednesday morning at 10:25."

Good. Two nights and a day for me to devise a suitable welcome. For once Bilal's people had me on a timeline that worked to my advantage.

And Saleem would know that.

"He must suspect Bilal might warn me he's coming," I said, "if they argued, and Saleem cut ties."

"That wouldn't be like Bilal to hand him over," Aura said, with a glance over her shoulder. "He prizes loyalty. He's mad at Saleem for going against his orders, yeah, but he gets Saleem's pride. They have that in common."

I thought about that. "Does your team have a secure way of communicating? If you're staying off phones?"

"Of course," Aura said, like the question was Hacker 101. "We use portable networks sometimes to share information and stay off the Internet. Or remotely, we can use private drop sites."

Like dead drops in espionage. One party leaves information for another to retrieve without direct contact. "Would Saleem be checking those?"

Her face hardened. "You're asking me to pretend to be Bilal."

"I'm asking you to help me. To prevent Saleem from doing something we'll all regret."

"But you already know where he'll be: King Street Station, Wednesday morning."

"And I could miss catching him there. If that happens, I want a contingency plan." I sent Aura coordinates of a location in Snohomish County. "Put this out on your drops for Saleem to find. Make him think it's from Bilal."

"He's my husband. It's like betraying him myself."

"We've both got a gut check here, Aura. Because I don't know how far I'll have to go to keep all of us safe. Your family and mine. If you want me to believe Saleem's acting alone, then help me stop him." That was as close as I would get to premeditation on an open line.

She was quiet for a long count. "I won't know if Saleem sees it."

"It's enough."

After another moment, she nodded. "All right. I'll do it. And I'll keep checking his brother's credit card and other accounts."

"Thank you. We'll get through this."

She nodded once more and hung up.

A few days before, Aura and Bilal Nath had been my worst enemies. Now events compelled us to cooperate. Those circumstances might include my holding their future over a barrel, and them trying to keep their unhinged bodyguard from blowing me away. Still, a reluctant ally was better than none.

I'd implied to Aura that I was wrestling with whether to kill Saleem outright. That had been a half truth. I'd already decided on a plan of action.

Tomorrow I would tip Lieutenant Guerin to the arrival of an armed individual traveling with false identification on the incoming Amtrak Wednesday morning. That should be enough to get Saleem arrested and likely deported after a long tour of various holding cells. Not a permanent solution, but enough to get the gunman out of the way while my attention was on Sean Burke and Liashko.

And if Saleem somehow slipped past Guerin at the station? The location I'd given Aura was Burke's barn in rural Snohomish. Isolated. And designed to make people vanish for good.

The idea of returning to that slaughterhouse, opening that vat once more to see what might remain within, made sweat rise on my scalp despite the outdoor chill.

But I could do it. For Cyndra and Addy, no question.

DRIVING UPTOWN, I WAS ABOUT to enter the underground tunnel when my phone rang again. Not Aura this time; the calling number had a 721 prefix. The burner that I'd tossed to Sean Burke.

Speak of the devil, and he shall telephone.

"You around?" he said.

"Depends what you mean."

"Get here. My apartment. You remember where."

And he hung up. Less than ten words, most of them sounding pulled from his throat. Was he drunk? Being forced to talk? Or was there something else going on?

I wouldn't waste any minutes getting there to find out. I did allow one extra second, however, to make sure the Colt had a round chambered.

FORTY-TWO

I RAN THE LIGHTS DOWN DEXTER Avenue and into Belltown until I reached the burnished spike of Sean Burke's building. I pressed 3-1-0-5 on the intercom and he—or someone—buzzed me in without a word.

I took the elevator off the residential lobby to the twenty-ninth floor, got off, and checked the stairwell. It was clear. Two flights up, the hallway outside Burke's door was equally quiet.

Without leaving the stairwell, I tapped the button to reply to my last call. Burke answered on the third ring.

"I'm outside," I said.

Ten full seconds later, the apartment door opened. Burke walked out into the hallway. He held a rocks glass full of ice and a dark brown liquid. It took him a second to find me and another tick to focus his eyes.

"Huh," he said. "Cautious cat, ain't you?"

He returned to his apartment. I followed. The double-paned French doors to the balcony were wide open and the wind at thirty stories brushed my hair back before I took my first step over the threshold.

It was my first look at the place with the lights on. Five grand a month in rent, easy, half of that paying for the view. The furnishings were slightly lower market, and so much of a piece I suspected Burke had bought them based on a catalog display. Sturdy and masculine and showing minimal signs of wear. I guessed Burke wasn't home a lot.

He plopped down in a leather club chair arranged where he could look out through the railing at the city beyond. Divots of perfect circles in the Persian rug marked where the chair normally stood. I shut the door and bolted it.

"You want coffee?" he said, brandishing his glass. "Something with teeth? Bar's over there."

It *was* coffee swirling around the ice cubes. A sharp aroma of burned beans persisted even through the breeze ruffling the curtains.

"You called me," I said, wondering if he might have forgotten.

"I did. Siddown."

There were no chairs near his. I crossed the expanse of living room to the dining area, taking an extra few steps to glance into the bedroom. No one there, unless they were hiding in the walk-in. I dragged a straight-backed chair from its place at the table and placed it where I could see the hall and the front door. The view could take care of itself. Cautious cat.

Burke sipped his coffee, licking stray drops from his lips. "You asked me why I didn't let Stepan kill you."

I nodded.

"If you found me, an' you know about Anatoly Liashko, that means you got some buddy-bud in the cops letting you peek at their files. Right?"

I didn't say anything.

"So I guess you must know all about Gus, too. My dad. Right?" The second *right* was spat out, like I'd insulted the man's memory.

"Gut Burke. Used to be a Westie in New York."

"That's Pops. Gus wanted me to have an education, which for him meant he spent stupid money for me to go to private school. Me with a buncha rich brats never walked more than a quarter mile at one time. I hated it. But I finished, 'cause that's what Gus wanted."

Some kind of painkiller in Burke's veins. Or maybe a muscle relaxant. No indicators of long-term addiction, no weight loss or tipsy balance. The action at the barn had proven Burke's reflexes were just fine.

Whatever he was popping tonight, it had relaxed his tongue well enough.

"After school I went back to what I'd been doing with Gus. Stealing, mostly. He'd started taking jobs for Russian multimillionaire fucks, looking to get their hands on American products that hadn't been cleared for export. After a few years he got in with Anatoly, and that was real money."

"Doing what?"

"Whatever needed doing. Gus kept me out of the hard stuff back then." Burke pointed in the general direction. "I think he still had ideas of me going legit someday. But I knew what he did. And he knew I didn't mind."

"Back then."

"Things change. Gus got older. Slower. Whether he changed his mind about bringing me in or jus' realized he needed my help, I don't know. Pretty soon I learned about everything, even the barn."

We both listened as a high, sustained whisper came into the room. The sound of a siren, some four hundred feet below us on the street, its wail stretched to the breaking point by the night wind.

"And you were still okay with all of it," I said. Making a connection between us I would have ignored if I could. "Sleeping soundly."

"Is that a crack?"

"No. It's a resemblance."

Burke shrugged. He didn't catch my meaning, but he didn't give a shit, either. "Anatoly had swerved from smuggling into selling weapons by then. Our job on this side of the water was about making deals run smooth. Cash drop-offs. Leaning on bent lawyers and money men who wouldn't take a hint. Sometimes there was work in Russia besides."

"So you got a passport."

"You know that, too, huh? Anatoly found Natalia for me, bribed somebody in the right directorate over there to approve my residency and attest to my living in Russia for years." Burke snapped his fingers, like describing a magician's illusion. "I bought a house with backdated estate papers. Only met the girl once, at the wedding. Never even fucked her. Done and done. But I'm getting ahead. All that came after."

He blinked, slowly. "Gus fouled up a job. A big one. Anatoly let it go. We thought."

Burke downed the last of the coffee and reached into his rocks glass to pluck an ice cube from the stack. He didn't put it in his mouth, just held it between thumb and forefinger, letting the melted drops fall to the rug. I waited.

"A year later Gus gets hit by a car in a casino parking lot. Crushed the whole side of him. Cops never found the guy. Never found the car. Don't know how hard they looked. Stupid Sean, I go on a tear trying to find Gus's killer by checking local body shops for repairs, before I wised up."

I was tracking Burke's tone, the pattern of his strange mood, as much as his words. "You stayed dumb. To stay close."

He grunted and tossed the ice cube out the window to a long, long fall.

"Sticking a blade right through Anatoly's neck was my first idea. *Whap.* Just enough time before he kicked so he'd realize why I'd done it. But getting next to him would be impossible in Russia. And Liashko comes to America about as often as I visit fuckin' Africa. He's a paranoid. Going to jail over there doesn't scare him. If they send his ass to a corrective camp, he's wired enough to buy himself a comfortable reeducation. But here? All the race shit and the other gangs? He'd be meat. He knows it. Our prisons freak Anatoly out."

"You've been waiting for a chance at him this long?" I said. According to the FBI file, Gut Burke had died almost a dozen years ago.

"I found other work." Burke couldn't help but glance at his fine apartment.

"Must pay well."

"Somebody owed. They signed their paid lease over to me instead."

Instead of the alternative. *Whap.*

"But I kept on bugging Anatoly," he said. "Telling him there was plenty of money to be made in the U.S. of A., the way the country's going to shit. And his cash flow's been squeezed ever since Putin started jailing his old sponsors on corruption charges. Now he's fucking frantic. It's beautiful."

"Stepan's crew was here to set up a deal," I said. "Is Liashko coming stateside?"

Burke sneered his affirmation, mouth a little slack from the pills. "I know that son of a whore. His mistrust cuts both ways. Any big transaction, Anatoly has to know every fucking thing."

He stopped, maybe noting how intently I was following his story.

"You an' me, we got—what do you call it? Commonalities. We can both keep it together when shit goes down."

"Yeah," I said.

"Plus I think I've got you scoped, Shaw. I tell you to take a long vacation away from Seattle, there's no better way to make sure you'll stay around. Keep stirring up trouble. And I'll keep trippin' over you." Burke laughed harshly. "So fuck it. You've already got me by the balls 'cause I let you live. If telling you to screw off doesn't work, maybe the truth will."

"Maybe."

"After too many years I finally figured out I'd never get my shot, a chance to take out Anatoly the way Gus might have. Dropping him into the vat still alive with his hands and feet tied. No gag, though. I'd wanna hear him."

He said it with the same flat tone he might have used when ordering the furniture from the catalog. Talk to Burke long enough, and you started to notice the shallow pools in his emotions.

He settled back into his leather chair. "I'd have to get Liashko another way. I needed help. So I called a friend of mine. A guy I've known since we were just kids. His life turned out different than mine. Better. I figured if there was anybody in this world I could trust, it would be him."

Holy shit. I gave the moment the space it needed, the space I needed to wrap my head around it.

"Burke," I said. It was the first time I'd called him by name. "Are you telling me you're working with the cops?"

He crushed the last ice cube between his teeth.

"Funny, isn't it? Gut Burke's kid, a fuckin' rat. Nobody knows about it except me and a coupla Feds. For my own safety. And now you."

"That's how you found me at the garage by the museum," I said. My face was probably stupid with astonishment, but right then I didn't give a damn. "The Feds have traces on my accounts. And your buddy is keeping you in the loop on my movements. In case—what, I might be hunting you?"

"You coulda been from one of Anatoly's competitors. Or who knew, maybe from the man himself. I wouldn't put it past that fucker to hire somebody to snoop into my business."

"I thought the task force was trying to nail you. For the dead ATF agent."

"Santora? Hell." Burke chuckled. "Marcus Santora's alive and kicking, somewhere. My guy put him undercover for months as a dealer. Had a whole trailer full of rocket grenades as bait. He got damn close, I'll give him that. But like I told you, Liashko's a bugout. He smelled something wrong. The next thing I know, he's fled back to Russia." Burke flipped the imaginary Liashko the finger. "I had to do something to save face. So we made the best of it. Santora vanished, and I told Anatoly I was the reason why."

"And he believed you."

"I had some cred. A few years ago, two Bratva shitheads ripped off Anatoly's summer house for spending money before they fled to the States. Busted up his housekeeper while they were at it. Anatoly sent me to find them. Wasn't hard. The idiots had holed up in a Long Beach fleapit owned by the brotherhood. But when I got there, they were already dead and stinking, overdosed on some laced heroin. Lucky opportunity. I made it look like I'd tied up the two punks and spiked them myself."

Burke had a different definition of luck than I did. If the two gangsters hadn't already been cold, would he have taken care of that minor detail, too?

Or maybe he had killed them after all. And lying to me about it was just second nature. Maybe he was lying about everything, including his status with the federal task force.

"So what now?" I said.

"Now you stay as low as the deepest roots under the tall trees, until Anatoly comes to America and we nail his ass. Don't say shit to anybody, just vanish. I can contact you when it's safe."

"No. Liashko's boys tried to burn my face off. Tell your guy on the task force that I want in."

"Get bent. He'll never go for it, and sure as hell I don't want you neither. You're gonna get me killed or something worse, stumbling around."

"So aim me where I can do some good. Even if it's watching your back in case your paranoid freak boss decides to have you whacked on general principle."

He slapped his glass down on the side table, hard enough to make the ice cubes jitter and bounce. "Fuck whether or not he takes me out. There's pressure here. My guy put his ass on the line, you understand? He's the only guy in the world would do that. I ain't taking him down with me."

Despite his loose tongue, Burke had kept his handler's name out of our conversation. But I could put the pieces together into a rough picture. The supposedly dead Santora had been ATF. And ATF Special Agent Rick Martens had offered me a similar deal as Burke's, to turn informant. Martens was in his late forties, about the right age to be a childhood friend of Sean Burke.

One plus one plus one. Burke had sent Agent Martens to Bully Betty's to offer me a deal, right after I'd told Burke about Moira.

Which might mean he wasn't as positive as he claimed about whether he might be my father.

"If you have enough faith to tell me all this," I said, "you can tell me about Moira."

Burke sighed. "I figured you'd circle back to her. You're like a pit bull on a fuckin' pork chop."

I waited. Without taking his eyes off me, Burke reached into the pocket of his trousers and removed a rectangular piece of clear plastic. A sealed bag. He unfolded it to show me. Inside the bag was a Q-tip. One tip of the swab was wet.

He held out the bag. I took it.

"You knew her," I said.

"Of course I knew her. I never forgot her. And before I spend the rest of my life in WITSEC, I guess you and I better sort this out, huh?"

FORTY-THREE

I CALLED PAULA CLAYBECK THE INSTANT I was back at the car. She picked up, thank God.

"Dr. Claybeck," I said. "Van Shaw. Hollis's friend."

"Oh, I'm aware. You said you would lose my number."

"I need a small favor."

"Color me surprised." Claybeck didn't seem too grateful that I'd helped extricate her from Ondine's clutches. But then, maybe the good doctor felt she'd traded the frying pan for the fire.

"I need to compare two DNA samples for paternity," I said.

"Honestly, dragging me into your baby mama troubles?"

In a few sentences I laid out what I needed. A long pause followed.

"That's not something I can do here at any rate," Claybeck said. "DNA comparison requires specialized equipment to separate the fragments and review the profiles."

"I guessed."

"I'll call a friend and see if he would be willing to fit the analysis into his day. Take down this address." She read it off. A street in the southern part of the Central District. "Unless I call and tell you differently, meet me there at seven o'clock in the morning. The process will require at least a few hours. Hours unencumbered by you hanging over his shoulder."

"Understood." I almost had to stop myself from adding "ma'am." Claybeck had that superior officer vibe down cold.

"Don't be late."

Un-damn-likely. I would be counting the minutes. Sleep might be impossible. It was like a twisted version of Christmas Eve as a child, agonizing through the hours until morning and time to see what presents had appeared under the tree.

Not that the yuletide had ever been so showy with Dono. My grandfather had kept our festivities to an extra slab of meat and some dessert on the dinner table, with a gift or two wrapped crudely in newspaper and garden twine as the centerpiece. Usually winter clothes or something I needed for school. But there was always cash on Christmas morning, too, and Dono never gave a crap what I spent it on. Spider-Man comics and a candy feast for me and Davey Tolan from the 7-Eleven later that same afternoon was the standard spree.

Now I held what might be the conclusive link to my father in my hand, and there was nothing to do but wait.

STANLEY SNUFFED FROM HIS TRACTOR-TIRE-SIZED bed in the corner, battling some dreamland adversary. Normally he'd be in Cyndra's room, occupying ninety percent of the mattress, but when I'd spread blankets on the couch around midnight he had padded out to join me, a yawn stretching his huge maw. The dog had apparently determined that he and I were guarding the castle gates together.

It was near five o'clock in the morning. For the past hour, my mind had been turning over what Burke had said about his buddy in law enforcement, how the Fed had put everything on the line to help Burke. That if the bust of Liashko went south, they would all be finished.

Burke saw his C.I. status as transactional. I had the same opinion. If Liashko wasn't caught, Martens's career might be flushed and Burke's chances of survival would follow it down the same drain. No criminal trial equaled no escape into WITSEC. The man in charge, U.S. Attorney Palmer Stratton, would wipe his hands clean of the whole debacle.

It was the smart move, politically. Burke would be abandoned, forced to run. Anatoly Liashko didn't seem to lack for trigger men to chase after him.

I finally tossed the sheets aside. Better to get something done than to fruitlessly pursue rest that I knew wasn't coming.

Addy kept her home computer perched incongruously on a delicate secretary desk that she'd owned for fifty years. Her original computer had been a creaker, close to joining the desk in antiquity, until Cyndra had insisted on a model that could handle a teenage-sized gaming habit.

I switched on the PC and pulled up a browser, searching for news on the recall election for governor.

The race had narrowed to three contenders. Stratton, the Democratic candidate, still showed a narrow lead in the polls. His Republican challenger, Fulcher, had made headway by trumpeting his ties to business growth as a congressman in Spokane. The independent third party, Barrish, had no chance judging from the poll numbers. She had barely pulled enough donors to be included in the debates two nights before.

I clicked on a KIRO-TV news video to skim through the latest debate. It was about as enlightening as I'd expected, meaning not at all. Every question the moderator threw to the candidates was quickly spun into whatever sound bites the politician wanted to repeat.

From what I saw, there wasn't a whole lot of difference between the two front-runners. Both white guys around fifty, with the sleek look of weekly grooming and well-rehearsed hand gestures. Stratton's money came from his family, Fulcher's from his corporate career before he climbed the rungs of the state and national legislature.

I focused more on the verbal combat. Fulcher was on the attack, implying Stratton was an entitled kid from a long line of career politicians. Stratton parried by emphasizing his job putting crooks behind bars and counterpunched with Fulcher's voting record, as evidence that Fulcher was far more right-wing than he claimed. Barrish ignored them both and appealed to the voters for action on corporate tax reform and housing inequality. Of the three, she seemed to be the one stressing her actual platform. Fulcher and Stratton were too busy fighting tooth and nail for every undecided voter.

Addy came into the room, swathed in her white Turkish robe with navy piping. Her silver hair stuck out in conical clumps instead of its usual slim spikes. Stanley's tail thumped the armrest.

"I didn't think you cared about politics," Addy said, closing one eye against the blue-white glare of the screen.

"I don't." I muted the video. The debate raged on in silence.

"Could have fooled me. It's usually Cyndra I'm telling to not sit so close."

It was true that I hadn't taken my eyes off the arguing candidates. Addy sat down on the couch, shooing Stanley to curl himself onto the remaining cushions.

"Have you learned any more about—your father?" she said.

My jacket was hanging on the dowel pegs by the door. I retrieved it and took the sealed plastic bag with the swab from Burke from the pocket to show Addy.

"He gave me this. To have it tested."

"Oh, my. That's huge. So he and your mother were a couple."

"I doubt Burke would put it like that. And," I admitted, "maybe Moira had other boys, too. But something makes me doubt it. If she and Burke hooked up as kids, my guess is that he's the only one."

"And your father. How do you feel about that?"

Like I'd opened a treasure chest to find that the gold doubloons inside carried a curse. Like I was sorry I'd ever asked.

"Burke's right in the middle of bad times, with bad people. I talked to Wren about him some last night. She implied knowledge is power. That by understanding the kind of person Burke is, I can make sure I'm different."

Addy didn't say anything. She knew me well enough to imagine that drawing that line could be so easy.

"Wren, eh?" she said with an upbeat tone. "She's quite something."

"Yeah. I like her. She's . . . direct."

"It's nice you're looking to the future. Not that I assume you two will become soulmates. But all of this"—Addy handed back the sealed bag—"is really just talking about what's already passed. It's not the same as leading your own life."

"Whatever happened, I'll find out the truth today." I pocketed the swab.

Addy idly scratched Stanley's ear. "You don't have to. I'm not sure I would, in your place."

The computer was still running the video of the debate. Candidates shook hands and waved to the crowd, each of them beaming a huge smile to communicate victory. I switched it off.

"I've come too far to let this go now," I said.

FORTY-FOUR

C LAYBECK WAS WAITING AT THE address she'd given me, a drably functional tinted-glass and chrome-steel building at the outskirts of a college campus. Its four stories had probably been the height of workspace design in the 1990s. Raised letters above the door read: SEATTLE STATE UNIVERSITY WEGNER HALL.

"Med school?" I guessed, touching a finger to the pitted metal frame around the keycard entry plate.

"Forensic sciences," Claybeck said, waving to a lanky man who was already hurrying from the back end of the lobby to meet us. "Don't let the facilities mislead you. The school produces some of the top analysts in the country."

The door's automatic lock clunked as the man drew within range of its motion sensor, allowing him to push the plexiglass door open.

"Paula," he said to Claybeck, shaking hands, "great to see you. And weird." He blinked happily at her, like the strangeness of our morning meeting was the most entertainment he'd had in ages. He was a touch over six feet, with long limbs and a neck framing a pronounced Adam's apple. In his plaid shirt and slim-cut jeans, a mannequin for the Northwest Professional Type.

"I appreciate the help," Claybeck said. "This is Mr. Shaw. He's the one in a hurry."

"Jay Corrigan," he greeted me. "I'm a professor of forensic biology here. Most of the time. I also do some consulting for state and King County police labs."

I caught the implication. Don't ask Corrigan to do anything that he would have to report.

"It's a paternity check," I said, handing him two baggies, one containing a swab from my own cheek, the other Burke's similar swab. Samples A and B. I explained what I wanted. His eyes took on that tickled expression again.

"How long will it take?" I said.

"Premium rush, right? I can start later this morning, and we can handle the short-tandem repeat here," he said, holding the samples against the light for a better look. "We apply reagents and heat to release the DNA. If there's enough to work with, I'll make a few million copies and separate those out. We've got a genetic analyzer on the third floor. To make a profile—"

"O'clock," I said.

"Ten o'clock," he said, with a staccato chuckle at my urgency. "About twelve hours after I start, we should be looking at the profiles and seeing if all twenty-one locations—that's half—match. That's proof of paternity. And that's as fast as the analysis can be done. Can't force it."

"I'll call you at ten." He told me his phone number. "What do I owe you?"

"It's a barter job," he said, jabbing a thumb at Claybeck. "Paula's gonna be a guest speaker."

Claybeck's mouth pursed. I was getting better at reading her moods. Less disapproval than concern. "I hope the results are worth the trouble."

The doctor had only a hint as to how much trouble obtaining that tiny swab had been. Or how much more grief it might lead to, if the results confirmed a killer like Sean Burke was my father.

I FOLLOWED CLAYBECK AROUND THE university building to the staff parking lot in the rear. The holiday break meant only half a dozen spots were occupied. Off to one side of the paved area, a large plot surrounded by ivy-covered wooden fences had been dedicated to a communal garden for the student body. Raised beds for vegetables and herbs were mostly just soil now, stiff and brittle with the night's frost. Waiting for the season of growth. I wondered if Wren knew of plants that would flourish in the cold months. Past the garden, a long row of groundskeeping sheds covered the space between the parking lot and the street beyond.

"I'll be staying in town tonight," Claybeck said as she removed her keys from her purse. "Once you hear the results from Jay, you're not obligated to let me know, of course. But I'd be lying if I said I wasn't curious."

Maybe it was the unexpected movement twenty feet ahead of Claybeck that sparked me. Or maybe I'd caught a ripple of something wrong on the light breeze. Either way, I was dodging left, behind the cover of the garden fence, before a cogent thought had formed.

Saleem stepped partway out from between the sheds to aim a large automatic at Claybeck's head.

"Be silent," he said. She stood frozen.

The Colt was in my hand and I was concealed, but the fence's wooden slats wouldn't be much proof against high-caliber rounds. Saleem and I were at a standoff. Doc Claybeck in the middle.

I didn't have a clear shot. Saleem took advantage and moved first, shifting his aim to me and closing the half-dozen steps to the doctor in a heartbeat.

"Move back," he said to me, wheeling Claybeck around and grabbing her by the coat collar. She was a tall woman. I had even less of a target than before. "Back. I will kill her if I must."

I retreated into the lawned garden. It was a stupid move, tactically. My cover went from inadequate to almost nonexistent in the open space. The walled plot of land offered more privacy for Saleem to finish us off.

But I believed him. He would risk a shootout in the open with Claybeck as his shield if I didn't comply.

My only chance would be to dive for the ground behind one of the raised planting beds. If Claybeck struggled, there might be a sliver of a second for a kill shot. I moved backward, stretching the yards between us as Saleem pushed Claybeck forward and into the garden. Stepping every time she stepped, as if they were dancing. She still clutched her purse and keys. In another few seconds, I would be out of room.

The doctor's fingers pressed urgently at her keyfob. Her eyes sought out mine, pleading, even as I leveled the Colt at a spot over her shoulder and prepared to jump.

I realized what she was doing. And kept walking, until my back was pressed against the ivy. Inviting Saleem to follow.

"Throw away your gun," he called to me as they took another step. He started to say more, but his time was up.

I already knew Claybeck's dogs didn't bark. And on the lawn, their sprinting feet were as silent and swift as the wind.

Saleem managed one stunted scream of terror and agony as they brought him down. He thrashed and kicked madly, not slowing the beasts for an instant. Claybeck recovered from her shock, tried calling them off. But nature would not be denied. Her dogs had smelled fear on their mistress, and that was enough. One lunged to clamp its jaws around Saleem's head. He kicked more, each time weaker than the last, and fell still.

Then all that remained were feral growls and the sounds of rending, like pork from bone and gristle. By the time the dogs finally responded to her commands, releasing their grips and running circles as they whined in horrible excitement, what was left on the dappled grass looked like a rag effigy dipped in carmine ink.

I didn't approach. In fact I had done my best impression of a stone, moving only to slowly hide my gun, in case the sight of it might be an attack trigger.

In another moment, Claybeck had them sitting, one hand on each of their heads. She was sobbing. Praising them. They panted and smiled behind their blood-drenched muzzles. They knew they were good dogs.

WHEN I WAS SURE CLAYBECK had them calmed, I walked around the edge of the fence to close the gate. Then I picked the clearest path I could through the reddened grass to Saleem's body. In one of his pockets I found the keys to an Impala, identifiable by a key tag that had the dealership's name along with the license number and model.

A locked shed at one side of the garden contained hoses and irrigation-system controls. I opened the valves and let the spray wash over the lawn, and Saleem's corpse. Claybeck took charge of the dogs, hosing each of them down. I went in search of the car. We hadn't said a word to one another.

The Impala turned out to be one of the handful of cars in the staff lot, and the oldest by at least half a dozen years. In its glove compartment I discovered Saleem's brother's passport and credit cards, along with a bill of sale showing the junker had been acquired for twelve hundred dollars in cash from the dealer in Salt Lake yesterday.

Saleem must have jumped the train and driven half the night to Claybeck's home before tailing her here. Maybe aiming to take her prisoner—once she was separated from her dogs—and ensnare me or Hollis by using her. Perhaps Saleem had planned to leave the train before it reached Seattle all along, or maybe my attempt at luring him to Sean Burke's barn had only served to arouse his suspicions. I guessed that he'd paid cash to keep the car off his brother's charges.

He'd probably paid cash for the plastic sheeting that lined the Impala's roomy trunk, too. Ready for our dead bodies. Now it would serve for his. I backed the Impala right up to the garden gate, grateful for the deserted campus.

Inside, Claybeck had finished cleaning her dogs and was doing her best to rinse blood from her sleeves and pants where they had brushed against her. The hounds lay on the dry grass to one side, watching curiously. Their black-brown fur stood out in lustrous wet spikes. I turned off the sprinklers and removed my jacket and shirt. Putting Saleem in the trunk would be messy work.

"Are you all right?" I said.

"No." Claybeck tugged forcefully at her pants cuff, wringing it out. "But as the gravedigger said, I'd rather be on this end of the shovel."

Her dark joke surprised me so much I nearly laughed. "Christ. You would have made a good soldier."

"Right now I wish I had been." She shuddered, not just from the cold water, and tossed the hose aside. The dogs rose to investigate and lap at the running stream.

"They were in your car," I said.

Claybeck nodded, a touch frantically. "I was planning to stay in the city overnight. I can't leave them at home. Of all the uses for a minivan with automatic doors . . ."

"I'm very glad. Thanks."

"What about—" Claybeck gestured but did not turn toward Saleem's body. She hadn't looked directly at it since she'd called the dogs off, I guessed.

"We can't tell the cops. For one thing, the courts would probably insist on putting your dogs down."

"I wasn't intending to involve them."

"I'll handle it."

"Yes. I suppose you would know how." Her expression was hard to read.

"You should stay with friends tonight," I said. "Don't be alone."

Claybeck nodded.

"Maybe not tomorrow, either. You're going to need some time, and somebody you can confide in."

"I'll be all right."

"Yeah. You will."

Her eyes were wet again. "Hollis asked if I would accompany him on a trip down the coast this week. I think I might just."

THERE WAS A QUIET MARSH off the Black River near Renton where I could dump Saleem. Wildlife and water would go to work on his remains. The blood-smeared plastic sheeting would be stuffed into a dumpster behind any grocery store with a butcher. The creaky Impala, clean and empty, I'd leave on a city street with the keys in it.

The corpse would be found eventually. But without papers—without much of a face either—it might never be identified or linked with the car.

Once the job was done, I'd call Aura Nath and tell her the gunman was no longer a danger. Leaving Claybeck out of the story.

Driving south in the Impala with the shrouded body in the trunk, I thought about the doctor and her dogs, and what they had done to Saleem. I pondered whether Stanley might have done the same, if it were Addy or Cyndra who had been in danger.

He would, I decided. The huge mixed breed was not a trained weapon like Claybeck's hounds. Stanley was friendly by nature. Despite that, the predatory instinct to bite and rip and kill lay just beneath, peeking out whenever Stanley tore after a squirrel or into a chew rope.

But killing a man would have changed Stanley. After such an experience, I doubted he could ever be the joyous overgrown pup that he was now, not completely. Dogs could suffer trauma, too.

Burke was akin to Claybeck's dogs. Merciless, and happy to be so. I wasn't quite as savage, but I knew full well I could get into that headspace when I chose. That I could live with the consequences and sleep well, just like Burke did. Maybe it was in our blood.

FORTY-FIVE

THE CLOCK ON THE WALL of the Sol Liquor Lounge read a quarter to ten, to the best of my knowledge. Hard to know for sure, because the interior light was soft and the wall entirely covered with a world map that perhaps explained why the lounge's décor was stuck somewhere between China and Polynesia. Also because the clock might not actually exist. My vision was a little impaired.

I tried focusing on the aged J. Baum of Cincinnati combination safe that rested in a place of honor atop the vintage glass-fronted cooler behind the bar. The safe was the main reason I liked the lounge. The bartender on my first visit had told me the staff had never succeeded in opening it. I was sure I could. Maybe I should do it right now.

To keep myself from trying, I called Professor Corrigan.

"You're a little early," he said. "But I got it done. You want the results now? Forget it, of course you do, I'm just wiped out." His stuttering chuckle did sound ragged. "It's definite. Matches across the board on the profile. Sample B is the father of Sample A. I'm guessing you're B? Is this congratulations or commiserations?"

"I'm A," I said, my voice sounding a long way away.

His amusement vanished. "Your dad, huh? Whoa. Okay. I suppose the same question applies."

It did. I just didn't have an answer.

"I've got the full profile; I can send that to you," Corrigan said. "It's not anything that can be used in court, just so you know. For that a lab tech would have to witness the samples directly—"

"Not necessary," I said.

"Cool. I gotta get out of here, get some sleep. It's been a minute since I've pulled an all-nighter."

I hung up.

Sean Burke, seventeen. Boyfriend of Moira Shaw, sixteen. A relationship doomed to fail, but it had lasted long enough to permanently change at least one of their lives, not to mention starting mine.

God.

Burke had wanted to know. I wasn't up for sharing the news. Not yet.

A notion of ordering another Boxer's Fracture tequila drink or six occurred. I let it slide past. Getting bombed—more thoroughly bombed—wasn't going to help my mood. I was still figuring out what the hell my mood was.

Of all the fathers I might have imagined, Burke wasn't even on the list. If the man had any redeeming qualities other than his faith in his friend Martens, I hadn't seen them.

I owed Burke my life. I wasn't sure I owed him the truth.

An hour later I surrendered my stool at the counter and wandered outside into an unexpected sleet. The slush fell at an angle that spoke of intentional spite, working its shivering way under collars and into gloves. While the cold didn't instantly sober me, it ensured my body would be burning every bit of fuel to stay warm, sugary alcohol included.

I needed clean clothes if I was going to stay at Addy's for any longer. I'd stop at my apartment, pack a bag.

But once I got there, I found myself sitting in my leather wingback chair, an extravagant piece that I'd bought because it reminded me of one Dono had once owned. I began looking up gubernatorial candidate Palmer Stratton on my laptop. He was the man in charge. The one who would decide whether Sean Burke—*my father*, my brain insisted on adding—would live or die, indirectly.

I didn't like Stratton's face. Or his Holy Order, Ivy League, yacht-and-country-club background. Even his mom, Margaret, pissed me off, with her endless causes, every one of them hyping the Stratton name.

I knew it was classist. I knew my opinion of Stratton was powered by booze. But fuck the guy. Whatever good he'd done as a prosecutor was just to balance the scales, make him more palatable to voters before he leapt into the political arena. He practically had CRUSADER stamped on his Botoxed forehead. With all the morally superior fervor that word implied.

Stratton was the man I needed to convince. Or barter with. I had knowledge that might be crucial to bringing down Liashko. Stratton was the only guy who could assure me that whatever happened, even if that didn't include the arms trafficker in handcuffs, the Feds would get Burke to safety.

His campaign webpage listed a private fund-raiser at the Alexis Hotel tomorrow night. For key donors and potentials, no doubt. Security would be tight. I'd have to think how to clear those hurdles, once my thoughts were back in full working order.

A text lit up my phone on the armrest of the chair.

ANYTHING?

It was from Burke. Maybe he was as curious, in his own sociopathic way, to know the results as I had been.

I could keep delaying the inevitable, or get it over with. I chose the latter.

Anderson Park reservoir. Half an hour.

The park would be closed at one o'clock in the morning, but I doubted Sean Burke would be put off by city ordinances any more than I was. Plus the reservoir was practically on my doorstep. Home field advantage.

HE CAME FROM THE NORTH side, past the volcano-shaped fountain that had
been turned off for the winter. Enough glistening frost from the earlier
rush of sleet remained that his shoes made crunching sounds on the
pathway.

"So?" he said, while still ten yards off.

I nodded confirmation.

He stopped short. "Damn."

"Can't put it better than that."

A curved concrete border around the dormant fountain served double
duty as a bench. We sat. Burke seemed no worse for wear from his binge
on downers the night before. His grizzly-brown hair shone wetly. Too long
since the sleet had fallen; maybe he'd showered before going out. In his
black windbreaker and khakis, he might have been about to tee off a very
late round of night golf at the Jefferson course.

"I dunno what to do about it, now that we know," he said.

"Now you tell me about you and Moira. No bullshit this time."

Burke took a long breath. "It's been thirty years. More."

I waited.

"Gus brought me along one day when he came to see your old guy,
Dono. Pops was buying something from him. Some sort of whatsit that
would help Gus get past a burglar alarm. That sound right?"

It did. Dono could make such a tool in his sleep. Though Gut Burke
must have been willing to pay a small fortune for my grandfather to bend
his rules and deal directly with a mob enforcer.

"Moira was at the house that day," Burke said. "Damn. Gut had to
slap my skull, I was staring so hard at her. I know she's your ma and all,
and I don't mean no disrespect, but shit, I was a teenage boy. I managed to
talk to her some. She wouldn't give me her phone number at the house.
But she said she'd call me."

And she had. Moira Shaw, straight-A student, apparently had a thing
for bad boys. I couldn't muster any surprise, given our family. My mouth
was dry.

"We had to sneak around," Burke continued, "and we hardly ever went anywhere when it was just the two of us. We'd go to the movies or hang with friends of mine from school."

"She ever talk about herself? Her plans?"

"College for sure, I know that much. But Moira was . . . her mom had died like a couple of years before. She was kinda distant."

"Not too distant."

"Well, yeah. When she, ah—when she said she wanted to get with me, it was a surprise, you know? I figured she still had her cherry. Sorry."

I shook my head. We were past protecting anyone's memory.

"Then she called me a week after and broke it off. That was it."

"What about later? The letters she wrote you?"

Burke's head snapped around. "Jesus. You've seen those? What, did she keep copies?"

"Her best friend caught her. That's how I learned your name."

He relaxed. "Well, shit. Yeah, she wrote me. I was wanting to get back together. She sent a letter: Thanks but No Thanks. Embarrassing as fuck. I'm glad you didn't see it."

"And that was all?"

"Almost." He took out his keys and began to remove something from the ring, slipping it off an inch-long ball chain of metal, like a tiny dogtag necklace. He handed the object to me.

It was a round brass disc about the size and shape of a fifty-cent piece. Tarnished half green from inattention. My religious education was nonexistent, but I recognized it as a Catholic medallion for a saint. The image etched in relief showed a bearded man standing ramrod straight, with a lighthouse in the background on his left side and a twin-masted sailing ship on the right.

"Saint Brendan," Burke said. "Built a boat and sailed around spreading the gospel. Moira sent that to me a few weeks after her kiss-off letter. She didn't explain why. I figured it was 'cause Gus and I got around a lot, we needed protecting."

She might have sent the medal to Burke after she realized she was pregnant with me. The timing was right. Stopping short of telling him about the baby—maybe she'd already judged Burke as a rock-bottom choice to raise a kid—but wanting her child's father to be safe nonetheless.

Moira had been sixteen. Hard to fathom exactly what she might have been thinking, or the stress she was under.

I could sympathize with her desire to keep Burke safe, though. Lousy daddy material or not.

He looked at the frost on the ground, sparkling in the lamplight. "I wish she'd said something."

The brass medallion fit in the key pocket of my coat like it had been crafted for it.

"What's Liashko bringing into the country?" I said.

Burke frowned. "I told you to keep out of that."

"Stepan and his team are dead, you're taking over. That makes you more valuable to the Feds now. Do you have any written guarantee they won't cut you loose?"

"Leave it."

"Not now I won't. Not after this."

"I'm askin' you. For Moira."

Angry as I was at Burke, laughter nearly won the moment. His cheap fucking ploy.

I tapped the medal in my pocket. "All this means is that a teenage girl gave a damn. Don't start pretending Moira was more to you than she was."

Burke looked at me like I'd sprouted antennae.

"I'm on Liashko's hit list, too," I said. "You want payback for Gus? Let's get it. Liashko will rot in a supermax cell twenty-three hours a day for the rest of his life. He'll know every minute that you're the reason. Give me something."

"You're crazy," he said. "I mean you're really fuckin' bughouse."

"But not stupid. I found you. I can do a lot more. What don't you know about Liashko's deal? Where can't the Feds go?"

Burke just kept staring. "I know what he's selling, but not where he's got them stashed. Yet. The paranoid fuck isn't trusting me." His hands tightened around his knees. "You really think you can find his stuff?"

"I got a knack for it. What am I looking for?"

He looked at the dry fountain, like it might help him decide. Grunted a laugh.

"Shit, I've gambled this far," he said. "Might as well go all in. You know what a Verba is?"

It was my turn to be stunned. "Russian surface-to-air missile launchers. Portable, for ground troops."

"That's right. When things really started to slide for Anatoly, he found a way to lift a bunch of those babies from some separatist group backed by his old Russian masters and blame their disappearance on the Ukrainian armed forces. Forty missiles with reusable trigger mechanisms and sights. I saw 'em myself, in Moldova, more than a year ago. Liashko's looking to close up shop. Everything he stole out of the war in the Donbass region, in one go."

Jesus. Like most modern missile launchers, the Verba had seeking and guidance tech built right in. Designed for infantry grunts who might have to fire the weapon after only a few spare minutes of training in the field. The missiles came with ultraviolet and infrared sensors both, to engage targets with even minimal radar signatures.

Just one of those could bring down a jetliner, or a military chopper, or a cruise missile. Damn near anything in the sky. Forty, deployed strategically, could temporarily cripple a nation.

Burke must have read my shock. "Ease up before you have a stroke. We're all over this."

"We?"

"Anatoly's buyer, the guy I've set him up with, is ATF." Burke spat on the ground in satisfaction. "An agent pretending to be a cartel go-between. We'll have a hundred Feds in combat gear swarming that piece of shit like ants on a dead rat the second he shows his face."

Because they didn't know where the Verbas were.

For once, I was ahead of Burke and the task force both.

"This could still go sideways," I said, "if Liashko never lets on where he's got the missiles."

"Like I said, I'll take that chance. Anatoly has fifteen million comin' to him, he thinks. That's a fucking big incentive. If you can really point me to those missiles, that's all we need. Once we nail this asswipe, you're home free."

"And you'll have a new name."

Burke grunted. "Yeah. It may not be much of a life in whatever podunk shithole they stick me in. But I'll be livin'."

He stood up.

"For whatever it's worth, I liked her," he said, and he pointed to my pocket with the medal of Saint Brendan. "Hang on to that. She woulda wanted you to have it."

"If I don't see you . . ."

"You won't." He smiled grimly. "One more week, and I'm as gone as gone can be."

BETTY CLOSED HER BAR EARLY on Mondays. I let myself in the back and went directly to the alcove where she kept the DVR that captured the feed off the security cameras.

The cameras had been a debate between us in the old location. Betty didn't want her customers to feel watched. I wanted a positive ID on anyone who made trouble. Taking that side had felt odd at the time: Van Shaw, Crimestopper. But I'd persevered. That same week a brawl had broken out in one of the U District watering holes, resulting in everyone threatening to sue everyone else. That had probably helped my argument.

The DVR stored a week's worth of high-def from eight different cameras I'd installed at key angles. Right now, I was concerned about the one to the right of the main bar. I clicked on last Saturday and sped through the captured feed until just before closing time.

There I was, with Special Agent Martens across the bar from me. His blue rep tie in full color. I let the silent video play at normal speed, as Martens gathered his coat and left the screen toward the back of the bar, as I went in the opposite direction to close up.

Martens returned almost immediately to the screen. Crouching very low, hiding from the rest of the bar behind the high counter. I watched as his image pulled out the recycling bin from underneath, removed something, and crept back the way he'd come.

A beer bottle. My beer bottle, the Reuben's Porter I had tossed during our little talk about me becoming an informant for the ATF task force.

Martens already had easy access to my fingerprints. I'd been booked before, plus my prints had been taken during military service. The only other use for that bottle was a sample of my DNA. But that could also be obtained by an official request to the Army. They had snagged a blood specimen from me when I was first inducted, same as any recruit. So what the hell was Martens after?

Burke might have confessed to his old friend why I'd sought Burke out, and that young Sean might have fathered me three decades ago. Martens and the task force could be checking that evidence for themselves. But if the task force wanted my DNA to find out the truth about Burke and me, why would Burke have given me his swab? Were the two sides operating independently, not sharing information?

There was another possible reason, besides my parentage. The task force was looking to match my DNA to evidence found at a crime scene. Maybe they didn't want to wait while the Army processed the request through its endless channels.

The break-in at Burke's house? Or somewhere else? I thought back, wondering if I had slipped up somewhere. I couldn't think of any crime I'd committed that might intersect with the task force's aims. But then, I'd broken into plenty of places since my return to Seattle. And my crimes hadn't stopped at B&E, either. Maybe Martens and his team had their sights on nailing me on another charge. Force my cooperation.

If a federal task force had added me to their list of suspects, I could wind up working for the law whether I liked it or not. That was the best-case scenario. The other would be a long stay in maximum security, maybe right alongside Anatoly Liashko.

FORTY-SIX

ONLINE REGISTRATION FOR THE NIGHT'S fund-raiser for Palmer Stratton, candidate for governor of the great state of Washington, had closed the day before. But a morning call to Stratton's campaign HQ produced a volunteer who had clearly downed plenty of coffee despite the early hour. He passed me on to a senior coordinator, to whom I breathlessly explained that I'd seen the candidate's performance in the debates and heartily *agreed* with his positions and would be *delighted* to purchase a pair of seats at one of the premier tables at tonight's little gathering, if any of those might still be available. She didn't squander a second in taking down my debit card number and held the line until the charge for ten thousand dollars cleared.

It did, barely. As fast as I'd made my substantial nest egg from selling my family land and from less legitimate means, it had evaporated.

Worth it, if my most recent spending spree got me close enough to Stratton to say a few words.

My next call was to Wren.

"How do you feel about incredibly overpriced chicken with a side of political speeches?" I said.

"I get enough punishment on the derby track. Is this our date to-night?"

"Sort of. A fund-raiser for the governor's race."

She made a humming sound of consideration. "You don't seem the type of guy to go to partisan rallies."

"No."

"Am I . . . camouflage?"

"Yes. But not for anything illegal. I need to speak to the candidate, and this is the fastest way."

"You take your activism seriously. This has something to do with your dad, yeah?"

"It does. Are you up for it?"

I heard her moving, then the sound of Janelle Monáe singing in the background dimmed.

"Two conditions," Wren said. "Tell me why this is so important."

"That's a long story, and I'm late to meet someone up in Everett. I'll call you after and tell you what's going on. If you don't like anything about it, you can bail. No hard feelings."

"You have a really weird way of flirting. How dressy is this fund-raiser?"

I hadn't even thought about clothes. The blue checked suit I'd acquired from the grumpy Giuseppe hung in my closet, back in its bag. "I'm guessing jackets and ties?"

Wren laughed. "Why is it guys never know? Doesn't matter. I have a dress that's conformist enough for any political stripe."

"Was that your second condition?"

"No. We'll get into that later. What time does the dinner start?"

"Six o'clock."

"Pick me up at five-thirty." She gave me her address, a house in Fauntleroy. "And don't forget to call me. This is a story I have to hear."

I'd already told Wren about my relationship to Burke and hinted at the kind of work he did. I could give her the rundown on Liashko and the task force without naming names or putting the investigation at risk.

Wren had seemed fascinated by my criminal past. I wanted to be up front with her about my life now, as harrowing as it was.

Would the truth push her away? Or was that part of my attraction for her?

THE REST OF THE DAYLIGHT hours were spent shopping, and cooking, after a fashion.

My early appointment in Everett was with a salvage yard owner, who'd been willing to open on his day off to let me purchase a small and barely seaworthy rowboat for a hundred bucks cash. I'd brought my own rope to tie the boat to the top of my truck's canopy. Secure while I made multiple stops in the northern tip of King County.

At each hardware store I bought a quart or two of kerosene. From pharmacies and outdoor shops and a janitorial supply company I acquired chemicals and other materials, including a box of shotgun shells and what eventually amounted to two full cases of antacid tablets. All purchased with cash. It took me two trips from the truck to carry everything up to my apartment.

Back in my kitchen, I filled the bottom of a large baking tray with clay cat litter and soaked it with a pint of gasoline mixed with cleaning solution, setting the granules to dry under the stove fan while I carried on in the living area.

The kerosene I poured one can at a time into five-gallon buckets, steadily adding the antacid tablets with their active calcium carbonate and a mix of other chemicals. What I was left with, after an hour of very careful stirring, was a thick pungent slurry roughly the color of a rotting peach, a byproduct of the rainbow assortment of tablets.

I had all the windows open and fans blowing to ward off the fumes. It helped, marginally. When my phone rang, I went out into the hall before I dared to take off my painter's mask and safety goggles to answer.

"Hollis," I said. "Are you where you can talk?"

"No one for a quarter mile but us, if you don't count the fish." Hollis was practically shouting. "I'm on the satellite phone, halfway up Juan de Fuca with the good Doctor Paula."

"How's she doing?" I'd filled Hollis in on the last moments of Saleem.

"A strong woman. She's quiet a lot, but that might just be her nature. Having the dogs at her side seems to help. The mutts and I are actually getting along, if you can believe that."

Believe it I did. Hollis Brant could make friends with a tiger shark.

"Hollis, I need to talk to your buddy Jaak today, along with someone who can translate the tougher parts. If you think we can trust him a short distance."

"You saved his life and his job, Van. I expect Jaak would take holy orders and become your father confessor if you asked. But, ah, you know he's still recovering—"

"There shouldn't be any danger. In fact, he might find it fun."

I explained what I had in mind. By the time I finished Hollis was laughing.

"Hell, I'd be up for that myself, if I were there. Sorry to miss it. I'll have Jaak's man call you."

I thanked him and returned to the miasma within my apartment. I sealed the buckets of flammable slurry, having already punched holes in the plastic lids with an awl to make sure the fumes didn't build up pressure. One more task, and then I would be ready.

The powder from the shotgun shells became the key ingredient in an oversized firecracker, packed into a cardboard tube with the dried and highly toxic cat litter. A long bit of waterproof fuse from the model rocket section of a hobby store capped the tube.

Not exactly a shaped charge with C-4, but I didn't have the Army providing toys for me anymore. It would serve just fine. Like Hollis, I was a little sorry I wouldn't be there to see it go off.

FORTY-SEVEN

THE LOBBY OF THE ALEXIS Hotel had been partitioned by velvet ropes and concrete security guards. A pair of crisp concierges in eggshell blouses and skirts ushered guests of the hotel toward the marble-topped reception desk. The rest of us, the politically minded affluent, were allowed past the ropes and welcomed into a barroom decked out like a bookseller's, with leatherbound editions lining the shelves in place of bottles. A cocktail reception was in full swing. A campaign staffer checked our names off a clipboard and handed us a card, which noted we would be at table 7.

Wren placed the card in her clutch purse. "A souvenir," she said.

She wore a beautifully simple midnight-blue sheath dress. With its sleeves covering her tattoos, and her dark hair gathered into a twist that managed to be both elegant and casual enough to allow stray curls to frame her face, Wren might have been a candidate herself. Only the bemused smirk at the corner of her mouth spoiled the effect.

"This is nuts," she said as she took my arm.

"Really? I feel right at home." We moved into the reception crowd, as two of the security guards changed position to get a better angle on us.

It had been a smart choice to bring Wren. Her earlier assessment was spot-on; I couldn't pass for a political patron. Nor even much like the clean-cut security detail in their blazers and gray slacks currently giving me the eyeball. Concealed weapons would be their main concern. Hidden cameras a close second. Indiscreet footage could be more damaging than a bullet, at least to a candidate's poll numbers.

Had I been alone, I would have been discreetly pulled aside, queried, probably searched, and almost certainly denied access once they performed a cursory check and noted that I had bought my seats the same day and had no connection to either the party nor anyone at the event. Better to refund a few thousand bucks than to invite very public outbursts from some disgruntled vet.

But Wren attracted the eye, to put it mildly. Once the guards had decided my presence was an acceptable risk, no one paid me any heed.

"Drink?" I asked. Wren agreed and we drifted toward a gold-draped table covered with trays of canapes and tiny quiches. Two servers stood at parade rest, offering prepoured champagne as guests drew near.

I didn't see Palmer Stratton among the fluted glasses and speckled neckties. Only five weeks until the election. I knew just enough about campaigns to assume Stratton would have an event scheduled every available minute of his day. He would probably appear through some private entrance after the dinner, make his stump speech and shake a few hands, half of his mind already on whatever function was scheduled right after this.

If all went well, I'd have ten seconds to grab his attention. Ideally without getting the rental cops involved.

"Ladies and gentlemen, if you'll take your seats," a staffer near us proclaimed, his arm outstretched toward the banquet room. Wren and I joined the migration and wound through a small jungle of circular tables to the front row. Table 7 was set near stage left, with an unobstructed view of the podium.

Hotel waiters circled, doling out bread baskets and pitchers of iced tea. The other guests at the table began to exchange names. They were all middle-aged couples, save for one lean older woman to Wren's left, in a dress-and-jacket combo whose shimmering gray color emphasized her nimbus of white hair.

"Margaret Stratton," she said to us as the introductions came around.

I'd already placed her, from the news videos. Palmer Stratton's mother. As the wife of the late congressman and mother of the Democratic hopeful, she'd been in front of the cameras nearly as much as her son recently. Breeding and probably something like equestrian sports had kept her posture youthful.

"I'm Van, this is Wren," I said.

"A Sounders game," Wren said with a note of surprise. "Sorry, but I just realized that's where I've seen you before, Mrs. Stratton. Last June. You were introducing a youth group at halftime."

"The Junior Strikers," said Mrs. Stratton. "You certainly have a good memory. My husband, James, started that team for underprivileged children, after he left Congress. Part of our Stratton Foundation."

"Soccer and sailboats," I said. "The Stratton Regatta was a few weeks ago. I saw the coverage." The cynical part of me wanted to ask if the deprived kids served as deckhands, but I figured that would be unproductive.

"Anything we can do for our city." Margaret Stratton nodded magnanimously. The royal "we," perhaps. "Are you involved with the campaign?"

"I aim to be," I said. "Your son is something else."

She smiled. "I happen to agree."

A three-person camera crew had set up at stage right, running prechecks at the podium. Ready to get a clip from Stratton's speech for the late news. The ambient jazz music dimmed and a woman with a blond pageboy and scarlet dress spoke into the podium's microphone.

"Good evening, and welcome," she said, beaming at the assembled donors. "I'm very pleased to announce a change for tonight. We've moved up our guest of honor's schedule so that he can take the time to meet you personally." A few people in the crowd murmured appreciatively. "Please welcome the next governor of the great state of Washington, United States Attorney Palmer Stratton!"

Stratton strode out of the wings and gave a big wave and even bigger smile to the room, as the guests obediently burst into applause.

In person, he looked tanned and nearly overflowing with good health. His indigo suit had been expertly tailored to encompass his college-wrestler shoulders and to conceal the stubborn few pounds around his middle that had accumulated in the quarter century since. Combined with a jewel-toned red tie and the gray at his temples that might have been tamed by a careful dye job, Stratton's whole image walked a line between old-money confidence and new-economy flash.

After a moment of Stratton soaking in the welcome, a brunette woman who was his equal for glossy attractiveness joined him onstage. I wondered if her dress had been chosen to match his tie, or if the tie had been made to match the dress. The blonde with the pageboy handed Stratton a microphone.

"Thank you for coming, everyone," he said. "Carolyn and I are delighted to be here, and even happier that we'll have a chance to thank you for your support in person. But I won't make you wait for your meals all the way through a stump speech. Not even mine." A ripple of laughter from the audience. "We'll say a quick hello while you enjoy the hors d'oeuvres and then get back to what's important." Stratton waved once more and took his wife's hand. On cue, the boisterous jazz music swelled again.

They came down the steps from the stage and immediately began shaking hands at the first VIP table. Everyone around us rose to their feet. Wren looked at me in amusement—*I guess this is how this works*—as we stood, too.

The campaign staffers quickly combined forces to herd the premier guests at the front into something resembling a queue. Rather than us filing past Stratton, he moved along the loose row, both preceded and followed at a discreet few feet by two of the blue blazers, who kept their eyes on the crowd. I pasted a smile on my face.

Stratton and his wife took no more than thirty seconds to greet each guest, and the donor had the full focus of his attention during that time. It seemed to be enough. Each guest went away looking a little dazed. I'd heard once that Bill Clinton had a similar effect on people, making them feel, however temporarily, like the most important individual in the room.

Busy with each VIP in turn, Stratton never looked to the next person. Never saw my face until he was already shaking my hand. Give him due credit. He had only seen me once before, in the state patrol station, but there was no question that he recognized me in that first instant.

"Mr. Stratton, Donovan Shaw," I said immediately, hoping security wouldn't notice the astonished expression that had swept the candidate's persistent smile away. "I've followed your time as our federal attorney, and it's made a huge impression."

"Well," Stratton said. His shake of my hand was much slower than the quick three-beat clasp he'd delivered to others. "That's very good to hear, Mr. . . . Shaw."

"Building a platform on your prosecution record, that's a solid foundation. I know a lot of people who put crime safety as their number one priority."

The candidate's eyes narrowed in calculation. This close, I could tell the suntan was mostly makeup, expertly applied for the cameras. Was I here to disrupt the event? Embarrass him somehow? "What sort of work do you do?"

"Freelance journalism. A new line for me, covering trade with Eastern Europe."

Stratton nodded, ignoring the staffer who was subtly trying to herd him onward. His public mask was back, but even as his body turned to greet Wren, his gaze stayed on me. "That sounds very interesting. Hello."

"Hello," Wren said, as poised as if there was no tension in the air at all. "Raina Marchand."

"Very pleased. How did you come to be involved, Ms. Marchand?" Stratton's laser attention had redirected to Wren, but I expected the question applied to us both.

"I'm active in environmental causes," she said. "My friends and I have a kind of task force."

I nearly snorted. Wren was a natural at sticking the jab.

"I see," said Stratton. His teeth behind the smile might have been gritted. "Very nice to meet you both."

After an extremely brief acknowledgment from Stratton's wife, Carolyn, who looked slightly confused by our exchange, the couple moved on to the next table. Wren and I sat. Margaret Stratton had disappeared during the receiving line—I imagine she'd had her fill of those recently—and we could speak without being overheard.

"That was strangely fun, poking the bear," she murmured to me. "Now what?"

I was watching Stratton. He glanced once in our direction, then leaned to speak a few quiet words in the ear of a campaign sheepdog. The staffer nodded briskly before hustling up the steps and backstage.

"Now we think about what restaurant we'll go to," I said. "I don't expect we'll be staying for dinner."

It took ten minutes for Stratton to finish greeting the donors at the premier tables. The blond assistant murmured in Stratton's ear, and he gave a quick wave to the camera crew before exiting into the wings.

A security man tapped my shoulder.

"Would you accompany me, sir?" he said.

I nodded as if I'd been expecting the summons since I first arrived. Our friends at the table looked uncertain, not sure if I was receiving preferential treatment or the bum's rush. Neither was I, but I smiled like I held the winning hand.

Wren cocked an eyebrow. "I'll make sure the champagne doesn't get lonely."

The security man led me around the far side of the stage to a door used by hotel staff. Beyond it was a short hallway with the sounds of a kitchen in full swing coming from the end, a melody of clattering pans and shouted orders. I was hit with the scents of vinaigrette and searing beef. The guard led me halfway down the hall and stepped aside to allow me to enter a side room, then closed its door behind me.

The room might have normally served as a meeting space for hotel staff, with framed Alexis promotional materials from years past on the taupe fabric walls. Now the furniture had been cleared to allow room for a studio-quality interview. Lamps and broad white fabric reflectors formed a loose circle around two high chairs at one end.

A makeup station, its mirror emblazoned with glowing bulbs, waited to one side. I walked over to it, noting the stained applicators and sweat pads and hairbrush neatly arrayed in case the candidate required a touch-up during the filming.

Stratton entered as I was adjusting my new tie in the mirror. He motioned to another guard in the hall before shutting the door.

"We can speak privately. And I'll spare two minutes, so let's dispense

with the bullshit." His natural speaking voice was flatter and less resonant than the baritone he used for the public. "Why are you here, Shaw?"

"To reach an agreement. About Anatoly Liashko, and your task
force."

"Stop there. I'm not discussing any part of any investigation with you."

"So I'll do the talking. Your ATF agent, Martens. He has an informant." I glanced at the door, conscious of the guard somewhere outside.
"I won't say his name out in the open, but you know who he is. You'd
have to know, as head prosecutor."

He stared. Hard to interpret the look on his face, but it might have
been dread peeking through.

"No matter what happens with your case," I said, "I want that inside
man protected."

Stratton reassembled his hard expression. "What's your interest?"

I shook my head. Burke and I could keep our questions of family to
ourselves.

"Martens already made you an offer," Stratton said. "You didn't follow
through. You've done jack to demand any concessions."

"What if I could find where Liashko is holding weapons? On U.S.
soil?"

His face tightened. "If you have information pertinent to this case,
you'll give it to us. Immediately. Or I promise I will bust you as an acces-
sory and find a way to make it stick."

"In which case you get nothing. My way, at least you secure the arms.
Maybe even get the drop on Liashko when he shows."

"This is national security, Shaw. You could wind up in ADX Florence
for the next twenty years, playing checkers using scraps of felt alongside
domestic terrorists. You lump yourself in with those traitors?"

My expression was another answer.

"So prove it to me," Stratton pressed.

"Your inside man," I said. "Arrest, no arrest, complete clusterfuck, I
don't care—no backing out on your deal with him."

"Just assuming there was a source, that person would be protected.
My word on it."

"Not enough. I want that protection guaranteed. Otherwise he's dead. You know that's the only outcome if Liashko goes free. And then you'll have a new problem."

"A threat," Stratton scoffed.

"I'd never threaten a federal prosecutor. But it's just as dumb to expect I'll keep quiet if this goes off the rails. '*U.S. Attorney Abandons Federal Informant to Mobster from Russia.*' It'll look like you manipulated the task force to try and score a political win in time for the election."

"That's completely false." The candidate's brow furrowed. His makeup would definitely need a retouch.

"I don't care. I have enough provable facts to point CNN and Fox and everyone else in the right direction. Like you said, I'll find a way to make it stick."

He crossed his arms. "There's a natural reaction to that action. State investigators will rake over everything you've done and everywhere you've been since the Army kicked your ass home. Including whatever went down in Oregon last year. Griffon County still has a few unanswered questions." He nodded. "There's no need for us to be on opposite sides. Give me what you have, and I'll do everything I can."

"Including the WITSEC deal in writing. If I locate Liashko's stash, I'll give you all you need to nail him. If I can't find it, you've lost nothing."

"Don't play brinksmanship with me, Shaw. You'll lose."

"We'll both go down." I knocked on the door, and the guard dutifully opened it. "You just have farther to fall."

FORTY-EIGHT

THE GUARD ESCORTED ME AROUND the back hallways of the Alexis, emerging at the lobby. Wren met me by the revolving doors.

"Well, you're not in handcuffs," she said, "and I didn't see a SWAT team run past while they were passing out the salads. Was it a win?"

"It was a draw," I said.

"Always take the draw. Tell people the refs made bad calls."

"Sorry if they hustled you out."

"They were very polite. The blond woman with the diamond studs and the DNC pin told me you'd be in the lobby in five minutes. I saw the entrees on a tray as I left. I'm sorry to miss out on the salmon."

"I'm hungry, too."

"Which raises the topic of my second condition for attending this crazy night with you."

"You want to pick where we have dinner?"

"I want room service."

"From the Alexis? I'm not sure we're *persona grata* here anymore."

"From another place. The Hotel Max is nice."

"So to get room service, we'd have to have . . ."

"A room. Yes. You said your place is kind of trashed, and I share my house with three other people. You're grinning. Is that good?"

"I told Addy you were direct. *That's* good."

"Then let's go. The sooner we're checked in, the sooner we order. I'm famished."

DINNER WAS DELAYED. BY THE time Wren and I walked to the Max and got a room and exchanged jokes about the dramatic black-and-white photographs that swathed every door on the hallway of the fifth floor, we'd distracted one another from the idea of food. Those intentions were sidetracked even further once she passed close to me entering the room, and I kissed her. Then all other plans went completely off the rails, as her dress slid off in one soft rustle to form a midnight-blue pool around her heels.

LATER, LYING ATOP THE BEDSPREAD we'd never gotten around to pulling down, I discovered that Wren's spiral of eponymous tattoos ended at her shoulder blade. I touched the last bird in the line—intentionally blurred ink mimicking watercolor paint—and traced the natural evolution of where future birds might join the procession. The line made a path down and across her spine, nearly touching the top of her childhood scar.

"If you left Seattle, where would you go next?" I said.

"Getting rid of me already? I see how this is," Wren murmured into the sheet.

"Do you keep heading west? Hawaii? The Philippines?"

She laughed. "I've never been to Alaska. Not sure what medicines I could grow there." She rolled onto her side and moved back to lean against me. "You came back to Seattle after the Army."

"Yeah. That was almost happenstance. I came home on leave, took up with somebody when I was here. So when my time was up, I came back to Seattle to keep seeing her."

"Are you still?"

"No."

"But you call it home."

"I guess I do. I never thought about where I'd settle once I was a civilian again, because I never thought I'd *be* a civilian again. Now that I'm here . . ." I shrugged. "It feels right. I like the city. I like how I can find almost anything but still run across people I recognize every day, like it's a small town. I like how insane the landscape is."

"Lettie says it's changed so much just in the past few years. All the industry coming in, people who started here can't afford to live here anymore."

"True. I sold a plot of land in the city last year for what would buy a new house most places."

Wren turned her head. The sharp outline of her profile looked like a cameo against the snow-white pillow we'd tossed aside earlier. Her hair smelled of limes and something like honey.

"You don't have to worry I'll vanish," she said. "If that's what you were asking."

"Good to know. Who would pay the hotel bill?"

"Not tonight." She laughed. "I mean Seattle. I don't do that, leave all at once. There's a whole decision tree and a lot of conversation with my tribe."

"Tribe?"

"My friends. You call your Rangers brothers, my friends are my tribe. Occasionally people decide to move together. A built-in support network when you get to wherever you're going."

"I hear Montreal is nice."

"It is. *Parles-tu français?*"

"Not a word," I said. "The Army had no plans to send me and my brothers into Quebec. At least not that they shared. How many languages do you know?"

"Five if I stretch the truth. My Spanish didn't get far after we left Morocco. Speaking of stretching . . ."

My hand had been cupping Wren's breast, and she unfolded her arms to reach splendidly toward the headboard. I trailed my fingertips lower.

"That's nice," she whispered after a few moments. "A little harder."

"Like that?" I said into the nape of her neck.

Wren hummed assent. "I'm getting the strong impression"—her breath hitched and gasped before continuing—"that we're postponing dinner for dessert again."

"I can wait."

She rolled over so that we faced one another. Her pupils so wide and dark, the irises showing around them were mere halos of chestnut brown, sparkling with amber.

"Prove it," she said.

FORTY-NINE

A T THREE MINUTES TO MIDNIGHT, the only sounds in the boatyard of the *Oxana M* were the deep rumble from a recycling plant farther up the stunted street and the almost musical clink created by the chain-link fence each time I cut one of its wires. Past the fence, towers of shipping containers in the gloom made a kind of huge metal maze, with each stack standing in for a hedge. Or a tombstone.

The tiny snap as the last wire parted was lost in the echoing boom of an explosion from the far side of the freighter. A rage of light threw the massive span of the *Oxana M* into dark relief and deepened the shadows for a quarter mile, including those around me.

Perfect. In black clothes and a balaclava over my head to hide my face, the dark was on my side tonight.

It wasn't much of a blast in terms of concussive force. But it was loud and blindingly bright, thanks to the flammable slurry I'd cooked up filling half of my new rowboat. New, and now destroyed. The fireworks had provided the boom and enough flame to ignite the rest of the boat into a miniature but very garish Viking funeral, lacking only the corpse.

Crude, but I'd needed something quick and easy for Jaak and his buddies. When we'd met that afternoon to discuss my idea over a lunch of meat pies and beer, Jaak's shipmate Harri had done the translating. The sailors couldn't keep the grins off their faces, and they toasted the audacity of the notion, or maybe just the chance to raise some hell.

His crew had used my speedboat to tow the rowboat up the Duwamish. When they were a few dozen yards off the *Oxana M*, they'd lit the long fuse on the giant firecracker, cut the rowboat loose, and hauled ass out of there. Right on time.

I twisted the fence aside and wormed my way under, ducking low to keep my small rucksack from catching on the cut wires. Then I ran like hell through the towers of cargo containers toward the looming hull of the ship.

The first burst of light from the explosion had dimmed into a flickering glow that danced off the *Oxana M*'s twin cranes. By now the freighter's crew would be gathered at starboard, staring at the impromptu show. I hoped. The fire wouldn't burn forever. Speed was as important as silence in getting aboard unseen. I took the steep gangway stairs to the deck three at a time.

At the top, the passage was clear. I could see the heads of crew members twenty yards across the deck at the far rail. Words in a Slavic language drifted my way in between laughter and shouts of encouragement to the blaze.

Between us, the broad gap of the aft hold yawned. A sharply sloped lip as tall as my shoulder ringed its edge, prevention against any sailor stumbling and falling a hundred feet from the deck to the very bottom of the open hold, well below the ship's waterline.

That was where I needed to be. I slipped away toward the bow, in search of the nearest stairwell.

Most of the ship's living and working spaces were housed in the three-story superstructure at the stern. Any crew not watching the burning boat from the deck should be there. Nevertheless, I cat-footed my way down an access corridor and four spiraling flights of stairs, then softly twisted both handles to unlock a watertight door to the aft hold.

It was like opening the door to a cathedral. A vast vertical emptiness seemed to extend high enough to touch the overcast sky. The lowest levels of the hold were stepped, three gigantic stairs on each side climbing the curve of the hull, adding to the sudden feeling of insignificance. I held on to the door for an extra moment to steady myself. Voices from the men high overhead might as well have been jeering at me.

This hold was empty, save for stifling vapors of fuel and oil that had sunk to the lowest part of the vessel. The *Oxana M* had two more holds the same size, each large enough to carry nearly a hundred forty-foot shipping containers in tight stacks.

I didn't need a hundred, just one, half that size. So long as it was the right one.

At the forward end of the immense interior was another watertight door, to allow crew to move between holds without retreating to the upper decks. I ran to it, conscious of the fact that any sailor who grew bored of watching the blaze outside might cast his eye downward into the hold and spot me scurrying around its sides like a mouse in an empty trash dumpster.

The door opened into a passageway cutting across the ship. I shut it behind me and tried the one opposite, to enter the midship hold.

There. One twenty-foot steel box, painted dark green, alone in the cavernous space. Liashko's smuggled container. I was sure I'd found it, even before my eyes had pieced together the identification code stenciled on its door. The white paint of each letter and number virtually glowed through the murk.

A C-shaped padlock sealed the container. I felt in my sleeve for the leather wrist brace I'd fashioned recently. The brace held my basic set of lockpicks on the inside of my forearm, for quicker access than fumbling in my pocket. I selected the right pick and opened the lock purely by feel.

Before touching the twin handles on the container door, I paused to listen. The voices above had quieted. The fire would have burned out, maybe even sunk the sorry rowboat entirely. I cautiously pulled at the handles to turn the door's lock rods, grateful to whatever dockworker had greased the rods half a world away.

The door came loose with a hollow reverberation, signaling that the steel box wasn't completely full. I entered and pulled the door closed behind me.

My arm brushed something flat and solid as I removed my flashlight from my belt. The beam bounced off long black crates stacked high on both sides. Plastic straps secured each individual crate to the container's sides, proof against foul weather. A gap down the center between the two stacks let me estimate their dimensions. Each crate was about seven feet long and eighteen inches square at the ends.

Just about the right size to hold what I'd expected.

I pushed the crate at the top, testing its weight. It shifted, barely. Two quick slices and its plastic restraints fell aside, allowing me to ease the crate—well over a hundred pounds, the cords in my neck standing out with the strain—silently off the stack to set it on the floor.

Twists of wire sealed the crate's latches. My blade cut those nearly as fast as it had the straps. I opened the lid.

The six-foot tube of the Verba missile launcher cushioned in molded foam padding looked deceptively innocent. Not much different than a length of metal pipe painted olive green. A trigger mechanism like an oversized pistol grip was detached and waiting in its own foam slot.

I lifted the tube out to look into its muzzle.

There was no mistaking the intent of the slim gray dart housed within. The surface-to-air missile was nearly as long as the launching tube itself, a malevolent needle packing enough speed and power to bring down damn near anything flying below fifteen thousand feet.

Under the tube, the crate held two more missiles just like it. Three to a box. Forty crates. One hundred and twenty in all.

That was three times as many as Burke had said the task force was buying. Which meant Liashko must have other customers. Jesus. Did Burke know?

There was something else here, too, at the very back of the container between the stacks. A silver metal case, smaller than the crates holding the missiles. Not much larger than my rucksack. I left the Verba to cut the case's straps and latches, then opened the lid for a look.

And nearly choked. I removed my hands from the case and stepped back immediately. A reaction as instinctive as if I'd opened the lid to find a cobra.

Nestled within the foam pads were twelve slim canisters of light, clear plastic. Every one of them bearing a large red-and-white label with the unmistakable tripod symbol for chemical weapons.

Nerve gas.

I told myself that it was safe to breathe. That the canisters couldn't be armed. My body didn't seem convinced, and my next few inhalations came shallow and quick.

Each canister was bisected by a slim metallic layer, with a pull-tab extending from it like a stubby tail. Their tops contained a blue-tinged liquid. At the bottom, a gray granular substance.

I remembered a few basics of bioweapon chemistry from the Army's defensive training. Nerve agents had a limited shelf life. Their components would have to be combined shortly before use. Pull the tab, allow the two halves to mix, and the canister was armed and ready to be deployed.

Deployed by missile, maybe. I comprehended an even more horrific use for the Verbas resting in their dark beds.

Anatoly's looking to close up shop, Burke had said. *Everything he stole, in one go.*

The task force had assumed they were buying Liashko's entire job lot. They weren't even close. The arms dealer apparently had other deals to make, other customers here in the land of opportunity. He'd kept Burke in the dark because that was the paranoid's MO.

What was the chemical? Sarin? VX? My stomach twisted, imagining how many dozens or hundreds of people would die in agony if even one of these canisters was detonated and dispersed over a crowded area.

Screw the arms deal. Time for the cavalry—ATF, National Guard, whoever could secure the nerve gas and transport it to where it could be safely destroyed.

I checked my phone. No signal. The steel container and the ship's hull beyond were impenetrable.

The whirring of an engine from above brought me out of my shocked reflection. I closed the case just as a second noise followed, a heavy reverberating clank of metal on metal. Close. Closer than something moving up on deck. I killed the flashlight.

Pushing the container door open an inch, I looked up toward the open hatch. The heads of crewmen at the lip of the hold showed as silhouettes against the deck lights and the night sky. I ducked back and silently shut the door again.

Shit. I would have to wait until they'd finished whatever work had them so busy at midnight. Maybe setting the rowboat on fire had prompted some kind of safety drill—

BANG

I flinched and nearly stumbled. The impact had been right over my head, on the roof of the container.

Oh, hell no. I realized what the sound meant, even as the sides of the container creaked with sudden pressure. I reached for the loose door and grabbed the retaining straps of the stacked crates with my other hand. Only an instant before the container with me inside it soared skyward, borne by the crane that clutched the big steel box like a scorpion claw on a doomed cricket.

FIFTY

T HE ABRUPT ACCELERATION THREATENED TO swing the container's heavy
door open. I threw all my weight into holding it shut. The missile
crates shifted against the straps, mashing my hand. I gritted my teeth
until the pain in them matched that in my finger bones.

In another five seconds the vertical motion abruptly stopped, only to
be replaced by a seesawing tilt and a feeling of acceleration that dropped
my stomach down to my knees. The Stygian dark inside the container
added to the sudden vertigo. But the slant of the huge steel box kept the
loose door closed. For the moment. Any tip in the other direction, and
the door would fly wide open, with me sailing out after it.

The container dropped in a barely controlled descent. I had an instant to brace myself before it hit the deck of the *Oxana M* with a scraping thud that must have removed metal along with paint. With another
creak and the whir of moving cable, the crane released its hold on the
roof.

I yanked my hand out from under the crushing straps, flexing my
fingers and willing some feeling back into them. A slender glowing line
appeared at the top of the container door, drawn by powerful deck lamps
high on the comm tower at the ship's bow.

Almost taunting, that sliver of light, with the rest of the interior so dark I couldn't see the wall inches from my face.

Someone might approach at any second. They couldn't miss noticing that the container wasn't locked tight. Then they would check the cargo.

Or, worse, just lock me in.

I would have to break for it the instant they came near the door. Count on surprise to buy me a second, maybe two. Run toward the gangway or jump for the water? Whichever direction looked less likely to get my head smashed in with a wrench.

A moment passed. I heard voices only yards away. I crouched, ready to spring.

Then the floor of the container buzzed, vibrated, rumbled. The feeling of the ship's propellers, surging into action.

The *Oxana M* was moving.

Christ. I was out of options. It would have to be the water. Jump off the port side and swim to shore. The river wasn't so wide that I couldn't make it, even through the bone-chilling cold.

I was about to launch myself out of the blackness when I remembered the nerve gas.

I couldn't leave the canisters behind. My escape and the havoc it would raise would undoubtedly force Liashko to change all of his plans. Including the deal Burke had arranged with Agent Martens and the Feds. Liashko would escape on the next flight across the Pacific, and who knew where his lethal stock would wind up?

Even if it meant never catching the evil bastard, I couldn't let this chance slip away. The nerve agent was too dangerous. Too easy to hide. Secure the chemical weapons now and let fate sort out Liashko. And Burke, too, if it came to that.

I moved to the rear of the container and knelt to open the crate again by touch. The steel floor quivered with the ship as the engines increased speed, pushing the freighter faster toward the Sound.

With my jacket wrapped around the flashlight to narrow its beam, I set each cylinder of nerve gas—very carefully—to one side. The foam pads I tore into chunks to line my rucksack. Working as fast as I dared, it took fifteen minutes to pack the canisters firmly into place.

I shone the beam around the container to make sure I'd found them all. My ruck stuffed full of padding and poison looked like a nest. I'd stolen real eggs, Aura's eggs, only a week before. Those had held the infinite promise of new life. These would birth only horror, and anguish, and death. I strapped the ruck to my back and peered out through the cracked door to the deck.

Empty. Maybe fifteen long paces to the starboard side. Beyond the rail, the lights of the city had receded into glittering specks, as if borne away in the freighter's wake.

Too far for me to swim to shore now. I would never survive, especially not loaded down with the rucksack. Its twenty kilos might not bear me under the waves immediately, but after a quarter mile or more, with the cold sapping my strength . . .

A boat. I would slip away to another part of the deck, steal a lifeboat with an engine or even just an emergency zodiac inflatable and some oars. Anything would do now.

I slipped out of the container, closed the door to refasten its padlock, and walked directly to the rail. Voices and the faintest hint of cigarette smoke drifted back to me. The wind so frigid that the skin around my eyes creased defensively.

A steel ladder led to the deck immediately below. I stole down the rungs and into a passage that led along the port side of the ship.

We were changing course. The curved phosphorescent wake off the stern showed our path turning northwest. Moving fast, fifteen knots at least, out of Elliott Bay and into the open Sound.

The *Oxana M* was in a rush. To where? To meet Liashko? Or had Liashko decided to abandon Seattle and the arms deals altogether?

It wouldn't change my plan. Find a boat and escape and call the cavalry. I crept along the passageway.

Footsteps. Clanging on stairs forty feet ahead, descending from the deck above. More than one person. I tried the nearest door. Unlocked. I ducked into the darkened room and shut the door again, just as the steps reached the passageway.

The steps were heavy but not fast. Two men, ambling along the deck, talking in what I took to be Russian. They halted just outside.

"I see you," the voice said in English.

I froze. My hand was on the Colt in its holster. I wasn't about to shoot any of the crew—hell, the sailors aboard may not even know who they were working for—but the sight of the gun might at least keep anyone from getting aggressive.

"Follow us out," the voice continued. A thick Slavic accent. "No, farther than so little. Another ten minutes. Anatoly is here."

Anatoly. The room had a porthole. I risked a look.

The one speaking held a phone to his ear with one hand and a powerful set of binoculars to his eyes with the other, looking somewhere northwest of the ship. I guessed him for an officer, probably the captain. He wore a brimmed cap and a thick blue coat and pants as wards against the cold, along with a bristly beard that started at his cheekbones and extended to his chest.

The second man stepped into view to snatch the phone. Big all over, with rolls of fat on the back of his bull neck and a belly that pushed out his fine black overcoat like it had been draped over a globe.

"Do you have it?" he said into the phone. I knew that resonant voice. The last time I'd heard it, I'd been covered in the gore of the killers he'd sent after me. Liashko.

An errant gust pushed his sparse black hair vertical, and he turned to impatiently smooth it back down. His head was round and his cheeks pink and hairless, like an infant's. But the glaring piggish eyes conveyed as much malice as the poison I carried in my ruck.

"And the landing?" Liashko said to the caller. "We will not be seen when the barge goes to shore?"

A barge. They must be rendezvousing offshore with another vessel, making an exchange there.

It made sense. The *Oxana M* had its own cranes to offload the shipping container, if that was their aim. In the dead of night, miles off land, the chances of being seen were minuscule.

I heard the captain speaking quietly into a radio. Almost simultaneously, the lights in the passage outside went out. Dimming the ship to running lights only for their clandestine meeting. The two men walked away. I exited the room a moment later.

The captain had said he could see the other ship, the barge. On the western side of the Sound. I couldn't spot it myself. Off the port rail, ebony water tipped with silver from reflected moonlight stretched for miles. A low strip of peninsula in the distance almost part of the horizon.

I tried my phone again. Nothing. Too far from shore. Liashko and the captain had been using a satellite phone. If I could find another like it on board, or get to a radio—

The steady hum of the engines lowered in pitch. We were slowing. Preparing to heave to and meet the barge.

Footsteps again, on the deck above. If I was too late to stop what was happening, I could at least get a look at who was taking ownership of the missiles. Enough to give the Feds a proper description as soon as I found a way off this heap.

The shipping container with the arms was near the bow. It followed that most of the crew would be either working there or staying warm inside the superstructure at the stern, walking a direct path back and forth on the main deck. This lower level should be clear.

But the long passageway on the port side offered no hiding places. I hunched low and headed forward on the ship, looking for a vantage point.

Farther along, the passageway opened out to span the full width of the ship. Two winches like huge toadstools, each as tall as my chest, flanked an open hatch on the deck floor. With the deck lights turned off, it took my eyes a moment to adjust and see what lay within the hatch. Heavy mooring rope, as thick as my arm. Another coiled pile of rope made a mound near the port siderail. The rail at this part of the deck had a two-foot-high gap underneath, to allow the mooring lines to run from the winches off the ship to a dock.

It would have to suffice for cover. Already the thrum of the propellers had changed again, becoming hollow. The engine in reverse, to stop the ship's leviathan momentum. I squatted beside the mound of coiled rope and looked out through the mooring gap in the rail.

A boat was drawing along the port side of the *Oxana M.* Liashko had called it a barge, and I had pictured something like a trash scow in my mind.

But this was something different. A vehicle ferry, made to transport a dozen or more cars and trucks. With the pilot's cabin at the rear and a ramp at the bow, almost the entire deck was usable smooth space for passengers.

The barge carried only two vehicles. A heavy-duty flatbed truck and a car.

A *cop* car. What the hell?

The cruiser was a chalk-white Chevy Caprice PPV, its push bumper and LED light bar on the roof readily visible from my bird's-eye view. I squinted to make out the dark blue insignia on its door: Washington State Patrol.

Was the sting already running? Had I stumbled into the middle of it?

Footsteps and voices overlapped on the deck above as the crew ran to throw lines to the waiting barge. A guy in coveralls emerged from the pilothouse of the barge to catch and secure one line to the barge's bow. A second man, a state trooper in a black winter coat and gray Smokey Bear hat, stepped out from between the vehicles to grab the line dangling at the stern.

No. Not a trooper. Just a man wearing the uniform.

Sean Burke.

FIFTY-ONE

BURKE WAS HERE. WORKING FOR Liashko, helping to smuggle the container of weapons ashore. He must have known the missiles were on board to prepare this rendezvous on the water. There would be no tactical team coming. If Burke had signaled Martens, they would have descended on the *Oxana M* before it cast off the first mooring line. He'd sold us out.

Above me, I heard the whir of cables and clank of the crane's jaws as it grabbed hold of the cargo again.

It wasn't tough to predict their next moves. They would place the container on the flatbed truck. Take the barge to shore. The boat had a shallow draft and the extendable loading ramp at its bow. They could set ashore at any boat launch, or even on a beach. And simply drive away, with Burke in his WSP disguise and stolen patrol car running interference, making sure that the truck reached whatever destination they intended. A hiding place? A buyer?

It didn't matter now. All that mattered was making sure I got the cops here before that truck reached shore. After that, the missiles might vanish.

A radio. There would be one on the bridge, and backup handheld sets around with the crew. I'd take the whole place hostage if I had to, set off every flare gun on board, just to hail the Coast Guard.

But I was already too late.

I never knew whether I had been spotted, or whether the four men had simply been taking an alternate path down the starboard passageway to cut across the deck. But they had been quiet. Even as I whipped around, they were already raising their guns, overcoming the shock of spotting me and yelling in multiple languages for me to halt.

Sailors, two of them, from their oil-stained weather gear. The other two wore street clothes, puffed vests and turtlenecks and woolen pants. Handguns for the sailors, AK-12 assault rifles in pixelated khaki camo for the city boys. Liashko's men, I was sure.

They grabbed me and threw me to the deck. Hands relieved me of my gun, emptied my pockets, and tore the balaclava off my head and the rucksack from my back. I yelled for them to be careful with it, and one of them kicked me in the side. After that I was no trouble at all. The crewmen hauled me to my feet and manhandled me up to the main deck.

Dazed, for an instant I thought I was lying on the ground again. But it was the container that was high, swooping overhead on its journey to the barge.

The wind at the bow whipped at our hair and clothes and even blew the last of my dizziness away. Liashko stood at the ship's rail, looking down at the barge as his steel box filled with one hundred and twenty Verba missiles was lowered to the waiting truck.

One of his men stepped forward to speak to him in Russian, before handing over the rucksack. Liashko's face, already glowering, began to seethe. He tore at the top flap, yanking the ruck open to look inside. His eyes went wide with terror. But he managed to keep a grip on the ruck and the canisters of death staring him in the face.

He turned to look at the green shipping container on the barge, then back at me.

"How do you have this?" he said, holding out the rucksack as if for me to look inside.

I didn't answer. Liashko said a word and one of his bodyguards punched me in the gut. I'd already tightened in expectation, but the blow still hurt like hell coming right after the kick to my ribs. I might have fallen if the sailors weren't still holding my arms. When I looked up again Liashko was pointing, ordering the crew to do something. The captain, standing behind me, spoke as well. From the side deck, a gangway began to lower to the barge.

Liashko and the captain got into a shouting match. The arms trafficker was furious about the stowaway and the near loss of his property. Around me, I could feel the bodyguards edging back, uncertain about the sudden tension from the crew all around them. Then the captain was marching down the gangplank to the barge, followed by Liashko and his two men, who herded me in front of them like a reluctant sheep.

Should I dive for it? The water here had to be something like forty-five degrees. A bullet would be much faster, and no less certain to end it all.

We reached the barge. A chop had risen with the wind, and the barge bobbed on the waves. Each man wavered unsteadily for a moment as they acclimated to the motion.

"Who the fuck is he?" Burke said, stepping forward. His eyes met mine. Rage? Or fear that I would give him away?

"It's him. Shaw, the thief," Liashko said.

"Can't be," Burke said. "Shaw's dead."

Liashko stared at me. Was I the same man? My scars hadn't been showing in the pictures he'd seen of my dead body. My standing here, very much alive, gave him cause to doubt his memory.

"Hiding aboard and looking to steal money," the captain said.

"No." Liashko brandished the rucksack. "He took these."

From his pocket he removed a set of keys and handed them to Burke. "Open it."

The barge pilot had been busy securing the container to the flatbed with chains and restraining straps. Burke stepped around him to climb onto the truck and remove the padlock. Liashko shouted at the pilot, who hurried to turn on the headlights of the state patrol car and illuminate the container just as Burke swung its door wide. Liashko stepped closer to see. I was shunted along by the muzzles of the armed bodyguards.

If the two thugs split up and I could take one by surprise, I'd have a chance. A lousy one, on this small boat with nearly no cover, but something.

Liashko swore at the sight of the open missile crate. He turned to grab me with both hands by the throat.

"Who are you?" he hollered, flecks of spit flying. He was strong. Even with my neck muscles tensed, his thumbs crushed my windpipe. Shining spots materialized in my vision, a mottled constellation on Liashko's enraged pink face.

Fuck it. Go down swinging. I went limp, sagging against the arms of the crewmen holding me, and just as abruptly sprang back up to headbutt Liashko in the teeth. He fell back and his hands dropped from my neck.

I didn't get to enjoy the moment. Something hard smacked me on the skull, and this time I folded for real. Another kick sent me over sideways.

"Don't!" Burke's voice. "Don't shoot him yet. He might have stolen more. Or booby-trapped it."

Liashko cursed again and spat on the deck. His men yanked my arms behind me once more and I felt handcuffs—probably taken from Burke's WSP service belt—click tight around my wrists. The sailors yanked me upright and frog-marched me to the patrol cruiser. One of the bodyguards opened the back door and I ducked just in time to save my head another bad knock as they tossed me headlong inside.

I wrestled myself upright. My side ached from the kicks. Looking through the clear plastic barrier between the backseat and the front compartment and the car's windshield I had a view of the back of the flatbed, and the collection of angry men standing between the truck and the freighter's massive hull. Burke and the captain were arguing now. Liashko held a handkerchief to his face. Red dappled the ivory cloth. Good. *A gift from me, you son of a bitch.*

Bravado. I'd failed, and now both the missiles and the nerve gas were back in Liashko's hands. And Burke's. My wave of hatred for both men almost overwhelmed the dread of the bad ending I knew must be in store for me. Soon.

Liashko shouted both men down, and now the captain seemed to be on the receiving end of his rage again. The barge pilot in the coveralls was inside the container, maybe checking the arms. He leaned out to show the Verba launching tube from the crate I'd opened, which seemed to infuriate Liashko further. His bodyguards had fanned out.

I saw what was about to happen before the crewmen did. Even before Burke did, and he began to move in the next instant. The bodyguards raised their rifles and fired. The two sailors didn't even have time for a look of surprise before they died. That left the captain, who lifted his hands as if to wave away the oncoming rounds half a second before they tore open his chest. He fell between the barge and his ship, into the water.

More gunfire now. Coming from above, from the deck of the freighter. I hit the floor of the cruiser. One bullet spider-webbed the car's windshield and another punched a tiny hole through the roof of the cruiser, two feet from my head.

I looked sideways out the window. The bodyguards had Liashko shielded from fire around the other side of the truck. They leaned out to exchange chattering bursts from their AKs with the continued assault coming from the ship.

Shifting in my seat, I tried to reach into my sleeve, to the leather brace with my picks. The cuffs hindered my hands. I could touch my wrist but no farther. I kept struggling, straining for a different angle.

In the corner of my eye, I saw the mooring lines fall limp from the freighter. They'd cut the barge loose. A few seconds later both sides stopped shooting. Engines surged and water frothed as the *Oxana M* began to pull away.

Liashko was screaming at his men. The barge pilot had wisely taken cover from the barrage inside the steel container. He obeyed his boss, jumping out and running to the pilothouse of the barge. The bodyguards checked the freighter's progress—too far away now to shoot at us again—before they risked moving to the open side of the truck.

They shouldered their rifles and bent down to lift something. Burke. Facedown and unmoving. Was he dead?

The two men dragged his limp body to the cruiser. They opened the back door and threw Burke inside with me, more onto the floor than the seat. The back of Burke's trooper jacket was torn in two places over his shoulder blades. The black fabric gleamed wetly. Blood. He'd been hit, probably in the first wild volley from the deck.

But he was breathing. Raspy, but there. I twisted to get my cuffed hands lower, to feel at his jacket. Yes. A lightweight ballistic vest, maybe stolen along with the uniform. He'd come prepared.

Body armor or no, Burke was wounded. Though he may not have enough time remaining for the bullets to prove fatal.

Liashko came to the open door.

"Your man is shot," I said.

He didn't bother to look. "Sean would die tonight, anyway. I know his plans. I know he is the reason you are stealing from me."

I didn't say anything.

"He is too excited to have me come here," Liashko said. "I know him, like his father. They smell blood. They turn on their masters." He spat on Burke's prone body, his lips stained red from my headbutt.

Liashko motioned to a bodyguard, who handed him an automatic pistol. He aimed it at my head.

"You will tell me who you are, if you and Sean have other partners. Then it will be quick. Instead."

He spoke to the bodyguards. One of them came around to the driver's side. I watched him through the clear barrier. He opened the door, leaned in to release the emergency brake, and shifted the car into neutral. The car eased fractionally on its shocks. Wheels ready to roll.

Liashko waited, his deep-set eyes expectant.

I didn't say anything. Just attempted a defiant grin, which was probably closer to a baring of teeth.

Liashko nodded like that was an answer he'd already known. He closed the car door and motioned. The bodyguards smiled and bent into the glare of the headlights to push at the front of the car, getting it rolling backward toward the open bow. A bump, as the tires hit the slight rise of the retracted loading ramp. It didn't slow our progress.

The back wheels rolled off the deck. The cruiser's chassis dropped to hit the bow edge with a grinding crash. I tumbled backward, Burke rolling from the floor onto the hard black plastic seat.

For an instant, it seemed like the car would be stuck there. Then the combined force of its momentum and the grinning bodyguards' shoves slid it one inch, three more—

We were falling.

FIFTY-TWO

THE BLACK WATER SPLASHED AND gurgled as if hungrily devouring the car's front compartment. It found tiny crevices, entry points between the seats and the caged rear. Icy gouts sprayed over me and the unconscious Burke. My feet were under now. So cold it felt like stepping on an electrified wire.

Ignore it. Set everything else from my mind and keep searching for the fallen lockpick. I'd had a hold on it, was already picking the handcuffs, when the car's rear tires banged off the barge and threw everything inside ass-backward. The pick was still here. It had to be. My fingertips brushed across the seamless hard plastic of the seat, even as the car tilted farther forward and the water rose to meet my touch.

Burke might have the keys to the handcuffs on his belt. Or in his pocket. Or not at all. No time and no way to search him now. Find the pick.

There. A tap of metal, brushing against my knuckles as a first wave lapped across the seat. I stretched, touched it, got the pick between two fingers that were already growing numb. I twisted around. The end of the metal pick scraped the cuffs, missing the lock. Water at my chest now, squeezing my ribs. Burke was half floating, his face bobbing just above the roiling surface. My head touched the roof, and the surface of the water rose fast to catch up.

Breathe, Shaw. You have all the time you need. Just like catching a line drive, or taking your shot at five hundred yards with iron sights alone. Nothing else exists. I closed my eyes.

The pick found the handcuff lock. Eased in. Turned, gently. All like my fingers had nothing to do with it.

My wrists were free. And my mouth underwater. I pushed with my legs, toward the last vanishing inches of air at the rear window. The car was near to vertical. Sinking fast. By turning my neck I found air, gasped twice, held it. Outside the window, I could see plumes of bubbles escaping from the car's trunk.

Burke was under now. His autonomic response keeping him from inhaling water into his lungs. I crawled hand-over-hand down his body to his ankle. Working by feel. The world was growing dark, and squeezing tighter.

He'd worn it. His backup Glock. *Bless your homicidal habits, you maniac.*

I yanked the gun from his holster and spun to shove it against the side window and began pulling the trigger, the explosions in the enclosed underwater space hammering on my ears. Two rounds, three, four. I reached out blindly to shove with both hands and the splintered window fell outward, more like fabric than glass.

Burke's legs were closest. I grabbed his foot and clambered out of the window. The cruiser's headlights still shone, silt and foam swirling frantically past the beams as we dropped. How deep were we now? I got myself free, and the sinking car immediately pulled at Burke, threatening to tear him from my grasp. It turned me upside-down, borne deeper by the car and my grip on Burke's pants cuff.

I reached in, finding his other leg, twisting to push against the car with my feet and force Burke's reluctant body from the car. Was he alive? The water pressure pounded at my skull. His legs were out, then his torso, and then suddenly we were floating loose.

Below us, the police cruiser flew toward the void, its headlights seeking, white paint as luminescent as some deep-sea creature returning home.

I kicked. Burke's body rose, too slowly. His body armor. I kicked harder, dragging at him. If there was an end to the water above, I couldn't see it. If the crushing pressure was lessening, I couldn't tell.

My heart stuttered in my chest, desperately pushing blood in search of oxygen that wasn't there. Somehow my head was expanding from the inside out. Everything was pain. Any second now I would lose the fight and my body would inhale, reflexively, and then there would be a moment of horrible agony before it was over.

Kick, damn you.

Was that a light? The moon? Or the light of the end?

Kick.

We broke the surface.

I coughed, retched, my lungs so desperate they had forgotten their job. Burke bobbed up next to me. His face to the sky. I grabbed at him, thumped on his chest.

He let out a strangled gasp. Clutched at me. Clawed my face. Pulled me underwater in his atavistic terror of waking to dark and pain and bone-deep cold.

I fought free from his thrashing limbs to surface again. He reached for me again, eyes wide and unseeing. I thrust him back with one arm, reached up with the other, and clubbed him as hard as I could.

Just enough. Burke went limp once more, floating on his back. I got behind him in a lifeguard carry, where I could keep him from drowning me if he revived.

If. I looked into the distance for the first time. I could see the sliver of black that signified land and sparse fairy dots from the brightest lights onshore. A long, long distance. Four miles or more to the closest point in the west.

Already my teeth had stopped chattering. I couldn't feel my hands or feet.

We were going to die.

And with that decision made for us, I swam.

It was a very slow process. My limbs like planks of wood. One arm, two legs, moving as well as I could convince them to move, a conscious debate each time. Towing Burke with me like driftwood.

A waspish buzzing sound filled my ears. An engine. Somewhere east of us, getting closer. Still out of my sight. I tried to raise my unfeeling arm to wave. It barely lifted above the surface. Tried again, and the arm pointed skyward.

The sound was coming fast from behind. I flailed to turn myself, just in time to see the spearhead of the gray hull bearing down on us. I blinked stupidly. I knew that boat.

A round bristled head appeared over the side.

Jaak.

"Shaw, man," he said, grinning. "You have crazy days, I tell you."

FIFTY-THREE

JAAK'S TWO CREWMATES FISHED US out, working in tandem to haul our soaked and uncooperative bodies aboard my boat. Jaak apologized for not helping. Given he'd been stabbed barely a week before, I could forgive him slacking off. I pointed more than I spoke to show them where clothes and towels were stored. My lips and tongue felt like so much dead fish.

West. The barge had gone west. Damn it, why hadn't I told them that first? I pushed my way past them to take the wheel, pushing the throttle forward with my elbow. The speedboat leapt forward and the sailors stumbled back, protesting.

"Shaw," Jaak said. "You're too cold."

"Nerve gas," I said. "They have nerve gas. Poison. You understand?"

Jaak's mate Harri translated into Finnish. Jaak blanched.

The gunfight between the ships might have been seen. Liashko must know he could put the barge ashore anywhere with a boat ramp or even a shallow beach. They'd headed west, toward the closest land. Probably aiming to get off the water before police boats or the Coast Guard came hunting.

That land was the Kitsap Peninsula. Did Liashko know the area? The peninsula would be quiet, with plenty of beaches. But it was also remote.

A long drive south and around the Sound until he'd be back on the mainland.

The cops could corner him. If we called it in now.

I told Jaak to take the helm while I stripped and fumbled myself into a dry turtleneck and paint-spattered jeans, my urgency and rage combining to warm my bones. My mouth still carried the taste of brine. I spat over the transom into the speedboat's thrashing wake. Jaak pressed coffee on me, and I gratefully downed half a pint straight from the thermos.

The Finns already had the groggy Burke half out of his sopping trooper uniform. The wounds on his back had bled but not profusely. Cuts and punctures. I guessed that the vest had mushroomed the rounds and Burke had caught a few splinters along with the impact that had knocked him cold. Lucky. Lucky that the gunfire had come from a distance, and that the rounds weren't jacketed with something harder.

"He's dangerous," I said, pointing. "Once he's in dry clothes, tie his hands and feet. And watch him close."

The VHF radio was on the shelf just inside the cabin door. I reached in to switch it to Channel 16 and handed the receiver to Harri, the one with the stronger English.

"Call for the Coast Guard. Say you saw a lot of gunfire between two ships on Puget Sound. A cargo ship and a smaller craft. The cargo ship headed out of the Sound and—" I checked our heading. The beam of a small lighthouse shone like a low star, maybe two miles off now.

"—and the smaller ship is going toward Point No Point," I finished. "Say that back to me."

He did, perfectly. The Finnish crew was adept at handling emergencies.

"Good," I said. "If they ask, tell them who you are and that you borrowed this boat from your friend Hollis Brant. There won't be trouble."

As Harri hailed the emergency line, I dove into the cabin, tossing the sleeping cushions aside to reach the compartment underneath. Inside was my worn set of hiking boots. And, wrapped in a waxed cotton sheet, a Mossberg pump shotgun and two boxes of shells. The shotgun was kept loaded. I filled my pockets with shells and grabbed a burner phone and a flashlight from the chart locker.

When I emerged, Burke was alert.

"Let me go," he said.

"I should've let you drown. You sold us out."

"The hell I did." He looked around at the sailors.

"You can talk," I said. "They're with me."

"Anatoly changed the plan tonight. The deal was supposed to go down three days from now."

"Then you should have told Martens. Called the task force in."

He sneered. "If I did that, I'd miss my shot at Anatoly."

The truth was so obvious I felt like my pounding head was some sort of divine penance for not realizing it earlier. "You were never going into WITSEC."

"Shit no. I'd kill Anatoly and his two pussies and call the Feds to come pick up the arms. My boy gets the bust, and I'm gone. Disappearing ain't hard when you've been preparing as long as I have." He showed me his bound wrists. "Cut me loose."

"Not a prayer."

Burke swore. At length, as I finished tying the laces on my boots. I imagined even Harri learned a few new words. "You owe me."

I glanced at the vast stretch of Sound to our stern. "Remember where you were ten minutes ago and say that again."

"You're going to take him out, right? I can help you. You can't do it without me."

Ahead of us, the torch of the lighthouse burned. It might have been my imagination, but I thought I glimpsed a reflection off green metal, at the beach mere yards from the short tower. I hefted the shotgun.

"Fuck I can't," I said.

FIFTY-FOUR

I HAD THE FINNS PUT ME ashore on the beach, half a mile south of the point. Or what passed for one. Point No Point had earned its name because, from a distance, it tricked the eye into thinking a mere bump in the land was something more substantial.

But it was enough of a bend that the short lighthouse was out of my view as I waded through the low surf. And I would be just as hidden, running along the beach.

Liashko and his men would watch the single road that led visitors to the lighthouse. With an eye on the water, too. Those were the places where cops might approach. They would pay less attention to the shoreline.

They couldn't have arrived too many minutes ahead of us. The speedboat was a hell of a lot faster than any barge, and I had pushed her throttle all the way open. How long would it take them to offload the truck? The pilot could run the barge hard into the shore—I guessed they planned to abandon the vessel—and then lower its ramp. Picking the right spot would be critical. If the truck with its heavy load floundered in loose sand, they were finished.

A path off the beach led to a hiking trail. Tall thickets and bramble bushes shielded me on both sides. Ahead, a flash of yellow light from behind the building. Too low for even the undersized lighthouse. Head-lights. I slowed my run, hunching over and keeping the shotgun butt tucked tight to my shoulder.

As I neared the end of the trail, the rev of a diesel engine temporarily covered the soft crunch of my footfalls on the gravel. I looked through a gap in the reeds. The truck, on the other side of the lighthouse. Already moving.

I kicked into high gear, tearing off the path, full tilt toward the stubby black-capped tower. Angling left to follow the moving target of the engine.

I stopped at the corner of the white building that abutted the light-house itself. The beams of headlights came into view. The truck was still on the beach, making its steady way forward on the harder-packed sand, parallel to the water. Steering to avoid chunks of flotsam and larger logs that had washed onto land over the years. Along with a line of small boulders, the timber formed a natural barrier that prevented them from simply driving straight off the shore.

Another hundred yards down the beach, lampposts illuminated a red-roofed house and nearby parking lot. The log barrier ended there. Liashko and his men would turn onto the paved lot and then to the road, and then they would be gone. The truck passed my corner at a runner's pace. They were careful. Not losing their nerve. Not getting stuck.

I sprinted out from the shelter of the building, racing toward the driver's side of the truck as it trundled away. Veering into an angle of approach I hoped matched the blind spot in its side mirror. Only thirty yards away from their taillights and closing fast. Jumping the boulders and the line of bleached logs like huge bones, my boots digging into the sand as I ran faster.

At fifteen feet they slammed on the brakes. They'd seen me. Too late for them.

The first blast from my shotgun exploded the left front tire of the truck. The second tore the side mirror from its brackets. I faded back, racking another shell and blowing out the two rear tires on the left side with one shot.

They floored the gas. Trying to escape the sudden onslaught. The big flatbed with its cargo sagged heavily to one side on flattened tires and dug in. Sand sprayed from under the shredded rubber for an instant before the front wheel became mired too deep to do even that. The truck's right tires pushed forward, the left side stayed stuck. The truck began to grind a slow painful circle in the dirt and sand.

I dove behind the nearest driftwood log. Knelt into shooting position. Over the howl of the straining engine I caught a loud creak from the passenger door on the far side. In another second, the silhouette of legs came into view under the flatbed. One of the bodyguards moving to the rear of the truck.

I shot the legs under the truck bed, racked, and fired again at the same spot over a scream of pain or fear I barely heard over the ringing in my ears. Half deaf and half blind on the dark beach with muzzle flashes still hot in my vision. I put one more blast through the driver's window. Not hearing the shatter.

Keep them guessing. Don't give the guards a chance to sight in with their assault weapons. I retreated, running to crouch behind one of the jagged boulders. The driver's door opened and the barge pilot fell out to scramble to his feet. He ran clumsily up the beach, into the beams of the headlights and away. I let him go, watching the truck as I loaded shells into the underside of the Mossberg by feel.

Liashko, and the second bodyguard. They were my concern. Both still in the cab?

I looked at the door of the steel shipping container. One thin black vertical stripe appeared on the wall of green.

The truck's engine stalled. My ears cleared enough to hear waves lapping on the shore. A gull screeched overhead, furious at the intrusion into its peaceful territory.

The stripe widened fractionally. A long tube extended out like a questing finger.

I hit the dirt, covering my head with my arms. But unable to resist the temptation to watch.

The Verba missile launcher was not designed for short-range work, by any stretch of the imagination. Aiming it by sight alone, at a ground-level target barely twenty yards away, was like tossing a grenade blindly in the same room in which you were standing. Maybe the bodyguard had fired a rocket launcher in the field and thought he had the procedure down. Or maybe he'd just reached for the biggest, baddest gun in his panic.

A searing orange flash of light erupted out of the open container door. The backblast from the launcher. It must have singed everything in the steel box, including the man. The missile itself ejected ten feet from the tube before its propellant engaged. That brighter glare of light had only an instant's life—which I barely glimpsed as I stuck my face into the crook of my elbow, my retinas already stinging—before the slender dart struck the logs from which I'd fired the shotgun a minute before, and the world erupted into flame and heat. Chunks of wood struck the boulder beside me. More pieces landed on the sand, blasted and smoldering.

I looked up. The logjam was mostly gone, replaced by a blackened and still burning shallow crater. A fire blazed in the grass farther up the shore, and leaves in a stand of trees just beyond glowed orange as they curled and died.

I waited.

Another minute passed. The door to the container widened. A figure slipped out, black against the red of the truck's taillights and the yellow bonfires the missile had ignited. He bent low, using the container as cover from where he thought I was. Wondering if he'd succeeded in blowing me to pieces.

Liashko's voice called from the front of the truck. The bodyguard didn't answer. Not giving away his location. As I watched, he moved around the truck on the water side, maybe to check his fallen comrade, maybe to whisper to his boss.

The truck's lights went dark. An instant later, the interior light of the cab followed.

I couldn't see them from here. I low-crawled toward the surf, the ground scraping my stomach. Sand fleas jumped and popped out of my path. The reek of rotten kelp grew stronger as I wormed my silent way forward, to a better position behind a low dune, fifteen yards from the rear bumper.

With the truck's lights off, the only illumination came from the small dying fires. And the moon. Near to full tonight, low in the sky on the western horizon. Its pale glow made the two men look like puppets in a shadow play. One huge and round, one lean and stooped and edging ahead of the other. Perhaps to check for the remnants of my corpse in the burning driftwood. The bodyguard's cautious steps as soft as rustling leaves.

I fired straight into the center of his shadow, racked to fire again. The shadow crumpled.

Liashko fled. A terrified and surprisingly fast run, over the smoking logs and toward the lighthouse. Instinctively seeking the nearest place to hide. I didn't shoot. In the firelight I saw the arms dealer clutching my rucksack to his chest with both arms, like an infant he was protecting from harm.

I caught him at the base of the lighthouse tower. He heard me coming, turned just as my shotgun butt was swinging for his bull neck. It clocked him on the cheek instead. He fell, even as I wrenched the ruck with its deadly nerve agent from his grasp.

I checked it. Nothing leaking. Nothing broken. I was breathing hard, but I still managed to exhale a little more in relief.

Liashko stared up at me from the ground. His face white around the punctuations of blood.

Of course. He'd last seen me half an hour ago, as the black waves consumed the sinking patrol car. Seconds from death. The second time I'd come back from the grave, a scarred and bloody specter haunting him.

Surprise, you evil fuck. I smiled at Liashko, and this time my grin wasn't forced at all. He shrank away from my reach.

I hauled the quivering man to his feet and marched him back to the truck to sit on his ass in the dazzling headlights, once I'd turned them on.

His bodyguards were alive. They might even stay that way, if the cops got here fast enough. Like Burke, they wore their own tactical vests under the seasonal outerwear, and the armor had saved them from the worst of the buckshot. One of them hung on to my arm and said something in Russian, maybe asking for help, maybe still trying to fight. The other might never walk right again. I handed him his own belt and motioned for him to make a tourniquet above his shredded quad muscles, not sticking around to see if he understood. I flung their rifles far out into the lapping surf.

While rifling through the truck cab, I found a long security cable with a padlock in the glove compartment. I used it to bind Liashko's wrists and ankles together behind his back and looped the cable around the truck's bumper before locking it. He wound up lying on his side, the damp sand and bits of seaweed painting one side of his big head. The padlock key followed the guns into the Sound.

I took out my burner phone and dialed a number I'd memorized.

Special Agent Rick Martens answered, his voice thick with sleep. "Wha—Whoizit?"

I held the phone out to Liashko and pointed the muzzle of the Mossberg at his groin.

"Say your name," I said.

It took him a few seconds to find his voice. "Anatoly Fedorovych Liashko."

I took the phone back. "Point No Point lighthouse. Get here fast."

The phone stayed on the truck's hood, the line still open in case Martens needed to trace the signal. My rucksack with the canisters of nerve gas next to it.

I ran back down the beach the way I had come, feeling exhausted, feeling unsteady, feeling like I could race the brilliant beam the lighthouse cast over the waves, and beat it.

FIFTY-FIVE

After some discussion with the anxious Finns, we agreed to chart a course south along the coast before turning across the Sound to Seattle. Giving the second wave of chaos at Point No Point a wide berth.

I watched the invasion through my set of field glasses. An SPD helicopter arrived first, then a sudden blossoming of lights onshore, red and blue and white, a second chopper, and what might have been a Coast Guard cutter. It was hard to tell; by that time we were miles away.

Burke had gone silent and pale. Aware that his opportunity for revenge was gone forever. And maybe his injuries and the near drowning had stripped everything from him but his defiance. Harri had patched his lacerations with gauze and tape from my well-stocked first aid kit in the cabin.

Now Burke sagged against the cabin wall, looking ten years older than he had an hour ago.

"What was your plan?" I said over the drone of the big outboard. "To get away after Liashko?"

Burke grimaced. "Anatoly was going to put the truck ashore at Edmonds. I'd ace him and his two lunks the second we touched land. Drive off in the cop car and call Martens to come get the weapons."

I hefted his torn WSP coat, my next question obvious.

"I already had the uniform," Burke said. "Looking like the law can be useful sometimes. The car I boosted earlier tonight from a substation in Auburn. Hardly anyone around during the regular week, they might not miss the car till Friday. After I was done with Anatoly I'd swap it for a clean vehicle I stashed in Shoreline with everything I need. Out of the state before dawn, out of the country by noon tomorrow. Spain to start. Maybe Mauritius once I got bored."

"Why was Liashko headed for Edmonds?"

"Anatoly had a plane at Paine Field, ready to fly with the sarin."

Sarin. So that was the chemical weapon that we'd been playing Capture the Flag with all night.

"You knew he had that lethal shit all along?" I said.

Burke nodded. "A bargaining chip for me, in case I needed some extra clout with the cops."

"You're insane."

He shrugged indifference. Jaak and his friends had found other places to be. Tough to do on a slim twenty-foot boat.

Burke looked toward the jagged line of lights that defined the city ahead. "You turning me in?"

"Why? You're a damned hero."

He looked at me, puzzled. I jabbed a thumb back toward the blaze of activity on the point.

"Liashko and the missiles in federal hands, and captured bioweapons as the cherry. You've disappeared. The prevailing theory will be that you took out Liashko and his men and drove away, almost like you planned."

Burke blinked. Started to say something, then thought about it for another few seconds. "He'll finger you."

"Maybe. But he's not a fool. If Liashko admits he knows me, he's also opening up the part where he tried to murder us. For all he knows, you're dead and deep underwater. The cops will find the sunken car only if they know to look for it. If he's shrewd, he'll claim he never got a look at the guy who shot up his truck and hog-tied him."

"The sailors on the cargo ship saw you, too."

"For a hot second. And the ones who got the closest look at me are dead now, thanks to Liashko's firefight. Maybe I was Sean Burke, and the guy in the trooper uniform was just another grunt. I think their stories will be confused as hell. The simplest answer is that you learned Liashko was moving the arms early, and you decided to handle it yourself and disappear. That seems about your level of crazy."

"The Feds will never buy it."

"I think they'll find a way to believe. Martens and the rest have what they want, and more. Why spread shit in front of the ticker-tape parade?"

"Now who's nuts?" Burke shook his head.

I took a diving knife from the cockpit locker to cut the bonds at his ankles and wrists.

"We'll let you off downtown," I said. "Get to Shoreline, get in your car, don't look back."

We watched the city manifest as the speedboat sliced through the soft chop. The Needle in the north, the stadiums south. A rough bell curve of skyscrapers between. The moon had dipped out of sight, and there was nothing to dilute the shimmering reflection of the city lights on the water.

"There's something I gotta tell you," Burke said, his voice barely carrying above the thrum of the outboard. "About Moira."

I looked at him.

"I already know," I said.

FIFTY-SIX

P ALMER STRATTON'S CAMPAIGN HEADQUARTERS OCCUPIED the first two stories of a narrow office tower near Denny Park, squashed between
apartments on one side and a medical center on the other. I counted
four different coffeehouses within sight of the entrance. Caffeine to
keep the volunteers going, and paramedics nearby when they finally
collapsed.

I let myself in through the small loading dock in the rear of the building,
took a freight elevator up four stories, found a stairwell, and walked down
to the second floor of the campaign offices. It wasn't difficult. Stratton had a
private security team, but they were downstairs now with the man himself,
along with all of the workers to hear Stratton's latest pep talk. No cops. The
U.S. attorney wasn't governor yet.

His personal office was in the rear. I knew that thanks to the half-
dozen videos of tours granted to news services and community organizations, all readily available on YouTube. I think the campaign's intent was
to demonstrate that despite his blue-blooded upbringing, Stratton's HQ
looked like almost any busy office in America, with cubicles and cluttered
desks and stacks of boxes and inspirational posters. All the volunteers
smiling as they worked the phones and checked the latest social media
impressions. One wall had been covered in pictures from rallies and other

appearances. Another displayed a variety of graphic designs for Stratton's official photos and his slogan: COURAGE—CHARACTER—COMMUNITY.

The office was locked. I opened the door, locked it again behind me, and drew the blinds. Stratton had allowed himself a large window and enough space for a small conference table and a couch. Clutter from the outside cubicle farm had not stormed the ramparts of the candidate's sanctum. The only pictures of himself here were framed family snaps of his wife, Carolyn, and their college-age twins, all smiling at the camera with an abundance of health and teeth.

His rolling chair behind the L-shaped faux-walnut desk was comfortable. I enjoyed it while I waited, looking out the window at the bright clear January day.

My birthday, as it happened.

Ten minutes later, a swell of noise on the second floor rolled steadily toward the back of the building. I heard Palmer Stratton's voice, talking jovially with his staff. The door opened and Stratton came in, with the blond campaign lead I'd seen at his fund-raiser and another two workers close on his heels.

He stopped midsentence. "How did you get in here?" he said. I smiled, all modesty.

The workers were staring, just as dumbfounded. The blonde turned to her boss. "Should I—?" She gestured back toward the office, and the guards who were no doubt minding the perimeter downstairs.

I held up the brass medallion of Saint Brendan that Burke had given me. Suspended between thumb and forefinger, like I was about to perform a magic trick for Stratton. Watch carefully. Something might just vanish.

Stratton stared, with the same look of foreboding he'd had when I'd told him to protect his inside man, Burke. Then he composed himself and turned to the staff.

"It's fine, Grace. I'd just forgotten our appointment. Would you tell Lyle and the others that I'll be a few minutes?"

Grace nodded, perhaps unconvinced, but she left nonetheless.

Stratton shut the door and waited until he was sure no one was hovering outside.

"We've been looking for you," he said. "You're more than halfway to an arrest warrant."

"Sounds like you're still undecided."

He frowned sternly. "This isn't a joke, Shaw. You'll answer our questions. Has Sean Burke been in touch with you?"

"I was wondering the same thing about you. Did Burke tell you he was going to disappear? That's the kind of thing you'd want a friend to know. So they didn't worry."

Stratton didn't say anything.

"My mother, Moira, gave this to my father, a long time ago," I said, setting the medallion on his desk. "And Burke gave the medal to me," I said, staying on course. "Saint Brendan. A patron of travelers, like Saint Christopher. But mostly of sailors."

"I read in your file that she died when you were a child."

"She'd been exploring her faith at the time, I've learned. I guess she wanted some reassurance. Tough on a girl, being knocked up in high school."

Stratton slid a chair from the conference table out, sat down across from me. Changing tack. "Liashko made noise about an American coming aboard the *Oxana M* and planting all of the arms, trying to frame him, before his lawyer buttoned his mouth. He may not persist with that alibi, but it's sure that his team will try to muddy the waters."

"Keep me out of it," I said.

"Sorry." He shook his head in mock regret. "You may not do time, but you have to be brought in. Tonight. It's up to you whether you leave here in handcuffs. And you'll testify if necessary. I want answers."

"Like father, like son."

His hand gripped the chair's armrest. "Excuse me?"

"I take after Moira's side. Black hair, black eyes. Burke is dark complexioned, too; it threw me for a while. But you and I are about the same size, and back in your wrestler days we were probably the same build. Plus there's this." I tapped the etched image of Saint Brendan. "Sailors. You and your family. Regatta races, service in the Navy. And you're Catholic. Why would she send a saint to protect an agnostic thug like Sean Burke?"

"That—that's a fantasy."

A rap at the door made him jump. The person on the other side opened it without waiting for a response. Margaret Stratton stepped partway into the room.

"Palmer?" she said, then realized it wasn't her son behind the desk. "Oh."

"Afternoon, Mrs. Stratton," I said.

"Mother, would you excuse us?" Stratton said. "We're just finishing up some business."

Instead of leaving, Margaret entered and shut the door.

"What was it you were discussing?" she said. To me, not to her son.

"Family legacies," I said.

Her minuscule smile evaporated entirely. "I don't understand."

"Palmer does. Tell her."

"Mr. Shaw," Stratton began, before clearing his throat. "Shaw seems to labor under the impression that I'm his father."

"Ridiculous," Margaret said.

"That's what I was about to tell him. Sean Burke has already admitted to being Shaw's father. He informed Agent Martens of that, when he explained why Shaw had sought him out. And Burke also informed us about the DNA test that confirmed his parentage." He nodded emphatically, back on message.

"The tests confirmed parentage," I agreed, "but it wasn't Burke's DNA on the swab he gave me. It was yours. He was covering for you."

"What are you saying?" Margaret's pallor came close to matching her silver-white hair.

"Burke told me that when he decided to turn informant, he reached out to the one guy in law enforcement he thought he could trust. Agent Martens was Burke's handler on the case. I'd just assumed Martens was also his childhood buddy. Martens couldn't have kept their prior history a secret from you, the man in charge of the task force. That would jeopardize any investigation."

Stratton and his mother exchanged a look.

"But I had it backward," I said. "You and Burke were the ones who knew each other in private school. Martens was his primary contact, as a go-between. Keeping things kosher for the eventual trial."

"I'm calling security," Margaret said, turning away.

"Don't," said Stratton. His mother stopped, one hand on the door-knob.

"When I started getting close, Palmer and Burke went over their options," I said to her. "It was clear to them that I wouldn't stop until I had answers. Burke knew that before long I'd steal a bit of food or a water bottle he'd tossed in the trash and have tests run. If that test came up negative for my father, I'd keep digging. Maybe I'd even find out the names of other friends of Moira's from back in the day. Like Palmer."

"That's wrong. Palmer never knew—your mother," Margaret said, as if that settled things.

"So they got out ahead of the problem," I continued. "Palmer gave Burke a swab from his cheek. Burke gave it to me. It would come up positive and I'd think Burke was my father. And it worked, for a day or two."

They were silent now. Waiting to see what cards I turned over, so they would know if they had any of their own left to play.

"I was already half convinced that Moira went for the bad-boy type. Then I remembered Burke had mentioned something else, about the two of them hanging with his friends from school. So I made some calls. Sean went to Whitaker Academy, I learned. Moira met someone else in that group, someone she liked more." I pointed at Stratton. "You. One of the academy's most distinguished graduates, and that's saying something."

"Whitaker has a lot of alumni," he said. "Your mother may have taken up with someone, but it wasn't me."

"There were other things that bothered me, too. Agent Martens had come to the bar where I work just a couple of nights prior to Burke giving me the swab. He lifted a bottle of beer I'd been drinking from out of the recycling bin. I have him on camera, skulking around. That got me puzzling. Why would Burke give me his swab if his C.I. handler had already stolen a sample from me? Unless someone on the task force was running a test for themselves. Maybe in private. Did you tell Martens you wanted my DNA for the case?"

"Conjecture," Stratton said, "and wishful thinking. I'm sorry Sean Burke doesn't meet with your image of what your father should be—"

"But he did," I interrupted. "Burke and I have more in common than I'd like. We're both raised by criminals. Both with a history of violence. And we're loyal to a damned fault. Burke was about to disappear into WITSEC. You two would work together to take down Liashko, who had killed his father, Gus."

I shrugged. "Tricking me, pretending to be my dad for a month or two, was a small price for Burke to pay. Especially since a shitstorm in the news about U.S. Attorney Stratton's out-of-wedlock kid could sink the task force, and ruin Burke's chance to nail Liashko right along with it."

"You've no proof—" Stratton began, and then stopped. Maybe guessing what was coming.

"Your makeup table at the fund-raiser," I said, pointing a finger-gun at him in confirmation. "I lifted a few hairs out of the brush. Too bad your dye job doesn't mask genetic testing. I've got a whole profile rundown. One of the state's leading authorities explained it to me earlier this morning, but I have to confess I only understood about half of what he said. The conclusion spoke for itself, though."

"If you say anything," Margaret said, "we will sue you into oblivion."

"That's the spirit, Grandma."

Her lips curled back. "Don't you dare call me that."

"What do you want?" said Stratton.

"Palmer—" said Margaret.

"It's over, Mother," he said, "except for the negotiating." He turned back to me. "How much?"

"You think this is a transaction? I'd say it's more of a plea bargain."

Margaret would not be denied. "I was sure this would come to pass. From the first moment I heard about that horrid girl. You're all malignant."

I stopped, and Stratton's mouth dropped open. Both of us caught off-guard this time.

"You knew about Moira," I said.

"Of course we knew. Do you imagine Palmer could be involved with people like you and we wouldn't know?"

Stratton stiffened. "Mom. What did you do?"

"What you should have. I told that girl to stay away from you. That if she didn't, James and I would make sure that monstrous father of hers went to prison where he belonged for the rest of his days. The child had just enough sense to know I meant what I said."

I looked at Stratton. He still stared at Margaret, aghast.

"Moira wasn't protecting you from Dono by breaking up," I said to him. "She was protecting Dono from you. Your family."

"James and I had people keeping watch after Palmer left for college," Margaret said, "in case she had lied. We found out she was *expecting*." The word was cyanide. "I couldn't believe it might be Palmer's. But I warned her again, in case the little witch thought she could lay any claim on you. I told her we would arrange for a medical procedure to clean things up. That if she even hinted that Palmer was involved she would regret it forever. She said—it doesn't bear repeating what she said."

Good for you, Mom.

"You knew," Stratton said to Margaret, as if his thoughts had become trapped at that point. "All these years. Moira was pregnant and had our child and you *knew?*"

"It doesn't matter," she replied, going to him. "It didn't matter then. Or now."

Stratton stood and brushed her questing hand away. "Don't. Don't pretend this is nothing. That what you tried to do . . ." Words apparently failed him.

She talked past him to me, an edge of desperation in her voice. "We will pay you a reasonable amount. But then it's done. Do you understand?"

I understood, all right. The teenage Moira was leaps and bounds tougher than any of them. I bet that had scared the hell out of Margaret Stratton and the honorable congressman.

"Get out," Stratton said to his mother.

"Palmer, this is unaccep—"

"Get out of my sight right now."

Margaret's face paled. She looked at her son, then back to me.

It was cruel, but I didn't even try to resist smiling at her.

"Dads and I have some catching up to do," I said.

Margaret went, immediately and directly, as if fury had given her wings.

Stratton closed the door behind her. When he came back to the chair I realized he was nearly as pale as Margaret had been.

"God," he said. With a tone of honesty directing his words upstairs. "How can this be?"

"The how explains itself," I said. "It's the why I'm wondering about."

Stratton was staring at the medal of Saint Brendan, still resting on the desk.

"Confession's good for the soul," I said.

He closed his eyes before he began speaking.

"Moira. She and I—we met when she came out with Sean. It was immediate between us. Even Sean saw it. He punched me in the gut, but he couldn't get too mad. It was just one of those things. And Sean had had a lot of girls. Moira was the first one I cared about."

He might be weaving me a story. Politicians were good at that, creating empathy out of nothing. But I didn't think so.

"We both accepted I'd be going east for college at the end of the summer," Stratton said, easing back into his chair. "We'd even talked about her coming to visit, once she got up the nerve to tell her dad she was seeing me. Then she stopped calling. I got a letter. Moira had sent it through Sean, and now I understand why. My parents might have intercepted it otherwise. Moira said she had to end things between us, that she hoped I understood. I didn't. At all. I suspected it was because of Dono, but I didn't care if he came after me."

Foolhardy. But Stratton had been young and in love.

"I went to her house one day, when I knew Dono was away, but Moira refused to let me in. I finally got the picture. She wasn't coming back. Then a couple of months later, at Cornell, I received another letter forwarded through Sean. With that inside."

He nodded to Saint Brendan. "I'd seen it before, the one time she allowed me into the house. Moira had told me then that the medal was a sort of heirloom she'd inherited, from back when the family were regular Catholics. Before Dono moved to America. I'd—encouraged her to start up again while we had been dating. But then . . ." Stratton folded his hands. "She wished me well in the letter and said she was okay. And that she hoped I'd keep it."

She had learned she was pregnant. And said nothing, to Dono or to Palmer, to keep the Strattons from using all of their influence to bury my grandfather.

"I nearly threw the damn thing into Beebe Lake the day I got it," Stratton said. "But no. The medallion was the only thing I had from her. Eventually I met Carolyn, and everything worked out." Stratton's interlaced fingers fiddled with his wedding ring, twisting it by habit around his finger.

"Until Burke."

"When Sean told me about you last week, I couldn't believe it. I thought it was a trick. Liashko trying to pull something over on Sean, getting him to trust you. I'd found out Moira had died years after it happened. I was still in the Navy, and overseas. It never occurred to me that she might have—that you might exist."

"Must have been a hell of a shock."

"The more I thought about it, the more I wanted to know the truth. Even if I couldn't do or say anything about it. Sean and I cooked up the idea of having you run the test on my DNA, believing it was his. I sent Martens to get a sample from you if he could, to find out privately for myself, and, well . . ."

"To keep me from upsetting the apple cart."

He had the decency to look abashed. "Yes. Moira was gone. Past helping. If I had known about you when you were young, perhaps—" He exhaled. "I gave Sean the medal to give to you. To sell the lie. And because of all people you should have it."

I picked up the brass disc. It felt heavier than I knew it was.

Stratton shifted uncertainly. "If you want money—"

"Not yours."

He flushed.

"You'll leave my name out of the investigation," I said. "No interrogation, no deposition, nothing. Sean Burke took down Liashko and his men and chose to disappear rather than suffer through life in WITSEC.

You make sure Liashko gets the worst hellhole the Feds can arrange for him."

Stratton hesitated. But his mind was back in gear. Making deals was his wheelhouse. "You'll have to sign nondisclosure agreements."

I laughed. "For what? I don't exist."

"That's all? Nothing more than to stay out of it?" said Stratton.

"What price freedom?" I said. "I don't like attention. Notoriety is even worse."

Updates on the Liashko case would be scrolling on cable news chyrons for weeks. A Ukrainian arms trafficker arrested with stolen Russian bioweapons on American soil. There would be think pieces and committees at every level of government. Seattle would become the temporary base of every national news service and true-crime podcast, and everyone remotely involved would have their moment in the spotlight. Like it or not.

"You should—you should have *something*," Stratton tried again.

He wanted to make amends, maybe feel absolved through his generosity if not his suffering. But Stratton wasn't the one who'd sinned, any more than Moira had.

I stood and put the medal of Saint Brendan in my pocket. "Good luck in February. Not that you'll need it."

Stratton nodded. When I closed the door, he was staring at nothing, still turning his ring around his finger like it might rewind time.

THAT NIGHT, I SLEPT. THAT night, I finally dreamed. Or remembered.

"MOM?" I SAID. "MOMMA? WHAT'S *this*?"

If the box had been on Mom's shelf before, I hadn't seen it. But she had a lot of little things, and I wasn't allowed to touch them unless she said.

"What's what, honey?" She was in the kitchen and couldn't see.

"This. Um." Like quarters but bigger, and yellow. "Coins. In the box?"

"Oh. Those are saints, baby. Do you know what saints are?"

"Nuh-uh."

"Well, they protect people, kind of. Each medallion there is a different saint."

I looked closer. There were—I counted—five of them. Four men and one woman. And one missing. Leaving a circle in the wooden box, like a puzzle that wasn't finished.

"Can I play with them?"

"Yes. But on the table and wash your hands after. You'll remember?"

"Uh huh." I lifted the box carefully over some little glass horses and brought it to the table, setting it down before I pulled out the chair and climbed up to see.

The coins fell out all at once when I tipped the box over, clinking and clattering real loud onto the table. Mom didn't say anything, so I guessed that was okay. I picked them up. They were much heavier than the loose change in my elephant bank. Like pirate money.

I lined them up to look at the pictures. One man held a book, and the woman carried something hard to tell, maybe flowers, but two of the men had long sticks like wizards. They all wore long clothes, and one man had a big tall hat, which was funny.

"Are you excited about first grade, Van?" The kitchen timer beeped like it was answering for me.

"Yeah." The coins spun best if I used two hands and pushed on them first with my fingers. Soon I could make them go for a long time, spinning upright until they started to tilt, making circles on the table and getting louder and faster. I counted to twenty-seven before the last one finally shuddered to a stop.

"The school's closed for the summer, so I'm going downtown to the district office tomorrow to get your forms," Mom said. "We'll find out who your teacher will be. And then I think you and I should get a lunchbox for you. Your kindergarten one is Worn. Out. Too many cookies broke the handle!"

I giggled. Maybe the lunchbox would have Hulk on it. Superstrong to hold more cookies. That made me laugh more. I spun the coins some more and stacked them and made them bounce off each other until Mom said over the sound of the oven closing that it was time for dinner. Something smelled good, maybe pork chops. When I put the coins back in the box with all their faces showing, I remembered the missing one.

"Um, Mom? There are only five. One was gone before," I said.

"I know."

"Did you lose it?"

Mom didn't answer. Maybe she hadn't heard. "Momma?"

"I didn't lose it, baby. I gave it to someone who . . . who could use a little help. That's what they're for."

"Help how?"

"Maybe . . . maybe knowing the right thing to do when they're not sure. We can all use that sometimes."

I looked at the coins again. Did they have powers? "Did it? Help them?"

"I'm gonna say yes, it did."

"Okay." Cool. I put the box back careful behind the horses.

"What were you going to do next?" She brought in plates and forks and set them on the table.

I was still looking at the coins in the box. One was tilted, and I fixed it. "Wash my hands."

"Right." She kissed me on the top of the head. "I love you, baby."

"I love you, too, Momma."

I went to wash up. The coins would be there tomorrow, after we came back from getting my new lunchbox. I bet I could get one to spin till I counted to a hundred.

EPILOGUE

B ULLY BETTY HAD ALLOWED ME to take over the back room for a private party. It was a small enough group that on a Tuesday night in early February we all could have easily gathered in the main bar, but putting it in a separate space allowed Cyndra to be present with some deniability. The kid, me, Addy Proctor, Oscar and Cannonball and Twelvetrees from the gym. My usual suspects Hollis, Willard, and Elana. Betty and A-Plus and Mo and a few others wandered through to say hello. Hollis and Willard sat across from one another, regaling my fellow gym rats with stories of youthful indiscretions. Which for them usually involved a large quantity of alcohol with a dash of felony.

And Wren. I looked across the room. She and Elana had hit it off, and Cyndra watched every move and joke the two women made with rapt fascination.

The party was supposedly for me, in honor of my thirtieth spin around the sun. I'd put Addy and Cyndra off planning anything until I was certain Palmer Stratton would keep his word and I wouldn't find myself in a holding cell, biding time between interrogations by everyone from Homeland Security to Parks and Rec.

Now Palmer Stratton's image appeared on the muted screen in the corner. Waving to the crowd in whatever hotel ballroom his campaign had rented for election night. A much larger room than for the fundraiser at the Alexis. The Stratton bandwagon had swelled exponentially during the month since Liashko's arrest.

It was only eight in the evening. Votes would be counted for hours yet, if not days. But every poll during the past week had shown U.S. Attorney Stratton leading the race, most by double-digit percentages. The candidate was just marking time until his acceptance speech.

On the screen, Palmer Stratton held his wife, Carolyn's, hand. He waved, she waved, their twins behind them beamed, both boy and girl looking a little dazzled by the lights and the adulation.

Margaret Stratton shared the stage with her family. She stood to one side, graciously leaning down to accept the proffered handshakes of people in the crowd. Was it me, or had she aged since I'd seen her at campaign headquarters? She moved hesitantly, responded to the well-wishers slowly. Maybe it was just the stress of the race.

I waved to Addy Proctor, who'd stepped out to use the restroom and had returned with a pint of stout for me and a shot of vodka for herself. Addy was the only person with whom I'd shared the truth about Palmer Stratton, and Moira.

She joined me at the wall counter, and both of us watched events unfold on the television.

"Your father is our new governor," Addy said softly after a few moments, shaking her head. "Isn't life amazing?"

"I always felt like a black sheep. Nice to know it's from a good flock."

She snorted. "Sheep's clothing, maybe. Scratch that. You don't look like anything other than what you are."

"Thanks."

"I meant it as a compliment."

"It is," I said. "I'm my mother's son."

Addy looked at me quizzically. "Perhaps that's why you broke away from your grandfather's way of life. Moira's influence, for however long she had you."

"I'd had that same thought. It occurred to me that all my stress about what I might have inherited from Sean Burke was a clue in itself. Burke's a damn sociopath, or spitting distance from it. Not capable of that kind of introspection. For all the similarities in our lives, at the core I've got something he's missing. Chalk that up to Mom."

The stout tasted like coffee and smoke. Perfect.

Addy nodded to the three young women laughing, slapping their hands on the table made from a repurposed door. "I like Wren. She's got focus."

"Yeah."

Me, too, it seemed. I knew what I wanted now.

Wren may have sensed our attention. She looked up and smiled at us. I toasted her with the pint.

"Addy," I said. "Your cabal of friends. You mentioned one of them used to run the United Way around here."

"That would be Connie," said Addy, "and she used to run the United Way. Of America."

"Ah." Addy's network never ceased to surprise. "So she would know something about setting up a charity."

"You could safely say that, yes. Why? Are you thinking of starting a benevolent fund for burglars?"

"Their children, actually."

She set down the vodka she'd barely been tasting. "You're serious."

"I am. Moira was a volunteer with something similar. Foster kids and others whose parents are doing time. Like Cyndra was. I was thinking about how to create an organization like that."

"Define 'create.'"

"Hire somebody who knows what to do. Give them funding."

"Funding from . . . ? You can't start a charity with stolen money."

"Depends on who it's stolen from. But let's work on the assumption that any proceeds can be legitimately explained."

"That sounds like a very gray area."

"I'm very comfortable with very gray. Can you help me?"

She took an actual drink of her vodka this time. "I'm willing to consult. That's as far as I'll go for now."

"Thank you." We clinked glasses, and I started a circuit of the room to say hello to everyone. Wren met me halfway, at the stained-glass window that gave the regulars a nicer thing to look at than the alley beyond.

"Hey," she said. "You throw a good party."

"I dunno. I might not stay too late."

"No? There's somewhere else to be?"

"A christening." I took a set of keys from my pocket, showed them to her. "I got a late birthday present. A lawyer contacted me yesterday. He asked me to come to his office to go over a mess of papers and other things, but the upshot is that for the next twenty months I hold the pre-paid lease to a high-rise apartment in Belltown. And a new truck. An inheritance, kind of."

She took the keys to give them a closer look. "This is . . . from the guy you thought was your dad? Burke?"

"Yeah. He's skipped town. For good. But after he left he arranged this little surprise. I'm still wrapping my head around it."

"So you have a new place to live."

"I do."

Wren stood close. She seemed to radiate something more than warmth. I could feel it down to my marrow. "And when you say you want to christen it, you mean . . ."

"I do."

"Hah. I'd better let Elana know we need to ease back on the tequila shots, then. Too many more and I'll be no good to you."

I grinned at her. Enjoying the challenge in her eyes.

"I have faith," I said.

ACKNOWLEDGMENTS

With gratitude to the people who unleashed *A Dangerous Breed*:

Lisa Erbach Vance of the Aaron Priest Literary Agency, a wonderful agent and first through the door in representing this and all my other works. Taking point takes courage and competence, and Lisa has both in spades.

Lyssa Keusch at William Morrow, a brilliant editor who hones and polishes every novel for the better, while making it seem like any improvements were my idea. And to the team at Morrow who steer and power the creative machine: our renowned publisher Liate Stehlik, Danielle Bartlett, Pamela Jaffee, Kaitlin Harri, Bob Castillo, Kyle O'Brien, and Mireya Chiriboga.

Caspian Dennis of the Abner Stein Agency, Van Shaw's top operative in the UK.

And to those who lent their knowledge and technical expertise. They offered their time and energy to make the story richer, sometimes only to find their hours of conversation distilled into a single line in the final draft. Any mistakes are my own darn fault.

Patricia Powell, MD, and Dave "Doc" Powell, USN, for specifics on field medicine, pharmaceuticals, oncology, and all things related to the healing sciences.

Christian Hockman, Bco 1/75 Ranger Regiment, for his military and tactical support.

John N. Nassikas III, Partner at Arnold & Porter and former federal prosecutor, for the structure and operations of joint task forces and their work with confidential informants.

Jeannette Wentworth and Betsy Glick of the FBI, for lessons on the science of DNA collection, profiling, and analysis.

Sheryl Moss of the Office of the Secretary of State, for insights into Washington State's political processes.

Los Anarchists Junior Roller Derby in Los Angeles, where our own young jammer skated hard.

And finally, for support both emotional and spiritual:

Jerrilyn Farmer, and the Saturday Gang—Beverly Graf, Alexandra Jamison, and John McMahon. Fighting the good fight, word by word.

Rick Martens, charity auction "character name" winner. Rick, for the benefit of anyone reading this first, I won't spoil whether your fictional counterpart makes it out alive.

My sincere thanks to every reader who gave this book a try; I hope you enjoyed the tale. And to the booksellers, reviewers, and fans who might have helped that reader find the novel in the first place. Your dedication transforms a solitary pursuit into a warm and welcoming community of friends.

Amy, Mia, and Madeline, I love you so much. Thank you for your unwavering faith and for making our home a peaceful harbor from any storm, including the occasional tempest inside my head.

AUTHOR'S NOTE

This novel is fiction, which means I get to make up anything and everything, including but not limited to businesses real or imagined, jurisdictions, history, or anything else that might keep the story moving, keep the lawyers bored, and keep potentially dangerous information where and with whom it belongs.

That said, it's worth recognizing a few of the more egregious liberties taken:

Sharp-eyed Seattle residents may have noticed that I've compressed and slightly accelerated the timeline of the long-awaited opening of the Alaskan Way underground tunnel, and the subsequent demolition of the old elevated viaduct. Neither had happened during January of the same year.

Washington State gubernatorial recalls, regardless of the circumstances, do not result in a runoff election between parties. The order of succession is a sedate process, where the duties would automatically fall upon the lieutenant governor. My way is more fun.

The beautiful Japanese Garden in Seattle's Washington Park Arboretum is closed to visitors during the winter months. Nor does it admit dogs at any time. Not even Stanley. These limitations aside, a peaceful hour spent in the garden is like a day's vacation anywhere else. If circumstances permit, I encourage you to see it for yourself.

ABOUT THE AUTHOR

A native of Seattle, Glen Erik Hamilton was raised aboard a sailboat and grew up around the marinas and commercial docks and islands of the Pacific Northwest. His debut novel, *Past Crimes*, won the Anthony, Macavity, and Strand Critics awards and was also nominated for the Edgar, Barry, and Nero awards. He now lives in California with his family, and he frequently returns to his hometown to soak up the rain.

Guiding Growth
in Reading

Guiding Growth in Reading

IN THE MODERN ELEMENTARY SCHOOL

SECOND EDITION

THE LATE

Margaret G. McKim

UNIVERSITY OF CINCINNATI

Helen Caskey

UNIVERSITY OF CINCINNATI

THE MACMILLAN COMPANY, NEW YORK
COLLIER-MACMILLAN LTD., LONDON

Library of Congress catalog card number: 63–8396

The Macmillan Company, New York
Collier-Macmillan Canada, Ltd., Galt, Ontario
DIVISIONS OF THE CROWELL-COLLIER PUBLISHING COMPANY

DESIGNED BY IRENE KEAN

Printed in the United States of America

To the teachers and children whose activities fill these pages and to my parents, Bessie Thomas McKim and Louis Thompson McKim, this book is gratefully and affectionately dedicated.

FOREWORD TO THE FIRST EDITION

A great many teachers will find this the most helpful book on the teaching of reading that has appeared in a long time. Whether the teacher is inexperienced and relatively inept or experienced and highly skilled, or any point between these extremes, she will find this book a treasury of helpful suggestions.

This volume is the result of a remarkably successful effort to survey all areas of research, practice, and theory for suggestions relating to the teaching of reading and then to organize and present them in a treatise designed specifically to help the teacher in her daily work. It is not a typical survey of research findings, but it is evident that the author has canvassed the fields of research and made use of all she regarded as pertinent. Although it is not a treatise on the basal, psychological theories of learning and teaching, it embodies a well-conceived system of psychological principles and uses them consistently.

The book is "practical" at every step, but it is not a mere collection of professional admonitions or lesson plans or descriptions of teaching devices, or procedures. It is a remarkable synthesis of information gathered from all sources and fashioned into a clear, lucid statement of the steps to take to become a better teacher of reading. It advocates no particular kind of curriculum, but should be equally helpful to teachers in all types of schools.

This book reflects the results of years of work in the classroom as observer of and adviser to many kinds of teachers in many types of schools, combined with the training of teachers, both experienced and inexperienced, in the author's own classes and with a diligent study of the literature. The book is remarkably free of vague generalizations and pedagogical jargon. The writing is simple and exact, unfamiliar technical terms are avoided, explanations are clear and pertinent, and practical suggestions are illustrated in a wealth of detailed reports of actual classroom activities, conversations, discussions, demonstrations, schedules, and other concrete data. Many teachers cooperated with Professor McKim to make this a *teacher's* book. The teacher can really understand it.

Professor McKim's book is a comprehensive report. Few are the problems or questions likely to be raised by a teacher which are not discussed frankly, fully, and constructively. The book advocates neither a new revolutionary theory nor a new practical "system"; it presents, rather, a sound and sensible guide to making the best use of the information and facilities now at our disposal for teaching reading. Let this statement not mislead anyone to assume that this volume is merely another report of "the same old stuff." It can be read with profit by anyone, not only the schoolteacher and principal, but also the reading specialist, and the most advanced reading investigator. This is a book which will do more than merely tell one how to make better use of all the available materials and methods of teaching reading. It will give a teacher new insights and equip her with general principles which will enable her the better to solve the many new problems certain to appear in the future.

ARTHUR I. GATES

January 10, 1955

PREFACE TO THE FIRST EDITION

This book is for classroom teachers.

It is not meant to add one volume more to the many now available which provide such excellent insights into the wealth of research in the field of reading and its bearing on the reading program in the modern school. Rather, it tries to answer the classroom teacher's frequent question, "Yes, but just how do I go about it with my children?"

Answers to questions of how to teach, while grounded in sound psychological principles and thoughtful consideration of existing research, reside, in their details, in the classrooms of creative teachers. The writer has tried to record and to interpret what she has been taught about the teaching of reading by the teachers and children with whom she has been privileged to work.

The focus of this volume is on the modern elementary-school classroom with its unit activities, its emphasis on pupil-teacher planning, and its concern for the maximum growth of each individual toward effective citizenship in the world of which he is a part. Most of the suggestions are not, however— the writer firmly believes—beyond the realm of possibility for the teacher who is working in a situation where resources are somewhat more limited or possibilities for grouping, scheduling, and program planning are not as flexible as those in some of the situations that have been used for illustrative purposes.

The discussion of teaching problems has been centered around three general stages of growth in learning to read: the prereading and beginning-reading period; the growth of primary children toward independent reading skills; and the development of the more mature techniques of the intermediate grades. A fourth section adds suggestions for appraising progress and for planning remedial help. Within this general framework, there has been no attempt to suggest a program grade by grade. Children will differ in their reading skills from that beginning September day when they walk into the kindergarten or first grade. Every teacher faces the problem of adjusting materials and methods to a wide range of abilities. Within the growth stages that have been indicated, an effort has been made to show how reading skill develops and to indicate how activities may be varied to meet differing needs.

Primary teachers may find some of the suggestions for work with older children appropriate to their purposes, while teachers of intermediate grades may find themselves using the simpler approaches more typical of work with younger children.

Teachers will need to skim to use this book effectively. It is not short, because the details of classrooms in action take time to spell out. It is repetitive in parts. Teaching reading is complex, and a single activity rarely contributes to one skill alone. Whenever possible, cross references to related sections are given, but an area of emphasis, a teaching technique, or a general principle is mentioned again when it seems that the full story cannot be told without it. Sections within chapters are organized around what seem to be major teaching problems. Section and paragraph headings, and in some cases side headings, have been used in an effort to provide help in the easy location of specific areas of interest.

This book is intentionally rich in the variety of detailed suggestions. It is the hope of the author that it will indicate goals that will challenge the experienced teacher as well as provide practical ideas for the novice. Beginning teachers should not expect to achieve immediately in their classrooms the complex organization of some of the situations that are described, and, if the book truly serves its purpose, experienced teachers should find more specific suggestions than they would use with any one class.

Although teaching suggestions have been given in detail, prescriptions have been avoided. Every classroom is different and the test of a procedure is its effectiveness in meeting the needs of a particular group of children. A conscientious effort has been made to identify underlying principles which the teacher can use as guides in making the adjustments appropriate to her situation. It is the writer's conviction that the ultimate success of a reading program depends upon the insights, sensitivity, and good judgment of the individual classroom teacher.

The typical lists of study-guide questions for students have been omitted. Instead, each chapter closes with questions suggested as a basis for appraising the aspect of the reading program under discussion. It is hoped that these may be of help to teachers studying the reading activities of their classes, and to school faculties as they go about their never-ending professional obligation of building better school programs for boys and girls.

MARGARET G. McKIM

Cincinnati, Ohio

PREFACE TO THE SECOND EDITION

The years since this book was first published have been years of rapid change and intensified interest in the problem of teaching children to read. In the light of these changes and of continued interest in the teaching of reading, this revised edition presents new resources recently made available. Also, it is hoped that there is an even more sharply focused delineation of the broad range of information available for teachers.

It should be emphasized that this book does not present a "system" for teaching reading; nor does it represent an attempt to repeat what others have successfully accomplished in summarizing research, and in reporting current practice in specific areas in the field of reading. The reader will find, however, that the detailed suggestions presented, and the emphasis placed upon the development of the individual pupil within the framework of a flexible program of group instruction, permits the kind of planning that frees both pupil and teacher to work purposefully and creatively in many kinds of school situations. Teachers and pupils, in the procedures outlined here, can plan together the kinds of procedures best suited to their needs, and can reap the benefits of the many suggestions for individual and group activities.

The revision of a presentation as comprehensive and carefully articulated as the one made by Dr. McKim in *Guiding Growth in Reading* is no light undertaking. Colleagues at the University of Cincinnati, especially Dr. Nancy Manney, Dr. Nancy Nunnally, Dr. Betty Beaty, and Dr. Gordon Hendrickson, have been most helpful in giving counsel. Gratitude is also expressed to Dr. Althea Beery of the Cincinnati Public Schools, and to Miss Helen Bertermann and the staff at Schiel School, Cincinnati Public Schools.

Permission to quote was granted by Dr. James Bryner for the experience records from his doctor's dissertation, quoted in Chapter VIII; by the Cincinnati Public Schools for the experience records in Chapter VIII taken from the *New Primary Manual;* by Ginn and Company for excerpts quoted in Chapter V from *The Ginn Basic Readers, My Little Red Story Book* revised edition, 1961 by Odille Ousley and David H. Russell; and by The Macmillan Company for the excerpts quoted in Chapter V from *Splash,* First Basal Preprimer of the Macmillan Readers, and from *Tuffy and Boots,* Second Basal Preprimer of the Macmillan Readers, by A. I. Gates, et al. The pictures are reproduced with the permission of the Cincinnati Public Schools.

It is the writer's hope that Dr. McKim's contribution through this book will continue to be of assistance to teachers as they go about the challenging task of helping pupils to become more able readers and wiser, more mature persons. No more appropriate memorial to a colleague devoted to the welfare of pupils and teachers could be devised.

HELEN CASKEY
Cincinnati, Ohio.

CONTENTS

xiii

Part III

DEVELOPING INDEPENDENT READERS IN THE PRIMARY GRADES

Part IV

EXPANDING READING SKILLS IN THE
INTERMEDIATE GRADES

Part V

ASSURING THE PROGRESS OF INDIVIDUALS—
APPRAISAL AND REMEDIAL HELP

Guiding Growth

in Reading

PART I

Learning to Read in Today's Schools

CHAPTER I

What Does It Mean to be Able to Read?

ADULTS READ IN TODAY'S WORLD

Adults read for pleasure. In a small town Mrs. Bairns finishes the supper dishes and settles down with the novel passed on to her by another member of the local book club. Her husband is looking at the evening paper. At the same moment three riders sitting side by side in a city subway train are reading—one reads a pocket book, another a comic book, and the third, a copy of a Broadway hit play. Travelers pause before magazine stands in the Union Station, choosing a magazine or paperback to read while they wait for train or bus to be announced. On an airplane high overhead, the stewardess gives magazines to passengers who settle down to read. A young woman in her suburban home picks up a magazine from the well-filled rack by the easy chair. There are copies of *Reader's Digest, Time, Life, The Saturday Evening Post*, and *Better Homes and Gardens* from which to choose.

In the house next door, Mrs. Newton sits down to read a recent popular biography, and looks forward to reading *Advise and Consent*. The sixteen-year-old son of the family has just discovered an anthology of the stories of Sherlock Holmes. Farther down the street, Mr. Jones, tense and weary from the strains and responsibilities of his rapidly expanding business, relaxes with a detective story. Mr. Johnson, "Grampa" to all the kids on the block, follows a pattern of long years' standing, as he reads a chapter from the Bible before he snaps off his bedside lamp. The community library, at the corner of Maple and Tenth Streets, is open. From its doors comes a small, but steady procession of borrowers, carrying home books of fiction, biography, travel, history and adventure. Each reader follows his own reading bent.

Adults read for specific information. In her farm kitchen Mrs. Martin locates her favorite recipe for blackberry jam. Then she reads the instructions on the bottle of special preservative she plans to use. Outdoors her husband is following the directions for assembling a new piece of farm equipment. Later in the day Mrs. Martin makes out an order from a mail-order catalog. In the city Mrs. Green looks at the bus schedule as she prepares to go shopping for the bargains advertised in last night's paper. Her husband reads the daily mail and checks several orders that have come into his office. He proofreads some letters, and then looks carefully through a set of new building regulations to see if they apply to him. Later in the day he reads the details of a new fire insurance policy. Dr. Allen brings home the latest copy of a medical journal, and looks for recent information on a new drug he is considering for one of his patients. The principal of the local school scans the *NEA Journal* and reads a new professional book with care to see if it should be purchased for the school library. His son, in the basement workshop, is following instructions for building a model nuclear submarine. In the evening in many homes, people turn to daily or weekly papers to keep up with local or world events, read editorials on a future election issue, check the standing of the local baseball team, look at gardening or beauty hints, or read weather reports.

Adults read to locate material bearing on a problem. Mr. Johns has spent the afternoon in the professional library of his firm doing research on a new chemical process. Mrs. Owen has a report to make to the parent-teacher association on the influence of television upon children's school work. She and the librarian have spent the afternoon tracking down studies. Mrs. Clay turns to the dictionary for help in spelling a word. Later she looks up a friend's phone number in the directory. On their vacation the Joneses follow road maps with care and turn to automobile club guide booklets for places to stay. Mr. Thomas uses the index in his paper to locate his favorite television programs. A little later he is interrupted by Betty, aged 10, who is trying to find information on the industries of the Eastern states for a school assignment. Together they consult the family encyclopedia. They also try the index in her geography text and check maps in an atlas.

Adults read aloud to share materials with others. Mr. Harte is in a secluded corner of the house practicing the speech he is to give to the local lodge. Mrs. White has put the children to bed and is reading them a bedtime story. Later she does some sewing, while Mr. White reads parts of the evening paper to her. At the meeting of the local agricultural society, Mrs. Nelson reads the minutes of the previous meeting, then Mr. Gardener reads the financial report. Downtown at the radio station, the announcer reads the news and then four local merchants refer to script topics for a panel discussion. On Sunday morning the Sunday school superintendent reads the lesson and parts of the hymns aloud. The drama circle meets once a month to read plays; the poet's corner meets to recite poetry; and a group of professional men meets to present papers.

These examples of the many reading activities in which adults engage are reminders that today's Western world is a reading world. Although radio, motion pictures, and television are popular means of communicating ideas, reading continues to be widely used, and so automatically that we are scarcely aware of the extent to which we use language in printed form. We turn to daily papers, to books and magazines for help in making up our minds on controversial issues. Vicariously, we ride with the test pilot in a new plane, or live the lives of personages in the public eye. We read a favorite book or magazine for relaxation, or for the esthetic satisfaction of reading beautiful prose or poetry. Our attitudes, levels of aspiration for our standards of living, and our judgments on moral issues are to some extent affected by what we read.

In a democratic society it is particularly important that citizens be skilled readers, not only in their ability to understand the printed page, but also in their ability and disposition to evaluate what they have read: the source, its accuracy, fairness, and the presence or absence of emotional tones in its presentation. On local issues an informed citizen has a direct influence—by his vote—on the composition of the city council and school board, the passage of a bond issue for local improvements, the success of a tax levy for the schools. On the national and international scene, the influence of the individual, though more remote, is still felt. A lasting peace may well depend on how clearly informed national groups are to understand the values, forms of government, and needs, not only of allied nations, but also nations with whom they find themselves in opposition on group attitudes toward the United Nations, the use of atomic energy, and the demands and obligations of international cooperation.

CHILDREN READ IN TODAY'S SCHOOLS

The reading problems of adulthood have their counterpart in the problems faced by children in elementary school classrooms. From the first day of school, teachers help children learn to use reading to serve the same types of purposes it does for their parents. The difference is in the degree of complexity, not in the type of problem. What reading activities would a visitor to a modern elementary school observe?

Children read for pleasure. Five-year-old Harry in the kindergarten has spent the last fifteen minutes examining the pictures in an alphabet book page by page. Similar experiences have occurred previously in Harry's home when he shared his favorite books with Daddy and Mother at bedtime.

Marian, in the first grade, is at the library table rereading some primer stories with which she has recently worked in a reading group. Children in this first grade, like those in other classes in the school, look forward to times when the teacher reads stories to them.

In one second grade, the children have just finished reading some Halloween stories. This is a special treat, but these children also look forward to the basàl-reader stories they read regularly. In another second grade, the most advanced readers have planned to work for the next two weeks on easy library books which their teacher helped them choose.

On a third-grade bulletin board is a letter from a classmate, now in another state. Another third grade has appointed a librarian to help keep the library table in order. This school has no access to community library facilities, but teachers have systematically added to room collections and there is some borrowing back and forth on special occasions.

In a fourth grade, the children prefer to keep their library books in their desks so that they can be reached more easily in spare minutes. One group of children in this class has just finished an interesting reading unit on folk- and fairy tales, using several basal readers at their reading level. They are planning to dramatize the ones they like best for the rest of the class.

In a fifth grade, over half the class is engrossed in fictional stories about pioneer days. The children became acquainted with these books when the teacher returned from the library with an armload of them at the beginning of a social-studies unit. On the bulletin board in another class are creative poems in free verse giving impressions of a recent snowstorm.

The poorest readers in one sixth grade have been reading an easy basal reader. They enjoy following the adventures of the characters in these stories, and look forward eagerly to the next story. On the library table in another classroom are copies of a class magazine containing creative stories and poems which class members have contributed during the year.

Children read for specific information. In kindergarten the children know which cloakroom hook is theirs for each has a child's name and a special picture symbol beside it. Many of these children can recognize their own mats for rest periods because their names are on them.

In a first grade, Sandy shows his mother the experience record his class dictated after a walk to the park. On the chalkboard in manuscript writing is a letter inviting mothers to a party. On the bulletin board is a list entitled, "What We Need for Our Party." Next to the easel in another class are simple instructions for cleaning paint brushes.

In a second grade, the children follow carefully the directions for making jelly. On the walls of their "store," constructed in one corner of the room, are a list of instructions for the clerks and a list of prices. In their basal readers they have found stories about stores. Pictures of stores in their neighborhood adorn another bulletin board, and captions tell what kinds of stores they are.

One third-grade group is working with separate stories on animals as part of a unit on pets. On the chalkboard is a list of questions the children are trying to answer. In another third grade, the children have summarized their information on post offices in a series of experience records held together with rings and placed on an easel for rereading. In another room a daily weather chart is kept up to date by various members of the group.

In a fourth grade, the children are working from books on several levels in a study of transportation. On the bulletin board are a number of pictures from magazines and newspapers. Lists of group plans and of committees have been posted. Nearby are fire-drill regulations. In another fourth grade, a schedule for the day is written on the front board. Next to it is a list entitled, "If You Finish Early." On a bulletin board in this room is a chart showing the income from this week's sale of seeds.

One fifth grade has most of its available table space covered with pamphlets on national parks. In another, children are reporting on interesting news events from a commercially published children's weekly newspaper. Posted on the bulletin boards in another class are group reports of a study of "Where Our City Gets Its Food."

In a sixth grade, children are reporting the suggestions in their language book regarding the correct way to punctuate a business letter. In another, a study of the United Nations is in progress. Each group is using textbooks, current articles from newspapers, encyclopedias, and materials secured from writing to the information centers of various countries. Pamphlets regarding the United Nations itself are also in evidence. A large wall map is in constant use.

Children read to locate material bearing on a problem. In kindergarten, Eleanor is able to tell which of the children's favorite stories her teacher is going to read today because she knows the pictures on the cover and the general look of the book. These children also know where to look on the bulletin board to see if anyone has a birthday.

In a first grade, Dora knows what her housekeeping responsibility is for the day because she can read her name, and the helpers' chart has pictures next to the words indicating the tasks to be done. In a reading group in another first grade, the children can find the title to their new story and know how to turn to the correct page.

In a second grade, the children enjoy looking through a picture dictionary. When they start work with a new basal reader they look over the table of contents to see what kinds of stories it will have. For another second grade, where the desire to write outstrips the ability to spell, the teacher has posted all the new words needed in alphabetical lists classified by first letters only.

One third grade has made up a telephone directory as part of some science activities in rigging up a play telephone. This group also knows how to use a simple index to locate information. In another third grade, groups reading independently find the information they want from a short bibliography posted by the teacher.

In a fourth grade, children build their own bibliography for a study of Mexico by looking through several social-studies textbooks and other materials borrowed from the library by the teacher and writing down the pages that seem to fit. Chapter titles and paragraph and section headings help as much as the index does.

In a fifth grade a "Manners Committee" has checked the contents of several language books for advice on how to behave when the class invites its principal to lunch. Children in this class made extensive use of the classroom encyclopedia in locating information about materials from which clothing is made. Another group is becoming quite adept in using the diacritical marks in the glossary in its basal-reader series. Children in this class made their first extensive use of maps in a study of the states in which they spent their vacations.

As part of the project of publishing their own paper, the children in a sixth grade have made a study of newspapers. They have been greatly interested in learning how to get information quickly from a feature article by judicious use of headline and opening paragraph. In another sixth grade the children are using the dictionary as an aid in their study of roots, prefixes, and suffixes.

Children read aloud to share materials with others. In the kindergarten the children enjoy joining in rhyming finger plays. Many of them also take great delight in supplying names and repetitive phrases when the teacher reads their favorite stories aloud. When they invite their mothers to visit them in the spring, Ronnie, as master of ceremonies, names the items on the program from a picture list.

Helen, in first grade, is practicing reading a primer story aloud so that she can take it home to read to her mother. Children in another first grade take pleasure in reading parts of a story in a basal reader aloud to each other just to show how well they are learning to read.

In a second grade, the children have just been invited to send a group to read stories to the kindergarten. In another class the children are getting ready to read their rainy-day poems to their mothers.

In a third grade, groups are getting ready to read their first social-studies reports to the rest of the class. In a reading group the children have enjoyed taking turns reading a story aloud while others in the group acted it in pantomime.

In a fourth grade, the children in one reading group are in the midst of getting ready for a make-believe radio program. They will read parts of a story from behind a sheet stretched over the cloakroom doorway. During social-studies work periods the children in this class have devised a system of letting the better readers read some of the harder books aloud while their group listens.

In a fifth grade, a heated argument has developed. Alex says, "My book says so, right here," and reads a passage aloud. Jim answers, "That's not in my book. It says . . ."

In a sixth grade, the children have been working with a tape recorder to improve their oral-reading skill. When the club meets in another sixth grade, Jim reads the minutes of the meeting. One group in this class had fun reading the parts of a play found in a basal reader.

These are modern elementary classrooms in action. They are rich in their invitations to read. Where there once were sets of forty copies of a single text, now there are likely to be smaller sets of several series, or at least other books to supplement an adopted text. This is true not only of basal readers but of textbooks in content fields. Children in these classrooms also have access to reference materials of many sorts. Classroom libraries provide for recreational and informational reading, and in many situations these are supplemented by resources in school and community libraries. Home resources of magazines and daily papers are tapped. Special materials, unavailable elsewhere, are sometimes written by the teacher, or by teacher and children together. In addition, bulletin boards and chalkboards provide many other types of reading experiences. Children live and work in a school world where it is important to be able to read.

Children in these classrooms know what they are about. They have had a part in thinking through what is to be done and why it is important. Among the most important skills they learn, from the kindergarten and first grade on, are those related to carrying forward a project independently, or, more often, as cooperative group members. The plans on the bulletin boards, the lists of jobs to be done, or the special problems to be answered through wide reading, all have meaning because the children have helped to set them up and have talked them through. Children turn to their reading in these classrooms with clear purposes in mind.

Teachers are important in these situations. They guide plans and identify new problems or areas of study. They are the ones who help to locate new materials, supply needed information, and teach new skills; who challenge the accuracy of a report or suggest a better way of working. It is part of their job to study the needs of the children in their classes and to make sure that a program of activities leading to well-rounded development is being provided. In these classrooms, however, teachers can often be found working with small groups or individual children rather than with the class as a whole. This freedom to give individualized attention is possible because children have been helped to develop good habits of independent and cooperative work.

These children must think while they read. From their first reading experiences, they are called upon to make thoughtful and critical judgments. This is as true of Dick, in first grade, helping to reread an experience record to make sure nothing important about a recent excursion has been left out, as it is of Ruth, in sixth grade, trying to decide if she has enough information to prepare her part of a group report; of six-year-old Billy, who complains that animals really don't talk, and eleven-year-old Don, who finds that the dates given in two of his history books disagree. It is important to read class plans accurately when your group is depending on you; to be careful about what you read to prepare a report when the whole class is going to look to you for information; and to have an opinion about why you liked a story in a basal reader when your group must decide whether to share it with the whole class.

Allowance is made in these classrooms for a range of needs, interests, and abilities; for capitalizing on strengths and for giving help where there are weaknesses. The children work together as a total class, but they also work in groups and undertake some individualized activities. Their reading materials are selected to care for a range in reading skills. When special practice is provided, it, too, is planned to meet specific needs. These adjustments to individual and group needs are possible partly because teachers take children into the planning process and partly because teachers work under flexible schedules.

These learning situations extend beyond the covers of books, the doorways of the classroom, and the boundaries of the school grounds. The children go into their communities to get information and invite community resource people to the school. Problems that are real to children in their daily lives find a place in their classrooms. Studies of other times and other lands are planned so that their bearing on the modern world, as children see it, can be explored. In these settings children find many purposes for reading, and many things to read about, but they also learn how to use their reading as one of many avenues to knowledge and personal satisfaction.

WHAT MAKES A SKILLFUL READER?

What skills does it take to meet the reading demands of the modern world? Toward what goals should the reading programs in today's schools be directed? The specific answer, for any one classroom, comes from the teacher's analysis of the abilities of her children and the reading problems that are being raised for them by their day-by-day activities. The suggestions that follow represent only one of many possible ways of looking at the problem as a whole.

A skillful reader understands what he reads. Reading is a tool. We read for something—to be entertained, to secure information, to follow directions, to solve a problem. The skilled reader has learned to turn to his reading with clear purposes. He possesses the experience background and the stock of word meanings that enable him to interpret accurately what he reads. He looks at words, sentences, and paragraphs in the light of what they have to offer for his purposes. He is alert and receptive to new ideas. When he reads to answer a specific question, he has learned to spot quickly those sections of the material that provide him the best answers to his questions. He skims new material quickly to see whether or not pictures, graphs, maps, and chapter headings look like promising sources. When he reads fiction he is able to follow a plot, sense the clues to character given by the author, and visualize the scenes described. He understands what he reads.

Therefore, beginning reading experiences start with the problem of clear understanding. A child first learns that words hold meaning for him, and he turns to books for pleasure and for information. As he does so, his teachers help him to take necessary steps toward developing the skills he will need in order to use printed materials quickly and easily. Reading for meaning continues to be basic to all his reading experiences through life, in school and out.

A skillful reader deals efficiently with the symbols he meets. Clear understandings can be obscured if the reader is not efficient in the way he works with printed symbols. Reading is one of the language arts. Long before he learns to read, the child learns to use words to express himself and to understand the words others are saying to him. Soon after he enters first grade, he begins to work with words in printed form. He must learn to recognize them, know what they mean, be able to tell them from other words with similar configurations, and eventually learn how to work out their pronunciation for himself.

Skillful reading calls for much more than mere identification of words. As the reader typically meets them, words are presented in phrases, sentences, or paragraphs. This is true even of preprimer materials. In one of the earliest studies of the way people read, Buswell [1] demonstrated that an effective reader senses the phrase units that best convey the meaning of a passage. The progress of his eyes across a line is irregular but forward-moving. The more skillful he is the less frequently he has to look back to restudy a word, to catch more accurately the beginning of a line, or to sense the meaning of a phrase. The skillful reader also learns to adjust his reading rate. He knows how to skim material from which he wants only general information and how to proceed slowly when every phrase in an article demands his attention. When he reads aloud, he has the added problem of conveying the meaning of a passage to others through skillful use of his voice.

Most reading matter calls for skills in addition to efficiency with words, sentences, and paragraphs. Paragraph headings, section headings, chapter summaries, pictures, graphs, maps, and other such ways of adding to the meaning of a passage, also have to be interpreted. Then, as the reader seeks to locate materials for himself, he must be able to use a dictionary, an index, an encyclopedia, a table of contents, and other aids to the location of materials.

These are not the abilities of the adult reader alone. A beginner works with sentences and very short paragraphs. He will meet chapter titles, and

[1] Guy Thomas Buswell, *Fundamental Reading Habits: A Study of Their Development.* Supplementary Educational Monographs No. 21 (Chicago: University of Chicago Press, 1922).

perhaps section headings. By the end of the first year he will have examined tables of contents. Even a first-grader has times when he does not want to read a story carefully, but skims it for a general impression. Sometimes he reads silently, and sometimes he reads aloud to a group. Every reader, at his own level, faces problems of working efficiently with the materials he reads.

A skillful reader adjusts his techniques to the purposes for which he reads. The most effective reading techniques do not operate automatically the same in all situations. They are flexible in terms of the reader's purposes and the material at hand. There is, for example, no one best way of skimming or of reading carefully. Skimming several books to see if they are likely to give help on a problem and skimming a single passage in a history text to recheck a date are different processes. Reading the details of an arithmetic problem for the first time and rereading a basal-reader story to get the details of a scene in order to draw a picture are done in different fashions. There is no one best way of analyzing a word. In one setting a complete phonetic analysis may be needed. In other, context clues and beginning letters may be enough. The skillful reader understands how to vary his approach appropriately for his problem and his material.

Children face problems of adjusting their reading skills as they read for different purposes. Even beginners work with a variety of materials and purposes as they move back and forth from various types of classroom records, signs, and notices to the simple story-type materials of their preprimers. In classrooms where children use materials in many ways, flexible adjustment of techniques to purposes is always part of the problem.

A skillful reader evaluates what he reads. The ability to make critical evaluation of the materials read has already been identified as an important reading skill in a democratic society. The skillful reader must decide whether the information given him comes from a trustworthy source. He is alert to the possible bias of the author: Who said this? What previous stand has the writer taken on this question? What experience has he had which would tend to qualify (or disqualify) him for writing on this topic? These are familiar questions to the good reader as he reflects upon his reading. He can judge when the materials at hand provide sufficient information, and when to seek for more. He is aware of emotionally toned words, specifically introduced to make him favor or disfavor a given proposition. He can alert himself to the possibility that only part of the information necessary to a clear understanding of the problem has been given, and is able to withold judgment until more evidence is in. He realizes that many "answers" cannot be final, and is willing to hazard a tentative solution and abandon it, when subsequent information makes it desirable to do so.

Children who are reading widely to solve problems have many experiences involving critical evaluation. To prepare reports they must select pertinent and accurate information. They find that older books may not have the up-to-date data that are needed. They note the special qualifications of an author to write about the Far East. They may question the ideas presented in the stories they read, raising such questions as: "Did the log cabin look like this picture?" "Is this the way people talked and dressed in those days?" "Would a young colt really leave good pasture grass to eat hay as the story describes?" These critical, thought-provoking, questioning aspects of reading are involved when children have opportunities to ready widely and freely for purposes that are clear and important to them.

A skillful reader likes to read. The reading program has fallen short of its

Cincinnati Public Schools

The joy of learning to read is found in getting pleasure from a story "on your own."

goal if it does not result in readers who enjoy books. All reading is not problem solving. Those who read widely have explored many types of literature—fiction, biography, science, philosophy, history, poetry, and drama. Through their reading experiences they have become sensitive to the impressions the author is giving as well as to the words he uses. They have learned to sense the mood of a poem and to despair or rejoice as a biography unfolds. Their experiences with good writing enable them to respond with esthetic satisfaction to apt choices of words and phrases and beauty of sentence structure. People who have learned to enjoy reading have developed standards of critical judgment regarding the literary, emotional, and esthetic values of what they read.

Children whose parents read stories to them begin to develop reading tastes and interests even before they come to school. Classroom libraries and school or community libraries help to expand their acquaintance with books. Stories in basal-reader series are planned so as to give many different types of reading experiences. Texts and supplementary books open doorways to their physical world, to their country, and to other lands. The modern elementary school is rich in opportunities to develop reading interests and tastes.

A skillful reader knows when to turn to books for help. Reading is only one means of communication. Printed words are abstractions. Their meaning depends, in part, on the kind of firsthand experience the reader brings to his reading. It is one thing to read about the Rocky Mountains, or even to see motion pictures of them, and another to motor through them. Going to visit the slums in one's city adds something important to newspaper editorials on housing. Reading about how to teach children to read and walking into a classroom to do the job are very different experiences. The skillful reader knows how and when to use reading effectively. He also knows how and when to turn to other sources of information.

Children in today's schools learn to explore their world through many avenues other than books. Even in the first grade they learn the difference between the trip they took and what they were able to record of it on an experience record, and the difference between reading about a rabbit and having someone's pet bunny in the school to watch. Older children learn what museums have to offer, evaluate motion pictures, and take trips to collect information. They live in a real world to which books make many kinds of contributions. Their reading experiences teach them how to read and how to be thoughtful about what they read. They also learn when to read and how to supplement their reading so that what they are studying comes alive.

A CHALLENGE TO TEACHERS

Reading is an important aspect of living, in school and out. It serves many different purposes and it calls for a wide variety of skills, attitudes, and understanding. To teach children to meet the varied reading demands of today's world is at once a crucial task for education and an undertaking calling for a high level of skill, insight, and resourcefulness on the part of the teacher.

SUGGESTIONS FOR FURTHER READING

Asheim, Lester, "What Do Adults Read," *Adult Reading.* Fifty-fifth Yearbook of the National Society for the Study of Education, Part II, pp. 5-28. Chicago: The University of Chicago Press, 1956. 273 pp.

Burton, William H. *Reading in Child Development.* Chapter 1. Indianapolis: The Bobbs-Merrill Co., 1956. 608 pp.

Gray, Lillian, and Reese, Dora. *Teaching Children to Read.* Second Edition, Chapters 1 and 2. New York: The Ronald Press Company, 1957. 475 pp.

Gray, William S., and Rogers, Bernice. *Maturity in Reading: Its Nature and Appraisal.* Chicago: The University of Chicago Press, 1956. 273 pp.

Hildreth, Gertrude H. *Teaching Reading.* Chapter 1. New York: Henry Holt and Co., 1958. 339 pp.

Hunnicutt, Clarence W., and Iverson, William J. *Research in the Three R's.* Chapter 1. New York: Harper and Brothers, 1958. 446 pp.

Russell, David H. *Children Learn to Read.* Second Edition, Chapter 1. Boston: Ginn and Company, 1961. 612 pp.

Waples, Douglas; Berelson, Bernard; and Bradshaw, Franklin R. *What Reading Does to People.* Chicago: University of Chicago Press, 1940. 222 pp.

Titles of books and names of magazines and authors in the examples on page 3 came from:

Hackett, Alice Payne. *Fifty Years of Best Sellers, 1895-1945.* New York: R. R. Bowker Company, 1945. 140 pp.

The World Almanac for 1961. New York: New York World-Telegram and Sun, 1961. 896 pp.

CHAPTER II

Guides for a Successful Reading Program

WHAT are the characteristics of reading programs that help children meet with success the reading demands of their daily activities? How are they helped to grow toward adult reading skills? From first grade on, children face varied needs for effective reading. Programs that meet these needs must be equally varied. They cannot be outlined simply. The general principles suggested in this chapter apply to all grade levels. Discussions of specific applications for differing levels of ability are given in the chapters that follow. Experienced teachers may find the guides proposed here useful as an overview, and perhaps as a basis for appraising the activities of their classrooms. Beginners may wish to reread this chapter after they have looked further into the detailed descriptions of programs in action.

EVERY SITUATION MAKES ITS CONTRIBUTION

All the child's reading activities have a place. A child's reading program needs to be thought of as composed of all the situations in which he reads. Some of these will be experiences planned to develop specific skills; some will consist of recreational reading; some will be activities calling for wide reading for information; some will be the experiences offered by the signs and notices around the classroom. Appraisals of the type of reading experience a child is receiving, the skills he is being helped to develop, and decisions regarding next steps need to take the full range of his reading into account. A group in first grade has just developed a book of experience records about helpers in its school. Here may be all the new vocabulary these children can take for the moment. A third-grade group has found in a basal reader some stories that bear directly on a classroom project. For a time this could be the best source of informational reading. A fourth grade has discovered the fun of independent recreational reading. This may well be the most significant experience in reading for them for a considerable period. Children in sixth grade read well when they are working silently but do poorly when they read aloud. These children may find preparing to present plays or engaging in choral speaking will provide the balance of activities they need. An ever-present problem in today's classrooms is that of finding time to give all children the help they need. Part of the answer lies in the skill with which use is made of every teaching opportunity and the degree to which activities are coordinated.

Classroom reading problems help to determine teaching emphases. In classrooms rich in opportunities to read, the way in which a child's skill develops, and the order and setting in which he meets new problems, are determined by his total reading experience. A reading program may be planned with a general sequence of experiences in mind, but as children venture farther afield in their independent reading it must become increasingly flexible in terms of these new situations and the needs they uncover. Jackie, in Grade One, is using the primer of a standard basal-reader series, but he is also in a classroom where bulletin-board notices and captions to pictures abound, and he has helped prepare several records of group excursions. Who is to say, for sure, what his reading vocabulary is and which of the new words listed in the basal reader will actually need a special introduction? Bob's name begins with *B*, Sidney's with *S*. Will this make a difference in the beginning letters to which they respond most readily in their first word-analysis activities? A workbook for a basal reader may put exercises with an encyclopedia late in the fourth grade, but Miss White's class may need to use this reference aid early in the fall. As they try to make an extensive report, children in a sixth grade may find suddenly that simple outlining skills will no longer do. Out of such situations come the day-by-day problems that children are trying to handle as they use reading for many purposes. Their reading programs must help them meet these problems.

All classroom reading materials serve a purpose. The materials used to teach children to read, then, are as varied as the problems they face. Basal readers are important, but they are only one source of reading experience. In first grade, children may also be trying to read several kinds of classroom records. Later in the year many of these children will read independently several easy books for beginning readers. In third grade, they may need help in their first experiences in reading books for information. In the fifth they may be working with copies of the classroom encyclopedia. At any level a wide range of possibilities exist for individual choices in reading. At one time the job may be to learn how to read arithmetic problems accurately; at another, how to find information in a science text without losing time; and at a third, how to interpret an article in a daily paper. A child's reading instruction must be planned so that he is given the help he needs to work with each new type of material successfully. Everything a child reads is potentially a basis for reading instruction, and everything he reads provides an opportunity for him to practice reading skills.

EVERY NEEDED SKILL FINDS ITS PLACE

Reading activities are planned to develop many types of skills. The effective reading program is a broad program. It will be broad, of necessity, if it is planned in terms of children's daily reading activities. It needs, also, to be planned consciously to give children an opportunity to develop the full range of reading skills, interests, and attitudes appropriate to their level of development. If it is important for children to learn to adjust the way they read to their purposes, then they need to read for many different reasons—to answer a specific set of questions, to enjoy the humor of a story, to follow directions, and to outline a story so as to propose appropriate scenes for a play. If they are to learn to make critical evaluations of what they read, they must face situations where judgments are important and where information from more than one source needs to be appraised. To be able to read aloud well enough to hold the attention of an audience is a skill that cannot be developed in the first two or three years of school alone. Since reading aloud is an important aspect of adult reading skill, it should find its place among other activities in the intermediate grades. Breadth of reading experiences can be planned from the beginning. Even primer materials can be handled so that children read for different purposes.

Conscious provision for varied reading skills needs to be made, not only through activities designed to focus direct instruction on reading, but also in related classroom activities. In primary classrooms, many types of class lists, plans, experience records, and captions to pictures can call for varied reading skills. With more mature readers, projects in science, social studies, health, and other areas can be planned so that children learn to use their textbooks and supplementary reading materials in many different ways. Recreational reading is important at all levels. First experiences will, of necessity, be simple and carefully guided by the teacher, but as children grow in independence they can be encouraged to capitalize on their increased skill.

Teaching materials are selected so as to raise many types of reading problems. Varied skills are developed more readily when children work with many types of materials. This is another reason for considering all classroom reading-matter as potential instructional material. Basal-reader series are planned, typically, to provide for variety both in content and style. Depending upon their general level of reading ability, children also need the experience of working with brief passages for directions or details; of reading an entire book; of looking for information in the chapters of several books; and of using indexes, tables of contents, dictionaries, encyclopedias, pictures, maps, graphs, and charts. Many types of classroom materials need to be used as a basis for reading instruction if children are to become efficient in their daily reading activities. This variety is equally important as a means of introducing them to new problems and as a method of developing needs for new skills.

Teachers' insights into the nature of skillful reading serve as guides to choice of experiences. Judgments as to what skills need to be emphasized in any given situation depend in large measure upon the insight of the classroom teacher. Johnny says he has read his story, but he comes up with very few right answers. What skills does he lack? It may be that he is reading too rapidly. Perhaps the material is too difficult and he only half-understands many of the words. Perhaps he does not know what he was looking for and needs more help in establishing purposes before he begins to read. What clues to the difficulty the teacher senses, and how she interprets them, depend on her insight into how reading skill develops. Children's reading activities need to be guided by a teacher who is competent to develop their reading experiences in terms of their needs, to use materials flexibly, and to provide the appropriate practice. This competence comes through understanding the reading process, the interrelationships among various reading skills, the nature of growth in learning to read, and the particular children in the class.

CAREFULLY PLANNED PRACTICE IS PROVIDED

Direct instruction is planned as needed to develop skill. In an effective reading program children are given definite instruction and practice. Although a child develops much proficiency by using his reading skills functionally from day to day, this does not mean that all instruction in how to read is incidental to these day-by-day reading experiences. One would not expect a tennis player or a pianist to perfect his techniques without help and without hours of practice focused on his specific needs. It is equally unrealistic to expect reading skill to improve without guidance. Some of the help will be provided in a planned sequence of activities developed around selected story and informational materials; some will be planned in relation to problems that have arisen in the course of other classroom reading activities; and some will be set up around work-type materials.

A program that provides for definite instruction and practice can still be responsive to classroom needs and individual growth problems. Typically, the highest degree of continuity from day to day is likely to be required for the activities of immature readers. As children become more skilled, their instruction and practice should become more flexible in terms of new reading needs and opportunities to practice reading skills arising from their classroom activities—first-graders decide to read some of their experience records aloud when their mothers come, and stop to practice; third-graders take time away from their basal readers to explore the books in their classroom library; fifth-graders discover that their social-studies textbook is one of their hardest books to read, and work at it as a reading group.

Practice is planned so that children work with reading skills in the way in which they will need them again. "We learn to do by doing" is a psychological principle that has definite implications for teachers of reading. Children need to practice reading skills in situations similar to those in which they will actually be using them. Activities of an artificial nature can be used with profit from time to time to focus a child's attention on a specific aspect of a skill or to highlight a process, but the bulk of his practice needs to be in a typical reading setting. The eventual goal of word-analysis activities, for example, is to help the child identify a new word in its context. His practice, then, needs to be planned so that he has ample opportunity to work with unfamiliar words in context. Work-type activities with guide words or alphabetical order can help to sharpen a child's dictionary skills, but he also needs to work with an actual dictionary in his hands. A skilled rapid reader must be able to see appropriate phrase units and key words without the benefit of mechanical equipment, flash cards, or paragraphs retyped so that there is an artificial gap from phrase to phrase. The more effectively teachers can capitalize on the child's daily reading experiences, the greater the amount of practice in a natural setting they will be able to provide. When it is important to supplement these experiences with special practice activities, they need to be planned with those situations in mind in which the skill will eventually be used.

Instruction and practice activities are planned so as to start where the child is. All children will not learn to read at the same rate. Factors such as general maturity, experience background, illness or physical defects, intellectual development, social and emotional maturity, and changing from school to school will have their influence. Within any classroom teachers need to be prepared for a range of three to five years in ability, or perhaps even more.[1] The reading program needs to be developed so as to take these differences into account.

While it is possible to plan so that the children are given completely individualized help,[2] many teachers will find it difficult to do so. The number of children in most elementary classrooms, the difficulties in finding time to meet with all pupils individually for guidance and discussion, lead most teachers to plan to meet individual needs largely through combinations of individual and group instruction. Teachers, however, are also individuals, and creative and skillful teachers will find many ways to meet the needs of children through adapting patterns of classroom organization to their own purposes. The most frequently used procedure is to plan for reading instruction and practice activities to meet the needs of groups working at several reading levels. This means not only finding time during the school day to work with these groups, but also equipping the classroom with reading materials for several different grades. It will be important, as well, to adjust recreational reading and experiences in reading for information to several levels of ability. Furthermore, the types of new reading problems raised by these activities will vary from one level of ability to another, and from child to child within a group. An effective reading program is not easily blocked out. Many types of adjustments are needed if children's reading problems are to be met.

Instruction and practice activities are planned so as to give the child the amount of help he needs. Children in the same class not only will read at many different levels, but they will require different amounts and kinds of instruction and practice. The slightest of suggestions will enable some to work on by themselves. Others will need patient explanations, many planned practice activities, and greatly extended experiences in working with easy materials. Effective instruction and practice need to be planned so that the child who is ready to move on to challenging classroom reading activities is not held up, while the youngster who is learning more slowly has the extended guidance and experience he needs.

Instruction and practice activities are planned with the sequence of development of reading skill in mind. Almost all the skills needed by an adult have their origin in the much simpler problems of the primary grades. Well-planned instruction does not seek perfection in one series of lessons. Instead,

[1] Albert J. Harris, *How to Increase Reading Ability*, Fourth Edition (New York: Longmans, Green and Co., 1961), p. 101.

[2] Readers interested in descriptions and detailed accounts of individualized reading programs may note the bibliography on this topic at the end of Chapter VI.

it provides for recurring experiences that enable a child to refine his techniques as he meets new situations that call for greater skill. In the early primary grades it may be the teacher who actually does most of the reading while the children gain their first acquaintance with a process. She reads the first experience records to children at the prereading level while they listen. She finds the first encyclopedia article for able third-graders to read. She makes out the bibliography as fourth-graders face the first project of the year that calls for wide reading. Later, children will be helped to take the initiative in such activities. Eventually they will learn to work independently, with only occasional need for assistance.

Planning for recurring experiences with the same skill does not mean that all children should be expected to take exactly the same steps, or to meet a more difficult problem at exactly the same point in their reading experiences. One group may acquire knowledge about a dictionary gradually; another may learn many of the same basic skills in one series of practice activities. Children in one fourth grade may face the problem of wide reading for information with a background of many such experiences as third-graders. In another school facilities for wide reading in the primary grades may be limited, and the task of handling reference materials in the fourth grade poses a number of new problems. The richer the child's total reading experiences, the more likely he is to encounter a wide variety of problems early and often. The key to deciding what is needed next lies in the efficiency with which children are meeting their present reading problems and the help that seems most likely to give them more independence in handling new situations. These decisions need to be made by the classroom teacher from her knowledge of how reading skill develops and her insight into the needs of her group.

PURPOSE IS CENTRAL IN ALL ACTIVITIES

Children turn to reading activities with clear purposes in mind. Children who are learning how to read critically, how to solve problems through their reading, and how to adjust their reading techniques to different situations need to read with clear purposes in mind. In their classrooms one seldom hears such assignments as, "Open your books and read the story on page . . . ," or "Let's open our books to page . . . Jill, will you start to read, please?" Instead, plans in which children share are heard. "Let's look at the pictures in our new story. What do you think it will be about? Let's read it and see." "John thinks this is a story we could dramatize. Do you want to think about that as you read?" "These stories about pioneers may help with your social-studies groups. Who has your list of questions?" "Do you remember that you asked for fairy stories like the one we read last week? Here are some in this new reader. Do you all want to report on the one most interesting to you?"

In these situations the material being read sometimes follows the order of the stories in a basal text and the problem of making the activity purposeful is one of helping children see a reason for reading that is meaningful to them and that guides their thinking as they read. In the reading done for unit activities in areas such as science, social studies, or health, the appropriate materials are those needed to solve the problems raised by teacher and children as they began the unit. If a classroom is equipped with many types of materials, it is usually possible, even with beginners whose reading vocabulary is limited, to make adjustments so that children read about a farm after they have visited one, or enjoy a group of animal stories after they have been to the zoo or have been talking in class about their pets. With increasing skill in independent reading, come endless opportunities to plan experiences with story and informational materials that take varied group purposes into account.

Children share in setting up plans for special practice. In their desire to have children interested in what they read and to help them find that reading is an enjoyable and profitable activity, teachers sometimes forget that the normal youngster can be much interested in seeing himself gain better skill. In an effective reading program children are helped to understand the skills they need and the purposes for which special practice is set up. "Here are some special stories that will help you remember your new words." "How did you like the way Allen read that for us? Could we make a list of things to remember when we read out loud?" "Today when you finish, I'm going to ask some questions to see how carefully you read." "Yesterday we took all our social-studies' time just to find what we wanted. Suppose you take out your books today and let's learn to use an index." Situations such as these help to develop children who sense their own problems, who enter willingly into plans to correct their difficulties, and who practice intelligently because they know what they are practicing for.

Incidental reading serves a real purpose. Purposeful reading extends to classroom bulletin boards, notices, and chalkboards. Rooms are not cluttered with signs and notices that are never read. Children look to class plans, lists of room responsibilities, notices of special events, bulletin-board displays, and captions to pictures because these records actually function in helping to keep the day's activities running smoothly. Notices are taken down when they are no longer needed, plans once made are actually used, lists of rules are reread as needed, and experience records serve a purpose after they are originally composed. The classroom environment plays a part in the total reading program because its reading materials are important in children's lives.

INDIVIDUAL NEEDS ARE MET

Grouping is flexible. The problem of meeting individual needs is generally met by placing pupils of approximately the same reading level in the same reading group. Such grouping alleviates but does not eliminate the problem of caring for differences, since children will not have exactly the same needs. Todd reads at fourth-grade level, but with such painful slowness that he seldom can be encouraged to read an entire book for recreation. Joanne also reads at fourth-grade level, but she tends to skim and misses important details. Sarah has an excellent visual memory for word configurations. With skillful use of context, she reads most second-grade material without trouble, but can work out few words for herself. Anne, who is also in second grade, is very proud of her ability to figure out a new word. Children such as these may work together on materials of the same level of difficulty, but they also need individualized help. Other children may start out together, but learn at different rates. Someone may be ill and need special instruction to catch up. On the other hand, a classroom problem that affects all groups may arise and children with differing reading abilities may need to work together on a project in social studies, science, or health. Meeting individual needs means providing for flexible grouping and individualized help that allow for these and similar problems.

Individual needs find a place within the activities of one group. Teachers who are skillful in meeting individual needs do more than provide for flexible grouping. They also find ways of working with children's special problems within a single group. In a prereading group, the children are dictating their story of their walk around the neighborhood near the school. Those who are almost ready for beginning-reading experiences with preprimer materials are commenting on the shapes of the words the teacher writes and trying to read some of the lines. Those who are least mature are suggesting what needs to be written but not making many attempts to read. In first grade, the teacher is giving a quick review of new words. "Jerry," she says, "this was the one that gave you trouble. Do you know it now?" In a fourth grade, the teacher asks a question that requires careful reading of the child who rushed through the story, and then says, "Do you think it would have helped if you had read more carefully?"

Other types of adjustments will need to be made during classroom activities when it is desirable for children of differing levels of reading ability to work together. In one situation the teacher may provide materials on several different levels. In another she may let the good readers help those who are likely to have trouble with hard words. When the only material available is an adopted text that is difficult for part of the class, it may be important to give special help to the group that needs it or to work with children individually. Group activities need to be planned with the problems of each group member in mind.

Opportunities for individualized reading activities are provided. All the child's reading experiences should not be in group activities. Children need to be encouraged to go ahead at their own levels and to develop their own reading interests and tastes. Many teachers have found, for example, that recreational reading is an important means of stimulating individual interests. Other opportunities for individual reading are provided through varied assignments as children read for informational purposes. The special needs and interests of the individual child have an important place in the total reading program.

Classroom records are used as guides to individual needs. Keeping the needs of thirty or more individuals in mind calls for the development of effective methods of appraising progress and keeping records. Simple testing devices, check lists of activities, and anecdotal records will all be important. In a busy classroom these will need to be planned so that they are a part of classroom activities, and an aid to enjoying them, not an extra job to be done. In a program where children have a share in planning their activities they also share in the appraisal process. "My trouble is that I repeat all the little words when I read out loud," says one poor reader in a typical fifth grade, "but I'm trying to remember it, and mother is helping me at home." "We put the names of our library books in our special notebooks," says a second. "I'm reading longer books now and more kinds of books." In a first grade, a child boasts, "Today I knew that word without any help at all." The recording and appraisal process in an effective reading program is a joint activity. Teacher and children together evaluate progress and plan next steps.

ALL TEACHING POINTS IN THE SAME DIRECTION

Growth in one type of skill does not hinder growth in another. An effective reading program is a coordinated program. The skills children need to learn are complex, and they interlock in many ways. Teaching needs to be planned so that growth in one area does not impede growth in another. Speed of reading, for example, cannot develop beyond a certain point if a large share of a child's reading activities are oral, or if he is held too closely to detailed reports on everything he reads. Careful reading to work out the analysis of unfamiliar words is difficult under pressure for increased speed. First-grade crutches of vocalizing and pointing can be discarded when there are opportunities to read simple materials silently. Many of the intermediate-grade skills of note-taking, outlining, and summarizing can more readily be developed if children work with informational materials where the vocabulary and general writing style are not difficult. Teachers need to identify potential conflicts and adjust their teaching emphases, types of material, or plans for practice accordingly.

All the child's reading experiences supplement and reinforce each other. The importance of looking at the child's reading experiences as a whole has been mentioned at several points. Decisions as to the balance of his activities need to be made in the light of all the reading he is doing. As he reads more widely, the problems he faces should play an increasing part in determining the emphases of his reading instruction. The amount of special practice he is given needs to be planned in the light of the opportunities to use the same skills being offered by his classroom reading experiences. The materials he reads for information or for recreation should be selected so that they are appropriate for his general level of reading skill. The activities in an effective reading program are thoughtfully coordinated. Every opportunity needs to be capitalized upon in such a way that the result is a unified series of experiences for the child.

Coordination is planned from grade to grade. The coordination of a child's reading activities needs to be planned not only for the class in which he now is, but from grade to grade, and from teacher to teacher, if he is in a school where more than one person works with him during the same year. Every teacher needs to be able to move children to the new experiences of which they are most in need. Skills stressed at one level should be picked up at the next, when their need recurs. If a child works with two or three teachers in special subject fields, each must be prepared to help him deal with the reading problems he faces in her room. This means that the several persons working with a child need to be agreed on how best to give him help. Furthermore, because children will not grow and learn at the same rate, every teacher must be prepared to handle a range of reading problems. There can be no such thing as teaching only a second-grade program, or a fourth-grade program, or even being a specialist in primary techniques or in techniques appropriate for the intermediate grades. Children's reading needs can best be met in a school where all teachers have worked together to develop a common philosophy and common goals and where there has been enough intervisitation and pooling of ideas on how to teach to develop mutual understanding of problems and methods.

SOME QUESTIONS TO THINK ABOUT IN APPRAISING THE READING PROGRAM AS A WHOLE

1. Is use being made of every situation in which the child reads?
2. Is the program broad enough to develop all the skills a child will need eventually in his adult reading experiences?
3. Is there provision for carefully planned practice at points of difficulty?
4. Are all the child's reading activities purposeful to him?
5. Is the program flexible enough to meet the needs of individuals and the demands of on-going classroom activities?
6. Is the program consistent and well integrated, from reading skill to reading skill, from teacher to teacher, from grade to grade?

SUGGESTIONS FOR FURTHER READING

HISTORICAL PERSPECTIVE ON MODERN METHODS

McCullough, Constance M. "Changing Concepts of Reading Instruction," *Changing Concepts of Reading Instruction,* pp. 13-22. International Reading Association Conference Proceedings, 1961. J. Allen Figurel, Editor. New York: Scholastic Magazines, 1961. 292 pp.
Russell, David H. *Children Learn to Read.* Second Edition, Chapter 2. Boston: Ginn and Company, 1961. 612 pp.
Smith, Nila B. *American Reading Instruction.* New York: Silver Burdett and Company, 1934. 287 pp.
Stone, Clarence R., *Progress in Primary Reading.* Chapter 2. St. Louis: Webster Publishing Company, 1950. 463 pp.

THE CHARACTERISTICS OF EFFECTIVE READING PROGRAMS

Betts, Emmer A. *Foundations of Reading Instruction.* Chapters 1-7. New York: American Book Company, 1957. 757 pp.
Bond, Guy L., and Wagner, Eva Bond. *Teaching the Child to Read.* Third Edition, Chapter 3. New York: The Macmillan Company, 1960. 416 pp.
Harris, Albert J. *Effective Teaching of Reading.* New York: David McKay Company, 1962. 387 pp.
Russell, David H. *op. cit.* Chapter 5.
Strang, Ruth; McCullough, Constance M.; and Traxler, Arthur E. *The Improvement of Reading.* Chapter 3. New York: McGraw-Hill Book Company, 1961. 480 pp.

THE PLACE OF SKILLS IN THE MODERN ELEMENTARY SCHOOL

Association for Supervision and Curriculum Development, N.E.A. *The Three R's in the Elementary School.* Washington, D. C.: The Association, 1952, 406 pp.
Caswell, Hollis L., and Foshay, Arthur W. *Education in the Elementary School.* Third Edition. New York: American Book Company, 1957. 430 pp.
Shane, Harold G.; Reddin, Mary E.; and Gillespie, Margaret C. *Beginning Language Arts With Children.* Columbus, Ohio: Charles E. Merrill Books, Inc., 1961. 286 pp.

Stratemeyer, Florence B.; Forkner, Hamden L.; McKim, Margaret G.; and Passow, Harry A. *Developing a Curriculum for Modern Living.* Second Edition, pp. 409-417. New York: Bureau of Publications, Teachers College, Columbia University, 1957. 740 pp.

ASSURING CONTINUOUS IMPROVEMENT OF READING PROGRAMS

Gray, William S. and Larrick, Nancy (Editors). *Better Readers for Our Times.* International Reading Association Conference Proceedings. New York: Scholastic Magazines, 1956. 176 pp.

Changing Concepts of Reading Instruction. International Reading Association Conference Proceedings, 1961. J. Allen Figurel, Editor. New York: Scholastic Magazines, 1961. 292 pp.

Hunnicutt, Clarence W., and Iverson, William J. (Editors). *op. cit.* Part I, pp. 5-259.

Language Arts for Today's Children. Prepared by the Commission on the English Curriculum of the National Council of Teachers of English. New York: Teachers College, Columbia University, 1947. 558 pp.

McKim, Margaret G., "Reading in the Primary Grades," *Development in and Through Reading,* pp. 270-287. Sixtieth Yearbook of the National Society for the Study of Education, Part I. Chicago: The University of Chicago Press, 1961. 406 pp.

Robinson, Helen M. (Editor). *Sequential Development of Reading Abilities.* Supplementary Educational Monographs No. 90. Chicago: The University of Chicago Press, 1960. 251 pp.

Robinson, Helen M. (Editor). *Controversial Issues in Reading and Promising Solutions.* Supplementary Educational Monographs No. 91. Chicago: The University of Chicago Press, 1961. 181 pp.

Persons interested in keeping abreast of research should consult the helpful yearly summaries of reading investigations compiled by William S. Gray for the *Journal of Educational Research,* and continued there in 1961 by Helen Robinson. The January 1962 issue of *The Reading Teacher* contains the summary for 1962. Also helpful are the appropriate issues on language arts and fine arts of the *Review of Educational Research;* and the section on reading, *Encyclopedia of Educational Research,* pp. 1086-1135, third edition, edited by Walter S. Monroe. Prepared under the auspices of the American Education Research Association. New York: The Macmillan Company, 1960. 1564 pp.

PART II

Laying Sound Foundations

PREREADING AND BEGINNING READING ACTIVITIES

CHAPTER III

What Makes for Success in Beginning Reading?

SOME BEGINNERS

IT IS the end of the first week of school in a first grade. The teacher still has much to learn about her class, but already she has found out enough about individual children to lay her first plans for the prereading and beginning reading program.

Three children are already in or beyond the stage of beginning reading activities, although the third has not yet shown a strong interest in learning to read:

BETSY has been trying to read independently since shortly after her fifth birthday.[1] Several of the preprimers in the room were already familiar to her. As the teacher wrote the children's names, Betsy stood by and named the letters as they were written. Free activity periods found her examining the books on the library table, smiling at some of the pictures and reading occasional words. She knew some nursery rhymes and quickly learned others that were part of group experiences in the first few days of school. Her great delight was to try to supply the rhyming word before the teacher said it.

JACK took a lively interest in everything in the classroom. He quickly learned to find his own name although he was apt to confuse it with Jim's if the two were used on the same chart. He enjoyed listening to stories, but he occasionally left

---

[1] For an interesting study by Dolores Durkin, see "Children Who Learned to Read Before First Grade—A Second Year Report," *Elementary School Journal*, **62** (October 1961), 14-18.

the group to go on with other concerns. He stopped to see if there was anything new on the bulletin board each morning, but he showed no great desire to know what the few simple notices said, unless an accompanying picture happened to interest him.

Louis brought his favorite story book to school on the first day. He could not read much of it except the title, but he could tell the gist of the story from the pictures. When the children were given an opportunity to paint, he was one of the few who could sign his full name to his picture. During the first week he was much interested in the few signs on the bulletin board and was delighted to be able to find his own name above a cloakroom hook and on a helpers' chart.

Two other children, Ted and Mary Lou, have as yet developed few of the skills that will be important as they learn to read.

Ted cried for the first few mornings when his mother left him at the classroom door. He was not concerned with the pictures and signs around the room. The play corner, the aquarium, and the blocks for construction activities held his attention. When a picture he had drawn was selected by the children to be posted on the bulletin board, he did not particularly care whether it had a caption, although several in the class thought that there should be one. At the end of the first week he had examined the books in the library corner only once. Although he joined small groups listening to stories for a few minutes, he soon wandered off to other activities.

Mary Lou was greatly interested in the easel. When asked to share her pictures with the class, she enumerated the objects she had drawn but seldom told a related story about them. She seemed to follow with interest the stories read to the group and enjoyed looking at the pictures. However, her own comments showed limited ability to make her ideas clear and a very meager vocabulary. At the end of the first week of school, she gave no evidence that she had discovered any clues by which she could recognize her own name.

The other children in this group will also have their own particular combinations of abilities and experiences, and, as the weeks go by, new strengths and new weaknesses will appear. Some are ready to progress rapidly; others will need a more extended program of enriched experiences before they can successfully undertake the tasks of learning to read.

How to work with these varied patterns of interests, abilities and backgrounds has long been of concern to all interested in the teaching of reading. Two features of the situation are widely accepted. First, all aspects of a child's development, as well as reading ability, are important in planning for him. Second, the wide range of individual differences would lead to the anticipation and the acceptance of differences in readiness for reading. However, teachers, parents, and children themselves are faced by the pressures and expectations that first graders will be able to learn to read quite promptly after they enter school. The premium placed upon this achievement is illustrated by the query of a seven-year-old, who walked into a new group of six-year-old playmates, and inquired condescendingly, "Any of you little children know how to read?"

What makes for reading readiness? What skills are needed for beginning reading, and how does a teacher discover the abilities of her group? The present chapter is concerned with the task a teacher faces in discovering what prereading experiences are needed by the children in her group. Once these needs are identified, an effective prereading or beginning reading program may be planned. The types of activities appropriate for a prereading program are discussed in Chapter IV. First experiences in learning to read are described in Chapter V.

DEFINING READING READINESS

That children differ—in height, weight, color of hair and eyes, intellectual ability, and even in the rate at which they mature, reach adolescence, and stop growing as adults—is as well established as any other psychological principle.[2] Progress in a skill such as learning to read is no exception. Two major types of studies have provided the research from which present-day concepts of reading readiness have been developed. One type has been concerned with investigating the factors that make for success in beginning reading.[3] The other has focused on the reasons why children have failed to make satisfactory progress in reading.[4] Many specific questions regarding the capacities and interests of first-grade children, the circumstances of their reading progress, and the types of activities most helpful in assuring their success in learning to read are still matters for investigation. For example, in

[2] See, for example: Anne Anastasia, *Differential Psychology: Individual and Group Differences in Behavior,* Third Edition, Chapter 2 (New York: The Macmillan Company, 1958).

[3] As examples, see: Millie C. Almy, *Children's Experiences Prior to First Grade and Success in Beginning Reading.* Teachers College Contributions to Education, No. 954 (New York: Teachers College, Columbia University, 1940). Arthur I. Gates, Guy L. Bond, and David H. Russell, *Methods of Determining Reading Readiness* (New York: Teachers College, Columbia University, 1939).

[4] As examples, see: Chester C. Bennett, *An Inquiry into the Genesis of Poor Reading.* Teachers College Contributions to Education, No. 755 (New York: Teachers College, Columbia University, 1938); Helen M. Robinson, *Why Pupils Fail in Reading* (Chicago: The University of Chicago Press, 1946).

the early years of the 1960's considerable interest was shown in children who learned to read before entering school. Durkin's[5] report concerned 49 children who learned to read before first grade. These children, whose I.Q.'s ranged from 91 to 161, appeared to have excellent memories, curiosity, persistence, self-reliance, and a high degree of ability to concentrate. Reported success in teaching two- to five-year olds to read[6] and the discovery that a considerable number of gifted children learn to read before age five[7] have led to some concern lest formal prereading and reading activities become unduly delayed. However, all that is known about these early readers and the evidence regarding readiness for learning suggests that parents and teachers of pre-school-age children should take care to provide enriching experiences, but should permit the child himself to initiate specific activities. The successful endeavors of a gifted child, the considerable curiosity of many children about words and their meanings need not lead us to stress unduly the development of skills which may be more easily learned later. Indeed the child who lives and learns in the second half of the twentieth century cannot help seeing many signs, advertising slogans, and printed directions. Many are gigantic and neon-lighted, others are on familiar packages from the grocery. In this setting many children ask about words and letters. It is one thing, however, to respond positively to requests for help—"Does this can of coffee say it's *regular* or *drip* grind?"—and quite another to insist upon learning skills not yet needed or desired by the child. One five-year-old, on his own initiative, hammered laboriously to make a sample alphabet out of scraps of wood. An interested adult thought he should learn the correct manuscript form for his letter-making, and produced a model for him to copy, saying that he could hammer in the nails, and also learn the letters correctly, so "killing two birds with one stone." The result was to kill a genuine interest in forming letters. The disillusioned youngster dropped his hammer and walked away, saying sadly, "But I don't *want* to kill two birds with one stone!"

The fact that children can be taught to read at four or five years of age does not thereby indicate that they should be. There are several factors to consider before planning for a child's first efforts to read independently.[8]

Readiness is an educational concept. The term "readiness," as distinguished from "maturation," typically refers to the time and the way in which certain activities will be taught, not to the inner unfolding of the child's

[5] Dolores Durkin, "Children Who Read Before Grade One," *The Reading Teacher*, **14** (January 1961), 163-166.

[6] "'Tis Time He Should Begin to Read." Carnegie Corporation of New York. *Quarterly*, **9** (April 1961), 1-3.

[7] "Preschool Reading of Gifted Children," *School and Society*, Summer 1961, p. 257.

[8] Agatha Townsend. "What Research Says to the Reading Teacher: Readiness for Beginning Reading," *The Reading Teacher*, **15** (January 1962), 267-270; 276.

capacities. Jersild[9] has described it as raising questions regarding the appropriateness of what is to be taught in terms of the child's ability to profit from it—his maturity, his background of experiences, and his possession of needed related skills.

Defined in this way, reading readiness refers not only to the beginning stages of learning to read, but to every step in the child's progress from simple reading tasks to those that are more complicated. Harrison[10] was one of the earliest to use the concept of reading readiness in this broad sense, and to attempt to outline, from level to level, the new reading tasks children might be expected to face. Although the term "reading readiness" is often used to refer specifically to those skills needed for success in beginning reading, it is a helpful orientation to the total readiness problem to think of the concept in its larger sense, and to use the term "prereading" for that specific aspect of readiness which has to do with these early primary skills.

The fact that reading readiness is an educational concept has implications for planning a prereading program. It raises questions regarding the skills the child now possesses and what he needs to be taught. The prereading program is not, then, a period of waiting until a certain stage of maturity is reached. Nor does it consist of a special series of activities that must necessarily be undertaken by all children. Rather, it builds the skills important to successful first steps in beginning reading, just as the later first-grade program develops readiness for work with second-grade materials, and experiences with fifth-grade reading problems prepare for the somewhat more complex activities taken on in the sixth.

What skills does a first grader need for success in learning to read? The evidence at hand shows he will need abilities related to working with words, stories, pictures, and books. These might be called basic prereading abilities. They are variously described, but in general these abilities include the following:

1. Facility in speaking and listening.
2. Interest in books and stories, and an awareness of the purposes they serve.
3. Ability to make gross discriminations in word forms, such as being able to see that "today" does not look at all like "September."
4. Sensitivity to rhymes and the sounds of words.
5. Ability to interpret pictures.

To these items might be added an understanding of the structural principles of word order in English, and a feeling for English sentence structure. It

[9] Arthur T. Jersild, *et al., Child Development and the Curriculum* (New York: Teachers College, Columbia University, 1946), p. 31. See also: James L. Hymes, Jr., *Before the Child Reads* (Evanston, Illinois: Row, Peterson and Company, 1958), pp. 7-16.

[10] M. Lucile Harrison, *Reading Readiness*, Revised Edition (Boston: Houghton Mifflin Company, 1939).

has been pointed out that teachers should be sensitive to the fact that many children six years of age speak in complex sentence patterns quite unlike the simple sentences of many primers.[11] These ideas further underline the great importance of language facility, particularly in speaking and listening.

If these are the skills most useful in the beginning steps in learning to read, it follows that an appraisal of a child's prereading status involves knowing to what extent he possesses them. Almost all reading readiness tests include tests of ability to work with words, rhymes, and pictures. These skills are also reflected to some extent in a child's general interest in printed matter. In her study of first-grade children, Almy[12] found that responses to many different types of opportunities to read, from looking at a story book while Mother reads it to trying to read the words on articles around the house, had a positive relationship to success in beginning reading. In a comprehensive study of factors that make for reading readiness, Gates, Bond, and Russell[13] found that tests asking children to interpret pictures, to match words, to give rhymes, to follow directions, and to follow the plots of stories in much the same way as in beginning-reading experiences, had among the highest correlations with tests of reading achievement given later in the first grade.

Experiences planned to develop prereading abilities must provide, then, many opportunities to work with words and pictures in varied settings. Some of these need to be oral. There also need to be contacts with printed words in books and stories, and many casual opportunities to respond to names, charts, labels, and special notices. Pictures need to be used—as sources of interest on the bulletin board, as part of the fun of sharing a story, as a record of an interesting excursion. Prereading activities and beginning-reading activities center around many of the same types of experiences.

Experience background is important. At one table may be Sally, whose parents have taken her to the Zoo, to the park, to the lake for picnics, or to spend a weekend on the farm. Sally owns a bicycle, a doll house, a pet kitten, and a phonograph, and lives on a street where houses have gardens. Next to her may be Jane, who has grown up in an apartment house, and never had a pet. Her parents rarely have time to take her on trips, and she plays in the narrow apartment court and on the street in front of her home. The influences of breadth of experience background in learning to read are pervasive. A child who has a wide background of experiences has more ideas about which to talk, to write, to read, and to interpret pictures. He also has a better background from which to understand preprimer stories. Simply written though these first materials are, they call for a working knowledge of subur-

[11] Harry R. Warfel, and Donald J. Lloyd, "The Structural Approach to Reading," *School and Society*, June 8, 1957, pp. 199-201.

[12] Millie C. Almy, *op. cit.*

[13] Arthur I. Gates, Guy L. Bond, and David H. Russell, *op. cit.*

ban family life, wagons and tricycles, and friendly postmen and firemen. Moreover, these preprimer experiences are but a small proportion of the total number of stories, books, and pictures to which a first-grader is expected to respond with understanding.

Prereading experiences need to be an integral part of a total primary program planned to develop a rich and varied background of experiences. In one sense they represent the verbal side of this program—the planning sessions, the sharing periods, the recording of what was seen on a trip, the experience of interpreting pictures, and the labeling of classroom exhibits. These are the contacts with words that meet prereading needs in settings where the importance of being able to read is kept to the fore.

Intellectual maturity plays a part. A number of attempts have been made to determine a mental age before which one should not try to teach a child to read. In one of the most frequently quoted of these, Morphett and Washburne[14] studied the reading achievement of first-grade children in relation to their mental ages. In this study there was a sharp upward rise in achievement for the group from 6-0 to 6-5 mentally, and another sharp rise for the group from 6-6 to 6-11 mentally. After this point increases were gradual. This led the authors to propose that beginning-reading instruction be postponed until the child reached a mental age of six years and six months. In this study, however, and in others in which a definite mental age for beginning reading has been proposed, little attention is given to exploring the possibility of varying teaching methods in terms of children's abilities.

Gates,[15] among others, went at the problem by studying adjustments of teaching techniques to varying levels of intellectual ability. In one situation, children above five years mentally made reasonable progress when materials and teaching methods were carefully planned to meet their needs. Other classrooms were reported where higher levels of intellectual ability were needed for successful progress. Studies such as this support the general conclusion that it is impossible to establish any single mental age as a crucial point before within limits, seems to be the way children are taught.
which instruction in reading should not be given. The determining factor,

Nevertheless, intellectual ability makes a difference. The fact that there seems to be no specific mental age that can be used as a determining factor in deciding when to start beginning-reading activities does not mean that pressure to learn to read can safely be put indiscriminately on all first-graders. Other things being equal, which they seldom are in situations involving human beings, children with high I.Q.'s are more likely to learn rapidly than

[14] Mabel V. Morphett, and Carleton Washburne, "When Should Children Begin to Read?" *Elementary School Journal*, **31** (March 1931), 496-503.

[15] Arthur I. Gates, "The Necessary Mental Age for Beginning Reading," *Elementary School Journal*, **37** (March 1937), 497-508.

children with low I.Q.'s. Correlations of scores on intelligence tests with measures of reading progress tend to fall between .35 and .65.[16] Furthermore, certain prereading skills are closely related to general intellectual ability. Tests of vocabulary and of picture interpretation, for example, are included in the *Revised Stanford-Binet Scale* at several levels as part of a composite picture of intellectual maturity.[17] Prereading activities can be used to supply many experiences from which a child can profit in terms of his general level of intellectual maturity. These activities can also, at times, serve to fill in important gaps in a child's pre-school background. However, there is little evidence to suggest that such experiences will make marked changes in the rate of a child's intellectual growth. This raises the question as to whether time is well spent attempting to force a child to extend himself to the limits of his intellectual ability in a struggle to learn to read when a few months later he may grasp the same concepts with relative ease. It is appropriate to question, also, whether the risk of discouragement and defeat is worth taking. Studies of retarded readers have identified attempts to introduce children to reading too soon as possible causes of later difficulty, and investigations of the permanence of the learning of immature children and of the amount of time needed to teach them suggest that the efforts of both teacher and children might better have been placed elsewhere.[18]

In general, studies of intellectual ability as a factor in reading readiness seem to support the proposal that the prereading program should be a program of active teaching, not a waiting period. They suggest, also, that this teaching needs to be paced to the individual child's capacity for growth. Able children, intellectually, if their specific prereading abilities are equally strong, may progress rapidly into beginning-reading activities. On the other hand, the lower the mental age, the longer the prereading period will need to be, the simpler the beginning material will need to be, the greater the amount of repetition in meaningful settings which will be needed, and the more highly individualized the teaching methods will have to be.[19] The simple, interesting, and informal experiences with words and stories provided in prereading activities may meet very well the needs of these children for a simplified and enriched beginning-reading program.

Other aspects of development may make a difference. Evidence as to the

[16] Guy L. Bond, and Miles A. Tinker, *Reading Difficulties Their Diagnosis and Correction* (New York: Appleton-Century Crofts, Inc., 1957), p. 42.
[17] Lewis M. Terman and Maude E. Merrill, *Measuring Intelligence* (Boston: Houghton Mifflin Company, 1937).
[18] Irving H. Anderson and Walter F. Dearborn, *op. cit.*, pp. 67-69. See also: Henry P. Smith and Emerald V. Dechant, *Psychology in Teaching Reading* (Englewood Cliffs, N. J.: Prentice-Hall, Inc., 1961), pp. 103-5.
[19] Samuel A. Kirk, *Teaching Reading to Slow Learning Children* (Boston: Houghton Mifflin Company, 1940), p. 83.

influence of physical, social, and emotional factors on success in beginning reading is not clear-cut. Children with defective vision, hearing, and speech have been successful in learning to read. On the other hand, studies have shown that such deficiencies do appear in a certain number of retarded readers.[20] Certainly, for individual children, physical difficulties will be a contributing, if not a deciding, factor in unsuccessful beginning-reading experiences. Focusing the eyes on the printed page is a complex task demanding both a degree of visual maturity, which may not always be achieved at the age of six, and specific skill in coordinating the functioning of the two eyes.[21] Not being able to hear, or not being able to pronounce words distinctly may make fine auditory discriminations difficult. Illness may also be a problem. The child who takes a trip to the farm, is out of school with a cold the next day and misses the class discussion and the writing of an experience record, and returns the day following to try to read the record, has missed a vital step in the sequence.

A child's general rate of maturation may also be a factor in his success in beginning reading. Olson[22] reports cases where growth in reading ability seems to parallel the child's over-all pattern of maturation. The question of maturation is also raised frequently in speculations as to why more boys than girls are found in remedial classrooms.[23] Considerable evidence has accumulated to show that girls, on the average, are about a year in advance of boys in general maturation by the age of six. There are, of course, many exceptions. What might this difference in growth rates mean in first-grade classrooms where both sexes are expected to perform the same visual tasks, to have the same span of attention, and to sit without wiggling for the same length of time?

Social and emotional factors may be involved, also, in the cases of individual children. In his study of poor readers, Bennett[24] did not find that, as a group, they were significantly different from good readers in areas of personal and social adjustment. However, a child may be so timid that he finds it hard to work with a reading group, or so anxious to make friends that he devotes his full time in a group to poking, talking, and making other kinds of social contacts, helpful in their own way, but not particularly conducive to

[20] Helen M. Robinson, *op. cit.*, pp. 7-33, 50-58.
[21] For a detailed discussion of visual readiness for reading see Emmett A. Betts, *Foundations of Reading Instruction* (New York: American Book Company, 1957), pp. 172-202.
[22] Willard C. Olson, *Child Development* (Boston: D. C. Heath and Company, 1949), pp. 121-134.
[23] Arthur W. Heilman, *Principles and Practices of Teaching Reading* (Columbus, Ohio: Charles E. Merrill Books, Inc., 1961), Chapter 11.
[24] Chester C. Bennett, *An Inquiry into the Genesis of Poor Reading*, Teachers College Contributions to Education, No. 755 (New York: Teachers College, Columbia University, 1938).

learning to read. In slightly over half of the thirty children included in Robinson's[25] intensive case studies of causes of reading failures, maladjusted homes were identified as contributing causes. Even more significant in this study is the evidence that the most severely retarded children tended to show the largest constellations of possible causative factors. This is another strong argument for considering the total growth of each child in appraising his readiness for beginning reading.

The prereading program, then, should be an integral part, but only one part, of a total primary program planned to contribute to the all-round development of children—physical, intellectual, social, and emotional. At times, meeting a need in one of these developmental areas may be an essential step in clearing the way for successful reading experiences. At other times, emphasis should not be placed upon learning to read, even if it seems likely that the child will be successful, because of a more crucial developmental need. The total growth of the child should be considered before his growth in any single skill or subject-matter area.

Individual differences in abilities will exist within one child as well as among children. Children do not grow evenly in all aspects of development. Profiles of scores on reading-readiness tests and broader studies of other aspects of growth indicate that each child will have his own particular pattern of strengths and weaknesses. Some children will be well on the way toward independent reading. Others will have little strength in any area—their language skills will be limited, gross discriminations among words will seem beyond them, and discussion of pictures will call forth only meager comments.

Prereading activities will have to be varied to meet individual needs. It will not be possible to set up an orderly arrangement of three or four prereading groups and to plan a definite series of prereading activities for each group. The pattern will have to be one in which many aspects of the primary program contribute to prereading skills—for individuals, for groups, and for the entire class. Nor will there be a clear-cut transition from prereading to beginning-reading activities. The difference between prereading and beginning reading is one of emphasis and the transition is gradual.

IDENTIFYING PREREADING NEEDS

As indicated in the previous section, individual children, small groups, or an entire class may need planned-for prereading experiences. What experiences? For whom? Appraisals of the present status of each child may be made

25 Helen M. Robinson, *op. cit.*, p. 222.

by day-by-day observations as children go about the normal activities of the classroom. Readiness tests, and cumulative records of children's growth, are additional sources of helpful information.

Such appraisals can help the teacher decide what day-by-day activities to plan for. They may also be the basis for deciding which children can work together most profitably, and can help to identify children who may move with success into beginning reading activities.

Decisions respecting the provision for prereading and beginning reading experiences are based upon the teacher's knowledge of the types of growth that are desirable. This means knowing, in general terms, how children will be called upon to use speaking and listening skills, and how they will be likely to work with pictures, stories, and books. There is considerable variation in points of emphasis among teachers, each of which is successful in helping children get a good start in beginning reading. It follows, therefore, that a child is ready for beginning reading activities when he has the skills he needs in order to be successful in his particular classroom setting.

Once a teacher has determined the kinds of growth to achieve, it is possible to study children's present status and to make plans for next steps. "Jane and the group who worked with her today could identify almost every word in the experience record without help. They should not have any trouble with a preprimer." "Tom scarcely gives anyone else in the group a chance. He will have trouble in a reading group until he becomes better able to work with other children." The discussion of yesterday's excursion revealed many gaps in experience. These children need many more such concrete contacts with the world around them."

APPRAISING PREREADING ABILITIES IN THE CLASSROOM SETTING

How effectively does the child express himself orally? Since reading is a problem of getting meaning from language in printed form, a child needs to have some facility both in expressing his own ideas and in understanding the ideas of others. When he starts to read, he will have to follow the thought from line to line, and remember a sequence of events. He will also need to be able to identify the speakers in a conversational passage.

Discussions used to enrich a story require facility in oral language. The child may be called upon to tell what he has read, guess what will happen next, or tell if anything similar has happened to him. Experience records, used as sources of beginning reading experience, are composed by children. Here the children discuss such topics as, What happened? What did we see? How shall we say this? What new words did we learn? The child who cannot make himself clear, or who has trouble following what is being said by others, is likely to be at a disadvantage.

In addition to being able to express himself clearly, the child needs a good stock of word meanings. Many of his first reading materials will be based upon trips actually taken by the class, or about home, school, toys or other familiar things. Even so, all children will have concepts limited by their own backgrounds. *Dog* may still mean the white woolly pet that is the special companion of one child. *Home*, for another, may mean the tenth story of an apartment house reached by an elevator, not the pleasant suburban home portrayed in most preprimers. As a child begins to read, he must be able to reinterpret his concepts in the light of the special way in which the author of his book is using the terms.

Facility in the use of oral language develops slowly. Little children tend to speak in simple assertive sentences, to ramble somewhat in long sentences connected with *and*, and to have ideas that are more complex than they can express. Their vocabulary is still increasing rapidly.[26] Helping children become more effective in language usage is one of the major objectives of the total primary program. Upon a child's growing ability to make himself understood rest not only his progress in reading but a number of his social relationships and his success in many other enterprises.

Beginning-reading experiences will not necessarily be postponed for children who have limited facility in the use of language, since the reading situation itself offers many opportunities for growth. However, the teacher must be prepared to work slowly, using many means of enriching their stocks of word meanings, and giving them many opportunities to learn to express themselves.

A typical primary classroom offers a wealth of opportunities to appraise children's facility in the use of language. The following suggest types of questions that may be raised. This list, and those given in subsequent sections, are intended to help in developing sensitivity in observing children in the classroom setting. No one, of course, would need or expect to collect evidence for all children on all the questions suggested.

How well does the child take part in class discussion? If he is given the opportunity to describe an exciting experience to the group, can he make himself clear? Is he able to relate events in a sequence roughly approaching the way they actually happened? If the children are trying to write a group report of an experience, what kinds of contributions does he make? Is he critical of the phrasing proposed by other children? In class planning sessions do his comments give evidence that he has been able to follow the discussion?

How does he respond to stories? When a story is being read to the class, does he listen or does he become unduly restless? When others comment upon the story

---

[26] Dorothea McCarthy, "Language Development in Children," *Manual of Child Psychology,* edited by Leonard Carmichael (New York: John Wiley and Sons, Inc., 1954), pp. 492-630.

and talk about what is likely to happen next, do his remarks give evidence that he has followed the story with comprehension? Can he identify parts of the story he thought were amusing or exciting? As he looks at the pictures accompanying a story, does he relate the picture to the story?

How well does he follow directions? When he is asked to put materials away, or to put papers on the teacher's desk, are they put where they should be? When plans are made for mid-morning lunch, dismissal, or some other routine activity, does he follow with reasonable understanding? How well does he follow the directions for a game, or for a new activity?

How clearly does he express his needs? Can he ask for materials or assistance in such a way that others can tell what it is he wants? When playing with other children, can he make his suggestions clear? In planning sessions, can he tell what part of the activity he would like to share?

How effective is his stock of word meanings? Does he know the names of common objects around the room? Can he identify some of the less common objects that other children bring to share with their classmates? Does he choose words accurately when trying to express his ideas? Does he show an interest in new words? How well does he describe a picture?

Is the child interested in books and reading? It is not always easy to understand why a child shows little interest in reading a colorful book or is unaware of the fact that the words he sees all around him serve a purpose, but such youngsters do come to first grades and kindergartens. Some have had little acquaintance with books at home. Parents may have been too busy to spend time reading stories aloud. Then, too, the surrounding environment that is simple to an adult is complex to a child. He is becoming acquainted with large objects such as busses, fire trucks, tractors, construction equipment, people, and animals. In the classroom he is surrounded with new kinds of play equipment, new types of furniture, and a much larger group of children than he is likely to have worked or played with before. Among these many new sources of interest, the printed words on street signs, book covers, chalkboards, and bulletin boards may not assume the significance that they have for the adult who can read. Furthermore, the child's interest in words may not have been encouraged by the adults around him. It takes both experience and maturity before these symbols begin to stand out.

In the group of children who are not interested in reading there must also be classified a small number who have had stories read to them for much of their lives, but who have no particular desire to read for themselves. Other opportunities in the first-grade classroom may seem much more exciting than the reading group. The aquarium, the objects brought in by other children to be put in a class museum, or the play corner may be sources of new learning more stimulating for the moment than books. Such children are aware of the purposes which printed words can serve, but they are content to let adults do the reading for them.

There is little justification for delaying beginning-reading activities on the basis of lack of interest alone, since interest can be developed through satisfying contacts with books and stories. However, prereading and beginning-reading experiences will need to be planned to supply many contacts with interesting stories, meaningful notices, and classroom records. This is important, not only for the children who need to learn that reading is a useful and interesting activity, but for the entire class.

A teacher may distinguish the child who is eager for more reading experiences from the one for whom reading as yet does not have much meaning by watching for evidence in areas such as the following:

Does the child seek out the library table? Can he pick out the book that is his favorite when the teacher offers to read a story? Does he spend time looking over pictures in the books on the library table? Does he ever suggest turning to a book for information?

Does he bring his favorite books from home to share with the group? Can he tell something about the stories in them? Does he discuss the pictures in them in such a way as to indicate some comprehension of the story? Does he give evidence that parents read stories to him?

Does he enjoy hearing stories read to him? Does he show an interest in a story hour, or in proposing a story he wants to hear? Does he show interest in the pictures in the book being read? Can he discuss the story or tell what happened in a story continued from the day before?

Is he aware of the signs and other informal bits of reading matter that surround him in the classroom? Does he try to find his own name? If a class record has been made of some interesting activity, does he turn to it for information, or point it out to his mother, or to an older child who visits the classroom? If captions have been added to some of the pictures, does he try to find out what they say? If a special note is posted on the bulletin board, does he show interest in what it says? If an object is brought to school with an advertisement or other writing upon it, does he show any curiosity about it?

Is he aware of reading opportunities in his out-of-class environment? As he goes through the halls, does he try to read the various notices? As he goes on excursions to neighboring points of interest, does he try to read the various signs that he encounters—the highway signs, the names of streets, the names of stores, the signs indicating bus stops?

Can the child make gross discriminations among word forms? As soon as a child begins to test his ability to read for himself the stories in his pre-primer or the lines of an experience record, he is going to need some techniques for telling words apart. Ability to make gross discriminations among words is all that is needed in the beginning. Materials for the beginning reader are written to avoid using words that demand many fine discriminations. The teacher's first concern, as a child starts to read, is to help him become familiar with the general configurations of enough words to begin to read two or three lines of a story or a classroom record for himself. Skill in word analysis is developed after the child has a stock of familiar words that he can use for the purposes of identifying similar sound elements or word-parts, although from the beginning the teacher points out similarities and differences as she helps a child who confuses words.

Some children will come to school skilled in the general techniques of word recognition. They will already know a number of words. New words will interest them and they will try to read them and pursue the teacher with requests for help. These are the youngsters for whom success in beginning reading can be predicted with reasonable assurance. Others will not have acquired the capacity to make needed discriminations among words. Some will respond to the general length of the word, but will see no difference between two words of approximately the same length. Some will see the general configuration of the word, but will reply with complete assurance that words like *color* and *mother* look just alike. Some will have no apparent bases for judgment. Suggestion has been made that children tend to notice similarities rather than differences, and that the major task of helping children to read is to help them to see how words differ.[27]

Children whose ability to make gross discriminations among word forms is limited need numerous prereading contacts with words in different settings. It is difficult to predict how many such experiences will be needed. The ability to discriminate among word forms is partly a matter of maturity. The child who is intellectually less mature may take longer to learn how to make such distinctions. Visual acuity may make a difference. Lack of experience with words may be another factor. The teacher must be prepared to extend informal experiences with words until the child reaches the point where his discriminations among words suggest that he can profit from more definite beginning-reading instruction.

Among the evidences of growth that may be of help in appraising a child's ability to make gross discriminations among words are the following:

Can the child recognize his own name? Does he know it when it is written alone to mark some of his possessions? Can he pick it out when it is on a list of helpers

[27] Henry P. Smith, and Emerald V. Dechant, *op. cit.*, p. 192.

for the day, or in some other place where similar names are likely to confuse?

Can he recognize signs that are being used regularly? Does he try to read notices on the bulletin board? Does he try to read the key words on a helpers' chart? Can he recognize other special charts—the weather, the news bulletins, the list of birthdays?

As the teacher writes charts or notices for the group, is he interested in the shapes of the words? Is he ever heard to remark on the lengths of words? Does he ever identify words that begin like his name, or look like some other word he knows? Does he ever point out words that begin or end alike?

Does he ever respond to key letters in words? Does he identify other words that start like his name? Does he show interest in initialed handkerchiefs or other objects where single letters are used? Does he show that he knows how the letters he uses to initial his work are related to his name? When looking at alphabet books, does he make comments such as "and my name begins with *B*, too, doesn't it?"

Does he recognize when the same word is used more than once? If a series of sentences in a class record all begin with the same words, does he note the similarities from line to line? If a word is repeated two or three times in one sentence, does he recognize this? If a word with unusual configuration is used in several places in the room, does he notice it, or can he find it when he is asked about it? If a word is used which was prominent in the title of one of his favorite picture books, does he remember it?

Does the child show an interest in differences in the sounds of words? Reading is not a visual task alone. A child soon comes to the place where the ability to hear likenesses and differences among words becomes important. A teacher can help him develop a valuable aid to word recognition if she can say, "Yes, *Sally* and *Billy* sound the same. Can you hear the part that is the same? Let's write them on the board and see if you can find the part that makes them sound alike", or "No, this one is *rides*. Let's put them both on the board and see if you can tell what makes it sound differently." To be able to hear that a word is long as well as to see its length, to be able to hear how words rhyme as well as to see that they look somewhat alike, or to hear the same word beginning three sentences in a story as well as to see it are skills that send a child well along the road to independent reading.

Unless the procedures used in beginning-reading activities rely heavily on a phonetic approach to words, children are not so likely to be handicapped in the very early stages of beginning reading if they lack skill in discriminating among the sounds of words as they are if they lack ability to make gross discriminations among the configurations of words. However, it is not long before weakness in ability to identify similarities and differences among sounds will make itself felt. Some of the necessary skill can be built through discussion of new words as reading activities proceed. Prereading experiences with rhymes, with words which begin with the same sound, and with words with interesting sounds can also help.

Ability to respond to the sounds of words may be appraised by asking questions such as the following:

How does the child respond to rhymes? Does he seem to enjoy the rhythm and rhyme of finger plays, poems, and rhyming games? If the teacher leaves a line unfinished, can he finish it? If she asks for several words which rhyme, can he name them? If words that rhyme appear in a class experience record, does he point them out?

Is he alert to similar sounds in words used in regular classroom activities? If his name sounds like that of another child, does he ever point it out? Does he ever make up rhymes about his name, or about the names of his friends? If two words begin the same way, does he comment on their sound as well as upon the way they look?

Does he show an interest in odd and unusual word sounds? If nonsense words appear in his story, or if characters are given peculiar names, does he enjoy the sounds? Is he ever heard laughing about words with unusual sounds? Does he ever remark about very long words, or exceedingly short words, or say them aloud to hear how they sound?

Does the child interpret pictures effectively? Anyone who has examined the preprimers, primers, and first readers with which most children begin their reading experiences knows how important a part the picture plays in the story. Often the title page suggests the contents almost entirely through a picture. In simpler materials the picture typically occupies one half to three quarters of the page, and occasionally, in a very easy preprimer page, the words of the story convey little meaning without the picture. The child who is adept in interpreting pictures brings to his first reading experiences a technique that suggests to him approximately what the story will say.

A picture is also important as an aid in identifying new words. If a story is illustrated with a picture of two children looking out of the windows of a plane, it is not very difficult for a child to deduce that the new word on the page is likely to be *airplane,* or perhaps *fly.* Having made this deduction, he inserts the correct word without much trouble in a sentence such as: *The children are in an* ————. *They like to* ————, would be equally plain.

Growth in picture interpretation appears to be a combination of maturation and experience. It is typical for the young child to pass through a stage where he enumerates objects in a picture before he begins to tell a story about it, and to tell a story about each of the characters separately before he weaves the total picture into one related tale. In the *Revised Stanford-Binet Scale,* Form L, picture interpretation appears among the test items as early as three years, six months and as late as twelve years. At the younger age, enumeration of three objects is sufficient to secure credit. However, Terman reports that children as young as three and four years gave interpretations of some of the pictures used in preliminary experimentations.[28] To be able to interpret a picture that relates to a situation within his experience, then, is a task that a six- or seven-year-old may reasonably be expected to perform. Children who have not acquired this ability need many interesting and realistic situations in which they can learn.

The typical activities of a kindergarten or first-grade classroom give many opportunities to judge a child's ability to interpret pictures. Children are drawing pictures themselves. They are also surrounded by many books with pictures, and by bulletin-board displays.

What does the child say about his own pictures and those drawn by his friends? If he is drawing an illustration for a group experience record, can he identify what he is trying to draw? Does he usually tell a story about his pictures, or does he point to objects? What does he say about other children's pictures?

How does he respond to pictures in classroom books? Can he identify the characters about whom he has been hearing? Can he tell which part of the story the picture illustrates? Does he comment upon interesting elements in the picture that throw light upon the story? Does he respond to the humor in a picture? Does he voluntarily spend time at the library table looking at pictures?

How does he respond to new pictures on the bulletin board? Can he tell what the picture is about? Does he make a story from the picture, or does he point to separate objects? Does he relate the picture to comparable experiences of his own? Does he ask questions that indicate that he has identified elements that are new and interesting to him?

Does he use pictures for information? Can he find an answer to his questions in an appropriate picture? Does he raise new questions as a result of studying a picture? Can he identify contrasts between a picture and his own experience?

Does the child know how to handle books? The beginning reader must know enough about handling books to be able to start at the front, turn the pages in order, read from left to right, follow the lines from top to bottom of a page, and identify the beginning of a new story by its title page. He also needs to know how to care for books properly. Of all the prereading abilities,

[28] Lewis M. Terman and Maude E. Merrill, *Measuring Intelligence* (Boston: Houghton Mifflin Company, 1937), pp. 204, 267-8.

these are the most easy to develop as children actually start their beginning-reading activities. However, adequate left-to-right orientation for the beginning reader is the technique most likely to take time to develop. Many first-graders will continue to have some difficulty as they begin to write, and as they try to read words that offer few configurational clues, such as *was* and *saw, on* and *no,* or *stop* and *spot.* Children who seem to be particularly confused in directional orientation will merit considerable help at the prereading level.

Teachers can look for evidences of skill in handling books such as the following:

How does the child handle the books on the library table? Can he find the name of the book on the cover? Can he open to the first page of a story he would like to hear? Can he point to the place in the page where the story begins? When he examines the book, does he turn the pages in an orderly sequence? How careful is he with books?

How good is his sense of directional orientation in classroom written activities? As the teacher writes a sentence on the board, can he tell at which side she should begin? If a caption is to be put under his picture, can he tell at which side it should start? If he writes his own initials on a piece of work, does he write them from left to right? As he copies letters, how many does he reverse? Can he point to the beginning of a line in an experience record, or to the place to start reading in a story in a book?

Can he identify the parts of a classroom experience record? Can he point to the title of the chart? Does he know where the first line begins? In helping to read the chart, does he take the lines in order?

USING READING-READINESS TESTS

Choose the test to meet the needs of a particular situation. Many school systems use reading readiness tests as another means of appraising prereading ability. They are not essential to an effective reading program, but can be of value in providing additional evidence against which a teacher can check her judgment of the probable success of individuals and groups. Therefore, the type of test and the time at which the test is given should both be planned with the needs of the teacher in mind.

Three main types of readiness tests are available. The first, of which the *Metropolitan Readiness Tests*[29] is one of the most widely known, is a test of educational readiness that explores broadly the skills needed for first-grade activities. In this test, certain of the subtests measure specific prereading

[29] Gertrude H. Hildreth and Nellie L. Griffiths, *Metropolitan Readiness Tests* (Yonkers-on-Hudson: World Book Company, 1949, 1950).

abilities—recognizing similarities and differences in words and pictures, choosing pictures that correspond to key words and sentences. Other subtests appraise general experience background, knowledge of numbers, and skill in copying numbers and figures. This type of readiness test is particularly valuable when the information needed is a general estimate of children's potential adjustment to typical first-grade work. Given late in the kindergarten or early in the first grade, it can be used as one guide in setting up groups of about the same ability level. Study of the subtest scores can help to diagnose particular strengths and weaknesses.

A second type of readiness test measures prereading skills specifically. These tests measure such abilities as interpreting pictures, recognizing similar configurations of words, identifying similar sounds, giving rhymes, recognizing the meaning of words, and following oral directions. Tests calling for knowledge of the names of letters and of numbers are sometimes included. Typically the child does little reading. He may be called upon to identify the two words that are alike in a set of four, or to find the word he has just been shown on a flash card. Ability to give rhymes is often measured by using pictures. Ability to understand oral language may be tested by asking the child to follow increasingly complicated directions. The *Gates Reading Readiness Tests*[30] and the *Lee-Clark Reading Readiness Test*[31] are typical of such tests. Tests of this sort are particularly helpful when the teacher is interested in specific knowledge regarding children's prereading skills. Profiles indicating the strengths and weaknesses of each child can be drawn, and prereading activities planned accordingly.

Reading-readiness tests are also provided along with other prereading materials in many of the present-day series of basal readers. These tests are designed to measure specifically the child's ability to progress into the beginning-reading materials of the given series. They are often developed around the same types of exercises as those included in the workbooks of the particular series. Frequently they test the child's ability to recognize the words that will be part of his next reading experiences. Such tests have special value for the teacher working with an adopted series who wants a guide as to whether her children are ready for more advanced work.

Other minor considerations need to be taken into account in choosing a readiness test. One is the question of how easy it is to administer. First-graders are not very skilled in following directions and are normally most cooperative in trying to help each other. It is usually wise to test them in small groups. The less help available to the teacher in giving the test, the

[30] Arthur I. Gates, *Gates Reading Readiness Tests* (New York: Teachers College, Columbia University, 1939).

[31] J. Murray Lee and Willis W. Clark, *Lee-Clark Reading Readiness Test*, Revised Edition (Los Angeles: California Test Bureau, 1951).

more important it is to have one that is easy to administer, with directions that are very clear for the children. Time is also a factor. Tests that have to be given to children individually may provide valuable information, but be difficult to use under typical teaching conditions. From the teacher's point of view, time consumed scoring the test should also be considered. It is often helpful to examine several tests and manuals before deciding on a test for a particular class.

Give the test at a time that will provide the most help in planning pre-reading experiences. In spite of the implication in the name, "reading-readiness test," such a test does not necessarily set a standard which all children must meet before they begin to read, nor does it necessarily separate the "ready" from the "unready." The chief use of a readiness test is to help the teacher decide what experiences to plan for children. Percentile scores indicate a child's status in relation to other children his age for the test as a whole, and for each subtest. Usually such scores may be used to predict potential success in reading. Such evidence is most useful early in the first grade as one aid in planning for the year's work.

A readiness test given in the kindergarten, while not as likely to be as accurate for the first-grade teacher as one given early in the fall, has the merit of being available for many children when school starts. The results of such a test may form the basis for tentative early groupings. Tests given in the early fall should be delayed until children are used to school routines, and can follow directions and use pencils and crayons. Usually two or three weeks will allow sufficient time. Tests which accompany a basal-reader series are usually most helpful if they are given at the place in the sequence of reading experiences where they are intended. Thus they may help to identify the children for whom the next materials are likely to be suitable, and those who apparently need a longer time with simpler activities.

In some school systems it may seem desirable to test all first grades at about the same time, in order to have comparable scores from class to class. However, there are also advantages in giving teachers freedom to decide when and how they will use readiness tests. At their best, these instruments serve primarily to provide another piece of evidence regarding children's growth. Teachers may differ in the times at which they feel this evidence is most helpful.

KEEPING OBJECTIVE RECORDS OF CLASSROOM OBSERVATIONS

Make anecdotal records. An anecdotal record is a brief description of a significant aspect of a child's behavior. The behavior could, of course, be any kind of behavior about which information is sought, and which the observer has the opportunity to record. In this instance, significant evidence is needed concerning the child's progress, or his difficulties in beginning reading activities. The teacher will not need to have information for every child about every aspect of growth, and the collection of anecdotes should be helpful, not burdensome. Many teachers carry with them a pad of paper upon which they can jot down brief notes as an incident worthy of special mention occurs. For the purpose of planning prereading activities, certain of these records should bear on the child's growing skill with words, stories, and pictures. These notes are dated, and dropped into the children's cumulative record folders at the end of the day. Later the folder may be checked and helpful summary statements recorded.

For example, a note may read: "Today Jerry found his name on the helpers' chart without being told. This is the first evidence that he is beginning to make discriminations among shapes of words." And later—"Jimmy had a story to tell about his picture today. This is the first time." There may be only two or three such anecdotes in the course of any one day.

The task of collecting anecdotal records can be simplified by watching for only one thing at a time in situations where children have the most opportunity for demonstrating their level of ability in this specific area. When the discussion follows a story hour, attention may be focused upon skill in interpreting pictures, or upon getting the main ideas of a story. It may also help to look for children who respond to shapes and sounds of words, as experience records are discussed. As plans are laid for independent activities, it is possible to watch for the children who are able to carry out the plans, and for those who need help.

Such anecdotal records may serve many purposes. They supplement the readiness-test scores, which are derived by the child's working with only one type of material. They give help in understanding children in the areas of social and emotional adjustment where test records are almost impossible to secure. They deal with a child's growing skill with words, stories and pictures, and are thus most helpful in planning for continued prereading activities in which pupils may engage.

Use informal test situations. Another method of securing an objective record of day-by-day growth is to set up an occasional informal testing situation. Children do not necessarily need to work with pencil and paper for this purpose. The teacher may plan an interesting activity where one particular skill predominates, and then work with a small group so that it is easy to note individual responses. Work with an experience record can be made the center of several types of informal tests. When a teacher wishes to appraise the ability of the group in identifying similarities in word forms, she can write words or phrases on cards and note which children can match the cards with the same words and phrases in the experience record. It is also possible to ask children to see how many places in a record they can find the same word or phrase. To tell how many children are beginning to read independently, note can be made of those who can read given lines without help. Games in which children try to supply rhyming words can be used to identify strengths and weaknesses in working with the sounds of words. An interesting picture book can be used to determine differences in picture interpretation. Brief notes can be made about the performances of individual children in such specially-planned activities and added to their cumulative records. Some teachers find it helpful and a saving of time to keep a chart on which children's names are listed across the top and significant areas of growth down one side.

In many classrooms, teachers will also be using a certain number of commercially-prepared or teacher-constructed work-type activities as part of children's prereading experiences. Performance on these materials can be appraised and typical samples of the child's work added to his cumulative file. Sometimes it is possible to select activities from several points in a prereading workbook so that the child works with exercises ranging from easy to difficult. Such exercises provide, on an informal basis, information similar to that secured from a readiness test.

Make effective use of records of classroom activities. In the normal course of the day, teachers make records of classroom activities which, if saved and analyzed, can add to the growing amount of information about a particular child. Listing the names of those who helped to compose an experience chart can provide a record of the children who took part in each such activity. Checking off, at the end of each day, the names of the children who worked at the library table can give a picture of those who are most interested in books. Adding the child's name to the object he brought to the museum corner, or to the picture he brought for the bulletin board, provides a simple way of telling which children are contributing most frequently. A record can be kept of some of the activities engaged in by an individual child by filing samples of his work—a picture he has drawn, a story he has dictated, or some of his written work.

Part of the secret of making effective appraisals of children's growth through day-by-day classroom experiences is to plan simple recording systems that serve the on-going activities of the group while they provide the teacher with a way of taking a more careful look at what is happening to individuals. Good records should not be a burden. They should be of use while they are being collected.

Study kindergarten records. Many children will come to first grade after a year in kindergarten. Teachers of five-year-olds are concerned with the same aspects of physical and social development that concern teachers of first-graders. Many activities are planned in kindergarten to encourage facility with language: books are read, stories told, and many pictures are used. It is helpful, in appraising reading readiness, for the first-grade teacher to know what kinds of experiences a child has had in kindergarten. Similarly, it is helpful to kindergarten teachers in planning their programs to know the types of activities in which children will be expected to engage in first grade. If kindergarten records are available, they should be studied with care in planning prereading activities in the first grade.

APPRAISING RELATED ASPECTS OF DEVELOPMENT

In the preceding sections were suggested ways of appraising the child's growth in skills and attitudes directly connected with working with books and stories. It is also important to study related aspects of a first-grade child's development. His physical and intellectual growth, his general experience background, the social and emotional adjustments he is making in the classroom setting should be studied. Cumulative records may supply evidence regarding these areas of growth. Some information will come from anecdotal records collected in a fashion to that just described. Additional evidence may be supplied by the school nurse or physician, or secured through visiting homes and talking with parents.

The sections which follow suggest ways of gathering, analyzing and using information about development in areas which relate to success in beginning reading.

What experience background does the child bring to his reading? Ways in which a beginning reader draws upon his background of experiences have already been described briefly. It contributes to his vocabulary and deepens his concepts. It is the basis from which he understands a story and interprets its pictures. It provides the impetus for oral-language experiences as he makes his suggestions for class plans, helps to dictate an experience record, or tells the group about something special he has done at home.

Experiences prior to first grade also influence the ease with which the child fits into the classroom. There will be differences in familiarity with such classroom equipment as paint brushes, crayons, scissors, construction blocks, and toys. Children will come to school with varied experiences in working and playing with other children. Ability to work with materials with reasonable independence and ability to get along well with other children without supervision both become important to the smooth functioning of the classroom when the teacher begins to work with reading groups for part of the day.

Activities that contribute to a broader experience background are important at all grade levels. For every first-grader there needs to be an environment where there are many new things to see, to handle, to talk about, and eventually to read about. For children whose background is limited, it may be important to supply more than the usual amount of concrete experience. Possibly for some weeks there will be few intensive prereading activities with words and stories while these children are encouraged to investigate their classroom environment, helped to learn to use various items of classroom equipment, given opportunities to work and play together, and taken on a variety of excursions to other parts of the school and to places of interest in the neighborhood.

The teacher can study the background of experiences with which children come to school by observing them in many different situations:

What home activities does the child report? When he comes back to school after the weekend, what does he say he has been doing? What does he bring to school to share with other children? Does he draw on home and community experiences in classroom discussions and interpreting pictures? Does he mention experiences of his own which parallel those of children in stories he hears, or those reported by other children?

What evidence of his background is revealed in his school activities? Does he mention that he has been on trips or has seen objects similar to those in pictures posted on the bulletin board? In a class discussion, does he draw on his outside experience? What do his pictures and creative stories reveal of his background? What can be learned about him from his dramatic play? What does he talk about when two or three children work or play together?

How much at home does he seem in the classroom? How well does he handle equipment? What kinds of equipment seem strange to him? How does he get along with other children? Does it seem easy for him to find his way around the school? Is he able to get out his own materials, put on his own coat or rubbers?

Are there physical factors that might impede reading progress? Evidence regarding a child's vision, hearing, and general health needs to be secured from a medical authority. At times this will be the school nurse, at times a family physician, and at times a specialist to whom the child has been referred. Certain tests of vision and various types of audiometers are available as a help in the screening process at school. However, care needs to be taken to avoid giving diagnoses on the bases of such tests. The responsibility of school personnel is to be alert to potential difficulties and to urge that further checks be made by specialists. Identification of speech difficulties is likely to be done by the classroom teacher unless there is a speech therapist in a school system. Here, too, medical authorities can help in locating actual physical malformations that may be causing the trouble.

Adjustments of the prereading and beginning-reading programs for children with physical handicaps will depend upon the advice of the specialist who has been consulted. Sometimes it may mean an extension of prereading experiences, in which pressures for day-by-day work with books and other materials that must be seen near at hand are not so exacting. At other times there may need to be adjustments of the materials and experiences of the beginning-reading period. A child with a visual handicap may be seated with special attention to light and to the size of print he uses, be taught with special care how to hold his book. A child who has trouble hearing may be seated close to the teacher and addressed directly. Special help may be given to correct speech difficulties and special care taken to provide supplementary activities for the child who has been absent because of illness.

Because of their daily contacts with children, teachers are in a unique position to identify health problems and to urge that a child be referred for further checks. It is important to be alert to the evidences of difficulty. These are often best caught during informal activities when there are opportunities to observe individuals or small groups—talking to children before school begins; working with individuals during an independent work period; or working with a small group for reading, language, or number experiences. It is particularly important to realize that a child often learns to conceal the fact that he does not quite know what is going on. He guesses, clowns, drops his book, talks to another child, or in some other way avoids the issue. The causes of undue amounts of such behavior need to be looked into with care.

Evidence such as the following may suggest the need for further checks by specialists:

Does the child show evidences of visual difficulties? Does he rub his eyes? Does he seem to shade his eyes from light? Are his eyes red, or watery? Are his eyelids granulated? Does he squint or turn his head at a peculiar angle? Does he seem to identify words at one distance, but have trouble with them at another? Does he complain of headaches, or say that his eyes hurt?

Is there evidence that he might not hear clearly? Does he appear to be listless, or daydream unless spoken to directly? Does he have a habit of turning his head to one side, listening with his mouth open, or cupping a hand over his ear when he is trying to hear? Does he confuse words with similar pronunciations? In repeating what a teacher has said, does he frequently substitute a word with a similar sound?

Are there noticeable speech defects? Are there sounds the child does not seem able to say? Is he consistent in his mispronunciation of these sounds, or does he have trouble only if they are at the beginning or the end of a word? Do patterns of "baby talk" persist?

Are there evidences of other types of health problems? How regular is his attendance pattern? Does he seem to tire more easily than most children? Is he listless? Are there any special physical symptoms of which parents do not seem to be aware?

What is the evidence of the child's functioning intellectual ability? It is not safe for a teacher to come to a definite conclusion regarding a child's intellectual ability without considerable test evidence. Many factors can influence judgments. A shy child is sometimes underrated, and a talkative child given credit for more reasoning ability than he actually has. Sometimes the slightly older child, who makes sensible suggestions out of more months of living, is rated as brighter than he really is. Illness, malnutrition, visual or auditory difficulties, or other health factors can affect a child's performance. Furthermore, the experience background with which a child comes to school may be highly educative in its own way, but may cause him to look confused and unintelligent in the first days of his acquaintance with his classroom setting.

Estimates of intellectual ability are likely to be more reliable if they are secured on the basis of an individual test, such as the *Revised Stanford-Binet Scale*.[32] The young child, particularly, is not always adept in following group directions. A qualified examiner working with a child alone is likely to catch such difficulties. However, such individual tests require training on the part of those who give them. Teachers usually do not have such training, and school systems rarely can afford the services of enough qualified psychologists to test every first-grade child.

Because of the practical difficulty of securing individual test scores for more than a limited number of first-graders, primary group intelligence tests are frequently used. References are suggested at the end of Chapter XIII to aid in locating such tests. In deciding on a specific test, school personnel need to take into account many of the same factors that are important in choosing a readiness test. If the test is to be given early in the first grade, care needs to be taken to select one in which the directions are as simple as possible and the method of indicating answers requires little dexterity in handling a crayon or pencil. Typically the test for the young child is untimed, or has a very generous time limit. Teachers are often urged by test authors to take groups of not more than ten children at one time, and to enlist the aid of a helper if possible. Care must be taken to make sure that children are not copying each

[32] Lewis M. Terman and Maude E. Merrill, *op. cit.*

other's work, that they are following directions properly, and that they are working on the correct page or exercise.

Even when a test has been carefully given, judgments about the intellectual abilities of first-graders should be very tentative. In a group test, some children may be handicapped by inexperience in following directions, handling pencil and paper, and turning pages. There is also evidence that raises questions regarding the adequacy of existing intelligence tests as measures of the potential ability of the child from an underprivileged area.[33] Because of the difficulty of securing accurate test scores for young children, some school systems prefer to postpone giving intelligence tests until the second grade. When this is done, teachers rely for the first year on evidence from reading-readiness tests and from classroom situations in which a child's ability can be roughly appraised.

An unusually low score on an intelligence test for a child who gives other evidence of above-average intellectual ability should always be questioned. Exceptionally good use of language, unusually strong prereading abilities, accurate use of number concepts, and logical reasoning are all evidences of intellectual ability in the light of which a low test score can be studied. A score on a reading-readiness test can also be used as a check on an intelligence test score.

Whatever the child's potential ability, the way in which he actually operates in a classroom is important to consider. Without making definite judgments that classify children as "dull," "average," or "bright," teachers can make many helpful observations of the ways in which children are functioning intellectually in the classroom setting. Skills such as interpreting pictures, identifying differences in the configurations of words, and following the gist of a story are in part dependent on intellectual ability. Increased attention span is another sign of functioning intellectual ability. So is capacity to follow increasingly complex directions and to carry out more complicated plans. All these types of growth are important to success in beginning-reading activities.

Immaturity in areas such as interpreting pictures and following the main ideas of a story does not necessarily mean limited intellectual ability. A child may lack the experiences which would have helped him develop these skills. It is possible, also, that short attention span or inability to follow directions may be the result of social and emotional immaturity, or of physical disabilities. The prereading program will need to be planned in terms of the cause of the difficulty.

Suggestions of situations in which to appraise growth in such skills as vocabulary and picture interpretation were made in earlier sections. Other

[33] Kenneth Eells *et al., Intelligence and Cultural Differences: A Study of Cultural Learning and Problem Solving* (Chicago: University of Chicago Press, 1950).

types of observations regarding functioning intellectual ability might be made in areas such as the following:

What seems to be the child's capacity for sustained attention? If he is working with a group, how long does he concentrate on the task at hand? How well does he listen to a story? If he is working on an independent project, does he stay on the job, or does he wander off to watch other children? How well does he keep plans in mind from day to day?

How clearly does he reason on classroom problems? Does he see simple relationships? Is he able to bring past experience to bear on a problem? Does he have logical reasons for disagreeing with other children? Is he able to identify why given suggestions would not work?

How well can he follow directions? Can he remember the equipment he needs? Can he tell clearly what he plans to do? Is he able to carry out a simple project without help? Does he still remember class plans after a short time lapse? How many steps in a project can he keep in mind?

How satisfactory are the social and emotional adjustments the child seems to be making? Behavior in the area of social and emotional adjustments is exceedingly difficult to interpret. It is often easy to see how a child is behaving, but to decide why he is behaving in that fashion, to determine what needs the behavior is satisfying in his life, and to tell how best to help him satisfy those needs through socially acceptable channels is another matter.

Learning to read requires a certain degree of concentration. The child must be willing to stay at the job. His attention must be focused upon the work at hand. He must be interested and willing to go on with independent tasks when his teacher is occupied with other children. He must be able to share in group discussions without demanding an undue amount of attention or being distracted by the people next to him. Children who are secure in the affection of their parents, who are happy with groups of their peers, who have learned to solve problems for themselves without an undue amount of assistance from adults, and who have learned to face failure or disappointment over a change in plans without undue concern are likely to be better equipped to profit from individual and group experiences at the prereading and beginning-reading levels than are children who are insecure, dependent on others, and unskilled in group relationships.

Human needs to be loved, to be accepted by a group, to be recognized as a contributing group member, and to be like others in a group are very strong. The means through which a child may satisfy such needs are many. Desirable growth will result in his learning to play happily with other children, to share materials with them, to take his part in a cooperative enterprise, and to accept criticism and suggestions without showing resentment or becoming unduly discouraged. Undesirable means of satisfying such needs will at times lead to behavior patterns that make it much more difficult for the child to learn to read. Teachers need to be able to identify such problems.

CHARLES has his first experience in playing with large groups of children. His only approach to them seems to be to poke them, pull their books away, tease them, and use other such devices for gaining attention. When a small group meets to discuss the writing of a class record, Charles' attention is almost entirely devoted to the children on either side of him. They retaliate and within a few minutes a little knot of children has been completely diverted from the task at hand.

SUSAN is the smallest and quietest child in the room. Previous to entering first grade, she has always played with younger children, and now her size has placed her at a disadvantage in all active games. To save herself from being pushed or knocked down, she has learned to retire quietly with her playthings to a corner where she is not in the way. Most of her class has been actively interested in helping dictate experience records of excursions. Susan has not yet volunteered a suggestion. When asked directly, she replies briefly in a timid voice. Although she apparently examines the books on the library table with interest she never brings a story for the teacher to read to the group.

JEAN has had few experiences in playing with other children. She has moved from one town to another with her parents. Most of her life has been spent in hotel rooms and at nearby parks with her mother. Large playthings were impossible under such living conditions. Now she is enjoying the activities of the first grade thoroughly. She plays well with other children and is expanding under the conditions of dramatic play which prevail in the playhouse. The easel, clay, building blocks, aquarium, and corner museum have all been fascinating to her. In the wealth of stimulating experiences, the printed notices, class records, and other incentives to read have received little attention. Jean has always had picture books. Her parents have read many stories to her. She comes readily to meet with the children who have just begun to work with a preprimer, but she is quite obviously putting in time until she can get back to more exciting activities.

Here are three children whose needs at present are not primarily concerned with learning to read. Problems of learning to play with other children, and of exploring other avenues of self-expression are more important. Until ways are found of helping these children meet such needs, progress in reading is going to be slow. As long as Charles has no other means of approaching children, the reading group will continue to be disrupted. Susan will not make her full contribution to the reading group until she feels more secure with other children. Until she has experimented with some of the other satisfactions which her previous home life did not provide for her, Jean will continue to give only half-hearted interest to reading.

Teachers should also be concerned with identifying the child who spends an undue proportion of his time with reading materials at the expense of other areas of growth. If home and community emphasis is upon rapid progress in beginning reading, the fact that such children may be developing poor adjustment patterns may not quickly be seen.

ALICE spends much of her time at the library table, although she is only reading material of a preprimer level. She enjoys turning the pages, looking at pictures, and arranging and dusting the books. If other children come to help her she moves away, or sits down with her own book and pays little attention to them. Her mother reports that Alice would much rather stay with her and listen to stories than go out to play. She enjoys drawing pictures to illustrate class records, but she rarely volunteers to share in anything which requires group activity. When the class gathers for group work, she sits to one side, a little apart from other children.

DOROTHY announced to the teacher the first day of school, "I can read almost every book you have here, I guess." She is not at all adept in any other kind of activity. Children do not want her in their games because she does not know how to follow the rules. Her attempts to help with the wallpaper for the play corner resulted in spilled paint. Her greatest joy and main source of satisfaction are to be able to read bulletin boards, preprimers, and other materials better than any other child. She boasts of her reading ability, and makes fun of other children when they make errors.

These two little girls are apparently headed toward successful reading experiences. Yet, like Charles, Susan, and Jean, they have needs that are more important to their all-around development than the need to learn to read. Little objective test data can be secured from very young children in areas of social and emotional development. Projective techniques have been used in which a child gives his own responses to a relatively unstructured test situation through such devices as a picture, a creative story, or dramatic play.[34] The responses of first graders can be studied by observing the child's drawings of his family; by studying themes, colors, and significant methods of work in pictures; and by listening to his dramatic play. Evidence secured from such observations has to be interpreted with caution, as it is relatively easy for the teacher to read into a child's responses implications that are not sound. However, in the hands of experienced persons, such devices are

[34] Arthur T. Jersild, *Child Psychology*, Fifth Edition (Englewood Cliffs, New Jersey: Prentice-Hall, Inc., 1960), pp. 348 ff.

proving of significant value. Teachers who are interested in their use should make an effort to read widely and to secure special training.

Identifying problems of social and emotional adjustment through classroom activities is a matter of studying the child in many different settings. It is difficult to suggest specific types of behavior at which to look without omitting others equally important, or giving the impression that a single piece of behavior provides evidence sufficient to conclude that the child is having difficulty. Five- and six-year-olds are in the process of taking an important step away from home toward working with people their own age. All immature responses are not symptoms of maladjustment.

In studying a child's social and emotional adjustment, questions such as the following may be helpful:

How well does the child get along with other children? Does he normally share with them and offer a certain amount of help? Can he work on a cooperative project? Is he unusually shy or aggressive in group discussion situations? Can he take turns? Does he share materials? Does he express sympathy when a child has trouble?

How dependent is he on adults? Does he seem overdependent on his mother or on an older child who brings him to school? How frequently does he turn to the teacher for approval? Can he solve a dispute with his peers without turning to the teacher for help? How well does he work independently? Does he seem to need more than the usual amount of reassurance?

What are his responses to frustration? Do there seem to be an undue number of tears, of temper tantrums when things go wrong? How does he go about persuading other children to do things his way? What kind of reaction does he give when plans have to be changed? What happens when he is asked to share equipment?

Total growth needs are the ultimate basis for decisions regarding classroom experiences and groupings of children for various types of activities. As suggested earlier when reading readiness was defined, the primary program needs to be developed as an integrated whole with the all-round development of children as its focus. Prereading activities are one part of the total pattern.

SOME QUESTIONS TO THINK ABOUT IN APPRAISING PROCEDURES FOR DETERMINING READING READINESS

1. Is every aspect of development taken into account?
2. Is special attention given to those skills with words, stories, and pictures that a child will need when he begins to read?

3. Is the child's growth appraised, in part, in terms of the ways in which beginning-reading activities are developed in the specific classroom?

4. Are the child's daily classroom activities used as a basis for appraising his progress toward successful beginning reading?

5. Are standardized tests chosen and administered so that they are of greatest help to the classroom teacher?

6. Do the various methods used to appraise reading readiness also help to guide the planning of daily classroom activities?

7. Has a system of records been planned so that objective evidence of a child's growth can be collected?

8. Is the system of record-keeping such that it grows out of, and contributes to, on-going classroom activities?

SUGGESTIONS FOR FURTHER READING

Anderson, Irving H., and Dearborn, Walter F. *The Psychology of Teaching Reading.* Chapter 2. New York: The Ronald Press Company, 1952. 382 pp.

Betts, Emmett A. *Foundations of Reading Instruction.* Chapters 8-13. New York: American Book Company, 1957. 757 pp.

Bond, Guy L., and Wagner, Eva Bond. *Teaching the Child to Read.* Third Edition, Chapter 5. New York: The Macmillan Company, 1960. 416 pp.

Dawson, Mildred A., and Bamman, Henry A. *Fundamentals of Basic Reading Instruction.* Chapter 3. New York: Longmans, Green and Company, 1959. 304 pp.

Dolch, Edward W. *Teaching Primary Reading.* Third Edition, Chapters 2, 4, 5. Champaign, Illinois: The Garrard Press, 1960. 429 pp.

Gates, Arthur I. *The Improvement of Reading.* Third Edition, Chapter 6. New York: The Macmillan Company, 1947. 657 pp.

Gray, Lillian, and Reese, Dora. *Teaching Children to Read.* Third Edition, Chapter 4. New York: The Ronald Press Company, 1957. 474 pp.

Harris, Albert J. *How to Increase Reading Ability.* Fourth Edition, Chapter 2. New York: Longmans, Green and Company, 1961. 624 pp.

Harrison, M. Lucile. *Reading Readiness.* Revised Edition, Chapters 2, 4, 5. Boston: Houghton Mifflin Company, 1939. 255 pp.

Hester, Kathleen B. *Teaching Every Child to Read.* Chapters 3-7. New York: Harper and Brothers, 1955. 416 pp.

Hildreth, Gertrude. *Readiness for School Beginners.* Chapters 1-4. Yonkers-on-Hudson: World Book Company, 1950. 382 pp.

————. *Teaching Reading.* Chapter 9. New York: Henry Holt and Company, 1958. 612 pp.

Monroe, Marion. *Growing Into Reading.* Chicago: Scott, Foresman and Company, 1951. 274 pp.

Russell, David H. *Children Learn to Read.* Second Edition, Chapter 6. Boston: Ginn and Company, 1961. 612 pp.

Smith, Henry P., and Dechant, Emerald V. *Psychology in Teaching Reading.* Chapter 4. Englewood Cliffs, New Jersey: Prentice-Hall, Inc., 1961. 470 pp.

Tinker, Miles A., and McCullough, Constance M. *Teaching Elementary Reading.* Second Edition, Chapters 3-4. New York: Appleton-Century-Crofts, Inc., 1962. 615 pp.

CHAPTER IV

Providing Prereading Experiences

A LOOK AT A TYPICAL FIRST-GRADE CLASSROOM

ONE of the most striking aspects of a first-grade classroom in the early fall is the amount of reading material around the room. Long before children have begun to do much reading for themselves, they are surrounded by stimulations to learn to read. Books, for the most part, are in large print. Signs and records prepared by the teacher are in manuscript writing or printed with a hand-printing set. Wherever possible these materials are hung low enough to be easily seen. What would a visitor find if he looked into a typical first-grade room?

Books are available in a library corner. In an attractive corner, away from the center of activities, is a library table, flanked by low bookcases. On the table are picture books, simple stories, alphabet books, and a few mimeographed copies of stories which the children themselves have dictated. Some preprimers, reserved for supplementary reading, are also in evidence.

Bulletin boards contain aids to classroom activities. The bulletin board is another attraction to those who would learn to read. On one corner is a poster labelled, *September Birthdays.* Under it are three names. Next to this is a chart marked *Helpers.* This is a list of room responsibilities—lunch, paper, plants, boards, and others. Beside each responsibility are the names of two children. In another part of the bulletin board is a sign, *To Tell Our Mothers.* At present, the only notice reads, *Party on Friday.*

Children's pictures have captions. Across the back of the room is a series of pictures painted by the children. Under many of them are simple captions—*This is Spot. He is Peter's dog; Marjorie lives in a house like this; Bob's kitten is white.* Another small bulletin board has a number of photographs of children, their homes and their families. At the top there is the large label, *Boys and Girls in Our Class.* Under the pictures are captions such as, *Betty and her brother; Sally Lou; Mike lives here.*

Special equipment has signs to guide its use. Posted near the easel is a simple color chart. Each color is represented by a circle of colored paper and has its name printed beside it. On some of the storage shelves and under some of the hooks are signs indicating where materials belong. Above the hooks in the cloakroom and on the backs of the chairs are the children's names. Near the library table is a sign saying, *We take care of our books.*

Experience records preserve the important aspects of group experiences. From the railing of the chalkboard at the front of the room hangs a report of a recent trip to a nearby grocery store, dictated by the children. On an easel is a chart labelled, *Today's News.* Posted on the bulletin board is a record titled, *Plans for Our Party.* On the back wall is another called, *We Are Good Housekeepers.*

What is essential to notice about this setting for prereading and beginning reading experiences? Briefly, these points:

1. All these various signs and captions refer to the on-going activities of the classroom. There is a reason why the children should pay attention to each one.
2. Children are not expected to read all of them; it is important rather that they live and work in an atmosphere in which reading is valued.
3. As the activities of the group move forward, the reading materials around the room will change accordingly.

In developing a first-grade program, teachers face several problems. First, what general objectives should guide the development of prereading activities? Second, how can the total primary program be made an effective setting for the child's prereading experiences? Third, how can the child's classroom activities contribute directly to prereading skills? Fourth, what is the place of commercially-published reading-readiness materials? Finally, how can the prereading program be varied to meet individual needs?

GUIDES FOR THE DEVELOPMENT OF PREREADING EXPERIENCES

What makes for an effective prereading program? In the discussion in Chapter III of factors related to readiness for beginning reading, general implications for the planning of prereading activities were pointed out. These suggest some definite criteria as guides for the development of prereading experiences.

The setting is a rich primary program. The broad objective of the modern school is to develop well-rounded individuals able to make maximum use of their capacities; socially and emotionally mature; sound in their understanding of, and ability to cope with, the world in which they live; and efficient in using the skills basic to solving problems, to calculating, to understanding the oral and written expression of others, and to making ideas clear to others. Learning to read is one of many areas of growth.

Prereading experiences were described in Chapter III as the verbal aspects of activities designed to help first-graders become better able to deal with themselves and their world. Looked at in this way, the prereading program is not an isolated part of the primary program for which special blocks of time are set aside, although there may be occasions when it is important to plan specific practice activities for individuals or for small groups. Every experience has a potential contribution to make.

All prereading skills find a place. A child's prereading experiences should provide for every skill that he will need when he begins to read independently. This means opportunities for oral expression, contacts with printed words, situations where it is important to distinguish among the shapes and sounds of words, and experiences in interpreting pictures and in handling books. Whenever there is need to discuss, to write a record, to post a notice, to turn to a book for help, or to examine a picture, there is an opportunity to build toward successful experiences in learning to read. Even an initialled purse or a new "T-shirt" with the picture and name of a television hero can play a part.

Interest and awareness, not reading itself, is the aim. In the classrooms that have been described, children read, in a sense, from the very beginning. They find their names on lockers. They use a combination of words and pictures on a helpers' chart to identify their special responsibilities. They point out the experience record composed when they talked about things to do on the playground and, with the help of the accompanying illustrations, they "read" the games they listed. However, the major teaching emphasis is not upon making certain that each child knows, for sure, each new word or phrase. Although teachers keep in mind the reading tasks the children will be facing a little later and stay well within children's stock of word meanings, the vocabulary load of the prereading environment is relatively heavy. The words used in classroom records are not restricted to typical preprimer vocabulary, nor is the amount of repetition provided that will be needed a little later to help beginning readers acquire a stock of words they can recognize at sight. What is sought at the prereading level is a child's interest in reading, his ability to follow the gist of a story when it is read to him, and his growing alertness to the configurations of words.

Individuals travel at different paces. All children will not be ready to profit from beginning-reading experiences at the same time nor will all need the same kinds of prereading activities. Then, there will be youngsters whose success in learning to read will hinge not as much upon experiences with books and stories as it will upon intellectual maturity, upon learning to get along with other children, upon health factors, upon ability to work independently, or upon richness of experience background. These needs must be taken into account, not only for the sake of the child's success in learning to read, but for the sake of his total adjustment, both in school and out. Indeed, the teacher who places success in reading above all other aspects of development often fails to achieve the very thing she most wants. The prereading program needs to be flexible—in the types of experiences planned for children, in the time at which children are encouraged to participate in beginning-reading activities, and in the emphasis placed upon the development of prereading skills.

PROVIDING THE SETTING FOR PREREADING EXPERIENCES IN THE TOTAL PRIMARY PROGRAM

The general nature of the first-grade program has much to do with determining the richness and variety of the child's prereading experiences. Three major aspects in the development of the child's total primary experiences deserve special consideration. First, there is the problem of helping the child adjust to school. Although some children will have had kindergarten experiences, many will not. All will need some help in fitting into the first-grade classroom and in learning to live and work together. Second, there is the problem of providing activities to widen first-graders' background of experience. Third, there is the whole area of helping children to become self-directing in their activities. How may these three important aspects of the total primary program be developed to provide the most effective setting for children's prereading experiences?

HELPING THE CHILD ADJUST TO SCHOOL

Identify the points of potential difficulty. Unless he has had experience in kindergarten, almost everything connected with school will be unfamiliar to the beginner and he may find adjustments difficult. Materials and equipment in his classroom, tables, chairs, bookshelves, lockers, chalk boards, may all be new to him. Even stacks of paper, clay, paints, scissors and crayons may not be familiar to some children.

Working in a large group of children may also present some problems. Being addressed as a member of a group called "boys and girls" may be a new and confusing experience. Comment about children's voices, as quieter conversation is necessary for comfortable classroom living, may be at first disturbing to some children. Adjustment must be made to regimentation in going to the toilet. A child may be unfamiliar with the techniques of sharing periods, story hours, group games and activities. He may lack experience in waiting for his turn, putting away materials, keeping his things neatly on a table, putting his hat and sweater in a new place, let alone facing the task of making statements heard by a large group of children. He may be unaccustomed to living by a schedule—time for play, time for lunch, time to listen, time to plan together. These are adjustments that may be difficult for the new learner.

The first grader has to find his way around an unfamiliar building, locating playgrounds, lunchrooms, halls, washroom, auditorium. He has to learn where things are, how to get there, and what the appropriate behaviors are in each instance.

Because it is important that first experiences in school be happy ones, teachers spend a considerable time in the early fall devoted to problems of school adjustment, and much emphasis is placed throughout the year on helping children to live and work happily together.

Provide a flexible and informal program. It is easier to help children to work and play happily together if the program is relatively informal and flexible. Children are seated in groups around tables or work in small groups in a play corner rather than in rows like an audience. There are many opportunities for a child to work alone or in small groups in painting, constructing, and manipulating materials. These informal groupings give children opportunities to work out ways of working together. Such situations also help the teacher to become better acquainted with the group.

Group projects, developed as unit activities, also provide opportunities to learn to work together. Such projects in the early fall may be concerned with decorating our room, planning our playhouse, arranging pictures for our bulletin board, finding how to care for the fish in our aquarium, becoming acquainted with other people in the school who help us, or planning for a

Halloween party. These activities, too, are flexibly planned. Each child finds a place both in contributing to class plans and in sharing in special aspects of the project on which he may be working alone or with a small group.

Talk out problems of how to live and work together. In most primary classrooms children are helped to feel at home quickly in the early fall because problems of living together are talked over with them, and they are helped to feel responsible for the smooth running of their school activities. "When we start to work, everybody can't come to the desk for help at once. How could we be sure that we each have what we need?" The first grade goes out to play at ten o'clock. The second grade comes out when we go in, so we must be ready or we will lose some play time. What should we do, then, when time comes to clean up?" "Before we go home today we want to look at your pictures, so when the clock says half-past two I am going to ask you to bring them here where we all can see." Time spent in the first few months helping children think through how to live together brings rich rewards later when the teacher wishes to work with a reading group or to give help on some other special project, assured that regular activities will continue as planned.

Give definite help in becoming acquainted with new materials and equipment. Children will adjust to school more readily in a classroom where time is set aside to help them learn how to use new materials and equipment. Help is usually given early with such general problems as how to carry chairs, scissors, paint jars, or other equipment that is hard to handle. Sometimes children assist in arranging the room, suggest where it would be convenient to keep certain equipment, and learn something of how to use and care for it in the process. When new media for creative expression are introduced, children are sometimes given help in small groups as they take turns experimenting. Additional assistance can be provided during individualized work periods. It is often an aid to devote special discussion periods to setting standards regarding how equipment is to be used—how many people may work at the easel at once, how large a group can play in the playhouse corner, what special precautions should be observed in working with the heavy building blocks. When time is taken to meet such problems as they arise, youngsters will be better able to proceed independently with their work later in the year, when the teacher needs uninterrupted periods for reading groups.

Plan a trip to become acquainted with the school. Many first-grade teachers find it helpful to take their classes on a trip around the school. The children go to the principal's office and talk to him about how he helps them. They locate the classrooms in which older brothers and sisters work. They may note playground boundaries and where school buses park. They talk to the custodian and ask how they can plan their housekeeping to be of the most help to him. They look into the kitchen and talk about good behavior in the lunchroom. They meet the school nurse and are shown the medical office. They look into the library. All such experiences help to build a feeling of at-homeness in the school. Over the year they may also serve to develop new interests and understandings.

BUILDING EXPERIENCE BACKGROUND

Provide a stimulating classroom environment. The problems involved in building experience background differ from child to child and group to group. Teachers need to study the children in their particular classes and then to plan appropriate activities that widen acquaintance with the immediate world. Many courses of study for first-graders recommend that such activities center around the environment near at hand—homes, school, and some of the more important community helpers. Some of these experiences are developed as extended units of work. Others may be planned as shorter projects. Some will involve the whole class, some groups, and some individuals.

The classroom environment itself needs to be one that stimulates new interests. Bulletin boards can be used for picture displays about holidays, community helpers, interesting pets, homes we live in, or toys we like. Window boxes or plants can be used to encourage science interests. So can an aquarium, a pet rabbit, or a terrarium. Building blocks offer possibilities for constructing a store, a lunch counter, or a post office. A table can be set aside to display special objects the children bring to school. The picture books on a library table can be used to develop many different interests.

Media for creative expression form part of a stimulating classroom environment. Even in classrooms where equipment is relatively meager, there can be many materials for children to explore. Poster paint and brown wrapping paper can be used for individual projects or for a group mural. Colored paper saved from Christmas wrappings, backs of book covers, and insides of candy boxes can be made into interesting designs or used instead of paint for parts of a picture. Cloth remnants can be fashioned into many different things—a mattress for a doll bed, a dress or apron for the doll, a costume for a dramatization, curtains for the windows of the playhouse. Wallpaper cleaner molds as readily as clay. Paper, paste, and patience are all that is needed for projects with papier-mâché. Even discarded tin cans have their uses.

Plan for wider acquaintance with the immediate community. Many first-grade teachers plan for activities that take children out of their classrooms into their local communities. These trips are not isolated experiences. They are planned as a result of group discussions, expressions of interest, and indications of lack of experience. In the fall the children decide to have a party to show their classroom to their mothers. With the permission of the principal the entire class goes to the nearby grocery to buy cookies for refreshments. They learn how to ask the clerk for what they want and they observe the cash register as they pay their bill. They see other articles for sale and perhaps note foods that are not familiar to them. When they come back, they talk about their trip and raise questions about the things they saw. Sometimes these questions call for a second trip or suggest that a guest be invited to school to provide more information. Needs for other trips arise in a similar fashion. From the classroom window, workmen can be seen laying the foundation for a new highway. The children keep a record of progress from day to day and learn about new materials, equipment, and ways of working. The immediate school neighborhood, whether it be the busy streets of a large city, the farms of the rural district, or the homes and gardens of the small town, provides many opportunities for enriching experience background.

Tap the resources in children's homes. A wealth of possibilities for enriching experience background can be found in children's homes. Someone lives in a house that is being remodeled. What can he tell about the carpenter and the plumber? Does he know whether the wallpaper paste is similar to the paste used in the classroom? Someone else tells about a new tractor or about caring for a lamb. Parents may come to talk about their occupations. A collection of the grains being harvested, a pet rabbit in the classroom for the morning, a description of the birds that occupied the bird house all summer and then disappeared in the fall, a favorite picture or story book, or an account of a favorite TV program, all may add to the experience background of the group and often contribute much to the development of the child who makes the contribution.

Make appropriate use of other types of audio-visual aids. Among the most effective audio-visual aids for beginners are the concrete objects they bring to the classroom or go out of the classroom to see. However, motion pictures, slides, exhibits, and records are also important in building experience background. A number of educational motion pictures now have the clarity of detail and simplicity needed for use with young children. Recordings may supply some of the musical experiences not provided in the home. Pictures clipped from magazines can become topics of discussion. Often the answers to questions can be found in the pictures of some of the books that are still too difficult for children to read. Museums sometimes loan exhibits that can be handled as well as looked at. Children may also build their own classroom museums.

Pictures are one step removed from reality. Size relationships, for example, can be confusing to the child who has not been to a zoo when an elephant and a bear, both the same size are presented in separate pictures. Such materials need to be appraised in terms of the maturity of the group and the experience background from which they will be interpreted.

HELPING CHILDREN LEARN TO WORK INDEPENDENTLY AND COOPERATIVELY

Provide for pupil-teacher planning. A rich and varied primary program in which the teacher has time to work with individual children and small groups cannot be developed unless children are able to take independent responsibility for many of their activities. The larger the class size, the more important it is for individuals to be self-reliant. Letting children share in planning their activities and encouraging their independence in carrying out their plans does not mean relinquishing leadership responsibilities. Rather, it frees the teacher to give more effective guidance at points where children cannot be expected to work alone. When reading groups are established, it makes for a program where many worth-while activities can go forward while the teacher is occupied with the children who are reading.

Planning periods can be used to help children decide which activities to undertake and to give them general suggestions on how to begin. These plans may involve either the entire class, small groups or individuals. In a typical planning session, needed materials, ways of working, and decisions as to which children are to take responsibility for various aspects of a project are thought through. The children then start to work with definite understanding of what they want to do and how to go about it. In the early part of the year, teachers usually circulate around the room after a planning session, helping individuals, noting where plans went awry, and identifying the children who seem to have most difficulty in following through on a job.

Evaluation periods are an important aspect of the total planning process. In these periods the children talk through what they have done. Difficulties are identified and suggestions for improvement are made; progress is appraised; and next steps are often projected. The work of today, in this way, becomes the basis for part of the plans for the activities of tomorrow. If the activities planned are within the understanding of children, have meaning for them, and seem to them to be worthwhile, it does not take long to develop, at least in the more mature members of the group, considerable ability to work without step-by-step supervision.

Provide for growing independence in working. There are several ways of helping children learn to work independently. One is to allow definite time in the daily schedule for individual work periods in which children may paint, play with toys, or look at books and pictures. These activities may develop desirable interests as well as help children become familiar with constructive activities in which they may later be engaged while the teacher is working with reading groups.

Another helpful procedure is to delegate housekeeping responsibilities, such as caring for some special materials, passing napkins for lunch, watering plants and the like. These are not just time-saving routines; they give children added practice in independently carrying out planned activities, and in doing things which add to the comfort and pleasure of classroom living.

Additional practice in working independently can be promoted by storing frequently needed materials within easy reach. If practical, one or two children may be put in charge of distributing and collecting crayons, scissors and other materials. The ability to take care of these responsibilities does not come without guidance. Children need to be helped to learn how to use and care for classroom equipment and materials. It is time well spent, however, if it makes possible the provision of a variety of activities, with time still available to give the special help needed to assure the development of fundamental skills through reading, arithmetic or science groups.

BUILDING PREREADING SKILLS

Activities designed to develop prereading skills were identified earlier as those aspects of first-grade experiences that call for oral expression; for the use of books, stories, signs, and other printed matter in meaningful settings; for gross discrimination among words by their shapes or their sounds; for interpretation of pictures; and for simple techniques of handling books. How can the varied activities of the first grade be used most effectively to develop these skills? How can teachers give the help needed to assure the desired growth without sacrificing the continuity of an experience to its prereading possibilities? What types of special practice activities might be provided?

Plan for sharing periods. Every aspect of the primary program offers opportunities for increasing the child's ability to express himself clearly and to understand the expression of others. However, there are certain key points where it is particularly easy to give help with language development. One of these is a group-sharing period, in which children tell of special happenings of interest to them. In these informal situations children can be helped to follow a sequence of ideas, and to express their own ideas in ways that may be clearly understood by others.

The entire class, or a small group with a common interest, may sit in a circle around the teacher's chair. Those who have something to tell stand near her where they can be seen and heard. A new birthday present, a particularly interesting picture, or a post card may be shown. A week-end trip, or the amusing antics of a pet may be shared. Contributions may be short. Some children will say only a sentence or two, although others will be able to relate a well-ordered series of events. Those who are listening are encouraged to ask questions and to join in the discussion.

In a sharing period the teacher, in leading the discussion, can assist the child who has difficulty. A well-timed question will help him put his ideas into words. "Why?" "What happened next?" "And then what did you do?" help to develop a sense of sequence. Children who are shy can be encouraged through the teacher's interest in their contribution, and by encouraging their sharing ideas in a smaller group. The shy child may also be encouraged to have something he can talk about—a leaf, a toy, or even a familiar home object like a thimble or a screw. Inadequate vocabulary can be supplemented by supplying the correct word, or by asking others in the group if they know what the right word would be.

Capitalize on planning and evaluation sessions. Planning periods and periods in which work is being evaluated offer other opportunities to build ability to communicate effectively. These sessions are particularly valuable for the development of clear oral expression because they relate to familiar topics close to the lives of the children. Almost everyone can have an idea about how to keep tables neat or what to do about the clothes that are falling off the hooks in the coat closet. It is relatively easy to put such a suggestion into a clear sentence because the suggestion itself is clearly understood. Acting as discussion leader, the teacher can help children learn how to keep their discussion to the general topic. Ideas that do not bear upon the problem at hand can be set aside and referred to later. Children can be helped to develop ability to follow the sequence of events as they outline step by step what they plan to do. Opportunities for vocabulary building often arise. In these informal situations where the teacher shares in the discussion there are many opportunities to develop better ways of putting ideas into words without embarrassing the child who is making the contribution.

Make use of the discussions centering around activities planned to broaden experience background. Activities that contribute to wider experience background also contribute to growth in ability to use language effectively. Excursions, trips to other parts of the school, new pictures on the bulletin board, new equipment in the classroom, the first snowfall of the season, the workmen on the nearby project, all provide new and interesting things to talk about. Freedom of expression is facilitated in these situations because children are commenting on things they know first-hand.

Many of the activities that broaden experience background offer opportunities to develop classroom records. These are times when children talk about what they have seen, tell what would be most important to remember, and suggest phrasing for the teacher to write. As these records are being composed, there are opportunities to discuss the importance of telling events in sequence and of giving complete sentences. These discussions also can contribute much to children's growing stock of word meanings. Each new object seen or handled and each new place visited can be used to clarify new concepts.

The pictures in commercially-prepared reading-readiness work-books offer another opportunity for small-group discussion. Children can discuss experiences of their own that are similar to those of the children in the picture, tell about their own trip to the farm, the store, or the zoo, or find pictures of objects or animals that are new and interesting to them.

Capitalize on needs to communicate with other persons in the school. Other opportunities to develop skill in oral expression arise because children are part of the larger school community. "We need to ask the principal if we may go for a walk tomorrow. What shall we say?" "We have a visitor today. What can we tell her about our work?" These are important reasons to express ideas as clearly as possible. Teachers seize such opportunities to discuss what needs to be said, how it should be said, and what the people being thanked or entertained would like to hear. At times the whole class shares in such discussions. At others, the teacher works with the group directly involved.

Make provision for sharing of stories. Stories are a rich source of language experience, and may be used in many different ways. Perhaps one of the most fruitful and pleasant procedures is for the teacher to build up a repertoire of stories to tell and to read aloud. Well chosen, well presented, and appealing to children, such stories provide a well-spring of new ideas, enriched word meanings, and deepened understanding. Stories may provide children with models for speaking, a sense that books may hold the key to wonder and delight, and a growing understanding of character delineation and plot structure, all aids to their own reading with understanding.

Children may themselves tell stories. Not the same story from a book, told over and over by each child, but a story heard at home, events of interest to them, accounts of their own experience, descriptions of things they have made, or seen, or done. They can tell about pictures they have drawn, or perhaps finish a story begun by the teacher or a classmate. They may tell stories about specially chosen pictures which suggest familiar experiences, or pose some question as to what might happen next. Sometimes a series of pictures may be found, either in readiness workbooks, or other texts, that show a series of happenings, and children may get useful practice in noting the sequence of events in a story.

Note that none of the stories told by children need be long; the important thing is to learn to express an idea to others, even if it involves only one sentence. Additional benefits in expressing ideas come from discussing what has just been heard. "How do you think he felt?" "What do you think happened next?" "What do you think he did?" "Would you like to have been there, too?"

Provide opportunities for dramatic play. Dramatic play offers other opportunities for language development. Many of the most worthwhile of these experiences develop informally, sometimes with little guidance from the teacher, as two or three children play they are the family in the playhouse, the clerk and customer in a store, or the driver and passengers on a bus. Children who find it difficult to express themselves before the group sometimes lose their self-consciousness in these make-believe situations. Children also can learn much about working and playing cooperatively, about taking turns, and about explaining ideas to others as the dramatic play progresses.

In addition to informal dramatic play, there are many opportunities for planned dramatizations of familiar stories or poems. These activities make their greatest contribution to skill in oral expression when they, too, are informal. Teacher and children talk over the story in order to become familiar with the characters and the plot. Then the children take turns acting the various parts. At times the teacher, or a narrator chosen from the group, tells the story while the characters act the parts in pantomime. At others, the characters speak for themselves, expressing the general idea of the story in their own words. Each time the story is dramatized, the conversation and the action are likely to be somewhat different. The aim is not a polished performance; it is to enjoy making a favorite story come to life.

Dramatic play offers opportunities to develop new concepts. "What would she say if she were very sad?" "What do you call the thing he was looking for?" These activities also can be used to develop sensitivity to the sequence of a story. Perhaps most important, they provide many opportunities for informal self-expression.

Find time for informal conversations. Most teachers find a few minutes during the day to talk with individual children. Some opportunities to talk with individuals come in the early morning and at noon as children are coming into the classroom and, again, as they are leaving school. Other opportunities come throughout the day. Sometimes in a planning session the children whose plans are clear go ahead with their work while one or two with special problems stay to talk with the teacher. Individual work periods offer time for the teacher to become better acquainted with one child at a time. If there is a lunch period, the teacher often moves to a new table each day to encourage conversation.

Children also grow in effective oral expression when they have an opportunity to talk with each other. Today's classrooms are not silent rooms. Children learn to give polite attention in audience situations. However, in work sessions, within limits that keep others from being disturbed, they are allowed to talk with each other as they work. They learn to ask each other for help, to give suggestions, and to share ideas. The buzz of conversation that is typical of a first grade at work is highly desirable from the standpoint of language development. It is highly desirable, also, from the standpoint of developing the skills of democratic living.

Encourage correct speech. Although some speech defects will require the advice and help of specialists, the experiences in every classroom can be planned so that they encourage correct speech habits in the majority of children. The teacher needs to be sure that her own pronunciation and enunciation are clear and distinct. Times when she is working with children individually offer opportunities to help those with faulty enunciation or pronunciation to speak more clearly. Small-group activities are often helpful for children who stammer or stutter. All-class sharing periods are times when children can be encouraged to speak clearly so that all may understand, yet the informal arrangement in which children typically sit for these group sessions means that the audience is not a formidable one. The opportunities for oral expression that have been described in detail in the preceding sections help to provide an atmosphere conducive to building correct speech patterns.[1]

BUILDING INTEREST IN LEARNING TO READ

Provide for varied uses of books. The typical first-grade classroom has been described as one in which there are many reading materials. These materials help to build interest in reading and develop the desire to read. They also provide the informal contacts with printed matter important for developing ability to identify similarities and differences among words, a sense of left-to-right direction, and other skills with printed matter that will be important when independent reading is begun.

A variety of books in the classroom provides one of the most natural stimulations to learn to read. Some of these will be stories that are read to the children. Others may be used by teacher and children together to locate needed information. Still others will be very simple books that children can enjoy by themselves. In most classrooms, books the children can explore independently will be found in a library corner. Here are picture storybooks, alphabet books, picture dictionaries, and perhaps simple one-word picture books made by the teacher to review important vocabulary items. Whatever the collection, it should be changed from time to time so that interest in new materials is sustained.

A commercially prepared reading-readiness book is another type of book

[1] For additional suggestions see Wilbert Pronovost and Louise Kingman, *The Teaching of Speaking and Listening in the Elementary School* (New York: Longmans, Green and Company, 1959), 338 pp.

that can be placed in children's hands. Although many pages of these pre-reading materials are given over to work-type exercises, they also contain simple stories which can be used to develop interest in books and to provide valuable experiences in picture interpretation, oral expression, and discrimination among the configurations of words.

Although the teacher carries the burden of reading the exact contents of a book at the prereading level, there are many ways of using books to build a desire to read independently. Children can be asked to choose from a story hour the books they liked best. This means being able to identify the title of a familiar tale. When a story is read to them, they can participate by discussing the pictures. They can also examine the pictures in an article providing needed information. When the names of characters in the book are the same as those of children in class, they can try to read them. Children who are beginning to identify other words or phrases may be encouraged to try their skill when these words or phrases appear in the story. All such experiences help children become interested in books.

Make use of experience records. In the early part of the first grade, the charts used as records of classroom activities offer at least as much stimulation to learn to read as do the books in the library corner. Not all experiences should lead automatically to a set of records. Any such routine emphasis is likely to make the reading side of the activity a burden. However, there are many genuine needs for records—a class book that contains the records of all the trips taken; poems the children composed during the year; the questions asked the bus driver and what he answered; a recipe for apple sauce; the daily news bulletin. Records such as these continue to serve a purpose long after children have begun to read. Detailed suggestions for their use with more skilled readers are given in Chapter VIII.

Teachers and children—the entire class, or the group specially concerned —compose such records together. This allows for many of the experiences in oral expression discussed in the preceding section.

MISS K:
 Who can think what we might call our story?
JOHN:
 We could say "The Store."
BETTY:
 No, it was our trip. Maybe it could be "Our Trip to the Store."
MISS K:
 Which do you like better? . . . How many would like to call it "Our Trip to the Store?" . . . Where shall we write it?
SALLY:
 It goes up at the top.

MISS K:

Then I'll write "Our Trip to the Store" up here. Now, what do you think it is most important to tell?

JOHN:

Well, first we should say we went there.

MISS K:

Where would I start to write that? . . . Yes, right over here. Should we tell what kind of store it was?

RON:

It was a grocery store.

MISS K:

Then shall I write "We went to the grocery store?" What might come next?

JOAN:

It was almost time to go home when we got back to school.

MISS K:

Do you think that comes next, or are there some things we saw at the store that we want to tell about?

SUE:

We should tell what we saw, because we wanted to know what the store sold.

BETTY:

They sell fruits. We saw some bananas.

After the record is completed at the board, it is often transferred to paper. It needs to be hand written, or printed with a hand-printing set. Lines should be kept short. Often each sentence is indented as a separate paragraph, much as the first sentences will be in the books used for beginning-reading activities a little later on. If the record is one that is likely to be reread during the year, it is often put on heavy paper or oak-tag so that it can withstand handling. If it is something that is needed only for a day or so, lighter paper may be used or the original record may be left on the board. Daily plans, reminders of dates, and notices of special events of the day, such as birthdays, are illustrative of temporary material. Records summarizing various experiences in a unit, songs or poems, and stories are more likely to be needed again. Insofar as possible, experience records are hung at the children's eye level. Sometimes oak-tag records are placed on easels and fastened together with steel rings so that children can turn easily from chart to chart.

In constructing and using experience records, teachers find many opportunities to develop prereading skills. As they begin to write, they may comment on where they begin and the direction in which they write. If the records are truly purposeful, there will be reason to reread them. When they are referred to again, the teacher has the opportunity to ask what the record was about, how it began, and what was said. Soon the children begin to identify the titles and to recognize words that are used frequently. Often teachers have the children illustrate a record by placing a picture next to its matching sentence. This makes it possible to "read" selected lines even though all the words are not recognized. As the children indicate the general gist of a line, the teacher may read exactly what it says.

MISS K:

Yes, we put down what we saw at the store so that we could tell our friends when they came to visit. Do you remember what we said first?

BETTY:

We told that we went to the store.

MISS K:

That's right. What kind of store was it?

JOHN:

A grocery store.

MISS K:

Can anyone remember how we said it? . . . Yes, we started by saying, "We went to the grocery store." Where did we put that part of our story? . . . Does anyone remember what it said up here just above the part that says, "We went to the grocery store?" . . .

RON:

That's the name of our story.

MISS K:

Who thinks he knows where we began the list of the things we saw?

SUE:

It was down here, where the picture is.

MISS K:

Shall I read them one at a time, and we'll see if we have planned for a picture of each one. The picture beside the first one tells what it was. . . . We put "bananas" first, didn't we?

In these discussions, the children see the teacher point to the appropriate lines and help her to find key words, using the clues she suggests. Soon, in their beginning-reading activities, some of them may see how many times they can find a given word, match the words on the chart with word or phrase cards, read whole lines for themselves, or engage in activities that have as their major objective helping children become able to recognize a specific number of words or phrases for themselves.

Capitalize on needs for special signs and notices. Many contacts with words, phrases and sentences can be provided in the typical first-grade classroom. For example:

1. Bulletin boards may contain notices of birthdays, holidays, plans, news items.
2. Pictures may be posted with appropriate captions. One such picture showed children listening to a story, with the caption, *We Like to Hear Stories.*
3. Records of committees and helpers, and short notices may be part of the bulletin board record.
4. Labels may help in using colors, paints, and in storing material.

5. Names of children can be written on pictures they have drawn, lists of persons who are to take special responsibilities.

In all of these notices, it is likely that a child will first learn to read his own name, and as he does so, he begins to look for similarities and differences among words. At the same time his interest is stimulated in learning to read the notices in which his name appears.

Classrooms should not be overcrowded with stimulations to read. Materials should be fresh and actually useful. It serves no real purpose, for example, to label common articles in the room, such as *chair* or *desk*. Teachers can judge the effectiveness of classroom reading materials by noting how much interest is shown in them. When the children seem oblivious to the printed matter that surrounds them, or seldom appear to have much need for it, the material and the way it is being used need to be re-examined.

Be alert to opportunities to read beyond the immediate classroom. The printed notices in the child's world beyond the classroom provide other opportunities to convince him that it is important to learn to read. Street signs and traffic signs, names of stores, and route signs on busses are all useful in developing interest in words. In the school there are other signs a child needs to learn. *Boys* and *Girls* help him tell the washrooms apart. *In* and *Out*, *Up* and *Down*, help him to tell which door and which stairway he is to use. *Lunchroom, Library, Principal, Janitor*, help him to find his way around the building. Sometimes the children themselves will ask about the signs. Sometimes the teacher will point them out. At times a picture that shows a highway sign, a street sign, or the name of a store will lead to discussion of other signs with which the children are familiar.

DEVELOPING THE ABILITY TO MAKE GROSS DISCRIMINATIONS IN WORD FORMS

Capitalize on the opportunities offered through classroom reading matter. At the prereading level, the objective of activities designed to help develop the ability to distinguish between words is to secure interest in the configurations of words and to build some general techniques for telling words apart. Prereading experiences have served their purpose if a beginner becomes interested in the shapes of words; begins to point out the same word when it appears again, even if he is not positive what it says; begins to identify similar beginnings or endings in words written near each other; reacts to the length of a word or to some unusual characteristic of its configuration; or makes other discoveries indicating that he is becoming aware of similarities and differences in the shapes of words. The children who acquire this skill quickly and who begin to recognize a number of words when they meet them again are ready for beginning-reading activities.

Activities that build ability to discriminate among the configurations of words are largely informal. As children work with books, experience records and signs, there are many opportunities to direct their attention to the shapes of words. As the teacher writes from the children's dictation she has opportunities to comment on particular words. "This one begins with a tall letter, doesn't it?" "Can anyone tell me whose name looks something like this?" "That's a long word, isn't it? See how much space it takes up. Say it, and see how long it sounds." Teachers do not, of course, try to say something about the configuration of every new word. Children cannot respond to more than a few comparisons at any one time.

Many children soon follow the teacher's lead and make their own discoveries about the configurations of words. They may begin to point out where the same phrase appears again, to comment on the length or the shape of the word, or to talk about the similarity between two words. Even though no particular effort is made to repeat words or phrases for the purposes of independent word recognition, the same phrase often recurs in the normal course of composing an experience record. A series of sentences, for example, may begin with *We went*, or *We saw*. Such repetition is helpful.

Activities calling for discrimination among words can be developed by using children's names. When a child finds his name on a list he can be asked how he knew it, what made it different from some of the others, or how many other names he knows. Teachers often construct their helpers' charts so that name cards can be inserted in slits and changed from week to week. The slips of cardboard upon which the names are printed may serve as word cards for a little informal practice. "Who can find his name when it is held up?" "Who knows whose name is being held up?" "How could we be sure to tell these two names apart?"

The use of manuscript writing or print helps to make similarities and differences among words as clear as possible. At the prereading stage, no particular effort need be made to assure that a child can recognize a letter in both capital and lower-case forms. Such distinctions are made more easily when a child can read the word. They do not have to be stressed in prereading experience unless a child himself asks about them.

Look for appropriate opportunities to point to individual letters. There is no particular need, at the prereading level, for a child to be able to name all the letters, and no need at all to know them in alphabetical order. Children will acquire this knowledge rapidly enough as they begin to read independently and start to use letter names as an aid to word recognition. Work with letters at the prereading level is mainly a matter of giving children another way of distinguishing the shapes of words. Alphabet books will arouse interest in beginning letters. Children may come to school with initialed handkerchiefs or other objects. Often, instead of signing their complete names to work being saved for them, children initial it. All such occasions provide opportunities to talk about letters, their shapes, and why particular letters are chosen to serve various purposes. Other discoveries regarding letters will come as children begin to try to see differences between words. If *Betty* and *Bobby* happen to be written under each other on a bulletin-board announcement, someone may point out that they begin or end alike. Certain children may even comment on the difference between the double letters in the middle. Experiences in making such distinctions provide useful background when the child faces the task of telling words apart in his preprimer or other beginning materials.

Use special practice activities as needed. Certain children will find it difficult to make any sort of comparison between words. While others are rapidly becoming able not only to point to differences in configurations, but even to recognize certain words independently, a few will not respond to the most obvious distinctions. These youngsters need more time to mature, and many more informal contacts with printed matter. They may also benefit from special practice activities.

Some reading-readiness workbooks provide opportunities for children to tell when two pictured objects are alike or different, and to make increasingly finer discriminations between figures. If such exercises are used, they should be accompanied by discussions where children can be helped to think about how to tell similar objects apart. When a series of perfect papers indicates that a group is having little difficulty discriminating among gross picture forms, it is safe to assume that more exercises with this type of material, even though the discriminations are somewhat finer, are not going to yield much further growth.

If activities calling for picture discrimination are used with immature children, they need to be followed by others where the discrimination must be made among words. Work-type activities can be found in reading-readiness workbooks, or hectographed by the teacher. The child may be asked to pick out the one word that is different in a line of four; to draw a line between the two similar words in a set of four; or to underline a key word whenever it appears on a list. Such activities use pictures in various ways along with the words so that the child must think about the meaning of the word while he is hunting for another that matches it. He may, for example, look at a picture of a ball, with the word *ball* under it, and then look for the word again in a set of four words, or sort word cards, placing each word under its correct picture. One of the distinct advantages of many of the informal classroom experiences with the shapes of words lies in the fact that the child is called upon to think about the message the word has for him while he studies how it looks.

DEVELOPING SKILLS IN DISCRIMINATING AMONG THE SOUNDS OF WORDS

Call attention to interesting sound elements in the course of daily experiences with words. Work with sounds at the prereading level does not concern itself with helping children attach specific sounds to exact letter combinations. However, building the ability to hear sounds is the beginning of phonetic analysis, and the aim is to build ability to listen to words with discrimination as the teacher says, "They begin the same way. Listen to them and see if you can hear how they begin." "This one ends in the same sound as a word you know." Or, "Say it and hear how long it is."

Comments on the shapes of words often can lead to comments on their sounds. When children discover that two words begin alike, it is a logical step to ask them to say the words to see if they sound the same. Discoveries of common endings can be treated in a similar fashion. So can occasions when children point out that two words are somewhat alike in general shape but have none of the same letters. At the prereading level, the teacher will be the one who reads the words. Later, as the children begin to read independently, they, themselves, will be able to read the words and often will identify new sound elements by comparing words they know.

Make use of poetry and rhymes. Poetry has many uses in the classroom, including a contribution to children's interest in and work with sounds. Nursery rhymes, songs, finger plays, and short poems written for and composed by young children can provide many experiences with sounds of words and letters. Children enjoy repeating together a favorite short poem, or they may say the rhyming words at the ends of the lines. Mother Goose rhymes contain excellent examples of consonant sounds. "Bye baby bunting," and "Sing a song of sixpence" are examples. Rhyming sounds are strongly marked, as in "Hark, hark, the dogs do bark," or, "Ding, dong, bell; pussy's in the well." Familiarity with these verses serves not only to provide enjoyable practice in hearing sounds, but also serves the excellent purpose of bridging the distance between home and school, providing something comfortably familiar in a new situation.

Care needs to be taken to be sure that children do not get the idea that all poetry must rhyme, and so limit the nature of their own creative expression. Much of what children say and write has a freshness and originality that are in danger of being limited and forced if a too self-conscious attention is given to strong meter and rhyme.

Provide special practice in meaningful settings. Some children will find it difficult to hear sound elements in words. If special practice activities seem desirable, they should, as far as possible, be in a meaningful and interesting setting. Activities such as listening for the different word in a set of four spoken by the teacher or telling whether two words spoken by the teacher are the same or different may help children to listen carefully, but they do little to encourage them to think about the meaning of the words they are hearing. Completing a two-line couplet or filling in the missing words in a poem read by the teacher provides a more meaningful setting.

Activities with word beginnings can be developed by games such as "I spy." The teacher, or a child as leader, says, "I spy something whose name begins like *paper*" and the children guess the correct word. Such activities must be kept very simple at first. Children at the prereading level cannot spell. The child who says that *city* and *sunny* begin the same way is correct, as far as sounds are concerned. Before children begin to read, such answers are accepted. However, if the teacher ever has cause to write such answers on the board she will need to point to the differences in configuration.

Prereading workbooks offer many experiences with sounds through picture activities. Children are asked to find the pictured object whose name ends like the one given at the beginning of the row; to find the object that begins with the same sound as the one pictured at the beginning of the row; to mark all the pictures of objects that begin or end alike in a given row; to mark which of a series of pairs of pictured objects begin or end alike. Teachers can build similar exercises by pasting on cardboard pictures clipped from magazines. These activities can be particularly valuable because they can be used to develop new concepts for some children while they provide experience with sounds.

Teachers should be on the alert for speech difficulties or hearing losses when activities involving sounds are undertaken. A child may fail to discriminate between *feather* and *weather* because he can not hear the difference in the sounds or because he himself has not been saying the sounds correctly. Speech difficulties are often readily apparent, and experiences in naming words that begin or end in given sounds may be helpful in correcting poor habits. Hearing losses may not be so easy to identify, especially if the child has more difficulty hearing some sounds than he has with others. Marked inability to respond to sounds should always suggest a test of hearing. If a hearing loss is discovered, special adjustments may have to be made. If no trouble with hearing is reported, the task then becomes one of providing enough experience to help the child learn to make the discriminations that cause him trouble.

DEVELOPING SKILL IN PICTURE INTERPRETATION

Make use of the opportunities in the typical classroom setting. Pictures are used in many ways on the bulletin boards of a typical primary classroom. These picture displays are to be used. Skill in picture interpretation grows when there is a reason for examining a picture, just as reading ability develops when the printed materials around the room serve a purpose. Often a helpers' chart has a picture of the housekeeping responsibility beside the word. A picture of a child painting may be posted near the list that indicates whose turn it is to work at the easel. Children may draw small pictures to illustrate each line in an experience record. Once in a while pictures may even be substituted for key words. As teachers work with these illustrated records they can help children learn how to use the pictures for meaning. "What is your job this week? Look at the picture, it will tell you." "Who can find the line that says we saw the ducks in the park? Do you remember the picture we put beside it?"

Children's books today are replete with pictures. These can be discussed as a story is read to the class. Children also can be helped to use the pictures in a reference book as a source of information even if they cannot read the words. After a trip to the zoo, for example, they may turn to a book of animal pictures to answer certain questions. Sometimes the teacher may read the accompanying text. At other times the picture itself may provide the needed information. Through such experiences children learn to look carefully at a picture in order to follow a story or to answer a question. "What do you suppose he will do next?" "Now do you see why everybody laughed?" "How big does it seem to be?"

Capitalize on the pictures drawn by children. The pictures that children themselves draw offer other opportunities for experiences with picture interpretation. Children do not always want to tell a story about their pictures, nor should they feel that every picture must have a caption. Freedom to be creative is important in artistic expression and this freedom should not be jeopardized because of the prereading need to develop skill in picture interpretation. However, many children will volunteer to tell about what they have drawn. In addition, there are opportunities to draw special illustrations. Children may make pictures of their homes or their pets. They may illustrate a story or draw pictures of what they saw on an excursion. These pictures can be used for many interesting bulletin-board displays and the resulting discussions can lead to considerable increased skill in picture interpretation.

Provide practice to meet specific needs. Special practice in interpreting pictures should not be needed often in the classroom settings that have been described. However, it may be helpful occasionally to have all the children in a small group talk about the same picture. It may also be helpful to provide experience in following a story in a picture sequence. Commercially-prepared prereading materials offer useful activities for such purposes. They are replete with many types of pictures that can be used flexibly for a variety of group discussions.

Pictures can be used for a number of exercises for independent work periods. The sequential picture stories that can be read from left to right and from top to bottom of the page are among the activities included in most prereading books that may be particularly helpful. These stories have already been discussed as a source of language experiences. Work-type activities can be developed by cutting apart a set of picture sequences and asking the children to put the pictures in their correct order. Games calling for picture interpretation can be made by pasting on separate cards small pictures of flowers, animals, birds, or canned goods clipped from advertisements in magazines, and asking children to sort them into appropriate groups. The picture interpretation skill, in this case, lies in identifying the classification to which the picture belongs. Time needs to be allowed for talk about such seat-work activities. With picture interpretation, as with experiences designed to develop other prereading skills, merely doing a practice exercise without discussing it reduces considerably the value of the activity.

DEVELOPING SKILL IN HANDLING BOOKS

Demonstrate how to handle books while they are used in regular classroom activities. Many of the skills needed to handle books are learned as children begin to use them regularly in beginning-reading activities. However, children can be shown how to handle a book properly in almost any situation in which a book is used. A teacher can demonstrate as she reads to the group. She may point to the title, ask children to show where she should begin to read, show how she turns the pages in order, and display the pictures one at a time in proper sequence. When children bring books from home they can be helped to handle them properly while showing them to the class. A few minutes' discussion before a child takes his turn will help him to point to the title on the cover of his book and to turn the pages properly as he shows the pictures.

Children's first independent contacts with books at school are with those on the library table. Here is another opportunity to talk about how to handle books. The necessity for clean hands, for not throwing books or snatching them, for leaving pictures unmarked, and for not folding pages can all be talked through. Children can demonstrate how to sit so that a book is held comfortably and how to turn the pages so that they will not be torn. Appointing librarians who help to care for the books and coming to agreements as to how many children can be at the library table at once and under what conditions books can be taken to other tables also help to arouse a feeling of responsibility for the proper care of books.

Use classroom experiences to demonstrate left-to-right orientation. Until they come to school, few children will have been in situations where the order in which they look at materials makes a difference. One does not examine a pet from left to right, or look over a new toy in any special direction, or start at the left side of a picture. Only as children begin to read and write does it matter where they start and in which direction they work. As they first enter upon these new activities most children will, from time to time, look in the wrong direction and write a letter or a word in mirror writing or read a word in reverse. Some will continue to have difficulty in being consistent in directional orientation for many months.

At the prereading level the experiences that build left-to-right orientation are largely informal. As the teacher writes while the children look on, and as she reads to them, she will have opportunities to say, "Where shall I begin?" "We begin at this side and up here at the top." "Where is our first line?" Often she can move her hand under the words she is reading to indicate direction, or point to the beginning of a new line. Care needs to be taken, however, to keep these gestures from becoming meaningless. Children need to be conscious of problems of directional orientation while the teacher points.

A certain number of writing activities may precede beginning-reading experiences. Children may be copying their own names or initialling their pictures. These first writing experiences need to be carefully supervised. Even in adding their initials to a picture, children may need to be taught which letter to put first and how to form the letters properly. The straight lines and circles of manuscript writing have greatly simplified the problems of learning to write, but care needs to be taken to make sure that left-to-right direction is followed consistently. The order in which the strokes are made in such letters as *b* and *d*, *p* and *q* is easily reversed.

Activities that teach the terms *left* and *right* may facilitate the process of developing directional orientation. Teachers can find occasions to suggest that a child use his right or his left hand, or go to the right or left. "As we go around the mural, let's go to the left so that we won't step on it." "We walk to the right in the hall and on the street." Needed objects may be described as located to the right or the left of the teacher's desk. Singing games, such as "*Looby-Lou*," may be helpful. Even with help, all children at the prereading level will not learn to use *left* and *right* correctly. Adults, too, on occasion, have difficulty in keeping their directions clear.

Provide special practice for the child who finds left-to-right orientation difficult. Many children will develop a sense of left-to-right orientation in the course of the regular classroom activities that have just been described. For those who seem to have unusual difficulty, special practice may be in order. Reading-readiness workbooks contain a number of activities. Others can be prepared readily by the teacher.

In providing practice activities to develop directional orientation, care needs to be taken to be sure that the child is practicing the skill he really needs. Picture stories in which the child follows a series of pictures from left to right and from top to bottom of a page in a workbook, call for the skill he will need when he reads. Another type of practice activity can be developed by cutting apart such story strips on separate pieces of cardboard and asking the child to rearrange the pictures in order. Some teachers keep sets of such materials for independent work periods. Work-type activities in which the child first looks at the key picture at the left of a line and then looks across the line to find a picture that rhymes or begins with the same sound can also be used for directional orientation. With all these exercises time needs to be taken to discuss the children's work.

Give the left handed child a good start. There is some evidence to support the suggestion that, if there seems to be no decided preference and a child seems under no strain when he is asked to try to use his right hand in such activities as drawing, writing, or cutting, it is often desirable to give the left-handed child a little encouragement to develop right-handed skills.[2] This is particularly true in activities such as writing, handling a knife and fork, and cutting, in which the left-handed person often finds that the world does not take his particular preference into account. However, it seems unwise to insist that the child try to use his right hand if he appears at all unhappy about it, and it is important to help him develop consistent handedness in writing.

It is not always easy to identify the left-handed child. While some children show a definite preference in all activities, others may seem to use either hand interchangeably, and a few may even have been required by parents to use the right hand when they prefer the left. Any activity in which one hand is used may offer clues. Which hand does the child prefer when picking up an object which he has dropped? He may catch a ball with two hands, but with which hand does he throw it? If he is offered a pencil held so that it is withing easy reach of either hand, which one does he tend to use? In an activity other than writing which demands considerable dexterity, which hand does he prefer?

It is at the prereading level, as children first begin to handle equipment, that special care needs to be taken to help those who are left-handed. If they are not watched, these children will follow the leads of their right-handed friends. This means that, as he begins to write, the left-handed child may try to tilt his paper in the direction which is more comfortable for one who is right-handed. Scissors may prove difficult for him. He may try to sew in the same direction as the child next to him and have trouble. Special help when such skills as these are first being learned will pay rich rewards later.

[2] Arthur T. Jersild, *Child Psychology*, Fourth Edition (New York: Prentice-Hall, Inc., 1960), pp. 109-110.

USING READING-READINESS BOOKS

Possibilities for supplementing classroom experiences with exercises from commercially-prepared reading-readiness books have been suggested at several points in the preceding section. Practically all basal-reader series provide these prereading materials. Typically they are in workbook form, although children do not necessarily have to mark or cut the books in order to work with them. Many of the exercises they contain are developed around pictures. Activities to build experience background are provided through pictures of home, school, and community life; of animals; and of children at work and at play. Picture stories give experience in following left-to-right sequence. Rows of pictures are used to give children an opportunity to find rhymes, to find words beginning with the same sound, to identify similarities and differences in configurations, and to match colors. Words are introduced through printed directions, in captions to pictures, and in single-sentence stories accompanying picture sequences. Sometimes a set of pictures is designed to introduce the vocabulary of the first preprimer of the given series. A certain amount of tracing and simple manuscript writing may also be included. Many types of language experiences are possible as the children discuss the various activities in these workbooks. It is also easy to give experiences in caring for books, in finding given pages, and in working from left to right. Reading-readiness workbooks, used wisely, can play an important part in the prereading program.

Evaluate reading-readiness materials in the light of the total prereading program. Reading-readiness books are not intended to supply all the child's prereading experiences, nor do they offer a magic gateway to sure success in beginning-reading activities. However, they provide for planned experiences which call for the development and utilization of prereading skills. The decision whether or not to use a reading-readiness book may be based, in part, on answers to the following questions:

1. Do children need more experience with words, rhymes, pictures, and stories that can well be provided in the regular classroom situation?
2. Is it likely that beginning reading experience will be more successful if children have some contact with the vocabulary and the personages presented in the preprimer being used?

If the answer to these questions is yes, it may be that judicious use of reading-readiness workbooks may extend experience and provide background. If reading-readiness workbooks are used, consideration must be given to their most effective use in meeting the specific needs of individuals or small groups.

Because reading-readiness workbooks are planned so that more complicated forms of the same activity recur at different points, it is possible to select a graded series of activities for children with special needs. For example, the children who seem to have the most difficulty interpreting pictures may work with a variety of picture stories. Those for whom rhyming is difficult may engage in the activities that stress sounds. Some of these exercises can be assigned for independent work periods. Others may be scheduled for group sessions. These groups can meet with the teacher while other members of the class go about various types of independent work. When they are used in this way, readiness workbooks can serve to provide practice activities that could be developed by the teacher only after many hours of work.

If reading-readiness workbooks are used selectively with small groups, there is rarely need to purchase more than ten to a dozen copies of a single book. Sometimes it is helpful to collect sets of workbooks from two or three basal-reader series. This expands the variety of practice activities available. It also makes it possible to extend the prereading program for children with special needs without obviously reviewing materials that other groups have already covered.

Use reading-readiness books to provide occasional group experiences. When a classroom is equipped with sets of ten or twelve reading-readiness workbooks, it is possible to give the children some useful group experiences in working with books. Working with experience records or listening to a teacher read a story do not give quite the same experience as having a book in one's hand, turning the pages oneself, and looking at the same page that others are also studying. This is another type of contribution to the prereading program that can be made by a readiness book.

Perhaps one of the most important contributions of a reading-readiness book is made to the children who are in need of extended prereading experiences. These youngsters often feel school and community pressures to begin to read, and they may be unhappy if they are not working with a book when others are reading preprimers and primers. Although the normal activities of the primary program may actually be meeting the prereading needs of these children, it may be very helpful, from the point of good morale, to plan for definite group experiences with a reading-readiness book. It may also be valuable to these children to have the additional planned practice that these booklets provide.

Even when children are using a reading-readiness book for group work on a daily basis, it is still helpful to be selective in the activities used. Teachers sometimes hesitate to vary the order in which they use work-type materials lest they lose the values inherent in the sequence of the materials. At the prereading level this danger is slight. Many other experiences are also contributing to the child's prereading skills, and his work with a prereading book is most effective when it is planned in the light of them. Sometimes it is helpful to vary considerably from the original purpose of an exercise. Children whose oral expression is limited, for example, may be encouraged to discuss the pictures in a readiness book in great detail. They may even go on to tell their own stories about the picture, or to dictate a group story for an experience chart. Reading-readiness books, used to best advantage, supplement and contribute to the total prereading program. They should not dictate the contents or the sequence of the program, either for a single child or for a group.

VARYING THE PREREADING PROGRAM TO MEET INDIVIDUAL NEEDS

How extensive should the prereading program be? How soon should children be encouraged to try to read independently? What adjustments can be made for the child who is immature, for the youngster who had difficulty making adequate social or emotional adjustments, for the child with a physical handicap? No teacher is ever completely satisfied with her efforts to meet the needs of individual children. However, the type of primary program that has been described offers a number of opportunities to adjust to special problems

Capitalize on the informality and flexibility of the program to meet individual needs. How can the program for primary children outlined in this chapter be used to advantage in meeting the needs of individual children? First, there is emphasis upon knowing what the children's needs are. A knowledge of their backgrounds of experience, their present interests, skills and abilities is the basis for plans which take individual needs into account. Second, there is general emphasis on helping children learn to work independently. This means that the teacher has more freedom to work with individuals or with small groups. Third, the day's program is planned to allow for independent work periods which may be used to provide for individual interests and needs. A child may enjoy books at the library table, work in paint or clay, or have the experience of working or playing in a group. The child may share in an aspect of a project best suited to his capacities, or may be steered into a group of children with whom he can work effectively. Wherever there is a choice of activities, or the teacher is free to work with individuals or a small group, there are opportunities to meet special needs. This informal setting provides an unusually good opportunity to give some help to children for whom school represents a difficult social or emotional adjustment.

In a flexible program, children with physical handicaps also can more readily find a place. It is not unduly difficult to seat a youngster with a visual handicap or a hearing loss in a front row when the class assembles. A youngster who should not be trying to make fine visual discriminations can be encouraged to join in the varied activities in which reading does not play a part. When he does read, he may work with the large print of experience records. Independent work periods may provide time for the teacher to give a little special help to the child who is handicapped in vision, hearing, or speech. It is also possible to plan individualized activities for such children without calling undue attention to their handicaps when all children are engaged in a certain amount of independent work.

The immature child in the classroom also raises problems. He may tire a little more quickly than his classmates, find it more difficult to sit still for long, lose interest in a project sooner, find pencils and scissors harder to handle, and prefer active experiences and playthings that can be manipulated without much fine muscular coordination. During group discussions, these children may be allowed a little more freedom in the amount of wiggling and stretching they do. Sometimes it may be desirable to have them make their contribution early in a planning session and then to free them to go on with other activities while more mature children wait their turns. If the immature child has difficulty in handling crayons, paint brushes, or scissors, he will need to be given special help. All such adjustments increase the variety and number of demands being made upon the teacher. However, the help provided at the prereading period will often save a child from much frustration and discouragement in succeeding grades.

Start beginning-reading activities as children demonstrate ability to profit from them. As children go about regular classroom activities, the teacher will have been continuously appraising their interest in books and stories, and their skill in handling work situations, and work-type materials. A group of children at approximately the same level in these areas may constitute a group for beginning-reading activities. Some teachers try out tentative groupings with experience records before the children are working with preprimers. With flexible grouping in the classroom for many different kinds of activities, children do not feel insecure if they are moved from one group to another.

Ideally, everyone in the class will not start to work in a reading group at the same time. As children demonstrate that they will benefit from beginning-reading instruction, room for this activity is found in the day's program. Meanwhile, those who still need prereading experiences go about the many other activities provided in the day's program. They work in various aspects of unit activities, participate in language experiences, use various media for creative expression, engage in dramatic play, and help to write and to illustrate experience records. In these activities, they are encouraged to work as independently with familiar words, phrases, and sentences as they are able. Whenever it seems likely that more children can profit from beginning-reading activities, a new group is set up.

To extend the primary program gradually until it includes three or more reading groups, and still to provide a wide variety of other experiences of equal educational value, is no easy matter. It calls for skillful scheduling and effective planning of group and individual activities. More detailed suggestions as to how this may be accomplished are given in Chapter V for the beginning-reading period, and in Chapter VI, for the later primary program.

Consider the possibility of different patterns of classroom organization. In most small schools adjustments for children who need extended prereading experiences, or who are already far ahead of the group when they enter first grade, will have to be made within the individual classroom. In large schools such adjustment may be made in other ways. One plan possible in schools where there are immature children in sufficient numbers is the establishment of junior primary or prereading classes. The youngsters in such classes sometimes may engage in prereading activities for much of the year.

When a prereading class is established, the children should not be selected on the basis of their prereading abilities alone. The informal activities of the prereading classroom have an important contribution to make to the child who, for any reason, is not ready for the regular first-grade program. This may include the child whose experience background is limited, the one whose health has not been good, and the one who has moved from place to place and does not possess the skills needed to work and play happily with other children.

The activities planned for a prereading class are very similar to those discussed earlier in this chapter. There are many stimulations to read but there are not necessarily reading groups. However, in many such classes some beginning-reading activities are undertaken before the end of the year. Activities to enrich experience background, language experiences, many opportunities to work informally with reading matter, many kinds of creative work, and time to learn to work and play with other children are all part of the program.

Some communities have recognized the need for flexibility beyond that possible within the usual pattern of three primary grades, and have established an ungraded primary unit.[3] In this plan of organization the primary years are divided into a number of levels of competence, rather than three grades. A child moves from level to level as he achieves the skills necessary to do so. No room carries a grade label, and no child "skips" or "repeats" a grade. The slower learner may take four years to move through the primary unit, while

[3] John I. Goodlad and Robert H. Anderson, *The Nongraded Elementary School* (New York: Harcourt, Brace, 1959).

the more able child may be ready to go into the fourth grade in less than the usual time. While there are many organizational and scheduling problems involved in this procedure, the emphasis it places upon the recognition given to pupil differences makes it worthy of thoughtful consideration.

Parents need to be taken into the plans when adjustments in the reading program are made. They need to understand why the adjustment is being recommended and how it can help their child. It is particularly important that parents, and sometimes teachers, be reassured about the child's eventual ability to learn to read successfully. Above all, parents need to be helped to see how to give the assistance at home which will supplement the school prereading program as effectively as possible. Because the problem of helping parents understand the reading program is an important one for all teachers, suggested ways of working together and a list of books and pamphlets of particular interest to parents are given in Chapter XIII.

The success of any modification of a school program to allow for individual differences depends ultimately on an all-school and community philosophy in which considered judgments about the needs and capacities of individual children and not arbitrary standards guide decisions. This does not make for a less challenging program or for lower standards. Rather, it enables teachers to take the steps needed to provide the most stimulating and the richest possible experiences for all children. In the field of reading there is ample evidence that some of the remedial problems of the upper grades arise from primary programs that were not adapted to the needs of individuals. Experienced teachers should be free to give the help they feel is important to children, and have the support of school organization, materials, and supervision that will provide maximum assistance in carrying out their plans.

SOME QUESTIONS TO THINK ABOUT IN APPRAISING THE PREREADING PROGRAM

1. Is the program one that makes for the all-round growth of the child—physically, mentally, emotionally, socially?

2. Are children growing in their ability to work independently so that the teacher can be free to help individuals and small groups?

3. Is reading being used as a functional part of the total classroom experiences, so that children see its purposes and develop interests in reading for themselves?

4. Are the prereading contacts with words, pictures, books, and language activities broad, so that the child meets stimulations to read in many settings?

5. Are children encouraged, from the start, to make as many independent discoveries about reading as they can, and do they enjoy so doing?

6. Have ways been found to provide special help to meet individual needs?

7. Are special practice activities planned so that they do not impede the ongoing experiences of the wider primary program?

8.   Are special practice activities chosen so that they focus directly on the skills needed by the child?

9.   Is effective use being made of commercially-produced teaching aids?

10.   Is it possible for an individual child to proceed at his own pace, with activities designed to meet his present maturity level?

11.   Do children move into the activities of beginning reading with interest and confidence growing out of many previous successful experiences at the prereading level?

SUGGESTIONS FOR FURTHER READING

PROVIDING A WHOLESOME ATMOSPHERE FOR LIVING AND LEARNING IN
KINDERGARTEN AND FIRST GRADE

Foster and Headley's Education in the Kindergarten. Third Edition. Revised by Neith E. Headley. New York: American Book Company, 1959. 499 pp.

Gans, Roma; Stendler, Celia B.; and Almy, Millie. *Teaching Young Children.* Yonkers-on-Hudson: World Book Company, 1952. 454 pp.

Heffernan, Helen (Editor). *Guiding the Young Child.* Second Edition. Prepared by a Committee of the California School Supervisors Association. Boston: D. C. Heath, 1959. 362 pp.

Heffernan, Helen, and Todd, Vivian E. *The Kindergarten Teacher.* Boston: D. C. Heath, 1960. 419 pp.

Hymes, James L., Jr. *Before the Child Reads.* Evanston, Illinois: Row, Peterson and Company, 1958. 96 pp.

Lee, J. Murray, and Lee, Dorris May. *The Child and His Development.* Part I. New York: Appleton-Century Crofts, Inc., 1958. 624 pp.

Wills, Clarice Dechent, and Stegman, William H. *Living in the Primary Grades.* Chicago: Follett Publishing Company, 1956. 416 pp.

DEVELOPING PREREADING SKILLS

Betts, Emmett A. *Foundations of Reading Instruction.* Chapters 14-19. New York: American Book Company, 1957. 757 pp.

Bond, Guy L., and Wagner, Eva Bond. *Teaching the Child to Read.* Third Edition, Chapters 6, 7. New York: The Macmillan Company, 1960. 416 pp.

Burton, William H. *Reading in Child Development.* Chapter 6. Indianapolis: The Bobbs-Merrill Company, 1956. 608 pp.

DeBoer, John J., and Dallmann, Martha. *The Teaching of Reading.* Chapters 5A and 5B. New York: Holt, Rinehart and Winston, Inc., 1960. 360 pp.

Dolch, Edward W. *Teaching Primary Reading.* Third Edition, Chapters 3-5. Champaign, Illinois: The Garrard Press, 1960. 429 pp.

Gray, Lillian, and Reese, Dora. *Teaching Children to Read.* Second Edition. Chapters 5, 6. New York: The Ronald Press Company, 1957. 475 pp.

Harrison, M. Lucile. *Reading Readiness.* Revised Edition, Chapter 3. Boston: Houghton Mifflin Company, 1939. 255 pp.

Hildreth, Gertrude. *Teaching Reading.* Chapter 9. New York: Henry Holt and Company, 1958. 612 pp.

Lamoreaux, Lillian A., and Lee, Dorris May. *Learning to Read Through Experience.* Chapters 1-4. New York: Appleton-Century-Crofts, 1943. 204 pp.

Meeker, Alice M. *Teaching Beginners to Read*. New York: Rinehart and Company, 1958. 76 pp.

Monroe, Marian. *Growing Into Reading*. Chicago: Scott, Foresman, and Company, 1951. 274 pp.

Russell, David H. *Children Learn to Read*. Second Edition, Chapter 6. Boston: Ginn and Company, 1961. 612 pp.

Tinker, Miles A., and McCullough, Constance M. *Teaching Elementary Reading*. Second Edition, Chapter 5. New York: Appleton-Century-Crofts, Inc., 1962. 615 pp.

CHAPTER V

First Steps in Developing Beginning Reading Skills

BEGINNERS START TO READ

IN THE early fall a visitor to the first grade described in the preceding chapter found books, charts, notices, and other reading matter serving many purposes in the classroom, but little independent reading by most of the children.

Some children could find their own names and could discover the same words in several places on a chart. They knew what lines had the same beginning and were able to tell, in general, the meaning of a line, but were not always exactly sure of the words in it. Others were much less interested in reading activities and showed less skill in making discriminations between shapes and sounds of words.

In a sense these activities are preparation for reading, yet the teacher is aware that in a very real way, reading is already a reality for some first-grade children. They are alert to the general configuration of words, they hear differences in sounds, notice likenesses in word beginnings, and are keenly aware of the fact that reading is a meaningful activity.

At the end of the first weeks of the fall term, the most advanced children have made striking progress. A visitor observing the activities of their reading group might readily see the growth that has occurred.

Children are eager to read. The most advanced group is working with the second preprimer of a basal-reader series. The children obviously look forward to their reading period. They find the right page for the new story, some using page numbers, others pictures. As they begin to discuss the story, it is clear that they remember the main ideas of what they read the day before. The title of the new story is *Tuffy and Boots*,[1] and the main characters are Boots, the puppy who was in the preceding preprimer, and Tuffy, who has just been introduced.

The children discuss the picture of the two animals on the title page, recall what they read about Tuffy in the preceding story, and speculate on how well he will get along with Boots. From their own experiences with cats and dogs, they propose several possibilities. The teacher suggests that they turn the page and read the little three-line passage to find out. *Likes* is a new word, but the children have recently used *like* in an experience record. After a brief interval, hands go up to report that Tuffy likes Boots. The teacher asks what Tuffy might like to do. After the children have made a few suggestions they read the three-line passage on the next page to see if they are right. Then, to discover with whom Tuffy likes to play, they turn the page and read the five lines accompanying the picture. The teacher gives a little extra help to three children who are using markers. Some murmur to themselves but many do little vocalizing. Reading and discussing in this fashion, they finish the story.

A word-recognition vocabulary has begun to develop. It is apparent that the children can recognize a good many words at sight. They read the little two- to five-line passages that accompany each picture with relative ease. In all, the first preprimer of the series[2] introduced fourteen new words. In its sixty-four pages these words were repeated many times over. It is apparent, also, that new vocabulary has been added through classroom experience records.

Several types of approaches to new words can be noted. *Tuffy* was introduced in the preceding story. Today, to help the children recall its configuration, the teacher writes it on the board. The children also find it in the title of the story. *Likes* is figured out because the children have had experience with *like*. *With* is another new word. The teacher points out that there is a new word on the page, and asks who can find it. Since the sentence is *Tuffy likes to play —— Boots*, several are able to supply it without difficulty. On the next page *with* is repeated three times. *Said* is the fourth new word introduced in the story. Here the teacher encourages the children to use the picture to decide what is happening, and writes *said* on the board after they have decided that Sally is saying something to mother. In the last four pages of the story, the new words are re-used in various combinations. At the end of the period the teacher holds up the four new words on word cards and the children take turns finding and reading aloud a line that contains each one.

Stories several lines in length are read with comprehension. These children can read several lines silently to answer a question. At the beginning of the story they read three lines to see if Tuffy likes Boots. When they are asked with whom

[1] Arthur I. Gates *et al.*, *Tuffy and Boots*, Second Basal Preprimer of the Macmillan Readers (New York: The Macmillan Company, 1951, 1957), pp. 9-16.

[2] Arthur I. Gates *et al.*, *Splash*, First Basal Pre-primer of the Macmillan Readers (New York: The Macmillan Company, 1951, 1957).

Tuffy likes to play, they read five lines. They read the last two pages of the story without interruption. Their comments indicate that they understand what they read. Oral reading is also used. It, too, is planned so that the children must think about what they read. Typically it follows the silent reading of the passage and supplements it. As the children report that Tuffy likes to play with Ted and with Sally they read the lines that gave them the answers. At another point several take turns reading what Sally said. The children enjoy testing their skill in reading aloud, but they also enjoy discussing what they have just read silently and enriching the stories by commenting on the accompanying pictures.

These youngsters finished a twenty-two-line story during their reading period. They learned four new words. In all, their preprimers have introduced nineteen new words, but this is not the full extent of their vocabulary, as they have learned others from the materials about the room. They still look to the teacher to tell them most new words and they still need discussion to guide their reading, even when it covers only four or five lines. However, they are well on the way to independent reading, and they are very pleased with their ability to read stories for themselves.

What experiences brought these children to the point where they could read with such evident interest and such growing skill in using the context to identify the meaning of new words? What kinds of reading responsibilities did they take on first? How did they become able to recognize so many words with so few errors? What kinds of practice were provided for them and how much practice did they have? The first few weeks of reading instruction do not differ greatly in general procedure from those which follow, nor do they differ greatly from the prereading period which went before. Yet the start is crucial for later progress. How do teachers go about it? Because the transition from prereading to beginning reading represents a special problem for many first-grade teachers, this chapter spells out in detail the possibilities for materials, classroom organization, and group reading activities for these early weeks. The development of the first-grade reading program beyond the first weeks of beginning activities is included in the discussion of the primary program in Chapters VI through IX.

CHANGING AIMS AS READING BEGINS

New skills imply new objectives. At the prereading level teachers work for interest in the message conveyed by printed material, but expect that they, not the children, will assume the major responsibility for reading it accurately. They welcome children's growing ability to identify individual words correctly but their aim is to develop general sensitivity to differences in configuration, and to give experiences with words which will lead to skill in word recognition. Now, as children reach the point where they are ready to take over more of the reading task, these aims change.

Responsibility for reading for meaning shifts from teacher to child. The first objective in reading, even at the prereading level, is to get meaning from what is read, and this remains a major objective throughout the entire reading program. During the first few weeks of reading instruction, the responsibility for meaningful reading shifts gradually from the teacher to the child. At first it is the teacher who reads the printed material, while the children listen, identify words, phrases or lines, and discuss ideas presented. As they take definite steps toward independent reading, children must learn how to get meaning from the printed message for themselves. The very short stories in the preprimer often contain pictures which convey the meaning almost as well as the words. Once introduced, the words are re-used frequently. After the children have learned these first few words and phrases, theirs is the major responsibility for finding what subsequent stories are about. The teacher is there to help them figure it out—by assisting with words that are not remembered, by introducing unfamiliar words, and by asking questions to direct their reading—but she no longer reads the materials to them. The aim now is to help children develop ways of getting the meaning for themselves.

Sentence and phrase units begin to be identified accurately. Part of the skill of getting meaning without help lies in deciding exactly what each group of words says. At the prereading level this does not matter so much. If the first line of a class record reads *Yesterday we went to the store* and somebody remembers it as *The line that tells that we went to Mr. Jackson's store*, he is close enough. The teacher can read the line correctly if it is important. When children begin to read for themselves they must identify the words exactly.

In the beginning the unit which conveys the maximum amount of meaning is often a complete sentence, and children, in effect, "memorize" some of their first reading. They know that the story on the page that has the picture of the little boy running says *Run, Ted. Run! Run! Run!* and that the story that goes with the picture of him jumping says *Jump, Ted. Jump! Jump! Jump!* [3] They may be able to tell the sentences apart when they are written on word cards, or to identify them when they are asked to draw pictures to illustrate them, but they may not always be certain, in the beginning, which word is *Run*, which *Jump*, and which *Ted*. They may say *Run! Run! Run!* correctly without seeing immediately that the word must be written three times if they say it three times. Teacher and children work together to learn

---

[3] The examples in this section are from Arthur I. Gates, *op. cit.*, pp. 17-32.

to recognize accurately sentence and phrase units. This is a second objective of the beginning-reading program.

Selected words become familiar friends. A child is not truly on the road to independent reading until he can recognize separate words in various combinations. Beginning-reading materials are written so that selected words recur. In preprimers, three or four words may make up the first few stories. Other words are added slowly and combined in various ways with those already familiar. For example, in the preprimer that has just been quoted, the children read such combinations as *Run, Sally; Ted! Ted!; Run, Boots, run; Run to Mother.* If experience records are used as the basis for beginning work, the total vocabulary load is likely to be more heavy. Here the teacher usually chooses certain words for special emphasis, while those that are not important remain temporarily as parts of larger phrase or sentence units. As selected words appear in different settings—now beginning a sentence and now ending it, now in the preprimer, now on a word or phrase card, and now in an experience story—children begin to recognize them accurately. Independent reading does not start with word drills. As the teacher gives the children the experience of actually reading short, interesting stories independently by recognizing phrase and sentence units, she looks for ways of sharpening their accurate recognition of individual words as rapidly as possible.

Prereading abilities continue to be strengthened as needed. Children who are ready for beginning-reading experiences will not all be equally proficient in the prereading abilities upon which successful reading depends. Prereading activities should not end when beginning-reading experiences start. The children who have begun to read will continue to share in many of the same types of experiences which are of benefit at the prereading level. The directed activities of beginning reading need as their setting many of the same stimulating primary experiences with books, stories, and words that provide the setting for the prereading program.

CHOOSING MATERIAL TO BEGIN

As children begin to read for themselves, all the materials which provided their initial contacts with printed matter continue to be useful. Books, items on the bulletin board, class records, letters received from other classes, captions to pictures—all have a contribution to make. Some will be used to supply supplementary experiences; some will be used to help develop precise recognition of words and phrases. Not all these materials will be read with complete independence in the beginning.

A "language experience approach" to reading has been reported.[4] In this approach to beginning reading, children's own writing and the teacher's recordings of the children's stories are used as a major source of reading materials for the classroom. The development of these materials gives large importance to meaning, to the clear expression of ideas, and to the provision of strong motivation for reading. The resourceful teacher may well encourage the reading of what children have written, where children have developed such skills, as well as of stories dictated to the teacher.

Experience records have a place. Of all the materials available, classroom records are probably the closest to the interests and experiences of the group. The children have shared in composing the record. It is in their words. It contains ideas with which they are familiar, and this familiarity is often a great help as the children take on more responsibility for reading lines, phrases, and words for themselves. Whether experience records are used alone or parallel with preprimers, they have a place among a child's beginning-reading materials.

Of all the records in a classroom, which should be selected for special attention in a reading group? Much will depend on the activities and interests of the given group. However, since it is important to help children become familiar with selected words, it is desirable to choose those records which have a relatively light vocabulary load. It may also help to focus on an activity that leads to a series of related charts in which the same vocabulary is likely to recur. For example, the children plan a trip to the firehouse. The teacher helps them write their plans. When they return they record the details of their trip. A little later they may dictate stories about the firemen, the fire engine, or the firehouse. There may be other reading activities. The children may draw pictures and add captions. They may find pictures of firemen and equipment in one of their library books and identify some of their new words in the context. They could build a fire engine and write rules for playing in it. They might compose a new song. They could invite another class to visit them and use their records to help in telling the story of their trip. Such a variety of related experiences usually results in considerable repetition of words and phrases. Precautions need to be taken, however, not to overwork a single experience for the sake of the reading materials that may be forthcoming.

The experience chart will typically have a somewhat larger vocabulary load than the preprimer. It is likely that attempts to reduce such charts to the generally accepted preprimer vocabulary or style would be inadvisable. The charts serve a valuable purpose in stimulating oral language develop-

[4] *Improving Reading Instruction: A Description of Three Approaches to the Teaching of Reading.* Monograph No. 2 (San Diego, California: Superintendent of Schools, Department of Education, San Diego County, California, May 1961), pp. 19-25.

ment, and in providing a record of experience which children can share with others, or help them to relate to some other new experience.

It will not destroy the vitality of experience charts, however, to do a bit of controlling of the number and repetition of new words. It will be useful if several lines can begin with the same phrase; indeed the children themselves often make repetitive simple sentences, beginning with such phrases as *We saw* or *We went*. Substituting simpler words and shortening long, rambling sentences is always possible. Constructing sentences only one or two lines in length, using manuscript writing, and the placing of a phrase to be read as a single unit on one line, will serve, in most cases, to develop useful and readable charts for beginning reading experiences.

Preprimers have a special contribution to make. Working with classroom records does not provide experience in handling reading matter in book form—paged, printed, and illustrated. Furthermore, although these records may have high interest value, their relatively heavy vocabulary load may prolong the period of partial dependence upon the teacher. In most classrooms part of a child's beginning-reading experiences is planned around preprimers, the first books in basal-reader series. These little books are paper-bound and light to hold; the print is large, and the lines well spaced. The stories typically center around children's activities—their pets, their family life, their games. Colorful pictures illustrate each page. These pictures are designed to give maximum help in word recognition. Indeed, at times much of the story is conveyed through the picture, not through the accompanying text. In all, a single preprimer may introduce as few as fourteen or fifteen, or as many as thirty or forty new words. Typically, a basal-reader series includes two or three preprimers of gradually increased difficulty. These little books are meant to be read rather rapidly. Vocabulary growth comes as the same words are met in a variety of simple, interesting settings.

It is not uncommon to find a first grade equipped with preprimers from several basal-reader series. Usually the argument given for working exclusively with the materials from a single series is that this procedure will result in a more carefully controlled vocabulary and in a more carefully graded introduction of new words. However, two factors suggest that this is not so important a consideration as it sounds. In the first place, the children are working in a classroom where they are using many other reading materials. Their word-recognition vocabulary, then, will be larger than that introduced by their preprimers almost from the start. Furthermore, the careful study that has gone into the construction of basal-reader series has resulted in considerable similarity in standards. While identical vocabulary will not be used in all series, there will be some words in common, and any new preprimer to which children might turn will use much the same type of controlled introduction and repetition of new words.[5] Therefore, strict adherence to the pre-primers from one basal-reader series does not seem, in actual fact, to be so important in securing a graded introduction to vocabulary as it sounds in theory, although it is true that new names for characters and pets may be confusing and that the ratio of new words to running words may be increased somewhat. Reading preprimers from several series before beginning a harder book may, at times, provide more desirable experience than progressing directly from one book in a series to the next. After several preprimers have been used for instructional purposes, and children have achieved a sense of familiarity and security with them, these materials may well serve for independent and recreational reading. At this time the greater challenge needed for continued instruction, however, would be more likely to be found in the basal primer of the series being used.

The fact that children will progress at different rates, and that all may not start beginning-reading activities at the same time also needs to be considered in selecting preprimers. Often it is desirable not to accentuate differences by using the same books with all groups. Although children occasionally may be eager to have an opportunity to read the books another group has finished, there is also the possibility that they will be discouraged to see others so obviously progressing faster than they are. It is possible, too, that just enough of the story will be overheard to detract from some of its interest value. Taking all factors into account, it is often desirable to reserve certain materials for children who are progressing slowly. These materials can be released for supplementary reading by other children after the group has used them for instructional purposes.

Every teacher has personalized her methods of teaching reading to a certain extent. The choice of materials for groups progressing slowly, or for those who are most advanced, may well depend on the teacher's own feeling of how she is able to use them most successfully. Other things being equal, children who make slower progress may benefit from beginning books that introduce a relatively small vocabulary and use a maximum amount of repetition. They may also profit from working with books from a series in which there are ample, easy, supplementary materials.

Plans need to be made so that experiences with materials supplement each other. When children are working both with preprimers and with a variety of classroom materials, care needs to be taken to be sure that these experiences supplement each other effectively. Undoubtedly the children will be working with a heavier total vocabulary load. This load is perhaps not as heavy as it first appears, since there is evidence that children tend to remem-

[5] A. J. Harris, *op. cit.*, p. 72.

ber long words with distinctive configurations more easily than they do small words with somewhat similar configurations. Thus, words that may appear on experience records, like *storekeeper, birthday, Halloween,* and *Santa Claus,* will not always cause undue difficulty. Even so, adjustments may be needed if the children's work with varied materials is to be successful.

There are several ways in which children can be helped to meet the heavier vocabulary load occasioned by the use of several types of reading materials. First, it is not necessary to work for independent recognition of every word the children meet. Beginning readers can be encouraged to read as much as they are able, but can be helped, as they would be during prereading experiences, with words that are not, for the moment, important for them to be able to read for themselves. Second, pictures can be used in experience records to give clues to key words just as they are in preprimers. For example, one group recorded a walk around the neighborhood in a series of short sentences. *We saw men fixing the street. We saw the post office. We saw Tippy's new puppy.* Each sentence was illustrated with an appropriate picture. Since *We saw* was familiar, it was easy for the children to read this chart independently. A third adjustment of total vocabulary load can be made by re-using the vocabulary of the preprimer, or, in some cases, previewing it. Preprimers and classroom records do not, then, need to make conflicting demands on the reader. When they are used skillfully, they supplement and reinforce each other while they help expand the child's ability to read independently in a wide variety of situations.

Special needs of individuals should be considered. The types of reading materials provided for beginners may require special adjustment in the case of groups with particular needs. Children who progress slowly, as mentioned earlier, may benefit from material with a light vocabulary load and much repetition. They may also benefit from much work with simple experience records that they, themselves, have helped to write. Children whose experience background is markedly different from that of the typical middle-class suburban child may need more classroom records developed around situations with which they are familiar. In some cases teachers may mimeograph or hectograph little stories so that the children may work with preprimer materials written specially for them. In a rural community, these stories may be about children in a rural school, farming, planting gardens, or raising chickens. If the children are from an underprivileged city area, their reading material may touch upon busses, traffic rules, or boats along the waterfront.

CLASSROOM ORGANIZATION FOR BEGINNING READING

Beginning instruction in reading needs to be given in small groups that are relatively free from interruption. In a typical first grade, children will have worked in groups of varying sizes and personnel from the beginning of the year. Youngsters who have had such experiences should be accustomed to working together and carrying out plans independently. They should also be used to a certain amount of regularity in scheduling. When group work in reading begins, it should not alter greatly the total pattern of classroom activities. The teacher will need longer periods of relatively uninterrupted time to work with groups. These should be planned so that it is possible for the children to continue to engage in the unit activities and in the individual and group projects which were of such great educative value at the prereading level. This section suggests some of the steps that may be taken to secure effective grouping and scheduling as first reading activities are begun. In Chapter VI are discussed some of the adjustments in grouping and scheduling that are possible as primary children gain increased reading skill.

GROUPING FOR BEGINNING WORK

Establish reading groups gradually. The practice of setting up one reading group at a time, as suggested in Chapter IV, is usually much less disrupting of on-going classroom activities than would be the procedure of starting reading groups with all children at once. Ideally, the first reading group simply offers another type of activity for a selected number of children, in a day already filled with interesting individual and group projects. If first experiences center around classroom records, the reading group may not seem very different from other groups that have worked with the teacher for a variety of other language experiences. As the children become accustomed to working independently while the teacher is at work with a reading group, and as others in the class seem ready for beginning-reading experiences, new reading groups are established.

In communities where a high premium is placed on learning to read early by parents, community, school administration, or even by teachers themselves, pressure may exist to begin formal instruction in reading as soon as possible. Children sense this pressure, and those who are not in the first reading group may be disturbed. In such a situation, school personnel and interested community members would work toward better adult understanding of reading readiness. However, this is a long process and not one that immature youngsters can understand. Under such circumstances, it may be wise to begin group work with all children whenever the first group is ready for beginning-reading activities. This is the place for the activities with reading-readiness workbooks described in Chapter IV, or for many simple activities with preprimers that provide for greatly increased repetition of new vocabulary.

Adjust the number, size and composition of reading groups to varying needs. Although three groups are commonly provided in beginning reading activities, the number of groups established actually depends on three factors, the range of reading ability within the class, the effectiveness with which children can work together, and the skill of the teacher in managing group work. The range of ability in any class may require four or five groups rather than three. One or two dominant personalities in a fairly large reading group may make it desirable to work with a smaller number. A group involved in first reading experiences should be small enough to allow for individual help and active participation. Persisting inattention and lack of participation in any group may indicate that the numbers should be reduced to allow for a greater amount of individualized help.

If the teacher consistently feels uncertain of the progress of specific children, or feels pressured to provide more help than the reading period allows, or is concerned lest all children did not have adequate opportunity to participate, these concerns may indicate there are too many children in the group. If the numbers are reduced, even by one or two, it may become easier to give each child the attention he needs. This benefit must be balanced against the amount of time available for each group when the number of groups is increased.

Change in group personnel is to be expected. Some children will spurt ahead; others will make regular, but slow gains. Some who did not seem likely candidates for the first reading group may progress rapidly once they have begun group work.

It is desirable to change group membership without making children unduly concerned about being moved to a slower or a faster group. A casual invitation to join another group with no special praise or undue commiseration may help prevent feelings of anxiety, and choosing special names for groups, preferably the name of the preprimer or primer in which they are reading, is probably better than labeling them first, second, or third. The beginning-reading period is an opportune time to establish the idea that instructional groups will change and that children may expect, from time to time, to be invited to meet with another group.

Use varied groupings for different reading activities. For example, as reading activities change from reading in preprimers to reading experience records, pupils may be working in different groups. If the experience record is one reflecting an on-going classroom activity, the entire class will want to share in reading it. If a smaller group had an experience which is recorded, this special group may be a reading group. Here are brought together children of varied levels of ability, who can be given different responsibilities in the reading activity. Those with most skill may take responsibility for reading to others, or in identifying key words or phrases, while those who are least advanced may use pictures to find given lines, or share in general discussion, or perhaps identify frequently repeated phrases.

Other activities may lead to other groupings. A story hour may involve every child in the classroom as a teller or listener. A small group may dramatize a familiar story for the rest of the class. There may be periods of time in which each child reads a book of his own choosing. The materials may range all the way from preprimers to teacher-made booklets or some of the trade books for beginners, some of which use only fifty different words.[6] Such cooperative reading activities involving many ability levels are important if units of work and other class projects are to contribute to increased reading skill. These varied groupings help, too, to break down the children's tendencies to classify themselves as being in the best or the poorest reading group.

SCHEDULING FOR BEGINNING WORK

Secure flexibility by using large time-blocks. Flexibility in use of time within large time-blocks is characteristic of scheduling in the modern elementary school.

Scheduling of beginning-reading groups within these large blocks of time will depend on how they best fit into the total day. Typically they are planned for periods when the rest of the class is engaged in activities which require a minimum of guidance from the teacher. Some teachers prefer to set aside one time-block in the schedule for reading groups to meet in succession. This is not the only possible organization. Sometimes it is desirable to work with one or two groups, then to go back to the class as a whole in order to help those children who are running out of things to do, or to give the entire class a break for recess, and then to come back to the other groups. On occasion it may help to meet with some groups in the morning and with some in the afternoon. In general, children need to work with reading material regularly in order to fix vocabulary, although even with beginners there may be days when it is appropriate to provide independent work-type activities or supplementary reading for some groups while others work with the teacher. Such adjustments need to be made in the light of the on-going activities of the particular group. They will not be made in the same way from one first grade to another, or even from day to day within one class.

Time should be allotted to each group in terms of what needs to be accomplished. An arbitrary time allotment of fifteen or twenty minutes for each group will often not actually guarantee that all groups will receive the

[6] Dr. Seuss, *Green Eggs and Ham,* (New York: Beginner Books, Inc. Distributed by Random House, 1960), 62 pp.

assistance they need. Some days a given group will need more time; other days less. For example, a given group will need more time if a new book is being introduced, or a new story presented, while in other cases less time is all that is needed. These variations in needed time may be kept in mind as the teacher plans for the next day's activities of three or four reading groups. If one group will need a fairly long time for considering and practicing new words, a second group may have a somewhat shortened time, and a third group may be busy with work-type activities. In general, the purpose is to give each group time to allow for real progress rather than to keep any rather rigid schedule.

Include varied reading activities in the schedule. In their anxiety to give beginners a good start in reading, many teachers feel that one period of reading instruction during the day is not enough. Although it is relatively easy to schedule two sessions with a preprimer for one or two groups, it is extremely difficult to find time for additional meetings of three or four groups if other valuable classroom activities are not to be neglected.

The system of using preprimers and experience records in combination offers one useful solution to the problem of supplying sufficient experience in reading without curtailing other classroom activities. Usually work with a preprimer is scheduled regularly, if not every day at least often enough that children do not lose the thread of the stories or forget the words or phrases they have learned. Then a second reading session is spent with chart materials. At times the members of a particular reading group will continue to work as a group for this additional reading; at times they may join other children with a special interest in the particular record. Often the work with an experience record or set of records fosters the on-going activities of a unit of work—developing a special report, sharing the report with other children, or rereading it in order to draw appropriate illustrations. In this way the same time-block is used to contribute to growth in several areas simultaneously.

In a typical first grade there are also opportunities for other reading activities related to special projects. There may be a period to check new notices on the bulletin board. If there is a daily news bulletin, it may be read as part of a group sharing period. Helpers' charts will need to be checked and birthdays for the week noted. Teachers who capitalize on opportunities such as these can find many ways of providing for additional reading experiences without curtailing other worth-while activities.

Work with preprimers and experience records need not be scheduled in exactly the same way every day. There may be times when it is important to spend full time on a set of records—to share them with another group, to use them in a program to entertain parents, or to make a report to another class. At other times the children may concentrate on a preprimer, explore supplementary materials, or share with other groups some of the stories they have learned to read aloud. As children become more skillful readers, there are possibilities for still greater variations in the types of reading experiences in which they engage. These are described in detail in Chapter VI. Even at the beginning-reading level, the child's total reading experiences will be the richer when many types of materials and many different situations are used to teach him to read.

Use pupil-teacher planning to help secure a smooth-running day. The time spent in the early fall helping children learn to plan their activities and to work independently bears fruit when it comes to adding reading groups to other class experiences. If concern for group activities in reading leads to an overabundance of seat work in order to keep the remainder of the class quiet and busy, many of the potential values of the primary program will be lost. Pupil-teacher planning is an important means of guaranteeing that children's total experiences will be as rich as possible.

Planning usually is done at several points in the day. Young children cannot be expected to remember plans over a long time span. Normally time will be taken to check the plans for the period ahead. After it is clear that groups and individuals have the materials they need and know exactly what they are going to do, the children start to work. The teacher may spend some time making sure that no unforeseen problems have arisen. When all is going smoothly she is free to call together the members of a reading group. Usually she will check with the children as the reading group disbands to make sure they know what they are going to do next. If they are to engage in follow-up activities related to their reading, these are explained. Often it is desirable to take a few minutes between reading groups to see that all is going smoothly.

The problem of securing a relatively quiet classroom while reading groups are in session often can be attacked through direct discussion with the children. "What kinds of things could we do, and what should we not try to do?" is the question. Various children may suggest painting, coloring, looking at library books, drawing, playing with toys, doing puzzles, working quietly on a special project, finishing classroom housekeeping responsibilities. They can be helped to see that hammering, handling heavy blocks, playing noisy games, and working on something where the help of teacher is going to be needed frequently are not appropriate for periods in which reading groups are scheduled. Before the first group work is begun, the children may even make believe that a reading group is at work and practice having a quiet period—walking on tiptoe, speaking in lower voices, and getting their own equipment without help. If the children understand the reason for such suggestions, and know that they, themselves, will enjoy their reading more because others will be equally thoughtful of them, they will enter willingly into such plans.

Place reading groups so that other children are not disturbed. In carrying out plans for the day, the teacher generally works with a reading group or, on occasion, with two or three pupils needing special help, or a single individual, in a place away from the center of on-going class activities. Low voices and a small circle of children give the larger group more freedom in carrying out their work. The low voices of the children and the teacher in the reading group in turn help other children speak softly and keep them from distracting, and being distracted, by other activities. Although reading experiences are important, it must be remembered that they are only one part of the total experiences which are valuable for the first-grade child. Restrictions and adjustments made to facilitate the work of the reading group may well be examined in the light of their effect upon other aspects of growth and experience.

DEVELOPING FIRST EXPERIENCES IN A READING GROUP

The work of a beginning-reading group is typically quite varied in nature. The most important experiences center around reading and discussing the preprimer story of the experience record. However, these need to be supplemented by a variety of rereading and review activities if children are to grow in independent recognition of sentences, phrases, and words. All these experiences need to be planned so that interest in reading is kept high and children have the satisfaction of making progress.

INTRODUCING AND READING THE STORY

Develop interest in the first reading activities. As children gather for their first day in the reading group with a new book, a major consideration is to arouse their interest in the story and to give them the satisfaction of feeling that they can identify some of the material and read the story for themselves. If a preprimer is to be read, activities usually center first in getting acquainted with the book. Children are given time to examine its cover. They are told its title. They look at the pictures and talk about the kinds of stories it is likely to contain. They discover that a boy and a girl, a father and mother, perhaps a baby, and a dog or a cat are going to be in the stories. When readiness books from the same series have been used, they may recall previous discussions about the same characters. If some members of the group still have difficulty in handling books, time is taken to help them learn how to hold their books comfortably and how to turn the pages. Once general interest in the book has been aroused and curiosity regarding its pictures has been satisfied, the children are ready to begin their first story.

When an experience record is used as the basis for the first reading-group activities, the situation will have less novelty, as the children will have participated in other discussions involving experience records. Arousing interest, in this case, may be largely a matter of helping them recall again the circumstances that provided the background for the record. They may discuss what they thought was most interesting about their experience, and they can talk a bit about how they wrote it—which ideas they put first, which ideas they wrote next, how their story ended. This discussion then leads into reading and talking about the contents of the chart. Depending on the nature of the chart, the teacher may read one or two lines at a time, or she may read it through entirely for the children and then direct discussion to individual lines. Sometimes the first experience of trying to read a chart independently develops directly out of the activities of writing it. "Who can remember how we wrote our first line? . . ." "Yes, that's what we said, and here it is on our chart." "What did we say next? . . ." "Where would it be on the chart?"

Give the help needed to make first reading experiences successful. When children first try to read, the teacher takes the responsibility for telling them many of the exact words. Children who have not seen their new preprimer before are not expected to be able to figure out the boy's name is *Tom*, or the girl's name is *Betty*,[7] although were there to be children in the class with the same names, the teacher would certainly capitalize upon it.

The first reading of the story is done so the children will think about its meaning and see how to use pictures and context to recognize exact words. They talk about the pictures. They are helped to raise questions related to the printed material and then the teacher helps them read the words.

In the preprimer under discussion, the first picture shows Tom fixing a wheel on his wagon. With this picture the simple text begins.

Tom's name is written right here under his picture. Can you find it in your book? Put your finger under it. What is he doing? . . . Do you think Tom is going to be able to fix the wheel? Let's turn the page and see. . . . The story tells what Betty is saying to him. She says, "Ride, Tom." Who would like to read it? . . . Look at the next page. Did the wheel stay on? . . . What do you think Betty is saying? . . . Yes, she is calling to him, "Ride, ride." Who can read what Betty tells Tom to do? . . . Do you think Flip wants a ride, too? . . . Do you think the wheel will stay on? Let's turn the page. What has happened? . . . Who can read what Betty said? . . . How would Betty sound when she said Tom's name? . . . Who can show us Tom's name in two places? . . . Who thinks he

[7] The lesson that is described is based on the first story in Odille Ousley and David H. Russell, *My Little Red Story Book*, pp. 3-11, first preprimer of the Ginn Basic Readers (Boston: Ginn and Company, 1953), copyright, 1957, by Ginn and Company. It does not follow the words of the teacher's manual exactly, nor would the authors expect a creative teacher to do so.

could read our whole story? Anthony, will you read it? . . . Who else would like to try it? . . . Whose picture is at the start of our next story? Her name is right here under her picture and it's just like the name of somebody in our room. Who can read it?

If an experience record is being read, the children will have some familiarity with the contents but there are likely to be many more words for them to remember. This may mean that the first reading is largely a repetition of sentences read by the teacher: "Who can remember how we wrote our first line? . . . Yes, we said, 'We went to the park' and here it is. Who would like to read it? . . . What did we say next? The picture will tell you. . . . Who will point to 'We saw a squirrel'? . . . What did we see next? . . . That's right, it was a man with a boat, and you remember we said 'We saw a man rowing a boat.' Here it is, right there. Josie, will you read it? . . . And what did our last line say? . . . It was fun, wasn't it? And we said, 'We had fun.' Who will read it?"

After this first reading the children may go back to find special lines. They may match a line on a word card with the same line on the chart and then read it. They may try to put their hands around the words that say, *We saw*. Several children may try to read the entire chart, with help from the teacher as needed.

In such beginning activities, much of the first independent reading may be almost an echo of what the teacher has just said: The first line says, 'We went to the park.' Who can read it? He is riding again, isn't he, and Betty is saying 'Ride, ride.' Jean, suppose you read it." In the process the children have been interested in the story and have felt that they had a real part in reading it. They have also looked actively at words, sentences, and phrases that they will meet again.

Develop habits of thoughtful reading from the beginning. Throughout all beginning activities a thoughtful approach to reading needs to be the major aim even though the materials are very simple, and often very repetitive. Children concentrate on understanding the story. They read to find out, for sure, what is happening in the picture. They find the line that answers a question. They find the name of the boy in the story. They use the picture to help tell them what the story is about. They may be inaccurate occasionally in their recognition of sentences or phrases, but this is not, at first, a matter of as much concern as is that of helping them get the meaning. The teacher can make corrections in such a way that the child is helped to feel that he has done the most important part of the reading job while his attention is called to the exact words. "That's right, he is riding, and what the story says is 'Ride, Tom.' It was Maryville Park, but we didn't write its name. Remember, we only said 'We went to the park.' " Such corrections help with accurate recognition, but they do not put undue emphasis on isolated words.

Give children more reading responsibility as they acquire a word-recognition vocabulary. After the first introduction of a preprimer story or the initial reading of an experience record, group activities are usually planned to allow for rereading of the story as a whole and of separate lines, and for reviewing selected words and phrases in various other ways. Through these activities children very rapidly become able to recognize the words and phrases that have been repeated frequently. They also develop considerable skill in using the picture and the context as aids to independent reading.

The more adept children become, and the more words and phrases they are able to recognize, the more independence they can be urged to assume in reading new material. Soon they become able to read several lines with very little help. "What do you think father will say? Read all three lines at the bottom of the page and see if you are right? Let's read the story under the picture. Now, do we have everything in our record that we wanted to say? Who will read it all for us so that we can tell? "There is something new on our bulletin board this morning. I wonder if anyone can read it?"

Introduce new words through context and discussion. Part of the skill of helping children begin to read simple materials independently lies in the way unfamiliar words are introduced. Beginning-reading materials differ from those which will be read a little later in that the number of new words introduced at one time is very small, and the picture and context are particularly well designed to give clues for word recognition. Since this is the case, it often enriches meaning to introduce the new word in the story context, or to use it as needed in an experience record, rather than to use some other device to introduce it before it is encountered in a story. This procedure also encourages children, from the beginning, to try to figure out the story for themselves. The use of preprimer pictures to give help with new words has already been illustrated. Context, also, can be used very early. For example, a few pages later in the preprimer that has just been used for illustration,[8] there occurs the sentence, "See Flip and Bunny." *And* is a new word, but *see*, *Flip* and *Bunny* are familiar. With this context, the children are not likely to have much trouble in deciding what *and* must be.

All new words do not have to be introduced in context. Sometimes the discussion preceding the reading of the story will provide an appropriate opportunity for the introduction of a new word or phrase, and the teacher may write it on the chalkboard. Occasionally a word first used in an experience record will reappear in a preprimer or vice versa and the children can be reminded of the setting in which it appeared before.

[8] Odille Ousley and David H. Russell, *op. cit.*, pp. 16-17.

The procedure of encouraging children to use context and picture clues to help in the identification of new words is not confined to the beginning-reading level alone. Later in the first grade, when three or four new words may be introduced on a single page, there will often need to be more definite plans to work with the new words ahead of the reading if the story is to be understood. However, whenever picture and context clues seem to provide sufficient help, the child should be encouraged to try to use them. As he becomes more skilled, the child will develop another important aid to word recognition in his growing ability to use word-analysis clues. As rapidly as a youngster develops new techniques, he should be encouraged to test them out. The process starts at the beginning-reading level.

Children should not be expected to remember every new word after the first time it is met. The new vocabulary will need to be repeated in many settings before they are sure of it. Often a word will be recognized on one page and not on another. It may be identified at the beginning of a line, but missed as part of the phrase in the middle. Sometimes it will be picked out accurately in one sentence and missed when the sentence structure is changed slightly. All this is part of becoming able to read. Teachers should expect the process to be uneven and should provide for ample repetition in meaningful settings.

USING CONCRETE AIDS WITH BEGINNERS

Use oral reading as an aid in understanding. The beginner needs all the concrete help he can get as he takes his first steps toward independent reading. Crutches are a handicap if a child relies upon them beyond the point where he needs them, but as he starts to read certain types of concrete help can prove useful. Oral reading is one of these.

Reading aloud has many values, particularly for the beginning reader. Although there is evidence to indicate that children can learn to read without reading aloud,[9] the advantages of such procedure seem limited. Up to the time when they begin to read, children have been using words orally. In the beginning, the reinforcement of hearing their own voices say the words they see seems to help in getting meaning. For some children, who have had stories read to them for many years, being able to read the story out loud may be convincing evidence that they actually have learned to read. Most youngsters enjoy the experience of being able to read to others. For reasons such as these most first-grade teachers provide for considerable oral work. This does not mean, however, that children need to take turns in reading one line at a time, or that all need to sit and wait while each child reads his special

[9] Guy Thomas Buswell, *Non-Oral Reading: A Study of Its Use in the Chicago Public Schools.* Supplementary Educational Monographs No. 60 (Chicago: University of Chicago Press, September 1945).

part. Even in the beginning there are many ways of providing opportunities for children to read aloud in more meaningful settings.

A certain amount of oral reading typically takes place as the story is first read and discussed. Children should be allowed to read silently first so that they may think about the meaning of what they are reading. Then, when all have had the opportunity to read for themselves, they may talk about what they have read, or read a line or several lines aloud. "What do you think he is saying? Let's read the story and see. . . . What did he say, Ann? . . . Will you read it for us?" As stories grow longer, children may find several lines, each of which contributes to the discussion. These may be told in the children's words, or read aloud. Other opportunities for the oral reading of short passages may be provided as children review the story, read phrase or sentence cards, or find phrases or words that answer specific questions. Many of the review activities suggested in the following section assume that children will answer aloud.

Even with beginners, it is not necessary to plan to read every story aloud. The teacher often can secure ample evidence of understanding and of accurate word recognition through discussion and review activities. Oral reading can then be used to share the story with other groups, or to give the members of one group the fun of reading aloud for their own entertainment. It is also possible to take well-studied stories home to read to parents. Oral reading can be a valuable aid to beginners, but the way in which it is used should be varied to meet the needs of the particular situation.

Oral reading occasionally serves another purpose for beginners. Some children murmur to themselves, even when they are reading silently. These youngsters seem to need a little of the reinforcement of their own voices to help them in understanding what they read. Vocalization becomes a handicap when children reach the place where their eyes can cover the material more rapidly than their voices. However, in the beginning a certain amount of this semi-oral reading may be helpful. As they become better readers, most children cease to use vocalization of their own accord. These who do not can be shown that the best readers do not need to say the words out loud, and encouraged to try to read without moving their lips.

Provide markers if needed. Following a story from line to line without losing one's place is not always easy for beginners. When reading materials are only one or two lines long and these lines are well spaced, markers do not have much value unless children are very immature. With slightly longer passages they may be helpful. Usually a strip of colored paper one- to one- and one-half inches in width and about as long as the width of the page is used. This the children slide down from line to line as they read.

All beginners will not need markers. Some will acquire the knack of reading from line to line without any difficulty. Others will start the same line twice, lose their places, or be unable to follow when others read aloud. Here the marker is of help. Holding books and handling markers at the same time often proves difficult. Sometimes it helps to allow those using markers to sit at a table where they can have support for their books, or to drop their books to their laps so that they have their hands free. This problem needs to be solved in a way that assures good posture and good light on books. A marker should be a temporary device. As soon as children become more skilled, it is possible to encourage them to read certain easy pages without markers. Gradually they discard them for all reading.

Use other devices to sharpen the child's sensitivity to the configuration of a word. Other concrete aids, such as putting a finger under the right answer or putting hands around the word or words on the chalkboard that answer the question, also help in beginning reading. The child who cannot read a phrase accurately when he sees it in a sentence sometimes can identify it when he blocks it off with his hands. A pointer slid under the words of a chart as the child or teacher reads may help to establish left-to-right orientation. Word, phrase, and sentence cards, as discussed in the following section, may aid in accurate recognition. All children will not learn with equal ease merely by looking at words. For some the experience of drawing a line around a word to show its general configuration may be helpful. As children learn to write, some may benefit from the kinesthetic experience of writing their new words in meaningful activities. In general, the greater the number of senses that can be appealed to, the greater the likelihood of successful learning on the part of the members of the reading group. No method should become routine. All children need not use the same aids or use them to the same extent. Whenever the opportunity presents itself for a child to read successfully without resorting to a special concrete aid, he is encouraged to do so.

PROVIDING REVIEW ACTIVITIES

Plan for purposeful rereading of the story. Study of a preprimer story or an experience record does not usually end with the first reading. When the children have the gist of the story, they discuss it and in the process they are helped to become more familiar with sentence, phrase, and word units. The skill with which these review activities are planned does much to determine how effectively children learn to get meaning from what they read.

As the first reading of the story typically proceeds, there are opportunities for a certain amount of rereading. The children read a two- or three-line story or a few lines of an experience record silently in order to answer a question. Then, as they discuss what they have found out, someone may read the exact line that gives the answer. Two or three other children may read the same line. There may be disagreement as to what the right answer is, and someone may read the entire story to make sure. As stories become longer there are more varied opportunities for discussion and rereading. The children may discuss how the characters felt and find the line or the phrase that proves their point. They may pick out the most interesting part of a story, the funniest part, or the most exciting part. With an experience chart they may read the lines they helped to write, reread to see if everything has been included, or pick out the parts for which illustrations would be appropriate. All such types of discussion provide opportunities to help children gain acquaintance with phrases or words while they concentrate on the meaning of the story.

Provide opportunities to test out growing skill in recognizing words, phrases, and sentences. Beginners delight in trying to identify words and phrases, merely to prove to themselves and to others that they have learned to read. Some very profitable review experiences can be provided by asking children to locate specific parts of a story or chart. Such questions can be phrased so that they have to think about what they are reading. The teacher may ask the children to find lines that answer specific questions. "Where is the part that tells us where we went? Who can find the line that tells what we did?" A little later the questions may refer to phrases or to words. "Who can find the two words that tell the name of the park? Put your fingers around just the one word that tells what mother did. It's up here on the board, too. Who can point to it? We talked about the pony three times in our story. Can anyone find the word *pony* in all three places?" After the correct word, sentence, or phrase has been located, several children may read it orally. If it is being confused with a similar phrase there may be some discussion on how to tell the two apart. Sometimes new words or phrases may be written on the chalkboard and the children asked to find the one read by the teacher, to pick out one they know and ask another child to read it, or to select one they know, read, and erase it.

At the beginning it may be helpful to provide a certain number of activities where children actually match words, phrases, and sentences. This can be of particular value to the child who is still having trouble noting major differences in configurations. The children may look at the child's name on the first page of their story, then see if they can find the same word on the second page and put their fingers around it. The teacher may hold up word cards and have the children point to the same word in their books, on the chalkboard or in an experience record. The teacher may read the first line of a chart and then ask the children to find another line which begins the same way. She may write a line from a preprimer on the board and then ask the children to find the same line in their books. When an experience chart is being read, a duplicate chart is often prepared and then cut apart to form cards consisting of whole lines, phrases or words. Children can take one of the cards and hold it under the matching word or phrase on the uncut chart. If the word or phrase recurs on the chart, they can see in how many places they can find it. A preprimer story can be reproduced in chart form and studied in the same way. All such activities should be accompanied by discussion which adds meaning to the task of learning to identify words or phrases accurately.

Card-holders in which word, phrase, and sentence cards can be placed are a help in review activities. These holders are sold commercially, but they also can be made easily in any desired length. Heavy wrapping paper may be folded back on itself to form pockets about one- and one-half inches deep, leaving about three inches between each pocket. After the paper is folded it can be taped or sewn in place. The result is a tiered series of pockets deep enough to hold the cards that make up a story, line by line. Such holders have a variety of uses for review purposes. A story can be rebuilt, one line at a time. As children begin to recognize lines, phrases, and words, they may build their own stories in the holder and ask other children to read them. They may be asked to find a word or a phrase designated by the teacher, and to take it out of the chart. Each child may find the phrase or the sentence which he wishes to read and lift out the card as he reads it.

Care needs to be taken not to overdo the review activities centered around a single story. Preprimer materials are meant to be covered rather quickly. The child is not expected to become absolutely certain of a word or phrase after he meets it in one story. It will be repeated in many different settings and in several easy books, and children need the satisfaction of going on to a new story. In general, quantities of interesting materials, presenting many of the same words and phrases in different settings, are preferable to intensive study of one experience record or of one preprimer story. Periodically, the teacher may check certain children individually to be sure that vocabulary is being mastered.

Use individual work-type activities to help provide reviews. From time to time it may be valuable to give additional reading experience through work-type activities. With beginners, these activities need not be very extensive. If many opportunities to read are being provided during the day it is not necessary to end every group session with hectographed, mimeographed, or workbook exercises. Particularly questionable is the policy of providing quiet work-type activities for all children as a way of keeping them occupied while the reading groups are meeting. However, there will be times when children need additional contacts with new words, or when it is desirable to have one group work independently while others read with the teacher. As children become more skilled, a greater variety of independent activities are possible. Examples of these are included in the chapters that follow.

Work-type activities should be planned so that children are challenged to read thoughtfully in order to carry out whatever task has been set for them. Activities involving pictures can prove interesting to beginners. Children can be given pages on which words or sentences similar to those in the materials that they have been reading are hectographed and instructed to illustrate them. They may choose the part of the story they like best and draw a picture about it. It is also possible to hectograph a series of pictures illustrating various parts of the story and to ask the children to choose the phrase or sentence that matches the picture. Sometimes teachers mimeograph an experience chart which the children have read or write a short story using the words of the preprimer. These can be stapled into little individual booklets which children may illustrate.

Small card-holders constructed like the one described earlier for use with beginners. Some of these may be based on materials read previously.

> Where did we go?
> ——————— to the park.
> ——————— to the zoo.
> ——————— to town.
> What color was the wagon? red blue green
> Did father laugh? Yes No
> Did mother laugh? Yes No

Often it is desirable to give children the experience of reading the new words in a different setting before they answer specific questions. If this seems important, a short paragraph using the same vocabulary can be written and followed by questions similar to those that have just been illustrated to check on comprehension.

Small card-holders constructed like the one described earlier for use with groups can be made for individual children. The youngsters themselves will enjoy helping to fold the paper and holding it as it is pasted down. With these holders and sets of word or phrase cards developed from words they have been reading, the children can construct little stories for each other, reproduce the lines in the chart story, put together phrases that begin with the same words, and think of other ways of amusing themselves with the words they know. A little later as the children begin to write, they may use these word and phrase cards to help them with words they wish to spell. Increased skill in writing eventually provides another source of review activities. The children may write short stories, riddles, or poems; illustrate them; read them to other children or have them read by others; or take them home to read to their parents.

The workbooks accompanying basal readers are replete with interesting work-type activities for beginners. These materials, like other work-type materials, need to be selected in terms of the particular group. Taking all children through a workbook routinely, page by page, is not likely to meet individual needs at any reading level. For this reason teachers often prefer to have small numbers of several interesting workbooks, and then to select activities as they seem appropriate.

All individual activities are more valuable if the teacher finds time to discuss them. Beginners, especially, are not far enough along to be able to identify their own difficulties and mistakes. Work-type activities need to be shared in the reading group. Papers merely corrected by the teacher and handed back do not serve the purpose.

Provide easy supplementary reading. Supplementary reading experiences provide another source of reviews for beginners. They need materials on the library table that they can read independently. Preprimers are a valuable resource for this purpose. Some of these may be supplementary books that repeat the vocabulary of the preprimers being used in reading groups. Others may belong to basal series not being used for group activities. Often it is desirable to release for supplementary reading a book which has been completed by a reading group. It is also possible to tear apart several preprimers and to bind the stories separately. These can be added to the library table as soon as the story has been finished by the reading group. Supplementary preprimers need not all be placed on the library table at once. If a few are added at a time, these simple, carefully written materials can provide worthwhile independent reading experiences long after children have progressed to primers and first readers.

The past few years have seen a greatly increased supply of easy books using a carefully controlled vocabulary.[10] While many of them are probably of greater interest to the more advanced first-grade children and well-established readers in the second grade, they may be considered for the younger reader for the stimulation they can bring to the beginner. A supply of favorite picture story books is, of course, an essential resource.

Also, it is not unusual to find a first-grader who already reads more difficult material. It is essential that he continues to grow in his reading ability and materials appropriate for him should be available. A teacher who read aloud a story about Halloween chosen from a second reader was later surprised to see one pupil pick up the book from the library table and read to several other children the last story in the book. He read easily and fluently. Previously, this pupil had been alert, but was not an outstanding participant in discussions in his reading group. Such children particularly need the stimulating resources of a variety of available reading materials.

Teachers can also find many ways of re-using new vocabulary in the ma-

---

[10] For listings of easy books for beginning readers, see p. 215.

terials they write for children. Some of these may be hectographed versions of experience records or of children's stories. Single-word books may also be made by folding a piece of colored paper, printing the word on the outside, and pasting the appropriate picture inside so that the child may check his reading. In addition to the teacher-made materials added to the library table, there are the experience records, signs, captions to pictures, and notices with which first-grade classrooms abound.

Continually, in a room that is plentifully supplied with reading materials, children face fresh proofs that it is important to learn to read. Interesting messages await them. Information they need is at hand. Records of their most exciting experiences are available for them to reread for their own pleasure or to share with their friends. Beginning readers start their activities in an atmosphere that is a rich source of stimulating opportunities to learn to read.

SOME QUESTIONS TO THINK ABOUT IN APPRAISING BEGINNING-READING ACTIVITIES

1. Is the transition from prereading activities gradual enough to assure successful beginning-reading experiences?

2. Are reading activities planned so that other aspects of the primary program continue to make their full contribution to children's development?

3. Do children read for meaning right from the start?

4. Are reading activities planned so that a wide variety of classroom materials make a contribution?

5. Are beginning-reading activities adjusted to a range of ability levels?

6. Are methods of grouping and scheduling flexible enough to allow for effective meeting of the needs of the group?

7. Do review activities contribute to habits of thoughtful reading while they foster accurate recognition of words and phrases?

8. Are children provided with easy, interesting supplementary materials from the start?

SUGGESTIONS FOR FURTHER READING

Betts, Emmett A. *Foundations of Reading Instruction.* Chapter 20. New York: American Book Company, 1957. 757 pp.

Burton, William H. *Reading in Child Development.* Chapter 7. Indianapolis: The Bobbs-Merrill Company, Inc., 1956. 608 pp.

Dawson, Mildred A., and Bamman, Henry A. *Fundamentals of Basic Reading Instruction.* Chapter 4. New York: Longmans, Green and Company, 1959. 304 pp.

Dolch, Edward W. *Teaching Primary Reading.* Third Edition, Chapters 9, 10. Champaign, Illinois: The Garrard Press, 1960. 429 pp.

Gans, Roma. *Guiding Children's Reading Through Experiences.* Chapter 2. New York: Teachers College, Columbia University, 1941. 86 pp.

Gray, Lillian, and Reese, Dora, *Teaching Children to Read*. Second Edition, Chapter 7. New York: The Ronald Press Company, 1957. 475 pp.

Hildreth, Gertrude. *Readiness for School Beginners*. Chapter 15. Yonkers-on-Hudson: World Book Company, 1950. 382 pp.

Hildreth, Gertrude. *Teaching Reading*. Chapter 10. New York: Henry Holt and Company, 1958. 612 pp.

McKee, Paul. *The Teaching of Reading in the Elementary School*. Chapter 8. Boston: Houghton Mifflin Company, 1948. 622 pp.

PART III

*Developing Independent
Readers in the Primary
Grades*

CHAPTER VI

Planning the Reading Program in the Primary Grades

CHILDREN AT WORK IN LATE THIRD GRADE

THE children described in the preceding chapter who were then at the beginning-reading stage are now completing the third grade. Although a few children have transferred to other schools and some new pupils have joined the group, about three quarters of the class have been together for three years. Some pertinent questions may be asked about their present reading abilities. Are there wide differences in reading ability? Do they read many different kinds of materials? Has their growth in reading been constant and even? What kinds of reading activities do these children now engage in? The sections which follow will present a picture of the present status of this third grade group.

The range of reading abilities is wide. For five children in this group, easy second-grade materials still present difficulties while several youngsters read fourth- and fifth-grade basal readers without any trouble. Between these extremes range the other members of the class. It is late in the spring and by this time over a quarter of the children can handle easy fourth-grade books. Most of the rest are still somewhat more at home with typical third-grade materials, but many of this group will be able to handle easy books written for fourth grade if the next teacher gives consistent help in the early fall. Some will need to be provided with second- and third-grade materials for almost another full year. This range in abilities is not unusual. The progress is about what might be expected, and the four-year range in ability between the best and the poorest readers is typical.

Growth has not been even. The children who are now the best readers were not all in the first group to begin to read in the first grade. Of the children who belonged to that original group, one started a little later but soon caught up, and spent a good part of the year with the most advanced readers. Another did not show outstanding progress in reading for the entire first year. He did the work expected of his group, but sought little additional reading experience. Much of his free time was spent with various media for self-expression, particularly the easel and clay table. In the second grade he discovered that books offered many exciting areas of exploration and soon became one of the most avid readers.

The five most retarded children had varied reading careers. Two learned to read very slowly and were given greatly simplified programs from the beginning. Jane, the third child, was kept home by recurring colds for most of her first year. In spite of much individual help she has not yet made up for the poor start, although from month to month her progress is more rapid. John comes from a home where a sister two years older reads very well. During his three years in school his parents have had many conferences with his teachers regarding his progress. They are beginning to understand why John feels no challenge to learn to read as well as his sister. The fifth child, Bill, transferred to the school at the beginning of the third grade. His family had changed residence several times during his first two years in school. Eight teachers had been involved in teaching him how to read. He is just now beginning to feel at home with books. These changes in status from the predictions of the prereading period are also what might be expected. Many factors influence progress in learning to read.

Many types of materials are read. The variety of ways in which reading is now used impresses the visitor. Charts are still in evidence, but they serve more often as records of class plans needed by all for easy reference. One contains the list of characters for a play and a brief description of important points about each character. Another gives the general plans for a mural. A third lists the responsibilities of committees planning an open house to entertain parents. A fourth, near a table containing boxes of plants, seems to be a running record of an experiment with soils.

The library table now contains a wide selection of books. A number are marked with the call number of the city library. Others belong to the classroom collection. A few science and mechanics books have been brought to school by the boys. Recreational reading, science stories, several types of social-studies materials, a book on how to care for turtles, and another on how to build birdhouses testify to the variety of interests.

A children's encyclopedia and several dictionaries, most of them picture dictionaries, are on a work table a little farther over. Textbooks are more prominent than they were in the first grade. The children recently have begun to use a simple language text and have several books that provide experience with arithmetic concepts. Half-a-dozen copies of the easier books in a popular science series can be seen. Two or three copies of each of several different books on aspects of community life are also in evidence. Basal-reading series show signs of constant use; about ten copies of each of several sets have been provided. Some are at first- and second-grade level and some as high as fifth grade.

The evidence from the materials in the classroom is that children are reading for many purposes and that they are capable of getting much information without the teacher's direct guidance. The children's activities confirm this. Several can be seen checking various parts of the class plans. Many turn to textbooks and to other reference materials to look up information. Two or three refer to a list of hard words to check their spelling as they write an invitation to their parents for their open house. A number have recreational reading at their desks. One pair are at work on an assignment arising out of the reading group of the day before.

Reading groups undertake a variety of activities. Observation of the groups at work on various reading activities helps to fill in the picture of the growth in reading ability. The least advanced children have been meeting together as a regular instructional group. The teacher customarily stays near these children when they read new materials. They can still profit from guidance in locating the answers to their questions, and they particularly need help when it comes to identifying new words. Even so, they now read a story from eight to ten pages in length, and are beginning to show considerable independence in working out simple words. Their recreational reading is largely in first-grade books and they read these easier materials for pleasure with a minimum of help.

Grouping is distinctly more flexible for the children who are the better readers. On the day of this visit, two group projects are under way. The children in one group have been reading a series of animal stories in a reader and are now getting ready to share their reading with the rest of the class. It is to take the form of a little program. Two youngsters in this group are planning to read parts of a story aloud, and have asked for some group criticism as they rehearse. Four others are to present a story in pantomime while selected paragraphs are read aloud. They need to have their choice of selections for the oral reading appraised to make sure that the audience will be able to follow the gist of the story. These are the performers. The other children in the group have studied the same stories and are acting as critics. The teacher makes sure that this group is well under way and then leaves the children to help each other while she moves on to work with the children who make up the second group.

The children in the second group have not worked with a basal-reading series for several days. They have assumed major responsibility for finding more about how to care for the plants in the science corner. Their first step was to list, with the help of the teacher, the questions they wanted to answer. All then took a day to look through the books in the classroom to locate information, making as much use of tables of contents and indexes as they could. They next read independently until they began to exhaust their resources. Today in the reading group they are pooling their information. Each child has come with very simple notes on what he has found. The books that were used are on the table nearby for ready reference. Over the past day or so the teacher has done little to help these children other than to check on progress and assist individuals. Now she works with them for the full group meeting, calling them together about ten minutes after the others have begun work so that she can be free from interruptions.

Later in the morning another group activity related to reading appears. This time it involves everyone in the class. The purpose is to learn to spell some of the more difficult words the children have been needing frequently in their writing. As the children discuss the pronunciation of the words and identify unusual letter combinations, they draw upon all they have learned about word analysis through their reading. Even the poorest readers know the most common phonetic elements, but combinations such as *ought, tion, ine, ight* are still difficult for many in the class and words of more than two syllables require considerable thought.

Reading is not an isolated activity in this classroom. Every situation in which children need to read contributes to their reading program. Already many of the children are beginning to read widely. Special help is planned to provide for continuity of growth in reading skill, but increasingly the demands of daily classroom activities are the determiners of what that help is to be.

This chapter presents an overview of the reading activities of the primary grades after children have become familiar with preprimer materials. The three major sections of the chapter present aims, suggest types of reading experiences appropriate for primary children, and summarize implications of these aims and experiences for grouping and scheduling. Each of the three aspects of reading instruction described in this overview is discussed in detail in Chapters VII, VIII and IX.

NEW AIMS AS PRIMARY CHILDREN GROW IN ABILITY TO READ INDEPENDENTLY

In three years the children just described have grown from almost complete dependence upon the teacher to a marked degree of independence in reading for a variety of purposes, in locating the information they need, in working with many types of materials, and in identifying unfamiliar words. The objectives of the primary grades cannot be listed easily grade by grade. Children will develop at different rates and meet new problems at different times. Each teacher has to make the final decisions as to when her children should be encouraged to tackle more difficult reading tasks and what help they need to meet their present reading problems. However, in the light of the ways in which reading is used in the first three grades, certain general objectives can be suggested.

Reading begins to serve a greater variety of purposes. One major objective of the primary grades is to help children extend the ways in which they use their reading ability. Even at the prereading level, youngsters are encouraged to look to experience records and picture books for help on a variety of problems. As they gain in reading skill, they need to expand the purposes for which they read. Among the wider reading purposes that should develop are the following:

First: Recreational reading should begin to provide an increasing number of satisfactions. With the development of reading skill, children should be encouraged to explore both fictional and factual materials, and have the pleasure of selecting and withdrawing books from the library. The typical third-grade reader enjoys reading for its own sake and has wide reading interests.

Second: Children should begin to read more widely for information, increasing gradually the number and kinds of informational materials read. Easy textbooks in the content fields, and simple books on a variety of topics should be used. Children's magazines and weekly newspapers may be explored. By the third grade, children should be able to use several resources to solve a problem.

Third: Primary children should make increased use of the signs and bulletins written in connection with daily classroom activities. They should become more effective in using daily notices on the bulletin board, special directions for games, daily plans, outlines of group responsibilities, and communications from other classes or from the principal's office.

Fourth: With wider reading should come the development of reading tastes and the ability to evaluate what is read. Children should begin to gain skill in deciding on the appropriateness of what they read in terms of the questions for which they are seeking answers. They should also begin to make discriminations regarding the accuracy of what they read—to tell a factual story from an imaginative one, and to check their reading against firsthand experience.

Reading techniques begin to be adapted to varied purposes. One does not read a story for his own enjoyment in the same way that he reads the directions for playing a new game. Although children at the intermediate and high school grades face more exacting demands for flexible reading skills, it is at the primary level that they first begin to adjust their methods of reading to the ends for which they read. Among the areas in which increased skill should develop are the following:

First: Children should be able to read several pages without help in order to get the general gist of the passage. As they begin to enjoy recreational reading they should be able to read stories and even small books without much help. As they approach third grade they should seek longer books for recreational reading. They should also be able to skim simple informational materials to get an idea of the contents or to locate information bearing on a special topic. At the end of third grade the ability to read independently for main ideas of simple material should be firmly established.

Second: Primary children should show gradual gains in ability to read carefully in order to follow directions or to note precise details. As they progress toward third grade, they should be able to read carefully to answer a series of simple questions raised in connection with a problem in a content field. The various classroom lists and charts should be used with more accuracy. Details upon which the plot of a story hinges should be caught. Although note-taking will be very limited in the primary grades, some children may begin to jot down important pieces of information for committee reports.

Third: There should be a gradual increase in reading speed commensurate with children's growing grasp of word, phrase, and sentence units. The problem of help-ing children learn to adjust their reading speed to varied purposes belongs largely in the intermediate grades when word-analysis techniques and comprehension skills are better developed. However, independent reading experiences with well-graded materials at the primary level should result in a gradual increase in ability to read smoothly in phrase units. Such beginning-reading techniques as pointing, using markers, and vocalizing have gradually disappeared.

Fourth: Oral-reading skills should improve. As they read longer passages aloud, primary children should develop increased skill in reading with expression. With longer passages and more varied material this will involve responding to phrasing and punctuation marks, and conveying a little of the mood of the passage. Tech-niques such as how to hold a book so that the voice is not muffled should be learned. Above all, young children should develop the attitude that others need to understand you when you read aloud, and should learn to enjoy the experience of reading to others.

Fifth: There needs to be some progress in varying reading techniques in terms of purposes. This problem will be even more important at the intermediate level. Primary materials are usually written in a simple narrative style that does not call for much variation in method. However, by the time children reach third grade, they should be able to sense when it is appropriate to read rapidly, and when care has to be taken to note details. They should be able to glance through materials quickly to locate information and then to read carefully to get the facts they need. They should experience the fun of reading recreational materials at a reasonably rapid pace.

First steps are taken toward independent location of materials. A child is not truly an independent reader until he can locate his own resource mate-rials. Primary children take only one or two steps in this direction, but by the time able children reach third grade a teacher should expect to help them begin to locate source materials, and then be free to leave them to secure the information they need from the various sources, confident that work will progress satisfactorily without her. Among the reference techniques with which children should become acquainted are the following:

First: There should be growing acquaintance with the standard reference books commonly used in the room. Children should know the general contents of the library corner. Very early they may have experience with a small class-made picture dictionary. By the third grade many will know how to use a simple standard dictionary. Many third graders will have some contacts with an encyclopedia. Insofar as textbooks are being used in the classroom, they should know how to work with them.

Second: Primary readers should know the purposes of the major reference aids in simple books. It is not long before children begin to identify the title of a story, and to learn the purpose of page numbers. Soon they may use a table of contents in order to find out what a book is about or locate a special story. Third-graders should be able to use a table of contents without difficulty, and many will begin to develop skills in using the index.

Third: Even though techniques are often crude, two helpful attitudes should begin to develop. The first is a growing disposition to search through several books for specific information. The second is a growing sensitivity to what is appropriate for the solution of problems proposed. First-grade children begin to note that a story in a reading text gives needed information. Third-grade children are typically able to use reading from several sources.

Fourth: Primary children should be acquainted with the school or local library. Although they are not likely to use the card index to locate materials for themselves, they need to know what help a librarian can give and they should be disposed to turn to the library for help on special problems.

The technical aspects of simple materials are handled effectively. There is a great difference between the simple page of a preprimer and the story in a typical third-grade reader. There is also a difference between the narrative style of a first reader and the textbook in arithmetic or spelling that a third-grader may read. Primary children must learn how to work with these increasingly complex materials. If their reading matter is properly graded, the children may not actually realize that they are facing technical problems of increased difficulty. The teacher, however, needs to be alert to the fact that new problems are being introduced and to the need for helping children deal effectively with the new situations they encounter:

First: Primary children must become accustomed to increasingly complex sentence and paragraph structure. Sentences, paragraphs and entire stories gradually increase in length. More difficult materials present phrases which extend to the line below, the top of the next page, or even at the top of a page which has to be turned. Pictures no longer carry the main thought of the story from page to page.

Second: Throughout the primary grades there will be increasing need to adjust to the format of different materials. Reading textbooks generally present a group of stories, whereas a book for pleasure reading may be a single long story. Textbooks in the content areas vary in organization, with different patterns of explanations, practice materials, and questions for discussion. Work-type materials will have variety in directions and kinds of exercises. Primary children need to be able to work with these different types of materials.

Third: By the third grade, children should use effectively the simple visual aids accompanying their reading material. Pictures and, occasionally, photographs occur most frequently in primary books. Sample exercises in workbooks and very simple diagrams and charts which illustrate both experience records and easy textbooks offer additional visual aids. Although complex problems of using visual aids are not encountered until the intermediate and higher grades, primary children should develop an interest in these aids to understanding and a disposition to make use of them.

Skill in working with unfamiliar words develops. An important aim at the beginning-reading level is to provide for enough contacts with selected words to help children become able to recognize them wherever they are met. These words are typically within the child's stock of word meanings. As he grows in reading skill, the primary child should amass an increasing number of words he can recognize at sight. But he will not be truly independent in his reading until he can work out the pronunciation of a word for himself. Useful skills in word analysis should be well developed by the time a child has achieved third-grade reading techniques. Most children will not be completely independent in word-analysis techniques when they reach the fourth grade, but all should have varied ways of helping themselves. The stock of word meanings should also increase. Specifically, growth in areas such as the following should be expected:

First: Children need to expand their stock of sight words, partly as an aid to wide reading and partly as a basis for the development of word-analysis skills. In third grade, and even in the intermediate grades, certain words will be better introduced and learned on a word-recognition basis. As increased skill in word analysis develops, these words are likely to be place names, words with unusually difficult phonetic elements, or technical terms.

Second: There will be a gradual increase from first through third grade in the number of structural and phonetic elements recognized by the children. Significant in this process should be increased interest in word-parts and growing satisfaction in being able to discover new sounds and to use them to pronounce unfamiliar words independently. By the end of the third grade, the child who has read broadly and has been helped to observe carefully the shapes and sounds of words should be able to use most of the common phonetic elements in pronouncing words. He will typically continue, however, to learn new word-parts as he encounters the increased vocabulary load of the intermediate grades.

Third: From first grade through third, there should be gradually increased flexibility in identifying the parts of words. In the beginning, the analysis may be largely in terms of initial letters, the similarity of the word to familiar ones, and endings such as *s*, *ed*, and *ing*. As a child meets words of increasing complexity, he must be able to vary his approach. In some cases he may use word-parts that are themselves familiar small words, in others, syllables. Sometimes he will need to pronounce a letter separately, sometimes to see it as part of a two- and three-letter combination. Most third graders should have reached the place where they will try a second or third breakdown of a word if the first attempt does not work.

Fourth: Throughout the primary grades, children should develop increased skill in using context clues to aid in word analysis. As children grow more skilled, use of the context should become one important test of a tentative analysis.

Fifth: The more widely children read the greater will be the number of words with unfamiliar meanings they encounter. There will also be an increased number of new meanings attached to terms they already know. By third grade a certain amount of this new vocabulary should come from the various content fields. Primary children need the firsthand experiences, the visual aids, and the opportunities for discussion to make these new terms real.

These aims had their roots in the prereading program. With varied emphases they also guide the program for intermediate-grade children. Some primary children will not have achieved these goals by the end of the third grade and some will have reached the status of typical fifth- or sixth-graders. Each teacher has to be able to take the child where she finds him and to provide the experiences that are the appropriate next steps for him.

PROVIDING READING EXPERIENCES TO MEET THE NEEDS OF PRIMARY CHILDREN

The reading program of the primary child may be thought of as including all the reading done by him. These reading activities may be considered, for the purposes of discussion, as having three aspects. First, there is direct reading instruction, which includes all those activities, either individually or in groups, through which children are given specific help in order to improve their reading skills. Second, there are informational reading activities in which reading is used in some way to solve a problem, or to advance the ongoing plans of a group or of an individual. Recreational reading may be considered the third aspect of the child's total reading activities. Children should have the experience of enjoying simple materials just for the pleasure and satisfaction that such reading offers. Taken together, these three types of activities provide for flexible and varied reading experiences.

Actually these three aspects of the reading program cannot always be separated in practice. A story used for discussion in a group meeting for reading instruction may provide the information needed to solve a problem arising in a social studies unit. A planning session in a science activity may be interrupted in order to develop skills necessary to locate needed information. A factual book about birds may be more challenging pleasure reading to a child than a fairy story. In their eagerness to share new library books with others, children may spend several days practicing oral reading. It does not matter how a particular reading experience is classified as long as all the child's reading activities are developed in harmony with his maximum progress.

As children grow from the beginner's almost complete dependence on the teacher to the relative independence of the third-grader, there should be a distinct change in the relationships among the various aspects of the total reading program. In the beginning, a large share of the burden of introducing new words and complicated sentences and paragraphs will be carried by direct instruction of individuals or groups. Even in early grades, however, instructional activities will often deal with reading problems growing out of classroom experiences. As children become more and more able to read independently, a larger share of reading experiences are related to finding information and to pleasure reading. It is important that the reading problems children encounter during these activities be reflected in their reading groups. How do these interrelated activities develop in the typical primary program?

PROVIDING NEEDED DIRECT INSTRUCTION

Regular group sessions provide continuity. First graders in particular, and the children in second and third grade who need the most help, are likely to meet regularly in relatively constant reading groups. These are the children who are in greatest need of sequential experiences with materials carefully chosen with regard to difficulty of vocabulary and of sentence and paragraph structure. Typically, books from basal-reader series provide a large part of the instructional material for these groups. However, it is not always necessary, and sometimes not desirable, to follow the stories in one text from beginning to end. Other texts, supplementary books of the same difficulty level, experience records, and easy recreational books can all be used so that they contribute to the desired continuity of experiences.

The number of groups with relatively constant personnel in later first, second, and third grades will vary with the situation. In first grade few teachers work with less than three groups, and many prefer four or five at times. Many of the same factors that influence the number of groups at the beginning-reading period continue to operate—size of class, range in reading ability, speed with which new skills are being learned, ability of children to work independently, presence or absence of personality problems, and the skill of the teacher herself.[1]

When the increased ability of second- and third-graders to read independently is capitalized upon fully, the activities of their reading groups will include a greater number of experiences with materials other than basal-reader series. The personnel of the groups, too, will become more flexible in terms of the special projects at hand. In the third grade described at the beginning of this chapter, for example, only one group—the most retarded—was engaged in sequential study of basal readers. Of the other groups, one was working out a program based on a special set of animal stories and the second was collecting information needed for science activities. These were groups that also worked together for activities with basal readers. At another time the grouping might be in terms of interest and the total number of groups might well increase.

As children develop greater ability to read independently, there should be more occasions when they read alone for a time. In this way, several groups may be actively at work without taking up an undue proportion of the teacher's total day. Then, as children venture into more extensive informational-reading activities, there should also be occasions when the teacher sets aside the work with a basal reader planned for an instructional group in order to help with the reading problems related to on-going classroom projects.

---

[1] The pattern of scheduling described in Chapter V may be referred to here.

This combination second- and third-grade group has many interests which lead to satisfactions in reading. Sharing the information found in a good book is a rewarding experience for both speaker and listeners.

Typically, the number of such flexible adjustments will increase as children gain in reading skill.

More skilled readers undertake unit activities in reading groups. If primary children are to learn to evaluate, to read critically, and to decide when information is important, their reading experiences need to include these activities. As their reading skill increases, the members of reading groups should be helped to plan experiences that have many of the characteristics of a typical unit of work.

The heart of any unit activity is its problem-solving approach to learning. With the teacher's help, the children clarify a problem of concern to them. They lay plans for collecting needed information, for carrying out the desired activities, for preparing the exhibits, or for taking the other steps that seem necessary for the successful solution of the problem. Next they decide how to go to work, allot responsibilities, and proceed to carry out their plans. Eventually they bring together all they have done and decide how close they have come to solving their problem successfully. Depending on the problem, they may test out their solution in a new situation.

The activities of a reading group take on the characteristics of a unit when the children share in posing the problems around which their reading is to center, and then read to solve these problems. At first, only one story may be used. The children may leaf through the story, noting its pictures. They may list some of the things they hope to find out. All may then read silently to find as many answers as possible. Discussion next may center around pooling the information that came out of the reading. The discussion has unity for the children because their questions helped to guide it.

A little later, a series of related stories rather than a single story may be the center of a unit. The children may discuss the topic about which the stories center. They may recall other stories on the same general theme. They may leaf through the section in the text, discussing the pictures and identifying the stories which most interest them. The reading then may take several forms. All children may read every story and share their opinions in discussion. Each child may volunteer to read a special story and report to the group. Like the third-graders described earlier, pairs of children may work on selected stories and plan for oral reading or dramatization to share their reading. Such activities as these may call for a day or more of independent reading before group sharing is begun.

Stories in readers are only one source of reading units. Children may develop their own series of experience records around a special class project. Plans for recreational reading may lead to a fruitful unit. Collecting information for other class problems may result in units based on nature or social-science books.

New groupings are not necessarily required when reading activities take on the characteristics of units of work. At times the same children will simply take on more responsibility for planning their work. There will be other times when children reading at different levels may work together to carry out unit activities centering around special interests. Such activities usually call for independent reading of stories on different levels selected with the special abilities of individuals in mind. It is also possible to plan so that several groups read about a single topic. Since many readers include sets of stories about such topics as animal life, child life in America, fantasy, and humor, it is relatively easy to provide materials on the levels desired. Such units make it possible to have certain all-class activities in the reading program even though children differ in ability.

Increased independence calls for special group activities. There will be occasions when it is important to supplement or to replace the regular activities of instructional groups with special sessions for group or individual guidance. These sessions help to provide the flexibility needed in the total reading program as children venture farther afield in their reading and encounter a greater number of special problems.

Some of the problems calling for special help are met during informational- or recreational-reading activities. It may be important to locate information about airplanes, but nobody may be very effective in using tables of contents. It would be fun to tell others about good library books, but how do you give the main idea of a story without spoiling the ending? When mothers visit us we should like to read them the records of our study of signs of spring, but that will take good readers. Such special reading problems will occur from the beginning, but they increase in number and complexity as children develop increased reading skill.

Special problems also arise because reading skill does not develop evenly in all children. At first all are likely to require help with many of the same words, and difficulties in reading are likely to center around similar problems. This soon changes. Among children reading the same five-page story with reasonable comprehension there will be wide differences in the words they do not know. There will also be differences in children's independent approaches to these unfamiliar words. Some will use the picture as a major clue. Others will rely largely upon the context. Several will be able to use phonetic elements. One type of help in word recognition no longer serves. Similarly, there may be some children who sense the general story line but do not read carefully enough to answer detailed questions. Others may find it easy to answer single questions but may need help to pull together two or three ideas into a comprehensive answer. Growth will not be regular, even though children may have worked together consistently in the same reading group.

Several types of adjustments can be made to meet special needs. Sometimes the activities of a regular reading group are planned to provide the help. Time may be taken to see how one would use a table of contents to locate information, to learn the terms needed in order to read a series of experience records, or to work on skill in reading for exact information. Sometimes special work-type materials will be used for such activities. At other times stress may be placed on the needed skill through the materials currently being read.

New problems are not all handled within existing groups. Regrouping in terms of special needs is possible. Children with oral-reading responsibilities for a program to entertain parents may meet for two or three days as a special practice group. The entire class may have difficulty deciding how to look through several books to locate special information and all may work on the problem together. Ernie, who has been ill, may need extra help to catch up. The teacher may plan a combination of work-type activities and easy reading for him and spend ten minutes a day for two or three weeks working with him alone.

How special groups are scheduled depends on how they are related to other classroom activities. If they have replaced existing reading groups, the time normally set aside in the schedule for reading activities can be used for them. If they are running concurrently with other reading groups, extra time will need to be found. Often there is room for such activities in a time-block set aside for independent work on skills. When the special reading problem is directly connected with an on-going unit, time for help may be found during the period set aside for work on the unit. Often, too, the teacher can give a few minutes' help to a special group or to an individual child while reading groups are working independently. These adjustments will be made differently from class to class, and from day to day within a single class.

Special reading activities do not complicate the total day unduly. In the first place, not many such groups are likely to be at work at any one time. Secondly, when such groups are set up, they often replace existing groups so that the total number of different reading activities is not always greatly increased. Then, many such special group activities are directly connected with on-going class plans. "We can't go any farther with our questions until we can find. . . ." "These are good stories, when can we. . . ." Once children themselves see the need for the special activity they often carry on with a minimum of help from the teacher. The pattern of reading activities that results when special needs are met is undoubtedly more complex than that in which a given number of groups work regularly with text materials. Perhaps the best justification of the additional time and effort needed to plan such varied activities comes from teachers themselves who bear witness that a little help focused directly on a problem at a time when it is crucial is worth many hours of practice provided when the need is not as urgent. The teacher has the responsibility, however, of seeing that such flexibility does not lead to haphazard experiences and to skills and vocabulary half learned because sufficient time is not devoted to them.

MAKING THE MOST OF WIDER READING EXPERIENCES

Provide opportunities for individual reading activities. Many kinds of reading experiences are essential to the development of mature readers who can work with increasing independence and can use reading to satisfy a wide range of interests. Among these experiences are those which each child pursues to satisfy his own desires for information, to practice skills in which he needs to develop higher levels of competence, or to take delight in books and stories which he reads for his own enjoyment.

Incidental reading activities provide for meaningful practice. In a typical primary classroom, children engage in many incidental reading activities in the course of a day. They read group plans for the day, check on responsibilities listed in a helpers' chart, look for new items on the bulletin board, read the bill for cookies from the grocery. In a classroom where reading serves many purposes, one or two children are reading at almost any time of the day. Almost every reading skill is represented—following directions, noting details, locating information, evaluating, summarizing, and reading aloud.

Planning sessions or sharing periods offer opportunities for reading announcements, for reading class news of the day, for checking plans. Doing housekeeping chores may call for following special directions for cleaning paintbrushes or feeding goldfish. Work periods may call for reading directions for number games, rules for using clay, or taking care of books at the library table. In second and third grades, an increasing number of activities in other skill areas, such as spelling or arithmetic, may call for reading textbooks, or directions for work-type activities. While many of these activities may be done as a member of a group, many are done independently. Individuals who use the library table, the number games, or the clay table are the ones who read the rules. The person who is responsible for duties looks for his own name and for directions for his special task. The truly functional reading matter around the classroom offers many opportunities for individuals as well as small groups to do purposeful reading.

Reading for pleasure expands horizons of all children. Primary children need time to read for pleasure. Recreational reading is highly individual, and should be an activity in which each child follows his own interests and tastes. Group experiences can be profitable, as children recommend books to others during sharing periods. Oral reading sessions, when a child reads a good story to a small audience, are greatly enjoyed. Unit activities which are developed around common interests can lead to wider experiences with reading materials. However, each child is free to read his own book and there is no particular need for him to be grouped with others who are reading materials at the same difficulty level.

Time for recreational reading needs to be definitely scheduled. Many teachers encourage children to spend time at the library table whenever they have a few free minutes, but this procedure alone does not provide for the child who works slowly and who seldom has free time, nor does it always allow enough time for better readers. Sometimes one or two recreational-reading periods are definitely scheduled during the week. Time to get acquainted with new books may be provided after a library visit, or a sharing period to tell others about good books planned before the books are returned to the library. Unit activities centering around recreational reading can be planned for the time usually allotted to group reading experiences. Story hours can be scheduled when children read to each other, or when the teacher reads to the entire group. Such activities are important to include in the weekly schedule if children are to be encouraged to read widely for their own purposes.

Even though the materials children read for pleasure are simply written, recreational-reading activities provide opportunities to help children develop increased reading skill. First-graders, especially, will need help with unfamiliar words. Even third-graders will encounter occasional words they do not know. Activities connected with sharing books with others may raise new problems. Children may also need help in locating the books they desire and in choosing books appropriate for their own reading level. Many will need to be introduced to new types of books. Then, too, the experience of reading widely, in and of itself, helps to develop increased skill.

CLASSROOM ORGANIZATION FOR THE READING ACTIVITIES OF THE PRIMARY GRADES

The methods of grouping and scheduling described in the preceeding section are flexible in order to allow for many types of reading. Groups are regularly scheduled, but on many occasions pupils also read individually. From the last half of the 1950's to the early 1960's, considerable interest has been shown in a plan of instruction that is completely individualized. Based on the concepts of "seeking, self-selection and pacing" contributed by Olsen,[2] the program provides time for the individual child to seek his own reading materials, to read them at his own rate, and to receive guidance from his teacher, who works with him in an individual conference. Group activities are not omitted in this plan, which may include sharing periods, as well as group instruction in specific skills as needed. Many reports of successful programs may be found,[3] as well as statements summarizing both the advantages and disadvantages of the plan.[4] While it is likely that further research is needed to

[2] Willard C. Olsen, "Seeking, Self-Selections, and Pacing in the Use of Books by Children," *The Packet*, (Spring, 1952), 3-10 (Boston: D. C. Heath and Company).

[3] May Lazar, "Individualized Reading: A Dynamic Approach," *The Reading Teacher*, 11 (December 1958), 76-83. Jeannette Veatch, *Individualizing Your Reading Program* (New York: G. P. Putnam's Sons, 1959).

[4] Helen Robinson, Editor. *Controversial Issues in Reading and Promising Solutions.* Supplementary Educational Monographs No. 91 (Chicago: University of Chicago Press, 1961). Paul A. Witty, "Individualized Reading—A Summary and Evaluation," *Elementary English*, **36** (October 1959), 401-412; 450. Note also the additional bibliography at the end of this chapter.

establish with some precision the exact nature of the outcomes which may be expected to result from a program of individualized reading, creative and resourceful teachers may find much of value in both the reports of practice and the evaluative comments concerning such procedures. Most writers warn, however, that the success of the program depends not only upon an alert and well-informed teacher, but also upon the presence of a considerable number of books in a wide range of difficulty and over a wide range of topics, if the needs of pupils are to be met. There is also some evidence that slower pupils make greater gains in reading when they are taught in a basic reading program than when their reading instruction is completely individualized.[5] Class size also has a bearing, since time is not likely to be available to give completely individual attention to large numbers of pupils. Suggestions have been made for combining basic and individualized reading in ways that may retain the excellencies of both approaches. Particularly desirable contributions of individualized reading appear to be the keen interest aroused, the greater amount of reading done by pupils, and the greater understanding and rapport between pupil and teacher as a consequence of the individual conferences that are a strong feature of an individualized reading program. These suggestions for achieving these desirable features in a basic program include, among others, the introduction of individual reading as a part of the regular reading program at specific times during the school year, as a part of the day's work, or as an aspect of a series of topical units. In this last instance, the pupils are expected to select materials individually from a wide range of materials bearing upon a topic of interest to them.[6]

The guides for a successful reading program described in Chapter II of this book, and the program for the primary grades, described in considerable detail in Part II, and for the intermediate grades in Part IV, assume a rich reading environment, flexibility of grouping, and a wide range of possibilities for giving the individual reader the help he needs at the time he needs it. Furthermore, the individual reader will have many opportunities for choosing, with appropriate teacher guidance, materials of particular interest to him as he takes part in the reading units, described in Chapters VII and X, and in the units in content fields as described in Chapters VIII and XI. No single kind of program, either individualized entirely or implemented through group instruction exclusively, is foreseen as being a complete answer to instructional problems. It is rather the responsibility of each teacher to discover where each child is in his reading development, and to plan experi-

---

[5] Harry W. Sartain, "The Roseville Experiment with Individualized Reading," *The Reading Teacher*, **13** (April 1960), 266-70.

[6] Harry W. Sartain, "Individualized Reading in Perspective," *Changing Concepts of Reading Instruction*, pp. 84-87. J. Allen Figurel (ed.), International Reading Association Conference Proceedings, 1961 (New York: Scholastic Magazines).

ences that will be most appropriate for him. Help is given whenever a problem arises and is planned whenever possible in relation to specific needs. Every new gain in reading skill is capitalized upon by providing new challenges to read and more freedom to use the increased skill.

ACHIEVING EFFECTIVE SCHEDULING

Large time-blocks allow for varied activities. The use of large time-blocks in scheduling primary activities has already been described in Chapter V for the beginning-reading level. In later first, and in second and third grades, the pattern is similar. Periods of as much as an hour or longer are set aside for a series of related activities.

Normally the day's activities will follow a fairly regular sequence. Allowing for flexibility in scheduling does not mean that all semblance of regularity in planning disappears, any more than adjusting the activities of a home to the lives of its members means that there will be no definite time for meals, for rising, or for going to bed. A well-planned program allows for emergencies while it establishes routines. As teacher and children work together, certain times will be set aside for definite activities. Evaluation and planning may come late in the day or first thing in the morning, depending on the children's abilities to keep plans in mind. Some detailed planning will almost always come immediately before an activity is begun. This helps to guarantee that individuals will be clear about their parts in activity. Time will be set aside for housekeeping chores. Definite periods will be devoted to group work on unit activities. Within this framework one or more blocks of time will be saved, rather regularly, for individual and for group activities planned to develop basic skills in such areas as reading, oral and written expression, and number.

Typically, a first grade teacher allows time for the following:

First hour in the morning	Planning and work period. Usually this time is used for strenuous work—building, playing in the playhouse, and other activities that are hard to do quietly. At the end of the hour, there is time allowed for clearing up and getting ready for outdoor play.
Half-hour period	Outdoor play, active games, lunch and rest periods.
One and one-half hour block of time	Work on fundamental skills, with time allowed for cleaning up, and for evaluation of the morning's work.

LUNCH HOUR

First afternoon hour	Planning and sharing group activities connected with a unit of work.
Half-hour period	Outdoor play, rhythms, music.
Second afternoon hour	Individual activities, group evaluation and planning. Preparation for dismissal.

This is the schedule of an experienced teacher. Beginners might well simplify the variety of activities and the number of groups at work. Depending upon the degree to which functional classroom activities are contributing to growth in fundamental skills, more time might need to be provided for specific instruction.

How might the activities of this first grade develop if one were to follow the children at work for a typical day? Four reading groups are at work.

The first hour, from 9:00 to 10:00, was usually a work period when strenuous activities connected with a unit of work were carried out. The children were concerned about remodeling their playhouse so as to have a model kitchen. The first few minutes of the period were spent checking attendance and collecting lunch money. One child at each table was responsible for telling how many children were present at his table. Later, the children helped the teacher add to see how many boys and how many girls were present, and helped her add the lunch money. Then active work on the playhouse began. The group who had volunteered to paint wallpaper worked on that. Several of the boys who had planned to make a stove and a refrigerator went to work with hammer and nails. Three of the girls laundered the curtains. Some children who wanted to plant a small window box worked with the teacher.

In the first hour, children who did not have any special responsibilities for the playhouse had notes for their mothers regarding a special program to finish copying, pictures to paint, and housekeeping tasks to carry out. Several spent time with some number games. The teacher worked with the class as a whole long enough to be sure that plans were clear and then circulated around the room, giving help as needed. The reading done during this period was an all-class activity, as the children helped to compose a short news bulletin telling what the weather was like and giving one or two other special events, checked a list of plans for the playhouse, and noted changes in the helpers' chart. On another day a reading group might meet for part of this period.

Work on various aspects of fundamental skills was the usual activity for the block of time consisting of an hour or more beginning at 10:30. During this period, practice in writing and number experiences found their place along with reading. Creative work in art was sometimes used as an independent activity for this period. On the day being described, the children undertook a variety of activities. Some worked on work-type exercises in number; some had the notes to their mothers, mentioned previously, to complete; two children worked at the easel; and those in one reading group completed work-type activities prepared by their teacher and planned in the preceding meeting of their reading group.

While individual work went on, reading groups met with the teacher. She took time first to check briefly with a group of advanced readers who had a story to finish reading independently, and with the group who had the work-type activities to complete. Assured that these two groups were at work, she called a third. After work with this group was completed the teacher took a few minutes to check on the progress of other activities. Children with problems had a few of their questions answered. Those who had finished reading their story independently were reminded that they had planned to draw a picture of the part of the story they liked best. Then the fourth reading group was called. The last part of the period was spent working with the children who were completing work-type activities in number.

On another day it might be important to spend more time during the 10:30 period with number activities, or to work as a class on thank-you notes to be written to another grade. If these activities took up a greater share of time, group work in reading might be planned for one of the two time-blocks in the afternoon. The last period in the afternoon, particularly, allowed for a variety of additional experiences in skill areas.

Work from 1:00 to 2:10 in the afternoon usually centered around experiences with a unit of work. If the early-morning period involved construction activities, the afternoon period was likely to stress language experiences. Three times a week, the first fifteen minutes were used as a sharing period for children to talk about interesting happenings at home or to show objects they had brought to school.

After the sharing period, on the day being described, the children discussed a recent trip to a farm. They checked the list of questions they raised before they took their trip and saw how many they could answer. The teacher helped them to make a list of things the farmer said he did. This she later printed as an experience record. Someone suggested that they could write a whole book about the farm, and they took a few minutes to suggest what might be included. The teacher jotted down this list of suggestions for posting later. Then each child went to his table to draw a picture about the part of the trip he liked the best. Later these pictures would be given captions and posted.

During the second afternoon time-block activities were largely individual, and the children turned to the easel, the play corner, and the library corner. As children become more adept at writing, this was a period when short stories were written, to be posted later on the bulletin board. In the early fall it was sometimes a period when the children told stories which the teacher took down and later mimeographed in simpler form. Dramatization and story telling were also scheduled for this period from time to time. Once a week, recreational reading was shared.

On the day being described, the teacher worked with children individually, giving constructive criticism, suggesting new approaches, and helping with special problems. Then she called together the children who had been doing work-type exercises in reading, checked their work, and introduced them to the new book they were to start to read. For the last few minutes of the period the children shared their farm pictures and checked on their plans for the playhouse for the morrow.

The general framework of a third-grade schedule will be quite similar to the first-grade schedule that has just been described. Two large time-blocks for unit activities, a third for individual or group work on fundamental skills, and a fourth for various experiences with creative expression are provided. Instructional groups in reading, as well as group or class activities in spelling, arithmetic, and written expression are scheduled during the first long period. The special emphasis will vary with the need. Children who are not working with the teacher will be working independently on various related activities. Additional help on skills will often be given during part of the last period in the afternoon. This help will usually be on an individual basis so that the teacher is able to move about rather freely.

Pupil-teacher planning provides for needed continuity. Time for planning and for evaluation is an important feature of the schedules that have been described. Children are able to go ahead with many types of activities without the teacher's direct supervision because they know what they are doing. Pupil-teacher planning not only guarantees that worth-while activities will proceed smoothly while the teacher works with a reading group; it also guarantees that the work of the reading group itself will proceed smoothly. Children are sometimes helped to lay plans calling for independent work lasting two or three days. The purposes of work-type activities can also be talked through with profit in the reading group.

As children carry out group plans, the teacher is free to work with the individuals or with the groups most needing her help. She does not try to direct every step of an activity. Her responsibility is to see that plans are clear, to give whatever help is needed as an activity gets under way, and then to work intensively at the points where her assistance is most important. At times this means that the teacher works with reading groups while the children who are not reading move ahead on the plans for a unit of work. At times she may work on a particular aspect of the unit. At times she makes sure that the entire class is occupied with various independent activities and then gives help to individual children.

Children develop increased ability to carry out plans independently as they mature, and as they are given successful experiences in planning. First-graders will not asume as varied independent responsibilities as will third-graders. Their plans will be simpler; their ability to work cooperatively in groups will not be as well developed; their projects are likely to be shorter; and they are likely to need more direct guidance from the teacher. With increased experience and maturity should come increased ability to carry out more elaborate projects.

Independent reading ability can be capitalized upon. In the classrooms described earlier, teachers are able to make maximum use of the time they have available to give help in reading because they capitalize on children's ability to read independently. Unless her help is needed, the teacher does not sit with a group of children while they complete the reading of a story. She may introduce hard words and help the children establish some purposes to guide their reading, but then she is likely to work with another group, and to come back to the first group for a discussion period after they have finished their reading. First-graders will not be able to do as much independent reading as third-graders, but even beginners should be expected to be able to work alone.

Part of the secret of enabling primary children to read independently is to use materials that increase in difficulty very gradually, or to provide for some experiences with supplementary books that review vocabulary that is already familiar. Recreational reading and informational reading, particularly, will go forward more smoothly if the materials available are well within children's grasp. Then, too, most children will profit from a variety of follow-up or work-type activities that call for rereading the story or for reviewing new words. These activities are usually done independently. They also are more readily carried out if the directions are easy to read. Children learn to read by reading. Their experiences need not be restricted to the times when the teacher is free to work with them.

Flexibility in day-by-day activities helps to increase the richness of the total reading program. Another characteristic of the schedules that have been described is their flexibility. There are no rigid prescriptions regarding the number of times during the week that a reading group meets with the teacher, the number of minutes a day to be devoted to the group, the sequence in which stories are read, or the extent to which a given group of children are to work together. As a result considerable flexibility and variety in children's reading activities is achieved without sacrificing the continuity of experience that is important for consistent growth. After a set of stories in a basal text has been completed, the children may go to stories on a similar topic in another book, or may take time to do some extra work with the experience records developing out of a unit of work. Work in reading groups may be stopped for a time to give help to interest groups working on reading problems related to a unit. Separate groups may not meet for a day or so while the class as a whole concentrates on a special reading problem. The children in a reading group may need an extended amount of the teacher's time today in order to become acquainted with a new book. Tomorrow they may work alone. There are only a limited number of minutes in the school day. If children are to be given varied reading experiences, their schedule should be planned with the need for flexibility in mind.

Many skills can be taught in relation to the unit in which the problem arises. A typical primary program provides for one or more units of work to help children become acquainted with their physical and their social environment; gives opportunities for creative expression through art, music, and other media; provides for active play and cares for other health needs; and, in addition, allows time for the development of ability to read, to write, to speak, and to use number concepts. At first glance this program seems likely to overwhelm small children with the multitude of its activities. Actually this is not the case. Individual activities of a creative nature are planned for definite times in the schedule. Games, lunch, and rest periods are also scheduled on a definite basis. Many of the child's experiences in language, reading, and number are integrated with on-going unit activities. As a result, the periods set aside for work on fundamental skills carry only part of the child's total experiences with these important aspects of his curriculum.

Unit activities offer time to develop new skills and, perhaps more important, they offer ample realistic opportunities for practice. Children write letters to a classmate who is ill. They come across words they do not know. They are given immediate help and then, after the letter is written, they may take time to add some of the most important of these words to their spelling list. Some young architects need information before they can rig the elevator in their model apartment house. For the entire period set aside for unit activities they hunt through reading materials looking for pictures and descriptions that will help. A group is making curtains for the playhouse. The children cannot measure the cloth accurately and time is taken for an arithmetic session in which they learn simple facts about using a ruler. Much valuable experience in every skill area can be secured through such integrated activities if the teacher is alert to the possibilities.

Time to work with individuals is considered important. Teachers find time to work with individual children in the classrooms that have been described. Time is taken for a few minutes' discussion with a child during a period when the entire class reads independently; during a free work period when many types of activities are going on; in recreational-reading periods when each child is at work with his own book; as work on a unit goes forward. These short contacts with single pupils are a natural outcome of the flexible planning and scheduling that has been described. They need to be thought of as making a valuable contribution to the total reading program.

GROUPING TO MEET SPECIAL NEEDS

Children who work together most consistently are at about the same level of reading ability. Reading groups, as described in this chapter, develop in terms of the needs of the situation. The children who work together the most frequently are usually those of about the same level of reading ability. They may also work in these same groups when a difficult informational-reading task is faced. Ability groups are used less frequently for recreational-reading activities, although certain reading units centering around recreational reading have been suggested as appropriate for group experiences. As suggested earlier, size of group and number of groups depend upon many factors in the immediate situation. No two classes will necessarily be organized in exactly the same way.

In the situations described, the regularity with which groups of the same reading ability work together on sequential activities with a basal reader decreases as children become able to work independently and competent to take on other types of reading activities. This does not necessarily reduce the number of group activities under way, but it results in changes in the personnel of groups and in the focus of their activities. Consistent growth in reading skill, in the classrooms described, is secured through the integration of all the child's reading experiences. The sequential activities provided for him in a reading group are not expected to provide completely for the orderly development of his reading skill.

Specific reading needs are the basis for short-term groups. A second type of ability grouping used in the classrooms that were described is the short-term group of selected children with a special reading problem—some first-graders who need a little more help with word recognition; five or six third-graders who still have not grasped the basic techniques of word analysis; several who have special trouble taking notes in reading several books for information; three children who were ill and who need a little extra help. Special sessions with such groups for a few days, a week, or a month may often prevent serious remedial problems. Not many such groups are likely to be meeting at one time, and not all children will be involved. These short-term groups should be considered as a means of giving individualized help, should be set up when a special problem arises, and continued only until the need is met.

Interest groups are possible when materials and guidance are individualized. A number of examples of regrouping in terms of special reading interests are given in the preceding section—a group specially interested in one aspect of a unit; a book club meeting to share stories; the people who went on an excursion meeting to prepare their report; the members of the entertainment committee getting ready to read class records to their mothers. The size of interest groups, the frequency with which they meet, and the length of time they work together varies with the problem at hand. They are one important way of securing a more flexible reading program, and of making the best use of informational- and recreational-reading activities.

All reading experiences do not call for groups. It is important to remember that considerable practice and some valuable instruction in reading can be given without setting up any groups at all. The programs described earlier make definite provision for all-class experiences, such as checking plans, reading bulletin boards, discussing how to locate information, sharing library books, and reading special books bearing on a group problem. In these classrooms there are also provisions for children to work alone, for recreational-reading, and for certain experiences related to informational reading. When all the child's independent reading experiences, as well as the times when he works in interest groups, are considered as part of his total reading program, there need not be concern if the schedule does not always allow for work in a reading group for every child in the room. There are many avenues for teaching reading, and the program is richer when they are all used.

Pupil-teacher planning makes flexibility in grouping possible. Just as pupil-teacher planning is essential in flexible scheduling, so it is the basis of flexible grouping.

A child can undertake several reading activities at the same time if he has shared in the plans. He may work with one group to complete a basal-reader story and then go to a second group where he helps to locate information in connection with a science activity. If he has shared in the decision that it is important for him to have some special help in word analysis, he is ready when his special practice group is called. When he has been one of the group to suggest that it would be fun to read a story to the kindergarten children next door, he knows what kind of preparation he needs when the teacher suggests that he reread the story to be sure he can recognize all the words. In classrooms, as in life out of school, it is possible to engage successfully in a complex set of activities if one's purposes are clear.

It is important for children to learn to identify their weaknesses as well as their strengths. Many teachers are concerned because typical instructional groups, no matter how carefully named, are quickly identified by children as having the best readers or the poorest readers. The stigma of being in one of the slower groups is largely removed in a classroom where the emphasis, not only in reading but in other areas is, "Where do you most need help, and where can you help others." Each child will be in certain situations where he realizes that he needs more practice, but he will be in others where he is the leader and other children turn to him. If the emphasis is correctly placed, children can gain just as much satisfaction out of being able to plan for further help as they do out of being classified as being in "the best group."

An effective reading program is a cooperative enterprise. Teachers contribute their technical knowledge of how growth in reading takes place, their instructional skill, their knowledge of the needs of individuals, and their command of materials. The children contribute their problems and interests, their advice in laying plans, their evaluation of their own strengths and weaknesses, their ideas of how to work together to help each other. Together they develop the activities which make for the greatest growth.

SOME QUESTIONS TO THINK ABOUT IN APPRAISING THE READING EXPERIENCES PROVIDED FOR THE PRIMARY GRADES

1. Are many types of reading activities being provided?
2. Is care being taken to integrate the child's reading activities so that he makes consistent growth in the development of skill in recognizing new words and in working with more difficult materials?
3. Is help in reading being given whenever a reading problem is faced?
4. Are children being encouraged to take on independent reading activities commensurate with their ability?
5. Are children being encouraged to take on more complicated and challenging reading tasks as their ability warrants it?
6. Are reading experiences planned in such a way that other types of important learning experiences are not curtailed?
7. Are reading groups flexible in terms of the needs of the situation?
8. Are schedules flexible so as to allow for varied types of activities?
9. Are children encouraged to share in planning their reading activities?

SUGGESTIONS FOR FURTHER READING

Dawson, Mildred A., and Bamman, Henry A. *Fundamentals of Basic Reading Instruction.* Chapters 4 and 5. New York: Longmans, Green and Company, 1959. 304 pp.

DeBoer, John J., and Dallman, Martha. *The Teaching of Reading.* Chapter 13. New York: Holt, Rinehart and Winston, Inc., 1960. 360 pp.

Harris, Albert J. "Reading and Human Development," *Development in and Through Reading,* pp. 17-34. Sixtieth Yearbook of the National Society for the Study of Education, Part I. Chicago: The University of Chicago Press, 1961. 406 pp.

Hildreth, Gertrude, "Reading Programs in Grades II and III," *Reading in the Elementary School,* pp. 93-126. Forty-eighth Yearbook of the National Society for the Study of Education, Part II. Chicago: The University of Chicago Press, 1949. 343 pp.

Hildreth, Gertrude. *Teaching Reading.* Chapter 12. New York: Henry Holt and Company, 1959. 612 pp.

McKim, Margaret G.; Hansen, Carl W.; and Carter, William L. *Learning to Teach in the Elementary School.* Chapter 6. New York: The MacMillan Company, 1959. 612 pp.

Primary Manual, Revised. Cincinnati: Cincinnati Public Schools, January 1963.

Robinson, Helen M. (Editor). *Reading Instruction in Various Patterns of Grouping.* Supplementary Educational Monographs No. 89. Chicago: The University of Chicago Press, 1959. 212 pp.

Russell, David H. *Children Learn to Read.* Second Edition, Chapter 7. Boston: Ginn and Company, 1961. 612 pp.

INDIVIDUALIZED READING

Brogan, Peggy, and Fox, Lorene K. *Helping Children Read.* New York: Holt, Rinehart and Winston, Inc., 1961. 350 pp.

Chatz, Esther E., and others. *Exploring Independent Reading in the Primary Grades.* Bulletin 2. Center for School Experimentation, Ohio State University, Columbus, Ohio, 1960. 70 pp.

Darrow, Helen Fisher, and Hawes, Virgil M. *Approaches to Individualized Reading Instruction.* New York: Appleton-Century-Crofts, 1960. 102 pp.

Groff, Patrick J. "Materials for Individualized Reading," *Elementary English.* **38** (January 1961), 1-7.

Lazar, May. "Individualized Reading: A Dynamic Approach," *The Reading Teacher.* **11** (December 1957), 75-83.

Miel, Alice. (Editor). *Individualizing Reading Practices.* Practical Suggestions for Teaching, No. 14. New York: Bureau of Publications, Teachers College, Columbia University, 1958.

Robinson, Helen. (Editor). *Controversial Issues in Reading and Promising Solutions.* Supplementary Educational Monographs No. 91. Chicago: University of Chicago Press, 1961.

———. "News and Comments," *Elementary School Journal.* **60** (May 1960), 411-420.

Sartain, Henry W. "Bibliography on Individualized Reading," *The Reading Teacher.* **13** (April 1960), 262-265; 270.

Stauffer, Russell G. "Individualized and Group Type Directed Reading Instruction," *Elementary English.* **37** (October 1960), 375-382.

Veatch, Jeannette. *Individualizing Your Reading Program.* New York: G. P. Putnam's Sons, 1959. 242 pp.

Witty, Paul, and others. "Individualized Reading—A Summary and Evaluation," *Elementary English.* **36** (October 1959), 401-412; 450.

CHAPTER VII

Providing Direct Reading
Instruction for Primary Children

WHAT activities are appropriate when children who have progressed beyond the beginning-reading stage meet in groups for reading instruction? As was indicated in Chapter VI, approaches to group reading activities will be as varied as the groups themselves, their needs, their interests, the materials available to them, and the reading skills of their members. Nevertheless, primary teachers face certain recurring problems for which general guides and illustrative procedures can be suggested.

First, there is the problem of finding appropriate reading materials. Second, the teacher must decide how to guide the work with a story or set of stories. Third, there is the question of how best to give additional help to meet the needs of individuals. How and when should work-type activities be provided? How can the children themselves be helped to become aware of their needs to develop special skills? This chapter is focused on these general problems.

Two other problem areas of concern to primary teachers are discussed in the chapters that follow. Chapter VIII contains suggestions of ways of guiding children's informational- and recreational-reading activities, and Chapter IX suggestions for helping them acquire effective word-study skills.

PROVIDING READING MATERIALS FOR THE PRIMARY GRADES

Providing the range, variety, and quantity of reading material needed for the extensive activities of an effective reading program is a major problem for most teachers at all grade levels. What factors might be considered in equipping classrooms with materials adequate for the reading needs of primary children?

Basal readers make an important contribution. The colorful books from basal-reading series are perhaps the best source of carefully graded materials. The stories are well illustrated, and usually grouped around topics of interest to children. They are written with careful regard for such problems as vocabulary load, sentence and paragraph length of total story.[1] When a classroom is equipped with sets of about a dozen copies from a number of series, it is possible for children to read at different levels. This policy also provides a greater total variety of well-graded materials for all children, and it is likely to result in a greater selection of stories on topics of particular interest to a class.

Basal readers need to be chosen to cover the three- to four-year range in ability that will be typical of most classes. Within one school, it is sometimes helpful to come to a general agreement regarding the allotment of basal series to specific grades. Often it is possible to designate one or two series as specially valuable for children who are progressing slowly, and to hold them strictly for this purpose. Similarly, other books may be reserved for children who are making rapid progress and be used regularly in a school grade lower than that for which the book is designated by its author. Some such system guarantees that new and interesting materials of the correct degree of difficulty will be available for all.

Providing basal texts of varied difficulty levels is not entirely a matter of adjusting to the range in reading ability in a given class. Every reader, at times, needs to work with materials simpler than those being used to help him develop new vocabulary and master more complex sentence and paragraph structure. Recreational reading calls for easy materials; so does oral reading before an audience. First attempts at locating specific information, too, are more successful when unfamiliar vocabulary and difficult sentence structure do not complicate the problem.

The quantity of carefully graded material in a classroom can be increased by systematic purchases of sets of supplementary readers. These readers, which vary in size from small paperbound booklets to full-length books, are designed to review the vocabulary of the basal texts. There are a number of ways in which they can be used. They provide one source of independent recreational reading. They also offer easy new materials for children who need extended experience with stories of a given grade level. Sometimes

---

[1] For a description and analysis of these materials see: Vergil E. Herrick, and others, "Basal Instructional Materials in Reading," *Development in and Through Reading*, pp. 165-188. Sixtieth Yearbook of the National Society for the Study of Education, Part I (Chicago: The University of Chicago Press, 1961).

they are the texts reserved for use with the children who are having trouble with the regular materials provided for their grade. Because the vocabulary in these supplementary books is familiar, they are often useful as relatively easy reading for dramatization, oral-reading, or informational-reading purposes.

Many materials for independent reading are needed. Children learn to read by reading. From the beginning it is important to have available as large a number as possible of attractive, easy, and interesting books which they can read independently.

Variety is necessary. Since there will be a wide range of tastes and interests, it is best to have books and selections on a wide range of topics, particularly in the area of informational books. There should be balance, too, in content. Factual materials as well as fiction, fairy stories, picture books, books of poetry all make a contribution. Although a range of difficulty is desirable, it is well to remember that the less able reader will need materials for independent reading which are significantly easier than those which can be used for instructional purposes, and the better reader will not be harmed by reading these easy books. He will learn from them the joy of reading, and can use them to practice his new skills at a more rapid, fluent and flexible pace.

Many teachers are at some pains not only to provide a satisfying number of attractive books, but also to promote a good reading atmosphere in their classrooms. An attractive library corner has already been mentioned. Perhaps the children themselves can help to plan and provide for such a spot for reading pleasure. The care of the books is important—how they are circulated among the group. It is not too early for children to learn to respect books, to classify them under simple headings, and to help "check them out" to readers.

For many teachers the great problem is how to get the books there! Some brief suggestions for building up a classroom collection may be helpful. Fortunately, some elementary schools are providing a classroom library although there is need for more generous provisions for libraries for each room. A school library from which books for classroom use may be borrowed is a fortunate addition to the resources of some elementary schools. In some localities a bookmobile service is offered and children may withdraw the books of their own choosing, as well as have a classroom collection. Local public libraries often arrange to have classroom collections made up; these may be kept several weeks. Less fruitful, perhaps, but still useful, is the practice of suggesting that children share their own books with the class. Such procedure requires some tact in playing down the titles that have less classroom value, but are still dear to their owners.

Often valuable materials, particularly good stories and some factual materials, are available in older and less frequently used textbooks in the classroom. Copies of supplementary readers, basal readers no longer needed for group activities, and informational magazines, especially those with large and attractive pictures, all add to the stock of reading materials.

Perhaps equally important to developing some resources for reading is the interest shown by the teacher. The attitude that reading is important, that time may be planned for just browsing and enjoying books, and sharing the pleasure and excitement of a new-found book, all contribute to the interest and enthusiasm shown by the learner.

Primary children need to become acquainted with reference books. To some extent in first grade, and increasingly in second and third, simple textbooks will be available in such content fields as science, social studies, health, and safety. These materials allow children to begin to use more than one resource in solving an informational-reading problem.

Children's encyclopedias, dictionaries, and other standard reference texts have a place, too, in the primary classroom, especially in the third grade. Picture dictionaries are useful almost from the beginning. With many groups it will be the teacher who does most of the actual reading of such materials, although advanced third-graders often take great satisfaction in being able to read an article in an encyclopedia for themselves. It is in the intermediate grades that skilled independent use of standard reference texts develops the most rapidly.

The variety of available material is increased if pamphlets and clippings are saved. Providing sufficient material for informational reading is often particularly difficult in the early primary grades. The total supply of informational material can be increased somewhat if a systematic effort is made to clip and save pictures and articles that give promise of remaining timely for a year or so after the date of the publication. Some of these may come from adult magazines, pamphlets, and travel folders; others from children's magazines and newspapers.

One system of saving pictures and short articles is to clip each one and to mount it on heavy colored paper or cardboard. Material that needs to be folded will wear out less quickly if it and its mounting are cut and hinged with tape. Folders for these materials can be classified according to topics representing typical areas of interest. A simple code of call numbers with which the folder and each article in it can be labelled is a help in keeping such a file organized.

A method of assigning call numbers that simplifies the task of keeping a file in alphabetical order as new topics are added is to put the folder for each new topic at the end of the file, giving it the next available call number, and then to keep in alphabetical order an up-to-date list of topics. Numerals may be assigned to major topics, such as animals, transportation, or weather, and the assigned numeral, together with a letter, be used to indicate sub-topics. Topics selected for classification purposes need to be large enough in scope to include a reasonable body of material, but small enough to make it easy to locate needed items. A portion of the file of folders might look as follows:[2]

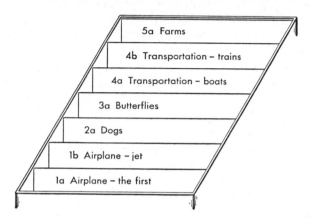

5a Farms
4b Transportation – trains
4a Transportation – boats
3a Butterflies
2a Dogs
1b Airplane – jet
1a Airplane – the first

The list of call numbers posted near this file or, if the collection grows very extensive, kept in a card catalog, would contain all the words that might possibly serve as key words in locating materials, arranged in alphabetical order as follows:

TOPIC	CODE NUMBER
Airplane	
The first	1a
Jet	1b
Animals	
Dogs	2a
Boats	4a
Butterflies	3a
Dogs	2a
Farms	5a
Trains	4b
Transportation	
Airplanes (see airplane)	
Boats	4a
Trains	4b

[2] This, and subsequent suggestions on filing are adapted from: Mildred English and Florence B. Stratemeyer, "Selection and Organization of Materials of Instruction," *Materials of Instruction*, pp. 129-148. Eighth Yearbook of the Department of Supervisors and Directors of Instruction of the National Education Association (New York: Teachers College, Columbia University, 1935).

The classroom library also can be increased if a systematic effort is made to save helpful parts of textbooks that have been worn out and are destined for disposal. Single stories or selected chapters from such books can be rebound with a stapled cover of colored paper and attractively titled. Several months issues of children's weekly newspapers or magazines can be saved and bound in the same way. In the primary classroom most richly equipped for reading experiences, good material is never discarded until it is completely worn out or its content obsolete.

Materials written by the teacher have an important place in the reading matter of the primary grades. Many teachers also write simplified materials for children which they mimeograph or hectograph. Some of these will be edited versions of stories the children themselves have dictated, some will be simplifications of materials found in resources too difficult for the children to read, and some may be simpler versions of fairy- or folk tales needed for purposes of dramatization or oral reading. Typically, materials written for one class have limited value a second year. However, there may be times when a story or chart that has proven to be particularly helpful will be saved and re-used with another group.

Available resources are used most effectively when they are cataloged systematically. A single book may serve more than one purpose. It may be an interesting story for recreational reading and, at the same time, a helpful authentic account of pioneer life. Similarly, a story in a basal reader may be helpful for informational reading, and at the same time provide recreational material about a special holiday; and a book in the public library that is difficult to read may contain excellent pictures for informational purposes. Full use of such resources can be made more readily if a systematic catalog is kept of them.

One simple method of keeping track of all available material is to develop an annotated card file, classified according to topics of interest to a given grade. The topical classification of each book or story would be placed at the top of the card where it could be seen easily. Below would be put the name of the book, the author and publisher, date of publication, library call number (if the book is located in the school or the public library), and a brief annotation regarding its readability, the helpfulness of its pictures, and any special information about its appeal to children. Often a single book will require several cross-reference cards. In one basal reader, for example, might be sets of stories providing information on animals, on farms, on children in other lands. A story about pioneer life might have a particularly good description of the furnishings in a pioneer home, and might also be classified as giving helpful information on transportation.

An annotated file makes available to the teacher a complete list of all the materials on a given topic to be found in basal readers, in other books in the classroom, and in the school or community library. Pamphlets and pictures stored in the teacher's materials file also may be annotated, if this is desired. Sometimes it is helpful to use colored cards to indicate the location of the material—white if it is in a basal reader, blue if it is in the school library, yellow if it is in the public library.

WORKING WITH STORY MATERIALS IN READING GROUPS

There is no one best plan for working with story materials in reading groups. At one time the children may be reading a set of stories; at another studying a single story. Some of the material they read will be humorous, some factual, some fanciful. Some will lend itself to oral reading, some to dramatization, and some merely to discussion. The teacher's plan for the lesson or series of lessons will depend upon the nature of the material and the purposes of the group work.

Even though the exact details of a group reading session will vary from story to story, certain general steps will still need to be taken. If the material contains many new words which the children are not likely to be able to analyze independently, there has to be some plan for introducing them. There also needs to be some preliminary discussion to arouse interest and to clarify the purposes for which the children are to read. Then time is allowed for the reading of the new material. Discussion of what has been read in relation to the original purposes usually follows. Questions suggested by the story, ideas for sharing it with other groups, for reading parts of it aloud, or for locating other stories on the same topic often lead to a variety of rereading or follow-up activities. Group work has unity and interest, in terms of agreed-upon purposes, even with the simplest materials.

GIVING HELP WITH NEW WORDS

Increase the number of new words gradually. Until children have developed a sufficient level of skill in word analysis to assure reasonable success in their independent reading, materials used in reading groups should introduce new words gradually and repeat them frequently. The less skill the reader has the more crucial it is to control the vocabulary he encounters. Even adults find the going hard when they read materials containing technical terms, and difficult concepts in a field which is new to them.

The control of new vocabulary is found in the carefully-constructed stories in basal readers, and the use of the readers is one guarantee that words will be introduced slowly and repeated frequently. It does not follow, however, that children need to read the stories in strict order in a single reader or keep only to the books in a single series. In the first place children in their earliest contacts with reading are working in a classroom environment intended to develop a larger word-recognition vocabulary. "New" words in any given reader may not be unfamiliar, nor may a different story in a different reader prove to offer more difficulties in recognizing words. There is also a common vocabulary from series to series,[3] and if children are reading in different books to find answers to questions about a common problem, there will be a natural repetition of words. Vocabulary basic to the unit topic is likely to be repeated in classroom-experience records or other projects. Finally, the proportion of new to familiar words even may be reduced if a group moves from a basal reader to a supplementary book which repeats familiar vocabulary, or to a somewhat simpler basal reader from another series.

If children are to make satisfactory progress in learning to read, teachers must be concerned about the amount of new vocabulary and the rate at which it is introduced. However, procedures for achieving control of new vocabulary should be guided by the abilities, backgrounds, and needs of the group, not by the technical aspects of the construction of a basal-reader series alone. The less able the group, the more important the sequential development of vocabulary in a single series may be.

Introduce new words ahead of time if difficulty is foreseen. When it is apparent that a number of new words are likely to make the reading difficult, they can be introduced before the story or the group of stories is read. How much time is spent on this activity and how it is done depend on the particular situation. Typically the new words are presented in such a way that the children have an opportunity to see them clearly and to think about their meanings. With a group skilled in word analysis, the teacher may merely list the new words and see how many of them the children can work out for themselves. If the pictures in the story are appropriate, they are sometimes used to develop new meanings, and the new terms are written on the board as they are identified. Sometimes a short paragraph containing the new words is written on the chalkboard and discussed. Occasionally an excursion or an exhibit precedes the story, and the new vocabulary is developed out of this experience. The preliminary discussion, extensive or brief, should serve to call children's attention to the configurations of the new words, to develop their meanings, and to do this in a setting that enriches the approach to the story.

Encourage independence whenever possible. In their zeal to make learning to read interesting and enjoyable to children, teachers should not be tempted to give more help with new words than is necessary. Children need

---

[3] Hildreth, *Teaching Reading, op. cit.,* pp. 384-386.

the experience of solving word-study problems for themselves. From the beginning they may gain considerable independence by adept use of context and picture clues. As their skill in word analysis grows, they need to be encouraged to use it. Further, children who read widely add to their word-recognition vocabulary so rapidly that extensive preliminary word-study activities are very likely to take up an undue amount of time on words already familiar to many in the group.

A safe rule in planning word-study activities prior to the reading of the story is to allow as much independence as possible. Difficult-to-analyze key words on which the meaning of the story hinges could well have some attention. So could unusual proper nouns. Context and picture clues need to be considered. For example, the word *flowers* would not be difficult if it were written in a sentence in which the other words were familiar and accompanied by an illustration of a boy with some pictured seed packages in his hand. *Ball* would be relatively easy in *Betty threw the* ——— *to Jim;* but it would be difficult in *Betty's* ——— *is on the table.* Consider also word-analysis skills; expect to spend relatively more time in preliminary word-study activities with children of first-grade reading ability than with typical third-graders. Special study of new words is, in a sense, a crutch, to be discarded gradually as children develop ways of working out their word-study problems for themselves.

Provide help as the story is being read. More opportunity can be given to a child to try his wings in word recognition if help is available when he gets into trouble. The teacher can work with a child quietly while the others read silently.

Help with a new word given to a child who is in the midst of reading a story should be reasonably prompt. However, this does not mean that he is merely told each word with which he has trouble. Eventually he must learn to puzzle them out for himself and the aid he is given should teach him how to go about it. A brief pause for a word-study problem will not destroy the continuity of the story. Sometimes the child can be reminded of the previous setting in which he met the word. Sometimes he can be helped to use a picture or a context clue. For more skilled readers the teacher may write the word on the board or on a pad of paper, and give a little help with word analysis. Typically, after a child has figured out the new word, he is asked to read it in context to be sure it fits. Whatever the exact nature of the assistance, it should have a dual emphasis: first, can you figure it out for yourself; and, second, does the word you arrived at make sense in the story?

Provide additional experiences to review new words. How easily children assimilate new words depends partially on how thoroughly familiar they are with the old ones in the same story setting. Once a word has been introduced, review should be provided to help the children remember it. Some-

Cincinnati Public Schools

Meanings of words are enriched by experience, and careful reading is important when success depends on following directions.

times the teacher may close a group session by a brief review of the words for which help has been requested. Many of the follow-up activities described later in this section provide an opportunity to re-use new vocabulary as the story is reread for specific purposes. Classroom experience records may sometimes review new terms. It is also possible to plan worktype activities to focus specifically on new vocabulary, such as those described in Chapter IX. In addition, it is important to capitalize on the typical construction of primary materials. There will be many times when the best review will come through meeting the new words again in a different story setting.

GUIDING THE READING OF THE STORY

Make it easy to read together. A most helpful arrangement is the grouping of chairs in a circle near the chalkboard. Word study is facilitated and children needing help are near to receive it. Such a grouping, helpful in the primary grades, is still useful in grades four, five, and six. However, if the children are working with large books or unwieldy materials, they may be able to work better around a table. The library corner may be a convenient work spot, or three or four groups may have need for working in different parts of the room, getting help from the teacher as needed, and perhaps meeting later for discussion. Fundamental to good work habits and to uninterrupted progress is the kind of pupil-teacher planning previously described, which assures opportunities for increasingly responsible and independent work on the part of children, not only in their reading groups, but in other activities as well.

Establish purposes for reading. Intelligent reading is purposeful reading. A first step, when a group starts to work with a new story or series of stories, is to make sure that interest in the story has been developed and that there are some agreed-upon purposes for reading. This usually means that a little time is taken to talk about the story before the reading begins. Occasionally the teacher takes the lead in raising questions or writes a series of questions on the board. More frequently purposes are arrived at jointly. The title of the story or the pictures are often used to stimulate discussion. "Here is a story about animals in the circus. Can you guess which ones?" "Our new story is called *An Adventure*. Does anyone know what an adventure is?" Sometimes the reading activities are planned around a holiday or a special event and the discussion helps to build background. "What does Halloween make you think of? . . ." "Here are some Halloween stories. Let's see which one looks the most interesting." Sometimes the story is chosen because it contains information needed for a unit of work. "We've been talking about people who help us. Here is a story about one of them." Often the story is one of a series all bearing on the same topic, and the children are helped to recall what they have already read.

Out of the introductory discussion should come some definite questions to point up the reading to follow. These questions should be thought provoking and, in most cases, rather general. Ideally, no two stories will be handled alike. Teachers sometimes feel they have not done full justice to a story unless the children are led to answer a carefully planned series of detailed questions. But this is not the only kind of reading children need to learn to do. They also need to discover that different types of stories can contribute to different kinds of interests. One can read rapidly when concerned with only a general understanding of the story, but one must proceed carefully if detailed information is required. Variety in approaches to new materials is important even for beginners. As the materials become more diverse, the purposes for which they are read also need to be expanded.

Plan for silent reading before oral work. Children trying to learn how a story got its name or discovering what the children in the picture are doing, need to read before much discussion is possible. This reading should be done silently so that each child has the satisfaction of grasping the ideas for himself without the distraction of trying to follow, line by line, as someone reads aloud who may destroy the sense of the passage by stumbling over hard words.

At first glance, an assignment to read a complete story may seem to be a heavy one for a primary child. However, basal readers are designed to make such an undertaking possible almost from the first. Stories increase in length gradually and, especially in the beginning, are planned so that the picture and context on a single page provide a unified center for discussion. Even at the end of the third grade, a story in a typical text is not often more than ten or twelve pages long.

Whatever the amount of material read, it should have some unity within itself. An adult does not get much satisfaction from his reading if he is required to lay down his book in the middle of a paragraph. Neither does the child who is required to stop reading merely because he has come to the bottom of the page, or because the time allotted to his reading group has been used up. It is important, also, to remember that the objective of the reading program is to develop skill in independent reading. Children should not be impeded in their efforts to forge ahead by themselves with unnecessary questions and discussion. There are many opportunities to talk after the complete story has been read, and follow-up activities can be used to provide needed experiences in reading aloud, in reviewing new words, or in noting details.

The longer the passage read silently, the more likely it is that one or two children will finish well ahead of the group. There are several ways in which the time of these rapid readers can be used to advantage. Sometimes the child who finishes early can be given a few minutes' extra help with words that caused him trouble. If his tendency is to skim carelessly, he may profit from a quiet discussion with the teacher to check on the thoroughness with which he has read. Often the original plans will include specific steps to be taken after the first reading is done. The rapid reader may proceed with these. "If you think it would make a good play, suppose you look back over it and think about the scenes we would need." "Remember, we were going to read the part that was the most exciting." Often the group proceeds to the discussion of the story before the slowest readers have quite finished. These children then complete the reading at their leisure.

The greater the amount of independent reading planned for the group the easier it is to occupy the rapid reader. He may go on to some other part of the plan for the group reading activity, to his share of the plans for a social-studies or science project, continue with recreational reading, engage in number activities, or take other steps to carry out his part of the class plans for the day. It is important to assure the good reader an experience both helpful and challenging. Merely rereading a passage will not usually be helpful for him.

Discuss what is read in the light of original purposes. Silent reading of a story needs to be followed by a discussion of what has been read. This may take place during the same session in which the story was introduced, or later, depending on the maturity of the group and the elaborateness of the original plans.

Children may be helped to give attention to the purpose that guided them to reading. If the purpose-setting question has been, "How do you think the story got its name?", the teacher's first question after silent reading might be "How many of you now know how this story got its name?"

In a typical reading-group situation, discussion then branches out to other aspects of the story. Some of these may be suggested by the children as they tell what they found, ask questions, or comment on parts of the story. Some questions will be raised by the teacher. When there is a dispute about facts or interpretations, the children turn back to the book. "There's another reason for the name of the story. Look on page 25." "Jack says it took all day to get to town, and Barbara says it was only two hours. Who is right?" "We said we would watch to see just what a corral looks like. Who can read the part that tells?"

Many opportunities for small amounts of oral reading occur during the discussion of a story. Children may read the sentences that support their points of view. If they are discussing the humor or the suspense in a story, they may read the parts they thought the funniest, or the most exciting. They may find and read key pieces of conversation or sentences containing new words.

In the interest of vocabulary development and accurate reading, it is sometimes a temptation to prolong the discussion of a story until all details have been covered and all new words re-used. Often the discussion is followed routinely by reading the entire story aloud. Such intensive study is not necessary. No single story is meant to guarantee accurate subsequent recognition of each new word or phrase. Furthermore, most primary materials are written with a simplicity of plot and style that yields only limited possibilities for truly interesting discussion. Many of the follow-up activities discussed in the section that follows will provide more vital reasons for rereading than detailed analysis of the story itself.

Help the children become sensitive to reading skills as they work. Even a beginner is more likely to be able to solve his own reading problems if he knows what skills he is trying to develop. Part of the discussion that accompanies the reading of a story should focus on what it means to be able to read. In a group of beginners, one is likely to hear, "We start at this side." "Watch that you don't skip a line." "That's almost the right word, but not quite; look very carefully at the way it starts." Third-graders may be discussing how and when to skim, what might help in finding specific answers to questions, or how to read aloud with expression.

Some consideration of how to read may be included as part of the introductory discussion of a story. "Suppose we all read it quickly, first, to see what happened." "Since we want to decide which story to read for our party, what should we think about as we read?" "When we finish reading let's try to make a list of all the animals they saw. Read carefully so that you don't miss any." Misinterpretations and incorrect answers can lead to further consideration of how to read. "How might you have told that the word couldn't have been *swimming?*" "Read it the way you would say it to your mother, so we'll know someone is talking." "John, did what you read really answer our question?" Children will often make their own discoveries. "People who read with their eyes and not with their lips go faster, don't they?" "I could tell from the picture." "I knew that word because it begins like *fast*." All such comments represent growing insight into the reading process.

PROVIDING FOLLOW-UP ACTIVITIES

Use follow-up activities for group and individual experiences. Work with a new story does not always end when its general contents have been discussed in the reading group. There are often values to be gained from activities that call for the child to rework some of the material for a new purpose. Some of these follow-up experiences will involve the cooperative efforts of the entire group, as when the children decide to read the story aloud to another group, to dramatize it, or to read other stories on the same general topic. Some will lead to independent reading. Some will involve answering questions based on the story, drawing pictures, or working with selected words or phrases. Follow-up experiences sometimes call for several days' effort on the part of the group; some may require an additional period of independent work, others may be planned as a quick review for the last few minutes of the reading period.

While there are many values in follow-up activities, they should not become a routine way of ending the reading of every story. Many times the intrinsic interest in a selection will be exhausted by the time the first lively discussion of its contents has ended. It may not lend itself particularly well to oral-reading activities, and there may be little in it to stimulate further reading. When this is the case, it is likely to be more beneficial to the group to proceed to another story, or to another set of stories. The practice of giving routine seat-work assignments to beginning readers was questioned in Chapter V. This practice is even less justifiable, if that is possible, in the case of more skilled primary readers who could be using the time with profit in many independent reading activities for informational- or recreational-reading purposes.

Use oral reading for follow-up purposes. Primary children enjoy the experience of reading aloud. This is typically more satisfactory as a follow-up activity after the children have become familiar with the story through silent reading than it is as an introduction to a new story. A certain amount of oral reading, as already mentioned, takes place during the discussion of the story while the children read sentences that prove their points, read answers to questions, or share parts of the story they liked particularly.

Follow-up activities can be planned to provide more extensive opportunities to read aloud. One of the simplest of these is for group members to take turns reading the story aloud just to see how well they can do it. At such times it is advisable for the children to provide a real audience, listening to the oral reading rather than following word by word in their own books. At other times stories may be practiced in the reading group and then taken home to be read to parents. There may also be times when the members of several reading groups work together on an oral-reading program to show their mothers how well they can read or to entertain another class. The members of one first grade took particular pleasure in reading their favorite stories to the kindergarten children.

Dramatization offers another follow-up activity of an oral nature. No effort is made to have children memorize the words of the book and the dramatization becomes a creative effort on their part.[4] Sometimes the children merely take a little time as they conclude the discussion of a story to act it out. More elaborate plans may call for rereading the story to decide what scenes might be appropriate and what characters would be needed in each scene. Children may also have valuable rereading experiences as they make sure just how a giant, a policeman, or a frightened little rabbit would behave. At times, oral reading can be combined with dramatization by having the story read while it is acted in pantomime. Puppet shows may also be developed.

Primary grade children should have many experiences with poetry as well as with prose. Since reading poetry aloud is a difficult task, most of the reading of poetry for an audience of immature readers should be done by the teacher. In this way a good model for reading poetry can be set and the delight of listening to verse enhanced. As children hear and enjoy poems, they will ask for favorites over and over. They can "join in" to say parts they know as the teacher reads or recites a poem. Often such repetition leads to memorization and to simple dramatizations of poems.

More mature readers at the end of the primary grades begin to develop skills in oral reading which enable them to enjoy reading poems aloud them-

[4] Suggestions for reading in the area of creative dramatics are given at the end of this chapter.

selves. One third grade reading group became keenly interested in poems and requested one day each week to read them. Various collections of poems were made available and the children listened to each other's reading with interest and enjoyment. They set up their own standards for good oral reading and evaluated their own growth in ability to read poetry effectively. In a situation in which poems are read and children have opportunities to hear and share them, understandings develop which preclude "sing-song" renditions and overemphasis upon rhyme and rhythm that obstruct the listener's grasp of the poem's meaning and destroy listening pleasure.

The larger the audience, the more important it is to safeguard a child against the embarrassment of making mistakes when he reads aloud. Often the members of the reading group preparing the story can form a helpful but critical audience for each other. Since all are involved in the final production, no one minds a suggestion for improvement. Skilled third-graders can work with each other in small groups with very little help from the teacher. It is possible, also, for the teacher to work individually with a child who seems unusually self-conscious. Sometimes the shy child is helped if he reads from behind a curtain in a make-believe radio or television performance. He takes courage, too, if he is one of a group taking part in the presentation.

Even with primary children, the teaching emphasis in preparation for oral reading can go well beyond accurate word recognition and good expression. Other problems may involve deciding how to cut a long story, where to break a story if several children are reading in turn, how to set up scenes for dramatization, at what point to stop reading if you wish your audience to read the story for themselves. Many of the skills needed for effective oral reading are difficult for children to attain until they have developed the comprehension and word-study techniques of intermediate graders. Primary teachers will find further suggestions for developing oral-reading skills in Chapter XII.

Stimulate wide reading through follow-up activities. There will be times when work with a group of stories in a basal reader will lead to a request for opportunities to do further reading on the same topic. For example, children in one class found in a set of supplementary readers a series of stories about American children similar to those that they had just finished in their reading group. Since these were easy books, each child chose the story he liked best, read it independently, and then read selected parts to the group. Members of another group went on from a set of "just for fun" stories to dictate their own to the teacher. These she hectographed in slightly edited form and gave back for the group members to read independently. Activities such as these add vitality to the materials in basal readers and help immeasurably in broadening reading interests and tastes.

Make use of selected follow-up activities of a work-type nature. From time to time it may be appropriate to use, after the reading of a story, a series of review activities developed with word cards, or phrased in multiple-choice, true-false, or matching form. Among the most stimulating may be the quick reviews of new words or of key phrases planned for a few minutes of the reading-group session.

Pictures can continue to provide interesting work-type experience beyond the beginning-reading level. The children may illustrate the parts of the story they like best, and bring their pictures to the reading group for others to identify. They may decide on scenes appropriate for a play and then draw them. They may illustrate given sentences or paragraphs. As they become more skilled in written expression, they may add their own captions to their pictures, or write their own synopses of the part of the story they are illustrating. Sometimes a group may develop a bulletin-board display, using pictures from its favorite stories.

Activities that ask direct review questions about the contents of a story can be made more interesting if a definite challenge or puzzle element is provided. Riddles referring to key characters are more exciting than yes-no questions. Various ways of numbering or of drawing lines may be used to match a character with a special action or event, or to match a new word with the part of the story to which it belongs. Sometimes the children can be given word cards and pictures to match, or work sheets to be cut up and repasted in the correct order. New vocabulary may be sorted into interesting categories—words that tell about the farm; and words that tell about the city. A new device for indicating a correct answer can enliven a set of questions—if the little dog was lost, draw his picture; if he was not lost, draw his home.

Plan so that follow-up activities focus on a variety of reading skills. Just as stories themselves can be used to develop a variety of reading skills, so follow-up activities can be planned to focus on many different skills. The suggestions following indicate typical experiences that help to develop specific skills. Some of these call for rereading the story for various purposes; some are special work-type activities based on the story. Most of the activities following are simple enough for first-graders, but there are those more appropriate for skilled third-graders. Teachers will need to select and adapt in terms of the abilities of their groups.

Critical evaluation is called for in: Rereading to decide on the appropriateness of a story for dramatization or for reading aloud; choosing from a set of stories the one that is most appropriate for sharing with another group; deciding whether a story is real or fanciful; checking the information in a story against that gained on an excursion; discussing the accuracy of the illustrations; deciding which of a series of stories is the most exciting, the most humorous.

Reading with careful attention to details is needed in: Answering specific questions based on the story; describing the costume or the manner appropriate for selected characters for a dramatization; drawing an accurate picture illustrating part of a story; making a list of facts learned from the story; making accurate statements as a story is discussed—telling correctly what happened next, how people felt, what an unfamiliar object looked like, exactly what the sequence of events was; matching a series of phrases to the appropriate characters; answering riddles; labelling a classroom exhibit or attaching appropriate captions to pictures developed out of reading-group activities; following group plans for producing a puppet show, dramatizing, playing a game.

Oral-reading experiences are afforded through: Reading specific points to answer a question or to support a statement; rereading a story just for the fun of it; reading passages in answer to questions; reading a story to another group; reading aloud as part of a dramatization; reading the phrase or the sentence that contains a new word; reading original stories to classmates.

Reference techniques are needed for: Examining the table of contents in a new book; using section headings to identify the parts of a story; using titles to identify groups of stories; skimming the titles of stories in a new book to find those appropriate for a special problem; discussing the title of a story as an aid to deciding what it will be about; using the pictures as an aid to interpreting context and recognizing new words.

Reading for the general idea of the story is called for in: Rereading a story to decide on scenes for dramatization; skimming several stories to locate material on a given topic; telling whether the characters in a story were sad, happy, worried; planning how to tell a story; suggesting another title for a story; placing a series of events from a story in the correct order; drawing a series of pictures to illustrate the plot of a story; deciding what parts of a story can safely be omitted in planning for oral reading or dramatization; writing one's own ending for a story.

Adjustments of reading speed are needed in: Reading a story for its general contents and then rereading to answer a specific question; following a rapid reading of the story with a work-type exercise that asks for specific details; going back over a story slowly in order to draw a picture or to describe a character; leafing through several stories to find one of interest and then reading it with care; rereading a story quickly to locate a specific piece of information and then reading the information carefully for correct details.

New vocabulary is developed through: Using pictures to help interpret new words; sharing in discussions which made use of new words as an aid to understanding the story; rereading sentences that contain new words; drawing pictures to illustrate sentences containing new words; classifying new words under categories appropriate for the story; answering multiple-choice questions in which possible choices make use of new words; answering or preparing riddles built around new words; working with word cards in reading groups; helping to develop illustrated word lists or picture dictionaries.

Broad interests in reading are developed through: Comparing several stories; participating in sharing periods where other groups tell about their favorite stories; reading additional stories on a topic of interests; sharing in group activities where stories are related to special events, such as Thanksgiving; working with stories in such a way that elements of humor, fantasy, excitement are highlighted in group discussion; preparing an illustrated booklet based on favorite stories to be sent to a child who is ill; writing or dictating creative stories after interest has been stimulated by reading.

DEVELOPING READING UNITS

Capitalize on increased reading skill by encouraging more complex activities. Reading units calling for work with a series of stories were proposed in Chapter VI as a means of capitalizing upon increased ability to read independently. Work with sets of stories can be developed in many different ways. Perhaps the simplest approach is to capitalize upon the fact that in a basal reader several stories are classified under a common topic. Sometimes the same characters appear throughout the entire section. These groupings make it easy to help children establish interests that carry through several days' work—we follow our characters from story to story; as we read each new story about transportation we talk about the additional information we have acquired; we compare what we like about each new fanciful story with what we enjoyed about the one preceding. Out of the children's interest in the series of stories can come plans for related follow-up activities and perhaps for a more elaborate culminating activity. As a set of animal stories is read, a bulletin board of pictures brought by the children may be planned. They may plan a Pet Day when they talk about their pets or even bring some of them to school; they may develop their own creative stories about animals, or compose several group-experience records. As the block of stories is completed each child may select his favorite to read to others in the class; the group may develop a display of its illustrations of favorite stories; a dramatization or a puppet show may be planned; perhaps parents or other classes may be invited to the program. Parallel with the group activities there may be independent work with library books about animals.

All-class units may be developed by using sets of stories on related topics. For example, all reading groups might have been involved in the unit on animals just described. Each would work with the stories in the appropriate section of its basal reader. All might share in plans for a bulletin board or for a Pet Day. As a culminating activity, each group might share the story it liked best, devise a means of telling about several stories or of reading appropriate passages.

As children become more skilled, there should be more flexibility in the choice of materials for unit activities and in ways in which the reading is done. To be able to read a story independently and to report on it to one's group or to be able to read several stories and to select the one best suited for a particular purpose, represents a distinct advance in reading skill. Children should be encouraged to undertake such projects.

A first-grade group became interested in "good stories"—largely folk tales and fairy tales. They found these stories in different sets of readers, in library books, and in books brought from home by the children for all to enjoy. Since many of the tales were too difficult for the children to read independently, the teacher read them to the class. Many children were able to read some of the easier stories for themselves, while others reread familiar parts.

The interest in these stories was expressed in various ways as the children planned how they might share their favorite story with others. They met in groups to plan their presentations. Some made puppets, others a "movie" of a strip of paper with appropriate illustrations in proper sequence and placed on two rollers in a carton. Dramatizations and original stories and songs were also a part of the contributions of various groups. The door to their classroom was covered with paper on which the children drew figures representing characters from their favorite stories. A notice said, "Come to Storyland." The reading, listening, and sharing experiences of these children deepened interest in books and reading and led to many language activities.

Stories from several basal readers may be used in a reading unit. A second-grade group became interested in a small number of humorous, fanciful stories in one basal reader. They asked if they could do more reading along the same line, and were able to locate similar stories in two other readers. In the discussion of how to get the most out of the materials available, the children suggested that each might read the story he thought was the most interesting and then share it with the group. The next few minutes were spent looking at the pictures and leafing through the stories. By the end of the period everyone had indicated his first choice. It was decided that each child would read his story silently first, and that children reading the same story would then get together and decide how to present it to the group. The next day's work was almost entirely individual. Group discussion took just long enough to make sure that each child remembered what story he had chosen. On the third day, the children decided on their contribution to the final program. There were two groups of three children each, one pair, and two children who worked alone. The teacher met with them to check on plans and make suggestions. Some children planned to read aloud, some to draw pictures about their stories and to share them, and one group to put on a short dramatization. For the next two days the small groups worked on their parts of the program, with the teacher acting as a special critic. Next, time was taken within the group for the presentations of the stories. Later the most interesting stories were shared with the class as a whole. This ended the unit, but many children went back to the readers to read independently the stories that interested them the most. They also found in several supplementary books a number of similar stories which they read for recreational purposes.

Find opportunities during reading units to work on specific reading skills. Children engaged in extensive and independent reading as they carry on units in reading will need help with problems they encounter. How may this help best be given?

Considerable help in developing greater reading skill can be given to the group at several points. An important part of planning for the work of the unit may include how to read the materials selected. Will everyone read every selection? What should each reader be prepared to report? How can we best find more material if we need it? If two people work together, how can they best help each other? When the group comes together to report on progress a second opportunity exists to give guidance. Bill's report is not too clear; how could people report more clearly? If we want to choose just one story to share with others, what standards should we use to decide? Plans for a culminating activity offer still more opportunities to focus on skills. Abilities in oral reading, dramatizing, and reporting are among those which may need extending.

Vocabulary difficulties may offer some problems for the entire group. In general, however, the children who do the most extensive reading, and therefore encounter the greatest number of new words, are typically those children who have already developed the highest level of ability in using context, picture, and word-analysis clues. The teacher may help by introducing special terms during the planning stages, by selecting somewhat simpler materials than the group encounters in guided reading, and by planning to give individual help during a time when all are working on some aspect of the unit.

Help to individual children can be given as the teacher sees need and opportunity. She may stop for a moment to help a child analyze a hard word, discover through questions in a short conversation how well a young reader has understood his story, check the simple notes being made by another youngster. Other items might include helping a child locate needed material or listening critically to a "trial run" of a dramatization or oral reading.

As children become able to work independently, the time available for this kind of individual help is increased greatly.

PROVIDING WORK-TYPE ACTIVITIES TO MEET INDIVIDUAL NEEDS

An effective skills program is an individualized program. As suggested in Chapter VI, the time soon comes when children, even those who started to read in the same group and worked with the same materials, develop different reading needs. Their progress will be dependent, in part, on the skill with which these needs are met.

A number of ways of meeting individual needs through grouping and scheduling and through wise choice of materials have already been discussed. Work-type activities, which children can carry out independently, are another aid to an individualized program. These exercises can be prepared by the teacher and hectographed or mimeographed, or they can be selected from the many workbooks prepared for use with primary classes.

Use work-type activities selectively. Even with beginners there will be wide differences in needs for special work-type experiences. Some will master each new reading task with ease and secure all the extra practice that seems necessary through the various follow-up activities undertaken by their groups. Others will benefit from rather regular experiences with the simplified, but interesting, tasks posed by work-type exercises. At no reader level does a workbook serve its purpose as an aid to an individualized program if every child is taken through every activity in the book. Such routine use is certain to doom some children who would otherwise be reading independently or be engaged creatively in another classroom project to reading activities that do not meet their needs. It is equally likely that routine experiences with a workbook will fail to meet the needs of other children, who would benefit from extra practice were this practice focused on their individual problems. Used selectively, the materials in workbooks at the primary level, as at other reading levels, can save the classroom teacher valuable time in providing the individualized practice required by her class.

Teachers may find it advantageous to purchase workbooks, like basal readers, in small sets of ten to a dozen copies. Usually it is helpful to have available the workbooks designed to accompany the basal readers given the most constant use. However, workbooks from other series are often equally valuable. There is a place, also, for materials not related to any particular series. Among the total selection may be some copies of workbooks that bear directly on a specific problem, such as the development of word-study skills. When such a variety of teaching aids is available, teachers must guard against the temptation to use more of these activities than children actually need.

Provide activities that challenge increased reading skill. Certain general criteria can be suggested as guides in the selection or preparation of work-type activities:

1. The activity should focus on a specific skill needed by the children. Work that serves mainly to keep children occupied and in their own seats is not helpful.
2. There should be maximum emphasis upon thoughtful reading, whether the activity calls for understanding a paragraph, reading a single sentence, or matching a word to a picture.
3. The activity itself should have high interest value. Paragraphs provided should be worth reading, questions thought provoking, and ways of responding sufficiently varied to make the activity fun.
4. The amount of time actually spent in reading should be high in proportion to the amount of time spent in coloring, pasting, drawing, keeping score in a game, or other such non-reading activities.
5. Directions should be simple enough that work can proceed independently once the teacher has given general instructions.
6. Activities planned as follow-up experiences should not be allowed to exhaust the interest value of basal-reader stories.

Teachers can save themselves time and effort and achieve greater interest in work-type activities if they plan materials that can be re-used in several ways. A single hectographed sheet may contain an illustration, a paragraph of text, and a series of questions. One activity might be to write the answers to questions, another to follow directions for completing or coloring a picture, and another to add to a picture all the appropriate objects mentioned in the paragraph. Fresh sheets with new directions can be passed out as desired for specific groups. Children themselves can help to prepare interesting and versatile materials. A series of riddles developed by various class members around key vocabulary in a unit of work could be mimeographed and used in several ways.

Word games and other work-type materials that can be used repeatedly by many children may be mounted on cardboard. In some classrooms a variety of these materials are placed on a table of reading games to be used during independent work periods. Such activities might include simple word games, card-holders, sets of word cards with which children can write stories of their own or reproduce experience charts, "surprise books" directing children to draw special pictures or carry out simple directions for construction, one-word picture books, sets of word cards that the children may read to each other, and sets of phonograms and letters for word-building activities. Generally speaking, one test of a good teacher-made activity is the amount of effective practice provided for the children in proportion to the expenditure of the teacher's time. Many teachers build files containing samples of easy, interesting exercises classified according to various reading skills, so that they have models from which new activities can be planned.

Plan activities for a variety of reading skills. In the beginning, many work-type activities may be designed to give experience with new words, since the problem of becoming thoroughly familiar with new vocabulary is basic to successful reading. More skilled readers may also need a certain amount of work with new words, and may benefit particularly from activities to develop word-analysis techniques. There also need to be provisions for experiences in following the thought of a passage, in noting details carefully, in following directions, in sensing a sequence.

Not all reading skills can be practiced effectively in a work-type setting. Learning to evaluate what is read, for example, is developed more successfully through actual experiences with stories or informational materials, although more skilled readers may be given a limited number of exercises requiring them to distinguish factual from fictional statements or tell whether a paragraph actually contains needed information. Ability to identify effective choice of words or skillful development of plot is also better developed when an actual story is under consideration. Work-type activities are of more use in situations in which a definite answer, rather than a judgment or an opinion, is needed.

Intensive practice of a work-type nature is more valuable after a child has developed some command of a new skill. Primary children are in the first stages of developing readiness for such reference techniques as using guide words, using alphabetical order, deciding on key words for work with an index, using section and paragraph headings and chapter summaries. They are also taking their first steps toward developing effective reading rate and may be still hampered at many points by their word-study skills. Intensive work-type experiences to build reference techniques or to develop effective reading rate, then, belong in the intermediate grades.

The suggestions that follow outline possible work-type activities for developing better skill in following the thought and sequence of a paragraph or story, in noting details, and in following directions. These activities should be supplemented by the suggestions for special practice to develop word-study skills included in Chapter IX. For children who are approaching typical intermediate-grade reading ability, the activities suggested in Chapter XII may also be helpful. No particular effort has been made to designate the suggestions that follow for particular grade levels. Teachers will need to adjust the vocabulary and the complexity of the activity to the abilities of their particular groups. As with the suggested activities in other parts of this book, this list is meant to be illustrative, not a prescription of activities for any given group.

Summarizing the general contents of a passage is called for in: Choosing the correct answer to tell how a character felt; reading a short paragraph and checking the best title, or the best statement of what the paragraph is about; matching a series of pictures to the correct paragraphs; drawing a picture or series of pictures to illustrate a paragraph; finding the answer to a riddle; checking the picture that best illustrates a paragraph; finding the key sentence in a paragraph; arranging a series of mimeographed paragraphs in the proper order to reconstruct a story.

Ability to note details is needed in: Choosing the right answer to questions such as *who, what color, how many, when, where,* after reading a short paragraph; circling *yes* or *no* after sentences giving details from a passage; answering riddles; crossing out a word that makes a sentence incorrect; drawing a picture to illustrate a particular event in a passage; matching pictures to sentences, words, or phrases; drawing a picture to illustrate the answer to a riddle; matching key words with appropriate phrases, key characters with descriptions; writing riddles for others in the class to guess.

Identifying the sequence of events in a passage is needed for: Placing in order a series of statements from a paragraph, story, or experience record; drawing a series of pictures that tell the events of a story or paragraph in order; reading a short story and listing the scenes that would be needed for a play; reading a short paragraph and checking the right statement to indicate what would happen next; crossing out a sentence that does not belong in a paragraph; writing the names of the characters in the order in which they appeared in a story; writing a new ending for a story.

Skill in following directions is important for: Setting up and playing a game according to written directions; following written directions for coloring or constructing; reading a series of sentences and following the directions given in each; drawing missing parts in a picture; coloring it, or marking it according to written directions; indicating the correct answer to a question by drawing a picture; helping to develop a picture dictionary according to agreed-upon plans; sorting sentences or words under appropriate headings—things that fly, things that go on wheels.

Help children become aware of the skills they need. The best work-type activity loses much of its value if it is merely handed in for correction. Children grow through identifying and correcting their mistakes. If a half hour is to be allotted to a work-type exercise, it is often more effective to have the children work for fifteen minutes and to discuss correct answers and analyze errors for fifteen minutes than it is to have them work for the full period and leave no time for discussion. A work-type activity need not always be discussed the day it is assigned. Children may work for one period and come to a group session to go over their work the next. It is also possible to find ways of giving help to individual children. If the work-type activities are planned for an independent work period, the teacher may be able to move around the room, giving a little help to each child who seems to be in difficulty. Sometimes it is possible to allow time for children to bring their work individually to the teacher's desk and to check it with her. Whatever the method used to give the help, the discussion should develop insight into reading skills. "You didn't look carefully at part of that word. Look again." "Read the sentence again, what word did you miss?" "Today you didn't have a bit of trouble with *was* and *saw*, did you?"

Children can also grow in their insight into their own strengths and weaknesses as they discuss the need for work-type activities. "Mamie, you were absent for our trip, and we learned some new words about airplanes. Suppose you work with this group who are practicing them." "Aileen, I think we could help you with your spelling if you did some special work with Pete's group." "Yesterday we had trouble guessing what would happen next in the story. Here are some questions . . ." "We weren't very good today in telling exactly what happened. Here is some work to help in reading more carefully."

When the reading program is planned effectively, children enjoy reading for its own sake—the interesting stories, the fun of follow-up activities, the excitement of exploring new books on their own, the challenge of locating information. They also find genuine pleasure in discovering how to read, in participating in practice activities designed to develop better skill, and in taking joint responsibility for their own growth.

SOME QUESTIONS TO THINK ABOUT IN APPRAISING THE WORK OF READING GROUPS IN THE PRIMARY GRADES

1. Are children provided with materials varied sufficiently in content, style, and level of difficulty to facilitate the development of reading skills?

2. Is the classroom equipped with materials appropriate to children of several levels of ability?

3. Are children encouraged to approach their reading of new materials in a thoughtful, purposeful fashion?

4. Are the activities of reading groups varied so as to make possible the development of many types of reading skills?

5. Are children encouraged to undertake as challenging independent reading activities as they are capable of handling?

6. Are follow-up activities related to a story interesting and purposeful?

7. Are specific skills, such as oral reading, developed in ways that do not

militate against the development of equally important skills, such as reading silently for information?

8. Are ample work-type activities provided to meet the needs for special practice of individuals and groups?

9. Are work-type activities used selectively in terms of special problems?

SUGGESTIONS FOR FURTHER READING

Betts, Emmett A. *Foundations of Reading Instruction.* Chapter 22. New York: American Book Company, 1957. 757 pp.

Dawson, Mildred A., and Bamman, Henry A. *Fundamentals of Basic Reading Instruction.* Chapter 5. New York: Longmans Green, and Company, 1959. 304 pp.

Durrell, Donald. *Improving Reading Instruction.* Yonkers-on-Hudson, New York: World Book Company. 402 pp.

Hildreth, Gertrude. *Teaching Reading.* Chapter 12. New York: Henry Holt and Company, 1958. 612 pp.

Kephart, Newell C. *The Slow Learner in the Classroom.* Part I. Columbus, Ohio: Charles E. Merrill Books, Inc., 1960. 292 pp.

Russell, David H. *Children Learn to Read.* Chapter 7. Boston: Ginn and Company, 1961. 612 pp.

Shane, Harold G.; Reddin, Mary E.; and Gillespie, Margaret C. *Beginning Language Arts Instruction with Children.* Chapter 13. Columbus, Ohio: Charles E. Merrill Books, 1961. 286 pp.

CREATIVE DRAMATICS [5]

Siks, Geraldine B. *Creative Dramatics.* New York: Harper and Brothers, 1958. 472 pp.

Ward, Winifred. *Playmaking with Children.* Second Edition. New York: Appleton-Century-Crofts, Inc., 1957. 341 pp.

Wilt, Miriam E. *Creativity in the Elementary School.* New York: Appleton-Century-Crofts, Inc., 1959. 72 pp.

[5] For a helpful annotated list of books and articles in this field see: George L. Lewis and Ann K. Burkhart, "Creative Dramatics: A Selective Bibliography," *Elementary English.* **39** (February 1962), 91–100.

CHAPTER VIII

Developing Reading Skills Through On-Going Classroom Activities in the Primary Grades

A GOOD primary classroom invites children to read. Day-by-day reading experiences in these classrooms are concerned with problems important to children. They read to find answers to a wide variety of questions; they read for pleasure in a wide range of materials. Many times a day it is necessary to read thoughtfully if an activity is to move forward smoothly. These experiences complement and reinforce the reading that goes on in reading groups.

How do teachers make the most of the opportunities for reading afforded by the varied activities of the primary classroom? This chapter is concerned with the problems related to two types of reading experiences. First, how can most effective use be made of informational-reading experiences? And, second, how can the foundations for interest in recreational reading be laid?

USING INFORMATIONAL-READING EXPERIENCES

Children's experiences in reading for information in a primary classroom range from pauses for a few seconds to note one's housekeeping responsibilities to the extended reading that often accompanies the development of unit activities that help children become better acquainted with the world in which they live.

A general picture of the activities of the primary classroom which provide the setting for children's reading experiences was given in Chapter IV, when readiness activities were described, and in Chapter VI, when the problems of planning the total reading experiences for more skilled readers in the primary grades were discussed. The activities described in this chapter assume the rich and varied total program, the experiences that build broad experience background, the planning with children, and the flexible scheduling and grouping described in earlier chapters.

This section is focused on three separate but interrelated problems. First, how can the most effective use be made of day-by-day opportunities to read signs and notices? Second, how can the reading experiences related to unit activities be developed? Third, how can both these types of reading experiences contribute to primary children's readiness for the more extensive reading activities in the content fields that they will undertake as intermediate-graders?

USING CLASSROOM RECORDS AS AIDS TO DAILY WORK

Use records that help in the problems of living together. Among the most prominent stimulations to read in the classrooms that have been described are the many signs and notices on the bulletin boards. Not every classroom experience requires a set of records, but they can be used in many ways as aids to more effective group living. In the early part of the first grade, these records are likely to serve as prereading materials. Gradually the children take over more of the responsibility for their own reading.

Helpers' charts are among the earliest and the most constantly used of the records of plans for cooperative group living. There may also be special sets of directions for such group responsibilities as caring for a pet, signing a book out of the classroom library, or carrying out the special jobs of the clean-up committee. These directions the children compose together and then recheck as they undertake the special responsibility.

Primary teachers devise various ways of making such records interesting and functional. Pictures drawn by the children frequently help to guide the reading. Charts listing room responsibilities are usually designed so that new names may be inserted. The children in one hospitable class planned a chart to hang outside their door telling visitors where they were—We are at home. Please come in; We are at the library; We are on the playground. To the left of this list ran a ribbon which could be set at the appropriate message.

Cooperatively derived rules foster happy group living in the classroom.

The following standards for work periods and for using materials were arrived at by a first grade:[1]

GOOD HELPERS
Work quietly.
Whisper.
Say "Please."
Say "Thank you."
Take turns.
Listen.

PAINTERS
Wear your apron.
Write your name.
Stir the paint.
Wipe your brush.

OUR LIBRARY
Have clean hands.
Read with your eyes.
4 children may read.

OUR PLAYHOUSE
Two may play.
Play quietly.
Have good manners.

Another first-grade group discussed their responsibilities and recorded their conclusions concerning proper procedure at a fire drill:[2]

FIRE DRILL RULES
Ring, Ring (2).
We walk in line.
We wait for Miss Stilt
in 108.
We follow Miss Stilt
quietly.
We have a nice line.

The members of a second grade summarized some of their safety responsibilities on the playground as follows:[3]

1. Be careful how you get off and
   on the teeter.
2. Don't do tricks on the merry-go-round.
3. Do not run into the streets after a ball.
4. Watch the traffic lights.
5. Keep away from between parked cars.

---

[1] These examples are from the classroom records of Mrs. Shirley Ohlhauser, teacher at Schiel School, Cincinnati, Ohio.

[2] From the classroom of Miss Lauretta Stilt, first-grade teacher at Schiel School, Cincinnati, Ohio.

[3] James R. Bryner, "The Content of Primary School Experience Charts," (unpublished Doctor's dissertation, Stanford University, 1951), p. 76.

Cooperative relations with other school helpers were recorded after the children in another first grade toured the school. These charts served as prereading materials in the early fall.[4] These two records illustrate paragraphing in regular basal-reader style.

Mr. Hansen is our janitor. He cleans the floors. He brings in milk bottles. This morning he cleaned the windows. We can help him by keeping the papers picked up.	Mrs. Green is Dr. Moore's secretary. She types the notes we take home. Mrs. Green counts the milk money. She rings the fire bell.

At another time the children in this class composed safety rules after they had talked through the problems of carrying umbrellas on the crowded school grounds.

RAINY DAY SAFETY

1. Look around before you open your umbrella.
2. Hold your umbrella high.
3. Walk slow.
4. Watch out for traffic.
5. Look around before you close your umbrella.

Records such as those that have been cited are written as the problem arises. Many of their values for the children come as the problem in group living is talked out. As reading-matter, they remain posted in the classroom as long as they are needed. Their vocabulary load is relatively heavy, but they are phrased in words the children themselves have used. When they are reread, the teacher is there to help with unfamiliar words.

Find ways of posting items of current interest. A primary classroom is a busy place. Birthdays have to be remembered, letters or cards sent to children who are ill, letters from travelers acknowledged, notice taken of holidays, and events of interest in children's homes given recognition.

In the classrooms mentioned at the beginning of this section, part of the bulletin-board space is given to these current interests. Sometimes a sharing bulletin board or a sharing table is used to display letters and clippings, or to set up a labelled exhibit of articles brought from home. Some teachers

[4] *Ibid.*, pp. 43, 44.

set aside a section of a bulletin board for special events—notices to be taken home, auditorium sessions to which the children are invited, paper drives. Such special bulletin boards are sometimes framed with a bright paper border so that they stand out as centers to watch.

A class news bulletin may be of help as a record of events of the day. Sometimes the writing of the day's news is used as a language activity. One such record [5] composed by a first grade read as follows:

> Today is October 2.
> Today is Monday.
> It is a chilly, chilly day.
> Kenneth had a birthday.
> Kenneth is 7.
> Happy Birthday, Kenneth.

After some second-graders, who were gaining skill in written expression, had had some group experiences in composing a class diary, they took turns writing the entries. When help was needed with spelling, the teacher supplied it. The following are typical of the excerpts appearing in children's handwriting on the long sheets of paper that made up the diary: [6]

> Wednesday, January 17, 19—   by Jimmy
>   Ruth is a Blue Bird.
>   She wore her Blue Bird suit to school.
>   Betty is a Brownie.
>   She wore her Brownie suit to school, too.

> Monday, January 22, 19—   by Marie
>   The Museum of Natural History sent us a
>   cowboy exhibit.
>   They sent a rattlesnake, two prairie dogs,
>   two pair of cattle horns, and an old time saddle.

> Thursday, January 25, 19—   by Kenneth
>   This was a snowy day.
>   So we made spatter paint snowmen.

Notices such as those described are usually read during a sharing period or a class-planning session. Brief news bulletins for the day may be composed during these same planning sessions. Longer autobiographies or class diaries are often written during periods set aside for more extensive ex-

---

[5] From the first grade taught by Mrs. Esther Allard, Bath School, Bath, Ohio.

[6] *New Primary Manual,* Curriculum Bulletin 300 (Cincinnati: Cincinnati Public Schools, 1953), p. 88. Copyright 1953, Board of Education, Cincinnati, Ohio.

periences in creative expression. Once the materials are put on bulletin boards, children are encouraged to refer to them again as needed or to reread them for pleasure when they have a few minutes to spare.

Make it important to read classroom records and notices. Some classrooms which, on first glance, seem to be teeming with opportunities to read, actually provide very little reading experience. Most teachers watch for occasions to refer to special notices. A group disagrees about the day on which Jamie brought his dog to school and someone looks back at the class diary to make sure. Betty glances hastily at the helpers' chart and does Billy's job. Here is a chance to spend a few seconds on the importance of reading carefully. Four children congregate at an easel where two should have been and spill a jar of paint. It is a good time to look at the rules again. As the children discuss a recent program, they check their list to see how good an audience they have been. Records become functional when they are used in ways like these.

When children have become familiar with a set of directions or a series of rules, the record need no longer occupy a prominent spot in the room. If there is a possibility that it will be needed again, it may be bound with others to form a class book, perhaps entitled *How We Work Together*. Children enjoy rereading such materials, and the accumulated series can provide a helpful picture of how the group has grown over the year. The materials posted in a primary classroom in which reading is functional change frequently. The reading experiences afforded to the children are not measured by the quantity of the reading-matter with which they are surrounded, nor by the beauty of the bulletin-board arrangements. The ultimate test is the use to which the materials are put.

DEVELOPING READING ACTIVITIES RELATED TO UNITS OF WORK

Help children to explore as widely as their skill will permit. The unit activities that help children become acquainted with the world around them play an increasingly important part in their total reading program as they progress through the grades. Beginners start their study of their world with questions about familiar aspects of the environment near at hand. With increasing maturity children venture farther afield in space and in time.

Throughout the elementary school, and even into secondary school and college, reading is only one of many methods through which learners secure information about their world. The younger the child the more important it is that he have firsthand experience. All the resources suggested in Chapter IV for enriching the environment of beginners need to be tapped throughout the primary grades.

Ways of summarizing information and of testing concepts are also varied. Not always is the summary in written form. Discussion helps to consolidate information. Often this discussion results in a series of experience records composed by children and teacher. More mature children may plan for oral reports or for simple panels. Pictures are used in many ways—children may paint pictures to illustrate information of particular interest; they may plan a mural; they may piece together a set of pictures to develop a class motion picture; they may illustrate their own stories; they may develop a picture dictionary of new and interesting terms; they may make slides for an opaque projector or plan special posters.

Many kinds of construction activities can be used to summarize what children have learned: small scale models; a classroom store or post office; dolls dressed to represent the people being studied; models of specific objects of interest; peep shows; simple maps. Dramatization may range from dramatic play in the play corner to a special program planned to share the unit with other groups or with parents.

Written summaries of information are used from the beginning. At first these are records composed jointly by teacher and children. Sometimes these records, together with children's pictures, are bound into large class books. Later, individuals or small groups may develop other types of summaries in booklet form—individual booklets, class newspapers, class magazines, travel folders, handbooks, scrapbooks which contain a combination of children's work, and pictures they have clipped from magazines. Information may also be summarized in riddles; bulletin boards may be devoted to creative stories; accurate records of science experiments may be kept.

The amount of reading done and the type of material read will vary with the nature of the unit, the ability of the group, and the materials available. With increased reading skill should come the use of a greater variety of material, and more independence in the way it is attacked.

Make the most of varied opportunities to read as units develop. How do units actually work out? What kinds of reading experiences do they offer? How are these experiences related to other types of activities? The following units from first-, second-, and third-grade classrooms are examples of the ways plans can develop. Four units are reported in all. The first, second, and third are typical of average groups in the late first, second, and third grades. The fourth represents the work of a group of superior ability in the third grade.

In the spring a first-grade class developed both social- and natural-science concepts in studying about farms. The children in this group lived in a small town and many were used to driving with their parents into the surrounding farming land. Many of the homes had gardens and a few families kept chickens. Nevertheless, there were interesting aspects of the farmer's work about which the children knew very little.

BEGINNING THE UNIT:

The unit started during a sharing period when a child who had visited a farm over the weekend came in bubbling over with information about the new lambs and baby pigs. Out of the discussion came the proposal that the group try to visit a large farm at the edge of town.

In preparation for their visit, the children talked more about trips to farms they had taken with their families. They also discussed what their fathers were doing in preparation for planting their gardens, and speculated as to whether farmers went about it in the same way. They made a list of the farm animals they particularly hoped to see, aided by the teacher who had by now taken an exploratory trip to the farm. Several books yielded clear pictures of farm animals. The discussion of these pictures helped to develop better concepts of sizes and led to consideration of safety precautions around animals. Stories of trips to farms were available in a number of basal readers and some of these were read. With this background of reading, discussing, and looking at pictures, the children took their trip.

UNIT ACTIVITIES:

Many new learnings were developed through the trip and through subsequent activities in the classroom. As a class, the children decided to build a model farm in one corner of their room. They divided into groups to build the house, the barn, silo, and tool sheds, and to lay out the fences and the fields. Everyone helped to supply farm animals from collections of toys at home. In order to enlarge children's concepts of the services performed by farmers, the teacher set up a special bulletin board and a sharing table. Many appropriate pictures were found in magazines. In addition, butter cartons, bread wrappers, empty breakfast food cartons, and labels from various appropriate canned foods were collected.

SPECIAL GROUPS:

Special interest groups also worked during this unit. Two groups planned to find out more about farm animals, a third to learn more about what crops the farmer's planted, and one group of boys to find out about tractors and other farm machinery. These groups were able to do considerable independent reading. They also combed magazines at home for pictures. In the end, each group developed a special project—scrapbooks of pictures and stories about farm animals; a small window-box garden planted with wheat and flax; a special exhibit of toys and pictures of farm machinery. Individual activities were also planned—children drew pictures, wrote riddles about farm animals, made their own collections of animal pictures, and read farm stories. As a culminating activity, parents were invited to visit. The children conducted a guided tour of their farm, told about their exhibit, and reported on the work of their special groups.

READING ACTIVITIES:

The reading activities for this unit were extensive. It was relatively easy for the children themselves to locate farm stories in the sets of basal readers in their room. This they did one day during the time normally set aside for group reading activities. Each story or set of stories was then marked with a strip of colored paper. Stories in the basal readers being used for group-reading activities were read by the regular reading groups. Some of the other materials were read in group sessions of the special-interest groups. Easy library books about farms were read independently. As the unit progressed, story hours were set up when the children who worked with these books read them aloud to small groups.

Experience charts were developed to summarize group plans, to record the details of the trip, and to summarize special information about such topics as farm animals, what the farmer plants, how the farmer works, how the farmer helps us. Some additional reading was provided through the labels on the bulletin-board displays and through the special books developed by the interest groups. Then there were such related writing activities as writing thank-you notes after the trip, inviting parents; writing riddles; and preparing a picture dictionary of special farm words.

SOME BOOKS ABOUT THE FARM

Collier, Ethel. *I Know a Farm*. New York: William R. Scott, Inc., 1960.
Daly, Maureen. *Patrick Visits the Farm*. New York: Dodd, Mead and Company, 1959.
Floethe, Louise L. *The Farmer and His Cows*. New York: Charles Scribner's Sons, 1957.
Horn, Gladys M. *Fun on the Farm*. Racine, Wisconsin: Whitman Publishing Company, 1960.
Ipcar, Dahlov. *One Horse Farm*. New York: Doubleday, 1950.
———. *Ten Big Farms*. New York: Alfred A. Knopf, Inc., 1957.
Lenski, Lois. *The Little Farm*. New York: Henry Z. Walck, 1942.
Stewart, Elizabeth. *See Our Pony Farm*. Chicago: Reilly and Lee Company, 1960.
Tensen, Ruth. *Come to the Farm*. Chicago: Reilly and Lee Company, 1949.
Tresselt, Alvin. *Sun Up*. New York: Lothrop, Lee and Shepard, 1949.
———. *Wake Up Farm*. New York: Lothrop, Lee and Shepard, 1955.

A SECOND GRADE STUDIES PLANTS

In a second grade, a study of plants and how they grow called for more specialized informational-reading skills, and gave experiences in interpreting simple charts and other visual aids.

BEGINNING THE UNIT:

This unit began as the children started to bring early spring flowers to school and to discuss what their fathers were doing about gardens. In some homes, seeds were already planted indoors. Several families were also growing bulbs. As the children talked, they began to share opinions about whether seeds should be started in the light or the dark, why it was important to water plants, and what seeds looked like when they started to grow. The teacher suggested that they might be able to answer some of their questions by planting some seeds in the classroom.

As plans began to develop, the children started to look through simple science textbooks. Here they began to find suggestions of types of experiments they might be able to carry out. Everyone could not read all the suggestions, but many pictures were clear. Eventually a list of questions regarding what plants need in order to grow were formulated. At the same time both teacher and children brought to the classroom different kinds of seeds. The collection eventually included samples from the smallest seeds to bulbs, acorns, and avocado pits.

SPECIAL GROUP ACTIVITIES:

As the children talked about ways of answering their questions, they decided to break into interest groups, each with special responsibilities. One group took charge of planting some beans so that they could be watched through the side of a glass as they sprouted. Another group was responsible for two sets of seeds—one placed in the light and one in a dark cupboard. A third group worked on the problem of whether plants need water, a fourth on the problem of whether soil makes a difference, and a fifth tried to get some carrot tops and a sweet potato to grow.

UNIT ACTIVITIES:

As a class, the children planted petunias, which they hoped would be large enough to transplant for Mother's Day. Special directions for tending this class garden were posted above it, and the children took turns acting as gardeners. While these activities were going on, the teacher helped to develop concepts by discussion, by encouraging observation, and using pictures and stories in science texts and special books on plants and gardening. The unit ran parallel with other projects for many weeks while the children charted the growth of their plants, watched special developments in their experiments, and reported on new information as they watched their fathers' gardens.

READING ACTIVITIES:

This unit was particularly helpful in the introduction of simple reading problems involving tables, charts, and diagrams. As the children found special pictures and diagrams in their reference books, they used them as guides in planning their own projects. They also measured the growth of some of their plants, and developed a simple graph to show the progress. The children with responsibility for particular experiments posted simple records indicating exactly what they had done, and what their daily observations were.

Classroom records were extensive for this unit as the children listed their questions, stated the plans for the various projects, and eventually summarized their conclusions, giving evidence obtained from their observations. A number of these records were composed by the groups who planned the special projects. As each new step in the story developed and was recorded, the teacher typed it in a primer type and hectographed it. As a result each group built, page by page, a story of its particular project. These the group members illustrated with as careful drawings of their plants as they could make. Copies of the books that were finally developed were popular reading at the library table for many weeks.

The reading in books that was done for this unit was not as extensive as the reading of the records the children themselves developed. The children turned to books for some of the activities later carried out by the interest groups. As their projects developed, they spent several group sessions with the teacher, reading the information related to their special projects more carefully, and interpreting it in the light of what they themselves were finding out. There were also available some simple stories about gardening which served for independent reading. Meanwhile, the work of the reading groups went forward with other types of stories.

SOME BOOKS ABOUT PLANTS AND SEEDS

Blough, Glenn O. *Wait for the Sunshine*. New York: Whittlesey House, 1954.

Fiedler, Jean. *The Green Thumb Story*. New York: Holiday House, 1952.

Jordan, Helene J. *How a Seed Grows*. New York: Thomas Y. Crowell Company, 1960.

Miner, Irene. *The True Book of Plants We Know*. Chicago: Childrens Press, 1953.

Podendorf, Illa. *The True Book of Weeds and Wild Flowers*. Chicago: Childrens Press, 1955.

Selsam, Millicent. *Play with Seeds*. New York: William Morrow Company, 1957.

Selsam, Millicent. *Seeds and More Seeds*. New York: Harper and Brothers, 1959.

Webber, Irma E. *Travelers All*. New York: William R. Scott, 1944.

Zim, Herbert S. *What's Inside of Plants?* New York: William Morrow and Company, 1952.

A THIRD GRADE STUDIES AIR AND WATER

Third-graders go farther afield in their quest for information. In one third grade, the study of wind and of related facts about air began on a warm day as the children sat fanning themselves after a play period.

BEGINNING THE UNIT:

The teacher began to ask questions. "Why are you doing that?" "Why does it make you feel cooler?" "Are you making a wind?" "Why does moving your hand make a wind?" With these questions to start them off, the children began to talk about the wind. What does it do? Why can it move things? What kinds of things can it move? Out of this and subsequent discussions came a list of specific questions. These were posted on a special chart titled "Let's Find Out." Meanwhile the children began to look through the books from a science series and other reference books to see what might be available to help them with their unit. Less-skilled readers looked for such obvious key words as *wind* and *air*. Those with better reference techniques were able to use indexes and tables of contents quite efficiently. Each new source of information was marked with a slip of paper as it was located. While the children hunted for material, they also observed effects of the wind and talked about what they were discovering. By the end of this exploratory period they had an extensive list of possible activities.

SPECIAL GROUPS:

For several days the various interest groups read and tried out experiments related to their particular questions. Then, for a series of class meetings, these groups used the equipment on the science table to demonstrate their findings. As they did so, they reported on what they had learned from their reading. Class projects also developed as the children built kites and tested out various shapes of darts, paper planes, and pinwheels. As they explored they wrote class summaries of their general conclusions and group summaries of special topics, individual stories, poems, and riddles. Eventually this unit, which started with interest in air in motion, led into related questions on moisture in the air, rain, and other topics related to weather. Several tornado warnings heightened the general interest.

READING ACTIVITIES:

Much of the reading done for this unit was carried out individually or in interest groups. The less-skilled readers worked with simple science books, while those who had the most skill explored a wide variety of materials, including several articles in the encyclopedia. Many of the children took advantage of the weekly trips to the branch library to ask the librarian for help. The teacher found time to work with individual children during independent reading periods when all were looking for information. Sessions when interest groups worked together provided time to work on group problems. These periods also made it possible for the more skilled readers to share what they had learned with those whose reading had been more restricted. Part of the time reading groups went ahead on other projects. Once or twice they worked on stories related to the unit. On a number of days they did not meet in order to allow more time for the reading problems of the interest groups.

SOME BOOKS ABOUT AIR AND WATER

Bell, Thelma Harrington. *Snow*. New York: Viking Press, 1954.
Black, Irma S. *Busy Water*. New York: Holiday House, 1958.
Blough, Glenn O. *Not Only for Ducks—The Story of Rain*. New York: Whittlesey House, 1954.
Fenton, Carroll Lane, and Adams, Mildred. *Our Changing Weather*. New York: Doubleday and Company, 1954.
Friskey, Margaret. *The True Book of Air Around Us*. Chicago: Childrens Press, 1953.
Goudey, Alice E. *The Good Rain*. New York: E. P. Dutton and Company, 1950.
Irving, Robert. *Hurricanes and Twisters*. New York: Alfred A. Knopf, Inc., 1955.
McCloskey, Robert. *Time of Wonder*. New York: Viking Press, 1957.
Rand, Ann. *The Little River*. New York: Harcourt, Brace and World, Inc., 1959.
Schneider, Herman. *Everyday Weather and How It Works*. New York: Whittlesey House, 1951.
Smith, F. C. *The First Book of Water*. New York: Franklin Watts, 1959.

Waller, Leslie. *A Book to Begin on Weather*. New York: Henry Holt and Company, 1959.
Wyler, Rose. *The First Book of Weather*. New York: Franklin Watts, 1956.
Zim, Herbert S. *Lightning and Thunder*. New York: William Morrow and Company, 1952.
Zolotow, Charlotte. *The Storm Book*. New York: Harper and Brothers, 1952.

A THIRD GRADE STUDIES HOUSES AND BUILDINGS

What may be expected of children of superior ability in third grade? The reading activities of one class in which the range in reading ability was from high second- to sixth-grade skill, were as broad as those that might be expected of a typical intermediate-grade class. These youngsters came back after Christmas vacation to find that an addition to their school was being built.

BEGINNING THE UNIT:

Questions began to be raised immediately. Which classes were to be in the new building? When would it be ready to be used? Would it be built of the same material as their school? Would the classrooms look the same? Other questions had to do with the workmen, and with the equipment that was beginning to roll into the school ground.

Out of this unusually good opportunity for firsthand experience developed a unit that lasted for a total of nine weeks. First interests were in the new school building. As the children began to acquire information, the teacher raised questions than encouraged them to think about underlying concepts—the importance of thinking about the purpose a building is to serve in planning its blueprints; the effect of new materials and ways of working on the type of building that can be constructed; the changes that have been brought about by modern architecture. From the discussions that helped to explore these concepts came questions regarding modern homes and their contrast with homes of other lands and of other times. For much of this unit the two interests—in modern construction and in homes in other lands—ran parallel.

UNIT ACTIVITIES:

Firsthand experiences for the children in this third grade were many. On the day they returned to find the ground being excavated, everyone bundled into outdoor clothing and went to watch. From time to time they went out again, and on several occasions they took paper along and sketched equipment from various angles. This, incidentally, provided this class with some of its first experiences with perspective. The children also brought in pictures and saw several movies depicting dwellings in other lands. For two weeks all who could watched a television program that described the building of a house.

People came to the classroom to answer questions. Information regarding how large the new school was to be and which classes were to be in it was supplied by the principal. The architect brought his blueprints. The roofing contractor brought samples of new materials, some still in experimental form. The carpenter let the children handle his tools, and later the physical education teacher loaned the group a large tray of his personal tools. One of the mothers took photographs of the building at various stages in its construction. These the children labelled and displayed on one of their bulletin boards.

Classroom displays were developed. One of the most extensive of these was an exhibit of building materials. Children also brought toys from home and developed quite a collection of models of building machines. As group work connected with dwellings in other lands began to be rounded out, the children constructed, at home or at school, small-scale models of the homes about which they had been reading—an Eskimo igloo, a jungle hut, a cave, a castle, a Swiss chalet, a Roman house, a Colonial home, and a two-story stucco house.

SPECIAL GROUPS:

The group organization for this unit was complicated. All worked together to raise questions, to lay general plans, to get ready to ask visitors questions, and to develop displays. Special groups were set up to study aspects of the school building process more carefully—one on materials, one on workmen, and one on equipment. At the same time the children worked in other groups to study houses of other times.

READING ACTIVITIES:

Reading related to the unit was part of the group activities almost every day. There was no one large block of several days in which the children read intensively for information. They were encouraged to raise specific questions, to hunt for the information they needed, to share it with their groups and incorporate it in their plans, and then to go on to other questions. While they labelled exhibits, planned the blueprints for their models of homes, and decided what kinds of materials they would need, they turned again and again to books.

The readers with which this classroom was equipped supplied only a limited amount of information. Supplementary books contained much that was of help, the library had a number of single copies of useful books, and the encyclopedia proved to be of definite value to the more able children. Some of the reading was done individually and then reported to the interest group. Some was done in the interest-group setting. Less-skilled readers read the materials available on their own level and learned much from listening as the groups worked together. Many of the children took long strides toward skillful use of reference materials as they hunted for the information they needed, took simple notes, examined blueprints, and drew plans for their own models.

The materials developed in the classroom offered many other opportunities to read. The children kept track of their complicated projects through class plans, daily schedules, and group plans. They labelled their exhibit of materials and their display of pictures. They developed illustrated vocabulary lists of workmen and equipment. For one week they used as a spelling list the words they felt they needed the most. As they studied words like *construction* they discovered how helpful syllabication could be, both for reading and spelling.

Individual records, reports, and stories accompanied every step in the unit. As many of these as possible were posted on the bulletin boards for all to read. Each child developed his own "Shelter Booklet." They kept track of the steps in the construction of the new school and wrote individual stories about it. They wrote other stories about the equipment and the uses of materials. They described the houses they lived in and wrote about the kind of house they would like to build. They reviewed the movies they saw and the television programs they watched. Toward the end of the unit each child wrote about the kind of job he would like to hold if he were interested in construction. This served as one basis for evaluating the growth that had taken place.

SOME BOOKS ABOUT HOUSES AND BUILDINGS

Bergere, Thea, and Richard. *From Stones to Skyscrapers*. New York: Dodd, Mead and Company, 1960.
Burns, William A. *A World Full of Homes*. New York: McGraw-Hill, 1953.
Liang, Yen. *The Skyscraper*. Philadelphia: J. B. Lippincott Company, 1958.
Miles, Betty. *A House for Everyone*. New York: Alfred A. Knopf, Inc., 1958.
Neurath, Marie. *Building Big Things*. New York: Lothrop, Lee and Shepard Company, 1958.
Norling, Josephine and Ernest. *Pogo's House*. New York: Holt, Rinehart and Winston, Inc., 1941.
Osmond, Edward. *Houses*. New York: The Macmillan Company, 1956.
———. *Villages*. New York: The Macmillan Company, 1957.
Riedman, Sarah Regal. *Let's Take a Trip to a Skyscraper*. New York: Abelard-Schuman, Inc., 1955.

Many reading skills are needed in units such as these. Children read for information. They read carefully to follow group plans and to evaluate group summaries. They learn new terms as they help to label exhibits and prepare lists of important words. They read for pleasure as they locate interesting stories related to the unit and as they share each other's creative efforts. Skill in oral reading is needed, too, as children plan ways of sharing what they have learned with other groups. These are situations that provide the extended purposeful practice that children need if there is to be maximum development of their reading skill.

Reading is a source of information in these units, but it is by no means the only source. Teachers whose classrooms are more meagerly supplied with reference materials than the rooms that have been described still have available for their groups the opportunities to go to see, to bring materials from home, to invite visitors to share their knowledge and experience, to examine pictures, to listen to stories. Furthermore, in the classrooms that have been described the materials written by teacher and children jointly, or by children alone, make up an important part of the total reading matter, even for groups in which there are able readers. Children need not be denied the satisfactions of working together and of exploring their world, nor need they be denied the experience of purposeful reading merely because they are in classrooms where one or two sets of adopted texts provide most of their opportunities to work with books.

Use group records of plans to help guide unit activities. Classroom records are used in many ways in the unit activities that have just been described. One of their functions is to preserve the plans that guide the unit. Several types of plans may be made. At the beginning of a unit, there is often a list of questions raised by the children. These are usually general, as the children do not yet have the background to explore fully the problem, and teachers expect to develop broader and deeper insights as the unit unfolds. The third grade, whose unit on wind was described earlier, was helped to phrase questions that implied science principles. In a second grade at the beginning of a study of where food comes from, the questions were stated somewhat more concretely.

LET'S FIND OUT

1. Can air keep things out like a wall?
2. Can air be poured like water?
3. Can air pick up a heavy thing?
4. Does air push, even when you don't blow it or pump it?

QUESTIONS ABOUT FOOD

How many families of foods are there?
What different kinds of vegetables are there?
What different kinds of fruits are there?
What meats do we eat?
What fish do we eat?
How many different food stores are in our neighborhood?
What is a good breakfast for a school child?
What is a good lunch for a school child?

Questions may become more specific when interest groups go to work, as indicated by the shorter list made by the subcommittee on meat from the second grade mentioned above.

Which animals give us meat?
What are the names of different kinds of meat?
Which animals are the poultry we eat?
Which fish do people eat?

Plans may also describe proposed activities. When the second-grade unit on food developed to the point where the children were studying dairy products, their list of proposed activities was broad. In the third-grade unit on wind, the plans contained an equally varied list of activities.

WHAT WE WANT TO DO	*OUR PLANS*
1. Visit a dairy.	1. Make experiments.
2. Make pictures and cartoons about milk.	2. Paint and draw pictures.
3. Write and read stories about milk.	3. Bring things from home.
4. Build a play dairy.	4. Invite someone to tell us about the wind.
5. Churn butter.	5. Write stories and riddles.
6. Mix some milk drinks.	6. Read stories.
7. Ask our mothers about foods that use milk.	7. Have a puppet show about wind
8. Make milk recipe books for our mothers.	8. Make a frieze.
9. Have a dairy party.	9. Make kites, planes, boats, parachutes, windmills, and pinwheels.
	10. Have a kite or plane contest.

Various types of written plans can also be used to guide the day-by-day development of a unit. Many teachers make a practice of planning the daily schedule with the children and then posting it, so that all understand the sequence of activities for the day and the suggested time limits. Lists of things to do for people who finish early can be useful. Sometimes a special list of extra jobs connected with the unit, to be undertaken only if everything else has been finished, will help to enrich the program for an able child. Committee responsibilities for parts of the unit are often recorded. Lists of committee members may be helpful. So may lists of items to be brought from home. Many of these written records are planned with the children so that all are clear about what needs to be done. They help children to be more independent about the day's work, and, by so doing, they free the teacher to work where her help is most needed.

Develop new vocabulary through special records. Children who read widely and independently to locate the information they need for a unit are certain to run into new and difficult words. In the units that have been described, classroom records are used in a variety of ways to bring new terminology to the attention of the class. Because the vocabulary load is likely to be heavy, charts that can be used for reference throughout the unit may be particularly helpful. Many of these records are composed during group discussions so that new concepts are clarified as the list of words is built. How thoroughly children are expected to learn the words on such lists depends upon the ability of the class and upon the importance of the words for future reading activities. In first grade, particularly, the most useful function of some lists may be to add the terms to children's speaking vocabularies.

Illustrations and articles for display are particularly helpful in developing the new vocabulary related to a unit. In the third grade whose study of the new building was reported earlier, the children learned new terms rapidly through their lists of workmen and equipment and through their exhibit of materials. Captions to the pictures on the classroom bulletin boards helped to review new terms.

Frequently, vocabulary lists serve as an aid both to reading and to creative writing. Some groups build picture dictionaries of words they need. Others may develop their own file boxes of needed words. Often the lists are posted. In one first grade, where a unit on birds led to considerable creative writing, a bulletin board contained pictures of common birds clearly labelled. To give added help the following word lists were posted:

WORDS ABOUT BIRDS		*LITTLE WORDS*	
1. nest	6. worm	the	this
2. lays	7. egg	is	we
3. grass	8. house	are	was
4. find	9. fly	our	come
5. white	10. yard	in	came
		on	play
		at	have
		it	see

These children were interested in writing other creative stories and several new lists were in the process of being built—words about kites, words about rain, words about boats. All of these lists were posted on one bulletin board, which was serving as a center for creative-writing activities.

In the classrooms that have been described, further assistance in acquiring new vocabulary is given through the many classroom records that use the new terms and through the materials in textbooks and supplementary books. It is this planned repetition of vocabulary in many settings that makes it possible for a teacher and a primary class to go so far afield in the reading activities connected with units of work.

Add to the available reading materials through records summarizing information. Mention has been made at several points in this chapter and in preceding chapters of the value of classroom records as summaries of information. These records may vary greatly in length. At times a single chart will tell the complete story, at others a series of charts will be composed. Typical of the varied records that can be developed in the course of a unit are those of the second grade whose plans to study food were reported earlier. These were able children, and the vocabulary load in the records is heavier than that with which second-graders of limited ability should be expected to cope. They summarized their trip to the dairy in the following news bulletin:

THE DAIRY

We went to a dairy.
We watched the men work
   at the dairy.
We learned about their
   work to give us
   good milk to drink.
We visited the dairy
   down the street.
It is interesting to see
   the dairymen pasteurize
   and bottle milk.
They work hard for us.

Later, with the technical knowledge of the teacher to help, they prepared the following more extensive record, which covered two large sheets of oak-tag:

THE STORY OF MILK

Farmers milk cows. They put the milk into big cans. They keep the milk cool until the milk truck comes. Then they send the cans of milk to the dairy.

At the dairy the milk cans are emptied and washed. Then the cans are put on trucks and sent back to the farmers.

At the dairy the milk is weighed and sampled. It is pumped up to the big storage tanks through long pipes.

Then the milk is strained to take out any dirt. Next it is pasteurized to kill any germs. Big paddles stir the milk while it is being heated.

Now the milk is cooled by letting it run down over refrigerator pipes.

After that the milk goes to a bottling machine. It is put into bottles which have been washed very clean in the bottle washing machine.

Then the bottles of milk have caps and tops put on them. They are put into cases, and the cases are stored in the great big refrigerator room.

Milkmen come to the refrigerator room. They take cases of milk out to the loading platform. They put the milk on their milk trucks.

The milkmen take the milk to homes, stores, schools, and other places. Then we drink the milk.

And that is the story of milk!

In the third-grade unit on wind, described earlier, a single chart summarized a rather extensive discussion. Evidence of growth in sensitivity to accurate choice of words shows in the terms the children used.

WIND

1. FLIES	Kites, ballons, planes, and parachutes
2. BLOWS	Hats, trash can lids, roofs, leaves, paper, hair, seeds, dirt, dust, snow, rain, people, doors, clothes, and umbrellas
3. MOVES	Clouds and water
4. KNOCKS DOWN	Signs, trees, wire fences, telephone poles, fruits from trees, and flower pots
5. DRIES	Wash, streets, and pavements
6. TURNS	Windmills and pinwheels
7. BREAKS	Glass
8. SPREADS	Fire
9. SWAYS	Trees and flowers
10. SAILS	Boats
11. COOLS	Things, people, and animals

Work-type reviews of information can be posted in chart form. In a fist-grade room a study of growing things was reviewed through a series of riddles printed on small charts. Some of these were written by the teacher and some by the children. In a second grade another form of riddle was used, for which the children were to draw the correct answer:

WHAT AM I?

I am green
I grow on trees
I am little in spring
Then I grow bigger.
   What am I?

AUTUMN ANIMAL RIDDLES

Who flies south in autumn?
Who goes to sleep?
Who stores food?
Who changes color?
Who grows a heavy coat?
Who makes a warm home?
Who swims way down to the
   bottom of the pond?

For additional work-type activities which may serve as reviews, children may also be given matching activities, where they draw lines from key words to the correct pictures. They may answer yes-no questions, choose the right answer in a multiple-choice statement, or mark statements true or false. If their study has involved a sequence of steps, they may rearrange phrase cards to put the steps in order. They may label pictures, or draw pictures to indicate the correct answer. These are devices that are used for work-type activities in connection with the work of reading groups. They can be equally helpful in unit activities, and the same general principles regarding the need for interest and for thought-provoking questions still hold.

Group summaries of information are not the only ones used in a typical primary classroom. Children also write their own materials. Typically, the less skilled the group the more likely pictures are to be used as the form of individual expression. However, short written statements are possible if the teacher helps. In the first grade whose lists of words about birds were given earlier, the available bird books were too difficult for the children to read. The teacher, therefore, provided the needed information by reading to the group. Then, with the help of the word lists and some individual guidance from the teacher, each child wrote and illustrated stories for his own bird book. Some of these were very simple; some conveyed considerable information.

CARDINALS	*ORIOLES*
Cardinals stay in winter.	Orioles have a hanging nest.
The cardinals are red.	Orioles are black and orange.
Can you see the cardinals?	They lay white eggs.

Children at the third-grade level have considerable command of writing skills. They can put down the essentials of an experience, especially with the kind of help that comes from talking through an idea with others. Teachers often give direct and specific help in these writing tasks. They provide first, opportunities to talk out ideas, to share experiences and pleasant recollections, and to check the accuracy of facts and interpretations. They can provide suggestions for ways of dealing with ideas, help with spelling of new words, and provide, generally with the help of children themselves, lists of terms most likely to be needed.

The materials produced may be rather extensive. In the Shelter Booklets compiled by the third grade whose unit was described earlier, were to be found lists of new words; chapters on workmen, equipment, and materials; and reports of the work of the group to which the child had belonged when he studied homes in other lands. Booklets may be combinations of group and individual work. Records made by the group may be copied by each child for his booklet. Then later creative stories and pictures may be added by each child individually.

The activities described here imply a unified approach to language learnings. Learning to write, speak and read are closely related activities, and are so regarded in the primary classroom. Children talk about what they have seen; they help to dictate records as a group; they write their own reports; and they read, both to locate information and to review the information they have helped to record.

BUILDING READINESS FOR THE READING PROBLEMS OF THE CONTENT FIELDS

Help children become acquainted with different formats of books. First steps toward reading the varied materials of the content fields are taken in the primary grades. One of the adjustments the reader must be able to make is to texts written in a style that is different from the stories in basal readers and from simple recreational books. Primary teachers help children develop readiness for this both through the way they introduce the first textbooks in arithmetic, spelling, science, health, and social studies, and through the varied classroom records they use.

Cincinnati Public Schools

All curriculum areas provide opportunities to develop reading skills. Arithmetic requires careful reading.

Children have many opportunities to read arithmetic materials in the typical primary classroom. Before they read numbers they have many experiences with concrete objects. Opportunities to read numbers soon present themselves. In the early fall, one teacher prepared a prereading chart giving the prices of the school lunch and of the extra milk so that her children could be sure they had enough lunch money. Children learn to watch a calendar for birthdays, or to count the weeks to special holidays. They may be given other experiences in reading numbers through following simple recipes, reading a short list of prices in a play store, following simple directions for scoring a game, and reading rules that show how many children may work in the playhouse or paint at the easel. First grade teachers also use many different charts to show number groupings, simple money values, and ways of telling time.

The same functional use of numbers found in first-grade classrooms can also be observed in second and third grades. However there should be less need of concrete number groupings and greater ability to read the Arabic symbols. Readiness for large numbers was developed in a second grade through a daily record of attendance and, at the beginning of the new year, in a summary of the class discussion of days, weeks, and seasons.

Science materials require step-by-step reading with careful attention both to details and the sequence in which they are expressed. Experience with such reading can be given by classroom records of science activities. Children in one second grade made an accurate report of their study of safety measures with icy streets:

A WINTER EXPERIMENT FOR GOOD CITIZENS

We put a pan of water
   out on the window sill.
The water froze into the ice.

We felt the ice.
It was slippery.

Then we put ashes on
   part of the ice.
The ashes made the ice rough.

Then we put salt
   on part of the ice.
The salt melted the ice.

Be a good citizen
   in the winter time.
Shovel snow off your walk.
Put ashes or salt on your icy walk.

Then your mother and father
   won't fall.
Then your friends and neighbors
   won't fall.

First contacts with the formats of language and of spelling texts can also be given through classroom records. Models of the correct form for a letter are frequently seen on primary chalkboards. Very early, the letter itself is likely to be a group composition that is copied by the children. Simple illustrative sentences to show the uses of periods and question marks may be posted. So may one or two rules that the children have learned about using capital letters or ending sentences with periods. First lists of spelling words may be built from the words the children in the particular group seem to need the most frequently for their own writing. One second-grade teacher previewed the style of the adopted speller by presenting new words in the following chart form:

YOUR CLOTHES

Does your mother say this?
"Where are your cap and coat?
It is almost time for school."
Does your father say this?
"Is that your new hat by the door?
You must take good care of what we gave you."

| hat | coat | new | say | cap |
| your | gave | where | school | door |

As children begin to use simple textbooks in the various content fields and skills areas, teachers frequently take time to work with these books as they would with a reader. The children may examine the book, look at its table of contents, and talk about its general format. Then, as the first materials are actually read, time is taken to help the children identify especially useful parts of the book. They may note where the list of new words is placed on the page of a speller, talk about the way a language or an arithmetic book sets a rule apart in a special box, or notice the use of section and paragraph headings in a science or social-studies textbook. This introductory discussion is followed by further help, both to groups and to individuals, as new problems are faced.

Develop familiarity with simple illustrative aids. The skillful reader of materials in the content fields must be able to use pictures, graphs, maps, and tables to interpret what he is reading. Readiness for these reading problems, too, is developed in the primary grades. Pictures are a source of information from the first day of school. First-graders learn to read a number of other simple legends. Among these may be clock faces to tell when it is time for recess, for noon lunch, and for clean-up and simple symbols to record the weather for the day. They may also become acquainted with tables as the teacher records their weights and heights, and with graphs as she develops simple devices to show how many mothers are members of the P.T.A. or how many children have visited the dentist.

As second- and third-graders grow, both in their reading skill and in their ability to use numbers, their contacts with various kinds of visual aids increase. They may keep more elaborate records in simple charts or tabular forms—a record of the weather; a series of drawings of plants to show how fast a window-box garden is growing; drawings of two plants to show size comparisons under different growing conditions; a bar graph made by pasting pictures of books or other symbols after names to show how many library books each child has read; a chart classifying objects in the classroom museum. More skilled readers may also work with simple diagrams. In the third grades for which the units were described earlier, there were opportunities to follow a diagram for making a kite, to examine the blueprints of the new school building, and to make simple diagrams of the dwellings the children themselves proposed to construct. Third-graders may also have occasion to draw a map of their school grounds or of the neighborhood in which their school is located. Even first- and second-graders may occasionally draw a very simple map as they make a model of their community or mark the streets on which their homes are located.

Many of the experiences in interpreting illustrative aids provided for primary children are those in which the children actually help to construct the table, the graph, or the map. They learn how these devices convey information because they have used them for their own purposes. Later they will bring this understanding to the more technical informational material of the intermediate grades.

Help children take their first steps in using reference techniques. Informational-reading activities expand manyfold primary children's experiences in locating information. By the end of the third grade, the children should have become acquainted with many kinds of reference materials. The start is made through basal readers, supplementary books, and a few easy library books. Teachers add new types of reference materials as soon as they feel children are ready for them. If the entire class is not ready for a new experience, time may be taken to work specially with the group of more skilled readers. Sometimes a new resource, such as an encyclopedia, which may be used occasionally is discussed by the group as a whole in third grade, so that all know its general purposes, and then better readers are given help as they work with it individually. Children may be given further help in exploring a variety of resource materials by being encouraged to read children's newspapers, to bring from home pictures clipped from adult newspapers and magazines, and even to write for pamphlets. Often the teacher builds readiness for later use of more difficult books by showing the pictures to the children and by reading appropriate parts aloud. Much of the child's skill in using reference books will be developed in the intermediate grades. However, because of his experience in the primary grades, he comes to this task already aware of the great variety of material that is available to him.

Children also make strides in learning to locate materials. Even the first-graders whose activities have been described are able to use pictures and titles of books and stories to help them locate the material they need. These youngsters typically know how to find page numbers and what help to expect from a table of contents. More skilled readers in second, and particularly in third grade, develop more effective techniques in hunting for the material they need. Many will use tables of contents and some will be able to find obvious topics in an index. Often, some of the first reading periods related to a unit are spent looking through books and marking appropriate stories. Sometimes children develop simple bibliographies by listing the titles of books and the page numbers appropriate to their groups. As the teacher works with groups and with individuals, there are opportunities to ask what the children are using as clues to the information they need, to help them think about related topics that might yield additional information, and to demonstrate the value of looking carefully at chapter titles and section headings.

First acquaintance with alphabetical order may come as beginners examine the alphabet books on their library table. More interest is built when children begin to look at a picture dictionary. By second grade, charts containing needed spelling words are sometimes put in alphabetical order. Better readers in third grade should develop increased skill with the dictionary and even with the alphabetical arrangement of the encyclopedia.

Summarizing and note-taking, too, begin very simply in the primary grades. Many of the children's first summaries are done as a group when they compose a record of a trip they have taken, or tell what they think is most significant about a motion picture they have seen. As more skill in written expression develops, they begin to write their own reports. At first these may be only a few lines long. Later three or four short stories on the same topic may be collected into the types of booklets that have been described as a part of unit activities.

Note-taking is not likely to begin much before third grade. Even here, one or two sentences expressing a general idea are about as much as can be expected. Sometimes the process can be facilitated by simple summary charts. In one third grade, for example, the children who were reading about Indians were given a hectographed sheet divided into columns for such information as clothing, houses, food, and games. In the appropriate column the children wrote one or two words to help them remember the information they had found. Later they met to compare their lists. Written expression is not easy for all primary children and note-taking is a demanding task. The thrill of finding needed information should not be spoiled by too difficult an assignment to write it down.

If the resources of a school or a community library are available, teachers make a practice of helping children become acquainted with it. In their own library corner they are likely to find books that have public library call numbers. As beginners they may take a special trip to see the library. A little later they may borrow easy books and perhaps enjoy a story time planned by the librarian. By third grade they are likely to enlist the librarian's help in finding books on topics of special interest.

Experiences with reference techniques are informal in the primary grades. This is, for the most part, a period for developing readiness. Children use as effective techniques as they are able. They may spend some group sessions discussing how to be more efficient in finding the materials they want and they may be given help from the teacher as they work, but they are not likely to engage in many work-type experiences to develop increased skill. Later, in the intermediate grades, it may be helpful to devote both group reading activities and work-type experiences to polishing reference skills. Examples of such activities are given in Chapters XI and XII.

Provide reading experiences that call for skill in adjusting reading techniques to varied purposes. The skillful reader is adept in his ability to adjust the way he reads to his purposes. Experiences with informational reading offer many functional situations in which it is important for children to adjust their reading techniques to the problems they face.

Teachers can be more effective in helping children learn to read for many purposes if they are sensitive to the opportunities offered in their classrooms. The summaries that follow indicate typical situations that call for varied reading skills.

Critical evaluation is called for in: Deciding whether a classroom record is accurate; telling other children what you think about a library book; rereading class plans to make sure all proposals have been included; deciding which of a set of experience records will best inform parents about a class project; rethinking classroom rules to be sure they really say what is meant; checking when two books disagree; deciding when the questions raised for unit activities have been answered; deciding which of several books is most helpful for a specific problem; recommending reading to other children; distinguishing between factual and fictional books related to a unit.

Reading with careful attention to details is needed for: Noting special information such as dates and times on messages to be taken home; checking on special regulations for use of classroom equipment; rereading an experience record to be sure a trip is reported accurately; checking the details of a chart before drawing illustrations for it; editing one's creative story; checking lists of materials needed for a special project; helping prepare a weather chart or a news record; checking class plans as work progresses; noting special signs on bulletin boards; making sure a classroom collection is properly labeled; doing independent reading to answer specific questions; knowing pertinent details in order to tell other children about recreational reading; reading independently to follow up a special hobby or interest.

Oral reading experiences are afforded through: Reading classroom rules aloud; reading plans a step at a time while others check; reading aloud an item on the bulletin board not easily seen by children at their desks; reading a story to a small group; practice in oral reading of poems for choral speaking poems related to the unit; reading special information to the group that needs it; reading an experience record aloud while others listen to check its accuracy; reading aloud the parts which provide the specific information needed to settle an argument; reading the caption under your picture to the class; reading the story you have written to the class.

Reference techniques are needed for: Finding information by studying pictures and reading captions; using a table of contents to locate needed information; finding an article in an encyclopedia; using chapter and section headings in deciding whether a book contains needed information; finding a word needed for spelling in an alphabetical class list; reading the headlines in a children's weekly newspaper; writing book reviews and reading the book reviews written by other children; reading simple maps related to school or community; preparing simple charts or graphs; taking one- or two-sentence notes; helping to compose a group or class summary of materials read.

Reading for the general idea of a passage is called for in: Enjoying recreational reading where the plot of the story is the main purpose for reading; reporting a story to other children; answering riddles made up by other children; illustrating a mimeographed story or an experience chart; rereading an experience record to be sure it has covered all pertinent points; skimming books or experience records to locate specific items of information; checking an experience record to be sure it reports events as they actually happened; following various classroom plans; planning the

scenes for a dramatization related to a unit.

Skill in following directions is needed for: Reading charts describing how to carry out various housekeeping responsibilities; carrying out unit plans in order; reading recipes; reading directions for work-type activities in various skill areas; carrying out school regulations regarding fire drill or safety on the playground; carrying out a special science experiment; making gifts according to simple written directions; checking the accuracy of the report of a science experiment; acting on special announcements from the principal's office; following written instructions for classroom games; checking daily plans to decide what activities to take on next.

Adjustments of reading speed are needed in: Skimming material to locate specific information; reading a long article quickly to see if it contains items of particular interest; finding needed material and then reading it carefully to report on it; rereading to locate the evidence when a point is disputed; reading carefully when directions are involved.

New vocabulary is developed through: Preparing and using vocabulary lists needed for a unit; preparing a picture dictionary of words appropriate to a unit; developing a list of spelling words needed for the writing activities related to a unit; drawing pictures illustrating new terms and concepts; labelling exhibits or pictures; developing lists that classify new terms.

Broad interests in reading are developed through: Becoming acquainted with various reference books; exploring library books in a search for information; enjoying fictional stories related to the general topic of a unit; writing group stories; sharing creative stories written by individual children; locating related topics in basal readers; listening to stories related to the unit read by the teacher.

ENCOURAGING RECREATIONAL READING

Children who come to the intermediate grades eager to read have been given their start by primary teachers. Library corners are important centers in the classrooms that have been described. Opportunities to read for fun and experiences to develop new reading interests and more discriminating reading tastes are considered to be an integral part of the reading program. What steps can be taken to help children learn to enjoy reading, just for the fun of reading?

Make the library corner attractive. In most primary classrooms the library corner is an inviting place to work. It is typically located in a part of the room where children can read quietly. When possible, bookshelves flank at least one side, so that books are easily available. Sometimes the bookshelves are used as a partial partition from the rest of the room. If there is a bulletin board near by, it may be saved for special displays pertaining to recreational reading—bright book covers, pictures to stimulate reading related to a specific problem, a poem, interesting book reports from the children themselves, or records of their reading. Sometimes a rocking chair or some wicker furniture adds to the homelike atmosphere.

Frequently, new books worthy of being "featured" items are prominently displayed on a special rack, shelf, or table, so that they are easily seen. Colorful jackets with transparent protective covers are powerful attractions to the prospective reader. The featured book may be one which the teacher, or an enthusiastic reader in the class group, has read and wishes to recommend. Such a recommendation may be made to a small group, to an individual, or to the entire class, and may include the reading aloud of a scene or two, to whet the appetites of prospective consumers.

Provide time and opportunity to enjoy recreational reading. Part of the problem of encouraging recreational reading is providing time for it. As the total primary program was described in Chapter VI, definitely scheduled periods for pleasure reading were foreseen and definite scheduled times were suggested to allow children to share their recreational reading with others in the class. In Chapter VII, were described reading units which developed aound recreational-reading interests. It is also possible to set up special story clubs where children of like interests meet to share their reading. One third grade was divided into three books clubs. Their reading-matter ranged from first-grade picture books to some fourth-grade material. The reading clubs met regularly to share their pleasure in *Chanticleer and the Fox*,[7] and the delightful pictures illustrating the old, and satisfying story of *The Wolf and the Seven Little Kids*,[8] and *The Old Woman and Her Pig*.[9] Their horizons moved out to include the gentle, kindly *Crow Boy*,[10] who went to school in a country different from their own, and the story of the discoverer in *The Columbus Story*.[11] They pondered over the feelings of Dionisio in *A Hero By Mistake*,[12] and laughed over the delightful nonsense situations in *The Perfect Pancake*.[13] They introduced new friends to other members of the group as they became acquainted with *The Biggest Bear*,[14] or *Little Leo*.[15] Factual materials also held interest. Even children who had never been at the sea shore were interested in *Houses from the Sea*,[16] and expanded their understanding of a part of the world they had not before known about. Accounts of space travel had ready audiences, and such books as *You Will Go to the Moon*,[17] and *The True Book of Space*[18] were popular. In addition to these opportunities for reading for pleasure, the reading activities related to the units described earlier in this chapter can be planned so that there is time to read fictional as well as informational material connected with the unit.

Reading for pleasure need not always be classified as such on the weekly schedule. The important thing is to provide an opportunity for children to enjoy books, whether it be in a special period, part of the work of a reading group, an aspect of a unit of work, or a free-time activity.

Plan for experiences to help to develop reading tastes. Out of his total reading experiences, a primary child should be expected to begin to develop

[7] Barbara Cooney, *Chanticleer and the Fox* (New York: Thomas Y. Crowell Company, 1958).

[8] Grimm Brothers, *The Wolf and the Seven Little Kids*, il. by Felix Hoffman (New York: Harcourt, Brace and Company, 1959).

[9] *The Old Woman and Her Pig*, il. by Paul Galdone (New York: McGraw-Hill Book Company, Inc., 1960).

[10] Taro Yashima, *Crow Boy* (New York: Viking Press, 1955).

[11] Alice Dalgliesh, *The Columbus Story* (New York: Charles Scribner's Sons, 1955).

[12] Anita Brenner, *A Hero By Mistake* (New York: William R. Scott, Inc., 1953).

[13] Virginia Kahl, *The Perfect Pancake* (New York: Charles Scribner's Sons, 1960).

[14] Lynd Ward, *The Biggest Bear* (New York: Houghton Mifflin Company, 1952).

[15] Leo Politi, *Little Leo* (New York: Charles Scribner's Sons, (1951).

[16] Alice Coudey, *Houses from the Sea* (New York: Charles Scribner's Sons, 1959).

[17] Mae and Ira Freeman, *You Will Go to the Moon* (New York: Random House, 1959).

[18] Illa Podendorf, *The True Book of Space* (Chicago: The Children's Press, Inc., 1959).

standards for evaluating what he reads. Reading tastes do not grow from one aspect of the reading program alone; every experience contributes. The richer the total program, the more likely it is that discrimination will be developed.

Standards are developed, in part, through work in reading groups. Here the children begin to make discriminations as they read for different purposes—this story was very amusing; this one kept you guessing right to the end; this was exciting because it really happened; fairy stories and tall tales are fun; they start you imagining. When group activities are developed as reading units there are opportunities to contrast several stories, to discuss why those by a favorite author are so well liked, and perhaps to go to the library to find others of his books. The stories and poems in basal readers are selected for their literary merit, as well as for the experience with new vocabulary and more complex sentence and paragraph structure that they provide.

Guidance in reading these selections can include experiences which develop appreciation for apt descriptions of persons and places, or smoothly flowing sentences, and delightfully light touches of humor.

Nothing helps to develop reading tastes more effectively than the quality of the books available for recreational reading. Library shelves need to be stocked with care. This is no easy task when the great numbers of new and old books published for children are considered. However, the problem of what to select is eased by the many current guides to children's books which are helpful to both teachers and parents. Reviews of current books are found in periodicals such as *Elementary English*, and the *Horn Book;* many helpfully annotated lists of children's books are available. These lists give suggested age levels and probable appeal to specific groups of readers. Among these are *Adventuring with Books*[19] and *Bibliography of Books for Children.*[20] A more highly selective aid is *Children's Books Too Good to Miss.*[21] Other lists will be found in the bibliography at the end of this chapter, and following Chapter XI.

Book lists are useful aids, but nothing takes the place of real acquaintance with the books themselves. Teachers find it helpful to read widely and critically in the field of children's books, as well as to use the bibliographical aids.

On occasion, it is helpful to have recordings of children's books and stories. If the narration is good, and reproducing instruments are adequate, new vis-

[19] Published by the National Council of Teachers of English, 704 S. Sixth Street, Champaign, Illinois.

[20] Published and revised every two years by the Association for Childhood Education International, 3615 Wisconsin Avenue, N.W., Washington 16, D. C.

[21] May Hill Arbuthnot, *Children's Books Too Good to Miss*, Second Revised Edition (Cleveland, Ohio: Western Reserve University, 1959).

tas in appreciation may be opened up, both for poetry and for prose selections. Often poems and stories require men's as well as women's voices for interpretation, and records can fill this need. Since recordings are numerous and lists are soon out of date, the best sources of information are probably current issues of professional magazines in the area of the language arts, or of audiovisual aids.

Times when library books are being shared give opportunities to develop standards. Enthusiasm about a story can be picked up by the teacher with such questions as, "Why did you like it?" "What made it exciting?" "Why do you think it was so funny?" Standards can be formulated as children decide which stories to read to another class, or to share with another reading group. Sometimes the period before library books are to be returned can be turned into an evaluation session. "Did you like your book?" "Would other children like it?" "To whom would you recommend it?" "Why?"

Children learn to appreciate good literature through satisfying experiences with their own creative writing. This means, in part, being sensitive to opportunities for creative expression. These opportunities present themselves in many ways—invitations and letters can be creative; the hum of the machinery seen on an excursion can suggest a song; a foggy day or a bright traffic light outside the window of a city classroom can bring forth some imaginative stories; holidays can call for poems, songs, and plays; even the information that goes into a social-studies or science booklet can be phrased in one's own way, and illustrated with one's own pictures.

The teacher also needs to be alert to opportunities to develop awareness of apt expressions. In composing a group record, someone may choose just the right words to tell what he saw. Two children may suggest lines that have the rhythm and rhyme of a poem. In writing a Halloween story a child may have the very phrase that makes the ending sound scary. Children need to be helped to become sensitive to these evidences of creative ability in themselves and in their friends.

Special care needs to be taken to expand children's interest in poetry. Throughout the primary grades, experiences with poetry are more likely to involve listening and sharing orally than they are to call for the reading of poems. However, by third grade, some children may begin to enjoy reading their favorite poems for themselves. In one class a teacher shared her collection of poems with the children by mimeographing favorites that were appropriate for special projects. These the children put into their own "poetry books." Soon the youngsters themselves began to bring in poems. Usually it was the teacher who read these aloud to the group. The resulting discussions did much to develop more sensitive listeners, and the best of these contributions, too, went into the poetry books.

Classrooms in which children develop broad reading interests and sensitive reading tastes are typically those in which children hear many stories and poems well read by the teacher. They grow to love good literature because they are under the guidance of someone who also loves it, and who expresses her appreciation in her voice and her manner. They catch her enthusiasm as they listen to her read *Finders Keepers* [22] or enjoy with her the sounds of the strange words in *Scrambled Eggs Super*,[23] and they share their delight in a new story with her because they are sure of an enthusiastic and sensitive response. Perhaps nothing is as important in the development of children's tastes as the attitudes and appreciations of the adults who introduce them to books.

Reading is one of the receptive language arts. Listening is another. Speaking and writing are the expressive aspects of the language arts program. In actual practice these aspects are closely interrelated. Children talk. They write their ideas or they watch while their ideas are being written. They share their own creative expression. They enjoy the creative expressions of others. They listen in appreciation when the teacher reads to them and they read with appreciation when they read to others. Love of reading, appreciation of good writing, and satisfaction in expressing one's own ideas in writing develop together in the classroom where the language arts program is guided the most effectively.

SOME QUESTIONS TO THINK ABOUT IN APPRAISING THE ON-GOING READING ACTIVITIES OF THE PRIMARY GRADES

1. Do the signs and notices around the classroom serve a purpose important to the group?

2. Are children encouraged to read as widely for information as their skill will permit?

3. In unit activities, is effective use made of classroom records composed by teacher and children?

4. Are unit activities scheduled so that there is time to give help with group and with individual reading problems?

5. In the informational-reading activities related to a unit, are both materials and help provided so that children are able to read with groups working on topics of interest to them?

6. Are children encouraged to use reference skills as effectively as they are able?

7. Are informational-reading activities planned to develop readiness for more extensive reading in the content fields?

[22] William Lipkind and Nicholas Mordvinoff, *Finders Keepers* (New York: Harcourt, Brace and Company, 1951).
[23] Theodore Geisel, *Scrambled Eggs Super!* (New York: Random House Inc., 1953).

8. Are the books on the library table selected so that they contribute to better reading tastes?

9. Are children helped to develop standards for their choice of books through their experiences in discussing and sharing them?

SUGGESTIONS FOR FURTHER READING

Bamman, Henry A., and Dawson, Mildred A. *Fundamentals of Reading Instruction*. Chapter 8. New York: Longmans, Green and Company, Inc., 1959. 304 pp.

Betts, Emmett A. *Foundations of Reading Instruction*. Chapter 13. New York: American Book Company, 1957. 757 pp.

Hildreth, Gertrude. *Teaching Reading*. Chapter 13. New York: Henry Holt and Company, 1958. 612 pp.

Robinson, Helen M. (Editor). *Sequential Development of Reading Abilities*. Supplementary Educational Monograph No. 90. Chicago: The University of Chicago Press, 1960. 251 pp.

Stratemeyer, Florence B.; Forkner, Hamden L.; McKim, Margaret G.; and Passaw, A. Harry. *Developing a Curriculum for Modern Living*. Chapter 8. Second Edition. New York: Teachers College, Columbia University, 1957. 740 pp.

Zirbes, Laura. *Spurs to Creative Teaching*. New York: G. P. Putnam's Sons, 1959. 354 pp.

EASY BOOKS FOR THE BEGINNING READER

Condit, Martha O. "Trade Books for Beginning Readers," *Wilson Library Bulletin*. **34** (December 1960), pp. 284-301.

Groff, Patrick. "Recent Easy Books for First Grade Readers," *Elementary English*. **37** (December 1960), pp. 521-27.

Guilfoile, Elizabeth. *Books for Beginning Readers*. Champaign, Illinois: National Council of Teachers of English, 1962. 73 pp.

Heller, Frieda M. "I Can Read It Myself," *Some Books for Independent Reading in the Primary Grades*. Columbus, Ohio: The Ohio State University Press, 1960. 31 pp.

Russell, David H. "An Evaluation of Some Easy-to-Read Trade Books for Children," *Elementary English*, **38** (November, 1961), pp. 375-482.

CHAPTER IX

Helping Primary Children Learn to Work with Words

WHENEVER children are reading they are meeting with problems of how to recognize words. A reader becomes truly independent only when he has techniques for working out the meaning and pronunciation of words for himself. This chapter is concerned with ways of helping primary children achieve an increasingly higher level of independence in recognizing the words they encounter in their reading.

The problem of how best to develop competence in word study skills has been the focus of much discussion. Some suggestions for teaching have come from the field of linguistics. Materials illustrating a linguistic approach to word recognition expose the learner first to words which illustrate specific vowel and consonant sounds.[1] Lists of words which illustrate a particular sound are followed by short sentences using the given sound, for example, *Nan can fan Dan.* Meaning is not essential; the purpose is to develop reactions to the symbols which represent specific sounds.

As this book is written, these materials have not been rigorously tested in practice. The authors assume that children will not be repelled by "purely formal exercises" if a sense of achievement is thereby secured. Certainly this is an assumption which needs careful checking.

Since the middle 1950's the place of phonics in the word-recognition program has been of keen interest to parents, teachers, and the general public. Many parents and teachers, aroused by announcements of the presumed utility of a greatly increased emphasis upon phonics instruction in the pri-

---

[1] Leonard Bloomfield, and Clarence Barnhart, *Let's Read* (Detroit: Wayne State University Press, 1961), 465 pp.

mary grades, became anxious about the teaching of phonics. Teachers themselves, in speaking of word-attack skills, mentally included in their discussions both structural and phonetic clues to recognizing words, but parents listening in the PTA meeting did not hear the word *phonics* and continued to feel uneasy. After reading many discussions of the problem in the press and popular magazines, many continued to feel that something was missing in the teaching of reading.

In this atmosphere, strongly phonetic approaches to beginning reading found considerable acceptance. Such programs are typically based upon early teaching of letter sounds and of phonics rules before the child learns words as sight words. It has been pointed out that one such program presents approximately 70 per cent of all phonics rules in the first grade. The major difference between this phonics system and a typical basal reader program is not in the total number of phonics generalizations introduced, but in the timing of the introduction.[2] The basal reader program usually followed depends upon the child's having acquired a considerable number of words he is able to recognize at sight before he is expected to learn phonics rules, and the number of these rules are gradually introduced; very few of them are placed in the first year.

Available research evidence suggests that, in the long run, the early introduction of phonics generalizations does not result in superior reading skill. In comparing two groups, one taught by a strongly phonetic method, and the other by the usual basal reader approach, the investigators found that tests of reading ability indicated superiority for the phonetic method in grade one. However, tests at the end of grades three and four showed no difference in the groups, except that the fourth-grade group using the basal readers were superior in accuracy.[3] A later report by the same investigators gives results of tests for these same groups through grades five and six.[4] They found no significant differences between these groups in either reading or spelling. One may conclude that the early introduction of an extensive system of phonics instruction, therefore, does not produce readers who are superior to those who gradually develop understandings of phonics generalizations as one of several ways to gain independence in word recognition.

Even when the introduction of phonics generalizations is gradual, word

[2] Arthur W. Heilman, *Principles and Practices of Teaching Reading* (Columbus, Ohio: Charles E. Merrill Books, Inc., 1960), p. 236 ff.

[3] Paul E. Sparks and Leo C. Fay, "An Evaluation of Two Methods of Teaching Reading," *Elementary School Journal*, **57** (April 1957), 386-90.

[4] Leo C. Fay, "A Look at Two Approaches to the Teaching of Reading," *Changing Concepts of Reading Instruction*, International Reading Association Conference Proceedings, J. Allen Figurel, Editor, pp. 161-63.

See Also: Arthur I. Gates, "Results of Teaching a System of Phonics," *The Reading Teacher*, **14** (March 1961), 248-252.

analysis is a complex intellectual skill requiring both analysis and synthesis. The process actually begins at the prereading level. Long before a child can recognize many of the words around the room, he begins to make general similarities and differences. "My name begins like Sally's." "Those lines all begin exactly the same way." He goes on to discovering helpful parts of words, such as *s* endings, and compounds, like *something, fireman,* and *into.* He uses beginning consonant sounds as cues. Some children will see quickly the general principles involved and make their own independent discoveries with little help from the teacher; others will require prolonged and careful guidance in a program of word study which provides for continuing growth toward independence.

Such a program for word study for the primary grades is here presented as having three phases; first, the development of an expanded stock of sight words; second, an increase in meaning vocabulary; and third, strengthened ability to use context clues and structural and phonetic analysis as means of growing independence in reading. These goals were outlined in Chapter VI, and specific consideration will be given to these three phases of word study in the sections which follow.

To achieve independence in reading, a child must first understand the meaning of words he is called upon to recognize. This calls for learning new words and for enriching the meaning of words already familiar. For the purpose of discussion in this chapter, this has been called the *word-meaning* aspect of word study activities.

Second, in order to be able to read, a child must recognize a word in its printed form. For skilled, rapid reading he must be able to make this recognition instantly from a rapid inspection of the word. Presented as whole words in a meaningful context, these words are learned by the primary child as he meets them in the vocabulary of pre-primers and primers. Visual discriminations based upon the general appearance, or configuration, of the word, its peculiar characteristics, and the meaning associated with it, make it possible for the beginning reader to build up a stock of words he can recognize at sight. These words the child perceives as wholes, and does not make any extended attempt to analyze component parts. For the purposes of discussion, this has been called skill in *word recognition.*

Third, the child must be able to break an unfamiliar word into whatever phonetic or structural elements he needs to work out its pronunciation. This, for the purposes of this chapter has been called a skill in *word analysis.*[5]

While it is helpful to consider these three aspects of the word-study pro-

---

[5] For a discussion of the relationships between the "instantaneous perception" of highly useful and frequently repeated words, and the phonetic and structural analysis of less familiar words, see: William S. Gray, *On Their Own in Reading* Revised Edition, Chapter Two (Chicago: Scott, Foresman and Company, 1960), 248 pp.

gram separately, they are closely interrelated in the actual teaching situation. When a teacher helps a child to recognize *firemen, truck, engine,* or *bus* in order to read a story, she also enriches the meaning of these words through the story itself, pictures, and class discussion. When a child looks carefully at a word in order to be able to recognize it again, he has made at least a partial analysis of it, even though he has done nothing more than to see it as "the one with the tall letters" or the "short one that begins like my name." When the child attempts structural or phonetic analysis, he depends also upon clues in the size and shape of the word, and upon his familiarity with the meaning of the word, or a part of it.

SOME CLASSES WORK WITH WORDS

As a means of understanding better what these ways of looking at words would mean to a group of primary children, some descriptions of their efforts may be helpful.

First-graders begin to discover ways of telling words apart. In the first grade early in September, Betty could recognize her own name. She knew that it began with *B* and so did Bobby. Archie also knew his name and was happy to spell it to anyone who would listen. Several children soon learned to recognize the word *Birthdays* because it was the longest word on the bulletin board. However, when it was first used in an experience record, only two or three were sure of it. When Sally began to work in a preprimer, she persisted in saying *Daddy* for *Father* for several days.

Now, later in the year, the word November is used in a class record. Although it is a new word to the reading group, Jean says, "That's where we put the date and it's November today, isn't it?" Nancy exclaims, "It starts with *N*." The children do not yet know all the letters of the alphabet, but they are familiar with many of them.

Second-graders show increased familiarity with structural and phonetic elements. In the second grade across the hall, the children do not puzzle long over the word *inside.* Someone says, "It starts with *in*" and another voice adds, "And the last part says *side*." Several children figure out *dancing* because they know it begins like *dance. Silly* causes difficulty for many, but someone points out that the *ill* is the same sound that is in *Bill's* name and with the teacher's help the children add the *s* and the *y.* When the children come to the word *squirrel* they remember it from its general configuration. *Fiddle* causes more difficulty because few children know what it is. After the teacher tells them how to pronounce it, they look back to the picture and decide that it looks like a violin.

Third-graders work with less common word-parts and longer and less familiar words. In another room third-graders are puzzling over the word *frighten*. Their teacher puts *right* and *sight* under each other on the board. They say the two familiar words and decide on the sound of *ight*. Then they try it with *fr* as a beginning and, having been successful that far, add the *en* to the end and reread the context to be sure it fits. They have little trouble with *suppertime* as they know the two words that make it up. The word *alligator* is one the teacher reads for them, but they have previously looked at the picture and know that there is an alligator in the story. Several are ready for it when they meet it in context. *Nonsense* is also new, but someone knows *sense* and someone else sees *on* at the beginning. Not everyone knows the meaning, but Janet says that is what her mother says to her when she's being silly. On the bulletin board are lists titled, *Our Pioneer Words* and *Words We Learned at the Post Office*.

Not all children in these classrooms will be able to respond with equal ease to the word-study problems they face. Some will have limited meaning vocabularies. Some will find the task of learning to see or to hear a common sound element in two words particularly difficult. Others will forge ahead with discovery after discovery, seemingly independent in their word-study techniques almost from the start.

The sections which follow are designed to point out ways in which interrelated skills in dealing with words may be developed. The first to be considered are those connected with developing word meanings.

ENRICHING WORD MEANINGS

The primary teacher needs to plan for three kinds of growth in helping children build new word meanings. First, they need to be helped to enrich concepts connected with familiar words. *Ride* may have meant to ride in the family car. Now a child learns that one can ride a scooter or a horse; that one rides in a wagon, in a boat, or in an airplane. A *farm* may have meant a few acres on the edge of town. Now a child reads about a dairy farm, a wheat farm, a tobacco farm. This sharpening and refining of vague or limited concepts continues well beyond the elementary school. The high school geometry student adds new meanings to terms like *circle, square*, and *triangle*. The adult puzzles over definitions of *democracy* or *faith*.

Second, new meanings are added to familiar words. *Dress* may have meant a girl's frock. Now the child learns to *dress* the doll, or to *dress* himself for recess. He may read about the unusual *dress* of children in another land. A *foot* may be something on which he puts his shoes, a measure of distance, or a special end of his bed. A dog can *bark* but there is also *bark* on a tree. These new meanings are not all developed at once. The teacher must sense when a word is in an unfamiliar setting and give help with it.

Third, the child is exploring a greatly enriched and widened environment. As he does so, he encounters many new terms. He learns the names of new pieces of equipment in school. He visits the airport or the creamery in the nearby town. He begins to read textbooks in which a few of the special terms of the content fields start to appear. All these experiences make for an enriched stock of word meanings and for a much wider experience background from which to read.

The problem of enriching and expanding a child's word meanings extends far beyond the reading program. Every aspect of the primary program contributes. This section discusses ways of developing word meanings, first through the total primary program, second through group reading activities, and third through special practice devices.

USING THE TOTAL PRIMARY PROGRAM TO ENRICH WORD MEANINGS

Develop meanings from experience. Suggestions for widening children's experience background and for developing general facility in language usage were included in Chapter IV. Firsthand experience is important if a child is to develop accurate concepts. When the children come back from a trip they talk about what they have seen. Here is an opportunity to develop new terms. The rabbit we saw has long fuzzy fur like the fur on the collar of Mother's coat. He is not a *wild* rabbit. He is a *domestic* rabbit. His home is called a *hutch* or a *pen*. Other opportunities come as the children develop an experience record of their trip. Such records of new terms were illustrated in Chapter VIII.

Objects brought to school by the children, collections made during the year, exhibits loaned from museums, and other means of enriching the classroom environment also enrich word meanings. Jack's grandfather has been on a trip to Mexico. He brought Jack a *serape*. What is it? In the fall the children begin to bring interesting nuts and berries to school. They use one of the simpler nature books to look up their specimens and to label them correctly with the teacher's help. A science exhibit, entitled "Things that Float," adds terms such as *cork, canoe, balloon, waterball,* and *raft*. A recipe for jelly calls for terms needed for measuring and for names of ingredients. Such classroom experiences can be particularly helpful in vocabulary building because they offer many opportunities for the children to use the new terms.

Pictures can supplement firsthand experiences as means of developing new concepts. A trip to a farm may not answer all the children's questions. After they return they may study a set of pictures to secure further information. The farm we visited has a small barn; here is one that is large. Our farmer grew corn; here is a picture of a wheat field stretching as far as you can see. Here is a farm where dairy cattle are raised; there seems to be more pasture land. Bulletin-board displays can be developed around such topics as *"Animals We Know," "Signs of Winter," "Things That Grow."* Even pictures drawn by children can be helpful in concept building. For example, the illustrations of an excursion can be checked for accuracy. Are the colors correct? Are relative sizes right? Have important details been left out?

Sometimes it is not feasible to take a trip to a farm or a bakery, and films may be used to advantage. Most school systems are able to use films and filmstrips from the visual-aids centers of nearby universities. Used as teaching aids which are carefully chosen and prepared for, they can enrich understandings which promote growth in reading in all stages.[6]

Children help to enrich the vocabulary of their classmates as they report on special experiences. Roland takes a bus ride to his grandmother's and tells about the trip. Roy has taken a long trip by jet and talks about the many things he has heard and seen at the big airport. Judy's family lives near a big urban redevelopment project; Bob plans a garden every spring, and several children have seen a new television program. All such activities that contribute to the richness of the total program also contribute to children's stocks of word meanings.

Use wide reading to supplement firsthand experience. Primary children soon reach the point where their reading helps to enrich their stock of word meanings. After a trip to the post office the children can read in more detail about the machines and men they saw. As they begin to study about how people lived at the time of the first Thanksgiving, they find stories describing costumes, telling how the first houses were built, and illustrating the kind of furniture that was used. All the types of reading materials suggested in Chapter VII as important to the child's total reading experiences can play a part in enriching his stock of word meanings.

Encourage children to use new terms. Children need to be encouraged to make new terms their own by using them in their speech and writing. The composing of classroom records helps to serve this purpose. "That long thing they used to reach the windows." "Yes, but can anyone remember what they called it?" "It was a ladder." "Any special kind of a ladder?" "I think it was something like extension." "Does anyone know, for sure, what extension means?" Helping to label a collection; putting the right caption under a picture on the bulletin board; writing a note to a child who is ill and explaining so clearly that he will not have to guess what you mean by "the thing,"

---

[6] For criteria for selecting and using auditory and visual materials see: George D. Spache, "Auditory and Visual Materials," *Development in and Through Reading.* The Sixtieth Yearbook of the National Society for the Study of Education, Part 1 (Chicago: The University of Chicago Press, 1961), pp. 209-225.

Cincinnati Public Schools

Children's interests in the Space Age can be a springboard for developing listening, speaking, writing and reading skills.

"something round," "sort of dark"; and being given special credit for using a new word, all help to give a child reasons for putting his new words to use.

USING GROUP READING ACTIVITIES TO ENRICH WORD MEANINGS

Plan for variety in the materials read. Children can add steadily to their stock of word meanings through their reading-group activities, particularly if there is variety in content in basal texts and in the many other kinds of materials they can use. In the varied opportunities for small group and individual reading described in previous chapters, children will encounter new words, and enlarge their understanding of word meanings. However, some planning and attention given to procedures designed to help children achieve clear and accurate understanding of words may be helpful.

In the first place, care needs to be taken that the use of a variety of reading materials does not result in the presentation of new terms so rapidly that the children are floored by many words they can neither recognize in printed form nor understand. With the beginning reader, the problem of selecting materials is not one of adding new meanings, but rather one of making sure that meanings are familiar so that children do not face the problems of recognizing printed words and learning new meanings at the same time. More skilled readers can branch out into new areas without being overwhelmed by word-recognition problems if the material is simple, and the proportion of new words to familiar ones is light. Several helps for lightening the burden of new words may be suggested. It helps to read several stories in sequence which use the same concepts. New terms may be used in experience records at the same time they are being read in books. Thanksgiving plans may be developed in class, or group Thanksgiving stories composed, while Thanksgiving stories are read; a list of means of transportation can be prepared as a class project while groups read stories about transportation. When such precautions are taken, the child's experiences in reading groups should be expected to add steadily to his stock of word meanings.

Use word-recognition techniques that stress meanings. Methods used to help children become acquainted with the configurations of new words need to make meanings clear at the same time. Several techniques for doing this were suggested in Chapter VII. New words can be presented on the chalkboard in one- or two-sentence stories that highlight their meanings. They may be listed on the board, and the pictures or the title of the story used to develop their meanings. "What do you call that part of a train?" "Yes, it's the *engine*. That's what our story is about. I'll write *engine* up here where you can see it. It will be one of our new words." Sometimes new words can be introduced in an experience record. Such presentations in context help to assure that the child is thinking about the meaning as well as the configuration of the word.

When children begin to use word-analysis clues to work out words in context, teachers typically check to be sure the meaning is clear. "Read it again now. Does it fit?" "What would it mean if it said he was *clumsy?*" "If her dress was *ragged*, how would she look?" Sometimes the words that cause trouble are written on the board and checked again, both for meaning and for pronunciation, at the end of the reading period. Such checks do not necessarily take much time, but they help to make certain that children understand the words they have been reading.

Review activities, planned to strengthen word recognition, can also help to develop meanings. Some of these will be simple games with word cards, but many others will call for the child to use the word in context—to choose the correct word in a multiple-choice exercise, to mark a sentence true or false, to solve a riddle, to make a sensible rhyme, or to match a list of words with the correct pictures.

Point group discussion toward clear meanings. Emphasis on thoughtful reading contributes directly to enriched word meanings. Whenever the meaning of the story hinges on the interpretation of a word or a phrase, there is an opportunity to develop clearer concepts. "What word tells you how Jane felt?" "There's a word that tells you how big it was. Who can find it?" "That was one of our new words. Can anyone remember what it meant?" It is also possible to use the discussion of the pictures accompanying the story and children's comments from their own experiences to enrich word meanings. Children read about a squirrel gathering nuts for the winter, and look at the picture to see how he does it. Those who have squirrels in their trees add their firsthand information. Such emphasis on word meanings does not interrupt the discussion of the story. It comes in naturally as the meaning of the story unfolds.

Plan for follow-up activities that enrich word meanings. In Chapter VII it was suggested that many of the activities following the first reading of a story be planned to encourage wider reading, or to call for thoughtful rereading of the story. This type of follow-up can make a contribution to clearer word meanings. Locating more information about turtles to answer the questions raised by a story in the basal text will help to add new concepts in the natural-science field. Drawing a picture to illustrate a story calls for accurate concepts. Dramatization calls for thought about how a princess or a wicked giant would behave, and for careful consideration of just how the stage setting should look. During follow-up activities such as these the teacher often has time to talk to individual children, to work with a small group whose concepts do not seem to be clear, and to help children relate what they have read to their own experiences. In the process, critical evaluation, thoughtful understanding, and enriched word meanings move forward hand in hand.

PROVIDING SPECIAL PRACTICE AND REVIEW ACTIVITIES CENTERED AROUND WORD MEANINGS

Plan practice exercises that develop interest in new words. The most important teaching of new words goes on during regular classroom activities. However, it is possible to use special activities to keep children alert to new meanings and interested in learning to use new words.

Much of the process of noting new words is an informal one, especially

Primary children can express themselves creatively in many ways. Word meanings are enriched as children share ideas.

with first graders. Interest in new words may come through challenging questions. "There is a special word we use for that. We say the string *vibrates*. Would you like to use that word in our story? Watch while I write it for you." "Bill just said that the water *condensed* on the window. That is a big word, and he used it correctly. I wonder how many of you know exactly what he means?" Time may be taken also, to make comment on an unusual word in a story being read to children, or to discuss a trip or pictures which develop new word meanings.

Occasional work-type exercises may be planned for second and third grade pupils who are acquiring new skills, not only in reading but also in writing and spelling. Such exercises may include for example:

1. Writing riddles about new words.
2. Illustrating new terms on an experience record.
3. Making a simple class picture dictionary.
4. Answering a series of questions about a short paragraph by choosing a correct word.

First graders are likely to be more successful when they engage in informal oral work. Among types of special activities that can help to develop interest in new words are the following:

Children's interest and attention can be called to new words by: Taking special time to comment on an unusual word in a story being read to children; making a special point of reminding children that they might like to use a new word in their reports or creative writing, and putting it on the board for them to spell; discussing an excursion to develop new word meanings.

Special practice in using new words can be provided in: Drawing pictures to illustrate new terms; matching a group of words with the correct pictures; sorting a set of pictures according to some special classification—things that are animal, vegetable, mineral, things that belong in the country or in the city; writing riddles about new words; answering riddles written by others in the class; illustrating the new terms on an experience record; making a simple class picture dictionary; seeing who can put all the labels in an exhibit back correctly; answering a series of questions about a short paragraph by choosing the correct word.

Plan special devices to keep new words in sight. The primary child is acquiring many new words in his speaking and listening vocabulary. He will know the meaning of more words than he can recognize in written work. Some of these words learned in the course of his classroom activities will have only immediate use; others will be important both to read and to spell. New words which are needed in current reading or writing activities can be kept before the children so that they may refer to them for spelling purposes, and develop gradual familiarity with their configurations.

There are many occasions for posting lists of words for reference. Special words to help with spelling, when children are writing letters or creative stories may be written on the chalkboard or on special charts. A list of new words may grow out of an excursion, or a science project, or a social-studies unit which uses new place names. A second-grade class enjoyed a bulletin board labelled, "Help Yourself to a Word." On it were pinned envelopes for each letter in the alphabet, and in each envelope were word cards of words which the child could take to his seat to help him spell.

Provide special activities to give initial contacts with the dictionary. While extensive dictionary work belongs to the intermediate grades, the foundations of interest in and understanding of the usefulness of this learning tool can be laid in the primary grades. Beginning readers can examine picture dictionaries and may watch while the teacher locates a word, then discuss its accompanying picture. Occasionally spelling or other textbooks will have helpful simple glossaries which provide initial experiences with the skills used in dictionary work.

By the third grade many children should be able to use simple techniques of alphabetical order to locate words independently. They may have some direct practice in this, or with lists of special useful terms that have been alphabetized, at least to beginning letters. These activities, however, are largely informal. Additional suggestions for practice experiences such as the following may be helpful:

Simple experiences with alphabetical order can be given through: Finding a needed letter on classroom alphabet cards; using a simple alphabetical filing system to locate a word card needed to help with spelling; helping to develop lists of spelling words classified alphabetically—words we use beginning with *a, b, c;* examining alphabet books; finding a word in a picture dictionary; finding a topic in the index to a textbook; playing games in which one is to tell what letter comes before or after a given letter; telling in which part of the dictionary one would expect to find a given word.

Contacts with a dictionary can be provided through: Having opportunities to examine picture dictionaries; helping the teacher look up a word in a picture dictionary; looking at a picture in a dictionary to help with the meaning of a word; making a simple picture dictionary for a special group of important words; making a class alphabet book; finding a word in the glossary of a spelling book.

DEVELOPING SKILL IN WORD RECOGNITION

It is one thing to know the meaning of the word *cat*, and to be able to identify the picture of a cat or to describe one. It is another to know that the symbol *cat* says cat. In the beginning, a child's word-recognition techniques depend largely on clues from the general shape of the word. The youngster who can recognize *cat* in a story may do so by its configuration without being able to spell it, or to tell that it begins with the sound of *c* and ends in the sound of *at*. He may even be able to recognize the word as a whole without being able to name any of the individual letters. Adults use configurational clues more than they sometimes realize. It is possible to recognize *Tchaikovsky* without giving a phonetic translation of each syllable. It is also possible to read it silently with accurate meaning without being absolutely certain of how to say it aloud. Few teachers will have any trouble reading the sentence *T ch g r d g s a c pl x pr c ss,* although no phonetic analysis can be made from the letters given. Adults could also learn to recognize * /Σ as a code symbol for *mother* without being able to name any of the separate symbols or to give any phonetic equivalents for them. Children begin the process of learning to read by responding to configurational cues. A first step in helping them develop word-recognition skills is to help them build a stock of words they can recognize at sight.

As a second step in developing skill in word recognition, children need to be helped to refine their techniques for identifying words. They need to learn to use elements that help in more accurate discriminations. *Bobby* learns to tell his name from *Billy* by looking for the two *b*'s in the middle. The children learn to tell *ball* from *balls* by the general shape of the words and the *s* on the plural form. They use the context to decide between *was* and *saw.* They discover that they can tell *mouse* and *house* apart because *mouse* begins like *mother.* At first such discriminations may even be made without accurate knowledge of the names of the letters, but frequently used letters soon are known.

Third, children need to be helped to develop word-recognition skills that serve as the foundation for word analysis. They discover that several words begin with *th,* and listen to hear how they sound. They see that the rhyming words in a poem end in the same letters. They talk about how nearly alike two words sound and study the way they are written to see where the difference lies. They see the root word in *comes.* At first, these will only be partial clues. A child may know that *mother* begins like *month,* and may be able to give the beginning sound without knowing how to pronounce *ther,* or even being sure of the sound of *m* when it is not combined with *o.* In time, if children are helped to take an active interest in the shapes and sounds of words, they will become able to make an exact analysis of an unfamiliar word.

Much of the direct guidance given to the primary child in developing word-recognition techniques comes during his work in a reading group. Because this is the case, suggestions for introducing new words were included in Chapter VII in the discussion of how to assure a successful first reading of a story. The general plan for word-recognition experiences proposed in that chapter was as follows:

> *First,* the selection of materials so that the number of new words introduced at any one time is adjusted to the child's reading skill.
> *Second,* the introduction of new words before the story is read if it appears likely that children will not be able to use context, pic-

ture, or word-analysis alone. These words will be relatively few in number, and the group may participate in an attempt to discover what they are.

Third, encouragement of the children to use all available clues to recognize new words for themselves.

Fourth, follow-up activities connected with the story are planned so as to provide some review of new words.

In addition to help given in reading groups, children learn many new words from the wealth of supplementary materials, and materials read independently for pleasure which are a part of a stimulating classroom environment. This section is concerned with the development of word-recognition skills through group activities in reading, through wider reading, and through special practice and review activities.

DEVELOPING WORD-RECOGNITION SKILLS THROUGH GROUP READING ACTIVITIES

Make sure that meanings are clear. One of the basic principles underlying all methods of helping a child learn to recognize new words is to make sure that he knows their meanings. Teachers use a variety of ways to be sure that children gain clear meanings. Sometimes they give encouragement in using picture and context clues, or promote discussion which focuses on the meanings of new words as they are encountered. If the concepts in the new material seem to be unusually difficult, teachers may even plan for special excursions or for other concrete experiences before a set of stories is read. Such experiences may be particularly useful for children in culturally deprived environments. Whatever the specific method, developing ability to recognize a word and making sure that the child knows its meaning go hand in hand.

Present new words so that they may be clearly seen. Whenever a child meets a new word for the first time, he needs to get a clear picture of the way it looks. Such words may be written on the chalkboard as they are discussed, directing attention to each one. They may be presented in sentences with the word to be studied underlined. A child who needs help with a word in his silent reading may be helped to see the word more clearly by "boxing it off," with his fingers around the word. Sometimes the word occurs in a sentence or phrase where it stands out because it is the only new word in the group and children can be asked to watch for it as they read.

Discussing the appearance of a word also helps children to see it clearly. As the teacher writes a word on the chalkboard, she may comment on its length, beginning letters that are already familiar, striking characteristics or similarities to words already known. Children will also be able to note distinctions: "This word is like *look,* but it has a different ending"; or, "This word begins the same as *candy*." Such discoveries point the way to independent word analysis a little later on.

Often it is helpful to use several methods of presenting a word. As the teacher first mentions the word she may write it on the board. Later she may ask the children to match a set of word cards with the words on the chalk-board. Then as they discuss the story, she may ask who can find the new word. If they have difficulty in recognizing it in the story she may ask them to look again at the words on the board. Helping children meet the same con-figuration often and in different surroundings serves to make the impression more lasting.

Develop active interest in learning new words. Devices that help to call a child's attention to a new word also should help to keep him actively inter-ested in remembering it. No single method for studying new words should be adopted and carried out in the same way every day. To do so is to risk turning what should be a live, challenging activity into an uninteresting, rela-tively meaningless drill.

If word-recognition activities are planned in relation to the stories in which the words are met, there is less likelihood that they will become routine. No two stories will make the same demands on the reader nor will they provide the same kind of help through pictures and context. Each new day's work with words will therefore have a slightly different emphasis. On some days the challenge will be, "Let's see if you can read this story without help. I think you can figure out the new words when you come to them. Would you like to try?" At other times, reading the story will be the culmination of sev-eral days spent in introducing new words through discussion, observation, or experience records. If two new words in the story are quite similar, activi-ties may focus on how to tell them apart. Sometimes children themselves will suggest activities. "May I read the list? I can find it somewhere else in the room." Such variety helps to make the activities centered around learning words as exciting as any other aspect of the reading program.

After the story has been discussed, it is appropriate occasionally to go back to read the lines containing the new words, especially if they are key words in the story, or to discuss the part of the story in which the new words ap-peared. Care needs to be taken to assure that such activities, too, do not be-come routine or take up an unduly heavy proportion of the time set aside for the purpose of discussing the story. Having fun with reading is more than learning to name new words.

At times, introducing a game element is helpful in maintaining interest in new words. Keeping word cards he is able to recognize, erasing a word he knows, or taking a turn as "teacher" to point to review words are activities which many children enjoy. New words may be written on "picture books" each book being a folded paper containing the word on the outside and the picture on the inside. Children may work with these books singly or in pairs, trying to read the word on the front, and then checking to see if they are correct.

In the last analysis, nothing is going to make for progress in learning to recognize new words in context more effectively than enjoying quantities of easy, interesting story materials. Group interest in quick review may be stimulated by gamelike activities, but such devices should be used with caution. Especially to be avoided are aspects which call for a great deal of time in highly competitive non-reading activities—standing in line, writing names, discussing whose turn it is, or who is to "keep score." Games may provide a dash of spice, but the reading "meat" will be materials that provide continuing interesting experiences with reading for interest and enjoyment.

Expect occasional errors. In some ways learning to recognize words is a great deal like remembering the names of people we meet. Mrs. Smith and Mrs. Jones are petite blonds, given to wearing blue. It is difficult to greet them with the right name after seeing them only once. Mr. Brown, who generally is known to us as he appears in a grocer's apron behind the counter of the grocery, presents an unfamiliar appearance dressed in his Sunday best. To be introduced to a dozen strangers at one time will be likely to invite confusion. Similarly children may find it difficult to remember words that look a great deal alike, in general configuration, or that appear in different places on the page adorned with capitals instead of lower-case letters. And too many new words introduced at one time will be likely to cause the young reader some further trouble in attempting to recognize them.

Working with words in context is a valuable aid in reducing error occasioned by the configuration of a word. If a child's word-study activities are planned so that he spends most of his time guessing words from word cards, working with lists of words on the chalk-board, and playing games with isolated words, he has less opportunity to learn to check for himself whether he is right or wrong. If he reads the word in a story or chooses the word that answers a question based on a short paragraph, he learns to ask whether the words he has chosen makes sense in his reading. On the other hand, errors occasioned by giving synonyms that make good sense in the story call for activities where the child has to think carefully about the configuration of the words.

PROVIDING SPECIAL PRACTICE AND REVIEW ACTIVITIES IN WORD RECOGNITION

Provide reviews through opportunities for wide reading. No matter how striking a first presentation of a word may be, most children will need to meet it several times in different settings before they are sure of it. Some of the most effective review activities are those that present the new word again in interesting stories. Work-type practice can be reduced in proportion to the amount of easy, interesting reading with which the child can be supplied.

The list that follows summarizes means of providing additional word-recognition experiences through wide reading of materials using similar vocabulary. These have been discussed in detail in preceding chapters. Variations of these suggestions can be worked out in many ways.

Repetition of words in varied story settings can be secured by: Gearing reading activities to a classroom project requiring experience records and informational reading on the same topic; using stories on the same general topic from other basal-reader series as supplementary reading; placing a book on the library table after it is no longer needed for group activities; using easy basal readers for recreational-reading purposes—putting selected first-grade materials on the library table in grades two and three, making pre-primers available after children have progressed to primer and first-reader materials; having children reread simplified mimeographed versions of their own creative stories in order to illustrate them; having children reread a story to write riddles, plan dramatizations, draw pictures of favorite passages; preparing to read a favorite story aloud to another reading group.

Plan special practice activities that call for thoughtful reading. Some children will need little more repetition of new words than that provided through wide reading. Others will need considerable additional help. What kinds of special practice activities are likely to be most useful and effective?

Two general principles seem applicable here. First, a major share of review activities should be planned to help the child use new words in context, so that thoughtful reading is encouraged. Second, variety in review activities is important. Just as children grow weary of the same method of introducing words if they are used routinely day after day, so they tire if the same type of exercise is used automatically as a review.

Short creative language experiences may be used to review new words. The children may arrange sets of word cards to "write" their own sentences. They may dictate a short story about characters in a selection, which can then be hectographed and given back for rereading or illustrating. Later on, children may be able to write their own stories.

Pictures also offer opportunities for practice with words. Pictures may be matched with words, or children may draw pictures of their own to illustrate words, sentences, or an enjoyable scene in a story. Caution has to be taken, however, in using pictures, to be sure these experiences provide actual practice in thoughtful reading, instead of "busy work" to keep pupils occupied with cutting and pasting while other groups are at work.

Various types of multiple-choice, true-false, and completion exercises can be useful for word-recognition purposes. Children may be asked to choose the correct sentence from such pairs as:

> The tree was green.
> The tree was brown.

This same question could be set up as:

> The tree was (green, brown).

A form that demands very little writing and therefore is useful for beginners sets up a series of statements for which the child encircles *yes* or *no:*

> The tree was brown.   Yes   No

A more complicated form might ask the child to fill in the correct words for several sentences:

> The children went to the ————.
> They wanted to see the ————.
> The man who made them laugh was a ————.
>
> Circus, clown, elephant.

Riddles are often particularly interesting:

> I belong in the circus.
> I am tall.
> I am big.
> I have a long trunk.
> What am I?
>
> Clown, elephant, parade.

A certain number of exercises of the type just described can be developed around a story that the children have read. When this is the case, they can be given some additional helpful review experience if they are encouraged to reread the story in order to locate the correct answer. However, it will sometimes take the edge off the enjoyment of a story to go back over it to answer specific review questions. Similar activities can be developed by writing short paragraphs using the new words and then asking the child to answer questions similar to those that have just been illustrated. This type of exercise reviews the word in a new context setting and reviews it again in the question.

Practice activities for word-recognition purposes can be planned so that they contribute to increased skill in word analysis. The degree and the kind of discrimination required can be varied by the choice of the key words to which the child responds. For example, choosing between *ball* and *door* calls for general configuration clues only. Choosing between *ball* and *bill* calls for ability to note middle letters, whereas *ball* and *bat* require a careful look at endings, and *ball* and *call* stress beginning letters. The more skillful children become in word recognition, the more important it is to plan their activities so that they employ word-analysis techniques to make their discriminations.

The workbooks accompanying basal-reading series offer a variety of ingenious word-recognition activities. Some workbook activities are planned to follow the story in the basal reader. These are helpful when specific review of the story seems desirable. Offering more flexible possibilities for exercises are the workbooks that are more nearly self-contained. These typically present the new words in picture-dictionary or story form and then provide a series of short paragraphs and questions that call for the child to use the new words in various settings. Materials arranged in this way also provide a certain amount of fresh and interesting reading, even though the paragraphs are very short.

Additional types of practice activities that illustrate the suggestions that have been made in this section are the following:

Creative-language experiences with new words might include: Drawing a picture of a character in a story and suggesting an appropriate caption; helping to construct a group story using the new words; dictating stories about topics related to reading activities, to be reread and illustrated when they are mimeographed.

Activities using words and pictures can call for: Drawing lines from words to swer a question based on the story; choosing the correct word to answer a question based on a short paragraph supplied as part of the work-type exercise; choosing the correct answers to a series of riddles based on the story, or a classroom experience.

Activities using words and pictures can call for: Drawing lines from words to appropriate pictures; choosing which of two sentences correctly describes a picture; choosing which of two words is the correct caption for a picture; making a four-page picture book by drawing the pictures suggested by mimeographed instructions; drawing pictures of key people, animals, or objects in a story in response to instructions printed on the chalkboard; illustrating blank pages in a mimeographed version of a child's creative story; making single-word picture books for the library table; placing a set of cards under the appropriate pictures in a series mimeographed by the teacher.

Use games with caution. All activities with isolated words need to be used with caution. Children easily may turn to random guessing if they are not supervised. They also may become so intrigued with the game element that the amount of actual reading they do is rather slight. Care also needs to be taken that the teacher does not spend long hours constructing a device that serves the children for only a few minutes. The best practice devices are those which are simple for the teacher to prepare and flexible enough so that children get many hours of use from them. Placed on a table where they are readily available, they can be turned to for a few minutes' relaxation by a single child or by a group of children. They enjoy helping each other, matching scores, and securing evidence of their own progress.

Rather simple games, with few rules, which permit new forms as new sets of words are added to the children's vocabulary are useful. For example, a fishing game has such possibilities. A cardboard box, a series of word cards with paper clips attached, and small inexpensive magnets hung on small fishing poles are all that are needed. Children dip their poles into the box, and then read the card they pick up. If they can pronounce it correctly they may keep the card. Variations of this game might include fishing for words having to do with Christmas, or animals in the zoo or for names of toys. As word-analysis skills develop, children may fish for words beginning with a specific sound, ending with a stated sound, or containing a given syllable. A card game can be based on Bingo, or Lotto, using words for review. A word is pronounced by the leader, and the children look for the word on their cards and cover it if they find it. The winner is the one who first finds five words in a row or in a column that he can cover and recognize. The words, of course, can be varied to suit any desired situation. Additional suggestions for reading games and devices may be found in *Reading Aids Through the Grades*[7] and in materials by Harris,[8] and Hildreth.[9] Many workbooks, both those accompanying basal readers, and those designed to be used independently, are excellent sources of suggestions for a variety of review activities.

Make use of a variety of audio-visual and instructional aids. In addition to developing basic skills in word-recognition through the games and devices mentioned in the previous sections, a variety of audio-visual aids for stimulating interest in words and stories may be helpful. When it is available, an opaque projector can be used to focus attention upon familiar words for the purpose of reviewing them in new contexts. The projector can be used to show pictures with appropriate captions, and accompany a tape recording of

[7] David H. Russell, and E. E. Karp, *Reading Aids Through the Grades*, Revised Edition (New York: Bureau of Publications, Teachers College, Columbia University, 1951).

[8] Albert J. Harris, *How to Increase Reading Ability*, Fourth Edition (New York: Longmans, Green and Company, 1961), pp. 378-83.

[9] Gertrude Hildreth, *Teaching Reading* (New York: Henry Holt and Company. 1958), pp. 322-25.

pupils' reading (or the teacher's reading) of a story. Film strips are available to accompany some readers, and a number of films and recordings may serve to initiate interest in words or in stories. These aids may add variety and interests, and, particularly in the case of films, they have the advantage of focusing attention sharply upon the subject at hand.

The early years of the decade beginning with 1960 were marked by interest in devices for individualizing practice in learning specific skills. These devices, popularly called "teaching machines" are really not machines that teach, but rather a means of presenting to the individual student selected, sequential items, carefully graded in levels of difficulty. To these programmed materials the pupil responds by indicating his answers. If a response is correct, the learner then goes on to the next item. Since the program may be developed in a book or pamphlet form, wide use of these learning materials is foreseen. Suggestions have been made for their use in a number of fields, including reading. Specifically, questions have been raised concerning the utility of such programmed materials in developing vocabulary from a context given in the items presented, or in developing phonics skills as a pupil matches letters to appropriate pictures.

Such programmed learning sequences appear to many to have promise, because the pupil is rewarded immediately by an indication that he has made the correct response. Furthermore, it is suggested that the teacher will be freed from routine checking of papers; and both the teacher and the pupil who needs little further practice on a particular skill can be free to go on to something which is of special interest, or is creatively challenging.[10]

Thoughtful evaluation of this new tool for instruction must be made before its most efficient use can well be determined. The alert teacher will not only watch reports of its use, but will—if opportunity offers—use such materials selectively. Of great importance is the awareness that a sound program for reading development is the first essential. Such a program may be implemented with whatever devices or materials are available and effective. To be avoided, however, is the changing of goals and instructional plans particularly for the purpose of fitting them to a newly adopted procedure or device.

DEVELOPING SKILL IN WORD ANALYSIS

The first time a child tells two words apart by noting differences in the letters of which they are composed he has taken a step toward eventual inde-

[10] For thoughtful discussion of these possibilities see: P. Kenneth Komaski, "Teaching Machines and Programmed Reading Instruction," *Controversial Issues in Reading and Promising Solutions*, Helen M. Robinson, Editor. *Supplementary Educational Monographs No. 91* (Chicago: University of Chicago Press, 1961), pp. 109-120.

pendence in word analysis. The time lapse between this first step and the point at which a child can pronounce for himself all the new words he meets is a matter of years. In this period he has several complicated skills to learn.

First, the child must become able to break the word he is studying into elements that are effective for pronunciation purposes. This may involve seeing structural elements such as roots, prefixes, suffixes, syllables, or the words making up a compound word; it may call for responding to single letters or other sound elements; or it may require a combination of any of the above, depending on the particular word.

Second, the child must be able to give a reasonable sound equivalent for whatever parts of the word he sees. This is more complicated than merely knowing the sounds of the individual letters. He may need to respond to whole words as he reads *school-room;* to syllables as he reads *com-ing;* to phonograms as he reads m*ake* or c*ake;* to individual letters as he distinguishes between *h*ouse and *m*ouse; to digraphs as he reads bla*ck* or *ch*ild; to blends as he reads *bl*ue and ho*ld;* to different sounds for the same letter combinations as he meets gr*ea*t, br*ea*d, and m*ea*n; to prefixes, roots, and suffixes as he reads *walk-ed,* or *in-side.* And he is likely to meet any combination of these sound elements in a given word.

Third, the reader must be able to blend the sounds of the parts of the word he sees into a recognizable whole. Children who can give the sound equivalents for separate word-parts cannot always take this step. Thus, *spring* may sound like *spurring,* or *first* like *forest.* Later, as two- and three-syllable words make their appearance, the reader also has to recognize where to place the accent and how to blend the syllables.

Fourth, to be skilled in word analysis, the child must be able to vary his approach from word to word. *Chin* may be analyzed conveniently as *ch-in;* but the sound element *in* is of no help in *shine,* or *again.* The child who sees the small word *his* in *this,* or *car* in *scare* is in trouble. Versatility of attack is important. The skilled analyzer of words knows the sound elements most likely to yield the correct pronunciation. He has had enough experience with syllables to sense where the syllabic division usually falls; he is accustomed to treating combinations such as *th, sh, ch* as units and to dealing with letters such as the silent *e* as part of larger sound elements; and he can use the sounds of single letters when he needs them. Most important, he is able to shift his attack if his first attempt does not seem to work.

Fifth, the skillful reader must be able to perform the entire complex task of analyzing an unfamiliar word as he meets it in context, checking on the accuracy of his identification through the sense of the passage, and capitalizing on whatever short cuts the context setting has to offer.

Finally, the child must develop the attitudes and skills requisite to effective use of the dictionary. These have only their beginnings at the primary level.

Word-analysis skills are not likely to develop harmoniously without planned guidance. A child who can recite word families or who can give the sounds of the letters of the alphabet without hesitation may not be able to see these elements when they are embedded in a larger word. Even if he can see them and can give the sounds for separate elements, he may not be able to blend them correctly. The problem is complicated still more by the fact that the ultimate goal is to help the child become able to use all these techniques together, flexibly, in a context setting. It is the teacher's responsibility to provide for smooth, all-round development.

In laying the foundation for word-analysis skills, primary teachers face several problems to which this section is addressed. First, how does one go about the job of helping children discover the sounds of parts of words? Second, how does one decide which sounds to stress? Third, how can group reading activities be planned to foster word-analysis skills? Fourth, what help can be given through on-going classroom activities? Finally, what kinds of special practice activities are appropriate?

HELPING THE CHILD DISCOVER THE SOUNDS AND PARTS OF A WORD

Start with familiar words. How does a teacher help a child learn to attach a sound to a given letter combination? How does a child learn to see combinations of letters in a word? The starting-point is a known word in which there is a familiar element or, more often, several known words containing a common element. The child meets *hat* in his primer story and exclaims, "The last part of that word says *at*." The words *We* and *Will* begin subsequent lines of an experience story, and the child says, "Those two words start like my name." He has trouble with *call* in his reading and his teacher says, "You know how that begins. It has the same sound at the beginning as *come* and *cat*." As she does so, she writes the two words under each other so that he may see the common element clearly. From studying words he knows, the child is helped to discover elements he can both see and hear.

As he begins to read, some of the child's first discoveries are likely to be of a structural nature.[11] That is, he sees elements related to the structure of the word—meaning elements such as a root and suffix, or the two words in a compound word. In his preprimer he learns the word *ride*. A few days later his story contains the word *rides*. The teacher may tell him what the new word is, she may cover the *s* and ask if anyone knows the word, or she may ask the child if it looks like a word he knows. Later, in an experience record, the children use *want* and *wants*. They may take time to talk a little about what *s* does on the end of a word. Perhaps their teacher writes *ride* and *rides*,

[11] For a detailed statement on the differences between structural and phonetic analysis see William S. Gray, *On Their Own in Reading* (Chicago: Scott, Foresman and Company, 1960), pp. 32-65.

and *want* and *wants*, under each other on the chalkboard so that the likeness and difference can easily be seen. Now the children are beginning to be able to use the *s* at the end of a word. Other opportunities to use structural elements also appear. In their experience record of a trip to the fire station the children use *fire, fireman, firehouse.* In another record they use *some* and *something.* These large word-parts that are actually themselves familiar words offer excellent opportunities to help children take their first steps toward word analysis.

In the first grade the process of comparing known words soon extends to other sound elements. Initial sounds are a help early. The children use *like* and *laugh* and *look* and note that these all begin with *l.* The teacher may encourage them to say the words and to listen for the beginning sound. They may then try to name some words that begin with the same sound and watch as the teacher writes *late, letter,* and *last* on the board. In the course of reading a story, someone reads *his* for *this.* Since he knows the *is* ending from his acquaintance with the small word *is,* the teacher takes the opportunity to help him become acquainted with the *th* beginning. She says, "Let's take another look at that one. It might be *his,* but it is a different word. It begins like *them* and *that* and *there.*" As she does so, she writes the words on the board. "Let's say them." . . . . "How do they begin?" . . . . "Now let's try *this.* What does it say?" This is an approach through phonetic analysis. That is, the child sees sound elements within the word—beginning letters, phonograms, consonant blends.

In second grade, children discover more of the common endings. Their group poem contains the words *ring* and *sing* and they look for the letters that make the rhyme. Then the teacher reminds them that this is the same ending they have seen on *coming, looking,* and *playing.* At the same time, they grow in their ability to use beginning consonants and consonant blends. They meet more compound words and they find they can read combinations like *cannot, schoolhouse,* and *somewhere.* Less common endings begin to appear, and they compare *walk* and *talk,* and *book, cook,* and *look.* As they read more widely they meet more words with similar configurations and single-vowel differences or differences in vowel combinations such as *well, will,* and *wall,* or *mail* and *meal.* These words provide an opportunity to develop more skill in using vowel sounds.

By third grade, children's command of the sounds of individual letters and of most common beginnings and endings should be reasonably sure, and they should be learning to find these sounds in longer words, growing more skilled in working with syllables, and learning less common prefixes and suffixes. One group may discover that they can read *leaves* because it fits into the story and begins like *leaf.* They talk about the plural form and then look at other words forming their plurals in the same way. Soon they find that they can read *loaves, knives,* and *wives.* They may work out *careful* because they know the beginning, and the end looks something like *full.* They dictate other *ful* words and examine their list, which may contain *cupful, spoonful,* and *painful.* Out of this experience they learn both the pronunciation and meaning of the suffix *ful.* In grade four, the words for comparison may be *attention, position,* and *station,* all learned originally by word-recognition techniques but now compared to develop the *tion* ending and to build more skill in syllabication. To teach a new sound, the starting point, at any grade level, is to help the child relate it to a word he knows.

Care needs to be taken to gear the help given a child in discovering new sounds to his present level of operation. If a third-grader is stumped by the word *engine,* and knows neither the *en* beginning, nor the soft *g,* nor the *ine* ending, he is facing too many difficulties in the one word to make for a useful experience in learning the component sounds. At this point he should probably be told the word, and should remember it from its general shape. Later in the year, when he has met several other words with the soft *g,* or with the *en* beginning, he may be able to identify these sounds, one at a time. The ending *ine,* as pronounced in *engine,* is so infrequent in primary vocabulary that little time is likely to be spent with it. Word-recognition devices are used to relieve the pressure when the analysis of a word is too difficult to be a fruitful experience for a child not only at the primary level, but on into the intermediate grades.

Help the child test out sounds he has learned in new settings. Learning to identify sound elements by finding them in familiar words is a first step in the word-analysis process. A second step is to learn to see the sound element in an unfamiliar word and then to combine it with other elements in the word so as to pronounce it. Usually these two techniques are stressed in the same activity, as when the teacher of the child who has mispronounced *this,* points out that it starts like *them* and *there,* and then asks him to try the sound in the word that was causing him trouble; or when a third-grade child says *letter* for *later,* and the teacher blocks off the first and last letters and says, "There's a word in here you know," or covers the *r* at the end, and says, "Look at this much of it," and then asks the child to try the whole word. However, there are times when children will benefit from additional practice with a new sound after they have helped to discover it.

One method of providing additional practice with a new sound is to ask the children to try it in several other new words. The reading of a story is usually not interrupted for long with such activities, but time can often be found at the end of a group reading session. If the children have compared *cow* and *now* and have identified the *ow* sound, the teacher may ask them to try to pronounce other words of which they are likely to know the consonant beginnings. What can they do with *bow* and *how?* In giving this practice, a word such as *vow* would not be used, partly because its meaning is likely to be unfamiliar, which would put the children in the position of naming what would be, for them, a nonsense word, and partly because the letter *v* is not as likely as some other letters to be a well-known consonant beginning at first.

Another way of giving practice with a new sound element is to ask the children to name other words beginning or ending with the same sound. This helps children learn to listen for sounds, but it is more risky than suggesting other words to them, as they may recall a word with different spelling, give a nonsense word, or occasionally give a word spelled the same but pronounced differently. For example, the children may be working with the *ate* combination in *late* and *gate*. When asked for other words ending the same way, someone may remember *bait* from last weekend's fishing trip with his father, or *wait*. When this happens the teacher is usually wise to write the new word on the board, and to acknowledge that it does sound the same. She may then ask the children if they can see the letter combination they want, and they may conclude that there are other combinations of letters which also say *ate*. At this point the *ait* combination would probably be set aside and returned to at a later date.

As children become more skilled in word-analysis techniques, sufficient practice with a new sound is often given by using it in the word that caused trouble. First, the problem word is written on the board. Then two or three familiar words containing the same sound are used as clues. When the child can identify the needed sound he tries it in his difficult word. Third-grade Sally encounters the word *likely*. She knows it begins with *like*, but she is not sure of the ending. The teacher writes *only* and *lovely*, both of which have been recently used in a class experience record. Sally says them, and identifies the *ly* on the end. Then, as the teacher runs her pencil under the syllables, Sally says *like-ly*. She tries it again and blends the two syllables completely. The teacher then asks what it means, and checks a little on Sally's understanding of the context. Later she may ask Sally to try the word again to be sure she has it. She may also take special care to check the next time an *ly* word apepars.

As children acquire a larger stock of letter sounds and phonograms, the problem may not be one of teaching a new sound, but of helping them identify sound elements they know in two- or three-syllable words. In this case, the teacher's help may be almost entirely directed toward the process of breaking down the new words. "How does it begin?" "What does this part in the middle say?" "Let's cover the rest of it so that you can see." "Now, can you put on the ending?" "Let's try them together again." At first the teacher may take on the burden of identifying the syllables in order to help the child see the correct parts to pronounce. However, it is helpful to encourage a child to try to find the needed parts himself whenever it seems likely that he will be successful. Sometimes group discussion will suggest two or three ways of breaking down the word, all of which lead to an acceptable pronunciation. Such versatility is to be encouraged.

Work-type activities, such as those suggested in a later part of this section, offer other means for providing additional practice with new sounds. The help that is given during group sessions when children are reading a story, or during children's independent reading activities, must of necessity be short so that they do not lose their train of thought. Work-type experiences provide an interesting setting in which children who need extra practice can concentrate on word elements and new sounds.

Make it easy to see and to hear sound elements. Part of the technique of making it easy for a child to identify sound elements in familiar words is to present them so that they stand out clearly. In pronouncing a group of words with a common sound element, it is helpful to stress the sound slightly. Telling the child the part of the word to which he is to give special attention as two or three words are pronounced is also helpful. If words are being written for children to study, common elements will be seen more easily if the words are placed one under the other, rather than side by side. If the common element is an ending, the words may be written so that the endings come directly one under the other. If word cards are being used as an aid to working with words written on the chalkboard or on an experience record, the child may carry the card to the appropriate word and literally place it underneath. If a child meets a new word in story materials, it is often desirable to write it on the board or on a pad of paper where it can be underlined or blocked off easily, rather than to ask him to look at it in his book.

In helping children discover word-parts, it is often desirable to block off the part under discussion by some physical means. In working at the chalkboard it may be helpful to cover with the hand all but the part of the word the child is trying to identify. A finger can be used on a word in a child's book. Children can be encouraged to use their own hands or fingers in similar fashion. Uncovering a word one sound element at a time by moving a hand or a piece of paper across it may help with the blending process. Saying the word with the child or having the group say the word in concert as a hand is moved under the syllables, may be useful. Since the final task is to learn to see word-parts in an unmarked word in context, the effect of devices that present the word with unnatural spacing or marking should be counteracted by seeing that, before he has finished, the child has taken several good looks at the word in its normal written form.

Help the child to use context clues to check. One of the most important checks on the accuracy of the analysis of a new word is to see whether it makes sense in context. The child who has learned to make maximum use of picture and context clues is often more independent in his reading than an inventory of the number of sound elements he can recognize in isolation or the number of words he can read in a list would lead one to believe. What could be planted in a garden and begin with *let*? *Lettuce* seems to be the only possible answer, and the teacher confirms that this guess is correct. Is the small word *was* or *saw*? It starts with *s* and it makes sense to say, "I *saw* baby." The word looks like *string*, but it doesn't make sense to say, "Jack was *string* the lemonade." What was left out? *Stirring* is a longer word and has *stir* at the beginning.

Because skill in using context clues is an important aid to word analysis, the child needs to meet many of his word-analysis problems in situations where context clues are available. This means that a good share of his help with new words needs to be given as he reads stories, informational material, or books for recreation. It also calls for a consistent policy of asking, "Does it fit in the story?" When work-type activities are used for added practice many of these need to be developed around short paragraphs and questions where correct answers can be checked in context.

Encourage independence. A basic principle underlying all the foregoing suggestions regarding the development of word-analysis techniques is to encourage a child's independent discoveries. The aim is to help him reach the place where he is able to, and disposed to, figure out new words for himself. The list of ways to study a new word included in the description of the second grade at the beginning of this chapter represents the discoveries of a group who are beginning to take command of their own word-analysis activities. When the problem of presenting new words before they are met in the story was raised earlier in connection with word-recognition activities, it was proposed that study of words before reading the story be reduced as rapidly as it seems possible for the child to work out the words for himself. "You know how that one starts." "Try it, I think you can get it for yourself." "Let's write it up here, I think you can tell what it is." "Can you think of one that begins the same way?" "Did you get it by yourself? Good!" These are the comments that make it fun to work with words and a challenge to try one's wings.

DECIDING WHICH SOUNDS TO STRESS

Use the child's word-analysis needs and discoveries as a guide to the order in which sounds are taught. To say that a child should be helped to learn sound elements by identifying them in familiar words is not much help in deciding where to begin and which sounds to stress first. Suggestions as to how best to plan the sequence of a child's word-analysis activities range all the way from proposals that a planned program be developed in a definitely organized fashion to recommendations for incidental guidance as the child reads widely.

Recommendations for teaching new sounds in a definite order usually presuppose one of two types of reading programs. Either the consistent use of a single basal-reader series is assumed, where there is an opportunity to foresee which words and which sounds will be used the most frequently and where the activities in an accompanying workbook are planned to stress new sounds in a definite sequence; or a planned series of word-analysis activities is proposed, based on special reading-matter and work-type exercises and often distinct from the child's other reading activities. Back of such proposals are the recognition that the techniques of word analysis are not easy to grasp and the fear that some children will fail to develop this important skill if the teacher does not work at it vigorously and systematically.[12]

The reading program that has been suggested in the preceding chapters has proposed wide reading experiences and contacts with many types of materials. Suggestions have been made of ways of keeping the child's word-recognition vocabulary within his grasp, so that he reads easily and with enjoyment from the beginning, but these proposals are not of a nature to restrict his reading to any given vocabulary list. When children are working with many types of material, there is no way of predicting exactly which sound elements they will meet the most frequently or what parts of words they will identify first. This suggests that the most effective order in which to teach new sounds is that which is based on the sounds that recur most frequently for a given class, together with the discoveries the children themselves are making. Even when a single basal-reader series is being followed story by story, the reading vocabulary appearing in other classroom materials adds many new elements. Teachers find frequently that the discoveries of children and the proposals of teachers' manuals and workbooks do not agree completely on which sounds are the easiest or the most important to learn first.

A second, and perhaps the most important, argument for teaching new sounds in the order in which they seem to be most appropriate for a given group lies in the fact that the objective of the word-analysis program is to help children gain independence in their reading as rapidly as possible. This means that they need to be given help in meeting every new word-analysis problm that seems within their present level of ability. One of the major reassurances to those who fear that the lack of a reasonably definite sequence of word-analysis activities may result in gaps in children's skills and knowledge lies in this ultimate objective. No sound element or word-part needed frequently by a child as he engages in wide independent reading should be left untaught for long, once he has reached the point where he seems able to

[12] See, for example, William S. Gray, *op. cit.*

learn to use it. A program of word-analysis activities arising from the problems and discoveries of a given group should not, then, lack thoroughness or vigor. It may actually take more careful planning to capitalize on the word-analysis opportunities offered by children's reading experiences than it would to follow a series of suggested lessons.

In order to capitalize fully upon the word-analysis opportunities offered by children's reading experiences, teachers have at least four types of responsibilities. First, it is important to be alert to the child's discoveries, and to help him refine them. "Yes, they both begin with *l*. What sound do you hear when you say them?" "That's right, there are two small words in it that you know. Can you put them together?"

Second, teachers need to be aware of word-analysis possibilities the child does not see. It is not always the youngster who first says, "They begin the same way, don't they?" Often the teacher asks, "Who can see any way in which these words look the same?"; or points out, "We made a rhyme, didn't we? Can you see the two words that rhyme?"; or challenges, "If you look carefully there is part of this word that is just like a word you know."

Third, it is important to encourage the independence that has been proposed as an ultimate goal. "Billy got that one without any help at all. Tell us how you did it." "Here are some new words that might cause you trouble in the story. I wonder how many of them you can figure out by yourselves."

A fourth responsibility is to sense when special practice is needed and to provide for it. This may mean spending a few extra minutes with three or four children, setting up a special combined reading and spelling group to work on word sounds, or providing the whole class with special work-type exercises stressing certain word-analysis problems. In the point of view that it is helpful to capitalize on the problems the child is facing, there is nothing to preclude providing extra practice whenever it seems needed.

Be alert to sounds likely to be useful early. Even though children's reading experiences are used as a general guide in determining the order in which sounds are to be stressed, certain word-parts are likely to have value early, and the teacher can be prepared to watch for opportunities to give help with them. They are likely to be the following:

1. The *s* ending. This lends itself to easy structural analysis, the child can see clearly the root words with which he is already familiar.
2. The endings *ing, ed, es.*
3. Small words that appear as syllables or phonograms in large words are useful parts to identify early. Such words as *it, in, arm, at, as,* and *is* appear frequently.
4. Certain large elements such as *ake, ack,* and *ell* appear in many relatively simple primary words. Such endings as *tion, ious, ment* can be left for older children.

It is not safe to teach a child to look for small words, such as *it*, *at*, in larger words as a routine word-analysis procedure, since the small word often appears in combination with other letters that change the pronunciation; for example, the *it* in *wait*, or the *in* in *ring*. But he can be encouraged to try out a structural analysis that takes account of the small word. If it does not work, he must look again for his clue. "There is *part* of this word that sounds like a word you know." This has proved to be useful phrasing.

Since an effective analysis of a long word depends on the child's ability to work from left to right, common beginnings and beginning combinations are useful early. Some of these are developed at preprimer and primer levels. Often the assurance of the beginning sound and the anticipated meaning are the easiest and most effective keys to pronunciation. Knowing beginnings also helps to distinguish words like *was* and *saw*, or *on* and *no*.

Teach sounds the child can both see and hear. Part of the difficulty in learning to read and to spell the English language is that the same letter combination may be pronounced in many different ways. For example *ough* is found as an ending in *cough, slough, through, thorough*, and *hiccough*. Even as simple a combination as *ow* may be met by the child first in *cow* and then in *slow*. The small word *in* appears clearly in *pin*, and is lost in *train*. Assuming that the *ine* sound has been identified, the child still has to recognize it in *pine, engine*, and *magazine*.

One basic principle is not to try to teach two sounds for the same phonogram in the same lesson. If the word is *slow*, the sound might be developed from words such as *grow* and *snow*. For the time, the child would be encouraged to try to work out for himself the pronunciation of other words in which *ow* has the same sound, but would be taught *growl, now, owl* by their general configuration. Later he can be helped to discover this second sound for the combination *ow*. If he gives an *ow* word which does not fit with the group he is studying, the teacher can always say, "Yes, it looks the same, but it doesn't sound the same, does it? Let's think of some words where we can hear the sound."

It is helpful also to teach the child to work with as large a sound element as he can both see and hear. Structural analysis—root and prefix or suffix, the two words in a compound word, the syllables in a long word—is usually a more rapid process than working from one- and two-letter clues. When a word needs to be broken into phonetic elements, the larger the element that can be used, the more efficient the analysis is likely to be. *Candy* is better seen as *can-dy* than as *c-an-dy; faster* as *fast-er* rather than *f-as-t-er;* and *something* as *some-thing*. Teachers can encourage children to look for large elements by choosing with care the words they use as a basis for teaching new sounds and by blocking off appropriate large elements in helping the child to see the part he needs to pronounce.

A suggestion, somewhat contradictory to the proposal just made that large sound elements be used, is to avoid breaking apart letters that will usually be met in combination. *Store* is better seen as *st-ore* than as *s-tore,* and *stop* as *st-op* rather than *s-top.* Similarly, *blow* is broken into more helpful elements for later use if it is seen as *bl-ow,* and *play* as *pl-ay.* Teaching sound elements is a process similar in many ways to the word-recognition methods used to teach the child whole words. Part of the problem is to see that he meets the same element over again in many settings until he is thoroughly familiar with it.

In spite of all the foregoing suggestions, versatility in attack is essential. It is more important to encourage a child to try out several approaches independently until he hits on the one that gives him the word than it is to hedge him in with too many rules about how to go about it. If, for the moment, he uses a less efficient analysis, it is a small matter in comparison with the incentive to study words for himself that comes from a successful performance. The group may be stumped by the word *string.* Mac may recognize *ring* and blend the *st.* Opal may see that it begins like *street* and add the ending. Adam may work out *window* because he sees *win* at the beginning and knows what is needed in the context. Alice may know *in* and *ow* and blend the remaining letters. Veronica may start with *wind,* as in *wind* thread, and then change her pronunciation when she sees that it will not work. Class discussion can sometimes be centered helpfully on such discoveries. Children may be encouraged to tell how they figured a word out. Often there are opportunities to point out the value of seeing larger parts, or of breaking a word into elements that have a familiar look. The ultimate check, in all word-analysis procedures, is the context. "Did it make a real word?" "How does it fit in the story?" "Does it make sense?" "What does it mean?"

Use research analyses as general aids. As general guides to the order in which sound elements are likely to become important for primary children, teachers may find it helpful to refer to research analyses based on primary vocabulary lists. Manuals to most basal-reader series provide analyses of the vocabulary of the specific series. These are often the most helpful lists of sounds for the teacher who is following one series rather closely. There have also been analyses of the frequency with which sound elements recur in primary word lists. These have been used to suggest the sound elements to be taught at different grade levels.[13] Teachers can use such lists as an aid in identifying the sound elements to teach, and in deciding whether to stress certain elements early or to leave them until children are reading more widely.

[13] As examples see: Donald D. Durrell, *Improving Reading Instruction* (Yonkers-on-Hudson, New York: World Book Company, 1956), pp. 231-237. Paul McKee, *The Teaching of Reading in the Elementary School* (Boston: Houghton Mifflin Company, 1948), pp. 254-257, 295-303. Albert J. Harris, *op. cit.,* pp. 351-353.

While these studies should not prescribe the activities of a given group, they may also serve from time to time as a general aid in checking on progress.

DEVELOPING WORD-ANALYSIS SKILLS THROUGH GROUP READING ACTIVITIES

Give help in working out new words as the story is being read. Interruptions to give help with unfamiliar words need not be long. If it is apparent that the child is going to have much difficulty working out the word, he can be told what it is and allowed to continue reading so that the sequence of the story is not lost. The teacher works in a low voice with a child who is having difficulty while the others continue to read.

As children talk about the story or read parts of it aloud to confirm their answers to questions, other difficulties with words will lend themselves to group discussion. "John said *stand*, but this is the word in the story." As she says this, the teacher writes *stay* on the board. "Who can tell the difference? . . . It could be *big*, because he certainly was a big dog, but our story uses another word that starts the same way. Watch while I write it . . . Who can tell, now, what the story really said about the dog? . . . How could you tell that the word was *bad?*" By upper-second or third grade, the discussion may center on finer points of meaning dependent on correct analysis. "It was *longer*, but the book tells us something else about that walk. Look at the word again. Who can say it? . . . Yes, it ends in *est*. What does it mean if it is the longest walk? Do you think they were tired?" Discussions of this sort do not detract from the meaning of the story. The word study helps to develop insights not possible as long as an incorrect word is used.

Encourage children to help each other. More mature readers can gain valuable word-analysis experience by helping each other. Reading partners can be set up for certain reading activities and each child be charged with the responsibility of helping the other with hard words. Children can talk about how to give help without telling exactly what the word is, and enjoy the experience of trying to give partial clues. When the two youngsters working as reading partners are of about equal ability, one may have a useful hunch about a new word when the other is baffled. Caution with regard to assigning children to help each other seems in order when children have limited word-analysis skills, as a certain amount of fruitless guesswork may result. Some question may also be raised about how often to assign a good reader to help one who has limited ability. Although such a procedure can at times be a helpful way of making it possible for a child to read independently while the teacher is occupied with another group, the actual teaching of new sounds to a child who is having trouble usually needs to be in teacher's hands.

Plan group help so as to allow for individual differences. Even children who are able to read material of about the same difficulty level will not learn word-analysis techniques with equal facility. There will also be differences occasioned by the discoveries they have made for themselves and by the word-parts they have been helped to identify in other reading experiences. Work in groups needs to be adjusted to these differences.

Help can be individualized in a reading group by allowing time for silent reading, during which the teacher can work with each child on the special words causing him trouble. In group discussions of new words, children who are less skilled sometimes can be encouraged to try to work out the words, while those who know how can serve as experts and withhold their comments until their help is needed. Children with greater skill can be kept interested in this process if the child who is having difficulty is not allowed to struggle too long before others in the group are invited to help him. Quick reviews of words can be managed so that children work on those which represent their special problems if the teacher has kept a record of who asked for help. Then, too, everyone need not learn a new sound the first time it is introduced. Those who are not quite sure of it this time may be able to get it the next. Often it is better to keep a group discussion of new words moving rapidly and then to use work-type activities, independent work periods, or special practice groups to give additional help to children who need it, than it is to try to prolong group activities until every child has mastered the new sounds.

DEVELOPING WORD-ANALYSIS SKILLS THROUGH ON-GOING CLASSROOM ACTIVITIES

Capitalize on classroom reading experiences. Opportunities to give help in pronouncing words arise whenever children are reading in the course of classroom activities. Children dictating a note to *Dear Mother* stop to comment on the *m* sound. Mary reports that *Bobby* is to help water the plants and is told that it is *Betty* and helped to see the difference between the two words. A child composing a poem seeks for a word that rhymes. The committee planning to report in the third-grade science activities decides to arrange the workers' names in alphabetical order. Joe misreads *Tuesday* for *Thursday* on the bulletin-board notice and takes a second look. Linda thinks her library book is going to be about a *big nose*, only to find that the word is *noise*. Teachers pick up such confusions as the day's work proceeds.

Often the help given with word analysis during classroom activities is on an individual basis as a child asks for a new word in his recreational reading or struggles with informational material. However, opportunities for group work also arise. Some of the words on lists developed in unit activities will be difficult to analyze, but others may be very useful for word-analysis purposes. If the lists are alphabetized, children can learn to respond to beginning letters. Sometimes several words connected with a unit will have a common root. Often sounds that have been learned in other reading activities will recur on such lists.

Help with word analysis given during on-going classroom activities is, for the most part, casual. Activities are not held up while children work laboriously with words. They take only a minute or two to get help with an unfamiliar word, to comment on the similarity of two words on a list, to note a familiar root as the teacher writes a new word on an experience record. However, the total amount of word-analysis experience is increased greatly by these many informal activities.

Give help as children begin to write and spell. Effective spelling and effective word analysis are two aspects of the same problem. To read a new word, the child must be able to see the parts that give the correct pronunciation. To spell it, he must produce the correct letter equivalents of these parts. It is ineffective spelling to memorize the letters in a word one at a time without reference to syllables, just as it is ineffective reading to try to blend one letter at a time without paying attention to larger word elements.

Beginning spelling activities are very similar to beginning activities in word recognition.[14] The first-grader begins to write before he knows the exact sound elements of all the words he is writing. First-grade teachers are likely to write the needed word for the child. He then copies the same configuration on his paper. His first spelling job is one of making sure that what he has copied is correct, not of remembering all the letters, just as his first reading job is one of remembering the total configuration of the word, not of responding to the separate word-parts. Thus, from the very start, spelling activities are planned so that the child thinks about the look of the whole word, and learns to sense that it is incorrect when it does not look as it should.

Children's first writing and spelling experiences are with words they can read, or with words they are taught to read as they plan to use them for writing purposes. Often, in the beginning, what they write will be composed as a group record. In the process of writing the word, or often the short message, on the chalkboard for the children, there are opportunities to comment on shapes and sounds. If the message is to taken home to mother, or to be sent to another class, the children then copy it carefully.

When the time comes to encourage a child to remember how to spell a word independently, the study procedure is one that calls for a thoughtful response to the sounds of the word. Modern methods in spelling advocate that the child be taught to look at the word while he says it clearly, thinking about each part as he speaks it. Next he may say it with his eyes shut, trying to see the parts as he says them. Then he may look back at the word to check the accuracy of his memory. Then he may cover it and try to write it, saying

[14] David H. Russell, "A Diagnostic Study of Spelling Readiness," *Journal of Educational Research*, **37** (December 1943), 276-283.

the parts as he writes. Last, he checks his writing, part by part, against the original word, pronouncing it as he does so. Primary teachers rarely leave this study job to the children alone. As they look at new words together there are opportunities to give help with word-analysis techniques—to find words that begin the same, to learn new letter combinations, to identify familiar endings, to break a word into useful sight and sound elements, moving systematically from left to right. Sometimes these spelling activities may involve the class as a whole, but there are many arguments both from the point of view of good spelling and from that of good reading for a certain amount of work in smaller groups.

Mention has been made at several points of the practice of developing lists of words children need for their writing but which they have not yet been able to learn to spell independently. Teachers who do not use such lists are usually prepared to write the needed words for the child. In some classes children file the words they have asked for in their own file boxes. All these systems of giving help make it possible to discuss the look of a word with a child as it is being written for him. When simple alphabetizing systems are used to file the words, another word-analysis skill is being exercised. Whether the aim is to spell the word for the child, or to help him spell it for himself, the methods of working with words in spelling activities should supplement and reinforce those used in reading, and vice versa.

Provide for some preliminary acquaintance with dictionary skills. While dictionary usage is largely a problem for the intermediate grades, primary word-analysis activities can, at times, make a contribution to simple dictionary skills. These skills, in turn, give the more mature reader another effective type of help with his word-analysis problems. The beginnings of alphabetical order, and general acquaintance with such terms as long and short vowels and silent letters may develop in the course of spelling and reading activities. Occasionally a third-grade textbook may have a simple gossary, or include a pronunciation key after a place name. Dictionary use, like other reading skills, starts very simply with readiness experiences. Primary word-meaning and word-analysis activities can help to provide some of these experiences.

PROVIDING SPECIAL PRACTICE ACTIVITIES FOR WORD-ANALYSIS SKILLS

Provide work-type activities that help children think about the meanings of words. The amount of special practice provided to help develop word-analysis skills will need to be adjusted to individual abilities just as the special practice in other reading skills requires such adjustment. The children who are making the most rapid progress in developing the knack of studying words by themselves may receive all the help they need through group reading activities, through the word study connected with spelling activities, and through the individual help they are given during independent reading. At the other extreme, children who find word analysis difficult in spite of the ample encouragement given in regular classroom work may, by the time they reach upper-second or third grade, be ready to profit from an extended series of systematic lessons planned around specially selected work-type materials. In between are the youngsters who have trouble with particular word-parts or who need a little more help than that given during group sessions in order to develop security in their approaches to words.

Since the child's ultimate task is to learn to use a word in context, it is important that his practice activities help him to think about the meaning of the words with which he is working. Some of the most valuable work-type exercises call for completing sentences, for answering questions based on short paragraphs, for completing rhymes, or for choosing the correct word to fit into some other context setting. Many of the word-recognition exercises described in the preceding section serve equally well to develop word-analysis skills. Ways of varying the choice of words so as to call for fine discriminations were given when those exercises were illustrated.

Sometimes it is helpful to use lists of words or sets of three or four words in which the child underlines given beginnings, endings, or phonograms. Special care needs to be taken in using such activities to assure that the child does not merely spell out the letter combination he wants without thinking of its pronunciation. Having children discuss their answers in a group session, read aloud the list of words with which they have been working, or even work together on the whole exercise may help to prevent thoughtless underlining.

Since children need to learn to hear sounds as well as to see word-parts, a certain number of word-analysis activities need to be oral. Some of these can be developed as group experiences where the teacher reads several words and the children listen for given sounds. Often the words are then written on the chalkboard so that children can see the common letters. Work-type activities that put major emphasis on sounds can call for giving rhymes, or for choosing pictures of objects whose names begin or end with a given sound.

Work-type word-analysis activities, especially for the unskilled reader, should present the word as a whole. He may choose which of three words answers a question or completes a rhyme, identify the two small words in a compound word, or underline a given root or ending in a list of words, but whatever his activity, he works with the total configuration of the word, and his task is to see its component parts. Later, as children develop skill in spelling, it is possible to have a certain number of word-building activities. They may build compound words, add prefixes or suffixes to form new words, or add the correct beginnings or endings to phonograms such as *ack, ight,* or *all* to form words that match given definitions.

Workbooks have a contribution to make to word-analysis skills. These commercially prepared materials provide activities using pictures and many other novel formats that hold children's interest. Among the available workbooks are some that focus entirely on word-study activities. These may be of special value for the child who needs intensive help. Workbook activities in word analysis, like those in word recognition, need to be used selectively. Time that children could be spending profitably in wide reading should not be used on work with sounds they know, or on workbook pages that develop no new skills.

Learning to analyze words is a matter of learning to think about the techniques one is using. Whatever the kind of work-type activity, time needs to be allowed to discuss it with the children; to talk about the new word-parts; to read the new words aloud; to discuss how individual children hit upon the right answer; to suggest other words that have the same sound; or to recall what part the word played in a recent story or experience record.

Typical word-analysis activities for primary children are given in the suggestions that follow. Readers should also refer to the activities suggested for word-recognition purposes given earlier and, for work with more advanced readers, to the suggested word-study activities for the intermediate grades, given in Chapter XII.

Activities that help the child identify sounds can ask for: Completing rhymes; choosing a picture that completes a rhyme; underlining in a set of pictures the ones that begin or end like a given word; finding and underlining in a series of sentences the words that rhyme with a given sound; reading a list of words aloud and underlining those that begin or end with a given sound; changing beginning, middle, or ending letters to form new words according to special instructions— changing *bell* to something you throw, to a boy's name; writing the beginning sound for each of a set of pictures; choosing from three or four letters the one with which a given picture begins; listening to a group of words read by the teacher and telling what the common sound is; reading a set of rhyming words and underlining the common sound.

Activities that help a child identify fine distinctions between words can call for: Choosing between three words calling for a careful look at beginnings, middles, or endings in answer to a completion or multiple-choice exercise; choosing the right answer to a riddle from three words that are very similar in form; choosing which of three or four similar words matches a picture; choosing which of a group of three or four similar words the teacher has read; choosing which of two or three sentences, in which a single word is varied, matches a given picture.

Activities that help in identifying structural elements in words can ask for: Finding the two single words in a series of compound words and trying to give the meanings of each of the compound words; drawing a circle around the root words in a set using a common suffix; making compound words by putting together two single words, and telling what they mean or choosing the sentence which they complete correctly; making new words by adding a prefix or suffix and using them in a sentence.

Use occasional word games and related activities. The same general precautions regarding the use of word games and similar devices for word-recognition purposes also hold true for word analysis. Used wisely, these materials have a contribution to make. For a group as a whole, they offer an occasional novel way of giving more practice with word-parts. Often, for the child who has found the techniques of word analysis particularly difficult, they sharpen insights into the job to be done.

Many of the gamelike devices discussed in the section on word recognition can be used for word-analysis purposes by varying the degree of discrimination required. Until children develop skill in spelling, word games will need to be built around the world as a whole. Later, simple versions of games such as anagrams may be used. From the word-analysis point of view, word-building activities such as anagrams are likely to be more helpful if they make use of phonograms and blends as well as single letters. Whatever the game, it needs to be used as a teaching device, not merely as a spare-time activity at which children work alone.

Word games focusing on sounds can be developed through: Fishing for words that rhyme, begin with similar sounds, contain a given sound element; playing bingo by covering words that rhyme or begin like the word read; seeing who can read all the words on a word wheel; seeing who can read through a booklet where a series of cards continuing different beginning sounds are fastened over a common ending—*bl-ack, st-ack, b-ack, p-ack*; seeing how many similar words one can get when they are flashed on word cards or in a tachistoscope; playing adaptations of the game of authors with sets of words with the same beginnings or endings.

SOME QUESTIONS TO THINK ABOUT IN APPRAISING THE WORD-STUDY PROGRAM IN THE PRIMARY GRADES

1. Is the difficulty level of children's reading materials adjusted so that the word-study problems they meet do not detract from their enjoyment of reading?

2. Are children's word-study activities planned so as to give a maximum amount of help with the problems they are meeting in daily reading activities?

3. Are children encouraged to meet their word-study problems in their day-by-day reading independently whenever they are able?

4. Are children's discoveries about words, and their interests in them, being capitalized upon so that they are growing in their interest in working with words?

5. Are word-meaning, word-recognition, and word-analysis activities planned so that they supplement and reinforce each other whenever possible?

6. Are word-study activities planned so that individual strengths and weaknesses are allowed for?

7. Is sufficient special practice being provided when it seems needed to strengthen special skills?

8. Are work-type activities being used so that they allow for a maximum amount of teaching and a minimum of busy work?

SUGGESTIONS FOR FURTHER READING

Betts, Emmett A. *Foundations of Reading Instruction*. Chapter 24. New York: American Book Company, 1957. 757 pp.

Beery, Althea. "Development of Reading Vocabulary and Word Recognition," *Reading in the Elementary School*, pp. 172-192. Forty-eighth Yearbook of the National Society for the Study of Education, Part 2. Chicago: The University of Chicago Press, 1949. 343 pp.

Bond, Guy L., and Wagner, Eva Bond. *Teaching the Child to Read*, Chapters 9 and 10. New York: The Macmillan Company, 1960. 416 pp.

Burton, William H. *Reading in Child Development*. Pp. 232-277. Indianapolis: The Bobbs-Merrill Company, Inc., 1956. 608 pp.

Dawson, Mildred A., and Bamman, Henry A. *Fundamentals of Basic Reading Instruction*. Chapter 16. New York: Longmans, Green and Company, 1959. 304 pp.

Dolch, Edward W. *Teaching Primary Reading*. Third Edition, Chapters 12, 13. Champaign, Illinois: The Garrard Press, 1960. 429 pp.

Durrell, Donald P. *Improving Reading Instruction*. Chapters 10, 11, 12. Yonkers-on-Hudson, New York: World Book Company, 1956. 402 pp.

Gates, Arthur I. *The Improvement of Reading*. Third Edition, Chapters 7, 9. New York: The Macmillan Company, 1947. 657 pp.

Gray, Lillian, and Reese, Dora. *Teaching Children to Read*. Second Edition, Chapter 11. New York: The Ronald Press Company, 1957. 475 pp.

Gray, William S. *On Their Own in Reading*. Revised Edition. Chicago: Scott, Foresman and Company, 1960. 248 pp.

Harris, Albert J. *How to Increase Reading Ability*, Fourth Edition, Chapters 12, 13. New York: Longmans, Green and Company, 1961. 624 pp.

Hildreth, Gertrude. *Teaching Reading*. Chapters 14, 15. New York: Henry Holt and Company, 1958. 612 pp.

Hester, Kathleen B. *Teaching Every Child to Read*. Chapter 11. New York: Harper and Brothers, 1955. 416 pp.

McKee, Paul. *The Teaching of Reading in the Elementary School*. Pp. 235-260; 292-303. Boston: Houghton Mifflin Company, 1948. 622 pp.

PART IV

Expanding Reading Skills in the Intermediate Grades

CHAPTER X

Planning the Reading Program in the Intermediate Grades

THE CHILDREN AT WORK IN LATE SIXTH GRADE

IF A visitor were to come back three years later to look in on the third-graders described in Chapter VI, now at the end of the sixth grade almost ready for junior high school, what reading abilities would he find? The personnel of the class has remained relatively constant over the intervening years. Two or three youngsters have moved to other schools; a few families have left town; but the variation in ages and intellectual abilities is about the same. How has their reading progressed?

The range in reading abilities has increased. The three years have done nothing to close the gap between the ablest and the poorest readers. The range is now from low fourth-grade ability to nearly tenth grade. Two children are most at home with easy fourth-grade books. Four score between fifth and sixth grade on standardized reading tests. About ten more are somewhat under seventh grade on standardized tests, but most of this group, given time and some guidance, can read seventh-grade materials if the need arises. Slightly over half the group have little difficulty with seventh-grade books, and two can deal with the technical demands of most adult materials if the concepts involved are within their experience.

Greater variation in specific skills is also in evidence. Of the two children who read adult materials, Allen is an extremely slow, careful reader. He still needs help in increasing his reading speed. Several others of varying levels of ability join with him in practicing rapid reading. Sue reads remarkably well. She adjusts her techniques effectively to the specific reading task—skimming when her work allows it and reading with the necessary accuracy when details are needed. She enjoys reading aloud and displays considerable skill in entertaining an audience.

Among the children whose abilities are the most limited there is also great variation in specific skills. Most are now sure of the sounds of common phonetic elements, but several still have difficulty with words of two or more syllables. As one of these youngsters tries to sound *resourceful* by breaking it as *re-sour-ce-ful*, it is apparent that he is not yet skillful in selecting the elements most effective for correct pronunciation. Another child pronounces the word correctly, but does not know what it means and misinterprets the passage he is reading because of this. Effective oral reading is difficult for these two children and for several others unless they are given ample opportunity to prepare simple materials ahead of time. The class as a whole enjoys reading aloud and finds many opportunities to participate in reading both stories and poetry.

Information-getting techniques also vary considerably. Among the relatively good readers, several children are skilled in reading rapidly for the main idea of the story but are inaccurate in reporting details. Others do well so long as factual reporting is needed but find it difficult to summarize the general import of an article. Many still tend to be encyclopedic in their reading and report all facts, pertinent or otherwise. Throughout the year all have worked on the problem of taking notes on their reference reading in suitable outline or summary form. Less than half the group is able to exhaust the reference possibilities of a given topic. Many still stop when the most obvious aspects of a problem have been covered. Most of the children know how to use their textbooks in the various content fields for reference purposes, but a few still have difficulty in reading accurately the descriptive and explanatory passages. There is a wide range in ability to use visual aids, such as charts, maps, and graphs, effectively. Equally great is the range in technical vocabulary.

Growth is still irregular. The children who gave the most promise at the prereading level were not all among the best readers when they reached the third grade. Similar shifts in position have occurred from third grade to sixth. The two children who are nearly adult in their reading ability have been consistently among the best readers. They are both somewhat above average in intelligence, and both have been given much encouragement to read at home. The remedial help provided for Jane, who was ill in her first year in school, and for Bill, who transferred to the school after a series of first- and second-grade teachers, has now shown its effect. Both children handle typical sixth-grade reading problems without difficulty. Jim, one of the slow learners in the room, is doing about as much, with his fourth-grade books, as he is able. He has had special adjustments in reading instruction and materials all along the way, has been encouraged to take leadership in group activities that do not demand much reading, and is regarded as one of the best athletes and most reliable helpers in the class. He is a happy and well-adjusted boy, in spite of his limited intellectual ability. Sally, the other slow learner in the third grade, was immature and very small physically. She found the active children of her own age increasingly overpowering, and was held for a year in the third grade. Now she is making a much better adjustment with children who are a year younger.

Uses of reading are now very broad. Even in the third grade the children were reading widely. However, they were limited both by their own lack of skill and by the scarcity of informational materials written simply enough to meet their needs. Now in the sixth grade there are few barriers to wide reading. The classroom testifies to the variety of the reading activities. A bookcase near a special reading corner and a bulletin-board display of colorful jackets give evidence that recreational reading is important. The contents of other bulletin boards indicate the extent of the reading demands of various class projects.

On one bulletin board are lists marked "Committee Problems about Housing Project." A glance at these indicates that the children are interested in a local housing development. Questions center around why the particular site was chosen, what determined the size of the apartments, how the tenants are to be selected for the new homes, and what made the project so expensive. Wide reading will be needed in newspapers, current periodicals, and technical books on health and housing. Next to this section of the bulletin board is a list labeled "Plans for Assembly." The class contribution is apparently to be a dramatization of an historical narrative. The reading assigned to various children includes such items as:

Reread the story to make suggestions for scenes	—Andy's group
Look up in the encyclopedia about flintlock guns	—Mary and Jack
Check history texts for suggestions on costumes	—Bill's group
Look up language text to find how to write conversation in a play	and Sunny's group
	—Writing Committee

Another bulletin board contains clippings from the local newspaper. Headings such as "New Inventions," "Our Town," "The UN" indicate that reading the daily paper is a regular activity. On part of this same board is a chart which indicates that learning to read is, itself, a center of activities. Over half the children are listed for one or more special study groups headed "Spelling and Word Study," "Practice for Speed," "Reading Accurately," "Using Graphs." Beside each list is a set of suggested practice activities for individual work. A tentative schedule on the chalkboard indicates that part of a long period set aside for individual work on skills will be devoted to group work on word study, and to the children in the "Practice for Speed" group. Children range far afield in their reading now. Books for fun, many types of informational materials and reference books, current magazines, textbooks, pamphlets, daily papers, are all used as the need arises.

Greater flexibility and variety characterizes the activities of the instructional groups in reading. In the third grade the work of the reading groups provided for large unit activities in reading and for special practice for skills. At the point where the children's reading activities were described, the least advanced readers were working regularly as a group on reading skills, using basal texts for their practice. One of the other groups was planning to share stories from a basal text, and the second was locating science information. Now, in the sixth grade, the variety of activities is even greater and the personnel of groups even less fixed. The most retarded readers have received instruction as a group on a regularly scheduled basis throughout the entire year. Even this group has not had constant membership. The children have been joined from time to time by others needing similar help, and they have occasionally separated to work in other groups designed to meet special needs.

The special practice groups listed on the bulletin board were set up for varying lengths of time. Of these groups, the one on word study has met all year, with varying membership. For a month it took in the whole class, when special study of root words and word origins was under way. The group practicing for increased speed started to work only two weeks ago, when certain children began to work with greater amounts of reference materials and found it difficult to read rapidly enough for their purposes. Earlier in the year other groups spent short periods working on the problem of speed. The children in the group working for accurate reading are rapid readers who have recently shown a tendency to skim materials too carelessly. Two weeks' concentration on the importance of going slowly when necessary will probably solve the problem. Three of the best readers have not been in a group for special help all year, although they have participated in many other types of group reading problems.

Other reading projects have run parallel with the special practice groups. At present, one of these is a unit on poetry which has now developed into a series of experiences in choral reading. The entire class has worked on this and each of the four groups into which the children are divided is preparing special materials to share with the others. Every child has also taken on some special reading responsibilities for the study of the housing project and for the assembly program. While these plans are under way, groups or individuals who encounter special difficulty will be given help. Some of the needed assistance may call for another special practice group, but it is likely that most of the help will be given as the work on the various units progresses. The choral-speaking presentations will call for the groups to meet for a number of practice sessions. The study of the housing project is likely to lead into some all-group instruction since never before, in the experience of this class, has the problem of locating current information and interpreting newspaper reports been as crucial. The dramatization will demand few new skills, although accuracy and authenticity in costuming will require considerable research work. Some children will need help both in locating the information and in interpreting it. Instruction in how to read goes on at many points in this classroom.

Meeting the reading needs of older children calls for a complex organization of classroom experiences. Large projects demanding many skills; small-group practice of varying extent when difficulties arise; changing personnel and changing foci of group instruction; and, above all, children who understand what they are doing and who feel responsible for carrying out their plans and improving their skill—these are the characteristics of the reading program in the intermediate grades.

This chapter gives the overview of the activities of the reading program for intermediate-graders. Like Chapter VI, which outlined the general nature of the primary program, it suggests aims to guide the choice of activities. Next, there is a general picture of the types of reading experiences appropriate for more skilled readers. Finally, suggestions for meeting the complex problems of grouping and scheduling occasioned by the wider reading activities of older children are summarized. Classroom procedures suggested in this overview are discussed in detail in Chapters XI and XII.

EXPANDED AIMS OF READING INSTRUCTION FOR THE INTERMEDIATE GRADES

There is no sharp dividing line between the reading programs of the primary and the intermediate grades. Children with primary abilities will be found in the intermediate grades, and the primary grades contain children who read intermediate grade materials with relative ease. Furthermore, the goals for the intermediate grades do not differ from those at the primary level. The aims continue to be:

1. Achieve wider reading purposes.
2. Gain more skill in adapting techniques to purposes.
3. Increase ability to locate information independently.
4. Become more adept in handling the technical difficulties of reading materials.
5. Grow increasingly independent in the recognition of words.

There is no change in ends; the levels to be achieved are higher. These expanded goals help to determine the materials, the reading experiences, and the kinds of instruction provided for maturing readers.

Children use reading as a tool to serve many purposes. In the intermediate grades there is a marked increase in the variety of reading done. Even by the end of the third grade some children will be skilled enough in analyzing unfamiliar words independently to allow them to read at will in new materials. Others will become independent in dealing with new vocabulary in the fourth and fifth grades, so that a much wider range and variety of reading matter is possible than was the case in primary grades. Although materials will be selected to meet the needs of these children, each new kind of material, and each new problem in reading will call for new competencies. Increased reading skill will be demanded in the following:

First—Broadened interests: Children should continue to enjoy recreational material, but their reading should include many kinds of fiction, poetry as well as prose, and a wide variety of factual, informational material. They can well develop standards for evaluating what they read, and become aware of the special contributions of individual authors and illustrators.

Second—Varied sources of information: Intermediate-grade children will be using a greatly expanded range of informational materials. There may be five or six books in a given subject-matter area. Encyclopedias, atlases, and almanacs will be used more frequently. The more mature children also may be able to follow much of the news in the daily paper, and can locate pertinent articles in current magazines and special pamphlets. Of all the new demands made on older children, those occasioned by this greatly increased variety of informational materials are likely to be the heaviest.

Third—Evaluation of materials: Intermediate-grade children should show increased skill in evaluating what they read in terms of their purposes. In their recreational reading they should achieve a wider acquaintance with authors and illustrators. They should be aware of differences in style, and be increasingly able to select books for varied purposes. In their informational reading intermediate-grade children should become increasingly skillful in deciding whether or not they have chosen the most appropriate selection in order to solve the problem at hand. They should be increasingly able to check when textbooks disagree, to determine an author's qualifications for writing on a specific topic, to know the difference between editorial writing and news reporting, and to distinguish fact from fiction.

Children become increasingly skillful in adjusting reading techniques to their purposes. The greatly increased variety of materials explored by older children makes a correspondingly heavy demand upon their ability to adjust their methods to specific purposes. This is complicated by the fact that materials are no longer written in relatively simple narrative style, and by the fact that greater amounts of material are often read. Among the most important reading skills that older children will need to learn to use more flexibly are the following:

First—Getting the idea of a passage: There must be increased ability to read for the general idea of a passage, which at the intermediate-grade level may vary in length from a single paragraph to a complete chapter or an entire book. Major ideas may come from sentences or paragraphs found in different places within a selection, or indeed from entirely different books. Grasping the ideas presented is not enough; the mature reader must also perceive their sequence and relationship.

Second—Reading accurately for detailed information: Intermediate-grade children need increased ability to read accurately for detailed information. Some reading tasks will call for accurate facts, others for the detailed step-by-step reading that is needed in following directions. Increased skill will be needed to select the exact details which bear on a problem, and to see how such details relate to the entire passage.

Third—Adjusting reading speed to purpose: Children should become able to change their reading speed as the occasion demands. They should be able to skim for the main idea of a paragraph, and to read slowly and carefully for directions and exact details. They should know when to read rapidly for the purpose of locating particular information, and when to change to a slower pace as the needed information is located. In recreational reading they should know when to read rapidly and when to use the slower, more careful reading needed to appreciate a style of writing or to enjoy the imagery and rhythm of a poem.

Fourth—Improving oral reading skills: As they progress through the intermediate grades, children show marked improvement in oral reading skills. They gain more mastery of the technical aspects of their materials, and thus become able to give more thought to the impressions they wish to convey to the audience. Both poetry and prose should be read with skill.

Fifth—Using a variety of techniques to achieve a purpose: More able readers will need to use several techniques in order to achieve a single purpose. To be able to report on a selection to a committee, an intermediate-grade reader may need to skim rapidly to locate special information; to read a specific part carefully; to re-read quickly to verify a first impression, or to check upon the accuracy of the material or its appropriateness for his purpose. Flexibility of reading method in terms of purpose is one of the clearest marks of a skillful reader.

Sixth—Making useful records: Older children face increased problems in recording what is read. Whereas a primary child will take only occasional notes, intermediate-grade children have many needs for accurate records of their reading. The skills required include learning to summarize a passage without copying it in entirety; making accurate lists; writing simple outlines; collecting information on the same topic from several sources; keeping simple bibliographical information.

Independent readers become more adept in locating information. Primary techniques of using the pictures, the title of the story, and the table of contents as major aids in locating information will not suffice in the intermediate grades. One of the most important problems for the teacher at this level is to help children develop more effective ways of locating desired information. Many new skills will be needed. These include:

First—Becoming familiar with resources: Children need to know, at least in general terms, the kind of help to be found in such books as a dictionary, an encyclopedia, or an atlas. They need to become familiar with the major functions of other types of resources to which they might turn—textbooks, special reference books, newspapers, magazines, fictional materials. In addition, they should begin to build standards for evaluating such resources—to know which ones are likely to be most helpful on current problems; to become aware of possible difficulties in using fictional material for information; to know how to interpret reports in daily papers and magazines.

Second—Using resources effectively: There needs to be gradual development of the techniques necessary to use common resource materials effectively. Intermediate-grade children need to feel at home with an index, particularly with the most important aspects of cross references and subtopics. They must build skill in determining which key words are most likely to lead them to information on a particular topic. They must be effective in using alphabetical order and guide words. They must be able to handle the special study aids in their textbook—summary paragraphs, chapter and section headings, and examples set in a special type.

Third—Using the library effectively: Of major importance in the location of information is ability to use the library. Wherever such facilities are available, independent readers need to know how to use them effectively. They should know how to locate books in a card catalog. While they may have little need for complete understanding of the cataloging system, they should know enough about the general location of materials to be able to browse at will. They should also begin to identify by name some of their favorite authors and illustrators. Major projects involving wide reading cannot be carried out with ease if it is necessary to wait for an adult to locate all the needed materials.

Technical difficulties of more complex materials are handled with relative ease. In the primary grades, the technical difficulty of the reading-matter lies to a great extent in the length and complexity of sentences, in the problem of following the thought of a passage through an increasing number of sentences in a paragraph and pages in a story, and in such special problems as the sentence carried over from one line to the next or from the bottom of one page to the top of the next. At the intermediate level, such problems are largely mastered. However, the more difficult materials of the upper grades present a number of new technical difficulties:

First—Using variations in printed materials: The intermediate-grade reader will need to learn how to use effectively such aids for the reader as section and paragraph headings, summaries, discussions especially spaced or set up in different print, and columnar arrangements of materials and other variations in style. Primary-grade materials are lacking in these variations and the more mature reader must achieve skill in using them.

Second—*Interpreting a variety of visual aids:* A great many new visual aids begin to appear, particularly in materials in the content fields. Middle-grade readers are likely to meet such visual aids as maps, graphs, charts, pictograms, tables, and the like. The skilled reader must be able to interpret these, to relate them to the information given in the text, and to move from print to visual aid and back again without losing grasp of the continuity of ideas or their relationships.

Third—*Interpreting unfamiliar symbols:* Although the more complex symbols of science and mathematics are reserved for secondary school readers, children in the middle grades must read numbers, simple arithmetical formulae, and the diacritical marks in the dictionary.

Children develop increased competence in working with unfamiliar words. The child who goes into high school still uncertain of how to work out the pronunciation and meaning of an unfamiliar word will be severely handicapped. Technical terminology appears in increasing amounts in the materials read by intermediate-grade and high-school students. In many cases the meaning as well as the configuration of the word is unfamiliar. Children in the intermediate grades need continued help with their word-study skills. Among the areas in which they should develop increased competence are the following:

First—*Increasing meaning vocabulary:* There needs to be a rapid increase in the child's ability to understand the vocabulary of his reading material. In the intermediate grades every content field will have a set of unfamiliar terms. Even recreational reading will introduce unfamiliar words. Many of the terms which cause the greatest pronunciation difficulties will also be unfamiliar in meaning. Concepts may be unfamiliar even though the word is easy to pronounce. The intermediate-grade child needs to develop a greatly increased stock of word meanings.

Second—*Continuing word recognition skills:* Some words will still need to be learned on a word-recognition basis. Even the skilled adult reader relies heavily on his memory of the general shape of a word. Once having worked out or looked up the pronunciation and meaning, he does not expect to have to go through this process with the same word every time he meets it. New technical terms, personal and place names occur with increasing frequency in the materials read by intermediate-grade children. If they are to be read with ease, they must become familiar with these words.

Third—*Extending knowledge of sound and structural elements:* Intermediate-grade children should build upon their primary grade experience with common word-parts. Of particular importance is a growing acquaintance with prefixes, suffixes, and roots. Older children should also begin to make use of some of the most important generalizations regarding pronunciation and spelling.

Fourth—Recognizing words of two or more syllables: In analyzing longer words, the intermediate-grade child needs to become skilled in selecting the word-parts that make for the most efficient analysis. He also must be able to identify word elements that aid both in recognizing the word and in determining its meaning. Ability to use context clues skillfully in determining pronunciation and meaning should also increase.

Fifth—Using the dictionary skillfully: The child needs increased skill in using a dictionary, both for pronunciation and for meaning. Intermediate-grade children need to learn to use this aid independently. Furthermore, they need to develop an interest in new words and a desire to use them accurately, an attitude which extends into adult life. Primary teachers may lay the foundation through their discussion of new and interesting words, but many of the most important experiences are given in the intermediate and upper grades.

These are the general objectives of the intermediate grades. The exact ways in which specific problems will arise will depend upon the abilities of the given group of children and the reading demands made by the materials in their classroom and the projects they undertake. Each teacher must take responsibility for identifying the present status and particular needs of her class.

PROVIDING READING EXPERIENCES TO MEET THE NEEDS OF CHILDREN IN THE INTERMEDIATE GRADES

The reading program for children in the intermediate grades needs to be planned to capitalize upon the increased ability to read independently and extensively possessed by these more skilled readers. This means, first, providing opportunities to use reading in varied types of challenging activities related to group or class projects. In many classrooms, such reading experiences will be developed as integral parts of units of work. Second, the children need to be encouraged to engage in wide independent reading. Third, instruction and practice need to be provided for groups and for individuals as they meet specific problems calling for new or better reading skills. Many of the most valuable reading experiences of children in grades four, five, and six are supplied by their on-going classroom activities. Often they have almost more reading to do than time will permit. All these experiences need to be seen as important aspects of their total reading program.

The instruction and practice needed for the development of increased reading skill should be provided on a flexible basis. There are several reasons why this is true. In the first place, intermediate-grade children are reading more widely, and it is almost impossible to predict exactly what new problem will arise, or when it will be encountered. As these problems come up, the most effective instruction in reading is that which helps the children carry on more effectively a variety of classroom activities involving the location and use of printed materials. Such instruction does not leave the development of reading skills to chance. On the contrary, the classroom teacher must take the responsibility for making continuous appraisals of the reading status of the pupils so as to discover where help is needed. Planning must also be done so that these experiences provided as a part of on-going classroom activities will also serve to raise new problems, and call, in turn, for a higher level of skill in reading.

The flexibility and variety of the reading activities in any one classroom will, of course, need to be adjusted to the abilities of the particular group of children. Some fourth-graders will be more like primary children in the degree to which they can engage in wide independent reading, and in their need to have the activities that introduce new words and provide practice in new skills developed in a definite sequence. Smaller groups in the fifth and sixth grades may find typical intermediate-grade materials difficult and may need to work with easier books and less elaborate activities. Increased independence needs to be capitalized upon as it is attained; more challenging tasks provided as children are ready for them; and special practice planned in the light of the type of problem the children have encountered.

USING UNIT ACTIVITIES AS A SOURCE OF READING EXPERIENCES

Reading units develop around interest in story materials. Group activities which relate to the story materials found in basal readers have a real place in the intermediate-grade classroom. Such activities make their greatest demands for increased reading skill when they are developed as units of work.

A reading unit may be developed through the same procedures as were suggested for the primary grades. The children concerned meet with the teacher; lay plans for what they would like to do with the story, or block of stories; spend a day or more carrying out their plans; and finally share their efforts, either with members of their own group or with the class as a whole. Such unit plans may be elaborate or very simple. Detailed descriptions of how such activities may develop are found in Chapter XI.

Children are typically engaged in other reading experiences as well as those connected with reading units, and all children may not be engaged in developing reading units at any one time. The pattern of scheduling and grouping in order to provide an effective balance between reading units and other kinds of reading experiences is more complicated than a traditional plan of providing for daily scheduling of a given number of reading groups.

However, the interests fostered, the type of reading experiences made possible, and the flexibility provided by planning for reading units are richly rewarding. Children have opportunities for reading experiences which would not be possible if reading groups met daily to read text materials, story by story.

Deciding how and when to provide time for reading units is influenced by the reading problems children are facing, their needs for gathering information, for developing wider reading interest, or for practice in a special skill. If children are facing pressing and immediate problems in some reading area, such as locating needed information, or selecting materials for a social-studies unit, time usually spent in group reading experiences may well be spent in working on these problems. It may be that wide reading in a content field, or enough time for pleasure reading to strengthen reading interests may have first demands on time scheduled for reading activities. Then, too, specific reading weaknesses, such as difficulties with word analysis, may call for time for special practice.

There are several ways of scheduling reading units to allow time for other reading needs. Groups need not move immediately from one unit to another. A unit may be completed, other types of reading activities may be planned for several days, then another unit may be begun. It is often possible for a group to work alone for a few days while the time set aside for reading instruction is spent on a different reading problem. When plans are clearly understood, it is also possible to make room for another reading activity, and then to return to the job of concluding the unit. There may also be times when an elaborate reading unit will occupy a large amount of class time and other activities will be curtailed to allow for it. Such projects as exploring a series of biographies, offering a choral-speaking program, planning a book exhibit, or producing a make-believe TV program provide not only an enriched reading experience but also many valuable related language experiences. They deserve a prominent place in the classroom from time to time.

The scheduling of reading units is also influenced by the level of reading skill already possessed by the children involved. More skilled readers are able to plan for a more elaborate unit, and to work independently for longer periods. Part of their reading activities can therefore be scheduled for times when the teacher is working with other children on other types of problems. More skilled readers are also capable of using a wider range of materials through wide reading for information and for recreation. More of their time may be scheduled for independent reading experiences. On the other hand, it is usually desirable for the teacher to work closely with children who have limited reading skill. It is also likely that these children will be helped by more consistent experience with the relatively simple materials in basal readers.

Adjustments in scheduling reading units to allow for individual differences in ability can be made in several ways. The children who need the most extensive experiences with materials in basal texts may work out a series of reading units, while others in the class spend more time on recreational reading or undertake more ambitious reading activities related to the content fields. Often groups of different levels of ability can be helped to plan unit activities requiring different amounts of independent reading. The teacher can then adjust her guidance to the problems of each group. Then, too, when several groups are at work, plans can be developed so that the teacher is not needed urgently by all groups at once. Thus, while all may work on activities connected with reading units for a full period set aside for reading, the teacher may check only briefly with the children in one or two groups and then spend her time with the others. As children grow in their ability to read independently, it becomes increasingly easy to have several worth-while activities moving forward smoothly.

Grouping for reading units is likely to vary with the particular purpose of the unit. In a classroom where there is a wide range of ability, children of like skill are apt to work together so that materials can be provided in terms of their general reading level. However, this is not always necessary. Groups of children with common interests may work together. In a unit growing out of recreational reading, children may work on a common topic, but read books geared to their individual abilities. Sometimes children who usually read together will divide into smaller groups to carry out parts of a plan— working in pairs to illustrate favorite stories for a bulletin board, or in groups of three or four to get ready to read aloud for the class. It is also possible for the entire class to plan together for a unit and for each group then to do its assigned part with materials of suitable difficulty. In the sixth grade described at the beginning of this chapter, for example, all groups were working on aspects of a unit on poetry. While these variations in grouping make for a complex classroom organization, they are not unduly difficult to achieve in situations where children help to plan their own activities.

Units in the content fields provide important reading experiences. Children in the intermediate grades face many of their most difficult reading problems as they read informational materials in the content fields and undertake a variety of reading activities. The activities are frequently parts of units of work in the various content fields[1] and call for successful reading of

---

[1] Unit activities centering around problems through which the child is helped to become better acquainted with the world in which he lives have been called *activity units, experience units,* and *subject-matter units.* To avoid specific curriculum connotations, the practice of most texts in teaching reading of calling the areas to which the child turns for information the *content fields* has been followed, and the term *unit in a content field* has been used in this book to refer to those unit activities in which the child reads for information to solve a problem, regardless of the particular focus of the problem he faces.

many new kinds of materials. The resulting reading problems will include dealing with vocabulary and writing style; evaluating what has been read; using library techniques; and interpreting charts, maps, graphs, time tables, and other illustrative aids. The reading program for the intermediate-grade child needs to be planned to provide specific help with these problems.

Time to give help with the reading problems of units in the content fields can be scheduled in several ways. Typically, a little informal assistance with reading is given during the time normally set aside for work in the specific content field. A few minutes may be spent discussing how to read arithmetic problems. Directions may be checked before a spelling lesson is begun. Time may be taken to discuss the pronunciation of some unfamiliar science terms before the children start to read a new chapter in their text. This type of informal, but consistent, help with reading problems does not require the allotment of special time in the daily schedule. It is, however, a valuable aid in the development of increased reading skill.

Often, reading problems in the content fields require more intensive instruction than that which can be provided incidentally as daily activities progress. Help with these problems is frequently scheduled as part of the activities of the unit. For example, a period at the beginning of a unit may be given to problems of locating reference materials and to developing a class bibliography. As the unit unfolds, a day's work may be devoted to problems of note-taking; time may be taken to learn how to interpret graphs or other visual aids; or a period may be given to discussion of how to evaluate conflicting sources. If an adopted textbook used by the whole class proves difficult, time may be taken to study parts of it together, and to discuss how to read it. It is a legitimate expenditure of the time scheduled for activities in a content field to set aside a period to give help on reading problems.

It follows, also, that time usually allotted to units in reading may well be used to develop skills needed by children who are encountering difficulties in using textbooks and related reference materials in the content fields. Practice sessions can be used to develop locational skills, or to help children read accurately for details, or to evaluate materials respecting their suitability for a specific purpose.

Unit activities in the content fields frequently involve a certain amount of small-group work. As these groups carry out various aspects of the unit, there are opportunities for the teacher to give help on reading problems. Note-taking techniques may be checked for one group at a time. Special problems of locating material may be discussed with the group directly concerned. A single child who is having trouble may be given special help. Such work sessions provide excellent times for concentrating on the specific problems in the setting in which they arose.

Grouping, for the reading activities of units in the content fields, is likely to depend on the plans for the unit and the difficulty of the reading task. Certain common problems, such as those of locating material or learning to use a new reference book, are likely to be attacked by the class as a whole. When the class is broken into smaller groups, the children who work together on a special aspect of a unit are likely to be those who have a common interest in it. If interest is the basis for grouping, materials of varied difficulty will be needed. If the reading task is very difficult, children may sometimes work in groups set up on the basis of reading ability. Some teachers have found it desirable to have the poorest readers work together as a group so that they may be given special help, even though the more able readers work in groups of their own choosing. Whatever the particular group organization, it should be planned to facilitate the progress of the unit activities while making it possible to give help in reading to those who need it.

Not all teachers in grades four to six teach in self-contained classrooms. Whether or not science and social studies are taught by the same person who teaches reading, children will need help with the reading problems these content fields present. Direct help in reading the material of that subject can be given by using part of the time scheduled for that subject. Groups similar to those which have just been discussed are helpful in any setting, whether work is departmentalized or not.

ENCOURAGING INDEPENDENT READING

Recreational reading is a source of expanded reading activities. With increased reading skill should come increased interest in recreational reading. Wide experience in independent reading of both fictional and informational materials is an important factor in building reading interests and tastes. It is also an excellent source of the type of motivated practice that develops increased reading skill. Intermediate-grade children need to be encouraged to go far afield in their independent reading activities.

Since recreational reading is a matter of individual interest, groups are not used as frequently as they are for other types of reading activities. Teachers are more likely to encourage children to select their own books and to read widely at their own paces, both at home and at school. However, with older children, as with those in the primary grades, a certain number of group activities can do much to encourage independent reading. Special reading clubs of children with common interests can be set up. All-class periods can be spent sharing opinions about library books. Story hours can be used to encourage children to share favorite books with groups of varying sizes. Since each child usually reports on his own book in such group situations, there is no particular need to set up the groups according to reading skill, although, if the purpose of such activities is to interest children in books, some thought has to be given to the difficulty of the books about which they are hearing. There is likely, also, to be considerable regrouping as new interests develop and new ways of sharing books are suggested.

In addition to special group activities designed to share recreational-reading interests, it is possible to help intermediate-grade children develop a certain number of reading units around their recreational reading. Even the unit activities in a content field can be used to provide recreational-reading experiences as children, individually or in groups, read authentic fictional materials or interesting factual accounts that bear on their particular problem.

It is as important to provide definite time for recreational reading in the classroom schedule of an intermediate class as it is in the primary grades. With books readily available, children who have no special duties at a given period may read, but time free for all to read is essential. Time set aside for browsing through new books, for library visits, for sharing periods is time well spent. Teachers who have regularly scheduled periods for exploring new books and for enjoying uninterrupted contact with them have found such investment of time brings rich dividends in broadened interests and shared enthusiasms for reading.

Regular classroom activities offer many opportunities for independent reading. Just as a primary classroom offers many day-by-day purposes for reading, so does the classroom of older children. Class plans call for careful detailed reading. A current events bulletin board, a daily school bulletin, or a series of brief descriptions of a science exhibit offer other opportunities to read carefully. Captions to pictures can provide information related to unit activities in the content fields. Children's stories or poetry can be posted for others to read. Even the directions for a spelling exercise, the description of the correct form of a business letter in a language textbook, or the discussion of fractions in an arithmetic text can make a contribution to increased reading skill.

The informal reading experiences offered by the typical intermediate-grade classroom are not normally given a definite place in the schedule, nor do they typically call for group work. Children turn to them as needed. The secret of encouraging these many short contacts with reading is to give the children a share in developing their class plans so that special bulletin boards, group plans, the daily schedule, display corners, letters from other classes, and special notebooks have meaning for them and play a real part in their daily activities. It is important, also, to have an informal classroom atmosphere that provides opportunities during the day when children can move about, check plans, read bulletin boards, or study exhibits.

Possibilities for individualized reading periods may be explored. The essential features of an individulaized reading program have already been described in Chapter VI. Since most intermediate-grade children have already achieved a considerable measure of independence in reading, an individualized approach to reading activities may be an appropriate way to encourage wide acquaintance with books, and strengthened interest in pleasure reading.[2]

The flexible plans for individual, small group and all class-reading activities described in this chapter allow for many opportunities for individual reading. However, larger blocks of time for individual reading activities may be provided for in several ways. A period of three or more weeks, or approximately the time usually assigned to a unit, may be given to individual reading for the entire class. As the experience proves to be effective and rewarding, additional time for individual reading may be arranged. Another procedure may be to provide for individual reading experiences, and individual guidance, for those pupils whose interests and levels of ability are such that they do not readily fit into a regular group.

In any event, the following considerations are important in planning for largely individualized reading activities for any group of pupils:

1. A sufficient quantity of appropriate reading materials to meet the needs of pupils with whom they are to be used.
2. An awareness of the specific reading skills which each pupil needs to develop.
3. A careful planning of time, so that individual guidance is possible.
4. Planning with pupils, so that they know how they can best use their time, and can work effectively without direct supervision.

PROVIDING SPECIAL PRACTICE AS NEEDED

Concern with better skill leads to short-term groups. The challenge of learning to read skillfully calls for still another type of group activity in the intermediate grades. Many children will need, from time to time, a series of experiences with work-type activities designed to develop specific skills. In the sixth grade described at the beginning of this chapter, short-term practive groups are scheduled on *Spelling and Word Study, Practice for Speed, Reading Accurately,* and *Using Graphs.* Each of these represents a separate skill. In these practice situations, the materials used bear directly upon the reading problem, as does the children's discussion of their work. Such help is an important supplement to the experiences provided by the many other types of reading activities that have been described.

Because of the many reading activities in which older children are engaged, they are even more likely to have varied needs for special practice than are children in the primary grades. No two classes, and no two children will face problems that are exactly the same. To be most effective, groups

---

[2] See also the bibliography on page 154.

will have to be established as needs are identified. At times the group will be a small number of children who have a common problem—a few who are having trouble with word analysis; several youngsters who are encyclopedic in reporting on their reading and who need to learn to summarize; five or six who are reading too carelessly. At other times it will be the whole class, in difficulty with their attempts to read poetry aloud or floundering with a new reference book.

Even with the more varied needs of older children, scheduling short-term practice groups is not so complicated as it sounds. In the first place, many opportunities for gaining skills and for overcoming difficulties will be found in the reading units, the reading activities of units in the content fields, and the recreational reading experiences which have been described. Furthermore, in a class of thirty children there will not be thirty different kinds of difficulties requiring thirty different kinds of practice. Many children will have little trouble with new reading tasks. When troubles are encountered, they are likely to be in such areas as word analysis, oral reading, reading for detailed information, evaluating materials, or using reference books effectively. Thus help will be needed in only three or four problem areas at one time, and all children are not likely to need to be in a practice group at the same time.

There are several points in the daily schedule where special practice activities can be given a place. When the need for practice involves the whole class, as it is likely to do when the reading activities of a unit in the content fields pose a new problem, help may be scheduled for part of the time usually devoted to the unit. Ways of finding time for this type of practice were outlined earlier when the reading activities related to units in the content fields were discussed. Time normally set aside for unit activities centering around the story materials in basal readers may also be used for special practice. Sometimes small groups set up for special practice meet during a block of time set aside especially for work on skills. In this period some children may be reading, others completing arithmetic assignments, studying spelling, or engaging in various types of written language activities. On occasion, time can be saved by integrating the reading practice with help on another skill. A group of poor spellers may work on word-analysis skills, or a group of children who read arithmetic problems carelessly may work on careful reading as part of their arithmetic activities.

When short-term practice activities are most effective, they are developed as units of work. Children help to analyze their own difficulties. They share in identifying the need for special practice; help to decide whether they belong in a special group; and talk through the purposes of suggested practice exercises and how to use them. Children also can help to set up the schedule for special practice so that they know when their group will meet.

It is not unduly difficult for a child to meet a special reading obligation when he understands its purpose and has helped to decide what his responsibilities are to be.

Individual work-type activities have a place. Individualized work-type exercises—workbook exercises, special exercises planned by the teacher, special activities suggested in basal readers—are also an effective means for developing specific reading skills. They are likely to be scheduled during an independent work period at a time when all children are working to improve basic skills. Such exercises may be planned for as the schedule of "things to do today" is worked out, or they may be written down as a part of an individual's work sheet. Check sheets of reading skills may be developed from which the children themselves can determine the kinds of practice they need. Teachers who encourage this kind of individualized practice are likely to discuss the purposes of each exercise, so that each child knows clearly what he is trying to accomplish.

Children who have special difficulty may need a more tightly integrated sequence of activities. Sixth-grade children who are approaching adult skill will, to an amazing degree, provide their own practice and teach themselves new skills as they read widely to serve their own purposes. Children who handle the classroom materials reasonably well, will need specific instruction from time to time to supplement their classroom reading experiences. There will also be children who have difficulty with typical classroom materials and who need relatively more guidance, both in handling the day-by-day reading demands of their classroom work and in securing the practice needed to improve their reading skill. Some of these children will be working far below their potential level of ability and will be in need of remedial help. Others will be youngsters who learn slowly and who will continue to need more than the usual amount of careful guidance to make progress commensurate with their ability. Both groups need a more tightly integrated sequence of reading activities.

The fact that the children who are having the most difficulty are likely to need a greater amount of carefully planned sequential activities in reading and more direct guidance from the teacher does not mean that they should be segregated and given a distinctly different program. They need to have experiences in working with reading units, to take part in groups locating informational material, and to engage in recreational reading. These activities are sources of much valuable practice in reading as well as important means of arousing interest.

A number of grouping and scheduling possibilities that allow for a more tightly integrated sequence of activities for children who are having unusual difficulty have been described. They may meet regularly to work with basal-reader series on reading units of varying degrees of elaborateness while children with greater skill engage in other and more varied types of reading activities. If it is desirable to give these retarded readers additional help, they may also form a special practice group. The poorer readers may work as a group for unit activities in the content fields, so that special materials and assistance can be provided for them. Selected workbook exercises for re-tarded readers may be given them to complete during individual work periods. Then, too, teachers often have been able to give a few minutes' extra help during independent work periods. In all these activities, the effectiveness of the reading experience depends in large measure on whether the retarded reader is provided with material appropriate for his ability, and has specific guidance at the time he is encountering difficulty.

It is easier to help poor readers engage in the activities they need if they are aware of their problems. When there is a classroom atmosphere of frank appraisal of individual difficulties, these children do not mind being placed in groups designed to give them special assistance or being asked to work with children who can help them. They know that in another area they themselves may be the helpers. In providing for special practice, teachers have often been able to challenge the children who need the most help to analyze their own difficulties and to share in planning their own remedial programs. Flexibility in the type of reading experience, and in grouping and scheduling, has been the keynote.

CLASSROOM ORGANIZATION TO MEET THE READING NEEDS OF THE INTERMEDIATE GRADES

The preceding section contains specific examples of methods of grouping and scheduling to provide for varied reading activities of the intermediate grades. In general, the basic principles that underlie effective classroom or-ganization in the primary grades are also guides for meeting the grouping and scheduling problems that result from the more complex activities of older children. In addition to these considerations, three major growth trends need to be kept in mind.

First—intermediate-grade children are better able to plan and to carry forward independently the activities agreed upon.

Second—the children are more skilled in independent reading.

Third—the children are better able to analyze their own needs and to under-stand the purposes of practice designed to develop better reading skills. The sec-tions which follow summarize possible ways in which classroom organization can be planned so as to capitalize on this increased maturity.

ACHIEVING EFFECTIVE SCHEDULING

Large time-blocks are still the key to effective scheduling. Large blocks of time are characteristic of schedules in the intermediate grades just as they are in the primary grades. Unit activities are not impossible when short periods are used, but they are more easily carried out under a schedule that makes it possible to plan, work on special activities, and evaluate, all within one time-block. Work with individuals or with small groups also progresses more smoothly when the teacher has enough time to move from group to group without cutting short needed explanations. In addition, the larger time-block makes it possible to extend activities a little when the task undertaken proves to be larger than expected, or to go on to other activities without loss of time if a problem clears up more rapidly than was foreseen.

For example, a fifth-grade teacher typically will plan times for developing skills, unit activities, and individual work. Supervised play periods and opportunities for experiences in art and music are also planned. In broad outline, the schedule will include:

First morning hour	A work period of about seventy minutes for the development of needed skills.
Quarter or half-hour play period	This may be a period for recess or supervised physical activity.
Second morning hour	Work on unit activities.
Half-hour free period	May be used to continue unit activities or reserved for help with fundamental skills.

LUNCH

First afternoon hour	Activities related to a unit centered around a second major group problem.
Recess	Usually a ten- or fifteen-minute break. On occasion it is increased to forty minutes to provide for physical education activities.
Second afternoon hour	Provision is made here for individual activities or work on a unit activity, as needed. Special help in art is scheduled for two days each week.
	A period of time before dismissal is used for a planning and evaluation session.

How might the activities of this fifth grade develop if one were to follow the children at work for a typical day?

The work period from 9:00 to 10:15 began with a brief check on individual plans. On the board were special assignments for various groups and a list of extra things to do for a social-studies unit and for a unit on health. Children turned to the activities on this list during the entire day as they had time. After general plans for the day were checked, spelling occupied the whole class for fifteen minutes. The words that were to be the basis of the next week's spelling activities were dictated as a pretest. As a group, the children took time to identify some of the most frequent errors. Then each child made plans to study the words he had missed. While some worked on with this, the teacher gathered the group having the most trouble with fractions and devoted twenty minutes to instruction, and to explaining some practice exercises. Others in the class had special work-type activities in arithmetic to complete.

As the arithmetic activities ended, the class was ready to go on to reading. Three group activities were under way. One group was completing the independent reading of a set of humorous stories, and needed no special help. The teacher spent five minutes checking plans with a group of advanced readers who had volunteered to organize the reference materials for a new social-studies unit. Then this group worked on alone while the teacher met with the four poorest readers, spending most of the time on work-type materials in word analysis. The last few minutes of the period were spent by the teacher at her desk, checking on individual and group progress.

On the following day a slightly different balance of activities would be planned for the 9:00 to 10:15 time-block. The children who have just read the set of humorous and imaginative stories would be ready to discuss them with the teacher and to plan how to share them with the class. Work with the poorest readers would continue, spelling might be entirely a matter of individual practice, and more time for all-class work in arithmetic might be found.

During the work period set aside for unit activities from 10:30 to 11:30, other needs for reading skills typically arose. The long period made it possible to give help without interfering with other plans. On the day being described, the class was just starting a new unit, and needed to locate information not readily available in its textbooks. The children first listened to the report of the small reading group that had volunteered to do some organizing of available materials. Other problems of locating materials were raised during the discussion that followed the report. Then each committee took time to examine the materials more carefully, and the teacher found a few minutes to work on special problems with each group in turn.

On the following day the children might read independently, using the books most suited to their part of the unit, and the teacher be able to devote the entire work session to helping one child at a time. The four poorest readers would be provided with simple materials and be given special help until they were well started.

In the schedule being described, the half hour from 11:30 to 12:00 provided a short, but flexible, block of time that could be used in various ways. For three days a week it was allotted to work in music. On other days it was used as an unassigned period for special work; a way of giving more time to the unit activities of the preceding period; a period for class discussion of some new problem in connection with a skill; or a planning and evaluation period. By stopping the preceding work on unit activities earlier, this period could be made long enough for work on a special reading unit; for a series of creative-language experiences; or for more extended activities on some other class project.

From 1:00 to 2:10, this schedule provided another long period for work on unit activities. This period was shortened twice a week to allow for more extended physical-education experiences. On the day of this visit, the children were investigating the nutritional values of some of their favorite foods, as part of a unit in health, and the need to read tables correctly and to interpret them in terms of the written content of the textbook was paramount. Since other plans for some experimental work had to be carried out, it was agreed that the period on the following day would be set aside for the whole class to explore further the problem of reading tables.

The forty-five minute period following the afternoon recess provided a fourth large time-block for group or individual activities. In this class, these experiences often centered around language and related reading activities. Once a week, part of the time was given over to reports on library books. On the day being described, a group of about ten children who were much interested in writing short stories met to read their efforts to each other. Another group, who served as the editorial board of the school paper, spent the period making preliminary selections of items to be approved by the entire class for final inclusion in the paper. Proofreading was a skill on which these children had worked particularly hard. Art activities came in at many places in connection with unit plans. At least twice a week, they were scheduled definitely for this last period.

In this class, the planning time at the end of the day varied in length with the problems that had arisen during the day. Although the immediate problems connected with the development of various activities were discussed during the period in which the activity took place, this session provided for a final check on work accomplished and for a look at the schedule for the morrow. Needs for special help were taken into account. Projects demanding all-class attention, such as approving the articles for the newspaper, were definitely scheduled. Jobs that needed to be completed, together with a tentative schedule for the next day, were listed in a special corner of the chalkboard.

The activities of this class are illustrative of the variety of experiences that can make up a day's work for intermediate-grade children. The large time-blocks allow small groups and individuals to check their plans with the teacher and then to move ahead independently. The teacher is free to give help to individuals and groups because she is not needed to guide every step of each activity. Relatively large amounts of help can be provided for some groups because others are able to work without direct supervision. Over several days, many types of group and individual activities can be included because the use of each of the time-blocks is flexible, and is planned in relation to the demands of on-going activities.

Every part of the daily schedule makes its contribution to reading skill. The problem of finding enough time for scheduling reading activities becomes less formidable when every reading experience in which the children engage is thought of as providing an opportunity for reading instruction and practice. Instead of deciding what type of activity to include, and how much time to set aside for specific reading instruction, the problem becomes one of determining what experiences are needed to provide a well-rounded reading program. In the situations that have been described, children are given special help with reading problems during units in the content field. Time is also taken to call brief attention to reading problems whenever work with textbooks or supplementary materials seems to warrant it. When small groups are at work on special problems of locating information, individualized help in reading is provided. In this way, every teacher in the intermediate grades becomes a teacher of reading, and every situation contributes to the reading program.

Effective use of every activity in the child's schedule as a basis for developing reading skill cuts down the amount of time that needs to be set aside for reading instruction as such. It also makes for effective motivation, as the need for the reading skill is clearly apparent to the children at the time they are given the help. Further, it augments rather than decreases the time available for other subject-matter areas, since it helps to develop more efficient readers and thus enables the children to do greater amounts of independent work and to explore a problem more extensively.

Flexibility in scheduling makes for more efficient use of time. It is possible to be even more flexible in the use of time in the intermediate grades than it is with younger children. This increased flexibility is an important aid in meeting the reading needs of older children. In the classrooms described, schedules are not haphazard. Time-blocks are set aside for specified activities. However, within these time-blocks the exact sequence of activities varies from day to day, and on certain occasions the entire block of time is given over to a problem not normally scheduled for that period. No one kind of reading experience is necessarily scheduled every day, nor is any one book necessarily followed story by story from beginning to end. The specific reading activities the children undertake are planned in terms of the problems they are facing and in the light of the balance in the reading experiences offered by their total program.

All children do not use the time for reading instruction in the same way. Part of the class may be working with stories in a basal reader while the rest are reading independently. Some may belong to a group meeting for special practice, and some may use the time for practice in other skills, or for other types of reading activities. Groups working with basal-reader series may read different amounts of materials, plan ways of sharing what they have read that differ in elaborateness, and need different amounts of guidance from the teacher.

The time devoted by the teacher to working with individuals and groups is also scheduled on a flexible basis. At one time she may work with the whole class on a common problem. At another, she may take a full period to help a single group lay plans. When several groups are working with basal-reader stories at the same time, their activities are scheduled so that all do not need the same amount of help on the same day. A few minutes may serve to check the plans of one group, ten more be devoted to starting an activity with another, and the remainder of the period be spent working closely with a third. Then, too, there may be days when help is entirely on an individual basis while the children read independently.

Flexibility in the use of time makes it possible to adjust more readily to individual needs. Special problems can be made the center of attention more easily and the amount of help can be adjusted more readily in the light of the problems faced and the maturities of different groups. Flexibility in scheduling activities also frees the teacher more often to give a few minutes' special help to individual children.

Periods set aside for special work on skills guarantee time for special instruction. Even though there is flexibility in scheduling the reading activities of intermediate-grade children, there also needs to be a definite plan for helping individual children improve their reading skill. An important aspect of the schedule described at the beginning of this section is the time-block set aside for work on fundamental skills. This period can be used to capitalize on the growing ability of the intermediate-grade child to analyze his own strengths and weaknesses, and to help him to direct his own practice, not only in reading but in numbers, language, and other skill areas. Plans for special activities during these periods are laid in terms of the problems that arise. Conferences with individual children or with small groups help to identify needs and to explain the purposes of the assignments. Individual assignment sheets, planned jointly by teacher and children, may help to guide the different activities. Sometimes a class planning session at the beginning of the period serves to help all children think through things to be done. Children may work alone during these periods; they may help each other as spelling partners, partners in number games, listeners and checkers in reading activities, or editors of written work; or they may be called together in groups of varying sizes.

In a time-block set aside for work on skills, the teacher may take time for an all-class discussion of a new problem; work with one or more small groups who are meeting for help on specific problems; or find time for a few minutes with a child who has a special remedial problem. Certain of these activities may be scheduled regularly, others adjusted to the needs of the particular day. These periods, which provide for considerable individual or small group guidance, are planned on the theory that a few minutes applied directly to a child's problem may be more valuable than a much longer period of time spent working with him in a large group.

Pupil-teacher planning helps to make a complex schedule effective. Throughout all the illustrations in this chapter, pupil-teacher planning plays an important part in keeping activities running smoothly. Even first-graders can take a responsible part in directing their own activities. Older children are capable of laying more complicated plans, keeping them in mind over a longer period of time, and working toward a goal more consistently.

Planning goes on at several points in a typical intermediate-grade classroom. Often the major activities for the day are blocked out in an evaluation period toward the end of the preceding day. Children think through how far along they are; decide on the actitivities which will need the most time; list special problems that have to be solved; and note things left undone which will need special attention. The resulting plans can be written on the chalkboard and referred to as the new day begins. An alternate time for this session is in the morning before activities start. Detailed plans for unit activities or for work-type exercises are often made just as the period for this work begins, and short evaluation sessions are often used to check on progress as the period ends.

Planning sessions offer unparalleled opportunities to learn the procedures of democratic discussion and group problem solving. But teacher and children have to work together to develop effective techniques. It is not easy to give children a share in planning without devoting an undue amount of class time to unnecessary arguments, wrangles, and reviews. In part, the success of the joint planning session depends on how carefully the teacher, as class chairman, has thought through topics to check, points to raise, suggestions to offer, and the implications of alternate possibilities which might be proposed by children.

Children need to be taught to take an effective part in the planning process. Individuals who are inclined to push for their own ideas have to learn when to yield to the majority. Ways of compromising have to be worked out. Willingness has to be developed to abide by a group vote so that discussion can proceed to another aspect of the plan. Children also have to learn how to weigh ideas thoughtfully—it would be fun to have the whole school see our play, but would small children really enjoy it, and should we take the time to repeat it so often; it sounds like a good idea to build our map out of clay, but what about the school custodian; can we have a pet in our room if no one can take care of it over the week end; writing thank-you notes does take time, but shouldn't we be polite anyway? Children also have to learn that certain areas do not call for much discussion—as members of a law-abiding school community, we do not vote on a fire drill, or a special request from the principal's office, or a plan agreed upon for the benefit of all classes; teachers have certain delegated responsibilities as members of a school faculty and merit cooperation in carrying them out; facts in books may be checked, but when facts are available, personal opinions that happen to disagree do not take up group time. Group planning is a skill; it does not develop without work.

Planning sessions are more effective when there is skillful use of preceding decisions. Every activity need not be talked through again every day. Once a decision has been made, the new planning problem is to see whether there are any difficulties in carrying it out. Giving children a share in planning a daily schedule does not necessarily mean that every time allotment will have to be agreed upon over again every day. Certain time-blocks can be accepted by general agreement, and the key question for the day may be only, "Is there any need to make changes in our usual schedule?" It is helpful, also, to post plans. These may include lists of committees; special committee plans or problems raised for committee consideration; a calendar of special events; a proposed set of deadlines for a unit; a list of extra work activities to be picked up by individuals as soon as regular assignments have been completed; a series of assignments for special practice groups. Individual work-sheets have been mentioned as a means of helping each child to keep a list of his special errors or to check off work as he completes it. Teachers and children who plan together effectively check such lists; cross off work accomplished; star jobs of major importance; and devote their planning session to as efficient as possible a survey of where they are, and what needs to come next.

GROUPING TO MEET THE VARIED NEEDS OF INDEPENDENT READERS

Pupil-teacher planning is the key to the grouping problem. Techniques of effective grouping and scheduling are not easily separated. Just as joint planning makes it possible for children to work under a complex schedule, so it is a major factor in helping them engage in two or three kinds of reading activities in as many different groups.

Planning sessions help to identify what groups are needed; to determine what their special responsibilities are to be; and to decide upon personnel. Among useful planning techniques is that of helping children analyze their own reading needs. Out of such discussions can come agreements as to the desirability of joining a special practice group; the importance of working with a reading group being given special help with informational reading;

or the value of going on with individual work-type activities. Children who know their own strengths and weaknesses can also be more effective in selecting materials that are within their abilities. Group work proceeds more easily when time is taken to get group plans clear, lists of questions to be answered set up, individual responsibilities agreed upon, and ways of working decided. Written memoranda of plans posted, where all may check, have been mentioned as a way of facilitating the planning process. Periodic evaluation sessions help to check on group progress and to identify problems. All such techniques help to free children to work ahead in many different group situations, or to adjust easily to a change in the method of grouping.

Flexibility in grouping is essential. In the situations that have been described, no one method of grouping governs all activities. Grouping is used which is appropriate to the particular problem. Children with similar ability work together frequently for unit activities in reading and in other fields. However, this grouping is not always followed. Other suggested possibilities are:

1. Working with the class as a whole when the reading problem is common to the whole group.
2. Grouping children according to interests or friendship, and adjusting the difficulty of the reading materials accordingly.
3. Grouping children according to interest and assigning good readers to be special helpers.
4. Keeping together one group of children who need special help while others are grouped according to interest.
5. Breaking larger groups of like ability into pairs or subgroups in order to concentrate on parts of a group plan.
6. Selecting from children who would normally work in different groups a special practice group to work on a common difficulty.
7. Providing individualized work-type activities for a child with a particular problem.

In these settings the particular need and the most efficient way of meeting it determine the group.

Independent reading activities are seen as an important source of increased skill. The teachers in the classrooms described in this book value independent reading. Reading activities are set up so that work is not done entirely in groups nor entirely under direct teacher guidance. Children go ahead on their own in many reading activities. They read for pleasure, look up infornation needed in unit activities in the various content fields, or do background reading for the culminating activities of a reading unit. They also read independently at home to locate information as the occasion demands.

The classrooms in which these children work provide stimulation for independent reading. Group plans are posted, also lists of questions, schedules of special events, directions for work-and-play activities, creative stories, articles or poems. New and attractive books are readily accessible as are reference materials. Textbooks in skill areas are used as reference books. They may be used to look up the correct form of a business letter or review the explanation of a process in arithmetic. As the need arises, work-type practice activities are used by individuals, or by small groups, and children proceed at their own paces.

To encourage children to share in responsibility for analyzing their own strengths and weaknesses, for developing their own skills, for deciding on their own sources of recreational reading, and for locating and evaluating the informational material they read is not to neglect them. This is the responsibility which mature adults will have to take in a society that looks for effective independent thinking and cooperative action for the common good. Children have the right to be helped to take as many steps in the direction of independent activity as they are capable.

SOME QUESTIONS TO THINK ABOUT IN APPRAISING THE READING EXPERIENCES PROVIDED IN THE INTERMEDIATE GRADES

1. Are children being encouraged to use reading in many types of comprehensive and challenging activities?
2. Are there opportunities for extensive independent reading?
3. Do the children's reading experiences call for a wide variety of reading skills?
4. Is instruction and practice provided for groups and for individuals in terms of the specific reading problems they are facing?
5. Is the scheduling of reading activities flexible enough to allow for many types of experiences?
6. Is the pattern of grouping flexible in terms of the needs of the particular problem as well as the abilities of the children?
7. Are children encouraged to share in planning their activities?
8. Are reading activities planned so the teacher is free to give help to individuals or to small groups?

SUGGESTIONS FOR FURTHER READING

OVERVIEWS OF THE READING PROGRAM FOR THE INTERMEDIATE GRADES

Bond, Guy L., and Wagner, Eva Bond. *Teaching the Child to Read*. Third Edition, Chapter 12. New York: The Macmillan Company, 1960. 416 pp.
Gray, Lillian, and Reese, Dora. *Teaching Children to Read*. Second Edition, Chapter 9. New York: The Ronald Press Company, 1957. 475 pp.
Hildreth, Gertrude. *Teaching Reading*. Chapter 17. New York: Henry Holt and Company, 1958. 612 pp.

Intermediate Manual, Revised. Chapters 5-8. Curriculum Bulletin 400. Cincinnati: Cincinnati Public Schools, 1962. 404 pp.

McCullough, Constance M. "Reading in the Intermediate Grades," *Development in and Through Reading,* pp. 288-304. Sixtieth Yearbook of the National Society for the Study of Education, Part I. Chicago: The University of Chicago Press, 1961. 406 pp.

Russell, David H. *Children Learn to Read.* Second Edition, Chapter 8. Boston: Ginn and Company, 1961. 612 pp.

GROUPING, SCHEDULING, AND COOPERATIVE PLANNING

Burton, William H. *Reading in Child Development.* Chapter 15. Indianapolis: The Bobbs-Merrill Company, 1956. 608 pp.

Cunningham, Ruth and Associates. *Understanding Group Behavior of Boys and Girls.* New York: Teachers College, Columbia University, 1951. 446 pp.

Durrell, Donald D. *Improving Reading Instruction.* Chapter 6. Yonkers-on-Hudson, New York: World Book Company, 1956. 402 pp.

McKim, Margaret G.; Hansen, Carl W.; and Carter, William L. *Learning to Teach in the Elementary School.* Chapter 6. New York: The Macmillan Company, 1959. 612 pp.

Miel, Alice and Associates. *Cooperative Procedures in Learning.* New York: Teachers College, Columbia University, 1952. 512 pp.

Robinson, Helen M. (Editor). *Reading Instruction in Various Patterns of Grouping.* Supplementary Educational Monographs No. 89. Chicago: University of Chicago Press, 1959. 212 pp.

Russell, David H. *Children Learn to Read.* Second Edition, Chapter 15. Boston: Ginn and Company, 1961. 612 pp.

Stratemeyer, Florence B.; Forkner, Hamden L.; McKim, Margaret G.; and Passow, A. Harry. *Developing a Curriculum for Modern Living.* Second Edition, Chapters 7, 8. New York: Teachers College, Columbia University, 1959. 740 pp.

Wrightstone, J. Wayne. "Class Organization for Instruction," *What Research Says to the Teacher.* No. 13. Washington, D. C.: National Education Association, 1957. 33 pp.

CHAPTER XI

Developing Reading Skills Through On-Going Classroom Activities in the Intermediate Grades

In the reading program outlined in the preceding chapter, the functional use of reading in a wide variety of classroom activities is seen as making an important contribution to growth in reading skill through the motivation for effective reading it provides, the new reading problems it raises, and the amount of meaningful practice it offers. In developing these activities the teacher's part is important. She must be able to provide new opportunities to read, to give children a part in planning for new reading experiences, to sense when practice on new skills is needed, and to coordinate the various reading experiences in her classroom. Specific problems of scheduling and grouping, and the general interrelationships among the child's varied reading experiences have been discussed. How can the reading activities suggested in the preceding chapter be developd so that there is maximum growth in reading skills, interests, and attitudes?

The present chapter is concerned with suggestions for the effective development of the unit activities and of the independent reading activities which are at the heart of the functional use of reading in the modern classroom.[1] Chapter XII suggests practice activities that can be used for individuals or groups needing additional planned experiences focused on specific skills.

PROVIDING READING MATERIAL FOR THE INTERMEDIATE GRADES

Teachers in the intermediate grades face even greater problems in supplying classroom reading materials than do teachers of younger children. It is difficult to provide situations calling for varied reading skills if the reading-matter in the classroom is overly restricted, either in level of difficulty or in scope. Sets of basal readers are very useful. However, these materials alone present only a limited number of the wide range of reading problems with which the maturing reader should be learning to cope. Many of the suggestions in Chapter VI for equipping a primary classroom with a variety of reading materials are also appropriate for the intermediate grades.

Variety in style and content is important. Since one of the characteristics of the skilled reader is his ability to adjust his method of reading to the type of reading-matter he is using, the intermediate-grade child needs to work with many different writing styles and formats of books. While it is possible to teach a child to adjust his reading techniques by helping him to vary the purpose for which he reads, the process is facilitated when the material to which he turns poses a new reading problem.

Basal readers, especially if ten to a dozen copies of several sets are available, help to provide this variety. Typically, the readers designed for the intermediate grades contain materials such as informational articles, fictional stories that are factually accurate, fanciful or humorous stories, plays, and poetry. They are planned to widen the child's reading interests. Stories of other lands, folk tales, stories about animals, transportation, invention, and other topics of common interest are included. It is often possible to extend still further the variety of experiences offered in basal readers by selecting series that supplement each other. Certain of these books contain a relatively heavy amount of informational material. Others lean toward the more imaginative type of story. A few are planned so that a continuous story is developed around the experiences of the same characters.

Textbooks in the content fields help to widen experiences with differing

---

[1] The examples in this chapter come from the work of Dr. McKim with her students and their teachers. Because more than one version of the same activity was seen in a number of cases, specific footnote credit is not given except where material written with children is quoted.

formats; differing styles of presenting informational material; and maps, graphs, and other visual aids. When these books make their greatest contribution to the reading program, they, too, are provided in several sets, so that children may have such experiences as learning to locate information in several books, adjusting to more than one style of writing, and summarizing information from several sources. This variety is particularly important in fields such as the social and natural sciences where the questions raised as a unit of work unfolds usually call for more information than can be found in one book. Even in the development of skills, such as correct English usage, or new number concepts, it is often helpful to have more than one resource. In some classrooms, where children's reading ability is limited and the available textbooks seem particularly difficult, teachers may prefer to have a sufficient number of copies of at least one text in each content field to allow the entire class to work together on common reading problems. When this is the case, a systematic effort is made to supply smaller numbers of supplementary texts.

Experiences with such common resource materials as dictionaries, encyclopedias, atlases, and almanacs are most easily given when copies are located permanently in the classroom. Older children need also to learn to use fictional materials for the detailed picture they often give of life in other times and in distant places. Basal readers provide short selections of this type which are particularly useful for the less able reader, and fiction of excellent quality is available in several levels of difficulty. Classroom collections of such books may be built or copies borrowed from the community library. Many classes also have children's weekly newspapers or magazines available. In addition, more use can be made of the information in newspapers and in adult magazines than is possible with primary children. Classroom bulletin boards are often the means of sharing such information.

Variety is also important in the type of recreational reading provided. If the skilled reader is to be encouraged to expand his interests to many types of fiction, to biography, to informational materials, and to poetry as well as prose, the classroom library must be extensive. School and community libraries, too, will be used even more heavily than they are in the primary grades.

Providing full-length books and different types of reference materials in the classroom library does more than help children develop ability to work with varying styles and formats. It also makes possible experience in reading materials of different lengths. The adult reader may peruse an entire book for pleasure, search through several chapters in two or three books to locate needed information, or read one short article with care. Children at the intermediate-grade level need to be encouraged to undertake such varied reading tasks.

Range in difficulty needs to be considered. The problem of choosing materials to provide for four or more grade levels persists into the intermediate grades. With the numbers of basal-reader series now available, intermediate-grade teachers will find it as easy as it is at the primary level to plan for this range in ability without undesirable duplication of materials. Some primary materials, preferably those unused in the first three grades, are likely to be needed in the fourth grade, and often in the fifth. Provision also needs to be made for those children who are reading beyond their actual grade placement.

Providing materials in the content fields to meet the needs of children of several levels of ability is sometimes difficult. While it is as important to challenge the able reader as it is to adjust to the reading level of the retarded child, the problem often resolves itself into the practical one of locating simple materials for the poor reader, since the more able youngster has a wide variety of supplementary reading available to him. Most teachers examine new materials in the content fields with an eye to adding those most simply written to the classroom collection.

There are also available some pamphlet materials on specific topics in social studies and in science, which are geared to the less able reader. An increasing number of books are being written for children which provide both easy reading and accuracy in presentation. Books in science areas might include materials which present objective, accurate descriptions of living things and of various natural phenomena.

Many titles in the *True Book* [2] series are very easy to read but present materials in which older children, as well as beginning readers, may be interested. Other series developing factual materials include the *All About Books* [3] and the *First Books*. [4] Easy fictional materials which illuminate a period in history or a region in the United States are also available. *The Courage of Sarah Noble* [5] shows the conditions of early settlements in the Northeast, while such books as *The Beatinest Boy* [6] or *The Cave* [7] give the feeling and flavor of a region. In addition, some of the techniques used by primary grade teachers to provide reading materials may be adapted to the intermediate grades. These include the preparation of experience records and the salvaging of selected chapters or sections from textbooks to be discarded. Rebound in colorful paper covers, they can be helpful for the child who reads slowly and are useful so long as the information given is not out of

[2] Published by The Children's Press.

[3] Published by Random House.

[4] Published by Franklin Watts, Inc.

[5] Alice Dalgliesh, *The Courage of Sarah Noble* (New York: Charles Scribner's Sons, 1954).

[6] Jesse Stuart, *The Beatinest Boy* (New York: McGraw-Hill Book Company, 1953).

[7] Elizabeth Coatsworth, *The Cave* (New York: Viking Press, 1958).

date. Articles in children's magazines and informative pictures with accompanying explanatory text may also be used. Intermediate-grade teachers, as well as primary teachers have need for card index files giving the location and contents of these collected materials, and suggesting the reading difficulty of the material.

The foregoing outline of the broad variety of materials needed for an effective reading program for the intermediate grades suggests that teachers will need to emphasize the desirability of books as well as more fugitive materials in the classroom. Teachers will also be aware of sources of information about books for children. A selected bibliography of such sources is included at the end of this chapter. Close collaboration with librarians in the community is also desirable. The library can serve the children more effectively if librarians know in advance topics likely to be investigated, reading levels of pupil groups, and current popular reading interests.

As in the primary grades, it is important to make sure that all children have some experience with easy books. In their anxiety to lift the level of a pupil's reading skill, teachers sometimes feel defeated if children continue to enjoy reading at a level lower "than he should be doing." Naturally, it is wise to keep growing in the skills of reading, but it is wise, also, to consider that the intermediate-grade pupil is dealing with some fairly complicated techniques in a setting which may be new to him. He is confronted with needs for adapting reading speed to varied purposes; reading aloud to hold an audience; taking notes, outlining and summarizing. The development of these skills is made easier if the materials used are well within his grasp. The full enjoyment of pleasure reading may be lost if the book is too difficult. Therefore, many of the materials provided, both for the development of reference skills and for enjoyment, should be easier than those with which a pupil is working to develop a stock of new words or to polish his comprehension skills.

The difficulty level of reading materials may be predicted with considerable accuracy by the use of statistical formulae. A number of these have been developed, generally using counts of unfamiliar hard words, sentence length, and number of prepositional or qualifying phrases.[8] The classroom teacher, however, can make a useful estimate of the difficulty level of a book by comparing its style with that of two or three basal readers. Generally speaking, also, the easier book will have fewer technical or unusual words, shorter sentences and paragraphs, and helpful illustrations. Writing which is closely packed with ideas per page, or which introduces unusual terms or new concepts without illustration and explanation adds to the level of difficulty. Often very simple words in short sentences can be

---

[8] Jeanne S. Chall, *Readability: an Appraisal of Research and Application* (Columbus: Bureau of Educational Research, Ohio State University, 1958), Monograph No. 34.

used to express an idea which is difficult even for an adult to comprehend. The kind and number of concepts introduced, therefore, need to be carefully checked. Included in the suggested readings at the end of this chapter are sources of information about very easy books on a number of topics.

TEACHING READING THROUGH UNIT ACTIVITIES

In Chapter X, two general types of units were identified in which reading interests, attitudes, or skills play a major part. The first is the unit developed around varied interests in books and stories, where children explore different types of stories in basal readers, dramatize, read aloud to other groups, or expand their interests in recreational reading. The second is the unit in a content field where reading skills are important as children locate information, read reference materials, interpret graphs and other visual aids, and make appropriate notes and summaries. The discussion in this section is centered around ways of developing reading skills through these two types of units. Because the reading materials of the content fields are likely to pose certain special problems regardless of the focus of the particular unit, a third topic has been included in this section to suggest ways in which these problems can be met as the reading activities in connection with the unit are developed.

BUILDING READING UNITS AROUND STORY MATERIALS

Develop activities around single stories in unit fashion. A reading unit need not always cover a large amount of material. Many types of unit activities can be used with a single story. As with other units, children help to plan activities which help them answer questions of genuine interest to them. "This story is funny. How can we read it aloud so that other groups may enjoy it?" "Here is a selection about bears. What are some things we would like to know about these interesting animals?" "This selection is about clipper ships. Will this information help us in our study of transportation?" Or, other stories may be read simply for the fun of enjoying a new and interesting story. The greater skill the intermediate-grade children possess gives them ability to undertake more extensive independent reading related to any of the questions or activities proposed.

When a single story is involved, the culmination of the unit is often merely a lively group discussion developed in terms of the original purposes for which the story was read. Favorites, or particularly interesting stories, may be shared with other groups through brief projects. Various types of oral-reading and dramatic presentations are possible. Children share in the development of these relatively simple unit activities by contributing to the preliminary discussion of the story that clarifies the purposes for which it might be read, by taking part in the discussion following the reading of the story, and by helping to decide whether it should be shared and how this might be done to best advantage.

Make use of the grouping of stories in basal readers. A set of stories centering around a topic in a basal reader offers more opportunities for varied activities than a single story because there is more material from which to choose. These books have many possibilities for unit activities, and teachers will find many suggestions for such activities in the accompanying manuals. Children in one group, who read a series of stories about famous inventions, prepared a bulletin-board display, each child depicting the invention he thought the most interesting. Reading a number of fanciful tales led another group into creative writing. The stories that resulted were shared both with other group members and with the class as a whole.

In a sixth-grade class, where most of the children were skillful readers, there was unanimous agreement that they wanted time to read for fun. Accordingly, units on folk tales, humorous stories, and fanciful tales were located in several sets of fifth- and sixth-grade basal readers. The children proposed that each group choose the story it liked the best and plan some way to share it with the rest of the class. The next several days were given over to silent reading. Group discussions of the stories followed, and planning sessions about how to present them. This unit called for little direct supervision. The teacher was free to work with groups when she was needed, but spent relatively more time with the individual children whose reading skill was the most limited. The resulting presentations made use of a variety of oral-reading and dramatization procedures.

Extend activities from basal readers to supplementary materials. Units calling for wide reading often develop out of activities that begin with a collection of stories in a basal reader. One group, which read a story about ocean life, next turned to the encyclopedia to find more information. Enthusiasm for a special author's story in a basal reader led another group to the library to find some of his books and to report on them to the rest of the class.

One rather elaborate unit calling for supplementary reading was developed in a fifth grade. It started with some basal-reader stories about wild animals. The children read these together, discussing each story with special attention to animals that were unfamiliar to them. Then they planned a trip to the zoo to see some of the animals for themselves. In preparation for this, individuals and small groups looked up other information about animals of particular interest to them. On their return there was more reading of supplementary materials as they checked on what they had seen and looked up answers to new questions. The teacher and the librarian helped to supply materials of varied levels of difficulty, and the encyclopedia came in for considerable use. The end product was a series of pictures and an imaginary trip to the zoo, to which the fourth grade was invited. Each child stood near the pictures of the animals of particular interest to him and reported what he had learned about them as the guide directed the visitors' attention from place to place.

Capitalize on possibilities for entertaining others. Plans to entertain other groups can lead to units calling for many types of oral-reading presentations. Make-believe radio or television performances can be used. Pantomime or dramatization can be planned so that the narrators read aloud. Oral reports can be used to share books, stories, or information. Poems can become the basis for choral-speaking activities. Special events during the school year often lend themselves to oral-reading activities. All groups may read stories about holidays and share the ones they consider the most interesting in a special program. Class parties at such times as Christmas, Halloween, or Valentine's Day can be devoted, in part, to reading special stories or poems. In such activities, each reading group may contribute from stories at its own reading level, chosen to fit into the general class plans.

Oral-reading skill does not develop by accident. The mature readers of the intermediate grades are better equipped to learn to read aloud than are the children of the primary grades. Suggestions of ways of providing for special practice in reading both poetry and prose are given in the section on oral reading in Chapter XII. In the units described in this section, procedures such as those discussed in that chapter need to be assumed as part of the preparatory activities.

One fifth grade decided to send Christmas greetings to other classes by way of a tape recording. The children selected one or two favorite poems, a story they particularly liked, and some Christmas songs. As an introduction they wrote out their own Christmas greetings. After several rehearsals for continuity, the entire performance was recorded. It was then shared with children in other intermediate grades, and the result was particularly gratifying in that interest in oral reading began to spread.

In a sixth grade, the children planned for their part in a school-wide program celebrating the growth of their state by reading all they could find about its early history. Then, with their stories of famous people and events well in hand, they invited small groups from other classes to take turns joining story groups. A visitor to the school during the week this took place found, scattered through the halls, knots of younger children grouped around two or three sixth-graders, listening and asking questions.

In one unit in which teacher guidance was quite detailed, a group of children of limited reading skill planned to present a story to the rest of the class as a television drama. The story in the basal reader was read originally just because it looked interesting. The discussion that followed the first reading traced the plot and gave individuals an opportunity to express their reactions to the story as a whole. In the course of the discussion someone said it would make a good play, and someone else added, "We could make it look like television." Over the next several days the plans were worked out. In these planning sessions the teacher worked closely with the children. Careful rereading for details was necessary in order to decide on the characters and the specifics of the action. Ability to outline was needed as scenes were set up. Skill in following the general gist of the story was required in order to eliminate unnecessary action without spoiling the plot. Conversation was finally rewritten to suit the production as planned, and pasted to the back of the box serving as the television set, so that the actors could do some reading of their parts. Oral-reading experience was provided for the announcer by writing out his part. Skill in reading aloud was developed in practice sessions in which group members helped to criticize each other's performances. The stage setting for the final presentation was a large cardboard box, cut and colored to look like a television set. By sitting on a piano bench, the actors were able to arrange themselves so that their heads appeared in the opening cut for the screen.

Develop units around recreational reading. Profitable units can be developed around recreational reading. Some of these may be organized simply; others may call for rather elaborate plans which may include sharing the results of the reading with other classes or with other reading groups within the one class.

The most skillful readers in one sixth grade class developed a three weeks' unit around biographies of American heroes and heroines. This came parallel with a social-studies unit centering around early American history. The teacher's first step was to collect appropriate books. Among these were several of the *Landmark Books;*[9] a number from the *Signature Series;*[10] a few of the *North Star Series;*[11] *Ride on the Wind;*[12] *Carry On, Mr. Bowditch;*[13] *Carver's George;*[14] *City Neighbor, the Story of Jane Addams*[15] and biographies of several presidents.

[9] Published by Grosset and Dunlap, Inc.
[10] Published by Random House, Inc.
[11] Published by Houghton Mifflin Company.
[12] Alice Dalgliesh (ed.) *Ride on the Wind*, told from *The Spirit of St. Louis* by Charles A. Lindbergh (New York: Charles Scribner's Sons, 1956).
[13] Jean Lee Latham, *Carry On, Mr. Bowditch* (Boston: Houghton Mifflin Company, 1955).
[14] Florence Crannell Means, *Carver's George* (Boston: Houghton Mifflin Company, 1953).
[15] Clara Ingram Judson, *City Neighbor, the Story of Jane Addams* (New York: Charles Scribner's Sons, 1951).

Next the teacher told the children a little about some of the books. There was general agreement that it would be interesting to read such books, and to report on the lives of famous Americans to the rest of the class. After the children had an opportunity to examine the books and to hear a little about some of the less familiar personalities, each child chose his book. Because these children were capable independent readers, the teacher's main responsibility while the books were being read was to check on progress, to help the few children who were not happy with their first choices, and to plan for enough discussion with individual children to be sure no one was skimming too rapidly for adequate comprehension. For the most part, during this independent reading period, the teacher's time was spent helping less able groups work on other projects. When the time came to prepare reports, more of the teacher's time was spent with the biography group. For the group who originated the unit, it concluded with the reports to the class, but biography continued to be a favorite type of recreational reading for the entire class for the remainder of the year.

In a school with limited library facilities the children developed a unit around library books brought from home, and worked out ways of calling new books to the attention of the class, protecting the books from injury, and cataloging them so that they could be easily located. All of the books that came in were not of equal literary value, and time was taken as the year went on to discuss well-liked books and to build standards.

Help children become conscious of reading skills as they work. Teaching reading calls for developing better skill as well as for encouraging positive interests and attitudes toward reading. In part, this increased skill comes because of the amount of purposeful practice provided through units such as those that have just been described. It is also important to plan specifically to help children become sensitive to the techniques they need and conscious of working to develop them.

For many children a certain amount of practice in developing specific skills will need to be planned through special work-type activities. These are discussed in Chapter XII. Specific help with reading techniques can also come at many points in a unit. Part of the preliminary plans for reading should include some consideration of how to read. "We have four stories to read. Suppose we read them quickly first to see what they are like." "If you think this would be a good story to dramatize, what could you watch for as you read to be sure you are right?" "If you're going to share your favorite story with the rest of us, how could you get some extra practice in reading it aloud?" "It takes time to read a whole library book. How could you tell quickly if it is one you might like?" The periods when children are reading independently offer time to work on skills with individuals. Group sharing of what has been read, or discussion of how preliminary plans are working out can lead to other opportunities to discuss reading difficulties. Inability to report the gist of a story may call for help on how to note important points. Inaccurate or sparse details may call for discussion of techniques of accurate reading. Plans to share a reading activity with the rest of the class can lead to special attention to many skills as children analyze each other's oral-reading performances, check on the accuracy of details in pictures, or argue about characterizations for dramatization purposes. Whenever a problem arises in the development of a unit, in other words, there is a possibility of helping children focus their attention on reading skills.

The amount of help provided, and to some extent the variety of reading skills developed, will depend on the teacher's insight into the possibilities inherent in the activities under way. The following suggest typical activities that call for specific types of skills. These may serve as a guide in analyzing children's strengths and weaknesses and in providing for additional experiences.

Critical evaluation is called for in: Discussing the merits of an individual story; comparing a group of stories; discussing the styles and purposes of various types of materials; identifying favorite authors and locating other books by them; checking the information in a basal reader against follow-up reading in reference texts; deciding on appropriate materials to share with another class; deciding which of several stories would make the best dramatization of oral presentation.

Adjustments of reading speed are needed in: Doing a rapid first reading for the general plot of a story; re-reading to locate a disputed point; reading carefully for the details needed for a series of reports or pictures; reading a story with care to decide which points to include in an oral-reading presentation.

Oral-reading experiences are afforded through: Reading parts of one's favorite story to other members of one's reading group; reading the part of the

story that substantiates an opinion; planning a dramatic presentation of a story through pantomime, a play, a radio broadcast, a television show; reading captions of pictures aloud in sharing a bulletin-board display; reading to other groups summaries of factual information developed from a story; presenting choral speaking or oral reading of favorite poems to other groups.

Broad interests in reading are developed through: Selecting one's favorite story; working with groups of stories representing different types of literature; exploring library books; identifying the works of favorite authors; sharing reading interests with others; deciding which stories to share with others; enjoying the reports of other groups on their reading interests; discussing the moods of poems as bases for oral reading or choral speaking.

Reading for the gist of the story is called for in: Doing a first reading for the sense of the story; surveying a group of stories to decide which one to read; outlining a story for purposes of illustrating or dramatizing; skimming a group of library books in order to decide which one to read.

Reading with careful attention to details is needed for: Defending one's opinion about a story; drawing a picture correct in its details for the bulletin board; locating details of costumes and characterization for a dramatization; locating specific words or phrases which provide humor or color in the story; discussing the information contained in a factual article.

New vocabulary is developed through: Learning to pronounce new place names and names of persons; learning new technical terms in informational materials; studying an author's style to decide how his choice of words helps to convey humor, description or suspense.

Reference techniques are needed for: Locating a story on a given topic in a basal reader; locating further information in a supplementary reference text; becoming acquainted with authors and illustrators; locating parallel topics in other basal readers; looking up new terms in a dictionary or textbook glossary.

DEVELOPING THE READING EXPERIENCES RELATED TO UNIT ACTIVITIES IN THE CONTENT FIELDS

Encourage wide independent reading. Unit activities in the content fields make one of their most important contributions, both to reading skill and to growing ability to solve problems, through the opportunities they offer to encourage children to read as widely as their level of reading ability and the materials available will allow.

In a fourth grade, a unit was developed around interest in how we travel today. Preliminary discussion indicated that most of the children had been on motor trips, that a number had ridden on busses, that a few had been on a train, and that one child had been on an airplane. When the teacher raised questions about how food and other products reached the community, trucks and boats were added to the list of means of transportation. As the children talked about their experiences, questions and areas in which more information would be helpful began to appear. "Why do people ship things in trucks instead of using trains?" "What kinds of trucks go by the school?" "Where are they going?" "Can you go to bed in an airplane the way you do on a train?" "How long a trip would you have to take before you would need to go to bed in an airplane?" "What would it be like to travel in a boat?" "Were there ever passenger boats on our river?" "How did people get out to this country before there were any trains or busses?"

These questions and others like them were evntually classified according to the means of transportation involved, and the children divided into groups according to the special mode of conveyance in which they were most interested. In all, five groups were set up—trains, cars and busses, trucks, planes, and boats. This provided a simple class organization that made it possible for the teacher to give considerable time to each of the groups, yet it did not result in groups so large that the children, who were inexperienced in group work, had trouble working cooperatively. It was agreed that each group would try to answer the questions raised by the class about its area of special interest, and that any new information would also be reported. Since there was interest in early modes of travel, all groups decided to watch for historical backgrounds.

These children used a wide variety of resources. There were a number of children's books about planes, trains, and boats. There were also pamphlet materials written specially for children. Many of these contained excellent pictures. Stories in basal readers provided both current information and historical background. Social-studies textbooks gave additional information about early ways of travel. Pamphlets, timetables, pictures, and a few maps were secured by writing to selected railroads and airlines. Some current information about air power was secured from the local paper, and some pictures of planes and boats from travel magazines that the children found at home. Special information learned through excursions was summarized on experience records.

In this unit the children did much more than read. As a class they took trips to the railroad station, to the bus terminal, and to the airport. During three consecutive recess periods the group interested in trucks noted the names of all the trucks that came past the school and ended with a comprehensive list of the ways in which trucks served the community. The visual aids department of the school system was able to supply a number of motion pictures, slides, and still pictures. Some simple science experiments were used to demonstrate why boats float and how an airplane can keep up in the air. Quite a collection of models was developed from toys children brought to school. One of the fathers had been a pilot and came to tell more about planes. Another was connected with the railway and helped to answer questions about trains. The teacher had several good sets of pictures which he added to the bulletin-board displays. The art teacher helped the children develop a mural depicting the history of transportation.

Group work in reading was planned as one part of the total unit activities. Some general reading for background was done by the class as a whole. Then, for several days, group-reading activities were the only planned reading experiences. The teacher was able to meet with each group to give help in locating information and in deciding what to include in each final report. Plans were laid so that the group reports added new information, but did not duplicate what had already been secured through some other means. Since these children were relatively inexperienced in the preparation of group reports, the teacher took time to hear the plans for each report and to act as a critic of the report in its final form. The final group reports were presented in a simple panel discussion in which each child told something special his group had learned. The teacher served as discussion leader to help to pull together all the information that had been secured about each means of transportation. Each group also prepared a notebook of pictures and interesting information regarding its topic. These were put on the library table for other groups to read. As final check, each group supplied four key questions about its special topic, to be used as part of an oral quiz session.

In the early fall in a fifth grade, a unit developed out of children's reports about where they had been on summer vacations. Out of the discussion came the proposal that it would be good to know more about different parts of the country. It was suggested that groups take imaginary trips and prepare diaries of what they would see. Since this was a unit designed to develop general acquaintance with different sections of the country, many of which were designated by the course of study for more careful attention during the year, the children were helped to raise the kinds of questions a tourist might raise. "What kind of clothing would you need?" "How many miles would you travel?" "What cities would you visit?" "What kind of land would you see— farms, trees, hills, mountains, deserts?" "Would you see points of historical interest?" "What industries would you notice?" Arithmetic became an important part of this unit as children calculated the cost of their proposed trips and estimated mileage. Written language experiences were many as they prepared their group diaries.

Because the children in this class were able readers and not likely to need step-by-step supervision, many small groups formed. Two children with special interests worked alone. The teacher helped to lay original plans with the class as a whole, used evaluation periods to check on group progress, kept an eye on the groups as she circulated among them, and gave help when she was asked, but she did not attempt to give close supervision to each step of the group work.

The reading-matter for this unit included several sets of social studies textbooks, materials secured by writing to Chambers of Commerce in various cities, road maps, advertising materials from airlines, bulletins and booklets about national parks, and articles in travel magazines. The teacher had a materials file which yielded a number of special pamphlets, pictures, and clippings. Atlases were consulted for information about locations of cities and populations. Motion pictures, slides, postcards, and sets of pictures helped to supply additional information. The children also interviewed parents and friends who had travelled to the localities in which they were interested.

As a culmination of this unit, each group summarized the contents of its diary, using pictures and maps to help clarify the report. The complete diaries, which contained maps and pictures and many additional details, were then placed on display for other groups to examine and to read.

In a sixth grade, the children embarked upon a science unit to study modern means of communication. Firsthand experiences were very important in this unit. With the teacher's help the children set up a simple telegraph key and sounder, and a simple electric telephone. They also used other types of equipment to learn about batteries, switches, and magnetic fields. Trips to the local radio and television stations helped to build a sense of the great complexity of modern means of communication. The telephone company provided booklets on good telephone techniques. It was also possible to visit the local telephone exchange. Several parents were able to supply more information. One group of boys, with the help of the teacher, went on after the unit was completed to build an amateur radio receiving set.

Since the science information in connection with this unit was unfamiliar to most of the children and required careful explanation and simplification, part of the reading was done by the class as a whole, using a set of science textbooks. The teacher led the discussion based on the reading and used various diagrams, models, and other visual aids to clarify concepts. Smaller groups then went on to do specific reading on simpler aspects of the telegraph, telephone, radio, and television. Their resources included a number of pamphlet materials, science textbooks, and children's books on electricity. Basal-reader stories helped to supply some of the historical background. Daily papers and magazines provided some up-to-date information on radio and television, particularly with regard to the less scientific aspects of sound effects, camera techniques, and proposed new developments. This unit was culminated with a program to which parents were invited. Each group told about its area of special interest, using science equipment to demonstrate underlying principles. Among other things, each group prepared a chart showing something of the historical development of its particular means of communication.

In each of these units wide reading played an important part. The teacher was at hand to explain, to lead discussions, to help to focus attention on important points, to challenge inaccurate information or inadequate concepts, and to provide new information. What the children read helped to fill in background and to expand upon what they had seen and heard. The reading became more meaningful because it was supplemented by information from many other sources.[16]

Make adjustments to meet the needs of immature readers. Children of limited reading ability need not be deprived of the wide reading experiences

[16] For descriptions of units in which children's reading skills are more limited, see Chapter VIII.

that have just been described. There are a number of ways of adjusting the total reading task to varying levels of ability. Among the most important is the selection of material. Poorer readers need to have books well within their grasp. Second, it is possible to guide the preliminary discussion that raises questions, or outlines problem areas, or lays plans for securing needed information so that the reading task is made as specific as need be. Children of limited reading ability may, in some cases, read for only a few definite and clear details. Third, there can be variation in the amount of help given children in locating material. Less skilled readers may even be provided with exact page numbers. Fourth, the number of adjustments the child must make to differing types of materials and varied formats can be reduced by controlling the amount and variety of material provided for reference and the points at which new types of materials are introduced. Then, too, the type of planning and group activity that has been described makes it possible for a teacher to work intensively with poor readers without neglecting other children.

One fourth-grade teacher solved the problem of helping the immature readers in her class work on a science unit on rocks, developed out of interest in several collections made over the summer vacation, by bringing from the library books graded on three levels of difficulty. The sets of science texts in her room also varied in difficulty, although all were recommended for the fourth grade. In their preliminary discussion the children outlined the information they were most anxious to secure. The teacher helped them phrase their questions clearly, and posted the list in a corner of the bulletin board for easy reference. Then the books were distributed to the children, who worked in the same groups in which they would normally be placed for reading activities. Each group thus received materials adjusted to its own level. In the reading periods that followed, the teacher worked with each group in turn on the problem of how to read carefully for information. Since the children were reading different books, some of the time given to each group was spent helping them pool their information, and some was spent working with individual children. In this class all groups read to try to find answers to the same questions. As a result, the sharing period that drew the unit to a close called for oral reports from individuals and from groups but for no tightly organized committee activities.

Another class of very limited reading ability partially solved its problem of handling difficult materials by planning definitely so that at least one good reader was placed in each small group. It was his special job to help with hard words, and, if necessary, to read the material aloud while the others listened. The teacher circulated to give extra help where needed, and at one point read a particularly difficult, but interesting, story to a group. Armed with some very definite questions, the answers to which were quite clear in the various reference books, this class came out with a good set of notes in single-sentence statements. Short reports on what had been learned during the reading period were made daily so that there was oral reinforcement of the reading.

Use a unit approach to content fields even when materials are limited. Even in classrooms where the variety of reading materials is limited, it is important to use a unit approach to work in the content fields. Regardless of how much or how little they read, children need to learn to think critically in order to solve problems rather than to accept without question the printed words of their textbooks. They need to turn to arithmetic, language, and spelling textbooks as resource materials to help solve problems just as they do to the reading-matter of social studies, science, and health. The children in the preceding illustrations have been described as working in groups with materials adjusted to their reading levels and interests, but unit activities can also be developed in situations where the class works as a whole.

One fifth grade using a single adopted textbook developed a helpful unit on the Far West. To most of these children, the states to be studied were unfamiliar. Before they began to work they leafed through the entire section in their textbook, commenting on the pictures, contributing other items of information from their own background, and asking questions. Then each child listed the one thing out of all that he had heard and seen that he wanted to know more about. Groups with common interests were formed, and, while all children read selected parts of their text for general background, each group was responsible for a more detailed report on its special topic. Although many of the groups found other sources of information in their classroom encyclopedia and in a few supplementary materials, their major reading experience came from the adopted text.

A single health textbook provided the material for a unit on food. After the children read about balanced meals and had an opportunity to discuss what they had found out, they used pictures cut from magazines and pasted on colored paper to prepare charts of basic food groups and to illustrate typical meals. Discussion next turned to how to set a table properly and how to plan for pleasant meals. Some of this information came from the health text, and some from the teacher. As a culmination of the unit, the children set a special table in the school lunchroom and invited some of the city supervisors and the principal to eat lunch with them.

At the beginning of the year one class discussed the purpose of the practice activities in spelling books and, with the teacher's help, decided that these exercises would be most useful to them if the ones that stressed unfamiliar elements in new words were done with particular care. From this time on, special attention was paid to deciding what each exercise was trying to teach. In another class, a speller was not used consistently as a source of spelling words, but the children helped to suggest the words they thought should be part of their spelling activities. Dictionaries were used extensively by this class for help in pronunciation, meanings, and syllabication. Textbooks are source of practice activities for groups such as these, but they also serve as reference materials to help in the solution of day-by-day problems.

Cincinnati Public Schools

These children have used materials found in their community to enrich their understanding of the past. The words they use have clear meanings derived from firsthand experience.

Draw on resources other than books. A perennial problem in the intermediate grades is that of finding enough material to answer the questions that children pose in developing a unit in a content field. Extensive information may be made available, even if the reading-matter is limited in scope or too difficult for a group, if the full resources of school and community are tapped. Furthermore, older children need to learn to use the natural and human resources in the world around them as an aid in solving their problems. They are capable of much wider use of such resources than are children in the primary grades.

Much can be learned about the modern world by going to see for oneself. One class developed a unit around problems of how the community was fed by visiting the local bakery, market, and dairy. In this unit the class as a whole raised the questions that needed to be answered and then the children went visiting in small groups, each accompanied by two or three parents. This plan enabled the teacher to stay at school with the remainder of the class and gave those who did the visiting a reason for reporting carefully and for preparing written records of their trip. Children in one sixth grade learned most of their information about how newspapers are published through a trip to the local newspaper. This was followed by a study of the papers the children brought to school. In time, the reading-matter was expanded by writing to other cities for editions of the daily papers. The city council at work, the town water works, the special industries of a community, or the experimental farm offer other types of firsthand experience.

Community members are usually willing to come to school to talk to the children. Information about industries, professions, and civil services can be obtained in this way. Often, too, people with hobbies can be of help—the man whose hobby is wildlife, the amateur radio operator, the woman who weaves. One fifth grade developed a safety unit by studying traffic conditions around the school and then enlisting the help of the police traffic department. When their questions had all been answered, these children set about passing on their information by developing a program for the rest of the school.

There are also possibilities of using picture displays, exhibits, slides, models, motion pictures, science experiments, and concrete arithmetic materials. The children in one class developed understanding of the general nature of a Southern plantation by constructing a model of their own. While they read for background, they also paid careful attention to the details in all the pictures they could find. Another group developed a unit on air transportation by building a model airport after the children had taken a trip to a real one. Much of the technical information was supplied by their teacher and by one of the fathers, both of whom had been Air Force pilots. In one fourth grade a Mexican exhibit was collected from children's homes. In a fifth grade, the children gained a good picture of some of the furnishings of pioneer homes through articles that had been stored in attics. Even when books are plentiful, such concrete materials lend reality to studies that are moving progressively away from the here-and-now, both in time and in space. Reading material is better understood and reading skills are more purposefully used when the classroom provides other ways to learn in addition to reading.

Help children become aware of reading skills. With units in the content fields, as with reading units, children should be helped to become aware of the reading skills they need. The teaching procedures that achieve this are essentially the same as those used when a unit develops around stories in a basal reader or around recreational reading. In the classrooms just described, teachers gave help at several points. Preliminary plans include discussion of how to read. Reading problems are discussed, along with other types of problems, in evaluation and in planning periods as the unit develops. Problems of concern to the entire group are given attention during special periods set aside for that purpose. Help is also given to individuals and to small groups as the unit progresses.

The more clearly the teacher can identify the points at which various types of skills will be needed, the more effective she is likely to be in giving help. The following analysis suggests activities in which specific types of reading skills may be important. The classification is the same as that used on pages 299 and 300 of this chapter to help identify the types of skills that are called into use by reading units. Comparison of these two analyses may suggest ways in which children's total reading experiences can be planned to supplement each other so that the result is a well-rounded series of activities, calling for many types of reading skills.

Critical evaluation is called for in: Discussing the problems the group is trying to solve; helping prepare a bibliography of appropriate material; discussing the appropriateness of group notes; telling the class which resource book was the most helpful; finding when it is important to use current materials and when older books are just as effective; deciding which of two conflicting statements is correct; deciding whether material read really answers the questions raised; comparing the points of view of two articles on the same topic.

Reading with careful attention to details is needed for: Checking details on such items as clothing or housing for a report, a picture, a dramatization; following directions in a science text in order to perform an experiment; reading arithmetic problems; looking up the way to punctuate a quotation; following class plans in a science experiment involving such things as taking temperature, watering plants, recording growth; following class directions for constructing a graph on spelling or reading progress; reporting accurately on daily news items on the bulletin board; keeping a bibliography according to an agreed-upon form; following directions for a game, a recipe.

Reading for the gist of the story is called for in: Skimming a chapter to locate a specific piece of information; looking over several books in order to decide which is the most likely to be useful for a given problem; reading several chapters for the general setting of a particular problem; reading a description of an arithmetic process, a science experiment, a rule of correct English usage, in order to get the sense of the total process before checking on details.

Adjustments of reading speed are needed in: Locating and reading carefully the special details that are needed for one's particular problem; reading such specific materials as an arithmetic problem first for the general plan of the problem and then for details; changing from the closely-packed style of an informational article to a fictional account in social studies in order to get details of customs or ways of earning a living.

Oral-reading experiences are afforded through: Sharing new information with others in one's interest group; reading group or individual reports to the rest of the class; reading to the class stories or other types of creative expression arising out of unit activities; presenting the culmination of a unit to other classes through reports, dramatizations, choral-speaking presentations; read in the minutes of a meeting.

Broad interests in reading are developed through: Becoming acquainted with new and interesting informational materials; exploring biographical materials; discovering science magazines, nature magazines, other special periodicals that bear on areas of interest; expanding knowledge of the potential contributions of daily papers.

New vocabulary is developed through: Learning the names of famous people; becoming acquainted with the correct names for various types of science experiments; sharpening concepts of time and space; seeing pictures which widen understanding of natural phenomena; of people in other lands, of customs.

Reference techniques are needed for: Using indexes, tables of contents, and library card files to locate needed information in a single text or a group of texts; finding appropriate articles in standard reference books such as encyclopedias, atlases, almanacs; interpreting maps, graphs, charts, pictures, and other visual aids; checking a class bibliography to locate specific references; looking up information in a magazine or newspaper; using a dictionary.

GIVING HELP WITH THE SPECIAL READING PROBLEMS OF THE CONTENT FIELDS

Provide for difficulties with new terms and concepts. In any unit which draws upon materials in the content fields specific reading problems relating to these fields are likely to arise. One persistent problem is how to deal with new and difficult vocabulary.

Each content area has its own special vocabulary—*isthmus, delta, feudal, government, numerator, divide, triangle, digestion, carbohydrate.* There will also be the confusing possibility of familiar common words, used with a completely different meaning—butter is *washed* before it is packaged, wheat is destroyed by *rust*, a number may be a *mixed number*, some states are located in a *corn belt*, and distances to stars are measured in *light years.* New place names and proper names will appear—the *Mediterranean, Socrates, Joan of Arc, Cortez, Thomas Jefferson,* the *Louisiana Purchase.* Science and arithmetic will offer new symbols and abbreviations. To all these special problems will be added the general increase in the vocabulary load of intermediate-grade materials.

The problem posed by vocabulary of the content fields may in part be erased by giving direct help with new terms before they are encountered in independent reading. This is particularly true if they are special terms which are essential to the understanding of reading materials in an area. Words may be listed on the chalkboard and discussed before the material is read. Such discussion is particularly helpful if experiences which would illuminate new meanings are shared. One group found a fairly extended discussion of all the ideas they had about the word "cell" was a most helpful beginning for reading in their health book about the cells of the body. Sometimes pictures, maps, or a quick sketch on the chalkboard will serve the purpose of clarifying meanings. Children can help themselves in expanding vocabularies by checking new terms in a glossary or dictionary, developing lists of useful words for a class vocabulary, or helping to decide what words should be added to a spelling list.

It is especially important for a teacher to realize that concepts may not be clear even though children appear to use the material without apparent difficulty. Computation can be accurate, yet be merely "flipping symbols," and inaccurate or completely erroneous ideas in this and other areas may prevent clear understanding of the materials read. A girl in a sixth grade thought that "in Colonial times" meant when her own grandmother was a girl, and fourth grader was surprised to find that Stalin was a figure in modern times, not a contemporary of persons described in the New Testament. A fifth-grade boy was convinced that all rivers near the polar regions flowed "uphill towards the Pole." The limits of children's experience with space and time and with verbal and other symbolic representations of experience, particularly in fields in which specialized knowledge is often presented by adult specialists, make continued help necessary in clarifying concepts of major importance.

Look for special problems with format and illustrative aids. The particular materials being used in a unit need to be examined for special problems occasioned by their general format and by the ways in which maps, graphs, tables, pictures, and other illustrative aids are used. Typically, texts assume that a child will interrupt his reading to examine them. Children may need to be reminded to study a picture in order to clarify a description of a manner of dress or a type of dwelling; to refer to a map in order to understand a discussion of climates, trade routes, or harbors; or to use section or paragraph headings to help locate information. In an arithmetic text it may be important to point out where an example has been included, and to take children through it step by step to help them see how to use it for themselves.

If a new book is being used for the first time, or a different type of reading problem is being undertaken, it may be helpful to take a period to work out effective reading techniques as a group. Special uses of graphs, maps, charts, or pictures may be noted. Time may be taken to work through a sample reading problem together—discussing how to handle the format of the book to advantage; how to use the maps, graphs, or pictures to help supply information; and what adjustments to make for general writing style.

Special help for individuals and small groups is usually most easily provided as the reading proceeds. Difficulties with format or illustrative materials can often be caught by watching for evidence of misinformation occasioned by not reading a map or graph correctly; by looking into the techniques being used by a child who says that he can't find any information; by asking children directly if they made use of a picture or some other illustrative aid; or by being alert to partial answers that could have been better rounded out by effective use of illustrative material.

It is important not to assume that children will always have the techniques needed to handle illustrative materials efficiently once their value has been pointed out. Children may not be accustomed to locating detailed information in a picture, or to giving attention to the minute details of an example in an arithmetic text or in a science experiment. Maps, graphs, diagrams, and tables are developed in many different styles. Such skills as reading legends, knowing how to compare relative sizes, responding accurately to number concepts such as fractions or percentages, are not learned quickly and are not always readily readjusted when a visual aid is constructed in a slightly different form. Each new type of illustrative material may require special attention. Teaching procedures will have to be planned in terms of the new problem as it arises.

There will be occasions during the development of a unit when one or more periods will need to be devoted specifically to the problem of learning to handle a new visual aid. There will also be times when a series of specially planned work-type activities will seem desirable. These are included in the section on providing for efficient reference techniques in Chapter XII.

Give help in adjusting reading techniques to varied purposes. In some units requiring extensive reading, the techniques developed in reading story materials are no longer adequate. Reading an interesting episode in a piece of juvenile fiction requires, among other things, noting sequence of events and the details of description of character and setting. Such an understanding of how to grasp both sequence and detail may need expanding to include the sequence of events in a science experiment, or the closely packed details of a mathematics text. Skimming quickly over a page of print to locate a definite point may now be complicated by the inclusion of paragraph headings. Fictional material may be read for the purpose of picturing more clearly the locale described, or gaining a fuller understanding of a period in history. In such instances a child may need to learn to differentiate between usable information and the imaginative plot of the story.

Some help in adjusting reading techniques to new types of materials and new purposes can be given by discussing how to read before a unit begins. If the children's first task is to skim in order to see what information is available, they may talk about how to do this most effectively. Less skilled groups may even work together on this problem for a while. When the children come to the point where they need to read carefully for specific information, discussion and demonstration may again be helpful. The most pointed guidance is often given while individuals and small groups are at work. Cues as to difficulties may be secured by watching for children who appear merely to be leafing through materials, for those who claim that they have been reading but couldn't find anything, for those whose notes seem inadequate, or for those who have encyclopedic notes that are not to the point. Often it is helpful to sit with a child or a small group who are having trouble and to guide their reading for a page or two, asking them how they might have been able to read more effectively and how they think they happened to miss the desired information when they worked by themselves. Class sessions in which children who worked out successful ways of finding information tell how they went about the job can sometimes be helpful. Sometimes problems of ineffective skimming or careless reading of details will call for special practice activities as well as day-by-day help as reading proceeds. Suggestions for planning these work-type experiences are included in Chapter XII.

Develop increased skill in critical evaluation. Parallel with other problems in learning to read for information, children have to become increasingly skillful in evaluating what they have read. In part, this is a matter of selecting appropriate information and deciding when sufficient information has been located to solve a problem or to answer a particular set of questions. Guidance as children raise preliminary questions, take notes, and plan how to report on their information will help to develop this skill.

Some of the help in making critical evaluations is given to a group, or to the class as a whole, as a unit begins. This is the time to sharpen questions, to help children raise appropriate subquestions, and perhaps even to read a few pages together and come to some conclusions on how to decide what is important. Typically, as a unit develops, there are evaluation periods when groups report on progress and difficulties. Such evaluation sessions are a help in getting a quick survey of group problems. "Does your group have all the material it needs?" "Are there any topics about which you have found little information?" "Is there any help you need from other groups?" Help in deciding on the adequacy and appropriateness of what has been read is also an integral part of the assistance given as the teacher works with individuals and groups as the reading activities of a unit proceed.

As a child reads widely, he will discover the need for critical evaluation of his materials. He realizes that textbooks conflict; even recommended methods of punctuating a sentence or of addressing a letter may not agree completely. Fictional materials may contain historical inaccuracies or scientific misstatements. If the child is reading more than one daily paper he may find that news is not reported in the same way or that commentators disagree. Unless a class is working entirely from a single textbook, such conflicts are inevitable. Furthermore, they are invaluable in helping to develop critical readers. Learning how to appriase the accuracy of a resource is a second aspect of critical evaluation.

Intermediate-grade children can be helped to build standards for evaluating the accuracy of what they read by discussion of such conflicts as they are discovered. It may help to learn to look at the date of publication, to talk about the qualifications of authors, and perhaps to do some exploring of how historical information is obtained and of how records are kept. "This book was published in 1952 and the almanac in 1962. Would that account for differences in population figures?" "Could you tell whether the writer of the article has ever really travelled in Europe?" "Read it again. Does it really say he did that, or does it say people thought he might have done it?" Current materials from newspapers and magazines need to be scrutinized in a similar fashion. These discussions can take place at any point where they seem appropriate in the reading activities of the unit. Sometimes the children involved will be those in the particular group where the problem arose. Sometimes the problem may be important enough to raise for consideration by the class as a whole. Of all the contributions to increased reading skill that can be made through unit activities in the content fields, one of the most important is the development of the ability to read widely in a thoughtful and critical manner, rather than to accept without question the statements in a single text.

Critical evaluation has a third aspect. The school is failing to make its full contribution if questions that help children think about democratic values are never raised. Does this action respect the rights of individuals? Is it honest? Is it fair? What are our obligations as citizens of the class, of the community, of the country? Intermediate graders face such issues in their daily lives as they say goodby to brothers entering the armed services, examine the wanton breakage of their classroom windows that has taken place over the week end, or view scenes of crime and violence on evening TV programs. Democratic values can come under consideration also as children read about the history of their country, follow the lives of its leaders in biographies, discuss newspaper clippings they have brought for the bulletin board. The entire elementary school program is dedicated to helping children develop the values and attitudes essential to the perpetuating of our democratic society. Children's reading activities have a special contribution to make.

Provide help in locating information. Depending on the type of problem, the task of locating the right materials may be a difficult one. Although they have typically had some experience with tables of contents, chapter titles, and indexes in the primary grades, immature readers in the intermediate grades may not be very skilled in using these reference aids, nor may they have had many contacts with standard reference books. They may also have limited ability in identifying the exact information they need even when they have found a discussion that bears on their general problem. More mature readers may have trouble using subtopics and cross references, determining the topics that relate to the question at hand, or deciding which key words to use in trying to locate the information they need. In one group, for example, the children looking for a list of British colonies, started their hunt under the word *colony*. Another group, less mature, had trouble finding information about Paul Revere because they looked up the name *Paul*. Depending on the organization of the school library, children may also need help in using the library card index. In addition, the children in a particular class are going to need to become acquainted with the specific types of help available in the reference materials in their room.

Teachers have developed a variety of ways of giving help in locating information. With immature groups it is often useful to shortcut the process by putting markers in the appropriate pages or by listing page numbers in a bibliography on the chalkboard. More mature readers may be given valuable experience if they are encouraged to take time at the beginning of a unit to skim available material and prepare their own bibliographies. These can be checked against the teacher's list and posted for easy reference. The first time an encyclopedia, an almanac, an atlas, or another reference aid is used, it may be advisable to plan a special lesson on how to use it. A new task calling for wide reading in several types of books may be begun by examining the books and talking about how to skim them quickly to appraise their contents and how to locate specific items of information without reading the entire book or article. Often the librarian is able to give special help with library techniques.

Although some of the most effective assistance in learning to locate information is given in the course of helping the children solve the problems they actually face as a unit proceeds, specific practice to polish such techniques as using alphabetical order or choosing appropriate key words may be of value. Suggestions for these activities can be found in the section on developing effective reference techniques in Chapter XII.

Plan to give help with note-taking and reporting. Unit activities in the content fields frequently call for skill in collecting information and reporting it to classmates, a task which may be either fairly simple or difficult and complex. A series of separate questions, each with a definite answer, poses a relatively easy problem of reading accurately to locate details, whereas a comprehensive report may require note-taking from several sources and a skillful summary. Outlines may be needed either to record the information being read, or to serve as a basis for a group report. If several books are being used, simple bibliographies may be required.

Skills in recording essential information develop through planning how best to share ideas. These pupils have chosen a clear way of presenting their findings.

One of the most important contributions to skill in good reporting is the statement of a clear problem. Children who are reading vaguely within a general area are not so likely to make critical evaluations of what is read, or to be so selective in their note-taking, as those who know exactly what they are looking for. Questions or problems need to be clarified before reading begins. As groups begin work, it is helpful to check on the adequacy of the notes before the reading has progressed very far. Until they have become skilled in note-taking, most children will also benefit from individual help as they work. Special reading problems that are hindering the note-taking process can often be caught in this way.

Questions to be answered can be kept before the group by a variety of recording devices. Some of these were indicated earlier as units in the content fields were described. Lists of questions can be posted on the bulletin board, or left in a corner of the chalkboard. Each child may copy the list for his own notebook, or a secretary may keep the list for the group. Periodic progress reports during which the original lists are checked also help groups to see what has been accomplished and to rethink purposes and identify what remains to be done.

Many teachers report that a major problem in note-taking is that of copying material word by word from the reference text. Often the cause lies either in the difficulty of the material, which may be so far beyond the child's level of comprehension that he is unable to state in his own words what he has read, or in limited ability in self-expression which makes it difficult for the child to rephrase the material, even though it has been understood. Too-general assignments may also lead to copying, especially if the information related to the area on which the child is to report clearly meets his needs without any changes.

Copying can be discouraged by specific questions, phrased in the child's words. For example, one fourth grade studying Switzerland asked, among other things: "Why do the people do wood carving?" "What is Switzerland well known for?" "Why do we connect the Red Cross with Switzerland?" It often helps, also, to say, "Read your material, but close your book when you begin to write. If you are not sure, put down your pencil, and reread the material." When facility with written language is particularly limited, it may be important to place less emphasis on written summaries, and to plan for reports that make use of oral statements, panels, discussions, dramatizations, pictures, models, or some other means of sharing information that does not require skill in written expression. It is also helpful to raise questions about reports that seem to be copied—asking a child to tell what he found in his own words; asking for the meaning of an unfamiliar word over which he stumbles in his notes; encouraging him to look up hard words in the dictionary; praising him when he chooses an expression that is meaningful to the group. Children who become conscious of the desirability of saying things their own way often challenge each other. "You couldn't pronounce that word—you just copied it from the book." "Did you really write that?" "Where did he get that? I couldn't understand it." "I liked Joan's report because she used her own words."

ENCOURAGING RECREATIONAL READING

Even with the varied experiences with different types of reading materials provided through the group and individual activities in reading that have just been discussed, special plans need to be made to ensure that children are growing in their enjoyment of independent reading, widening their reading interests, and refining their reading tastes. Encouraging recreational reading is an important aspect of the total intermediate reading program, just as it is in the primary grades.

Provide a classroom atmosphere that encourages independent reading. In the classrooms that have been described the entire atmosphere is conducive to independent reading. Children start with a single story they enjoyed and go on to locate others on the same topic. They read a group of stories in a basal reader and are given opportunities to discuss the ones they like best and to share them with other groups. Reading units are sometimes developed around recreational-reading activities. In a unit in the field of social studies, the children read not only basal reference texts but also historical novels and biography. On classroom bulletin boards are special articles of interest. Children are encouraged to explore daily papers, to read family magazines, and to enjoy children's newspapers and magazines. Time is provided for individual hobbies and encouragement given to read about them. Materials are selected so that the retarded reader can find some he can enjoy.

Make special efforts to acquaint children with books. Reading is infectious. When everyone is doing it and everyone is talking about what he likes, the child who has not had any particular interest in wide reading is more likely to start to read. It is helpful to use as many ways as possible of acquainting children with recreational-reading possibilities.

Book jackets can be placed on classroom bulletin boards. Librarians can often find time to tell about new books of particular interest. If there are classroom funds available for purchasing books, children can share in selecting them. The books on the library table can be changed from time to time so that new stories are available. Library reading periods can be used to let a child with an interesting book read it to a small group of friends. Time just before children return books to the school or community library is often well spent asking children what they have enjoyed about their reading and having them suggest others in the class to whom they think the book would be interesting. One teacher engaged children in informal discussions about what they were reading as they arrived in the morning. Often she could be found surrounded by a knot of early-comers, each anxious to tell about his book. When a new unit in a content field is begun, many teachers make a practice of borrowing related books from the school library and devoting a period to telling children about them. Then movies, radio, and television programs may center around outstanding fiction and provide opportunities to talk about the book. The most successful promotion of wide reading is likely to be done by teachers who themselves enjoy reading and who have a wide knowledge of both the "classics" of children's literature, and fine books published in more recent years. Aids for locating these materials will be found in the suggested reading at the end of this chapter.

One of the problems faced by a busy teacher is knowing exactly what children have been reading so that it is possible to comment intelligently on their interests. There are many kinds of classroom and individual charts that serve to show at a glance how the reading is progressing. One group kept reading lists in correct bibliographical form in individual library notebooks. Other children set up a target and wrote their names around the outer circle. As each new book was read, the child wrote its title on a small arrow and pasted it on his line leading to the bull's-eye. The children in one fifth grade did illustrated book reviews, bound them in wallpaper, and tucked each new one into pockets bearing their initials on a wall chart. Children in another group wrote book reviews on small cards and attached these, one after the other, behind their names on a special chart. The result was a simple bar graph. At stated intervals, the chart was cleared and the reviews were transferred to a card file and placed after the child's name. A sixth grade used a map of the world and pinned the title of the book and the child's name on the correct site. In addition to providing a record of the reading done, these extrinsic devices sometimes prove the starting point for a child when other means of encouraging him to read have had little effect.

Provide opportunities for reading that may lead to enriched personal living. There are many excellent books for children, excellent in format and design, as well as style and content. To see and appreciate them is an esthetic experience. Unhappily, the tawdry and garish surround children and are proclaimed in neon lights for all to see. There may be no escaping the raw hillsides surrounding the newly developed shopping center, the rusty piles of abandoned junk metal, the littered and unlovely streets on which some children live. It may be that the only opportunities many children have for appreciating order and beauty will be available to them chiefly or even solely in books. The balanced design of many illustrated books, the skillful use of line and color may offer to the child of this century a much-needed oasis of ordered beauty which will be for him a "joy forever." The appeal of a well-designed and well-illustrated book is not limited to the young; the language of form and color is universal, and speaks to all ages.

The book which has something worth saying, and says it well, is a source of enrichment for children. Many books for children develop a key idea which all young persons may use to help them achieve depth and stability

Time to read books and to share them with others is an important aspect of developing wide reading interests.

in their stretching toward the maturity of responsible adults. They may read *Blue Willow*[17] or *Tobe*[18] to make them more aware of people whose lives differ from their own. Courage in the face of physical handicap is seen in *The Door in the Wall*,[19] and the conviction that life is stronger than any disaster, no matter how overwhelming, can be found in *The Big Wave*.[20] And for more able mature readers, there is the hauntingly beautiful *Island of the Blue Dolphins*[21] with its heroic story of self-reliance and the development of inner spiritual resources. Nor would one wish children to miss the beneficent gift of laughter offered in books, from the quiet chuckles that point up the wisdom of the spider in *Charlotte's Web*[22] to the rib-tickling guffaws of *Homer Price*[23] or *The Jack Tales*.[24]

Prejudice may be etched too deeply in a young person's experience to be erased by print, yet the sympathetic and honest treatment of problems relating to minority groups is at least a reasonable attempt. *Bright April*,[25] *Melindy's Medal*,[26] *Call Me Charley*,[27] *All-of-a-kind Family*[28]—all offer the reader a balanced and wholesome view of intergroup relationships. Teachers of middle-grade children will find an increasingly rich supply of books for children which will help to build more stable personalities, and aid in the development of a self-reliant person who is aware of his share in the ideals of a society which truly values the worth of each individual member.

Help intermediate-grade children achieve a well-balanced reading "diet."
Books suitable for readers in the nine-to-twelve group are available in abundance, and in many different areas. Fairy tales, myths, legends, folk tales, fictionalized biography, historical fiction, modern fanciful tales, mysteries, stories about animals (wild and domesticated), and regional books—these are some of the areas in which supplies of interesting and well-written books are available for the taking. Poetry, gay and lilting, or poetry for more

[17] Doris Gates, *Blue Willow* (New York: Viking Press, 1940).
[18] Stella Gentry Sharpe, *Tobe* (Chapel Hill, N. C.: University of North Carolina Press, 1939).
[19] Marguerite DeAngeli, *Door in the Wall* (Garden City, New York: Doubleday and Company, 1950).
[20] Pearl S. Buck, *The Big Wave* (New York: The John Day Company, Inc., 1948).
[21] Scott O'Dell, *Island of the Blue Dolphins* (Boston: Houghton Mifflin Company, 1960).
[22] E. B. White, *Charlotte's Web* (New York: Harper and Brothers, 1952).
[23] Robert McCloskey, *Homer Price* (New York: The Viking Press, Inc., 1943).
[24] Richard Chase (Editor), *The Jack Tales* (Boston: Houghton Mifflin Company, 1943).
[25] Marguerite DeAngeli, *Bright April* (Garden City, New York: Doubleday and Company, 1943).
[26] Georgene Faulkner and John Becker, *Melindy's Medal* (New York: Julian Messner, Inc., 1945).
[27] Jesse Jackson, *Call Me Charley* (New York: Harper and Brothers, 1945).
[28] Sydney Taylor, *All-of-a-kind Family* (Chicago: Follett Publishing Company, 1951).

serious reflection, is another aspect of the literature which is the heritage of all children. Intermediate-grade children with their ability to read more widely and independently need to be encouraged to explore many kinds of the great numbers of books available to them. The teacher is an important guide. She may sometimes stimulate interest in poems as favorite ones are read aloud, or help the enthusiastic reader of "dog stories" to achieve wider reading interests. Modern writers as well as authors long known— Kipling, Alcott, Mark Twain, Stevenson, and the creator of the ubiquitous *Black Beauty*—have much to offer children, and the wise teacher will use every opportunity to bring both new and old books and this year's group of eleven-year-olds together. They will never be eleven-year-olds again, and the chance of creating this kind of felicitous arrangement of good book and eager reader is truly a golden opportunity.

One way of assuring a delightful introduction to good books is to hear them read aloud. Merely because they can read independently does not mean that intermediate-grade children should be denied the opportunity to hear some things read to them. Such books as *The Wind in the Willows*[29] or *Miss Hickory*[30] or *The Borrowers*[31] are well worth the savoring by ear as well as by eye. Reading aloud is for many a child listener, an excellent way to stimulate new interests, and to raise the level of expectations in reading.

Book reviews can be useful as ways of developing reading tastes, if they are not routine assignments. Children can review books orally as part of a book club meeting. They can tell briefly about their books before they return them to the library. The children in one class decided to try to "sell" others on new books by seeing how good an advertisement for the book they could give in their reviews. Another group kept a class notebook. As each new child read the book he added his comments. In a sixth grade this procedure was modified by placing each new set of comments in an envelope in the back of the book. Activities such as these serve the purpose of book reviews without causing the activity to become routine.

In all these experiences, evaluation of the quality of what is read plays an integral part. Every time children spontaneously and enthusiastically talk about what they would like to read next, or ask to share a particularly good story, or go to the library with a special request for books, another step has been taken toward the development of adults with sound reading interests and tastes.

[29] Kenneth Grahame, *The Wind in the Willows* (New York: Charles Scribner's Sons, 1954).
[30] Carolyn Sherwin Bailey, *Miss Hickory* (New York: The Viking Press, 1947).
[31] Mary Norton, *The Borrowers* (New York: Harcourt, Brace and Company, 1953).

Scenes from familiar stories are fun to dramatize. Simple properties may be used if they are available, but the experience in thinking through the action of the scene, in planning and evaluating, is of great importance.

SOME QUESTIONS TO THINK ABOUT IN APPRAISING CLASSROOM READING ACTIVITIES IN THE INTERMEDIATE GRADES

1. Are the children reading with clear purposes in mind?
2. Are experiences planned and materials chosen so that many different types of reading skills are called into play?
3. Are children being encouraged to take on increasingly complex reading activities?
4. Are reading activities planned so as to encourage greater independence in reading?
5. Are reading activities adjusted so that children at various levels of ability can proceed at their own paces?
6. Are children learning to enjoy recreational reading as well as learning to read for information?
7. Are children learning to use firsthand experiences to supplement their reading, and vice versa?
8. Is help being provided as new problems arise?
9. Are children gaining clearer insights into how to read as they engage in various types of reading activities?
10. Are children developing sound standards for evaluating many different types of material?
11. Are children gaining acquaintance with their heritage of prose and verse?

SUGGESTIONS FOR FURTHER READING

SELECTING READING MATERIALS

Burton, Dwight L., and Larrick, Nancy. "Literature for Children and Youth," *Development In and Through Reading*. Chapter 11. Sixtieth Yearbook of the National Society for the Study of Education, Part I. Chicago: The University of Chicago Press, 1961. 406 pp.

Burton, William H. *Reading in Child Development*. Chapter 11. Indianapolis: The Bobbs-Merrill Company, 1956. 608 pp.

DeBoer, John J. and Dallmann, Martha. *The Teaching of Reading*. Chapter 11B. New York: Holt, Rinehart and Winston, 1960. 360 pp.

Gray, Lillian, and Reese, Dora. *Teaching Children to Read*. Second Edition, Chapter 15. New York: The Ronald Press Company, 1957. 475 pp.

Herrick, Vergil E., and Associates. "Basal Instructional Materials in Reading," *Development In and Through Reading*, pp. 165-188. Sixtieth Yearbook of the National Society for the Study of Education. Chicago: The University of Chicago Press, 1961. 406 pp.

Hildreth, Gertrude. *Teaching Reading*. Chapter 22. New York: Henry Holt and Company, 1958. 612 pp.

Robinson, Helen M. (Editor). *Materials for Reading*. Supplementary Educational Monographs No. 86. Chicago: The University of Chicago Press, 1957. 231 pp.

Russell, David H. *Children Learn to Read*. Chapter 13. Boston: Ginn and Company, 1961. 612 pp.

Walraven, Margaret K., and Hallquest, Alfred L. *Teaching Through the Elementary School Library.* New York: H. W. Wilson Company, 1948. 183 pp.

Whipple, Gertrude. "Desirable Materials, Facilities, and Resources for Reading," *Reading in the Elementary School,* pp. 147-171. Forty-eighth Yearbook of the National Society for the Study of Education, Part II. Chicago: The University of Chicago Press, 1949. 343 pp.

WORD LISTS

Buckingham, B. R., and Dolch, E. W. *A Combined Word List.* Boston: Ginn and Company, 1936. 184 pp.

Dale, Edgar; Eichholz, Gerhard, and others. *Children's Knowledge of Words.* Columbus, Ohio: Ohio State University Bureau of Educational Research and Service, 1960. 188 pp.

Gates, Arthur I. *A Reading Vocabulary for the Primary Grades.* New York: Teachers College, Columbia University, 1935. 29 pp.

Horn, Ernest. *A Basic Writing Vocabulary.* University of Iowa Monographs in Education, No. 4. Iowa City: College of Education, University of Iowa, 1926. 225 pp.

Murphy, Helen A. "The Spontaneous Speaking Vocabulary of Children in Primary Grades," *Journal of Education.* **140** (December 1957), 2-104.

Rinsland, Henry D. *A Basic Vocabulary of Elementary School Children.* New York: The Macmillan Company, 1945. 636 pp.

Thorndike, Edward L., and Lorge, Irving. *Teachers Word Book of 30,000 Words.* New York: Teachers College, Columbia University, 1944. 274 pp.

DEVELOPING READING INTERESTS AND TASTES

Gray, Lillian, and Reese, Dora. *Teaching Children to Read.* Second Edition, Chapter 14. New York: The Ronald Press Company, 1957. 475 pp.

Harris, Albert J. *How to Increase Reading Ability.* Fourth Edition, Chapter 17. New York: Longmans, Green and Company, 1961. 624 pp.

Hildreth, Gertrude. *Teaching Reading. op. cit.,* Chapter 21.

Huck, Charlotte S., and Young, Doris A. *Children's Literature in the Elementary School.* Chapters 11-13. New York: Holt, Rinehart and Winston, 1961. 522 pp.

Intermediate Manual, Revised, Chapter 8. Curriculum Bulletin 400, Cincinnati: Cincinnati Public Schools, 1962. 404 pp.

Robinson, Helen M. (Editor). *Developing Permanent Interests in Reading.* Supplementary Educational Monographs No. 84. Chicago: University of Chicago Press. December 1956. 224 pp.

The Reading Teacher. October 1958, issue has the theme, "Stimulating Personal and Social Growth Through Reading." The April 1959 issue is devoted to the theme, "Developing Lifetime Habits in Reading."

Smith, Henry P., and Dechant, Emerald V. *Psychology in Teaching Reading.* Chapter 10. Englewood Cliffs, New Jersey: Prentice-Hall, 1961. 470 pp.

Witty, Paul A. "The Role of Interest," *Development in and Through Reading.* Chapter 8. Sixtieth Yearbook of the National Society for the Study of Education. Part I. Chicago: The University of Chicago Press, 1961. 406 pp.

DEVELOPING UNIT ACTIVITIES

Blough, Glenn O.; Schwartz, Julius; Huggett, Albert J. *Elementary Science and How to Teach It.* Revised Edition. New York: Henry Holt and Company, 1958. 608 pp.

Grossnickle, Foster E., and Brueckner, Leo J. *Discovering Meanings in Arithmetic.* Philadelphia: The John C. Winston Company, 1959. 442 pp.

Heilman, Arthur W. *Principles and Practices of Teaching Reading.* Pp. 275-282. Columbus, Ohio: Charles E. Merrill Books, Inc., 1961. 465 pp.

Hanna, Lavone A.; Potter, Gladys L.; and Hagaman, Neva. *Unit Teaching in the Elementary School.* New York: Rinehart and Company, 1955. 592 pp.

Intermediate Manual, Revised, Chapter 3. Curriculum Bulletin 400, Cincinnati: Cincinnati Public Schools, 1962. 404 pp.

McKim, Margaret G.; Hansen, Carl W.; and Carter, William L. *Learning to Teach in the Elementary School.* Chapter 6. New York: The Macmillan Company, 1959. 612 pp.

Michaelis, John U. *Social Studies for Children in a Democracy.* Second Edition, Chapter 12. Englewood Cliffs, New Jersey: Prentice-Hall, 1956. 523 pp.

Miel, Alice, and Brogan, Peggy. *More Than Social Studies.* Englewood Cliffs, New Jersey: Prentice-Hall, 1957. 452 pp.

Spitzer, Herbert F. *The Teaching of Arithmetic.* Boston: Houghton Mifflin Company, 1961. 352 pp.

Stratemeyer, Florence B.; Forkner, Hamden L.; McKim, Margaret G., and Passow, Harry A. *Developing a Curriculum for Modern Living,* Second Edition, Revised. New York: Bureau of Publications, Teachers College, Columbia University, 1957. 740 pp.

Wesley, Edgar B., and Adams, Mary A. *Teaching Social Studies in Elementary Schools.* Boston: D. C. Heath and Company, 1952. 466 pp.

Tiegs, Ernest W., and Adams, Fay. *Teaching Social Studies, A Guide to Better Citizenship.* Boston: Ginn and Company, 1959. 562 pp.

READING IN THE CONTENT FIELDS

Bond, Guy L., and Wagner, Eva Bond. *Teaching the Child to Read.* Chapters 13, 14. New York: Macmillan and Company, 1960. 416 pp.

Dawson, Mildred A., and Bamman, Henry A. *Fundamentals of Basic Reading Instruction.* Chapter 11. New York: Longmans, Green and Company, 1959. 304 pp.

DeBoer, John J., and Whipple, Gertrude. "Reading Development in Other Curriculum Areas," *Development in and Through Reading,* pp. 54-74, Sixtieth Yearbook of the National Society for the Study of Education, Part I. Chicago: The University of Chicago Press, 1961. 406 pp.

The Reading Teacher. **11** (February 1958). Theme of entire issue is "Efficient Reading in Each Curriclum Area."

Smith, Henry P., and Dechant, Emerald V. *Psychology in Teaching Reading.* Chapter 13. Englewood Cliffs, New Jersey: Prentice-Hall, Inc., 1961. 470 pp.

Spencer, Peter L., and Russell, David H. "Reading in Arithmetic," *Instruction in Arithmetic,* pp. 202-223, Twenty-fifth Yearbook of the National Council of Teachers of Mathematics. Washington, D. C.: The Council, 1960. 366 pp.

Fay, Leo; Horn, Thomas, and McCullough, Constance. *Improving Reading in the*

Elementary Social Studies. Washington, D. C.: National Council for the Social Studies, 1961. 72 pp.

Gates, Arthur I., "The Nature and Function of Reading in the Content Areas." *New Frontiers in Reading,* pp. 149-153. International Reading Association Conference Proceedings. Y. Allen Figurel, Editor. New York: Scholastic Magazines, 1960. 176 pp.

Gray, Lillian, and Reese, Dora. *Teaching Children to Read.* Second Edition. Chapter 13. New York: The Ronald Press Company, 1957. 475 pp.

Gray, William S. *Improving Reading in All Curriculum Areas.* Chapters 5, 9-14. Supplementary Educational Monograph No. 76. Chicago: University of Chicago Press, 1952. 262 pp.

Tooze, Ruth, and Krone, Beatrice P. *Literature and Music as Resources for Social Studies.* Englewood Cliffs, New Jersey: Prentice-Hall, Inc., 1955. 457 pp.

AIDS FOR LOCATING READING MATERIALS: ELEMENTARY SCHOOLS

I. REFERENCE BOOKS AND BIBLIOGRAPHIES

Brewton, John E., and Brewton, Sara W., Compilers. *Subject Index to Children's Poetry.* New York: H. W. Wilson Company, 1942. 969 pp. (Supplement 1954).

Children's Catalogue. 10th Edition. New York: H. W. Wilson Company, 1961. 915 pp. (Annual Supplements).

Eakin, Mary K., and Merritt, Eleanor. *Subject Index to Books for Primary Grades.* Second Edition. Chicago: American Library Association, 1961. 167 pp.

Olson, Barbara V. "Aids for Librarians in Elementary Schools," *Elementary English.* **38** (May 1961), 336-341.

Rue, Eloise, Compiler. *Subject Index to Books for Intermediate Grades.* Second Edition. Chicago: American Library Association, 1950. 493 pp.

Subject and Title Index to Short Stories for Children. Compiled by a subcommittee of the American Library Association. Chicago: The Association, 1955. 333 pp.

II. GENERAL BOOKLISTS

American Library Association. *Basic Book Collection for Elementary Schools.* Seventh Edition. Chicago: The Association, 1960. 123 pp.

Arbuthnot, May Hill, and others. *Children's Books too Good to Miss.* Second Revised Edition. Cleveland, Ohio: The Press of Western Reserve University, 1959. 64 pp.

Association for Childhood Education International. *A Bibliography of Books for Children.* Bulletin No. 37. Washington, D. C.: The Association, 1960. 134 pp.

Association for Childhood Education International. *Children's Books for $1.25 or Less.* Revised Edition. Washington, D. C.: The Association, 1961. 31 pp.

Eakin, Mary K. *Good Books for Children.* Chicago: University of Chicago Press, 1959. 294 pp.

Eaton, Anne Thaxter. *Treasure for the Taking.* Revised Edition. New York: Viking Press, 1957. 322 pp.

Larrick, Nancy. *A Teacher's Guide to Children's Books*. Columbus, Ohio: Charles
E. Merrill, 1960. 316 pp.
National Council of Teachers of English. *Adventuring with Books*. Champaign,
Illinois: The Council, 1960. 189 pp.
Tooze, Ruth. *Your Children Want to Read, A Guide for Teachers and Parents*.
Englewood Cliffs, New Jersey: Prentice-Hall, 1957. 222 pp.

III. LISTS ON SPECIAL SUBJECTS OR IN SPECIAL AREAS

Blair, Glenn M. *Diagnostic and Remedial Teaching*. Chapter 8, "Reading Materials
and Practice Exercises." New York: The Macmillan Company, 1956. 409 pp.
Carr, Constance. "Substitutes for the Comic Books," *Elementary English*. **28**
(April-May, 1951), 367-68.
Harris, Albert J. *How to Increase Reading Ability*. Fourth Edition, Appendix B:
A Graded List of Books for Remedial Reading, pp. 594-607. New York: Long-
mans, Green and Company, 1961. 624 pp.
Heaton, Margaret M., and Lewis, Helen B. *Reading Ladders for Human Relations*.
Revised and Enlarged Edition. Washington, D. C.: American Council on Edu-
cation, 1955. 215 pp.
Horn, Thomas D. "Periodicals for Children and Youth," *Elementary English*. **34**
(May 1959), 342-44.
Huus, Helen. *Children's Books to Enrich the Social Studies*. Washington, D. C.:
National Council for the Social Studies, N.E.A., 1961. 196 pp.
Kambly, Paul E. "The Elementary School Science Library for 1958," *School Sci-
ence and Mathematics*. **59** (April 1959), 294-302.
Kircher, Clara J. *Character Formation Through Books: A Bibliography*. Wash-
ington, D. C.: Catholic University of America Press, 1952. 103 pp.
McCauley, Virginia C. "Out of This World: A Bibliography of Space Literature
for Boys and Girls," *Elementary English*. **41** (February 1959), 98-101.
Maib, Frances. "A Suggested List of Literature Books," *Elementary English*. **36**
(April 1959), 253-265.
Schewitzky, M. "Children's Literature About Foreign Countries," *Wilson Library
Bulletin*. **32** (October 1957), 142-48.
Serviss, T. R. "Books to Widen a Child's World," *National Parent Teacher*. **52**
(December 1957), 26-30.
Spache, George D. *Good Reading for Poor Readers*. Revised Edition. Champaign,
Illinois: Garrard Press, 1960. 175 pp.
Tooze, Ruth, and Krone, Beatrice P. *Literature and Music as Resources for Social
Studies*. Englewood Cliffs, New Jersey: Prentice-Hall, 1955. 457 pp.

IV. HELPFUL BOOKS ABOUT CHILDREN'S LITERATURE

Arbuthnot, May Hill. *Children and Books*. Revised Edition. Chicago: Scott,
Foresman, and Company, 1957. 684 pp.
Duff, Annis. *Bequest of Wings*. New York: Viking Press, 1946. 204 pp.
———. *Longer Flight: A Family Grows up with Books*. New York: Viking Press,
1955. 269 pp.
Fenner, Phyllis. *The Proof of the Pudding, What Children Read*. New York:
John Day Company, 1957. 246 pp.
Frank, Josette. *Your Child's Reading Today*. Garden City, New York: Doubleday
and Company, 1960. 391 pp.

Fryatt, Norma R. (Editor). *A Horn Book Sampler*. Boston: The Horn Book, 1959. 261 pp.

Hazard, Paul. *Books, Children and Men*. Boston: The Horn Book, 1944. 176 pp.

Mahoney, Bertha E., and Field, Elinor W. *Caldecott Medal Books: 1938-1957*. Boston: The Horn Book, 1957. 329 pp.

———— *et al. Illustrators of Children's Books 1744-1945*. Boston: The Horn Book, 1947. 527 pp.

Meigs, Cornelia, *et al. A Critical History of Children's Literature*. New York: The Macmillan Company, 1953. 624 pp.

Miller, Bertha Mahoney, and Field, Elinor Whitney (Editors). *Caldecott Medal Books: 1938-1957*. Boston: The Horn Book, 1957. 329 pp.

————. *Newbery Medal Books: 1922-1955*. Boston: The Horn Book, 1955. 458 pp.

Miller, Bertha Mahoney, *et al. Illustrators of Children's Books: 1946-1956*. Boston: The Horn Book, 1958. 299 pp.

Smith, Irene. *History of the Newbery and Caldecott Medals*. New York: Viking Press, 1957. 140 pp.

Smith, Lillian H. *The Unreluctant Years*. Chicago: The American Library Association, 1953. 193 pp.

CHAPTER XII

Developing Reading Skills Through Special Practice Activities in the Intermediate Grades

PRACTICE activities to be used both by individuals and by groups are provided for in the reading units described in the preceding chapter. These activities are not suggested, however, as a routine part of the reading program, but as a means of individualizing instruction and focusing it at points where new needs develop or weaknesses become apparent. They are seen as a way of supplementing the help given during the progress of reading units. The extent to which these special practice exercises are used, as well as the skills upon which they are focused, will depend both on the nature of the on-going classroom activities, and upon the capabilities of the pupils. For some children the reading units and other functional classroom activities that have just been discussed will provide a large share of the practice needed for the development of efficient reading techniques. Others will require much supplementary help. Every child is likely to reach one or more points in his progress in learning to read when he will benefit from a series of work-type experiences.

Suggestions for scheduling practice activities and for establishing needed groups were made in Chapter X. For some immature children, procedures similar to those suggested for the primary grades in Chapters VI and VII may be more appropriate. As indicated in these earlier chapters, special practice sessions will be most effective when they, too, are developed cooperatively, with many of the same elements of planning and evaluation that characterize the development of a unit of work. Children can be more intelligent and self-directing about their work if they understand what purposes it is to serve and why it is needed. This understanding is important whether the situation involves a single child engaged in a series of work-type exercises, an entire class practicing to establish a new skill, or a group at work on the activities of a unit in a content field.

A first step in developing a practice activity cooperatively with children is to help them see the value of the additional practice. Identification of special reading needs can come in many ways. Children themselves may report a problem. "Our group couldn't find any material we needed." "It takes such a long time to do all that reading." "It's hard to understand him. He reads too fast." Teachers, working with groups or individuals, may identify weaknesses of which children are unaware. "Most of the groups are missing important pieces of information as they read." "As I check your notes, it seems to me that you are copying the whole chapter. I wonder if you could learn how to write down just what you need to answer the questions." "Look at the list of the words we didn't know. They all have three or more syllables. Wouldn't it be a good idea to work on pronouncing longer words?" Sometimes a problem can be foreseen as a new activity is undertaken—the first major project calling for an encyclopedia; the first systematic use of the dictionary; the first extensive experience in choral reading of poetry; or the first time an outline is needed. Short informal tests are a help in identifying difficulties. Standardized tests can be analyzed in order to discover patterns of errors. All such concrete evidences of difficulty can be used to help children see the need for special practice.

Just as children developing a reading unit or a unit in a content field share in planning next steps, so children working with a series of practice exercises should share in planning their activities. It is usually the teacher who suggests the appropriate exercise, but the children need to see why it was suggested and what skills it is likely to serve. "You are the people who read so fast you miss things. Here are some work-sheets that ask you questions you can't answer unless you read carefully." "When you can't break a word into syllables, you often have trouble learning to spell it. Here are some exercises that will help you with syllables." "All of us had trouble yesterday finding the topics we wanted in the encyclopedia because we didn't know what words to look for. Here are some questions to try."

If they are to be self-directing about their activities, children also need to share in setting up the proposed schedule for practice. "We are all going to lose time in our reference reading unless we learn how to take better notes.

Shall we plan to work on that first tomorrow morning?" "Suppose for the next week our practice group meets for ten minutes right after recess." "If I leave the practice exercises out on the table, could you work ahead? Suppose I post a chart, and you can check off each exercise as you finish it." "That would be a good activity for spelling partners. Could you do it then?"

Continuous evaluation is as important in the development of a special skill as it is in any other type of activity. Children need the opportunity to discuss new difficulties, to check the accuracy of the work they have been doing, and to decide on next steps. It is this type of participation that builds a classroom atmosphere in which there is pride in being able to identify one's needs and willingness to accept help without feeling inadequate or defeated by one's lack of skill. Part of this evaluation usually takes place as children meet to check on work-type assignments. They discuss right answers, tell how they secured them and why they are right, help the child who was wrong figure out his difficulty, and decide whether progress has been made and how much more practice is likely to be needed.

At a number of points in the discussion that follows, basal readers are suggested as one source of interesting practice material. These books do not serve their full purpose if they are used only for the unit activities described in Chapter XI. On the other hand, precautions need to be taken to avoid turning almost every story into a practice exercise by placing upon the chalkboard a list of questions to which the children routinely write answers, or even by having the children work systematically through the questions which are found at the end of each story in some series, intriguing though these questions may be. The most effective integration of children's total reading experiences will be achieved when their teacher takes the responsibility for appraising their present status and for deciding on their needs.

One of the most difficult problems for the teacher of older children is to decide precisely what is the need for practice exercises in reading. It is easy to say that this individual, or that group, reads too slowly, or reads inaccurately. It is not easy to know *why* this is so. Slow reading may result from poor techniques of word analysis, inability to use chapter and paragraph headings as a guide for skimming, a lack of clear purpose regarding what is to be located, or a tendency to vocalize. Inability to read accurately for details could result from too slow or too rapid reading, from not having a clear purpose for reading, or from inattention to key words. The more effective the practice, the more clearly the exact nature of the problem is seen, and the more precisely the activity is designed to meet the child's need.

In the sections that follow there are, first, an analysis of the nature of the skill under discussion; second, suggestions of possible interrelationships with other skills; and, third, a discussion of typical activities that might be used for special practice. No attempt has been made to designate activities for particular grade levels. Most of those suggested can be adapted to several levels of ability.

DEVELOPING TECHNIQUES OF EFFECTIVE COMPREHENSION

For the purposes of discussion, the skills involved in effective comprehension have been classified in three groups: Those concerned with making a critical evaluation of what is read; those related to following the general gist of a paragraph in order to summarize it, follow its sequence, or predict an outcome from what has been read; and those centering around reading carefully for details, either in isolation or in the step-by-step process of following directions.

DEVELOPING TECHNIQUES OF CRITICAL EVALUATION

Identify the skills involved in making critical evaluations. Because the ability to make critical evaluations in terms of reading purposes is, in a sense, the basis of all intelligent reading, problems in this area were discussed or implied at several points in Chapter XI. As suggested in that chapter, critical evaluation calls, first, for ability to think through a problem so that the reader knows exactly what information he needs. This includes not only being able to make a clear statement of a general problem, but also being able to identify a number of definite subproblems. "We are studying about how the Indians lived, and here is our list of questions." "These are the things we are going to look for to help plan our mural." "This is what we need to know before we start to build our birdhouses." In the realm of appreciation, the problem may be one of setting up criteria for selecting an appropriate story to dramatize, for choosing a story to recommend to another group, or for deciding which of several poems to use for choral speaking.

As he begins to read, the child must be able to cope effectively with several problems:

1. Does this piece of information answer my question, or is it merely a general statement about the topic?
2. Is this a statement of fact; or is it fiction, or someone's opinion?
3. Which of these conflicting statements is more likely to be correct?
4. Does this selection meet the standards selected for choosing stories (or poems or plays)?
5. Does this material give me enough information, or should I look for more?

Essentially, the problem of developing skill in critical evaluation is one of helping the child think as he reads—about the authenticity of his information; about its appropriateness to his problem; and, from the standpoint of appreciation, about the way in which it is written. A beginning may also be made at this level in appraising an author's point of view or special bias.

Make sure the child has the background and the related skills important in making critical evaluations. Many related factors can complicate the problem of making critical evaluations. Experience background may be limited. If a child has never tried to dramatize a story, he is not going to be sensitive to the criteria to use in deciding on the appropriateness of a story for effective dramatization. If he has little experience with farms, he may not know what questions to suggest if his group is embarking on a study of what the farmer contributes to our welfare. Lack of experience also influences a child's sensitivity to the accuracy of what he reads. If he has no experience against which to check his reading, he may not sense inadequacies in descriptions of other countries, people, or ways of living and working. Part of the problem of helping children become able to make critical evaluations is to provide the background that enables them to understand clearly what they read.

Inadequate reading skills also get in the way of critical evaluations. Sometimes a child may lack the reference techniques he needs fully to explore the material available to him. If the material is difficult, either in concepts or in sentence structure, a child may have trouble recognizing the answers to his question. Even when easy material is provided, the youngster who is unskilled in varying his reading approach may have trouble. If he does not think of the general significance of the paragraph as he goes along, he may miss certain details because he does not see how they fit into the pattern. If he does not read carefully for details, he may miss some of the points he is looking for or he may not catch an inaccurate statement or a misleading implication. Speed of reading may also be involved. The slow, careful reader may not cover enough material to see its full possibilities for his problem, while the child who reads too rapidly may miss the implications of key details. All such potential problem areas need to be studied when a child has difficulty in making critical evaluations of what he reads.

Generally speaking, the type of help provided for children who have trouble making critical evaluations will be of two kinds, depending upon the need. The first kind of help may be given through providing assistance in developing a reading skill, such as skill in close, accurate reading, as opposed to the too rapid, inaccurate reading which may prevent critical evaluation. Here, the help provided would be through practice for appropriate reading speed, or through provision for easier material.

The second kind of help may be given through specific practice in critical evaluation, both through work-type activities and by means of group discussions of how to decide when material is pertinent and accurate. Short selections are excellent sources of practice of this kind, since they provide sufficient interesting material to make a number of types of critical judgment possible. Questions may be devised which may help to analyze these materials. The reader may respond to such questions by checking, such as: *helps, does not help;* or by classifying the selection as *factual* or *fictional; proven in the text* or *not proven.* Discussion questions on these materials may call for decisions regarding motives and feeling of a character, harmony of presentation with materials previously read, or with personal experience, as may be suitable to the material and to the problems the group is encountering in their various reading activities. As many teachers have observed, pupils differ widely in ability to handle these more penetrating questions. The ability to evaluate critically grows slowly, as children meet a variety of materials and a wide range of challenging problems. Practice exercises are useful but do not take the place of broadly challenging situations, nor will they assure equal proficiency for all children. The following suggestions can be adapted for use with many different reading materials, and a variety of situations.

Deciding on the appropriateness of materials can be practiced through: Sorting a set of newspaper clippings according to their bearing on a series of problems; choosing from a list of chapter titles those most likely to be helpful in a given problem.

Telling factual materials from fiction or from opinions is called for in: Reading a story and listing statements which could be true and statements which are probably make-believe; checking a group of statements from a basal reader in terms of such standards as *story proves this true, this might be true but story does not tell, story proves this false;* analyzing newspaper reports for statements of fact and opinion, for the special biases of the writer; analyzing appropriate newspaper advertisements.

Deciding on the appropriateness of specific pieces of information is needed in: Filling in missing points in a partially constructed outline; selecting paragraphs to read aloud to answer specific questions; choosing from a group of mimeographed paragraphs the ones which bear on a particular problem.

Standards of appreciation are called for in: Listing the points to consider in choosing a story to read to another reading group, parents, or younger children; developing bases for deciding which of two stories could best be dramatized; deciding which of a small group of stories on a similar topic one likes best and why; preparing a special report on one's favorite author; discussing the mood to be created in developing several choral-speaking presentations.

HELPING CHILDREN FOLLOW THE GIST OF A PASSAGE

Identify the skills involved in following the gist of a passage. Ability to get the general significance of a passage is needed in most wide reading.

It is basic to the enjoyment of recreational reading. It is an important aspect of locating information, since it provides the reader with a framework within which to operate. It is the skill needed in identifying cause-and-effect relationships, tracing the sequence of events, or predicting the probable outcome of a series of events. It is used when the reader gives a title for a paragraph or story, decides how a character felt or predicts what he might do next, outlines scenes for dramatization, or gives the plot of a story as a book report.

The reader who is able to grasp the general significance of a passage must be able to deal with these questions:

1. What are the key ideas of this selection?
2. In what order does the author place them?
3. What ideas are used by the author to illustrate a main point, or to support his argument?
4. What conclusions can be drawn from the ideas in this selection?

Many reading problems which prevent accuracy in critical evaluation also get in the way of following the gist of a passage. Difficulty in pronouncing key words, confusion in meaning of words, and the painfully slow analysis of unfamiliar words may cause the reader to lose sight of the meaning of the passage as a whole. Details may be seen in isolation rather than in relation to the total meaning of a passage. Words that signal relationship of ideas, such as *next, the first, or on the other hand,* may be overlooked. As the amount of material to be covered increases, reference skills, such as using section or paragraph headings, and chapter summaries, are important aids in getting the general significance of what is read.

Provide practice that calls for a general impression of a passage. Some of the most valuable practice in following the gist of a passage comes as a child goes about purposeful reading activities—skimming to locate needed material, reporting on recreational reading, deciding on the scenes needed to dramatize a story. Special practice activities can be developed around basal-reader stories or around other relatively short passages. It is important that the passages selected be varied in content. A story written for entertainment is in a different style than an informational article, and an article giving directions is likely to be phrased more precisely than one giving general information. Children need to have the experience of reading for the general sense of such varied types of materials. Furthermore, they need to engage in activities that help them learn to adjust their reports in terms of their purposes. The items chosen to summarize the same adventure story are different, depending on whether one is thinking of it as a story to read aloud to others, a book to recommend to a boy who likes adventure stories, or a source of information for children who want to know what animals live in the mountains.

Questions calling for a reaction to the general idea of a passage should require answers that summarize, titles to paragraphs, or statements of main points. Children may write the answer in their own words or check various types of objective-test forms. The following suggest typical practice activities.

Summarizing the general contents of a passage is called for in: Giving titles to a series of mimeographed paragraphs; choosing the correct one of three proposed titles for a paragraph; choosing one of three or four statements answering the question, *What is this paragraph about;* choosing the correct answer to tell how a character felt, acted, looked; choosing which of several questions is answered in a given paragraph; sorting paragraphs clipped from newspapers or mimeographed, according to the topics they cover; writing single paragraphs on a given topic in terms of whether they are factual or fictional, whether they would help to answer a given question or not.

Identifiyng the sequence of events in a passage is needed for: Making an outline; putting in the missing points in a partially finished outline; listing the steps given in a story to describe the unfolding of a special activity; deciding on the scenes for a play; rearranging a series of statements from a story in the order in which they came; writing a brief book review or telling the class briefly about a favorite book; choosing the correct statement to answer such questions as, *Which came first, What came next.*

PROVIDING EXPERIENCES IN READING CAREFULLY FOR DIRECTIONS OR DETAILS

Identify the skills involved in reading details. Reading for directions or details depends, as do other comprehension techniques, on a clear purpose. It calls for enough exactness to assure the precise noting of a date, an event, or a description. It is a precise, accurate approach to materials. This is the reading skill that is needed to follow group plans effectively, to collect the detailed information needed for a group report, to perform a science experiment, to read an arithmetic problem, or to report accurately on daily news items on the bulletin boards.

The abilities needed in reading for details are those involved in the following:

1. Noticing carefully modifiers which give indications of quantity, quality, extent, comparison.

2. Observing clues to sequence, such as *first, before, after, then, in the meantime*.
3. Noting the orderly sequence of procedures in directions.
4. Being willing to re-read in order to check a specific point.

Make sure the child has related skills important in noting details. Skillful detailed reading is dependent both upon the techniques of critical evaluation and upon those of following the gist of a passage. Because the skillful reader of details knows what he is looking for, he uses many of the same techniques he would use to get the general idea of a passage, both in order to locate the details he needs and to understand them in their setting. Change of pace also has been identified as an important aid in activities such as following directions, reading arithmetic problems, or tracing the historical sequence of events, where it is often helpful to skim for general understanding of the passage first. As the job of locating information becomes more complex, the related reference skills of using tables of contents and indexes become important. In addition, the general difficulty level of the material to be read and the learner's experience background influence the effectiveness of detailed reading just as they affect other aspects of comprehension.

Provide practice that calls for precise reading. Practice activities centering on detailed reading ask questions such as *what, when, how, what time, where, in what order, how many, what kind.* These are the types of questions with which the child turns to his social-studies report, his science textbook, or the article he has clipped from the daily paper. Work-type materials can be developed around short mimeographed passages or stories in basal readers, accompanied by a variety of multiple-choice, true-false, or completion questions. Because reading for details is particularly important in informational reading, a number of the practice passages should be factual in nature. The difficulty of the reading problem can be governed somewhat by the question. The answer to a question worded in almost the exact phrasing of the book is easier to locate than one that calls for an inference, or for seeing the relationship between two facts.

These questions relating to precise details are generally quite easy to prepare. Hence many children have already had considerable practice in reading to find answers to them. More than in any other area, therefore, it would be likely to be most rewarding to use a pretest, or to make some kind of analysis of pupils' responses and backgrounds to discover whether a need exists for more activities of this type, before preparing to use them extensively with an individual or a group.

Because it is important to teach children to read with clear purposes in mind, the child should know the questions he is to answer before he starts to read. It is sometimes argued that the youngster who knows what he is to look for will merely turn pages until the right answer appears. This is not likely to happen if questions are phrased so that the answer is not immediately apparent and if children have been helped to become truly interested in learning to read well. Furthermore, if this procedure leads to correct answers, it can be argued that such intelligent skimming is more effective than indiscriminate noting of all the details in the passage, pertinent or otherwise. Except for an occasional demonstration of the importance of reading with care, children should not be given an assignment to read a passage without knowing, at least in general terms, what they are reading for. This applies equally to special practice and to assignments in the content fields. Typical practice activities are suggested in the paragraphs that follow.

Practice in locating separate details can be given by: Answering questions asking, *who, what kind, what color, how old, when, where;* answering factual statements about a passage with *yes* or *no, true* or *false;* completing factual statements about a passage; choosing the correct word to complete statements of details from a passage.

Practice in discovering related details can be given by: Listing important details about the characters in a story; matching the names of several characters with appropriate descriptions; classifying facts in two or three columns according to a scheme suggested by the contents of the passage—list the animals that hibernate and those that do not, list the methods used by pioneers and those used today.

Experience in following directions may be given through: Carrying out mimeographed directions for construction, cooking, making charts, making classroom decorations, or some other appropriate activity; putting in order a set of statements indicating a sequence of events; listing, step by step, a process described in an informational story in a basal reader; answering *true* or *false,* or completing key statements about a set of directions from a workbook, an arithmetic problem, or a description of a science activity.

DEVELOPING EFFECTIVE READING RATE

Identify the techniques needed for effective reading rate. Consolidation of the skills that make for effective reading rate comes largely at the intermediate-grade level after primary techniques of comprehension, and particularly those of word analysis, have been well established. Many adults today are faced with so many reading tasks that accurate, rapid reading is essential for many persons. Speed, however, is not the sole basis for excellence in reading. Actually, as indicated in the objectives of the intermediate-grade reading program in Chapter X, the most efficient reader is the one who can vary his speed appropriately in terms of the reading task he is undertaking.[1] Rapid reading is effective for locating needed material, for certain types of recreational reading, for skimming to appraise the potential value of material, for rechecking familiar material for needed information, and for getting the general idea of a passage. The reader must go more slowly if he is paying attention to details, looking for a specific piece of information, trying to follow a set of directions, or working out an arithmetic problem. Slower rate is also needed for recreational reading when the enjoyment of the passage depends on being aware of its descriptive qualities or its cadence.

The effective reader varies his rate not only from one type of material to another, but within a single reading task. He skims to locate needed information, slows down to read carefully when he has found it, rereads rapidly to be sure he has understood it correctly, and takes notes on one point at a time. It is this flexibility in approach that is the ultimate objective in helping children develop effective reading rate.

Because rate of reading is dependent upon the purposes for which the child is reading, it is not possible to set up standards in terms of numbers of words a minute against which the child's reading can be checked. Many of the standardized reading tests published for the intermediate grades have checks of reading rate from which the child's position in relation to others of his reading level can be secured. Even these scores must be used with caution, because they indicate the child's performance only when he is working with materials and with questions similar to those used in the test.

A rough picture of the range in reading rates can be secured by noting the order in which the members of a reading group complete a given selection. Children who consistently finish last are likely to be those who will benefit from activities designed to increase their speed. Other evidence of unduly slow reading can be secured by watching the order in which children finish other assignments; by looking for a pattern of well-done but unfinished work on standardized or classroom tests; by studying oral reading for poor phrasing, which is sometimes a clue to a word-by-word approach to reading matter; and by watching for signs of vocalization or pointing. Children who finish well ahead of the group can be studied in a similar fashion for evidence of too rapid reading—not being able to report at least the general gist of what is read, missing obvious details, making a hit-and-miss pattern of errors which bears little relationship to the increasing difficulty of the questions on a test, or reading aloud in a fashion that shows little sensitivity to meaning.

Change of pace is also important to note. Does the child who does such a satisfactory job of careful note-taking shy away from long recreational

---

[1] For a further discussion of rate of reading, see A. J. Harris, *op. cit.*, pp. 504-511.

books because it takes too much time to finish them? How effective is the avid reader of stories when he reports his share of a group project calling for exact information? As a child works his way through a single reference book for information, does he start at the first page and read his way ploddingly through to what he actually needs or does he use some short cuts? Such surveys will indicate some children who need special help, but will identify many others who have learned to adapt their reading rate to their needs in the normal course of learning to handle materials of increased variety and difficulty.

Make sure the child has related skills important in effective reading rate. Causes of ineffective reading rate are many. A lack of clear purpose may cause the child to skip important details because he does not recognize their value, or to plod laboriously through his reading trying to pay attention to everything. With a clear purpose in mind the reader can more effectively adapt his rate of reading to that purpose. The ability to achieve an effective rate of reading also depends upon such skills as:

1. Using the author's aids to his readers, such as chapter headings, section headings, topic sentences, summaries.
2. Using adequate techniques of word analysis.
3. Effectively relating new ideas to the reader's background of experience.
4. Reading in phrase units, rather than word by word.

As all adult readers who have skimmed a newspaper and read the fine print in a legal contract are aware, the more difficult the material the slower the reading speed. But even though materials are easy and purposes clear, some children have established a habit of word-by-word reading, sometimes accompanied by vocalizing or pointing to each word. These immature techniques, which serve a useful purpose at the primary level, may linger on.

Although poor eye movements are occasionally listed as a cause for slow reading, further investigation has shown that the pattern of these eye movements in reading is affected by the level of the reader's skill, rather than causing it. The unskilled reader sees one word at a time, looks several times at a word to pronounce it or get its meaning, or loses his place and has to go back over what he has read.[2] Activities designed to secure more effective reading rate need to concentrate then, not on devices to help the eyes move in mechanical rhythm, but on experiences which make for better word recognition and ability to see key words and phrase units as reading progresses.

Provide practice in reading rate focused at the point of difficulty. All the foregoing sources of difficulty need to be kept in mind in planning practice activities to secure more effective reading rate. Again, a basic first step is to

[2] A helpful recent summary of the studies of eye movements can be found in Henry P. Smith and Emerald V. Dechant, *op. cit.*, pp. 124-128.

make sure that children know the purposes for which they are reading. In the interests of effective speed, it is often helpful to discuss with a group how they will need to read in order to achieve their purposes. "There are many books for you on the library table. How could you skim so as to find those which will be most helpful to your group?" "Before you do anything else, suppose you read this story, just thinking whether it would be a good one to share." "This is a good description of lobster fishing, but you are going to have to read carefully or you will miss some of the steps." Such discussions not only help children become aware of good reading techniques, but they help the teacher identify inadequate ones.

A second fundamental aid to the development of effective reading speed is the provision of quantities of easy, interesting material. If the words of a story are well within a child's grasp, the sentence structure is simple, and the story is one that holds his attention and pulls him along because of his interest, he is much more likely to increase his speed. Easy recreational reading provides useful experience in rapid reading because the child is not slowed by the need to look for special information or to check carefully for details. In the content fields, also, a child can develop more effective reading speed if he is not hampered by unduly hard words and complicated style.

When slow reading is occasioned by inadequate word meanings or poor word-analysis techniques, there can be little pressure for increased rate until such time as the word-study problem has been solved. If it is desirable to help the child develop techniques of rapid reading at the same time that he conquers a word-study problem, he will need to be provided with very easy material for practice purposes.

The too rapid reader also needs help. Some of the most effective activities to teach such a child to read more carefully are those that require reading for details or following directions. This is one case where it is sometimes helpful to use a series of detailed questions to check on the accuracy of the child's reading without giving him any advance warning of what he should have been looking for. Sometimes more difficult reading or more challenging problems are helpful if the too rapid reader happens to be an intelligent child who is relying mainly on his general intellectual ability and on minor context clues. Once in a while, the child who is seemingly a careless rapid reader is actually one who finds the material difficult and who is hiding his inability to handle it by seeming to skim through it. Diagnostic insights based on a study of each individual are a first step in planning for practice.

Activities for the slow reader whose problem seems to be a laborious word-by-word approach should, for the most part, be planned with interesting passages—basal-reader stories, workbook paragraphs, articles from children's newspapers.

The question is sometimes raised whether or not to use mechanical devices such as tachistoscopic training and rate controllers of various types to improve rate of reading. Most investigators have worked with college or adult groups, with a few reports at the elementary level. The studies available suggest that mechanical devices for improving reading speed do not produce better results than strongly motivated reading of easy materials.[3]

The type of question that encourages rapid reading calls for a general reaction to the passage. Detailed reading, unless the details are very obvious, requires slower speed. Since part of the skill is to learn to read for specific purposes, questions are more useful if stated before the child begins to read. If ability to vary pace is desired, the questions can call for several specific details, which the child first skims to locate and then reports accurately. Often timing the reading so that the child is under a little pressure to read rapidly and graphing progress so that he can see himself improving are devices helpful to the slow reader. If the timing can be arranged so that a child is allowed to finish a selection, it makes for better comprehension than if the reading is stopped arbitrarily at the end of a given number of minutes. Among the specific activities that are helpful are the following:

Questions helpful as checks on comprehension when rapid reading is desired ask for: Checking how the main character felt; answering obvious questions of fact; answering obvious questions about what a key character did or what kind of person he was.

Children can be helped to see the value of reading in phrases by: Reading aloud to the child while he follows silently, if his silent speed is slower than the teacher's oral speed; demonstrating phrase units by word cards; typing all but the climax of an interesting sentence, and flashing this to the child in a phrase; asking him to find the answer to a question phrased in the words of the book by looking down the page as rapidly as he can until he reaches the correct place; reading conversation, or other oral-reading activities where it is natural to use good phrasing.

Methods of timing convenient for classroom are: Writing the time on the board in ten-second intervals and letting the child copy the numbers he sees as he finishes; having the children raise hands as they finish a selection and jotting down the time; allowing the group to read for a determined amount of time and then counting the words each child has read; using a standardized reading test of speed; letting reading partners time each other.

Vocalization and pointing can be reduced by: Working with very easy material; having a group discussion on why one can go faster without these crutches; having the child put a finger to his lips as he reads; having the child hold his book in both hands so that pointing is not possible; asking the child to glance rapidly down the page looking for an obvious piece of information.

[3] *Ibid.,* pp. 224-234.

Activities to sharpen the use of reference techniques in developing more effective skimming are: Skimming a list of chapter titles and checking those that might be of help on a special problem; seeing who can find a stated section in a standard reference book the most rapidly; locating a paragraph on a given topic by looking for topic sentences; listing the topic sentences; listing the topic sentences in a series of paragraphs; using the index or table of contents in a given book to see who can find a stated topic the most quickly.

Habits of overly careful detailed reading can be broken down by: Cutting down, if necessary, the number of classroom demands for detailed information; making assignments that call for the general impression of a paragraph—checking to see if these books might help us, leafing through the library books and seeing which one sounds the most interesting; asking the child to sort a group of newspaper clippings with clear headlines as rapidly as he can in terms of a given classification of topics; having children predict what an article in a children's newspaper will be about by skimming the headline and the opening paragraph; leading a class discussion about ways of finding information more rapidly.

IMPROVING SKILL IN ORAL READING

Consider the purposes served by oral reading. One of the recurring problems for many intermediate-grade teachers is that of the appropriate use of oral reading. Teaching techniques have varied from those that make much use of oral work to those that allow very little. A common-sense solution to the problem can be arrived at by considering the uses of oral reading in everyday life. Two clear-cut types of oral reading demand an audience. First, reading aloud is used in a discussion to confirm or to illustrate an opinion. Second, the oral reading of a longer passage is used to inform or to entertain others. Much of the oral reading done by adults is of the first type, in which the reader discovers a passage in a newspaper, magazine, or book which illustrates something of interest, and asks his audience to listen to it. He does not practice the reading, although he has already read the material silently. The effectiveness depends more upon the appropriateness of the material than upon the artistry of the reader. In the second type, the audience is prepared to sit and listen to more extended reading of a story, a poem, a play or the minutes of a meeting. The materials have been selected ahead of time, and the effectiveness of the presentation depends not only upon the care with which the material is chosen but also upon the skill with which it is read.

From the teacher's point of view, the diagnostic function of oral reading may be listed as a third purpose it can serve. Often the most helpful way of identifying the exact trouble when a child is having difficulty pronouncing words or is using poor phrasing is to have him work aloud. This type of oral reading is not meant for an audience. It is an experience to be shared by the child, his teacher, and perhaps the members of a sympathetic reading group interested in helping each other.

A fourth use of oral reading, for many readers, is to aid comprehension and word recognition when materials are difficult. Primary teachers are familiar with this need. Many beginners seem to benefit from hearing, as well as seeing, what they read. Adults often mumble to themselves when reading becomes hard. Vocalization is properly frowned upon as a hindrance to reading speed, but it is not necessary to become disturbed if a good reader occasionally resorts to this device. The child who needs help is the one who uses it as a regular habit. There will even be times when the teacher may encourage a child to try a difficult passage aloud or read it to him, if he seems unable to correct an error in pronunciation or in emphasis by rereading silently. Like oral reading for diagnostic purposes, this type of oral reading does not call for an audience.

Teaching of oral reading needs to be planned to allow for experiences both with the reading of short passages to illustrate and confirm opinions, and with the reading of longer selections to entertain or inform. The responsibility of the teacher is to provide the opportunities where each is appropriate, to know the kind of material that is suitable in each case, and to vary the audience situation with the purpose for which the material is being read. With intermediate-grade children the development of skill in reading longer stories, poetry, and drama in audience situations is a particularly important point of focus, since these older children now possess the underlying word-recognition techniques and the other reading skills needed for effective oral presentations. This is the type of oral-reading activity in which practice to develop new skills is most likely to be needed. Reading to confirm or to illustrate an opinion does not require so high a degree of competence in reading aloud, although it provides valuable practice in selecting appropriate passages for special emphases.

Many intermediate-grade teachers feel that it is important to do a certain amount of oral work for diagnostic purposes in reading-group situations. While it is true that much can be learned about a child's difficulties by this procedure, the very fact that errors are anticipated means that difficult materials have to be read. This makes for a situation in which a child is likely to be embarrassed by the presence of an audience and in which the members of the audience have little interest unless they, too, are concerned with the diagnostic process. Although it is possible to develop in a group a spirit of helpfulness and a willingness to let others point out errors, intensive diagnostic work through oral reading is usually best done when the child and teacher work together away from the rest of the group.

Teachers who may be confronted with the problem of having fairly difficult reading materials and less able readers may occasionally feel that comprehension will be assured if children take turns reading textbook assignments
aloud rather than having the material read silently. This conviction is often
strengthened by the enthusiasm of children who feel in this procedure the
comfort of a relatively undemanding routine. While it is undoubtedly true
that the child who is reading aloud is being helped with some hard words,
other readers are pacing their silent reading to the slow speed and inaccurate
phrasing of their inept colleague. It is quite likely that telling the information outright, of having the pupils listen to the teacher's reading would prove
more effective in helping them grasp the ideas intended for them.

Even less than in the primary grades is there need for the round-robin approach to a story where each child reads aloud, often without previous preparation. Not only is it important to set up reading activities where the child
learns to use silent-reading techniques but it is equally important to keep
out of the oral-reading situation the possible negative attitudes associated
with listening to oneself and one's friends make mistakes, waiting one's turn,
taking too long to finish a story since it would go much faster silently, or
waiting patiently while a story that has just been read silently is read again
aloud. Diagnostic clues can be secured in sufficient number as children report on what they read silently, pronounce unfamiliar words listed for them
on the chalkboard as part of the introduction of a new unit, read aloud short
passages in answer to questions, or work together aloud for the legitimate
purpose of preparing to share a story with another group. There will be,
however, occasions when a reading group will take turns in reading a story
aloud, just for the fun of participating, without any particular regard for developing a presentation for an audience and without undue concern for the
degree of skill shown by each of the group members. Usually this sight oral
reading will be with relatively easy material, or with stories in which the
hard words have already been studied through silent-reading activities.

Identify the skills needed for oral reading. Oral reading has its own set of
techniques. These were outlined in brief when the objectives of reading instruction in the intermediate grades were discussed in Chapter X. It calls,
first, for successful pronunciation of unfamiliar words. In silent reading the
child may take time to work out the analysis of a difficult word. In an oral
presentation he loses his audience or fails to make his point if he hesitates too
often or too long. The practices of using simpler materials when a long selection is to be read aloud and of giving the reader an opportunity to scan the
material silently before he reads aloud, and in many cases to rehearse, provide
safeguards at this point.

The skilled oral reader must have adequate command in a number of areas.
He must, for example, be efficient in the following tasks:

1. Recognizing words fluently and accurately. The audience is lost if the reader hesitates too often or too long.
2. Reading in phrase units. The reader's eye must be far enough ahead of the voice to foresee both phrasing and difficult pronunciations.
3. Interpreting the mood and meaning of the selection. Humor, sadness or suspense should be conveyed without drawing undue attention to the reader himself.
4. Delineating character clearly, especially in reading conversation.
5. Controlling volume and pitch of voice so that the audience can hear easily.
6. Gaining suitable "stage presence." This may include looking at the audience, holding a book correctly, knowing what to do if a mistake is made, knowing what to do in a group presentation.

Speed, in oral reading, is a matter of achieving a rate which is effective in conveying meaning. Typically a child's oral-reading rate should be approximately that at which he normally speaks. Only rarely will there need to be any pressure for increased speed. More often the task will be one of encouraging him to read more slowly and distinctly.

It is often helpful to prepare a check list of oral-reading skills to serve as a guide in working with a group. For diagnostic purposes such a list would concern itself chiefly with the child's ability to pronounce difficult words, his attack on new words, where and why he repeats, how well he phrases, and other evidences of reading skill. For guiding growth in audience situations the list would center more upon techniques that are needed to hold an audience—ability to read with expression, poise in front of an audience, clearness of enunciation, quality of voice. Children will grow in their insight into good oral reading if they help to prepare such lists. Classroom bulletin boards often display charts entitled *How to Make a Good Report,* *What Makes a Good Story Teller, How to Be a Good Audience, Things to Remember When We Read Aloud.* Such lists can serve both as a guide for preparing an oral presentation and as a basis for subsequent evaluation.

Provide materials and settings appropriate to the oral-reading task. Problems of choosing the materials and settings for oral-reading activities are more easily solved when the type of oral reading is kept in mind. Reading a few lines to answer a question or to confirm an opinion seldom needs any special adjustment of material or special plans for the audience. Children read from the books they have been using to solve the problem at hand. The audience is the particular group interested in the problem. All may have their books open, if a common text is being used, and all may check on the reader or read other statements in their turn. Typically, the reader has scanned the material silently, but he seldom has done much careful preparation for his oral contribution. Little tension is produced by the audience situation because the selection read is very short and others are doing the same thing.

Often the group is sitting in an informal circle and, while the reader may stand to be heard, he rarely needs to assume a lonely place in the front of the classroom.

When the situation is one of presenting a story, a report, or a dramatization to an audience, more care is needed in choosing materials and in planning for the oral-reading experience. The task of holding an audience demands interesting material. Insofar as possible, it should be unfamiliar to the listeners—a story or play in the basal readers reserved for a particular reading group, a library book that is new to the group, a play written by the children themselves, social-studies reports developed by a small group for presentation to the class as a whole, the minutes of the meeting of the class club, or the report of the special group who went on an excursion. Never should an audience in this type of situation sit with open books checking on the performers. Since skillful reading is important to hold the attention of the audience, the materials should be easy for the performers to read. Reports growing out of units of work in content fields usually meet this criterion if the children are encouraged to use their own words and to avoid copying verbatim from their reference books. Stories from basal readers, plays, poems, and selections from library books can be evaluated for difficulty as one step in deciding whether they are appropriate to share with the class. Choice of reasonably short selections is another aid in holding an audience. Even with careful selection of materials, performers should not go before the audience unprepared. This is the type of oral-reading situation most likely to produce tension. The participant deserves to feel thoroughly at home with what he reads, and he owes it to his audience to be well prepared.

Adjust teaching emphases to the needs of each oral-reading situation. The type of help given by the teacher will vary with the demands of the particular oral-reading situation. When the selections read are very short and the setting informal, there is not much opportunity to emphasize the fine points of phrasing and inflection. Stress is likely to be upon appropriate selection of what is read in terms of the problem. "Where did you find it?" "Can you prove that?" "I don't think that's what it meant." "What part of the story was it in?" "My book said . . ." are the types of questions and comments that call for the brief oral report. However, this informal situation offers an opportunity to give help in many of the fundamentals of good oral presentation. Children can be expected to make themselves heard, to use acceptable phrasing, and to pay attention to punctuation. In this informal sharing, suggestions designed to help the audience understand can be offered without unduly embarrassing the reader. "Would you read that just a little louder, it was hard to hear." "Didn't he read the wrong country? My books say Australia, not America." "Try to read your choice of the scary part so that it really scares us." This informal give-and-take also helps children get used to the idea of making their points before an audience without the pressure that comes from a more lengthy presentation.

When longer selections are being prepared for an audience, much effective practice can be secured in the small group in which the project arose. If several children are to share in the presentation, they form a natural group to set standards, to act as a critical audience for rehearsal purposes, and in other ways to help to polish the performance. Many insights into good oral reading can be developed in these group sessions. In making their plans the children may discuss what makes a good report, a good story to share, or a good dramatization. Insights into different methods of presentation can be developed— a story could be dramatized, each child could read a selected number of paragraphs, one person could read to a climax and ask the audience to guess what would happen next, a series of climaxes could be used this way, people could read the conversation, reports could be given in panel form, pictures might help the presentation, a solo and some choruses could be used in a poem. In practicing for the oral performance the group members can help each other. Sometimes two or three persons may try out a part or a method of presentation. Group discussion can analyze the strengths and weaknesses of the various interpretations. These intensive work sessions can do much to help a child become accustomed to listeners while he receives help with his part of the presentation.

Of all the oral-reading situations, those calling for reading poetry aloud are among the ones requiring the most skill. There are several reasons for this. In the first place, the poet has little space in which to develop his ideas. Therefore, if a key word is slighted or a shade of feeling misrepresented, the meaning is blurred or lost completely. Word order is often transposed, meanings are evoked, rather than specifically represented; and to add to the reader's burden, lines are arranged on the page in a way that leads him to drop his voice at a spot where prose writers would have placed a period, only to discover too late that meaning has been wrenched out of shape, and the rhyme has received undue emphasis. When it is observed that these difficulties exist in even the simplest verse, the conclusion may well be drawn that the most mature reader should be generally the reader of poetry in an audience situation. This mature reader is, of course, the teacher, who shows by example how poems may be read aloud to give pleasure to all hearers. Given thorough familiarity with a poem, and many examples of good reading, children should undertake to share with others a favorite poem. Choice of material and preparation for audience reading should assure an enjoyable situation for both hearers and reader.

One teacher enhanced the pupils' understanding of their poems and their pleasure in sharing them by inviting all who knew any part of a poem to join her in saying it. A group of children dramatized the action and events of a short poem, adding incident and dialogue where necessary. In so doing they committed the poem to memory, and spoke it with enjoyment and conviction. Another group agreed to set aside time for reading aloud those poems which they particularly enjoyed. Careful preparation was made on the part of each reader to assure a competent presentation. Another group of children discussed possibilities for choral reading of poems, giving attention to meanings, mood, tone, and ways of speaking to make these clear to the hearer. This experience greatly aided in the development of reading skill, both silent and oral.

Provide for an attentive audience. An appreciative audience makes an important contribution to good oral reading. In part, this can be achieved by discussing with the children standards of good audience behavior. Sometimes at the end of a presentation the participants can be asked how the audience helped them. Sometimes an audience can evaluate itself. Situations when the class is invited to a program given by another room can be used for discussions of how guests should behave. Assembly programs offer other opportunities for consideration of audience behavior.

Some consideration needs to be given to the quality of the performance presented to an audience. Well-prepared performers, interesting and new material, and a reasonably short presentation have been suggested as aids in securing a successful presentation. At times a group has been helped to set better standards by a frank discussion of why the audience became restless.

Tension before an audience can be reduced if critical comments are not requested. When a small group has worked hard on a presentation, there will be ample opportunities for critical interactions among those directly involved. The larger audience can then confine its comments to questions on points of interest, statements about things especially well done, questions about how the group worked, contributions to general discussion from their own related experiences, and other types of participation which avoid direct criticism of the performers.

Help the shy child gain confidence. Even with an informal situation and a sympathetic audience, a shy child may have difficulty reading before others. There are many ways of giving support. It is often helpful to encourage participation in a small group first. Experiences in answering questions and reading short selections in an informal discussion group can provide an easy start. If the child is one of the poorer readers, it may be well to encourage him to begin by telling what he has read in his own words rather than by reading aloud. Thorough preparation when oral reading is undertaken will also help. On occasion, the teacher may work with the child alone in order to be sure that his performance before the group is successful. Easy materials and short selections often help.

In coming before the class as a whole, the shy child may first have a nonspeaking part, perhaps as one of a group—one of the seven dwarfs, one of the mischievous children in the family, or even one of a grove of trees whose sole responsibility is to sway in the wind. First oral attempts before the entire class may also be easier if the child is with others—reading part of a story, telling about one of several pictures, or reading one part of a report on a social-studies panel. Something to hold or point to can help—a picture one has drawn, a piece of science equipment, a chart, or the illustrations from a favorite book.

In a classroom where a relaxed and cooperative atmosphere has been developed, children can be helped to understand each other's problems and to give sympathetic help. One group promised not to look at a shy child as he spoke his first lines on a large stage so that they would not make him nervous. The child's delight in his success was no greater than that of his friends. Another group took care to give generous approval of each success of a child who was gradually overcoming oral-reading difficulties. A third group divided to form practice partners in such a way that good readers could help the poorer ones. In these atmospheres the shy youngster is not so hesitant to try his wings.

Supply ample opportunities for oral reading. An essential element in the development of skillful oral reading is a genuine need to share with others, whether it be a line or two to settle an argument or a favorite book. These oral-reading experiences do not represent an isolated expenditure of time since, in many cases, they help to culminate silent-reading experiences growing out of unit activities, provide outlets for creative-language experiences, or make it possible to share recreational reading. Many types of oral-reading activities are suggested in the reading units discussed in Chapter XI. Opportunities such as the following deserve consideration:

Opportunities for reading stories are found in: Sharing recreational reading with other groups; reading original stories developed through creative-writing experiences; planning a special program for another class; sharing appropriate stories as part of a holiday celebration.

Experiences with poetry can be secured through: Sharing poems during a poetry period; developing a program for other classes by means of a tape recorder; using poems as part of a Christmas program; reading favorite poems to other reading groups as choral-speaking presentations; reading original poetry; developing original choral-speaking presentations as part of the summary of a unit.

Oral reading related to dramatization can be encouraged through: Reading a story aloud as group members pantomime the action; reading parts of a story or a play as a reading-group activity; sharing a favorite story with other groups as a play, a radio performance, a television show; summarizing a social studies unit with a play.

Reading reports aloud is called for in: Reading current news articles; reading the minutes of a club meeting; reading individual or group reports as part of the summary of a social-studies unit; reading special announcements to other classes; sharing book reports during a library hour; reading aloud group plans for a special activity.

DEVELOPING MORE SKILLED APPROACHES TO WORD STUDY

Word recognition, meaning, and analysis are the three-fold emphases of the word-study program of the intermediate grades, just as they are in the primary grades. However, the relationships among them change for the child who has made typical progress. Words with unfamiliar meanings, which were carefully controlled in primary reading materials, appear in increasing number now. This heavier vocabulary load is occasioned not only by the new concepts of the various content fields but also by the greatly extended scope of the topics included in basal readers, the wide range of books available for recreational reading, and the many types of incidental reading done by older children. Whereas the task of learning to recognize a word at sight or to work out its pronunciation is, for a first-grader, rarely complicated by an unfamiliar meaning, the more skilled reader often finds his problem a combined one. Word-recognition techniques now serve mainly to help secure the instant recognition of words, by configuration and small clues, that makes for the skilled, rapid reading of the adult. Word-analysis skills, which become a gradual point of focus as primary children gain the reading background needed for the identification of word-parts, now are indispensable as the reader makes independent attacks on his varied reading problems.

All three of these areas call for planned activities in the intermediate grades. The reading tasks undertaken by older children require word-study skills that could not have been developed completely through the reading-matter of the primary grades. Furthermore, these more mature readers have the intellectual ability to understand technical aspects of the construction of the English language that would have served little purpose earlier.

In many classrooms, and particularly in fourth grades, the word-study problem will be complicated by the fact that some of the children will not have grasped the fundamentals of word analysis typically developed in primary grades. Immaturity, illness, moving from school to school, unfortunate experiences when the first steps toward word analysis were taken, and habits of relying too heavily on the general configuration of the word and on context clues may be among the causes. For these children, the word-study program will need to be begun at the level that represents their present accomplishment. This may mean using some of the procedures suggested in Chapter IX for work with primary children.

BUILDING WORD MEANINGS

Help children meet the word-meaning demands of daily reading experiences. The trends that characterize the growth of the primary child's stock of word meanings also characterize the growth of the vocabulary of the older child. New problems, too, can be identified as children face the increased vocabulary of intermediate-grade materials. First, the number of new terms continues to increase as children read about the far West, a trip to the moon, the animals of Africa, how to keep a simple budget, how to care for pets, or how to build an amateur radio set. Second, familiar words continue to take on new meanings. A period may be a punctuation mark or a time block in the day's schedule. A governor may be someone at the head of a government or a device to control the speed of a car. Third, a single meaning for a word continues to be enriched. A wagon may be a child's toy, something used by a farmer, a mode of conveyance in pioneer days, or a police car. Fourth, derivatives of familiar words begin to appear more frequently—care*ful*, care*less; mis*place, *re*place, place*ment; dis*cover, *un*cover, *re*cover. Fifth, many abstract terms begin to be used—*democratic, dictatorial, cooperative, sympathetic.* Sixth, because English is a living language, new terms are being coined. Some of these meet the needs of our changed social and scientific world, some are made popular by sports or other feature writers, some represent the gradual adoption of slang expressions—*telecast, blitz, orbit, O.K., a grounder.* Finally, as the maturing reader explores the daily paper he meets terms that have acquired emotional tones for advertising, propaganda, or other purposes—*drastically reduced, liquidate, un-American.* There may also exist the added problem of lack of the experience background that makes these new terms live. How does it feel to ride in a *covered wagon?* How tall would a *pyramid* be? Is our school ground larger or smaller than an *acre?* Does *democracy* mean more than merely taking a vote? What is it like to live in a *slum?* If we had *German, Japanese, Canadian* visitors, would they be different from ourselves?

Children grow in their grasp of new terminology partly through their wide reading, and partly through the sensitivity to new words that is developed in a stimulating classroom atmosphere. The teacher who helps children develop a rich vocabulary and a precise choice of words is, above everything else, alert to the day-by-day possibilities for vocabulary development in her room. Children can be helped to sense when one of their classmates has used a particularly apt expression or when their reading has introduced an unusual term. They can talk about words that are unfamiliar in a basal-reader story. After an excursion, new terminology can be listed and in some cases additional reading done to clarify concepts. Effective choice of words can be noted in creative writing. In oral-reading situations it is often helpful to check on the child's understanding of the meaning of a word that he is having difficulty pronouncing, since part of his pronunciation problem may lie in the fact that he is trying to read a word he has never heard before. "Tell it in your own words." "What do you think that means?" are useful checks. Children, too, can learn to listen for unfamiliar words in an oral report and to challenge the speaker if he seems to be using terminology of which he is unsure. Encouragement to see if one can get the meaning of the new term from the context, its root, or its prefix or suffix is stimulating. Children can be given special recognition when they use a recently learned term in their conversation or written work. Consistent use of the dictionary and the attitude of "Let's look it up" are other useful teaching aids. Occasional check tests built in the pattern of the typical vocabulary test may be used. Children may also help to decide which of a group of new terms are important enough that they should be added to the class spelling list. All the words that are part of a child's reading vocabulary will not, of course, become part of his writing or his active oral vocabulary. However, the general classroom atmosphere should be one that encourages interest in learning to use new words, not merely passive acceptance of meanings in a context setting.

Make special provision for the new vocabulary of the content fields. The problem of developing word meanings in the content fields differs from the general problem of vocabulary building in degree only.[4] Many of the techniques that have just been discussed will serve equally well for a unit of work planned around experiences in science, social studies, or arithmetic. However, the problem has several complicating factors:

1. New terminology in a content field is likely to be met in quantity. The words are needed in order to talk or write about the new topic at all.
2. These new words are likely to be key words, essential to a satisfactory grasp of the meaning of a passage.
3. If the child's experience background is limited—and it can hardly be anything else—the reader is unable to use his personal experience as an aid to meaning.
4. The word-analysis task, particularly of personal and place names, may be difficult.

[4] See Chapter XI for descriptions of typical problems of word meanings occurring in the materials of the content fields.

5. Even if materials are chosen carefully so as to present as few vocabulary difficulties as possible, the reader must still cope with new terms.

These special problems make it necessary, then, to give help with the words in content fields. How may such help be given effectively?

Suggestions for introducing new words ahead of time so as to simplify the problems of reading for information in a unit of work in a content field were given in Chapter XI. Classes can also participate in word-meaning activities as reading proceeds. Often the children help to extend a word list as they encounter new terms. One such list contained all the words that the children felt were especially important to Mexico. In another group, each child made his own glossary, with picture illustrations, of the words that most interested him. The children in one sixth grade made a picture dictionary of their most important words, small groups being responsible for a card with a clear picture, a written meaning, and the pronunciation key for each of the words on their list. A fourth grade made a pronunciation key of Spanish words learned in a study of Mexico and gained additional experience by putting the words in alphabetical order. The committee groups in another class agreed that as part of each report all special terms, with the proper pronunciation keys, would be written on the chalkboard so that they could be referred to as the report was being given. One science group prepared diagrams to illustrate a set of new terms. Another made labels for each object in a classroom display. All these activities help to keep new words before the children until they are thoroughly familiar with them. They also help the children to become sensitive to the need to expand their stock of word meanings.

Review activities can be of many sorts. In one social-studies group the children prepared a series of riddles about the people on whom they had reported. Members of the listening audience were to answer the question, "Who am I?" Another group varied this approach with "What am I" riddles about important places, buildings, and objects. One teacher provided interesting factual reviews by typing descriptions on one side of a card and the name of the person, object, or place on the other. Children with free time played with these cards in pairs, one child asking the questions. The game was to see how many correctly answered cards one could amass. Another class worked out a "Twenty Questions" type of review. One remedial group with special word-recognition difficulties worked out a Bingo game with some social-studies words. To have credit for one's Bingo, one had not only to recognize the words on one's chart, but to answer any informational question about them asked by a member of the group. The Bingo idea was worked out more elaborately by a fourth-grade teacher whose children needed special help with word meanings by putting the words on the cards for the players and then reading the definitions of the words to them. Simpler checks can be made by preparing vocabulary tests in multiple-choice or completion form as part of the final evaluation of a unit. The more ways in which a child can be helped to work with a new term in an interesting fashion, the more likely he is to make it his own.

Give special consideration to concept formation. In the matter of vocabulary building, it is particularly important to create a classroom environment which provides the concrete experiences, the visual aids, and the freedom of inquiry needed for the development of clear concepts. Many of the community resources discussed in Chapter XI can be helpful. Sometimes it takes only a simple comparison to clarify a concept. "A mile is about as far as from here to the post office." "Those trees would be about as tall as our building." "How many of us would it take altogether to weigh a ton—let's add up our weights and see." "How long would a whale be? Let's hold hands down the hall and see how many it would take to stretch from its head to its tail." Words are abstractions. The reality lies in the object; the actual place with its noises, odors, and sights; the living animal. Concepts become clearer when children can have firsthand experiences or, next best, can see a film, a picture, or a model.

Plan practice activities that keep interest in word meanings high. One of the problems of planning special practice activities to enrich word meanings is that of keeping interest high and avoiding routine assignments to look up the meanings of lists of words or to write out lists of unfamiliar words encountered in reading. Boring activities with words affect not only interest in new terms but often attitudes toward reading itself.

Special practice with word meanings can be of a work-type nature or it can be provided through short unit activities. Intermediate-graders can become much interested in studying word origins, in learning the history of place names or personal names, or in studying the special choice of words of a favorite author. Such short units can be independent of other activities or developed in relation to on-going projects. Creative-language experiences offer other opportunities to concentrate on effective use of words. Several kinds of work-type activities that can be planned as part of a unit of work have already been described. Other typical activities are given in the suggestions that follow:

Special short-term projects can focus on: Studying word origins and the history of interesting words; studying current school slang and its history; studying class first names or surnames and their origins or meanings; making a history of interesting place names in the community.

Special test situations can be set up by: Making simple crossword puzzles; playing anagrams; choosing the correct meaning for a word after reading it in a sentence context; seeing how many new meanings one can develop by adding prefixes and suffixes to given roots; taking multiple-choice or matching tests where one checks synonyms or antonyms; matching meanings in two sets of sentences illustrating different uses of a word.

Creative-language experiences can develop sensitivity to word meanings through: Making a class list of "Quotation Helpers" to replace the word *said* in writing stories; dramatizing a list of quotation helpers to show where each would be most appropriate; studying a basal-reader story to identify effective choice of words; listening to records and writing down descriptive phrases to convey one's impressions of the music.

DEVELOPING MATURE TECHNIQUES OF WORD RECOGNITION

Meet the word-recognition needs of daily reading activities. Recognizing a word by its general configuration is sometimes thought of as a technique used only in the primary grades. Although the mature reader should be able to work out the analysis of a word for himself, he, too, often uses instant recognition of a word from context and from obvious structural clues. Both rapid silent reading and skilled oral reading depend, in part, on the reader's ability to go ahead smoothly with few pauses for detailed word analysis. Most adult readers also have a stock of words—foreign place names, unusual personal names, unfamiliar technical terms—which they recognize by general configuration, but for which they find it difficult to give any adequate phonetic analysis. The intermediate-grade child has many of these typical adult needs for word-recognition skill. In addition, he has the particularly difficult problem of acquiring rapidly the vocabulary of the content fields.

Two general approaches used by primary teachers in building word recognition techniques are useful, with appropriate modification, for older children. One is to develop acquaintance with new words before they are met in context; the other is to provide many repetitions in varied settings until the child is thoroughly familiar with them. The middle-grade teacher may show a film about ancient Egypt to a group about to investigate the contributions of this area to modern civilization. The words *pyramid, Sphinx, Nile, hieroglyphics, lotus* and the like are heard, illustrated, and may be seen written as captions to pictures on the chalkboard. These words which will appear in later reading have thus become somewhat familiar to the group. Many subsequest contacts with words will help to build familiarity with their general configuration. Lists of new terms, special labels on exhibits or pictures, individual notebooks, and word games help to provide needed repetition. Care needs to be taken in all these situations to be sure that words so introduced and repeated are key words; that is, that they are essential to understanding, and are subsequently used with some frequency.

In the intermediate grades, the approach to the first pronunciation of a new word should be, as far as possible, through word analysis, since the ultimate aim is to help the child become independent in his recognition of new words. With the controlled vocabulary of a basal reader, it should not often be necessary to tell a child the pronunciation of new words, although immature fourth-graders may still need this help if the story contains many unfamiliar names or technical terms in an area in which the children's experience background is limited. Materials in the content fields may cause more difficulty. If only a few words seem likely to be unfamiliar, the first reading of material will not be seriously impeded if the children are encouraged to stop to work out the pronunciation of new words as they come to them. Since this first reading is almost always silent, the teacher is free to help individuals who are having undue difficulty. When it seems wise to present words likely to cause trouble ahead of the time at which the material is read, the use of word-analysis skills can be encouraged by asking the children to see how many words on the list they can pronounce for themselves. With proper nouns, particularly, this is not always a desirable time expenditure for children with limited word-analysis skills, but more skilled readers can be given many legitimate lessons in the interpretation of diacritical marks by being asked to use a pronunciation key placed on the chalkboard next to a list of new words, or to look up the words for themselves in a glossary or a dictionary.

In deciding how much help to give a child in the pronunciation of an unfamiliar word, his eventual use of the word needs to be kept in mind. A word that is likely to become part of a child's regular speaking and writing vocabulary, or one that presents word-analysis problems typical of those he will meet again, merits the time spent helping him to make a structural or phonetic analysis of it. On the other hand, a word that seems likely to have limited use, or presents a rare word-analysis problem may well be handled quickly by telling the child the pronunciation. Adjustments will also have to be made in the light of children's present word-analysis skills. Those who are still using primary techniques will need more help. Furthermore, the greater the gap between any child's general reading level and the difficulty level of the particular material he is trying to read, the more likely it is that he will need additional help with unfamiliar words.

Plan practice activities that focus on mature word-recognition techniques. When special work-type activities are needed to develop skill in word recognition, they should serve one of two purposes. They may provide the repetition needed to develop easy familiarity with new vocabulary; or they may serve to sharpen those word-analysis techniques that enable the reader to use context clues and large word elements, such as roots, prefixes, and suffixes, as an aid to quick recognition of unfamiliar terms. Ways of repeating new words are essentially the same as those that help to develop new word meanings through using the printed word in many settings and types of activities. Special practice to develop skill in rapid recognition of words by means of word-analysis clues should be given, for the most part, in exercises in which the reader can use context clues. Various word-card devices can help to demonstrate the word-analysis techniques that are the most useful, but the task facing the reader ultimately is to be able to recognize the word in context, not in an isolated list.

The following are activities that help to build word-recognition techniques. In addition, many of the activities suggested for developing word meanings and word-analysis skills also help with word recognition. Teachers should refer to these other sections as well. Activities for less skilled readers are found in Chapter IX.

Cincinnati Public Schools

Increased skill in word analysis comes with guided study.

Acquaintance with unfamiliar terms can be built through: Building a class list of new terms; labeling exhibits, diagrams, or pictures; writing reports or experience records using the new terms; taking matching or multiple-choice vocabulary tests;

learning to spell selected new terms; working with riddles and other games focusing on the new terms.

Ability to respond to key elements in words for rapid recognition can be developed through: Breaking compound words apart; or building compound words; building words by adding prefixes and suffixes to a given root; telling apart two similar words seen on cards or other tachistoscopic devices; telling which of two flashed words would end a given sentence correctly; filling in the correct words in blanks in a paragraph where only the key letters of the missing words have been supplied.

DEVELOPING ADVANCED WORD-ANALYSIS SKILLS

Identify the word-analysis skills needed by mature readers. Even less than in the primary grades is it possible to foresee exactly what word-analysis problems skillful readers will face in the vocabulary load of their widespread reading activities. However, a general picture of their problems can be secured by examining the kinds of new words the children are meeting. What are these words like? What difficulties are involved?

1. They are longer and call for working with two or more syllables.
2. They contain sound elements not common in the primary grades, such as the prefixes *pre, ante, trans, sur, ad, ex;* and suffixes such as *tion, ious, ful, ible, less, ance.*
3. They demand understanding of the meaning of prefix and suffix, and its function in changing the root to an adjective, a noun, or an adverb—*repeat, repetitive, repetition, repeatedly.*
4. They tend to carry unfamiliar meanings and to relate to concepts beyond the children's experience.
5. They generally are met in independent reading where skill in using a glossary or dictionary is essential if the reader is to pursue his task unhindered.

The exact problems faced by the children in a given classroom will need to be identified as they work. There are several ways of keeping a tally of where the greatest difficulties lie. In giving help during silent reading the teacher can jot down on a pad or on the chalkboard the words which cause trouble. This system makes it easier to underline syllables, to mark prefixes or suffixes, or in some other way to help the child to see key word-parts, and it also provides a list of the day's difficulties. Children working alone can be encouraged to write down difficult words and bring them to group sessions for help. As children try out their pronunciation skills on new words listed on the board for special study it is possible to make a record of the problems causing the most trouble. Sometimes difficulties in spelling give clues to unfamiliar sound elements. Children who are having the most trouble with word analysis may display an over-all weakness that suggests the need for systematic help with the word-parts usually learned in the primary grades. Out of such surveys should come a picture of the present status of the group —weaknesses where special help would be useful, points where incidental guidance is likely to be sufficient, or adeptness which suggests that a child is making satisfactory independent progress.

Encourage independence in daily reading activities. Since the ultimate aim of the word-analysis program is to help children become completely independent in their attack on new words, it is important that their experiences encourage independence as daily reading activities proceed. Because word-analysis techniques are interrelated both with word recognition and with the development of new meanings, a number of ways of building word-analysis skills were suggested in the two preceding sections. Whenever it does not interfere seriously with understanding, it is proposed that children be allowed to meet new words in context and to try to work out the pronunciation for themselves. When it seems desirable to present the new terms ahead of the reading, the suggestion is that children can be encouraged to see how much of the list they can pronounce without help and to use the pronunciation keys in dictionaries or glossaries. On-going reading activities can be used in other ways to foster an independent approach to new words. Oral-reading experiences in small groups prior to sharing a presentation with an audience can focus, in part, on word pronunciation. Sometimes reading partners can be given the responsibility of helping each other. Disagreements about how to pronounce words in a committee report can be settled by referring to a dictionary. Children reporting on current events can be held responsible for looking up unfamiliar words. Committee groups reporting on unit activities can be encouraged to give the audience special help with the pronunciation of difficult terms. Lists of spelling words can be studied so that word-analysis skills are stressed.

In helping children with word-analysis skills during on-going classroom activities, the teacher's responsibility is partly one of encouragement and partly one of giving whatever help seems to be needed at the moment. "Cover the end of that word and see if you don't know the rest of it." "I think you can get that one if you'll look it up." "This ends the same way as station. Now can you get it?" "This part is a small word you know. Does that help?" "Remember what we said an e on the end of a word often did?" "You're almost right but it has three syllables. You skipped the part in here." Much depends on the credit given to children when they succeed. Children can learn to compliment each other, to take pride in their use of the dictionary, and to give special credit to the reader who is just beginning to show progress if the teacher's attitude is one of enthusiasm and frank appraisal. "I'm proud of you, Irene, you got that all by yourself." "I don't think you'll need special help with many of these. Let's see if you can't figure them out." "This is a hard book, could we have someone who is a good reader volunteer to work with this group so as to help with the hard words?" "That's right, Jim. Tell us how you figured it out."

Correlate word-analysis activities with spelling. Poor spelling in the intermediate grades is sometimes explained by blaming poor word-analysis techniques. In actual fact, well-planned reading and spelling activities should supplement each other. Furthermore, spelling lessons often provide ideal settings for added experiences in word analysis, since they offer a purposeful opportunity to study the makeup of words.

Techniques suggested for learning to spell a word focus on correct pronunciation and careful attention to sounds and syllables. The following set of directions is illustrative of those given to older children in most spelling textbooks:[5]

1. Say the word, look closely at it as you say it and be sure to say all parts of the word distinctly.
2. Close your eyes and try to recall how the word looks, part by part, as you pronounce it in a whisper. Be sure to say all the parts carefully.
3. Open your eyes and look at the word again. Say it again distinctly as you look at it.
4. Close your eyes again and try to recall it, then open them and check again with the correct form of the word.
5. Write the word, saying it clearly to yourself as you write it.
6. Check the correct form to see if you wrote it correctly.

When this approach is used consistently, there are many opportunities to help children think about the proper analysis of a word.

Spelling activities can be used to build the habit of listening and looking for sounds and syllables. In one class the children worked as spelling partners, with a child who was good in word analysis assigned to help a child who was having trouble. In another, a group having trouble met regularly to work on spelling and word-analysis problems. One device that children enjoy is the dictation of a long, phonetically-easy word as a "bonus" word on the spelling list. Study of new words can be directed to elements helpful for word analysis. Children can be asked to list groups of words ending or beginning in the same sound. Prefixes and suffixes can be studied. Children can be encouraged to break words into syllables, to identify familiar roots, and to work out simple spelling and pronunciation rules. However, both in reading and in spelling children need to learn that all words do not follow rules. Here again, an approach that concentrates on significant pronunciation ele-

[5] Adapted from Arthur I. Gates and David H. Russell, *Diagnostic and Remedial Spelling Manual,* rev. ed. (New York: Teachers College, Columbia University, 1940), pp. 24-25.

ments can be helpful. Special attention can be given to letter combinations such as *ight, ough, tion*, for example, and children can be helped to see that it is important to look for combinations such as double letters and for relatively rare sound combinations, such as *eo* in *people*, and *ai* in *aisle*. Many of these activities will be planned by the teacher to meet the special needs of her class. Most spelling textbooks offer other possibilities for word-study exercises. These are often used most effectively if the teacher will choose from among the entire set of activities proposed for a given lesson a few that focus on needed word-analysis skills.

If word-analysis techniques are to operate effectively in spelling, it is important that spelling activities be planned so that children do not violate the word-analysis principles they are trying to learn. Studying words by spelling them aloud, one letter at a time, or by copying them a given number of times may break down the habit of thinking of sounds or syllables in writing a word. Approaches to sound elements sometimes suggested in spelling textbooks do not agree with the corresponding reading approach. Sound elements such as *ea, ie, oa* are treated as phonograms in reading. Occasionally in spelling exercises the child is asked to look for a "silent letter" in such words as br*e*ad, gr*e*at, rec*e*ive, bel*ie*ve. Teachers need, also, to use cautiously activities that ask children to fill in missing letters when these are written so as to break up a typical phonetic element, for example, *spe-l, c-arge*. Caution is also needed when a spelling exercise is so designed that the child need only read across the letters of the key word in the word list and then write a missing letter or syllable without thinking of pronunciation. Good word-analysis techniques are essentially the same for reading and spelling. It is important to plan so that the activities in these two fields reinforce each other.

Plan practice activities that assure independence in word analysis. There are many sources of practice activities in word analysis. Workbooks to accompany basal-reader series are replete with exercises. Sets of workbooks focused entirely on word-study skills are available. Selected activities in spelling textbooks have also been mentioned. Many of these exercises are readily adaptable to the particular word-study problems of a group.

Because the reader's eventual task is to be able to pronounce the word in its contextual setting, practice activities should include much work with words in context. Short work-type activities that call for the child to use context clues can be developed by asking him to complete a rhyme, to choose the word that correctly answers a riddle, to choose the word that correctly answers a question based on a short paragraph, or to determine the meaning of a compound word from its use in a paragraph and its component parts.

Various types of games and other activities with lists of words can also have value, particularly for children who need inducements to participate in extended word-analysis experiences. Many of the games and similar devices appropriate for primary children can be adapted to the needs of better readers by varying the difficulty of the words being used. In choosing or preparing such activities, it is just as important as it is in the primary grades to appraise the amount of actual reading experience provided for the children in proportion to the amount of time it takes to prepare the exercise, and the number of extraneous activities in which the children engage.

The skilled reader needs to make efficient word-analysis skills his own as rapidly as possible. This means that he needs to be helped to become conscious of what he is doing. Word-analysis activities lose much of their value if they are not discussed in group situations so that children can think about what they are learning, compare different ways of working out words, and develop simple pronunciation rules.

Typical activities that help in developing word-analysis skills are given below. Teachers should also refer to the activities suggested for primary children in Chapter IX. Many of these are easily adaptable for more skilled readers.

Practice with sounds can be secured through: Completing rhymes; trying to pronounce all the words on a word wheel; trying to spell an unfamiliar word by listening to its sound elements; making up rhymes that stress a given sound; making special studies of prefixes, suffixes, or roots; choosing the correct word to complete a sentence or answer a riddle; studying spelling words in order to note unfamiliar sound elements.

Work with syllables can be given through: Looking up the pronunciation of a list of words needed or a unit in a content field; completing exaggerated rhymes where the number of syllables needed in the missing word is obvious; listening for the syllables in order to spell an unfamiliar word that is phonetically easy; studying a spelling word so as to identify its syllables; trying to count the syllables in a word by pronouncing it very distinctly.

Experience with roots, prefixes, and suffixes can be secured through: Helping to develop a short unit on word origins; building compound words and using them in a sentence to test their meanings; breaking apart lists of compound words; figuring out the meaning of compound words from their parts; trying to give meanings of words from the root and the context; seeing how many words one can make by adding prefixes or suffixes to a given word, and telling the meanings; making a list of opposites by adding a prefix such as *un* to a given list of words.

DEVELOPING SKILL IN USING THE DICTIONARY

Survey the needs for dictionary usage of intermediate-grade children. Learning to use the dictionary is largely an intermediate-grade problem. Primary children are likely to become acquainted with a picture dictionary; second- and third-graders may have some experience in putting words in alphabetical order; but extensive dictionary use comes as children face a wider vocabulary load and become better able to spell the words they want to look up. One of the first important early uses of the dictionary is in looking up the meanings of words. Soon it becomes a resource for checking on spelling. As children become able to use diacritical marks a dictionary also becomes an aid to pronunciation. Gradually there may also be a certain amount of use of special features—pictures; lists of proper names; lists of abbreviations; information about roots, prefixes, or suffixes.

Because of the special format of a dictionary, teaching children to use it calls for the development of a number of new techniques. They must be able to place words in alphabetical order. Habitual use of guide words, while not essential, makes for much greater efficiency. Readers must also be able to choose, from three or four definitions, the one that is appropriate.

This involves choosing between meanings given to a word used as different parts of speech. If the word is a verb, the seeker is obliged to understand that the infinitive phrase usually given must be changed to the tense and form of the verb required in the sentence in question. In the sentence, "He *staked* his life upon the quality of his boat," the child who knows the word "stake" only in his listening and speaking vocabulary as a kind of sharp stick must do the following things: (1) Locate the word. (2) Note the pronunciation, using the key words, if necessary. (3) Change the infinitive form, *to wager*, given as one of the definitions, to the appropriate past tense, since "He to wager his life" makes no sense. (4) Finally, if *wager* is not a familiar word, he may turn to a definition of *wager* to discover that it means "to bet." Now the reader may well say, "He betted his life," only to be told that "bet" is also the past tense. These sequential steps with related problems suggest that some needs can be anticipated, and directed helpful experiences used to develop necessary skills. Other problems can probably be best handled in the settings in which they occur.

Skillful use of the dictionary can be impeded by lack of other reading skills. Poor spellers are hampered. Children who cannot follow the gist of a paragraph often cannot choose an appropriate meaning. Those with limited experience background sometimes find meanings phrased in terms too difficult for them, unless the definition is accompanied by a picture or a concrete illustration. A meager word-recognition vocabulary can also cause trouble if the meaning of a given word is phrased in terms equally unfamiliar. Because of the difficulties caused by lack of these related skills, it is sometimes desirable to start dictionary work with the glossary in a basal reader or in a speller where the total problem may be less complicated. A primary picture dictionary or a simplified beginners' dictionary may be of help in the first dictionary work of a fourth grade. Habitual use of the dictionary is not likely to develop until children have the related skills to handle it easily.

Make use of classroom opportunities for dictionary usage. Special work-type exercises will do little to build good habits of dictionary usage if the teacher does not take pains to encourage it in daily classroom activities. Routine assignments, such as writing the dictionary meanings of a list of spelling words whether one already knows them or not, copying the dictionary pronunciation keys for a list of hard words, or looking up the syllabication of lists of words, should be avoided. Children need to learn to turn to the dictionary when there is a genuine problem. Dictionaries need to be available, if not in every desk at least in sufficient numbers that several children can work at one time. Even such a simple technique as placing dictionaries where they are easy to reach and in a place where it is convenient to work for a few minutes can be helpful.

Provide the special practice needed to develop efficient dictionary skills. Practice with the dictionary should come, in part, as children work with the actual books. When it is not possible to put one in the hands of each child, they may work in pairs, or groups may take turns. Some activities can be planned by using the smaller dictionaries in basal readers or in spellers which are often more readily available to every member of the class. Work-type exercises focused on such problems as learning to use alphabetical order can be set up by placing practice lists on the chalkboard. More elaborate practice sheets can be prepared by hectographing or mimeographing a sample of part of a dictionary page. Some children's dictionaries contain sets of special exercises designed to help children use them better. A basic guide in planning experiences with dictionary skills, as it is with other types of practice activities, is to provide exercises which focus as directly as possible on the type of skill the child will actually be using in solving a real problem. Among the activities that can be of help are the following:

Practice in choosing correct meanings can be secured through: Telling which of several meanings will best fit into a given sentence; trying to give sentences which use each of the meanings of a given word; matching several meanings for the same word with sentences using the word in various ways; deciding which of several meanings is correct for a word encountered in classroom reading.

Ability to use diacritical marks can be developed through: Marking the long and short vowels in a list of familiar words; putting in the accents correctly after pronouncing a list of familiar words; looking up the pronunciation of unfamiliar words; making a simple pronouncing key for a list of important classroom terms.

Skill with alphabetical order and guide words can be developed through: Placing lists of words of varying degrees of difficulty in alphabetical order; seeing how close one can come to opening a dictionary at a given letter; telling which letter comes before, after, or between given letters; telling which of several pairs of guide words would be used to look up each of a list of words; seeing how fast one can find a given word by using the dictionary guide words; looking up a given word and telling what guide words it was between.

Acquaintance with other aspects of the dictionary can be secured through: Spending a class discussion period examining the way in which a dictionary is made up; looking up the meanings of prefixes, roots, and suffixes; discussing the use of pictures or other aids as they bear on a classroom problem that took the child to the dictionary.

PROVIDING FOR EFFICIENT REFERENCE TECHNIQUES

Since many of the problems of effective use of informational materials must be solved as classroom activities develop day by day, suggestions, both of types of problems and of ways of working with children, were included in Chapter XI. The discussions that take place as purposes are clarified for a new unit and plans are laid for the reading that needs to be done, and the individual and group guidance that is provided as the unit develops, are at the heart of the activities that build effective reference techniques. These daily experiences are the more valuable because children are reading for purposes that are important to them and learning ways of adjusting their study techniques to real problems. Specially planned practice activities can serve to give intensive experience with new techniques and can help to focus discussion sharply on specific problems. This section suggests ways of providing this additional practice for three groups of reference techniques— problems of reading informational materials in the content fields; problems of locating information; and problems of outlining, summarizing, and note-taking. Among the suggested activities will be found some that can be developed as work-type experiences and others that are new ways of using classroom experiences to develop specific reference skills.

PROVIDING SPECIAL PRACTICE FOR EFFECTIVE READING IN THE CONTENT FIELDS

Identify the reading demands being made by the materials in the individual classroom. A general description of the types of problems encountered in the reading matter of the content fields was given in Chapter XI. Each teacher has to decide the exact ways in which these problems are being faced by her class. Such questions as the following may help in uncovering the problems to be solved, and in suggesting first steps in helping children as they encounter various kinds of reading materials in the content fields.

1. How are the children expected to use these materials?
2. What difficulties do these materials offer in terminology, concepts, format, visual aids, writing style?
3. What range of reading skills exists within the class group?
4. Are these pupils in possession of adequate word-analysis techniques, or will further help be needed?
5. How will these children use maps, graphs, pictures, diagrams, illustrations?
6. How efficient are these children as they try to locate answers to an easy set of questions?

With a picture of the present status of her group and the types of materials they are going to have to read, the teacher is able to plan how to give them special help.

Provide practice in reading materials in the content fields in the light of specific needs. One important over-all solution to the problems of reading informational materials is to adjust the reading task to the child's present ability. A typical fourth-grade reader will not be expected to read as widely as a sixth-grader. The questions he tries to answer will be less complicated. The material he uses will be more simply written. Then, too, the amount of help given to individuals and groups can be adjusted to the demands of the special problem. Ways of making these adjustments were outlined in Chapter XI.

Certain problems may well be the center of attention for several days for a group or for the entire class. In one class, need for help arose because of careless reading of arithmetic problems. The children took their textbooks and studied selected problems together, talking about why it was important to read carefully, and what to look for. Reading errors that had been common in a previous series of exercises were used as a basis for the discussion. Then the children went on to some special reading activities—telling what the problem asked them to find; telling whether the final answer would be larger or smaller than the original numbers, and why; making special lists of key words that usually indicated subtraction, addition, multiplication, division; estimating what the final answer would be, and telling why; telling what processes would be needed to solve the problem, and why. Some of these activities were done orally in class and some were carried out as work-type experiences planned in multiple-choice and true-false form.

Problems of securing information from graphs were tackled by the children in one sixth grade who discovered that some of the material they needed was presented in three or four simple but unfamiliar graph forms. Few of the children had much experience in interpreting material of this kind. In this situation the entire class worked together. The children discussed the purposes of graphs and how they are constructed. Two of the graphs from the reading material were placed on the chalkboard so that all might examine them together. After the children felt they knew how to read a graph, they went back to the context and tried to interpret it in the light of the graph. As they used different textbooks, they discovered that the same information in a graph could be evaluated differently by different writers, and learned more about interpreting specific information in its broader setting. This study, which began as a problem of understanding the visual aids in a specific piece of material, developed into a broader study of graphs through parallel arithmetic experiences. At this point arithmetic textbooks became a new resource, and the children eventually did several small school and community surveys on problems that interested them and presented their information in charts and graphs.

In a fourth grade, a special project developed the first time the children began to make extensive use of maps. This was a relatively new experience to many in the group. Parallel to other reading activities in social studies for two weeks ran a study of types of maps. These were selected so as to pose problems typical of those the children were meeting in their reading. They learned the difference between a political and a physical map. They worked with various types of legends and learned how to find items such as rivers, mountains, and important cities. A trip to a tall building in their city helped them get a picture of how a countryside actually looks from a distance. After this visit they made their own map of their neighborhood and developed their own legend. This group also spent a little time thinking about the difference between maps and globes. This unit by no means taught these children all they would eventually need to know about maps. It aroused their interest and gave them certain basic techniques that served their present purposes. As the year went on, new problems with maps were solved as they arose.

Another class learned how to use authentic pictures effectively through a unit planned to help other children in the school develop interest in visiting the zoo. The children in this class had little difficulty reading typical reference materials, but they wanted more information about the appearance of some of the animals, and they found it in a series of large color photographs. Here the information had to be secured by reading a rather meager caption and then examining the photograph for details. At first the children were baffled. Their reports tended to contain only summaries of what they found in the captions, and their questions indicated that much more information was needed. The teacher raised the problem of how effectively they were using the pictures. First it was pointed out that the pictures were authentic and could be trusted. Next the children were helped to take the accompanying captions apart, phrase by phrase, looking at the picture to see what each phrase meant. Then they tried to work out together a comprehensive statement taking in both what they read and what they saw. After this day of class discussion, each small group went back to work on its particular set of pictures. The teacher followed the lesson by helping one group at a time.

In a sense, all the methods that have been suggested in preceding sections for helping to develop better reading skills also contribute to the child's ability to handle the materials of the content fields. When special practice activities are needed for a problem occasioned by the style or format of particular materials, they will be most effective if they are built around the same type of material and make the same type of reading demands as those made by the classroom situation in which the original problem arose. The amount of material in any one exercise needs to be long enough to pose a genuine reading problem, but short enough to allow practice with several questions in one work period. Workbooks accompanying basal readers usually contain short selections of typical arithmetic, science, health, and social-science materials. Children's newspapers and magazines often have usable articles, sometimes accompanied by excellent test questions. Short two- or three-paragraph selections can be mimeographed. Often a short selection from the regular textbook can be used with test questions mimeographed or written on the chalkboard. When the problem is one of learning to use particular aspects of format, such as section headings or summaries, a selection in the textbook itself is by far the most effective basis for practice. The type of question raised about these passages can vary with the particular skill that needs to be developed—choosing correct information; reading numbers accurately in an arithmetic problem or telling what one is asked to find; responding to precise terminology in science; distinguishing fact from fiction in a supplementary book. Completion, short answer, multiple-choice, true-false, and matching forms of test questions are all useful.

Activities for interpreting graphs, maps, and other visual aids can be developed by asking questions based on textbook materials. This is also an area where typical intermediate-grade workbook materials and tests of study skills suggest many types of activities. Materials for practice can also be mimeographed for children. Much additional helpful experience can be given through the illustrative materials produced by members of the group —maps on which they are at work, charts they are making of their reading progress, diagrams they are developing to illustrate a committee report.

The suggestions that follow include ways of helping children learn to work with different types of material, and methods of giving experience with visual aids and with special aspects of format. Special activities for vocabulary development were included in the preceding section on word study.

Ways of adjusting reading techniques to special purposes can be learned through:
Answering a variety of questions on a set of arithmetic problems—which of the

following did the problem ask you to find, will your answer be larger or smaller, which of the following processes will you use; answering questions calling for ability to read carefully the materials in a science text—putting the directions for an experiment in proper order, answering questions about diagrams or charts, preparing lists of special terms or checking special definitions; answering a series of questions on a social-studies assignment calling for details or for the general sequence of events; checking a series of statements in terms of whether they help or do not help with a problem; checking a series of statements in terms of whether they are proven true in the text; choosing which of a series of paragraphs bears on a specific problem.

Experience with visual aids can be secured through: Answering a series of simple questions calling for interpretation of symbols on a map common to the group; sharing in the preparation of a class map of the city, the school ground, the state; writing answers to questions developed around a graph in common use; preparing a graph using data collected in a class project; comparing the values of several types of graphs used in familiar material; telling as much as one can about an event from a bulletin-board picture; reading daily weather charts; preparing a class weather chart; preparing a graph of one's progress in reading speed, spelling test scores, or arithmetic marks.

Ability to use special aspects of format such as section and paragraph headings can be developed by: Seeing how rapidly one can locate a special topic or piece of information in a textbook or basal-reader story by using chapter or section headings; predicting whether a chapter will be of help on a problem by reading the chapter summary; testing the section headings in a story as possible bases for scenes in a play; discussing the style in which special examples are written in an arithmetic or a language textbook; identifying the devices used in a textbook to present rules, illustrations, or other special types of information.

IMPROVING ABILITY TO LOCATE INFORMATION

Identify the skills involved in locating information. Problems of locating information were identified in Chapter XI as centering around the use of such aids as tables of contents and indexes; knowledge of such standard reference books as encyclopedias, atlases, and *The World Almanac;* and ability to use the library. Just how these problems will arise in particular classrooms depends upon the materials the children are actually using. The skills needed in locating information may be identified in three areas; first, those relating to familiarity with reference sources; second, those relating to the format of reference books; and third, those relating to selecting key words and topics in order to find what is wanted. Specific questions may be helpful in noting these abilities more exactly:

1. What reference sources are familiar to the group? Can they use each efficiently?

2. Do pupils know how to use guide words? cross references?
3. Are pupils familiar with the position and purpose of items of a bibliographical entry?
4. Do pupils know how to use the author, topic, and title cards of a library card file?
5. Are the children versatile in choosing topics for locating information? If "farming" is not helpful as a key word, can they move on to "agriculture" or "crops?"

Just as all reading skills start very simply and gradually become more complex, so do reference skills. Many technical refinements may not be learned until college or graduate school. The teacher needs to help the children learn whatever techniques they require to be efficient with the problem at hand. As more complicated aspects of the same skill are needed, new help can be given.

Make sure the child has related skills important for locating information. Inadequate reading skills can block the effective location of information in many ways. One major hindrance may be the child's general reading level. Much progress has been made in the writing of easy reference books for children. However, many children will still have difficulty in finding easy materials on topics of interest. Relatively more efficient use of typical reference books will be made by skillful readers. Another skill, difficult for many children, is that of defining exactly what questions they are trying to answer. This calls for all the teaching techniques related to helping children set up purposes, clarify problems, and learn how to make critical evaluations that have been discussed in preceding sections of this chapter and in Chapter XI. In some cases, it may also be important to build general experience background, and, in some, to help a group develop a more extensive stock of word meanings. The more the reader knows about an area, the more likely he is to be able to suggest key topics for reference purposes. Any technique that develops depth of insight into a problem is likely to help in developing skill in independent location of materials.

Provide practice in locating information in the light of specific needs. Many of the specific skills required to locate information lend themselves well to work-type exercises. Again, the most effective work-type activities are those that teach the child how to use the materials in his own classroom. Acquaintance with the general contributions of different types of reference books, particularly, is best built as the child tries to use the books to solve a problem. Often the actual encyclopedia, index, or table of contents that the children are using regularly is the best source of practice. Commercially prepared workbook exercises and mimeographed sheets that reproduce sample items from indexes or tables of contents are also helpful. Librarians can sometimes supply models of catalog cards suitable for group study.

Elementary grade children take a trip to learn how books are made, and gain a new appreciation for the importance of these sources for their own learning.

Special questions based on these practice materials can be developed in a variety of completion and short-answer forms. As nearly as possible they need to be representative of the sort of question the child will have to answer as he uses reference materials from day to day. Since it is important for the child to think about why he chose the book or topic he did, it is particularly helpful to plan practice sessions so that there is time to discuss procedures used, to appraise bases for choices, and to decide where one would turn next if one does not find all the information one needs.

Identifying key words is needed for: Choosing from three possible answers the word most likely to be helpful in looking up the answer to a question; naming the topics under which the answer to a series of questions would most likely appear; checking a given problem in an index and reporting the key words under which it is listed; underlining, for a series of proper names, the part that would be the key word—United States, John Paul Jones, British Empire, Santa Fe Railroad.

Using an index is called for in: Locating the page on which one would find a list of topics and subtopics phrased in the same way they appear in the index; a list phrased differently from the way they appear in the index; placing a list of topics from the index in alphabetical order; telling how many pages in the book contain references to a topic area; going from the index of one's text to the pages indicated to decide which reference actually provides the needed help; telling which topic in an index would be most appropriate for locating a specific piece of information.

Using a table of contents can be learned through: Seeing how quickly one can find a special story in the basal reader; checking the tables of contents of several books to list the chapters available as references for a given topic; estimating from a table of contents how many pages are likely to be devoted to a given topic; examining a new book and predicting its probable nature from the table of contents; taking a new book and listing all the things one can find out about it from a table of contents.

Ability to choose among standard reference materials is developed through: Indicating which of a list of texts will answer a series of questions; finding an article in a classroom encyclopedia and answering simple questions based on it; comparing several classroom reference texts and listing the special uses of each; starting with a given topic in an encyclopedia and following the cross-reference suggestions; providing a bibliography of available materials for one's committee to use; studying and reporting on the parts of the daily paper as background for publishing a class paper.

Skill in using a library can be developed through: Answering completion or multiple-choice questions about a sample library call card; choosing which of two or three suggested topics would be most helpful in locating information to answer a list of questions; keeping a simple bibliography of the references used during a unit activity; seeing how many titles one can find by one's favorite author, or about one's favorite topic; locating classroom materials in a classroom card file or school materials file; helping to set up a simple file of classroom materials; serving as librarian for the class library.

DEVELOPING SKILLS IN OUTLINING, SUMMARIZING, AND NOTE-TAKING

Identify the skills involved in making written records of what is read. Outlining, summarizing, and note-taking go on in relation to a specific problem. In providing special practice it is important to give attention to the immediate task being faced by the reader. This is particularly true of note-taking where the usefulness of the notes depends largely on their bearing on the problem at hand. Outlines and summaries, while they may in some cases give the sense of the total selection, more often are developed to meet a special need. It is almost impossible to supply the reader with a standard formula that will produce effective notes, summaries, or outlines for all situations.

Note-taking, outlining, and summarizing all require the reader to put what he has read into his own words. This is often a difficult task. Fourth-graders will do well if they are able to give in logical order the four or five main points of an outline. Their summaries are likely to be simple, and their notes are likely to be a series of statements of fact centered around one or two very definite problems. More mature readers should be able to identify the subpoints in an outline. Their summaries should show greater ability to distinguish between important points and unnecessary details. They should be able to make a series of notes bearing more directly on the subpoints of a complex problem. Furthermore, they should begin to show more versatility in attack—better ability to judge when full notes are needed and when a brief record is sufficient, when many details should be included in a summary and when only main points are needed, and how complete an outline should be.

Make sure the child has related skills important for making written records of what is read. When a child seems to be having unusual difficulty making an outline or summary or taking adequate notes, several areas will bear further investigation. As indicated in Chapter XI, a first check may well be upon the child's conception of what he is looking for. Vague purposes usually result in vague reporting. A second check should be on the difficulty of the material. Even a competent reader is likely to come to unfounded conclusions, or to resort to copying or to paraphrasing the words of the book, if its terminology or the strangeness of its concepts makes him uncertain as to what it actually means. Lack of comprehension is often betrayed by copying meaningless sentence fragments, or by misquotations, transpositions, or omissions that destroy the meaning. It is important, also, to look at the child's general reading skills. Outlining and summarizing, particularly, call for ability to follow the gist of a paragraph or a longer passage and to see details in their proper relationship. Note-taking adds the task of selecting details appropriate for the problem at hand. The job of reporting what has been read in written form, whether it be an outline, a summary, or a set of notes, is a difficult one. Foundation skills can be laid in the elementary grades, but proficiency is not likely to be developed before high school or college.

Provide practice that calls for written expression. Because the problems of note-taking, outlining, and summarizing are closely related to the child's on-going reading experiences, much of the help he receives should come through the type of day-by-day guidance discussed in Chapter XI. Sometimes a special problem can be made the center of several days of intensive work. In one fifth grade with exceptionally strong reading skill, the teacher developed note-taking skills through a study of pioneer life. This class eventually used every resource book in the room and brought many items from home. The first notes were encyclopedic. This became apparent during the first day's work as the teacher checked the progress of each group. The note-taking problem was raised with the entire class at the beginning of the next work period. Under the teacher's guidance the children evaluated some of their notes in the light of their original plans. It was agreed that too little attention was being paid to the purpose for which they read. One child pointed out that he didn't know exactly what his committee was looking for. Someone suggested that committees should have raised more definite questions before they began to read. Some groups did have lists of questions, but they were in the secretaries' notebooks and were not being used. As a result of the discussion, each group drew up a specific list of *Things to Look For*. The teacher helped to appraise each list as she visited the groups in turn. After the lists were checked, they were printed on large sheets of paper and pasted on cardboard so that they could be propped up and studied as the groups worked. One more evaluation period was devoted to reports on whether the lists were helping and to a discussion of other note-taking problems that were still causing trouble for the class as a whole. From this point on, the teacher gave individual help as needed.

Special practice activities should be planned so that the child is helped to think about the purposes his notes or outlines are going to serve. In most cases, the child should have the experience of writing his answers, since one of the skills he needs to learn is that of putting what he has read into his own words. Any short, clearly written story or piece of informational material can serve as a basis for practice. Single paragraphs can sometimes be used for purposes of summarizing but, since the reader is trying to learn how to report on several points in relationship, a short article with several paragraphs is often more useful. Many of the shorter basal-reader selections can be used effectively. Children will have a better opportunity to concentrate on the desired note-taking or outlining skills if they are working with relatively easy material so that lack of related reading skills does not get in the way. Reasonably high interest value in the materials being used also helps.

The difficulty of the note-taking or summarizing task can be varied by the phrasing of the assignment. Listing the four main points in a story is simpler than listing subpoints under each. Filling in one missing subpoint is easier than filling in all of them. Telling in one sentence the most important fact in a paragraph is easier than trying to include subpoints in a three- or four-sentence summary. Often it is helpful to work through several activities with the children as a group so that they can discuss the basis for the points they have chosen and the teacher can help to develop insights into what makes for an effective outline, summary, or set of notes. The following suggest possible types of activities to use for practice.

Skill in outlining is needed for: Filling in two or three points missing in a four- or five-point outline; filling in one or more subpoints in a partially finished outline; filling in completely an outline where only the framework of numbered points is given as a guide; helping group a series of questions, suggested by the class for the development of a unit, into three or four main topics; finding topic sentences in a series of easy paragraphs; writing an outline of a clear article by giving the topic sentence of each paragraph; matching a series of topic sentences with the correct paragraphs; rearranging a series of topic sentences into the original organization of the story; reading a basal-reader story and dividing it into acts and scenes for a play.

Ability to make a summary is called for in: Writing a brief review of a recreational book; taking part in a group discussion of what points to include in a class report; preparing a summary of a basal-reader story by writing one clear sentence to give the gist of each paragraph; giving the main idea of a passage by looking for the topic sentence in each paragraph; rearranging a set of sentences so that they summarize the steps in a process or a sequence of events in the correct order.

Note-taking skills can be developed through: Taking notes with other members of the class on an agreed-upon topic and discussing why each member included the points he did; discussing what makes for good notes; writing in one's own words the gist of information located; discussing strengths and weaknesses of the notes taken by various group members as they are pooled to prepare a report; taking notes on an oral report given by another group and then comparing them with those of other class members; discussing how to take brief notes on an excursion.

SOME QUESTIONS TO THINK ABOUT IN APPRAISING SPECIAL PRACTICE ACTIVITIES IN THE INTERMEDIATE GRADES

1.   Are practice activities planned so that they supplement and reinforce the experiences provided by regular classroom experiences?

2.   Are practice activities based on diagnostic evidence of the types of related skills that are needed?

3.   Do children understand the purpose for the practice and the skills they are trying to develop?

4.   Is the amount of practice adjusted to the needs of individual children?

5.   Is the type of practice exercise such that it calls for purposeful, thoughtful reading on the part of the child?

6.   Are practice activities planned so that children learn skills in the way in which they will actually use them later?

SUGGESTIONS FOR FURTHER READING

IMPROVING COMPREHENSION

Bond, Guy L., and Wagner, Eva Bond. *Teaching the Child to Read*. Third Edition, Chapter 11. New York: The Macmillan Company, 1960. 416 pp.

Burton, William H. *Reading in Child Development*. Chapter 9. Indianapolis: The Bobbs-Merrill Company, 1956. 608 pp.

Dawson, Mildred A., and Bamman, Henry A. *Fundamentals of Basic Reading Instruction*. Chapter 10. New York: Longmans, Green and Company, 1959. 304 pp.

Gates, Arthur I. *The Improvement of Reading*. Third Edition, Chapter 15. New York: The Macmillan Company, 1947. 657 pp.

Heilman, Arthur W. *Teaching Reading*. Chapter 9. Columbus, Ohio: Charles E. Merrill Books, Inc., 1961. 465 pp.

Hester, Kathleen B. *Teaching Every Child to Read*. Chapters 12, 15. New York: Harper and Brothers, 1955. 416 pp.

Hildreth, Gertrude. *Teaching Reading*. Chapter 19. New York: Henry Holt and Company, 1958. 612 pp.

Preston, Ralph C. *Teaching Study Habits and Skills*. New York: Rinehart and Company, Inc., 1959. 55 pp.

Russell, David H. *Children Learn to Read*. Second Edition, Chapters 11, 14. Boston: Ginn and Company, 1961. 612 pp.

Sochor, Elona. *Critical Reading, An Introduction*. Champaign, Illinois: The National Council of Teachers of English, 1959. 37 pp.

Smith, Henry P., and Dechant, Emerald V. *Psychology in Teaching Reading*. Chapter 8. Englewood Cliffs, New Jersey: Prentice-Hall, 1961. 470 pp.

Tinker, Miles A., and McCullough, Constance M. *Teaching Elementary Reading*. Second Edition. Chapters 8, 9. New York: Appleton-Century-Crofts, Inc., 1962. 615 pp.

DEVELOPING EFFECTIVE READING RATE

DeBoer, John J., and Dallmann, Martha. *The Teaching of Reading*. Chapters 8A, 8B. New York: Holt, Rinehart and Winston, 1960. 360 pp.

Figurel, J. Allen (Editor). *Changing Concepts of Reading Instruction*. International Reading Association Conference Proceedings, pp. 214-230. New York: Scholastic Magazines, 1961. 292 pp.

Harris, Albert J. *How to Increase Reading Ability*. Fourth Edition, Chapter 18. New York: Longmans, Green and Company, 1961. 624 pp.

Smith, Henry P., and Dechant, Emerald V. *Psychology in Teaching Reading*, pp. 224-236. Englewood Cliffs, New Jersey: Prentice-Hall, 1961. 470 pp.

DEVELOPING·SKILL IN ORAL READING

Burton, William H. *Reading in Child Development*. Chapter 10. Indianapolis: The Bobbs-Merrill Company, 1956. 608 pp.

Dawson, Mildred A., and Bamman, Henry A. *Fundamentals of Basic Reading Instruction*. Chapter 9. New York: Longmans, Green and Company, 1959. 304 pp.

DeBoer, John J., and Dallmann, Martha. *The Teaching of Reading*. Chapters 10A, 10B. New York: Holt. Rinehart and Winston, 1960. 360 pp.

Durrell, Donald D. *Improving Reading Instruction.* Chapter 8. Yonkers-on-Hudson, New York: World Book Company, 1956. 402 pp.

Gray, Lillian, and Reese, Dora. *Teaching Children to Read.* Second Edition, pp. 241-246. New York: The Ronald Press Company, 1957. 475 pp.

Ogilvie, Mardel. *Speech in the Elementary School.* Chapter 4. New York: McGraw-Hill Book Company, 1954. 318 pp.

Pronovost, Wilbert, and Kingman, Louise. *The Teaching of Speaking and Listening in the Elementary School.* Chapter 6. New York: Longmans, Green and Company, 1959. 338 pp.

DEVELOPING MATURE WORD-STUDY TECHNIQUES

Betts, Emmett A. *Foundations of Reading Instruction.* Chapter 24. New York: American Book Company, 1957. 757 pp.

Deighton, Lee C. *Vocabulary Development in the Classroom.* New York: Bureau of Publications, Teachers College, Columbia University, 1959. 62 pp.

Dolch, Edward W. *Better Spelling.* Champaign, Illinois: The Garrard Press, 1942. 270 pp.

Durrell, Donald D. *Improving Reading Instruction.* Chapter 12. Yonkers-on-Hudson, New York: World Book Company, 1956. 402 pp.

Fitzgerald, James A. *The Teaching of Spelling.* Milwaukee: The Bruce Publishing Company, 1951. 233 pp.

Gates, Arthur I., and Russell, David H. *Diagnostic and Remedial Spelling Manual.* Revised Edition. New York: Teachers College, Columbia University, 1940. 50 pp.

Gray, William S. *On Their Own in Reading.* Revised Edition, Chapter 7. Chicago: Scott, Foresman and Company, 1960. 248 pp.

Harris, Albert J., *op. cit.,* pp. 350-355; 396-422.

Hester, Kathleen B., *op. cit.,* Chapter 11.

Hildreth, Gertrude. *Teaching Reading.* Chapter 20. New York: Henry Holt and Company, 1958. 611 pp.

———. *Teaching Spelling.* New York: Henry Holt and Company, 1955. 346 pp.

Horn, Ernest. *Teaching Spelling.* What Research Says to the Teacher, No. 3. Washington, D. C.: National Education Association, January 1954. 32 pp.

Russell, David H., *op cit.,* Chapter 9.

Strang, Ruth; McCullough, Constance M.; and Traxler, Arthur E. *The Improvement of Reading.* Third Edition, pp. 360-376. New York: McGraw-Hill Book Company, 1961. 480 pp.

REFERENCE SKILLS

Bond, Guy L., and Wagner, Eva Bond, *op. cit.,* pp. 232-244.

Burrows, Alvina T. "Reading, Research and Reporting," *Social Studies in the Elementary School,* pp. 187-213. Fifty-sixth Yearbook of the National Society for the Study of Education, Part II. Chicago: The University of Chicago Press, 1957. 320 pp.

Carpenter, Helen McCracken (Editor). *Skills in Social Studies.* Chapters 4, 5, 8, 9, and 10. Twenty-fourth Yearbook of the National Council for the Social Studies, N.E.A. Washington, D. C.: The Council, 1954. 282 pp.

DeBoer, John J., and Dallmann, Martha. *The Teaching of Reading.* Chapter 9A. New York: Holt, Rinehart and Winston, 1960. 360 pp.

Durrell, Donald D., *op. cit.*, Chapter 9.
Gray, Lillian, and Reese, Dora, *op. cit.*, pp. 299-306.
Hester, Kathleen B., *op. cit.*, Chapter 14.
Hildreth, Gertrude, *op. cit.*, pp. 450-454.
McKee, Paul, *op. cit.*, Chapters 13, 15.

PART V

Assuring the Progress of Individuals

APPRAISAL AND REMEDIAL HELP

CHAPTER XIII

Appraising, Recording, and Reporting Progress

SUCCESS of the reading program depends upon the insight and good judgment of the classroom teacher. Hers is the responsibility for developing new skills in the order and at the rate most appropriate for the maximum growth of the children in her particular class. This places upon her the major share of the burden of appraising progress and of deciding upon next steps. How can she be sure that her decisions are sound?

Appraisal of children's progress in learning to read has two interrelated aspects. First, and perhaps most important, it provides the insights that guide the planning of day-by-day reading experiences. Second, back of these immediate decisions are more general considerations regarding the degree to which the children in a particular group are making satisfactory progress toward the eventual mastery of adult reading skills. This little group of first-graders is still struggling with a preprimer. Is this to be expected or should more intensive practice be provided? Several children in this second grade cannot name the letters of the alphabet in order. Should they be given more practice now or should the teaching of this skill be left until later? What about the reading interests of the children in this fifth grade? Should they be encouraged to read more library books, even if it means spending less time with basal-reader series? Answers to questions such as these call both for insight into the immediate problems faced by children at their present levels of ability and for understanding of the goals toward which the total reading program is directed.

Since appraisal has been regarded in this volume as a necessary first step in planning every reading experience for children, the preceding chapters contain many examples of the appraisal process in action. This chapter summarizes suggestions related to four main problem areas. First, what standards can the teacher use to corroborate her judgments regarding children's progress? Second, what techniques can she use to appraise and to record day-by-day evidence of progress and problems? Third, how can standardized tests be used most effectively in the appraisal process? Fourth, how can children's progress be interpreted to parents?

School faculties are also professionally interested in appraising the effectiveness of their total reading programs. Guides for such appraisals can be found in Chapter II, where general principles underlying the total reading program are proposed, and at the end of each of the subsequent chapters in the questions suggested for appraising the effectiveness of the aspect of the program under discussion. These guides may be helpful to teachers desirous of taking a look at the reading program for the school as a whole.

ESTABLISHING STANDARDS FOR APPRAISAL PURPOSES

An appraisal is a value judgment. This implies standards. Statements of goals such as those given in preceding chapters suggest general objectives, but each child is likely to be at a different point in his progress toward these objectives. What further guides may the teacher use as she tries to determine the needs of her particular class? How can she be sure that the children are making progress commensurate with their abilities? On what can she base her decisions as to when to push and when to move slowly, when to increase the difficulty of the job to be done and when to simplify it?

A number of guides can be suggested for the appraisal process. Some relate to the objectives of the reading program, some to accumulated knowledge regarding child growth and development, some to the child's performance in the classroom, and some to his ability to handle such standardized reading materials as reading tests or basal-reader series.

Does the child's progress follow a pattern typical of the normal sequence of development of reading skill? Thorough understanding of the way in which reading skill develops under modern teaching methods is essential in appraising progress. This means not only knowing the general sequence in which children can be expected to develop increased skill but also having insight into the interrelationships among specific techniques. The discussions of changing goals from the prereading program to the intermediate grades and the analyses of interrelationships among specific techniques given in earlier chapters are included as aids to this understanding.

In the light of her understanding of the process of learning to read, a teacher can make an appraisal of the general status of a child or of a group —they are typical second-graders; they work more like primary children although they are in fourth grade; they are exceptionally able readers for sixth-graders. This understanding also helps in appraising specific techniques. These children are first-graders; their knowledge of sounds can be expected to be limited. This third-grade group relies too heavily on the configurations of words; by now they should be more independent in word analysis. This youngster is still polishing his word-analysis techniques; he should not be urged to read more rapidly. There is no reason for this sixth-grader to read so slowly; he needs help to overcome his habit of word-by-word reading. Teachers should also seek other more objective evidence regarding the progress of their classes, but they should not distrust their own professional judgments.

The teacher's professional insight plays an important part in the day-by-day appraisals that govern her decisions regarding next steps. As she works with the children she notes a situation in which skills are inadequate, a tendency to turn to her for help on a problem where independence could be expected, an area in which the group seems to be making unusual progress. These types of observations guide her discussions in reading groups, her choice of work-type or follow-up activities, her work with individuals.

Is the child's pattern of growth typical of that which might be expected of children of his general level of maturity and ability? The statement that and eight-year-old's reading skills are typical of those of a third-grader is not an evaluation of his progress. Whether his achievement is to be appraised as exceptional or as limited depends on many factors.

Chronological age or its corresponding school grade is not an adequate standard against which to appraise achievement. Children who have lived for the same number of months have inherited different capacities to learn. They mature at different rates, grow up in homes that provide different types of experience background, suffer from different childhood illnesses, and struggle with different physical handicaps and emotional tensions. They cannot be expected to meet a single standard in their school achievement.

Various alternatives to chronological age have been proposed as bases for evaluating progress in reading. For remedial cases, Gates[1] suggests using a child's mental age based on his performance on the *Revised Stanford-Binet Scale*. This is an individual test that must be given by a qualified examiner. It has the advantage of requiring a minimum amount of reading from the

[1] Arthur I. Gates, *The Improvement of Reading*, Third Edition (New York: The Macmillan Company, 1947), p. 583.

child and yet of posing for him questions that have proven valuable in predicting school achievement. However, school systems do not always have the personnel trained to give this test, and rarely is there sufficient psychological service to give it to children other than those who have remedial problems or who, for some other reason, are the subjects of intensive study.

Group intelligence tests also yield mental ages. As indicators of a child's potential ability, these scores have to be used with caution. This is particularly true when the child is a poor reader and the test score is based on items that demand reading skill. In the intermediate and high school grades, especially, poor readers may be classified as dull children because of their low achievement on verbal intelligence tests. Some group intelligence tests are built around items that do not demand reading skill, and some provide separate subtest scores for items involving language and for those that measure such factors as number and spatial relationships. These non-language scores may be of help in estimating the potential ability of a poor reader, although there is evidence to suggest that there is not always a high correlation between a child's language ability and his reasoning ability in situations in which language is not of primary importance.[2]

Olson[3] reports considerable thought-provoking evidence regarding the relation of children's over-all patterns of maturation to their achievement in school subjects. He suggests the child's organismic age—an average of separate age calculations for such factors as intellectual development, height, weight, dentition, grip, and skeletal growth—as a basis for evaluating his achievement. Although such extensive information about children's growth patterns is not always available, the suggestion that general maturity be considered in appraising children's school achievement is a helpful one.

There are also available reading achievement and capacity tests for the late primary and intermediate grades.[4] They measure word meaning and paragraph meaning both in the typical format of a reading test and in an oral version where the children listen as the examiner reads to them, and then mark pictures to indicate the correct answers. For children whose normal language development has not been retarded, scores on these tests may be helpful in revealing discrepancies between ability to read and ability to understand through listening to materials of the same difficulty level.

Even without test scores, an experienced teacher can often make a reasonable estimate of a child's potential ability. Observations of the way in which he operates in problem-solving situations are particularly helpful. In group

[2] L. L. Thurstone and Thelma Gwinn Thurstone, *Factorial Studies of Intelligence* (Chicago: The University of Chicago Press, 1941).

[3] Willard C. Olson, *Child Development*, Second Edition (Boston: D. C. Heath and Company, 1959), pp. 141-154.

[4] Donald D. Durrell and Helen B. Sullivan, *Durrell-Sullivan Reading Capacity and Achievement Tests* (Yonkers-on-Hudson: The World Book Company, 1937, 1941, 1945).

discussions does he see relationships quickly and draw sound conclusions? Is his speaking vocabulary rich or impoverished? How well does he handle arithmetic problems? Does his curiosity about the world around him center on aspects that are simpler or more complex than those that interest most children of his age? Care needs to be taken, however, to avoid a "halo effect" resulting from a specific aspect of a child's behavior. Impoverished experience background does not mean that a child is incapable of learning. Sometimes the common-sense comments of an over-age child give the impression of greater intellectual ability than he actually has. Children who are ill or emotionally disturbed may not display their full potential ability. Even when there are intelligence test scores to support the teacher's judgment, it is not safe to classify a child too quickly. Often it is a helpful safeguard to match opinions with other teachers who also work with the child, or with the principal or a supervisor who are not so directly involved in the day-by-day situation.

Maturity and potential learning ability are not the only factors to consider in appraising a child's progress in learning to read. His growth needs in areas other than reading also have to be taken into account. From kindergarten on, there will be children whose general language ability is limited, and who need unusually broad experiences in writing and speaking as well as in reading. There will be some for whom the school must supply the breadth of experience often provided by the home. Others may need special experiences to develop health habits normally taught at home. There will be children who need help in learning to get along with their peers and children who seek in the school the affection that others find at home. There are only a limited number of minutes in the school day, and they must be expended to assure the greatest possible total development for each child.

Progress in reading, then, needs to be appraised with the maturity, the range of potential abilities, and the total growth needs of a class in mind. Are the majority of these fourth-graders more nearly like typical third-graders in maturity and in general intellectual ability? Then the fact that they are just now beginning to approach fourth-grade reading skill is not a matter of concern. Are they a very able group, many of whom operate like typical fifth-graders? Then low fourth-grade reading ability suggests that there has not been adequate stimulation and guidance in learning to read. The assumption that children are doing satisfactory work because they have the skills typical of the average child in the grades to which their chronological ages have assigned them is unsound. It sets for the child of limited ability a standard that is likely to lead to frustration and defeat and, perhaps more serious, it asks of the gifted child only a minimum use of his full potentialities.

The teacher's insights into a child's potential ability and his related growth needs also guide day-by-day decisions regarding the type of help he should be given in learning to read. There will need to be special adjustments of materials and methods if the slow learners in the room are to make maximum progress in terms of their abilities. Equally, every effort will need to be made to provide experiences that will challenge the full powers of children of high potential ability.

It is particularly important to look at a child's potential ability when making decisions regarding his need for remedial teaching. All the youngsters whose work is below that which would be considered average for their grade are not candidates for remedial programs. The child who is most likely to profit from intensive remedial help is the one whose potential ability is distinctly above his actual performance. Such help is not likely to bring about marked gains in the case of the child whose achievement is already close to the expectancies suggested by his own growth patterns and potentialities.

Is there reasonably steady growth in ability to handle new reading problems? Under a reading program that is well adjusted to children's capacities there should be reasonably steady growth. This is another way in which the progress of a group may be evaluated.

The concept of reasonably steady growth needs interpretation. All reading skills will not necessarily improve at the same rate or at the same time. Some depend upon the development of others. Furthermore, there will be plateaus in learning when a child seemingly consolidates and learns to use efficiently his present skills. Nevertheless, it is appropriate to ask whether a child is gradually becoming able to handle more difficult reading problems. Six weeks ago Joe needed help with a primer; today he is reading for recreation a book of about the same difficulty. Three weeks ago Kate was baffled by three-syllable words; last week she was able to break several words into syllables, but was not too sure in blending them; today she worked out several words without help. At the beginning of the year Norma's tendency was to copy notes directly from the science book; today she had clear statements in her own words. These are the types of evidence from day to day that show that children are gaining increased reading skill.

Reasonably steady growth also means that more mature ways of working are developing, not that a child is getting better and better at using laborious techniques. It is not progress in the primary grades to become so skillful in remembering the configuration of new words that word-analysis techniques are seldom employed. Neither is it progress to grow so painstaking in reading for details that techniques of skimming are rarely used, or to become so adept at reading aloud that silent reading speed is affected.

Another evidence of progress is a child's insight into his reading skills. With increased maturity should come increased understanding of effective reading techniques and increased ability to identify difficulties and needs for special practice. "If you don't know a word, it helps if you think how it starts and whether it fits in." "You save time if you look to find just what you want before you start to read." "I'm trying to slow down when I read out loud. People couldn't tell what I was saying." Insights such as these indicate that children are learning how to solve their own reading problems, and becoming sensitive to the skills that make for efficient reading.

The teacher's judgment regarding the types of experience needed to assure progress helps to determine the kind of challenge she places before a group. Sometimes it will seem important to consolidate present gains by providing ample experience with reading problems of the same complexity as those with which children are now working. Sometimes it will be appropriate to simplify one aspect of a reading activity in order to achieve gains in another aspect—as when a teacher provides materials that pose few technical problems for the first note-taking efforts of a group. At other times the group will seem ready for a more challenging activity, for more difficult materials, or for a new way of working.

Does the child make active use of his reading skill in solving classroom problems? Perhaps nothing provides a surer guarantee that children will make progress commensurate with their abilities than a classroom in which there are ample materials of varied difficulty levels and many opportunities to use reading to solve genuine problems. In such a setting the range of reading opportunities extends far beyond the capacities of the most able child, and there is virtually no limit to the standards he may set for himself.

One basis for appraising children's growth in reading, then, is the degree to which they are disposed to use their skill. Do they enjoy their activities in reading groups? Do they take pleasure in testing out new skills—in finding new words on the bulletin board; in making independent analyses of new words; in finding articles in the encyclopedia without help; in locating at home the information needed for a special project? Do they ask permission to read favorite stories to their friends, or to take books home? Such active interest is evidence that the program is vital and challenging even to the less skilled readers. It means, too, that the children with greater skill are finding opportunities to tackle problems that call for the full use of their abilities.

Increasingly, as children engage in wide independent reading, the problems they face help to determine their next reading activities. Playing a part in the choice of activities, also, is the teacher's professional judgment regarding the kind of guidance that will result in progress toward the eventual mastery of adult reading skills. As she watches children in reading situations throughout the day, she notes strengths and weaknesses—work with these spelling words indicates phonograms that need to be stressed; this group is going to need more practice with the vocabulary in the last experience record; this youngster should be more efficient in using an index; the notes taken by the members of this group indicate weakness in reading for precise details. These problems then become centers for instruction—in reading groups; in special practice groups; in a class activity as part of a social-studies unit; as part of a spelling lesson; in work-type activities planned for individuals or groups; in special conferences with the teacher.

What is the nature of the child's performance on standardized reading tests? In many school systems children's scores on standardized reading tests are used as one basis for appraisal. Occasionally they outweigh other evidences that children have made progress. Their value lies in the fact that they provide, through their norms, evidence regarding the typical performance of large numbers of children who have worked under standardized conditions with the materials which comprise the test. Test scores are, therefore, useful objective measures against which the teacher can place her more subjective judgments regarding the progress of her class.

Because standardized tests are in common use, a later section in this chapter is devoted to problems of selecting, administering, and interpreting them. It is sufficient to say, at this point, that a grade score of 4.0 on a reading test represents a statement of what the average child at the beginning of fourth grade might be expected to accomplish. It is not a minimum score below which no beginning fourth-grader should be expected to fall, nor is it a maximum which would represent satisfactory work for a child who is exceptionally able. The grade score of any particular youngster needs to be appraised with the factors mentioned previously in mind—his maturity, his mental age, his other growth needs. For a fourth-grader with approximately third-grade intellectual ability a grade score of 4.0 on a reading test would be very good indeed. For a fourth-grader with intellectual ability of approximately fifth-grade level, this same score represents limited achievement in reading. In looking at class averages, teachers need to keep these same factors in mind.

Standardized reading tests fail to serve their full purpose unless they, too, help to guide daily classroom activities. Methods of studying test performances for this purpose are also included in the section on tests later in this chapter.

How well does the child handle the basal-reader series constructed for his grade level? Perhaps no measure of reading achievement is used as frequently as that which expresses a child's ability in terms of the basal-reader level at which he is working. "He is still reading primers." "These are the poorest readers in this fifth grade. They are still reading third-grade books." "Some of these fourth-graders can handle sixth-grade readers without any trouble." Such statements are frequently heard and, because the difficulty levels of basal readers do not differ greatly from series to series, they give a reasonably clear picture of a child's reading ability.

The grade level of the basal reader that a child can handle with ease tells no more about whether his achievement is to be appraised as superior or limited than does a grade score from a standardized reading test or a teacher's judgment regarding the general level at which he is working. This measurement of a child's achievement, too, has to be appraised in terms of his potential learning ability. Authors of basal texts have designated them for the grade level at which they are most likely to be useful for the average child. There is no intent to propose these materials as standards which all children in a given grade must attain or to use them to hold an able reader to a level of achievement that is below his capacity. When related factors have been taken into account, the grade level of the basal reader which a child can handle with relative ease is another useful objective check on a teacher's professional judgment regarding his present status and the types of experiences that will be most effective in contributing to his growth.

APPRAISING AND RECORDING EVIDENCE OF PROGRESS AND PROBLEMS FROM DAY TO DAY

It is not easy to provide the necessary guidance for the varied activities of a large group of children and still to be sure that the needs of each child are being met, not only in reading but in all the other areas of experience that make up his school curriculum. The preceding chapters contain many examples of techniques that are helpful in studying the problems and progress of a class. These may be grouped, for summary purposes, in three areas. First, there are problems of finding ways of studying children as regular classroom activities proceed. Second, there are problems of devising a system of record-keeping which provides the needed objective evidence about a child but which is not so cumbersome and time-consuming as to be virtually impossible to maintain in a typical classroom. Third, there are problems of helping children share in the appraisal and the recording process. A variety of possibilities is explored within each section. No one teacher will necessarily use them all, nor will she need all the evidence suggested in order to appraise adequately the progress of an individual child.

STUDYING CLASSROOM ACTIVITIES FOR CLUES TO PROBLEMS AND PROGRESS

Identify the problems arising in functional reading situations throughout the day. It is not as difficult as it may seem to appraise children's reading skills as they go about their daily classroom activities. In fact, any teacher, even a beginner, gives a very clear picture of the abilities of her group as she talks about her work and her problems to her colleagues, her principal, or her supervisor. One of the most helpful techniques described in preceding chapters is that of providing opportunities for children to work independently. Even in a first grade this gives the teacher a certain amount of time to talk with individual children or to observe the ways in which various group members approach a new reading problem. With more mature children the teacher may have time to talk to small groups having special difficulty; to quiz a youngster about the way he worked out the pronunciation of a word or to ask him how he went about finding it in the dictionary; to move from group to group observing children's reference techniques. These short contacts with individuals and small groups highlight strengths and weaknesses in a way that is not possible when thirty or more youngsters are taught as a total group.

Another device that is particularly fruitful in identifying the needs of older children is that of talking over problems of how to read before a task requiring extensive reading is begun. This not only prevents certain problems from occurring, but it also helps the teacher to identify efficient procedures or confusions and inadequate approaches as children discuss how they will go about the job.

The times when special help in reading is planned as part of a unit of work offer opportunities to take a look at specific skills. Some first-graders work on the new words learned on an excursion; which are the ones that are the hardest for them to remember? A third-grade group takes a period to learn more about locating the information for a science project; what techniques do they lack? Everyone in a fifth grade shares in a discussion of how to locate topics in an encyclopedia; what confusions exist?

It is helpful, also, to be sensitive to regular classroom activities that are most likely to yield evidence regarding specific skills. Lists of such situations were given in Chapters VIII and XI. Spelling activities, for example, often reveal word-study problems. Times when children are using class plans, following the directions for a special project, or following the written rules of a new game provide opportunities to observe differences in ability to follow directions. Recreational-reading periods can be used to study a child's reading interests, the grade level of the book he chooses to read independently, and his ability to report on the gist of a story. It is not necessary to try to appraise growth in all reading skills at once. More effective observations will be made by studying the range of abilities in the skill that is focal at the moment.

Study children's responses in reading groups. Reading groups provide opportunities to study children's strengths and weaknesses very directly. Here, too, the policy of encouraging children to read independently is helpful in the appraisal process. As a group reads a story silently it is possible to observe differences in reading rate, to spot habits such as pointing or vocalizing, to note tendencies merely to leaf through the story. Often, during this silent-reading period, the teacher has time to explore a little the word-analysis approaches of children who ask for help or to check briefly on the comprehension of those who finish first.

In the discussion that follows the reading of a story it is possible to ask questions that reveal ability to follow the general thread of a story, to note important details, or to predict what will happen next. Opportunities to read parts of a story aloud can be used to appraise oral-reading skills. Follow-up activities can be used to explore strengths or weaknesses in such areas as recognizing new words, outlining the story for dramatization or illustration purposes, or listing important details. If these activities are planned originally with definite reading skills in mind, the process of appraising the abilities of the group is simplified.

When children are working to improve a specific skill in a reading-group situation, it is easier still to note progress and problems. These practice sessions are often planned around work-type activities. When this is the case, the child's paper provides further evidence of his skill or the lack of it.

A certain number of useful records can be made in reading-group situations. Lists can be kept of the words for which help was requested. Sometimes the group member engaged in special practice will keep records of their progress through check lists, records of questions missed, or graphs of progress. Anecdotal records of reading habits may be made as children work silently. Such systematic collection of significant bits of evidence can result in a helpful accumulation of information.

Analyze work-type activities. Other evidence of children's present status in reading can be secured by studying their work-type activities. Some of this analysis goes on as teacher and children talk over the particular activity. "Why do you disagree with Jerry's answer?" "Can you see why you made your mistake?" "Why did you have trouble with that word?" Such discussions help the teacher to see where some of the difficulties lie, and they also help the group members to grow in their understanding of reading skills.

When more information seems to be needed, work-type activities may be collected from time to time and made the subject of more intensive analysis. What pattern of errors seems to emerge? Is there a group problem revealed or are the difficulties mainly those of individuals? Does lack of related skills seem to be complicating the task at hand? Where do these related problems seem to lie? If a permanent record is desired, diagnostic notes from such analyses may be added to the mimeographed exercise or the workbook page and the material dropped in the child's cumulative record folder.

Set up informal test situations. When further evidence of children's strengths and weaknesses is needed, it is possible to set up informal test situations. Work-type activities serve this purpose, insofar as they focus upon a particular reading skill. The suggestions in Chapters VII, IX, and XII of ways of setting up work-type exercises in objective-test form will provide the patterns for informal tests of various silent-reading skills. Workbook pages can serve the same purpose. Children may complete these exercises independently so that the picture of each child's work is accurate. Later they may be used for teaching purposes.

It is also possible to plan group activities so that they yield informal test evidence. Review activities with words in the primary grades can be planned so that children's special problems are revealed. A problem such as "Let's see how long it will take you to find . . ." sets up a situation requiring speed of reading and skill in locating details. Asking children to tell how they would change the ending of a story will reveal differences in ability to predict outcomes. A dictionary game in which children race to find the meaning of a given word can give evidence of skill with alphabetical order and guide words.

Oral reading was mentioned in preceding chapters as a source of diagnostic evidence. A reasonably well-graded informal test can be set up by selecting paragraphs from near the beginning and the end of basal readers covering three or four grade levels. With an oral-reading test planned in this way the level at which a child begins to have trouble with unfamiliar words gives a reasonable indication of the difficulty of the material with which he should be working. It is possible to get evidence of a child's comprehension of a passage by asking him about it after he has finished reading and also by noting the types of errors he makes. If he substitutes words that make sense, repeats in order to correct errors, and reads in recognizable phrase and sentence units, he is sensitive to the meaning of what he is reading. If his errors destroy the meaning of the passage, it is less likely that he is able to think about what he is reading. Such evidence needs to be checked against a child's silent-reading performance, however, as the task of reading aloud is, in itself, sometimes difficult enough to cause misreadings that would not occur in a silent-reading situation. It is important to remember, also, that the more difficult the material becomes the less meaning the passage is likely to have for a child. Oral reading of extremely hard material is perhaps of most value in revealing a child's approach to unfamiliar words.

Additional helpful insights into a child's word-study skills can be secured by asking him to read aloud a list of words that increase gradually in difficulty. Often it is revealing to ask him to tell what he is doing. Some children can describe quite accurately the methods they use. "First I look for all the little words I can find. Then I try to put them together." "It's like spelling. If I say the letters to myself I sometimes remember what it is." "It begins like *stay* and the last part says *shun*. It's easy when you can find parts you know." "I sort of squint at it. Sometimes you see it better that way." When their word-study habits are analyzed, some children who seemingly are good readers will be discovered to have excellent memories for the configuration of words but very little skill in word analysis. Others will be relying on routine use of a single technique—small words, word families, beginning letters. These insights into a child's methods of work can be helpful in planning his next word-analysis experiences and sometimes in explaining his difficulties in comprehension.

Check lists can be of value in analyzing oral-reading skills. These often serve as useful teaching aids if teacher and children develop them together. Extensive lists have been provided in the pupil's record booklets that are part of the diagnostic test batteries prepared by Durrell [5] and by Gates. [6] However, these lists are very detailed and a selected number of crucial items are likely to be more appropriate for typical classroom use. As suggested in Chapter XII, check-list items used to appraise a child's ability to handle the technical aspects of the material he reads will center around the types of errors he makes, the words he misses, the points at which he repeats, and his ability to sense phrasing and to respond to punctuation marks. Items to appraise a child's skill in reading before an audience will put relatively more emphasis on enunciation, ability to convey a desired mood, effective rate for the listening audience, and poise. Check lists also may be useful in recording a child's skills in word analysis—his general approach; the sounds he knows; the parts of words he responds to most readily; his ability to break words into syllables. Some teachers have found ways of using such check lists as a regular part of group practice sessions. Eventually the completed records may be added to the child's cumulative folder.

KEEPING ADEQUATE RECORDS

Add representative samples of work systematically to the child's cumulative record folder. Many plans for reading experiences from day to day are made on the basis of observations that are not recorded. However, teachers also face the problem of interpreting a child's progress to his parents and of supplying to the teacher to whom he is promoted a reasonably clear record

[5] Donald D. Durrell, *Durrell Analysis of Reading Difficulty* (Yonkers-on-Hudson: The World Book Company, 1937, 1955).

[6] Arthur I. Gates, *Gates Reading Diagnostic Tests,* Revised Edition (New York: Teachers College, Columbia University, 1945, *Manual,* 1953).

of his growth and his present status. It is important, then, to make a systematic effort to collect objective evidence of a child's achievement.

In many school systems a cumulative record is kept for each child. This record is begun when he first enters school. Often the record form is printed on a folder in which a variety of evidences of the child's growth can be filed. Usually there is space on the folder itself to record such data as birth date, names and address of parents, siblings, medical record, scores on standardized tests, and records of transfers from school to school. On this record form each teacher notes her appraisals of the child's work for the year. Sometimes this is in the form of letter grades, sometimes in descriptive statements. A busy teacher needs simple ways of collecting the evidence that substantiates these appraisals.

A certain amount of evidence can be collected by dating and filing samples of the child's work from time to time. Some teachers file a sheet listing the books the child has read under guidance during the year. A number of other appropriate materials have already been suggested. Work-type activities or workbook pages can be chosen so that the child's growth over the months can be seen. Check lists of oral-reading skills can be filed. It is often helpful to keep in the child's record for at least a year the actual test booklets of any standardized tests he has taken. For older children it may be of value to file typical samples of the types of notes they take or the summary reports they write. If such materials are dropped into the file at reasonably regular intervals, the result can be a well-rounded picture of a child's progress and an excellent collection of concrete material to use in parent conferences.

Eventually cumulative folders can become cluttered with a child's work. It can be helpful to go over the material at intervals and to summarize the evidence on a permanent record sheet. These summary statements need to contain facts as well as judgments. "Sue is becoming much more interested in recreational reading," is not as informative as "Last month Sue read. . . . Her selection of library books today includes. . . ." If conferences with parents are foreseen, representative examples out of the total collection of the child's work may be important to leave in the file.

Save records of group activities. Because pupil-teacher planning is an integral part of the development of activities in the modern classroom, the bulletin boards are likely to contain many records that can provide a helpful picture of children's reading activities. Such records do not have to be transcribed to a child's cumulative folder to be useful. They may be dated and kept in a single file until special information is needed. If the collection becomes too unwieldy it, too, may be analyzed at intervals and the most important information summarized for the folders of individual children.

Records pertaining to unit activities in the content fields can give a picture of the breadth of children's informational reading. In the primary grades some of these records will be experience charts. Affixing the names of the children who shared in composing particular charts provides information regarding special contributions to the unit. Lists of committees, bibliographies, class notebooks containing group reports, help to record the parts older children have played in the development of a unit. At both levels, lists of unfamiliar words will help to show the type of vocabulary building that was needed.

There may also be group records of reading projects. Among these may be summaries of class discussions of reading problems—how to be a good audience, how to read aloud, what makes a good book report, what steps to take to find new materials. Then, too, there are likely to be lists signed by people who have given book reports, lists of volunteers for oral-reading story parties, and records of plans for reading units. All these can help to fill in the picture of the breadth of the total program and of the participation of individual children.

Many ways of developing class records of recreational reading have been suggested in earlier chapters. These can be studied to determine the quantity and the quality of the child's independent reading. Some of these records may be planned in such a way that the child classifies his book as he records it. When this had been done he, his teacher, and his parents can see at a glance where his reading interests lie.

Collect occasional anecdotal records. From the prereading level on, anecdotal records can be a helpful addition to other information collected about a child. These are the teacher's special observations of a child's attitudes, behavior, and ways of working. The fact that Janice read three books this month whereas last month she read only one may not be so revealing as the teacher's report that Janice was so entranced with her latest book that she had to be pried away from it to complete other work. Bennie's low score on a word-recognition test may conceal the fact that he has recently been trying out word-analysis techniques on all the new words he meets, even though his methods are not always accurate. Sandra's love of poetry and the fact that she reads it well may not appear in the files of her written work. These pieces of evidence are important to the total picture of the child's reading skill.

As suggested in the earlier discussion of the use of anecdotal records in appraising reading readiness, it is not necessary to try to jot down something every day about every child in order to collect helpful anecdotes. What needs to be recorded is the significant evidence of progress or the anecdote that illustrates a typical problem. In the earlier discussion it was also suggested that the collecting of anecdotal records can be facilitated by identifying points in a typical day's program when specific reading needs are likely to be most clearly apparent—a library period studied for evidence of reading interests; a group activity of composing an experience record studied for evidences of differences in oral expression; an informational reading period studied for evidence of ability to work independently. It is virtually impossible in a typical classroom setting to write extensive anecdotal records about all children, but it is possible to collect a limited number of them to supplement the other evidence accumulating about a child when the full story can not seem to be told without them.

HELPING CHILDREN SHARE IN THE APPRAISAL PROCESS

Provide a classroom setting where children enjoy the challenge of a hard job. Children need to be given a share in appraising their progress. This is important if they are to grow in their insight into their own needs and in their ability to give direction to their own practice activities. The classroom atmosphere that encourages children to look at their weaknesses as well as their strengths is one in which credit is given to those who have insights into their own difficulties, and one in which it is obviously more important to be tackling a new skill and improving, even though progress is slow, than it is to turn in a perfect paper.

Many examples were given in preceding chapters of ways of involving children in discussions of their own reading problems. "That was the word that was hard for you, wasn't it, Jill? I'm glad you remembered." "Andy was really trying to hold his book so that we all could hear him, wasn't he? Don't you think he did better?" As suggested in preceding chapters, such appraisals go on at many points—in planning sessions, in evaluation periods, in group reading periods, as teachers work with individual children. Reading, in itself, is interesting and challenging to children. Discovering what one needs to work on next in order to read more skillfully can be just as interesting and challenging if it is made an integral part of children's reading activities.

Give group members an opportunity to work cooperatively in the appraisal process. Children grow in their insight into their own strengths and weaknesses by participating in group activities where they appraise each other. This is particularly true of more mature readers. In these group activities the teacher does not relinquish her responsibility as leader. Typically, she works with the children until desirable standards are established, leaves them to help each other while she works with other groups, and then returns to pick up special difficulties. In one intermediate-grade classroom five groups laid plans to read stories aloud. After a discussion of what makes for a good presentation to an audience, each group went to work. While the teacher divided her time among the groups and gave help wherever she could, the bulk of the improvement came as group members made suggestions to each other. In another class the children talked through standards for good reports based on extensive reading in social studies. Then each child read his report for criticism by others in his small group. In a third class, spelling partners worked to help each other develop better skills in analyzing words. This, too, involved a mutual effort to figure out where present techniques were inadequate.

Teachers are sometimes fearful lest group criticism embarrass and discourage a child. However, this is not likely to happen in situations where all group members have a common concern, and the generous approval frequently given to a child who has shown improvement often can be very helpful in morale-building. Furthermore, the cooperative appraisal process increases manyfold the total amount of help available to each child and helps all group members to grow in their sensitivity to a job well done.

Help children share in keeping records. Record keeping is another aspect of the appraisal process through which the members of a class can be helped to develop insight into their own strengths and weaknesses and to build standards for their work. Here, too, the degree of participation increases with increasing maturity.

Many types of records in which children may share have been mentioned in preceding chapters. They may keep records of their reading—lists of library books, simple bibliographies of books used for informational reading, lists of basal readers with which they have worked. They may share in a number of types of diagnostic records—notebooks of difficult words, check lists of oral-reading skills, notebooks containing spelling pretests and final tests kept as an aid in identifying word-analysis difficulties, check sheets indicating the results of periodic tests of silent-reading skills, collections of work-type activities. Older children may also make simple graphs of their progress—records of reading rate, the percentages correct in series of work-type exercises, graphs of the numbers of special work-type practice sheets completed. In addition, children can share in deciding on typical samples of their work to file or on materials that should be kept to help parents understand their activities—notebooks containing reports of unit activities, collections of book reviews, special outlines or summaries.

Just as teachers need to analyze and to summarize the evidence accumulating in children's folders, so teachers and children together need to look for signs of progress and for needs for help. Some of this appraising is done informally as the record-keeping process moves forward. As children enter new books in their library records, they talk about the number and the kinds of books they have read. As they complete a check of oral-reading skills, they look to see how last week's record compares. As they study their errors in a spelling pretest, they make a list of the phonograms they need to learn. As they decide to save a special piece of work to show their parents, they look at earlier work to see how much they have improved. Some appraisal goes on in individual conferences, as teacher and child talk over what should go into a report to parents, or plan for special practice. Records that do not contribute to on-going classroom activities have little place, whether they are collected by the teacher alone or by teacher and children jointly.

USING STANDARDIZED TESTS

Many standardized tests are available for use in the appraisal process. They can be classified in two main categories: *group tests* and *individual tests*. Group tests can be given to the whole class at one time. They are designed to survey various silent-reading skills, and the children work with them quietly after some simple group directions. Individual tests must be given to one child at a time. The child answers aloud and the examiner records his responses in a special record booklet. An individual test is needed to measure such skills as oral reading, certain aspects of word recognition and word analysis, ability to give sound equivalents for letters and letter combinations, and ability to hear likenesses and differences among words. Both group and individual tests can be diagnostic if they are designed to provide subtest scores for several skills. In most situations group tests are used to survey the abilities of a class. Individual tests, or informal diagnoses from classroom performance, may then be used for a more careful study of children who are having difficulty. Group tests are constructed so that they can be given by the regular classroom teacher whereas individual tests call for somewhat more training on the part of the examiner.

Reading tests measure the same skills that a child is using in his daily reading activities. Primary group tests typically get at the child's ability to recognize words and to read simple sentences and easy paragraphs. Often the test items use pictures in questions similar to the exercises in a typical primary workbook. Usually the time limit is generous. At the intermediate level, where children can be expected to use flexible reading techniques for a greater variety of purposes, tests are available to measure more aspects of reading skills. Frequently a single test yields several subtest scores. A subtest of ability to read paragraphs of increasing difficulty is often included. So is some measure of reading rate. Subtests of vocabulary are common. These may assess a child's general stock of word meanings or his special knowledge of terms in the content fields. Evidence of the flexibility of the techniques of more skilled readers may be secured through tests of such specific skills as following directions, noting details, getting the general impression of a paragraph, or predicting outcomes. In addition, teachers of older children may get measures of their reference skills—ability to use an index or a dictionary, to read maps and graphs, to make outlines.

Because reading tests merely provide another way of looking at the same reading skills that teachers are appraising from day to day, it is not essential to plan elaborate testing programs in order to provide effective reading experiences. However, many teachers feel that tests are a helpful objective check on their judgment. Often tests are used as part of a city-wide testing program and provide useful information about the child who transfers from school to school. When standardized tests are part of the appraisal process, it is important that they be used effectively. A teacher needs to be able to select the test appropriate for her particular situation, to administer and score it properly, and, perhaps most difficult, to interpret the test scores, both for the class as a whole and for individual children.

SELECTING APPROPRIATE TESTS

Does the test measure the abilities the teacher wishes to appraise? Because standardized tests measure different skills or different combinations of skills, a person who is responsible for selecting tests needs to examine more than one before making a choice. Subtests of word meaning and of sentence and paragraph comprehension measure basic abilities on which any class appropriately may be tested, but there are distinct differences from class to class in the times at which such specific techniques as using a dictionary, outlining, summarizing, and using other reference skills are stressed and in the point at which reading rate becomes important to measure. A teacher should choose the test that will provide objective evidence in the areas in which she most wants to corroborate her judgment. It is not a reflection on the type of reading program provided for a group of children if a standardized test happens to measure skills which, for the moment, are not a point of focus. Tests are not serving their proper function if the particular selection of subtests made by the author determines the reading program. The responsibility of deciding which skills are of immediate importance to a group needs to remain in the hands of their teacher.

Does the test include sufficient items to measure the abilities of the best and the poorest readers? Choosing a test that measures the skills about which a teacher needs information does not mean selecting a test that covers exactly what children have been taught. A standardized test should provide a measure of a child's full ability. It is important to choose one that contains ample material to challenge the best reader in the class. If a child makes a perfect score or even comes within a question or two of a perfect score, it can usually be assumed that the test is too easy for him and that the full extent of his reading ability has not been measured. It is important, also, not to discourage the child who is a poor reader. For example, the poorest readers in a third grade will have a distressing time with a test recommended for grades three through six if the norms are such that a child need have only three questions correct to secure a grade score of 3.0. If, on the other hand, a test is designed so that a child needs to answer eight or ten questions correctly to secure a grade score of 3.0, even a third-grader with limited reading skill will have some success before the test questions become too difficult for him. Sometimes to secure an adequate measure of children's abilities it is desirable to give, first, a test that seems appropriate for the average and below-average readers in the room, and to follow this with a more advanced test for the children who make perfect or near perfect scores.

How much additional help is provided in the test manual? Tests vary in the amount of help provided for the teacher in the test manual. It is appropriate to consider this factor in choosing between two tests that otherwise seem equally usable. Clear directions for administering and for scoring the test should be expected, and should be followed exactly. In addition a teacher should expect to find a reasonably detailed description of the purposes of the test and some information about the groups upon which the norms were developed and the degree to which the test has proven reliable and valid. Discussions of how to make out class record lists and how to interpret the test norms can be helpful. Sometimes norms for different population groups will be provided—private schools, urban schools, rural schools. Suggestions of how to use subtest scores to diagnose the strengths and weaknesses of a particular child or a group may also be given. In some manuals it may even be possible to find illustrative case studies of individual children and suggested remedial activities. The use of a standardized test should rarely stop with the making out of a class list. The teacher needs all the additional help a test author can provide.

INTERPRETING TEST SCORES

Interpret grade scores in the light of related information about children's growth. The test norms of most reading tests at the elementary school level are given as age and grade scores. Since it is customary to think of a child's ability in terms of the grade level at which he reads, a grade score often conveys more meaning than the corresponding age score. The related factors that need to be considered in evaluating test scores were discussed earlier in this chapter. A teacher needs to ask what the general intellectual level and the maturity of her class seems to be; to consider what other areas of growth have needed to be stressed; and to ask whether the test has measured skills that have been important points of focus for her group.

It is also important to study a child's test scores in the light of his performance from day to day. Tests are not completely reliable. The progress of a child who has made a full year's growth, or better, may not be apparent in his test scores. He may, for example, by a combination of skill and lucky guesses perform at the top level of his ability on the first test, and on the second make a minimum score because of a few careless errors or unfortunate guesses. Then, too, tests do not measure all the factors that go into increased reading skill. A child may make marked gains in interest in reading and in the ease with which he handles certain types of materials, without making appreciably higher test scores. Furthermore, all tests are not standardized on exactly the same population groups, and slight variations in norms from one test battery to another may operate to exaggerate or to minimize the gains that have actually been made. Teachers who work with the same test over several years often develop helpful insights into its particular strengths and weaknesses. These insights are important in the interpreting of scores.

When due allowance has been made for other factors, test scores can be enlightening. Sometimes the weaknesses of a child who has been covering up his confusion by answering obvious questions, clowning, or bluffing will become apparent. Sometimes a child who has been indifferent will display ability that has not been revealed in his classroom work. The results of standardized tests should not be brushed aside merely because they do not correspond with the teacher's judgment. It is always important to take a careful second look.

Study the profiles of subtest scores. Helpful information about a child's strengths and weaknesses can be secured by studying the patterns of his subtest scores. This may also be done for a class by calculating mean or median scores. In one first grade the class average on a test of word recognition was high. On a test of paragraph reading, however, the class average was relatively low. This was a situation in which there had been an overemphasis upon isolated word-study activities, and the test scores revealed clearly the limited experience in working with story-type materials. In another first grade differences in subtest scores provided helpful diagnostic evidence about a youngster who had unusual ability to make shrewd guesses from context. This child earned a high score on a test of paragraph reading, but his inability to distinguish clearly between words of similar configuration when he met them in isolation was revealed in a low word-recognition score. In the intermediate grades it is often helpful to compare a score on an untimed comprehension test with that on a test of reading speed. Sometimes differences in subtest scores will enable the teacher to identify the child who grasps the general idea of the passage but who does not read accurately for details, or the reverse. Often a low score on a word meaning subtest helps to explain errors on the more difficult items of a test of paragraph meaning. Typical interrelationships among reading skills were analyzed at several points in earlier chapters. A study of subtest patterns can lead to many insightful diagnostic hunches if a teacher is aware of these interrelationships.

Take a look at the way the child worked. It is often helpful to go back to the child's test booklet to study the way he worked. This is the same procedure a teacher might use in studying any work-type activity, and the patterns of errors to look for are much the same. In primary tests of word recognition it may be possible to note consistent errors, such as failure to look carefully at the middles of words or insufficient attention to endings. A pattern of correct answers on items containing words known to be within a child's reading vocabulary and consistent errors on those containing words known to be unfamiliar may indicate limited word-analysis skills. In a test of paragraph comprehension that increases gradually in difficulty, a sprinkling of errors from the easiest to the most difficult paragraphs may suggest careless reading, too rapid reading, or perhaps limited word-analysis skill that results in errors whenever the context contains words that the child cannot recognize at sight. Correct answers on a test of paragraph reading if only a limited number of questions are completed suggest slow reading speed. Such insights are helpful as guides in planning for special practice activities. They are also helpful in appraising a child's test scores.

Use a sliding scale in deciding on the seriousness of retardation. Discrepancies between a child's performance on a reading test and his potential ability need to be interpreted differently for different grade levels. This is true also in using test scores as a guide to the grade levels of books a child is likely to be able to handle with ease. If a test score is reasonably accurate, it can be used as a rough indication of the basal-reader level with which a child might be expected to work. For easy reading without help, he probably should have a book graded somewhat lower than the grade score he made on a test. How much trouble he will have with more difficult materials depends on the grade level at which he is reading. In the early primary grades, reading material increases quite rapidly in difficulty of vocabulary load, sentence length, and paragraph length. A child whose reading achievement is grade 1.5 could be expected to have considerable difficulty with a second-grade book. By the end of third grade a half year's retardation would not be as great a handicap. In sixth grade, a test score of grade 5.5 does not usually predict that a child will have insurmountable difficulty in working with sixth-grade books. In terms of practical classroom planning, then, retardation of a half year to a year in the lower primary grades will usually call for special adjustments of materials and teaching methods. In the fifth and sixth grades the degree of retardation should be somewhat greater before special adjustments need to be given serious consideration.

Consider the use of individual diagnostic tests to investigate special difficulties. Extensive diagnostic test batteries, such as those of Durrell [7] and of

---

[7] Donald D. Durrell, *op. cit.*

Gates[8] can be used to supplement the evidence secured from group tests if children appear to be having unusual difficulty. These batteries provide, in standardized form, the tests needed to make a detailed inventory of those aspects of reading skill that cannot be measured by silent reading tests. They include subtests of oral reading, of word recognition, of phrase reading, of ability to respond to syllables, phonograms, and letters of the alphabet, of ability to hear sounds, and others. The record booklets that accompany these batteries include check lists of special difficulties and suggestions for case studies.

Diagnostic test batteries are instruments that a classroom teacher can learn to use. As mentioned earlier, they require more skill on the part of the examiner than do group tests. There is nothing magical about the types of insights into a child's difficulties that they yield. The evidence is essentially the same as that secured by an experienced teacher as she studies a child's pattern of errors as he reads difficult paragraphs aloud, listens to him work out the analysis of unfamiliar words, or works with him on a series of work-type activities that reveal his problems with phonograms, syllables, and letter sounds. Although the scores from diagnostic tests may sharpen patterns of weaknesses and strengths, they should agree at many points with what a teacher already knows about a child.

Some follow-up, whether it be through the appropriate parts of a diagnostic battery or through informal classroom tests, should be made when the child's performance on a silent reading test suggests that he is having unusual trouble. This is particularly important if the pattern of his subtest scores does not seem to offer any particular explanation for his difficulty. Many helpful insights can come from asking a child to do a little work aloud. A word-by-word approach to silent reading sometimes reveals itself in poor phrasing when a child reads aloud. A hint that a child can read with good comprehension if he knows the vocabulary of the material he is reading at sight but that he is hampered by poor word-analysis skills can be followed up by watching his pattern of errors when oral-reading paragraphs become difficult. Flashing a list of words to a child for instant recognition and then seeing how many more he can get when he has all the time he needs to study them also helps to reveal word-analysis difficulties. Asking a child how he works, as suggested earlier, often reveals where his techniques are inadequate. With children who are remedial cases, particularly, such a careful systematic look at possible sources of trouble is essential.

Compare classes or schools with great caution. There are few procedures capable of arousing more tension and unnecessary concern on the part of teachers than that of calculating class averages and making public at the end of the school year comparisons of schools or of classes. These figures do not

[8] Arthur I. Gates, *op. cit.*

necessarily reveal the fact that the program for an able group of children has provided little of challenge or that a program for a group with limited ability has resulted in remarkable gains. Furthermore, even an extensive battery of standardized tests will measure only a limited number of the total objectives of the reading program. A sure way to destroy a good program for a group of children is to give their teacher the feeling that the most important result of the year's experiences should be a set of high test scores in May.

If standardized tests are to be an aid in developing the reading program, they should be given at a time when the scores will be of the greatest help to the teacher in planning experiences for her group. Often this means testing in the early fall rather than in the spring so that there are fresh scores available as an additional guide in selecting reading materials and in setting up reading groups. Even when no comparisons of classes are being made, teachers sometimes tend to blame themselves if their class averages on a set of tests given in the spring do not come up to expectancies. There may be less unfortunate feeling of personal involvement if a teacher faces the strengths or shortcomings of her group with a year's work still ahead of her.

Help children share in the testing program. Children have a right to know the purposes of a test. Often considerable anxiety can develop if a child begins to suspect that a test will affect the grade on his report card, or perhaps his promotion to the next class. Even able readers may become concerned if parts of a test prove difficult for them. The more mature the group and the more general sophistication they have about school procedures the more important it is to take steps to allay apprehensions such as these.

There are many ways of helping children understand the purposes of a testing program. If they are accustomed to discussing their own strengths and weaknesses objectively, a test may be introduced as "another way of helping us to decide just where you need help the most." It can be made quite explicit that the purpose is to see how the children's work compares with that of boys and girls in other parts of the country, not to secure a grade for a report card. Anxiety about difficult parts of the test can sometimes be prevented by saying, "This test is planned for boys and girls of several grades. Don't worry if you find some of it hard." Giving a test in the fall, preliminary to the year's work, rather than in the spring when nothing is ahead except grades and promotions may reduce children's anxieties as well as those of their teacher.

Some teachers who are accustomed to appraising strengths and weaknesses objectively with their groups have found it possible to discuss exact grade scores. One teacher began with a small group of retarded readers by talking about the general purpose of the test and then saying, "Allen, where do you think your score was?" "Pretty low," said Allen. "You're right," said his teacher. "It shows that we were right in starting you with a third-grade

Often a difficulty can be smoothed out quickly if help is available, and the reader knows what his own problems are.

book. Now let's plan how your special work in reading can help you." This same teacher also discussed high scores, taking care to point out areas other than reading in which the better readers could recognize that they, too, needed special help. Another teacher, whose children knew they were assigned to her because of remedial needs, posted actual test scores. Across from each child's score on the fall test was a question mark, to be filled in when the group was retested in the spring. "It's not where you started but how far you can go and how hard you work," was the motto in both these classrooms.

REPORTING TO PARENTS

Home-school cooperation plays an important part in a child's school adjustment. Parents need to have a clear picture of a child's progress, his strengths, and his weaknesses. Furthermore, if they are to give intelligent cooperation to the teacher, they need to understand, at least in general terms, the methods by which he is being taught. In return, parents can supply much helpful information about their children.

Use methods of reporting that give the full picture. One of the problems of great concern in schools today is that of developing satisfactory methods of reporting to parents. No matter how carefully they are thought out, ratings or letter grades, whether the system is one of grades from *A* to *F* or ratings of *Satisfactory, Improving,* and *Unsatisfactory,* cannot tell the complete story. One of their greatest disadvantages is that they cannot convey, at the same time, an estimate of the child's progress in relation to his potential ability and a picture of his present status in his group. For example, who should receive the *A,* fourth-grade Joan with the mentality of a sixth-grader who is coasting with good fourth-grade work, or fourth-grade Sammy, with the intellectual ability of a third-grader who, through outstanding effort, can now cope with a fourth-grade book? It is sometimes argued that the child's actual achievement is the important consideration, but are Joan's parents really content to know that she is only a little ahead of her group when her potential ability is so great? Is the important information for Sammy's parents the fact that intellectual tasks are not his forte? And what of the attitudes of Joan and Sammy as they carry home their report cards? Do Joan's parents want her to learn to set standards for herself in relation to the average achievement of the group? And do Sammy's parents want him to classify himself as inadequate and inferior because in one area he does not have as great a natural endowment as some of his friends?

Letter grades based on potential ability can be equally misleading and equally productive of undesirable attitudes. Suppose, in terms of achievement in relation to potential ability, Joan receives the *C* and Sammy the *A*. Are Joan's parents not to be helped to see that their child has unusual ability? And should Sammy's parents not be helped to understand that college is likely to be very difficult for him, that careful choice of high school courses may be needed, or perhaps that it may be desirable to hold him in the same grade for a year in order to let him work with younger children? What of Joan and Sammy? Will this grading system help them to grow in realistic understanding of their own abilities?

Teachers, too, have difficulty as they try to interpret the letter grades on children's cumulative records. Ranges in ability will differ from class to class. Is a teacher of a class, all of whom have limited potential ability, to defeat them time after time by giving grades of *C* and *D* to their best efforts? How high a standard should be expected of a group of able children if letter grades of *A* are to go upon their permanent record cards? What interpretations are teachers to place upon the letter grades on report cards of children coming from several classes within one school, or from several schools?

The mental hygiene considerations connected with the problem of recording and reporting progress are important. It is not conducive to a child's ultimate well-being to evaluate his work in such a way that he builds an unrealistic picture of his ability. He needs to know where his strengths lie and where he has weaknesses. As an adult he is likely to lead a more useful and satisfying life if he has learned to accept himself for what he is and to set goals for himself that are within the realm of possible achievement. Furthermore, it is not a defeating experience for a child to face his inadequacies as long as he also faces his strengths and as long as he participates actively in plans that he knows will help him improve. Children have a right to be helped to understand themselves, to accept themselves, to learn how to solve their own problems, and to learn how to make the most of their abilities. This means using a system of recording and reporting progress that conveys clear information to a child as well as to his parents.

Many examples have already been given of ways in which children can be helped to make objective appraisals of their work. To share these insights with parents, teachers in many school systems have begun to use letters or other written statements, or, better still, conferences with parents as means of reporting. In some school systems these devices have replaced letter grades completely; in others they supplement and help to interpret the letter grades.

In the give-and-take of a conference situation it is easier both to answer a parent's questions and to learn from a parent information that will be helpful in working with a child. Remedial measures or special adjustments of materials and methods can also be interpreted more readily. "Yes, she did get a bad start last year when she was ill, and she was very discouraged when she came this fall. We started with very easy books so that she could be successful and she is just about ready now for third-grade books." "No, he hasn't been working much with basal readers. He reads very well and most of them are too easy for him. The group he is with has been exploring a great variety of library books. Here is a record of his reading for the past month." "Her group has been doing a lot of special word study. You could help with her spelling if you would dictate the words very distinctly for her so that she can listen for the sounds."

Letters home do not offer the flexible give-and-take and the opportunity to show actual examples of a child's work that are possible in a conference, but they can convey much more information than a grade. They need to be specific. If they become stereotyped much of their value is lost. "Mary is improving" or "Jerry needs more help" are statements that are, in some ways, less informative than ratings of *Satisfactory*, *Improving*, or *Unsatisfactory*. Furthermore, they need to be phrased so that parents do not have to struggle with technical terms and pedaguese. And, to convey the necessary information, they sometimes have to be long. The comments on a first-, a fourth-, and a sixth-grader's progress in reading included in such letters might read as follows:

JOAN started to school this fall and had many adjustments to make, as you know, She now works and plays with other children very well. Just recently she was the one the children chose to be the princess in some dramatic play. You will recall how much trouble she was having with the activities in our readiness book when you visited us at Thanksgiving? Now she is doing quite well with the stories in a preprimer. She will need to start with easy first-grade books next year.

MARY started the year reading third-grade books. She rarely went near the library table. This month she has taken home four library books. She has worked all year with a group who were given special help in reading. Now they are tackling their second fourth-grade book. This represents excellent progress. You may help by encouraging her to borrow library books. Do not worry if she chooses short ones that do not seem to be at fourth-grade level. She needs to learn that reading is fun.

ART is an excellent reader. However, he does not always make full use of his ability. Over the year it was hard to keep him supplied with library books, but in his social studies and science he sometimes failed to take the time to get the full information he needed. Once in a while the children accused him of bluffing. Art tells me that he is going to build an amateur radio set this summer. The detailed reading he will have to do could be helpful. It might also be a challenge to him to be given some easy interesting adult nonfiction, such as the advanced books on the enclosed summer reading list.

Reporting to parents through conferences or letters is very time-consuming. Many teachers who would prefer to report by these means have given up when faced with the almost impossible task of doing the job without help two or three times a year for as many as forty youngsters. Administrators need to experiment with various methods of facilitating the process. Sometimes the children in one class can be taken by a substitute or by other teachers for an afternoon while their teacher confers with parents. Even the provision of secretarial assistance to type letters to parents can provide considerable relief.

What of the teachers in school systems where letter grades or similar ratings are the accepted and the expected means of reporting progress? There is no completely satisfactory resolution of the dilemma of how to convey several kinds of information in a single rating. In some schools a partial solution has been to use a second grade to indicate effort, and then to stress to children that this is the important rating. Certainly, whatever the decision as to the meaning of the rating, it should be adhered to uniformly throughout the school system. It is helpful, also, to interpret the general basis of the rating system to parents. This may call for conferences, letters, or perhaps discussions in meetings of the Parent-Teachers Association. Whatever the rating system, parents need to be informed when a child is having trouble. It can be very disturbing both to parents and to child if a series of *A's* and *B's*, for a child of limited ability, are followed at the end of the year by the recommendation that he spend a second year in the same grade.

Methods of reporting to parents are more easily revised when parents and teachers work together on the problem. It is just as important to involve those who are to interpret reports in the preliminary planning as it is to involve those who are to write them. Often a joint effort to revise the reporting system is more successful if the opening question for discussion is, "What do you want to know about your children?" rather than, "What rating system should we use?" After there is a clear picture of the type of information desired, proposals about how best to give it can be examined in sharper focus.

Give children a share in the reporting process. Children need to be involved in the reporting process. It is an important aspect of the appraisal of their work, and their attitudes toward their own achievements will necessarily be influenced both by the type of report that goes home and by their parents' reactions to it. They can often help in the process of interpreting to parents if they have shared in preparing the report. Even young children can have a part in dictating a letter to tell their parents about their school activities. Older children can write their own letters, to be included with those of the teacher, or can help the teacher decide what information her letter should contain. A child can also share in a conference by showing a parent his work or by telling about some of his activities. In addition, children can help to collect typical samples of their work to show their parents, and can sit down with the teacher to evaluate the evidence in a cumulative folder before a report is sent home. If a system of letter grades is being used, it is often helpful to talk over with a child the meaning of his grade. These activities do not necessarily call for much additional time expenditure. They can be planned so that they contribute to the appraisal process from day to day while they serve the larger purpose of bringing children, parents, and teachers closer together.

Interpret the principles underlying modern teaching methods. Parents can interpret reports of their children's activities more effectively if they have a background of general understanding of the philosophy of the school and of the psychological principles underlying modern teaching methods. While no one would dispute the importance of a teacher's professional background to her effectiveness in the classroom, the fundamental principles underlying good teaching are no more difficult for intelligent laymen to understand than they are for intelligent teachers. Nor do these principles seem any less reasonable to one group than they do to the other. Parents have a right and an obligation to understand the reasoning back of the methods being used to educate their children and school personnel have an equal obligation to help them to acquire this understanding.

Many helpful joint steps have been taken. Parents and teachers have worked together in study groups. Parent-Teacher Associations have planned programs focusing on teaching methods. Often teachers have developed helpful displays of children's work or have planned demonstrations for such meetings. In some schools, large parents' meetings have alternated with smaller sessions where mothers have met in discussion groups led by the teachers of their children. Some schools have made effective use of spring meetings of parents whose children will enter first grade in the fall. Interested community members have been invited to spend a day in school. Sometimes parents have been invited to visit classrooms for the hour preceding afternoon Parent-Teacher Association meetings. It has also proven helpful to have parents visit individually to watch their child at work before they have a conference with his teacher. Modern methods explain and justify themselves when they can be observed.

School personnel have also experimented with written interpretations of their programs. In one first grade this was a one-page hectographed bulletin *About Ourselves*, written jointly by teacher and children and sent home once a week. Leaflets describing aspects of the school program have some-

Parents can better understand a modern reading program when children illustrate for them the many ways they learn to use reading materials.

times been included with report cards. Use has also been made of some of the recent bulletins written for lay people, of which typical examples are given in the suggested readings at the end of this chapter. These may serve as study guides for discussion groups, or as helpful reading for individuals.

Children can help to interpret modern methods if they, themselves, have been encouraged to think about the reasons for their work. One teacher took time at the end of a unit to ask the children what they had learned. After they had made a list, the length and variety of which surprised them, she asked if they thought their parents would be interested in seeing copies. This suggestion was met with enthusiasm and the children went home with their lists, eager to explain. Another teacher helped her class to think through their learnings in a social-studies unit in terms parents would recognize. For an open-house, this group prepared charts analyzing the unit—*What We Read; What Arithmetic We Needed; What We Needed to Write; What*

Facts We Learned; How We Worked. Children have also learned to interpret their school activities by helping to decide what kinds of work should be on display for an open-house in order to give parents the full picture of their work. Then, too, individual classes can plan special activities to share aspects of their work with their parents. Examples were given in Chapter XI of reading units planned by the children to show their parents how they learned to read and what kinds of stories they liked. Often teachers have used part of the time given to such special programs to allow children to tell in their own words how they worked and what they thought they learned.

Teachers, themselves, must understand modern methods if they are to interpret them. This implies a critical and intelligent appraisal of classroom procedures. It means participation in professional organizations, in curriculum committees, and in other groups concerned with the continuous evaluation of the educational program. It implies also that administrative personnel will take pains to keep the school library of professional books well stocked.

The teacher, then, is at the heart of the appraisal process. In the classroom she is the one who takes major responsibility for setting the goals for her group and for evaluating their progress toward these goals. It is her insight into the child's performance from day to day that plays a major part in determining the skills he needs and the experiences that will be most profitable for him. The way in which she works with her children determines the degree to which they develop insight into their own problems and interest in developing better skills. As a member of the school faculty, she shares in the appraisal of the total school program and helps to take leadership in involving parents and interested community members in providing more challenging learning situations for boys and girls.

SOME QUESTIONS TO THINK ABOUT IN APPRAISING THE APPRAISAL, RECORDING, AND REPORTING PROCESSES

1. Does the appraisal process make a maximum contribution to on-going classroom activities?

2. Have children been given a share in the appraising, recording, and reporting processes?

3. Is children's growth being appraised in the light of broad understanding of the skills needed by effective readers in a democratic society?

4. Do the standards held for individual children take their maturity and potential ability into account?

5. Do the standards held for individual children take their related growth needs into account?

6. Have ways been worked out for studying progress and problems in on-going classroom situations?

7. Does the record-keeping process make a functional contribution to daily classroom activities?

8. Are standardized tests used in such a way as to be of maximum help to the classroom teacher?

9. Does the system of reporting to parents provide them with a clear picture of the child's progress and his potentialities?

10. Are parents and teachers together making a critical appraisal of the total reading program?

SUGGESTIONS FOR FURTHER READING

IMPLICATIONS OF CHILD DEVELOPMENT FOR THE APPRAISAL PROCESS

Almy, Millie C. *Ways of Studying Children: A Manual for Teachers.* New York: Bureau of Publications, Teachers College, Columbia University, 1959. 226 pp.

Anderson, Irving H. and Dearborn, Walter F. *The Psychology of Teaching Reading.* Chapter 1. The Ronald Press Company, 1952. 382 pp.

Jenkins, Gladys Gardner. *Helping Children Reach Their Potential.* Chicago: Scott Foresman and Company, 1961. 200 pp.

Jersild, Arthur T. *Child Psychology.* Fifth Edition. Englewood Cliffs, New Jersey: Prentice-Hall, Inc., 1960. 506 pp.

Jersild, Arthur T. and Associates. *Child Development and the Curriculum.* New York: Bureau of Publications, Teachers College, Columbia University, 1946. 274 pp.

Olson, Willard C. *Child Development.* Chapter 6. Boston: D. C. Heath and Company, 1959. 497 pp.

Russell, David H. *Children Learn to Read.* Second Edition, Chapter 3. Boston: Ginn and Company, 1960. 612 pp.

APPRAISING GROWTH IN THE CLASSROOM SETTING

Austin, Mary C. and others. *Reading Evaluation: Appraisal Techniques for School and Classroom.* New York: Ronald Press Company, 1961. 256 pp.

Betts, Emmet A. *Foundations of Reading Instruction,* pp. 456-475. New York: American Book Company, 1957. 757 pp.

Bond, Guy L., and Wagner, Eva B. *Teaching the Child to Read.* Third Edition, Chapter 12. New York: The Macmillan Company, 1960. 416 pp.

Gans, Roma. *Guiding Children's Reading Through Experiences.* Chapter 6. New York: Teachers College, Columbia University, 1941. 86 pp.

Gerberich, J. Raymond. *Specimen Objective Test Items: A Guide to Achievement Test Construction.* New York: Longmans, Green and Company, 1959. 436 pp.

Gray, Lillian, and Reese, Dora. *Teaching Children to Read.* Second Edition, Chapter 16. New York: The Ronald Press Company, 1957. 475 pp.

Hester, Kathleen B. *Teaching Every Child to Read.* Chapter 22. New York: Harper and Brothers, 1955. 416 pp.

Hildreth, Gertrude. *Teaching Reading,* pp. 466-474. New York: Henry Holt and Company, 1958. 612 pp.

The Reading Teacher. **14**, No. 1, September 1960. The theme of this issue is "Diagnosis of Reading Problems with Classroom Materials."

Robinson, Helen M. *Corrective Reading in Classroom and Clinic.* Chapters 3, 4. Supplementary Education Monographs, No. 79. Chicago: University of Chicago Press, December 1953. 256 pp.

Robinson, Helen M. (Editor). *Evaluation of Reading.* Supplementary Educational Monographs, No. 88. Chicago: The University of Chicago Press, 1958. 208 pp.

Russell, David H. *Children Learn to Read.* Second Edition, Chapter 16. Boston: Ginn and Company, 1961. 612 pp.

Strang, Ruth; McCullough, Constance, and Traxler, Arthur E. *The Improvement of Reading.* Third Edition, Chapter 14. New York: McGraw-Hill Book Company, Inc., 1961. 480 pp.

Tinker, Miles A., and McCullough, Constance M. *Teaching Elementary Reading.* Second Edition, Chapter 16. New York: Appleton-Century-Crofts, Inc., 1962. 615 pp.

SELECTING AND USING STANDARDIZED TESTS

Bond, Guy L., and Tinker, Miles A. *Reading Difficulties, Their Diagnosis and Correction,* pp. 461-68. New York: Appleton-Century-Crofts, Inc., 1957. 486 pp.

Buros, Oscar K. (Editor). *The Fifth Mental Measurements Yearbook.* Highland Park, New Jersey: The Gryphon Press, 1959. 1292 pp.

Burton, William H. *Reading in Child Development.* Chapter 14. Indianapolis: The Bobbs-Merrill Company, 1956. 608 pp.

Harris, Albert J. *How to Increase Reading Ability.* Fourth Edition. Chapters 7, 8. New York: Longmans, Green and Company, 1961. 624 pp.

Gates, Arthur I. *The Improvement of Reading.* Third Edition, Chapter 3. New York: The Macmillan Company, 1947. 657 pp.

Kottmeyer, William. *Teacher's Guide for Remedial Reading.* Chapters 4-6. St. Louis: Webster Publishing Company, 1959. 264 pp.

Traxler, Arthur E. "Values and Limitations of Standardized Reading Tests," *Evaluation in Reading.* H. M. Robinson (Editor). Supplementary Educational Monographs, No. 88. Chicago: University of Chicago Press, 1958. 208 pp.

RECORDING AND REPORTING PROGRESS

Dawson, Mildred A. and Bamman, Henry A. *Fundamentals of Basic Reading Instruction.* Chapter 15. New York: Longmans, Green and Company, 1959. 304 pp.

D'Evelyn, Katherine E. *Individual Parent-Teacher Conferences.* New York: Bureau of Publications, Teachers College, Columbia University, 1945. 99 pp.

Hester, Kathleen B., *op. cit.,* Chapter 20.

Hildreth, Gertrude. *Readiness for School Beginners.* Chapter 12. Yonkers-on-Hudson: World Book Company, 1950. 382 pp.

Hymes, James L. *Effective Home-School Relations.* Englewood Cliffs, New Jersey: Prentice-Hall, 1953. 264 pp.

Langdon, Grace, and Stout, Irving W. *Helping Parents Understand Their Child's School.* Englewood Cliffs, New Jersey: Prentice-Hall, 1957. 508 pp.

McKim, Margaret G.; Hansen, Carl W., and Carter, William L. *Learning to Teach in the Elementary School.* Chapter 11. New York: The Macmillan Company, 1959. 612 pp.

Rothney, John W. M. *Evaluating and Reporting Pupil Progress.* What Research Says to the Teacher, No. 7. Washington, D. C.: National Education Association, 1955. 33 pp.

Russell, David H., *op. cit.,* Chapter 17.

Stout, Irving W. and Langdon, Grace. *Parent-Teacher Relationships*. What Research Says to the Teacher, No. 16, Washington, D. C.: National Educational Association, 1958. 31 pp.

Wrightstone, J. Wayne; Justman, Joseph; and Robbins, Irving. *Evaluation in Modern Education*. New York: American Book Company, 1956. 481 pp.

Wrinkle, William L. *Improving Marking and Reporting Practices*. New York: Rinehart and Company, 1947. 120 pp.

INTERPRETING THE READING PROGRAM TO PARENTS

Many of the references suggested for preceding chapters will also be of interest to parents. In addition there are a number of books and pamphlets planned particularly for parents as well as teachers. They are designed to:

A. *Help answer the question: "How does my child learn to read?"*

Artley, Sterl A. *Your Child Learns to Read*. Chicago: Scott, Foresman and Company, 1953. 255 pp.

Bond, Guy and Wagner, Eva. *Child Growth in Reading*. Chicago: Lyons and Carnahan, 1961. 156 pp.

Department of Elementary School Principals, National Public Relations Association. *How to Help Your Child Learn: A Handbook for Parents of Children in Kindergarten Through Grade 6*. Washington, D. C.: National Education Association, 1960. 40 pp.

———. *Janie Learns to Read*. Washington, D. C.: National Education Association, 1954. 40 pp.

Gans, Roma. *Reading Is Fun*. New York: Bureau of Publications, Teachers College, Columbia University, 1949. 51 pp.

Hymes, James L. *Before the Child Reads*. Evanston, Illinois: Row, Peterson and Company, 1958. 96 pp.

Mackintosh, Helen K. *How Children Learn to Read*. Washington, D. C.: Superintendent of Documents, U. S. Government Printing Office, 1952. 16 pp.

Monroe, Marion. *Growing Into Reading*. Chicago: Scott, Foresman and Company, 1951. 274 pp.

B. *Help answer the question: "How can I provide my child with enjoyable reading experiences?"*

Association for Childhood Education International. *Literature with Children*. 1961-62 Membership Service Bulletin, No. 3-A. Washington, D. C.: The Association. 56 pp.

Association for Childhood Education International. *Reading in the Kindergarten??* Margaret Rasmussen (Ed.). Membership Service Bulletin 1962-63. Washington, D. C.: The Association, 1962. 40 pp.

Duff, Annis. *Bequest of Wings*. New York: Viking Press, 1946. 204 pp.

———. *Longer Flight*. New York: Viking Press, 1956. 269 pp.

Frank, Josette. *Your Child's Reading Today*. New York: Doubleday and Company, 1960. 391 pp.

Larrick, Nancy. *A Parent's Guide to Children's Reading*. New York: Doubleday and Company, 1958. 316 pp.

Tooze, Ruth. *Your Children Want to Read*. Englewood Cliffs, New Jersey: Prentice-Hall, Inc., 1957. 222 pp.

CHAPTER XIV

Caring for the Child Who Needs Remedial Help

CHILDREN WITH PROBLEMS

Children struggle to overcome accidents that caused them to fall behind their groups. In fourth grade, Tony is working with a second-grade book. Two intelligence test records of I.Q.'s over 115 confirm his teacher's judgment that he is an able child. Recurring colds kept him at home for much of the winter in the first grade. He was then promoted to an overcrowded second grade where he made little progress in learning to read. His third-grade teacher was able to help him overcome some of his discouragement and frustration, but even now in fourth grade his progress is still slow. In class discussion he has much to contribute because he and his family have traveled extensively in the summer. In spite of his limited reading skill, the children like Tony and look to him for leadership.

Karen, across the hall in third grade, is new to the school. In her first two years of school she had twelve different teachers as she and her mother moved from town to town in order to be near her father. She is just beginning to read a first reader with success. Karen faces the added problems of having few friends and of being very shy with other children, although she gets along well with adults.

Children attempt difficult tasks with inadequate techniques. In fourth grade, Monica seems to get the general idea of a passage quite well, but she makes occasional surprising mistakes in reporting specific details. In reading aloud, she stumbles over many of the longer words. In her spelling tests she shows little ability to recognize syllables or other sound elements. Her third-grade teacher reports that she showed remarkable skill in recognizing words by their general configuration. This approach to new words seems to be the only one she is using this year with the more difficult vocabulary of the content fields.

418

In the sixth grade, Dennis is a painstakingly slow and accurate reader. His work is usually well done, but his mother is worried because he spends three or four hours a night on his homework. Many emotional scenes have developed at home because his parents insist that he go to bed while he protests that he will be given a low grade if his work is not done.

Children struggle with personal handicaps. In grade five, Mike has just come with new glasses. For the past month he has been complaining that it hurt his eyes to read. Although both his parents and his teacher suspected that this might be an excuse to avoid situations in which he needed to read, they had a specialist check. A pronounced visual difficulty that had not been caught in the screening tests used by the school nurse was uncovered.

Scottie, in second grade, has a Stanford-Binet I.Q. of 84. He is just now ready to do successful work with first-grade materials. His progress will depend on whether easy books are available for him and on whether his teacher is skilled in the techniques of beginning reading. Other teachers are also going to have to adjust to his limited ability if his progress is to be assured.

Children try to live up to discouraging expectations. Joel is just ending his year in first grade. His sister was in the same room a year before and progressed rapidly in learning to read. Everyone expected Joel to do equally well. Now, at the end of the year, he is still immature. He has difficulty working with other children and has shown no particular interest in reading as yet, although he has worked his way through several preprimers. His teacher advises that he be allowed to develop at his own pace, but his parents are wondering if he might not be given some special tutoring over the summer.

Roberta's parents are already planning for her college career although she is only in fifth grade. She has only average intellectual ability, but she takes endless pains with her work. She is unduly tense and anxious whenever she makes a mistake. Her parents take great pride in her report cards and plan a special family party whenever she brings home an *A*. Roberta seldom reads for pleasure. When she does, she selects a book that looks grown-up and difficult. She does a good job when she has an assignment that calls for exact reporting of details, but she is fearful of expressing her own opinion lest she make a mistake.

Jeff's teacher does not believe children should be promoted to the next grade unless they can handle the books normally read at that level. She has used many extrinsic devices to encourage her children to read. There is a special ceremony when a child is moved to a reading group working with harder materials. Children who choose difficult library books are praised. Jeff is in particular disfavor with some of his classmates because his low grades in reading have kept his row from coming in first in a weekly race. Recently he has taken to finding excuses to leave the room during reading activities. In his reading group, he clowns and disrupts the group in other ways.

Children have trouble because of emotional pressures unrelated to reading. Phyllis made excellent progress through the first two grades. Now, in third grade, she is facing the fact that her parents are planning a divorce. For a time she has been living with her grandmother. On a number of occasions she has awakened with an upset stomach and has been unable to come to school. When she does attend, she is likely to daydream unless her teacher is right at her side. After one prolonged crying spell, her teacher was able to elicit the information that Phyllis was interpreting a quarrel she had overheard to mean that nobody wanted her. All her school work is suffering.

George is a confused and unhappy first-grader. He was given no warning that his little sister was on the way and faced the problem of adjusting to school and that of learning to share his parents' affection at the same itme. He is constantly at the teacher's side with special requests for help. He gives up and cries after a feeble attempt to tie his own shoes or to button a difficult button. The other children have not accepted him because he snatches their things. Although he gives evidence of being an intelligent child, George has not been able to concentrate on reading activities well enough to make much progress.

In spite of skilled teachers, interesting and well-graded reading materials, and genuine concern on the part of parents, some children have far more difficulty learning to read than they might be expected to have. These youngsters are to be found in every grade, even into high school and college, working laboriously at tasks that should be easy, feeling discouraged and often out of place because others have so much less trouble, and avoiding as often as they can situations requiring them to read.

An effective reading program for a school or for a single classroom must be planned so that there are provisions for identifying problems early and for giving efficient help. Although specialists in diagnostic and remedial methods may be available in some school systems, there are many in which the full responsibility for the child who needs remedial help will fall to the classroom teacher. This chapter is focused on two problems: what causes a child to become a remedial problem, and what steps can be taken in the regular classroom setting to give him the help he needs.

WHY DOES A CHILD HAVE TROUBLE LEARNING TO READ?

The word *remedial* stems from *remedy*. The child who presents a remedial problem is the one whose reading capacity is appreciably greater than his present level of reading achievement. Suggestions of ways of adjusting reading experiences to meet the needs of children of a wide range of ability, all of whom are making full use of their potentialities, are given at many points in preceding chapters. Such normal adjustments for varying levels of ability are not remedial. In the case of the child who is given remedial help, there is the expectation that skilled teaching, together with intensive practice, will result in marked progress. As the term is typically used, not all children whose achievement falls short of their potential ability are classified as having remedial problems. A very able child, who handles the typical reading activities of his classroom well, actually may be operating several grades below his potential ability. This youngster needs help. However, he does not need the carefully planned practice and the adjusted reading materials that are typical of a remedial program. The focus of this chapter is upon the child who fails to make the progress that might be expected of him and whose lack of skill also causes him to have major difficulty in participating in the reading experiences of his class.

There is no simple explanation of failure to learn to read. In Robinson's[1] intensive case studies of individual children, referred to in Chapter III in the discussion of reading readiness, no one factor was found to account for the difficulty in all thirty cases. Thought-provoking, too, was the evidence that the retarded reader is likely to be struggling with a combination of other difficulties, not necessarily identifiable specifically as causes of the reading difficulty, and that the most retarded readers tend to have the greatest number of added difficulties. Other investigations reinforce these findings. In trying to understand the causes of a child's difficulty in learning to read, teachers must be prepared to take a case-study approach. Factors in home and in school are as important to consider as are factors of physical and intellectual development.

In making a case study of a child with reading difficulty, classroom teachers may wisely plan to draw upon as many resources as possible. Most teachers will have neither the time nor the specialized training necessary to make the complete case study which is possible to a clinician. However, the thoughtful collection and interpretation of relevant data regarding a child who had difficulty in reading are essential to giving him adequate guidance, and the classroom teacher holds a key position in this respect. A complete outline for making a case study has been given by Harris.[2] Essential information can be provided by parents,[3] and by teachers who have previously worked with the child. The family doctor and oculist may be consulted. A scout leader or a Sunday school teacher may have helpful insights. In large school systems it may be possible to draw upon the resources of a bureau of psychological services. Wherever help in understanding a child is available it should be tapped.

[1] Helen M. Robinson, *Why Pupils Fail in Reading* (Chicago: The University of Chicago Press, 1945).
[2] Albert J. Harris, *op. cit.*, pp. 313-14.
[3] *Ibid.*, pp. 272-273.

Physical or intellectual factors may be involved. Visual, auditory, and speech defects all need to be taken into account in looking for the cause of reading difficulty. So do health factors that might have kept a child out of school or have prevented him from responding with full alertness even if he was in school. As suggested in the earlier discussion of reading readiness, there is evidence that children have learned to read successfully in spite of various physical handicaps, but there are also on record cases where the physical difficulty seemed to be related directly to the reading problem.[4] However indirect the relationship appears to be, anything that will assist a child in seeing or in hearing more clearly, in pronouncing words more distinctly, or in responding with more alertness and vitality in the classroom is likely to facilitate the ease with which he learns.

The evidence regarding the relation of left-handedness and of mixed dominance to reading difficulty has been conflicting. While the exact significance of these aspects is difficult to assess, most careful analyses of causal factors in reading retardation include a check on hand and eye dominance. Harris[5] has noted a higher proportion of cases of mixed dominance among a group of pupils having reading difficulty than among an unselected group. Although teachers do not need to give great emphasis to handedness, some analysis of the factor should be made in a diagnostic study of an individual child.

Children have learned to read in spite of limited intellectual ability. However, there is always the possibility that the reading program will not be flexible enough to meet the needs of the child who learns slowly. When this is the case, he may be confused and bewildered by experiences that make sense to the more able members of his group. Should such a child be so unfortunate as to be promoted to a second teacher who also fails to provide the help he needs, he can soon be far below the level at which he might be expected to achieve.

Home and community pressures may result in unfortunate attitudes. Learning to read often assumes great importance in the eyes of parents. Schools, in the early history of this country, were established to help children learn to read and to write. Today, most parents occasionally may say without much tension, "His handwriting cannot be read," or "He spells just like his

[4] Guy L. Bond, *A Study of the Auditory and Speech Characteristics of Poor Readers,* Teachers College Contributions to Education, No. 657 (New York: Teachers College, Columbia University, 1935).

Paul Fendrick, *A Study of the Visual Characteristics of Poor Readers,* Teachers College Contributions to Education, No. 656 (New York: Teachers College, Columbia University, 1935).

Helen M. Robinson, and C. B. Huelsman, Jr., "Visual Efficiency and Progress in Learning to Read," *Clinical Studies* in Reading II, pp. 31-63. Supplementary Educational Monographs No. 77 (Chicago: University of Chicago Press, 1953).

[5] Harris, *op. cit.,* p. 254.

father," or "He takes after me, I never did like arithmetic." Many become genuinely concerned, however, if it becomes apparent that their child is not progressing as rapidly as they expected him to when he started to read. This concern is not necessarily a cause of difficulty in learning to read, but it often can add to the child's problems if he begins to have trouble. Unless there is great wisdom and forbearance in the home of the child whose progress in learning to read is temporarily slow, there may be emotionally charged tutoring sessions and worried exchanges of remarks over the dinner-table in the child's hearing. Sometimes there is open crticism of the school, which forces a child to divide his loyalties between his parents and his teacher. All this concern may magnify a child's difficulties in his own eyes which, in turn, may lead to more unhappy experiences and to still greater concern.

Every child needs to feel secure in the love and affection of his parents. Sometimes a child is unwisely compared with older siblings or with neighbors' children. If he discovers that he is not considered to be making satisfactory progress in a skill that is apparently important to his parents and easy for his brothers and sisters, he may feel that he has failed in an important competition for parental affection. Sometimes it is easier not to compete than it is to try to learn and have the failure made even more apparent.

Learning to read can assume other undesirable emotional meanings for a child. One mother of an only child took great pleasure in reading to him. For several years beyond the time when he should have been reading independently he used his reading difficulty as a means of assuring her continued attention. Even when parents scold or punish, a youngster who is deprived of normal affection unconsciously may fail to learn in order to cling to this one proof that his family is concerned about him. Sometimes a child will be pulled between two parents. Mother is overanxious about his reading ability, and father jokes about the whole situation and points out that he, himself, never liked to read. Which parent is to be satisfied? Such problems are the more serious because the child has no conscious recognition of the meanings he is attaching to the process of learning to read, and parents and teachers frequently do not realize what is happening.

Concern about a child's progress in learning to read may extend beyond the home to the community. The little girl next door may say, "Can't you even read that book yet? That's baby stuff!" A neighbor remarks sympathetically over afternoon tea, "Don't worry, my dear. I'm sure he will soon be getting along all right." Grandmother says, "We learned to sound all those words when I went to school. I don't see how he will over be able to read or to spell the way they teach today." Such pressures need to be reckoned with as possible factors contributing to a child's discouragement, to his panic when he cannot do all that the best readers in his class are doing, and to his conviction that skill in reading is beyond his power. Emotional tensions are not necessarily the original causes of failure to learn, but a large percentage of children who are retarded reveal emotional problems.[6]

Schools may set up unfortunate learning situations. Schools cannot be absolved of all responsibility when children fail to learn to read. Although the policy of adjusting materials and teaching techniques to the varied needs and abilities of a group is becoming widely accepted, it is by no means universal. There are still many classrooms poorly equipped to meet individual needs. Teachers who must work with a single basal reader or a single set of textbooks in a content field are greatly handicapped in giving the retarded reader the experience he needs, and almost as greatly handicapped in challenging the able child to make full use of his ability. The situation for the retarded reader is made no better if he fails to be promoted and must work with the same books the following year.

Teachers, themselves, are not always prepared to meet the needs of retarded readers. Sometimes there are conflicting philosophies regarding how to meet individual differences. A youngster who is just beginning to make progress with easy materials in first grade under a teacher who believes that a range of abilities should be expected in every classroom is in immediate difficulty if he is promoted to a teacher who feels that children should not be sent to her unless they can read second-grade books. Sometimes teachers who are anxious to adjust to the needs of individuals are not sure how to go about it—second-grade teachers may not know the methods of beginning reading; intermediate teachers, the techniques of the primary grades; high school teachers, the problems of teaching fourth- and fifth-graders. Sometimes, too, teachers overestimate the ease with which a child learns to read and assume erroneously that the teachers who worked with him in previous years did not do a good job. Word analysis, for example, is an important point of emphasis in primary classrooms, but it is a complicated skill. Most children will need some additional help in the intermediate grades, and a few may just be beginning to work independently with words. If a fourth-grade teacher assumes that word analysis should not be part of her job and that this extra burden has been placed upon her because of the poor teaching of her primary colleagues, her attitude toward a child's problem is more than likely to add to his feeling of failure. The concept of reading readiness needs to be accepted throughout a school if children are to make consistent progress.

In spite of the greatest of care, transitions from the primary to the intermediate grades, and from the intermediate grades to the junior high school, may not be smooth. The difficult level of reading materials often increases too rapidly for the child who has marginal ability and, in some cases, the

---

[6] Helen M. Robinson, *Why Pupils Fail in Reading* (Chicago: University of Chicago Press, 1945), pp. 76-90

reading problems he faces also increase in complexity too quickly. Teachers in these transitional grades have a special obligation to watch for signs of trouble. Often a few more months of intensive help with problems of word analysis, some carefully planned sessions on how to handle textbooks in the content fields, or some special guidance in how to use reference aids may make the difference between success and failure, discouragement, and gradual retardation.

Children's tensions and anxieties about poor work are sometimes increased by the grading system used in a school. When grades from *A* to *F* are used, the child who begins to have trouble may find himself receiving *C*'s, *D*'s, and *F*'s. Over a series of report cards he may accumulate an overwhelming amount of evidence that there is no use trying. In her study of the school adjustment of delinquent children Edwards reports on one boy who, by the time he was nine years old, had received a total of 106 failing marks for all subjects for all report periods.[7] Conferences or letters to parents, as discussed in the preceding chapter, are often much less anxiety-producing both for parents and for children.

Sometimes a very understandable anxiety on the part of school faculties to develop an effective reading program can place unfortunate pressures on a child who begins to have trouble. The tensions that may be created when averages from standardized tests are used to rate teachers were discussed in the preceding chapter. Overzealousness to give beginners a good start can sometimes result in the establishing of reading groups before children have developed sufficient readiness to have a successful year. Sometimes there may be unfortunate pressure on a child to work toward the best reading group or to choose recreational books that are "up to grade." Sometimes, without intending to, a teacher will give more praise and recognition to the good reader than to the child who has equally good achievement in another field. In classrooms where no other achievement results in the status that comes from being among the best readers, the child who cannot read may turn to undesirable means of securing recognition from his peers. One of these may be to gain fame unconsciously as the person about whose reading difficulties everyone is concerned.

Evidence from classroom work that a child is having difficulty, concerns of parents, or critical reactions from community members, need to be examined with care. It is too easy merely to assume that the school program is sound and that critics are uninformed, parents are overanxious, or a child is lazy, careless, or indifferent. One of the professional responsibilities of those planning a child's activities is to continue to appraise the total program, to

[7] Vera C. Edwards, "A Study of the School Adjustment of Fifty-five Delinquent Children," unpublished Doctor's dissertation (Cincinnati: University of Cincinnati, 1954), p. 121.

identify weaknesses as well as strengths, and to work cooperatively toward more effective reading experiences.

Problems may develop from lack of continuity in school experience. Learning to read is a complicated process. The child who, for any reason, is not able to work consistently at the job may begin to have trouble. Recurring illness has already been mentioned as a possible source of difficulty. Moving from school to school is another. Conditions which result in a series of changes in staff during a single school year may also break the continuity in the learning process. Remedial problems do not have to result from lack of continuity in experience. If parents are patient, and teachers provide special help, it may not be long before the child is again working up to capacity.

Unfortunate habits sometimes go uncaught. Occasionally a child will learn one reading technique exceptionally well and then cling to it. Since his performance is often acceptable for the moment, his teacher does not always realize what he is doing until new material has become so hard that the immature method fails completely. The child who is particularly adept at remembering the configurations of words and who suddenly begins to have trouble with word analysis in the upper third or fourth grades is an example of this sort of persistence of an inadequate way of working. Group discussions of reading skills, pupil evaluations of their own progress, and reading experiences that call for many types of skills are of help in catching such inadequacies early. Prevention of remedial problems is, at least in part, a matter of continuous appraisal.

Difficulty may lead to dislike of reading. Practice is a vital factor in good reading. Once a child begins to have difficulty, he may avoid further reading experiences if he can. He cannot read the new poster on the bulletin board because there are several words he does not know, and next time he does not try. He cannot read rapidly enough to enjoy a story, so he does not do much independent reading. He finds informational material hard to locate, and he substitutes his own experiences or studies pictures without reading the accompanying context. The problem is complicated because it is not always obvious that a child is avoiding situations calling for him to read. He chooses easy books and gives the appearance of being interested. He dawdles over his reading and is scolded for wasting time. He develops hobbies and other special interests in the classroom and is far too busy to find time for recreational reading. A first step in giving remedial help often is to develop a child's interest in reading and to convince him that he can learn.

MAKING REMEDIAL HELP COUNT

How does a teacher in a regular classroom go about giving remedial help? Essentially, the teaching methods are the same as those that would be used with any child with the same reading needs. However, the child who needs remedial teaching is one who has not profited from these methods in the past. Several adjustments in normal classroom procedures may be needed before he will profit from them now.

First, special attention needs to be given to the complicating factors that may be operating to make it difficult for the child to learn. This would include taking such steps as making sure that physical defects are cared for, helping the family understand the problem, and working with emotional tensions caused by unfortunate situations either at home or at school. Second, the retarded reader faces the task of acquiring new skills more rapidly than the child who has made regular progress. He may be several years retarded and he needs to catch up. This means providing greater amounts of practice, and more practice directed toward specific weaknesses than is needed by the typical youngster. Third, because he is retarded in his reading skills, the child is likely to be more mature intellectually than the average child reading at the same level. This means that he has relatively more ability to understand the purposes of his reading activities. This should be capitalized upon by giving him more opportunities to analyze his own shortcomings and to discuss the purposes of his practice exercises. Fourth, the remedial case has often developed a hearty dislike of reading and sometimes a definite fear of it. Far from seeking opportunities to learn to read, he avoids them. These negative emotional overtones have to be dispelled.

Problems of providing remedial help in the regular classroom setting center, then, around finding time to give the additional help, developing confidence and interest in learning to read, and focusing practice activities as effectively as possible upon a child's problems.

FINDING TIME FOR REMEDIAL HELP

Capitalize on the full possibilities of a flexible classroom organization. When the general classroom organization is designed to meet the needs of individuals, there are relatively more opportunities to give special help to the child with a remedial problem. He is not usually as much alone in the classroom as his retardation would lead one to suppose. Often there are three or four children working at approximately his reading level. Some of these may be slow learners who are making satisfactory progress in terms of their abilities. Others may be youngsters who also need special help. These children may form a small reading group. As suggested in earlier chapters, this group may work together regularly throughout the year, using basal readers and work-type activities in a somewhat more systematic fashion than will the more able readers in the room. At times, these youngsters may continue to work as a group for special help in the reading related to unit activities in the content fields. Children who need remedial help may also fit very well into special groups meeting for short-time instruction. Sometimes a remedial spelling group will provide added help with word analysis. There may be another group working directly on word-study problems, or a group practicing to develop more effective reading speed. A first step in finding time to give remedial help is to fit the child into groups that most nearly meet his particular needs.

Flexibility in materials is possible as well as flexibility in grouping. If all the books available for a unit of work are at fifth-grade level, the retarded reader will have great difficulty sharing in any of the reading activities. If there are some second-grade books, he has a reading task within his power, and as he works on his part of the unit he secures some of the additional reading experience he so badly needs. Even if materials have to be written in experience-record form for the children who are the poorest readers, it is important to capitalize on every opportunity to encourage them to read.

In the schedules described in preceding chapters, there is time allotted for independent work. In these periods, when all the children are working on arithmetic, studying spelling, writing letters or reports, or concentrating on other skills, the retarded reader can put relatively more emphasis on reading. Some teachers have found it helpful to provide workbooks through which these children can proceed systematically, or to hectograph graded series of work-type activities for them. Teachers have also set up special game tables with various types of word wheels, flash cards, and other games at which children can work with reading partners. All such activities help to add to a child's total amount of practice in reading.

In a flexible classroom organization, teachers have relatively more time to work with individuals. Even five or ten minutes' help at regular intervals can make an appreciable difference in a child's progress. Some of this can be given during independent work periods. Some may be provided while the children are reading independently to locate the information needed for a unit of work. Some may be given as the other members of a child's reading group work silently. A few minutes may also be found by dismissing the children in a reading group one at a time and holding for a little extra practice the youngsters who have been having the most trouble. It takes planning to find time for the children in a room who need remedial help, but it can be done to a reasonably satisfying degree if full use is made of the possibilities for individualizing a teacher's help.

Make the most of special help from other teachers if it is available. In some school systems there will be teachers employed to give remedial help.

Sometimes the most severely retarded children from several grades are grouped in an adjustment class and remain together for a year or more. This plan makes it possible for a teacher to set up a very flexible schedule and to concentrate on children's special problems, but it may result in giving to one teacher a group with a wide range of reading needs and sometimes in throwing together many children who are emotionally disturbed. Such classes need to be small, and need to be in the hands of someone who has great talent for helping children to feel loved and secure. Precautions may also have to be taken to keep such groups from being filled with children who are slow learners or with those who have emotional problems but who are not in need of remedial help.

A plan for remedial help that involves the classroom teacher more directly is the one in which three or four children are sent to a remedial teacher for a special period each day. Usually the schedule is arranged so that the children go for help during the time when others in the class are also working on reading activities. This provides the intensive help a remedial case needs, but it may raise problems in coordinating his work with that of his class.

There do not always need to be teachers specially employed in order to develop a remedial center. Occasionally a school schedule is planned so that primary children are dismissed early. If this is the case, their teachers may be able to give a period to remedial teaching. Such plans to use the time of existing personnel need to be set up with care, however, if overheavy schedules are not to be the result. It is important, also, to remember that all teachers do not have equal insight into children's emotional problems and equal command of the techniques of primary reading that are likely to be needed for remedial teaching. A free period in a schedule is not an adequate basis for selecting the person who is to give special remedial help.

When help from someone outside the classroom is provided for a child, his teacher's responsibility is to supplement this help as effectively as possible. The remedial teacher can do a better job if she can coordinate some of her work with what is going on in the classroom. In turn, her help may be enlisted in finding materials of the right difficulty level for use in regular classroom activities. She may also be able to share her diagnosis of the child's difficulty and be helpful in outlining steps that can be taken in the classroom to supplement her work.

Other children in the class will be aware of the fact that a child is being given special help. His activities need to be interpreted to them in a positive way. Sometimes work done in the remedial session—stories written, recreational reading, interesting games—can be given special recognition in the classroom. Well-timed comments such as "Wouldn't it be fine if we could have Miss ——— here to help us with that." "Paul has been reading such an interesting book." "Sunny, you've been learning a lot about dividing words into syllables, can you help us?" can also do much to help to establish the prestige of a remedial center.

Help the home share the responsibility. When parents are genuinely concerned about a child's progress, it is sometimes difficult for them to sit back and let the school carry the full responsibility. From the teacher's point of view, opportunities for valuable additional reading experience are lost if the child never takes any of his reading home. While it is important that a child not be confused by conflicting teaching methods, whether they be the methods of home and school or those of the remedial teacher and the classroom teacher, there are many ways in which parents safely can give help.

An important first step is to help parents understand the remedial process. They may have a tendency to expect progress too quickly. Sometimes they do not understand the need for easy materials and are heartsick if a fourth-grader comes home with a second reader. Occasionally parents misinterpret genuine evidence of progress. They may, for example, be critical of inaccurate oral reading without realizing that a child's tendency to substitute words that fit in the context actually indicates that he is comprehending what he reads, or be concerned because he is uncertain of the sounds of some of the less frequently used letters, without realizing that he has grown tremendously in his ability to use larger and more helpful word parts. The time parents and teachers spend together studying the reading program is well invested, whether the child be in need of remedial help or one of the best readers in the room.

Some of the most effective help from parents comes in situations in which they can share without direct attempts to teach. They may give lavish praise when a child brings home a story he has practiced and reads it aloud. They may allow him time for recreational reading, take him to the library, help him to arrange bookcases and a special desk in his room, and perhaps, with the teacher's advice, buy him books. Occasionally they can play simple word games with him. Sometimes, too, parents can help a child to gain status in his classroom in areas in which it is difficult for him to contribute from his reading. They may be able to take him on special trips so that he can report from firsthand experience, or help him find pictures or locate objects to take to school for an exhibit. Above everything else, cooperation between home and school may aid in convincing the child that all the people he likes the best are back of him, and are sure that he is going to make satisfactory progress.

DEVELOPING CONFIDENCE

Have a confident attitude in working with a child. Many remedial cases will need to be convinced that they can learn to read. Every teacher who gives remedial help must be prepared to sound interested, encouraging, and genuinely confident, even though progress is painfully slow. She is the one to whom the child looks for help. When he feels discouraged, her word may be about the only proof he has that he is making progress.

Several procedures can be helpful in convincing a child that his teacher has confidence in him. One is to be genuinely interested in him as a person, so that he will feel free to express his discouragement and to talk about his concerns. A second helpful procedure is to give a child a part in planning his activities so that he can share in his teacher's feeling that he is making progress. "You did very well with these today. Perhaps we don't need any more exercises like that." "You really are beginning to like to read, aren't you? Here's another book you should enjoy just as much." "You can time yourself on this one and see how much faster you are reading." A third technique that helps to build confidence is to discuss a child's problems with him frankly. If he had particular trouble with an exercise, it is usually better to admit it and then to proceed in a matter-of-fact way to make plans for more practice than it is to pretend that he has done well. Akin to this, a fourth technique is to provide businesslike practice that helps him feel he is getting somewhere. "You surely did have trouble with this page. Let's see if we can figure out why. There's another page like it that you may try." These confidence-building procedures are important to use with any child. They assume special significance in the case of a youngster who is receiving remedial help because of his unique need to be convinced that he can learn.

Start with material with which the child can have early success. Since the retarded reader often comes to the new classroom sure that he is going to fail again, it is important to provide early concrete evidence that this time things are going to be different. One way to do this is to start with very easy practice materials. Care may need to be taken, however, to make sure that such materials are not too obviously intended for much younger children. Some youngsters will not mind working with books that are meant for lower grades if they are convinced that the practice is worth while, but others may be defeated from the start by this indication that their work is below grade.

Several procedures may be helpful in providing a child with the materials with which he should be working without embarrassing or discouraging him. One is the policy, suggested in earlier discussions of reading materials, of reserving at least one basal-reader series for retarded readers so that there can be no chance that a younger brother or sister is working with the same book. Sometimes it is even desirable to mimeograph materials so that the primary format will not be obvious. Often a special remedial workbook that contains easy materials written in upper-grade form may be useful. In informational- and recreational-reading activities, the fact that the retarded reader is using very easy books may be made less obvious if all children are given an opportunity to enjoy the pictures and stories in these same books. One tutor of a child who did not mind reading a preprimer in the classroom provided a special cover for the times when the child carried the book home on busses. The adjustments needed in order to provide the materials with which a child can have successful experiences will vary. The important thing is the way the particular youngster feels about his work.

Consider the use of professional-looking materials. Not all children who need remedial help will respond to typical classroom materials. Some will have had so many unsuccessful experiences, perhaps even to struggling through the same book twice because they have failed a grade, that their confidence in most regular teaching aids is shaken. There is very little evidence that mechanical devices, special sets of word cards, word games, or workbooks labeled *diagnostic* or *remedial* are actually any more helpful in developing reading skills than are regular classroom materials. However, the psychological effect on the learner may be positive. Here, at last, is something new, and the child may approach the strange material with confidence and hope. Such special devices probably serve their most important function when a child is first beginning to make progress. Once he has had some feeling of success, that, in itself, can provide powerful motivation.

A device need not be expensive to look professional. A workbook different in style from those used by other children may serve. Writing one's own stories on a classroom typewriter may help. Using specially prepared word cards such as the Dolch cards,[8] keeping a file of hard words, trying to read words flashed with a simple hand-made tachistoscope, may all help to build the feeling that new methods are being used.

The kinesthetic, or tracing, approach used with success by Fernald[9] with severely retarded readers is another device that may appeal. This is a system where the child starts by tracing a word written for him by his teacher as he studies its configuration. When he feels that he knows it, he writes it without looking at it. Then he is given opportunities to use it in composing his own sentences and stories. These are typed before he has forgotten their contents and become part of his reading activities. This approach uses another sense as an avenue to learning. It provides novel reading matter, because the child reads his own stories, and it also gives him a certain amount of quick success which may help to break down his defeatist attitude.

Use records to help convince a child of his progress. Gold stars, charts of work accomplished, graphs showing the percentage of questions done correctly, and other concrete evidence that progress is being made have more place in the life of the remedial case than they do in that of other youngsters. Such devices are not primarily to stimulate a child to work, but to show him

[8] Edward W. Dolch, *Basic Sight Cards* (Champaign, Illinois: The Garrard Press, 1949).
[9] Grace M. Fernald, *Remedial Techniques in Basic School Subjects* (New York: McGraw-Hill Book Company, Inc., 1943).

concretely that he is getting ahead. Even if he seems to be progressing slowly, his book list gives the evidence that he actually read five books this month. If his score is not good on today's exercises, the chart in the back of his workbook demonstrates that he usually does a very fine job. One teacher placed all the new words with which an eight-year-old was working on separate cards. After a specified number of review checks the child destroyed, with great ceremony, the cards he could read. Even this simple proof of his progress had definite encouragement value. Typically, the more insight a child has into his own progress the less he will need such extrinsic devices. In the beginning, such concrete evidence that he is on his way can be helpful.

Help a child begin to interpret errors as signs of progress. Once a child has had some successful experiences, it is important to take him into more difficult materials without having him lose confidence. As his work gets harder he is certain to make more mistakes, and he needs to be prepared for this. Positive comments are usually more effective than negative ones. "You're doing this so well, I believe we can try you on something harder." "No trouble at all with that one? It looks as if it was a little easy for you, wasn't it?" "This page is quite hard, but it will help us see where you need more practice. Would you like to try it?" Techniques such as these help a child to face his errors, not as signs that he is again failing but as evidence that at last he is learning to read.

Help the child feel that he is a contributing class member. One important way to convince a child that his reading skill is improving is to help him to take his full share in classroom activities involving reading. Providing easy informational materials upon which the retarded reader can report is one step in this direction. Sometimes it is worth while to devote a remedial session to helping him locate and read the material he needs. Once in a while a situation will arise where it is important to spend considerable time helping a child perform a difficult reading task. In one Christmas assembly a retarded reader wanted very much to read the description that accompanied the class tableaux. In a fourth-grade play, read behind the scenes as a radio production, a youngster set his heart on reading the part of his favorite character. In each case the teacher took extra time to help the child learn the hard words and practice the oral reading so that he could do a creditable job; and in each case the gain in confidence far outweighed the time spent.

The emotional concomitants of not being able to read well are lessened in a classroom where there are many other ways of becoming a contributing group member. When a book is difficult, a poor reader may sometimes report on the pictures. Again, he may be the one to tell about a firsthand experience or to make some other contribution that does not call for extensive reading skill. In a classroom where the total program is broad, a child's achievement in number or in music, his special collection of beetles, or his science demonstration may gain him recognition. Achieving group status is a basic human need. It is important to make a special effort to help the child who has reading difficulty find some means of becoming an accepted group member.

DEVELOPING INTEREST IN READING

Provide many pleasant contacts with books. When a child who has been given remedial help begins to read widely for enjoyment, he is well on the way toward rapid growth in reading. He needs to be given many pleasant contacts with books. Hearing stories read by the teacher, participating in story groups where children are doing the reading, and listening to parents read stories at home provide some of these contacts, but the child also needs every encouragement to read for himself. In the beginning, the literary quality of the book is not as important as a child's interest in it. Within limits, even comic books may be acceptable. It is particularly important that many of the books be very easy for the youngster whose reading is retarded. Even length sometimes makes a difference. This is especially true if a child is a slow reader who normally plods for days, or perhaps weeks, to finish a book. Often it is helpful to rebind stories from basal readers so that the retarded reader can have the satisfaction of finishing a small "book" quickly. Even less than other children in the class should the remedial case be under criticism if he builds a long recreational-reading list by choosing very short books. The important thing is to start him to read.

Choose materials that capitalize on a child's special concerns. Occasionally a severely disturbed child will resist all efforts to interest him in reading. "I'm going to work with engines. I won't need to read." "Books are sissy stuff." "I'm not going to take courses in high school where you have to read." Such attitudes are not easily changed by argument, even though it may be suspected that they are in large measure a protection against failing again. Sometimes it is necessary to start with the only purpose for reading that the child can see. One youngster said that he was not interested in anything except airplanes, and pulled out of his pocket a collection of pictures. Some of the planes he could recognize, but there were others whose names he wanted to know. For the first few weeks these cards became the center of various word-recognition activities. Once this boy saw that he could learn to read the names of the planes, he began to try to pick out some of the words in the descriptions on the backs of the cards. Weeks later he started into a simple book on planes. Another severely retarded boy, approaching high school age, said that he would never bother to read except that he wanted to get a driver's license. Materials from the Automobile Club started the reading sessions. If a child will attempt to read nothing else, lotto, authors, or other games may at least start him looking at the configurations of words.

Write materials for children to meet special needs. On many occasions a teacher will write material herself in order to have something that is of interest to a retarded reader. One nine-year-old, sophisticated beyond her years, said that she didn't care to read anything except beauty columns. Since few of these are written at second-grade level, the teacher cut out advertisements from popular magazines and rewrote the beauty suggestions. For a time, this child's reading vocabulary was somewhat overweighted with terms related to beauty culture, but she gradually began to read stories about girls whose homes had some of the glamor that her own did not provide. When the poorest readers in a third grade wanted to dramatize the story the teacher had been reading to the class, she hectographed a simplified version for them. It is time-consuming to prepare such materials, but they are well worth the investment if children begin to read.

Sometimes a child's own stories serve as his first reading-matter. These may be dictated to the teacher or written by the child with the help of a file of spelling and vocabulary cards in a variation of the kinesthetic approach described earlier. Usually they are then typed so that the child can read them more easily. These materials may find their way eventually to a class newspaper, to a class notebook on a special project, to a story corner of the bulletin board, or just into the child's special notebook. The tasks of proofreading, learning new words, and perhaps preparing to read the story aloud to other children all provide useful practice. No opportunity to encourage a child to read can be overlooked in planning remedial work.

MAKING SPECIAL PRACTICE ATTRACTIVE AND EFFECTIVE

Direct the child's practice to his specific difficulty. Remedial activities need to be focused directly on a child's difficulties. This calls for the use of all the techniques for studying children's strengths and weaknesses discussed in Chapter XIII. However, the child who is in need of remedial help is likely to have had trouble over several years. This often means that his difficulties have not been obvious. It means, too, that he may have peculiar gaps in his skills and, in self-defense, have developed ways of bluffing that hide some of his weaknesses. His successes and failures need to be studied without prejudice to see exactly what he can and cannot do. Persons skilled in the diagnosis of reading difficulty are often remarkably adept at catching minor clues to inadequate techniques. This adeptness comes in part because skilled diagnosticians have had experience in studying patterns of errors and in part because they understand thoroughly the process of learning to read. Teachers develop the same sensitivities through their study from day to day of the reading needs of the children in their classes.

Careful diagnostic study of retarded readers will reveal some children who are victims of general retardation and whose ways of working are typical of those of youngsters in much lower grades. There may be, in fifth grade, a child whose pattern of skills is very much like that of a second-grader. There may even be an occasional child who has not progressed much beyond pre-primer materials. Children who show general retardation will need reading programs that, in many ways, are typical of those planned for primary children reading at the same level. However, the amount of intensive practice with work-type activities designed to develop word-study skills and to build comprehension skills is likely to be greater than it would be in the corresponding primary program, and the amount of discussion and follow-up of basal-reader stories somewhat less.

Other youngsters will have specific weaknesses—an inefficient approach to new words, a word-by-word style of reading, ineffectiveness in establishing clear purposes for reading, inability to select appropriate details, and others. In such cases, practice needs to bear directly upon the inadequate skill. How direct this help sometimes needs to be is illustrated by the case of the youngster who had had considerable remedial work and who exclaimed in a diagnostic session, "Word families, *at, cat, mat, bat,* I know them all!" This he did, when the words were of one syllable. His problem, however, lay in seeing the parts of two- and three-syllable words and in blending them. This particular skill had not been stressed in the simple word-study activities with which he had been laboring. On the other hand, children can have combinations of difficulties. For example, a youngster who has been struggling with materials in which the vocabulary has been much too difficult may develop poor habits of comprehension. Such a child will need some experiences with very simple materials to encourage him to think about the meaning of what he is reading, and some with materials with more difficult vocabulary to help him develop effective word-study skills. Part of the art of remedial teaching lies in achieving a proper balance in activities.

A child who is reading at a grade level lower than his actual grade in school is likely to make errors typical of younger children. Intermediate-grade teachers who work with severe problems of retardation need to develop a primary teacher's point of view. Mistakes that seem baffling to a teacher of older children actually may be quite typical of the performance of a youngster reading at the level at which the remedial case is working. Practice can be fitted more readily to a child's needs when his difficulties from day to day are correctly interpreted.

Finding enough interesting practice material at the correct difficulty level for the remedial case is not always easy. In many classrooms the problem is complicated by the fact that the materials must be such that the child can work alone, counting on his teacher for rather brief periods of help. Sometimes a regular primary reader and workbook will serve. However, typical primary materials do not always interest an older child. Often it will be more effective to use workbooks in which the activities are developed around a short article with which the workbook page begins. Teacher-made work-sheets have been suggested as a means of supplementing these commercial materials. The actual form of the work-type exercise need be no diffrent from that which might be used with a child who is making regular progress. Descriptions of activities appropriate for specific skills are included at a num-ber of points in preceding chapters.

It is just as important to be selective in using workbook materials for reme-dial purposes as it is to be selective when they are part of the regular reading program. A workbook is usually planned to give well-balanced practice in a variety of skills. This is effective for the child whose retardation is general, but not for the one who has a specific weakness. A slow reader, for example, might well be assigned workbook activities calling for the general gist of a paragraph, but he should not be expected to do word-study activities that may reinforce his present tendency to work with painstaking attention to de-tails. Only someone who has worked with a child can determine the experi-ences he needs.

No matter what other skills are developed, a remedial program has missed its mark if a child does not also begin to enjoy reading for its own sake. Time needs to be scheduled definitely for activities designed to develop interest in reading, such as those described in the preceding section. When these recre-ational-reading activities are planned around books of the correct difficulty level, they, too, help to provide the extensive reading experience that is im-portant in the progress of a retarded reader.

Plan practice activities that call for thoughtful reading. The child who is severely retarded typically has had many experiences where the materials he tried to read made little sense to him. His practice activities need to be planned so that he has maximum opportunity to learn to read for meaning. This implies that the proportion of games or other activities in which words are met out of context usually would be light in comparison to those in which the child reads a short paragraph, answers a riddle, answers questions based on a short story, follows directions in order to draw a picture, or does something else that requires him to think about the meaning of what he has read. This is essentially the same basis on which work-type activities would be chosen for any child. It is of particular concern in planning remedial work only because the child's previous reading experiences are likely to have de-veloped unfortunate habits and attitudes.

Keep the child's practice interesting and varied. It is important to keep the many hours of practice needed by a retarded reader from becoming bor-ing. This is another reason for using materials where thoughtful reading is required—short stories, paragraphs that provide interesting information, rid-dles, workbooks that present a new story with each new page. It is another reason, too, for exerting every effort to interest a child in recreational read-ing so that some of the experience he needs is supplied by stories of his own choosing. In providing practice activities, it is often important to plan to in-troduce a new challenge from time to time. Sometimes a reading game can serve. It can be helpful, also, to allow a child to choose some of his own prac-tice activities. He may even help to prepare some of the materials—make his own word cards, plan his own games, develop his own file of words to help with his spelling, devise a simple tachistoscope. The graphs, stars, and other concrete records of progress discussed earlier can also be of use in keeping interest high. If a child comes to a tutor for extended practice sessions it may be possible to read to him, to take turns with him in reading aloud, to interest him in construction activities for which he must read the directions, or even to stop work entirely for a day in order to take a special excursion. For many children who are retarded, reading has been a confusing, meaningless, and frustrating experience. Remedial activities need to be in sharp contrast.

Provide for consistent practice. Part of the secret of making remedial work effective is to give consistent guidance. Small amounts of daily help are usu-ally preferable to remedial sessions twice a week, and these, in turn, are pref-erable to longer weekly periods. In the earlier suggestions of ways of find-ing time for remedial help, a pattern was proposed that would give the child several kinds of reading activities within the classroom, in each of which he would participate regularly, and through each of which he would receive some regular guidance. When materials are adjusted so that full use can be made of every situation in which the child may be given an opportunity to read, his day's activities often can add up to a surprising amount of excellent experience.

Continue with special help until new techniques are thoroughly mastered. A child who has once faced frustration and discouragement in learning to read should not be placed in situations where he may be defeated again. Es-pecially in the beginning, a slow pace and ample practice may be most im-portant in building confidence. As a child's skill begins to approach that of his classmates it is often better to continue to adjust the difficulty of the books he reads and to keep him in a group where he can be given special help than it is to push him into activities that may cause him trouble. If he is in a special reading center or is working with a tutor, this may mean letting him continue to have the help even though there seems to be a chance that he might be able to handle regular classroom work without it. When the special help is discontinued, the teacher should take particular pains to help the child fit into the regular classroom work successfully. Many suggestions have been made in preceding chapters of ways of giving a little extra assistance to a child who is learning slowly so that he may be able to participate successfully in regular classroom activities. These same techniques can help to bridge the gap for the remedial case.

Help the child share in appraising his progress and in planning next steps. The most interesting practice loses much of its force if a child goes at it blindly. The same procedures that help other children to analyze their strengths and weaknesses and to understand the purposes of special practice will also help the retarded reader. The reasons for practice activities can be talked through before a child undertakes them. He can help to analyze his successful experiences so that he knows what he has done well, and to study his failures so that he knows where he needs more practice. Three or four children working together may discuss what helped them to recognize a new word or how they located the answer to a question. In areas such as word analysis, their greater maturity may make them able to deduce rules which may facilitate their progress. Eventually the retarded reader should develop the same healthy interest in taking an objective look at his achievement and in sharing in plans for his next activities that is displayed by the child who is making normal progress.

Independence is the final goal for all children. When a child begins to understand what it means to be a good reader, takes an active interest in learning to read more skillfully, and, most important, finds in being able to read a way of solving his problems and a source of personal satisfaction, he is well on his way toward the eventual mastery of adult reading skills.

SOME QUESTIONS TO THINK ABOUT IN APPRAISING THE REMEDIAL HELP PROVIDED FOR CHILDREN

1. Is a careful study made of all possible factors that might be affecting a child's progress in reading?
2. Is the classroom program flexible enough to allow time to give special help to individuals?
3. Are administrative problems in the school, such as class size, solved in such a way as to facilitate the teacher's efforts to give help to individuals?
4. Are there sufficient easy recreational and informational materials to provide the successful and enjoyable reading experiences needed by the retarded reader?
5. Is the atmosphere in which the child works one of enthusiasm and confidence?
6. Is every effort being made to interest the child in reading?
7. Are practice activities planned in terms of the child's special needs?
8. Are there ample interesting work-type materials for special practice?
9. Is the child given a share in planning his own program and in appraising his progress?
10. Is there continuous study of the effectiveness with which the total school program is meeting individual needs?

SUGGESTIONS FOR FURTHER READING

ADDITIONAL RESOURCES FOR REMEDIAL HELP IN THE CLASSROOM SETTING

Burton, William H. *Reading in Child Development.* Chapter 17. Indianapolis: The Bobbs-Merrill Company, 1956. 608 pp.

DeBoer, John J., and Dallmann, Martha. *The Teaching of Reading.* Chapter 12. New York: Holt, Rinehart and Winston, 1960. 360 pp.

Durrell, Donald D. *Improving Reading Instruction.* Yonkers-on-Hudson: World Book Company, 1956. 402 pp.

Fernald, Grace M. *Remedial Techniques in Basic School Subjects.* Chapters 3-12. New York: McGraw-Hill Book Company, Inc., 1943. 349 pp.

Gray, Lillian, and Reese, Dora. *Teaching Children to Read.* Second Edition, Chapter 12. New York: The Ronald Press Company, 1957. 475 pp.

Heilman, Arthur W. *Principles and Practices of Teaching Reading.* Chapter 12. Columbus, Ohio: Charles E. Merrill Books, Inc., 1961. 465 pp.

Intermediate Manual, Revised. Chapter 9. Curriculum Bulletin 400. Cincinnati: Cincinnati Public Schools, 1962. 404 pp.

New Primary Manual. Chapter 16. Curriculum Bulletin 300. Cincinnati: Cincinnati Public Schools, 1953. 496 pp.

Robinson, Helen M. "Corrective and Remedial Instruction," *Development In and Through Reading,* pp. 357-375. Sixtieth Yearbook of the National Society for the Study of Education, Part I. Chicago: The University of Chicago Press, 1961. 406 pp.

Smith, Henry P., and Dechant, Emerald V. *Psychology in Teaching Reading.* Chapter 15. Englewood Cliffs, New Jersey: Prentice-Hall, 1961. 470 pp.

BOOKS WITH MAJOR EMPHASIS UPON THE DIAGNOSIS AND TREATMENT
OF READING DISABILITIES

Blair, Glenn Myers. *Diagnostic and Remedial Teaching.* Revised Edition, Chapters 2-5. New York: The Macmillan Company, 1956. 409 pp.

Bond, Guy L., and Tinker, Miles A. *Reading Difficulties: Their Diagnosis and Correction.* New York: Appleton-Century-Crofts, Inc., 1957. 486 pp.

Dolch, Edward A. *A Manual for Remedial Reading.* Second Edition. Champaign, Illinois: The Garrard Press, 1945. 460 pp.

Gates, Arthur I. *The Improvement of Reading.* Third Edition. New York: The Macmillan Company, 1947. 657 pp.

Harris, Albert J. *How to Increase Reading Ability.* Fourth Edition. New York: Longmans, Green and Company, 1961. 624 pp.

Kottmeyer, William. *Teacher's Guide for Remedial Reading.* Chapter 14. St. Louis: Webster Publishing Company. 1959. 264 pp.

Monroe, Marion. *Children Who Cannot Read.* Chicago: University of Chicago Press, 1932. 205 pp.

Reading Teacher, The. **14,** September 1960. Entire issue is devoted to the diagnosis of reading problems.

Robinson, Helen M. (Editor). *Corrective Reading in Classroom and Clinic.* Supplementary Educational Monographs, No. 79. Chicago: University of Chicago Press, 1946. 257 pp.

Robinson, Helen M. *Why Pupils Fail in Reading.* Chicago: The University of Chicago Press, 1946. 257 pp.

Strang, Ruth, and Bracken, Dorothy Kendall. *Making Better Readers.* Chapters 3 and 4. Boston: D. C. Heath and Company, 1957. 367 pp.

Vernon, Magdalen M. *Backwardness in Reading: A Study of Its Nature and Origin.* London: Cambridge University Press, 1957. 227 pp.

SOURCES OF PRACTICE ACTIVITIES

Dawson, Mildred A., and Bamman, Henry A. *Fundamentals of Basic Reading Instruction.* Appendix A. New York: Longmans, Green and Company, 1959. 304 pp.

Gates, Arthur I., *op. cit.*

Hester, Kathleen B. *Teaching Every Child to Read.* Chapters 10-19. New York: Harper and Brothers, 1955. 416 pp.

Hildreth, Gertrude. *Teaching Reading.* New York: Henry Holt and Company, 1958. 612 pp.

Russell, David H., and Karp, Etta E. *Reading Aids Through the Grades.* New York: Bureau of Publications, Teachers College, Columbia University, 1951. 120 pp.